MW01674946

John Wilson, R. Shelton Mackenzie

Noctes Ambrosianae

Vol. 5. February, 1832, Feb., 1835

SALZWASSER
VERLAG

John Wilson, R. Shelton Mackenzie

Noctes Ambrosianae

Vol. 5. February, 1832, Feb., 1835

Reprint of the original, first published in 1863.

1st Edition 2022 | ISBN: 978-3-37500-473-6

Verlag (Publisher): Salzwasser Verlag GmbH, Zeilweg 44, 60439 Frankfurt, Deutschland
Vertretungsberechtigt (Authorized to represent): E. Roepke, Zeilweg 44, 60439 Frankfurt, Deutschland
Druck (Print): Books on Demand GmbH, In de Tarpen 42, 22848 Norderstedt, Deutschland

NOCTES AMBROSIANÆ

BY THE LATE

JOHN WILSON

"CHRISTOPHER NORTH," OF BLACKWOOD'S MAGAZINE, PROFESSOR OF MORAL PHILOSOPHY IN UNIVERSITY OF EDINBURGH, ETC.

WM. MAGINN, LL.D., J. G. LOCKHART, JAMES HOGG, AND OTHERS.

REVISED EDITION

WITH

MEMOIRS AND NOTES

BY R. SHELTON MACKENZIE, D. C. L.

VOL. V

FEBRUARY, 1832—FEB., 1835

NEW YORK

1863.

William Maginn

MEMOIR

OF

WILLIAM MAGINN, LL.D.

BY DR. SHELTON MACKENZIE.

William Maginn, one of the most distinguished writers of his time, and very eminent for his knowledge of ancient and modern literature, was an Irishman. His father kept a classical academy in Marlborough-street, Cork, where William (the eldest son*) was born on the 10th July, 1793. From the earliest age, he had a great aptitude for acquiring knowledge—so much so, that before he had completed his tenth year, young Maginn was sufficiently advanced to enter Trinity College, Dublin. The entrance examination there is nearly as difficult, after four years' study, as that on which students obtain their degrees at the Scotch and many other universities. Maginn's answering was so good, on this examination, that (the rank being invariably given according to merit) he was "placed" among the first ten, out of more than a hundred competitors, two-thirds of whom were double his own age.

The distinction which he thus obtained, at the commencement of his university career, he preserved to its close. He passed through all his classes with credit, obtained several prizes, appeared to learn without an effort, and graduated before he was fourteen. No one (since the brilliant career of Cardinal Wolsey, at Oxford) better merited the appellation of "The Boy-Bachelor." His college tutor, Dr. Kyle, then a fellow and afterwards Provost of the University,† repeatedly declared, in after years, that Maginn, while in his teens, had more literary and general knowledge than most men of mature age whom he had ever met.

* John Maginn, the second son, is now a beneficed clergyman in the South of Ireland. Their sister, Miss Maginn, was mistress of a school for young ladies, in Cork, and, being erudite and a blue-stocking, wrote a novel—which made no sensation when published. This was before my time, and if I ever heard, I have forgotten the name of this fiction.—M.

† In 1830, on the death of Dr. St. Lawrence, Dr. Samuel Kyle was made Bishop of Cork and Ross, at the head of which See he remained until his death in 1848. It was his friendship which provided John Maginn with church-preferment.—M.

Returning to Cork, Maginn became principal assistant in his father's school. In 1813, his father died, and William Maginn, at the age of twenty, on whom was now thrown the necessity of supporting his family, determined to carry on the school,—a course which he pursued, with marked success, for ten years, when he retired, his brother succeeding him.

While Maginn resided in Cork, it obtained the name of "The Athens of Ireland," and was highly distinguished for the energy and success with which its sons applied themselves to the cultivation of literature. Among the most eminent Irishmen of the present day, at least one-half belong to the city or county of Cork. An eminently social man, Maginn soon became "the life, grace, and ornament of society," in his native city. Nor did he spare the quip and the jest, the epigram and the satire, upon his townsmen's vulnerable points. In his youth, he as freely and fearlessly hit at them, right and left, as, in riper years, at statesmen, publicists, and authors. Throughout his life he never could understand how, when the arrow had hit the mark, it was possible for it to rankle in the wound. That, after the writer had forgotten the squib, the victim whom it had ridiculed could feel annoyed, was wholly out of his calculation,—almost beyond his comprehension. Never was satirist less influenced by ill-nature. There was no motive of malice in his wittiest sarcasms. The subject tempted him—he dashed off the impromptu—laughed at it, as others did—dismissed it from his mind—and saw no reason why he should not be as friendly as before with him whom he had made ridiculous.

In 1816, being then only twenty-three years old, Maginn received the degree of Doctor of Laws, from his Alma Mater.* His standing in the university was over thirteen years, and the degree—which never before had been obtained by one so young—was his, of right.

Dr. Maginn, with some leisure, his head filled with learning and miscellaneous knowledge, and teeming with wit and frolic, took to authorship, almost as a matter of course. It is not worth while to notice his contributions to the local newspapers. His first communication to any periodical out of Ireland was sent, in 1819, to the *Literary Gazette*, which had been commenced not long before, and, from the peculiar character of its critiques, (giving full and well-selected quotations from the newest books,) had obtained a large provincial circulation. He did not write, for a long time, under his own name, but signed his letters "P. J. Crossman." His articles for the *Gazette*, at this time, consisted chiefly of miscellaneous scraps in prose and verse, parodies of well-known songs, translations from and into several languages, bagatelles of all sorts, notices of books, and discussions on classical literature. All this

* It may be proper to state that though the degree of Doctor of Laws is conferred, by right or favor, ("causâ honoris,") by the principal universities of Great Britain and Ireland, Oxford alone makes Doctors of Civil Law. Hence, all others affix the initials LL.D. to the recipient's name, while D.C.L. peculiarly denotes the Oxford man.—M.

was sent gratuitously. One of his hardest hits was a lively review of the errors of Debrett's Peerage, a reply to which drew forth a longer and more sarcastic notice. Thus early, also, had he begun to exercise his great mastery of classic lore. One of his earliest *Gazette* articles was "The Second Epode of Horace done in a New Style," by which, he said, the powers of the translator and the original could be both fairly represented in one book. It commences thus:

Blest man! who far from busy hum,
Ut prisca gens mortalium,
Whistles his team afield with glee
Solutus omni fœnore:
He lives in peace, from battles free,
Neq' horret iratúm mare;
And shuns the forum and the gay
Potentiorum limina.

Blackwood's Magazine was rapidly making way, at this time, and it has been stated by Δ (D. M. Moir) that Maginn's first contribution was the translation of the old ballad of Chevy Chase into Latin verse, which appeared in the number for November, 1819. This is a mistake: Mrs. McWhirter's song, on the Powldoodies of Burran, (*vide* "Christopher in the Tent," vol. I. p. 98, of the present edition,) was certainly Maginn's. It is Irish all over, and has the Doctor's mark upon it.

The translation of the first part of Chevy Chase into the universal language of Europe, Latin, was sent anonymously to *Blackwood*, and the writer, who simply signed O. P., boasted, and not without cause, that he had "retained the measure and structure of the verse most religiously." It opens thus:

1.	1.
THE Percy out of Northumberland, And a vow to God made he, That he would hunt in the mountains Of Cheviot within days three, In the manger of doughty Douglas, And all that with him be.	PERSÆUS ex Northumbria, Vovebat, Diis iratis, Venare inter dies tres In montibus Cheviatis, Contemtis forti Douglăso Et omnibus cognatis.

Here is Roger Withrington's gallant boast, spiritedly rendered:

23.	23.
I wot ye be great lords two, I am a poor squire of land, I will never see my captain fight in a field, And look on myself and stand; But while I may my weapon wield I will not fail both heart and hand.	Vos estis magni comites Et pauper miles ego, Sed pugnaturum dominum, Me otioso, nego: Sed corde, manu, enseque, Pugnabo quamdiu dego.

The concluding portion did not appear until June, 1820. In it, Percy's apostrophe over the body of Douglas runs thus:

14.

The Percy leant upon his brand,
And saw the Douglas die;
He took the dead man by the hand,
And said, "Woe is me for thee.

14.

Persæus nitens gladio
Douglasi vidit mortem,
Et manu capta mortui
Ploravit ejus sortem.

15.

"To have saved thy life I'd have parted with
My lands for years three;
For a better man of heart nor hand
Was not in all the north countrie."

15.

"Tribus annis agros dederem
Servare virum talem;
Nam fortior nemo fuit per
Regionem borealem."

The quaint stanza, on Withrington's gallantry, is rendered in this manner:

30.

For Withrington my heart is woe,
That o'er he slain should be;
For when his legs were hewn in two,
He knelt, and fought upon his knee.

30.

Pro Withringtono doleo
Quem fatum triste stravit;
Nam binis fractis cruribus
In genibus pugnavit.

In a note appended to the first *fitte* of Chevy Chase was a statement that the writer had also translated the poem into Greek, of which the first verse was given as a specimen:

Περσαῖος ἐκ Νορθύμβριης
Εὔχετο τοῖς θεοῖσι,
Θηρᾶν ἐν τρισὶν ἡμέραις
Εν οὔρεσι Χεβιατοῖσι,
Κἂν ἀντέχῃσι Δύγλασος
Σὺν πᾶσιν ἑτάροισι.

The translator added, "I was thinking of translating old Chevy into Hebrew—for I am a Masorite; but as Professor Leslie has declared Hebrew to be a 'rude and poor dialect,' in his book on Arithmetic, I was afraid to come under the censure of that learned gentleman. To be sure, he does not know (*as I can prove from his writings*) even the alphabet of the language he abuses, but still I am afraid he would freeze me if I had any thing to do with it."

At this time, Professor Leslie had just succeeded Playfair in the chair of natural philosophy in the University of Edinburgh—he had been elected to the chair of mathematics in 1805, and met with great opposition from the strict Presbyterian clergy, on the ground of his supposed scepticism. He was a very strong Whig partisan, also, and a contributor to the *Edinburgh Re-*

view. From these causes, and probably others more personal, *Blackwood* strongly opposed Leslie, and the challenge, as to his scholarship, thrown down by Maginn, induced Mr. Blackwood to write to his new and unknown contributor, begging that he would prove Leslie's ignorance, as to Hebrew. A letter, headed "Leslie *v.* Hebrew," accordingly, appeared in *Blackwood* for February, 1820, in which the accusation was fully proved. This was followed, in November, by another letter signed O. P. (which *Blackwood* changed into "Olinthus Petre, D.D., of Trinity College, Dublin,") which repeated the charge that Leslie "did not know even a *letter* of the tongue he had the impudence to pretend to criticise," ridiculed his pretensions to be considered a great mathematician, alluded to *Brewster's Journal* having accused him of "conveying" his doctrines and discoveries respecting Heat from the *Philosophical Transactions*, and glanced at his presumed disbelief of the Scriptures and Revelation. All this, boldly written and fearlessly published, in a manner compelled Professor Leslie to vindicate his character in a court of law. He commenced a libel-suit against Blackwood, and obtained—a farthing damages!

In the interval, Maginn continued to contribute extensively to the Magazine. The quantity, variety, spirit, and value of his articles made him an excellent assistant. His private letters to Mr. Blackwood were signed "R. T. S," but, being urgently solicited, he relaxed, so far as to subscribe himself Ralph Tuckett Scott. He had never alluded to remuneration. Blackwood, who was very liberal, entreated him, if he would not accept money, to receive such books as he might require to complete his library. When, as he thought, he had at last got his contributor's name, he sent a cheque for a large amount, payable to Ralph Tuckett Scott, or order, and Maginn (who still maintained his incognito) wrote him an amusing letter, detailing the difficulties which he encountered in getting cash for a cheque drawn in favor of and endorsed by an imaginary person.

From the appearance of the Latin version of Chevy Chase, scarcely a number of *Blackwood* appeared without one or more articles by Maginn. He soon assumed the *sobriquet* of Morgan Odoherty—a sketch of whose (pretended) life had been given in 1818.

In May, 1820, when vacation was so near that he could leave the management of the school to his brother, who now was his assistant, Dr. Maginn visited Edinburgh. Mr. Blackwood, writing to Delta, said, "I have living with me just now, my celebrated Cork correspondent, who pummelled Professor Leslie in such a grand style. He has come over quite on purpose to see me, and, till he introduced himself to me on Monday, I did not know his name, or any thing of him, except by his letters under an assumed signature, like yourself."

His introduction to Blackwood was original and amusing. He called at Blackwood's place of business; assumed a very strong Irish brogue; presented himself as a gentleman from Cork, who had been grossly libelled in Maga;

demanded the writer's name, inquired whether "one Tuckett Scott" did not contribute; nearly frightened Mr. Blackwood out of his wits; and finally said, pulling out a bundle of letters, "I suppose you will not deny your own handwriting; may be these letters are not written to Scott, and may be you'll say that I am not the man? I am Dr. Maginn, of Cork." They shook hands, and the result was, for the six weeks of Maginn's stay in Edinburgh, he was Blackwood's guest, and was introduced to, and became familiar with, Wilson, Lockhart, Gillies, Captain Hamilton, (Cyril Thornton,) William Harrison, (the M. de Peudemots, so much praised in "Peter's Letters,") and the other leading writers in Maga.

Maginn returned to Cork in the middle of July, 1820, and resumed his pen, with his wonted industry and ability. In 1823, he married a lady named Cullen, and determined to give up his school, and make literature his profession. His *Blackwood* articles, the authorship of which was now well known, had won him considerable reputation, and he was received in London as a well-known writer, of great wit, readiness, learning, and Toryism. Theodore Hook invited him to conduct a Wednesday's newspaper, which the proprietors of the *John Bull* intended to raise on the ruins of half-a-dozen nearly defunct journals. He was employed, also, on the *London Literary Journal*, (a weak and short-lived rival to the *Literary Gazette*,) and wrote several articles in the *Quarterly Review*. Indeed, so high did he stand, at this time, that when it was determined, on what was called "the destruction" of Lord Byron's autobiographic manuscripts, that Moore should not write the Life of the noble Childe, it was Maginn that Murray selected for that purpose. Mr. Kenealy, the friend and biographer of Maginn, says, "Nothing can more clearly show the high opinion of those best qualified to judge of his abilities, than this fact. A young man, from an Irish provincial town, who had never written a book, and whose name was little known, intrusted with the biography of the greatest of England's poets, by one of the shrewdest booksellers that ever lived, is a spectacle not often seen, and Maginn used to speak of it with no little satisfaction. The papers and letters of his Lordship were accordingly placed in the Doctor's hands, and remained in his possession for some time, but no steps were taken in the biography, and it was finally intrusted to Mr. Moore."

In 1824, when John Murray started his daily journal, called "The Representative," he sent Maginn to Paris, as foreign correspondent; he remained there for some months, returning when the speculation became a decided failure.

Whether in Cork, London, or Paris, he maintained his fealty to *Blackwood*. The NOCTES AMBROSIANÆ were his suggestion, and he occasionally contributed largely to that brilliant series. The whole of No. IV., where Byron and Odoherty, at Pisa, are the only speakers, was written by Maginn. His poetical compositions are scattered over the series;—most brilliant among them are "Cork in the Aiden, for you, love, and me"—the slang song from Vidocq's

Memoirs,—the Latin version of "Back and side go bare,"—the Irishman, and the imitation (of which Peel was the hero, not Brougham, as stated in the *Irish Quarterly Review*) of Béranger's "Monsieur Judas."

The London evening newspaper, called *The Standard*, was commenced in 1828, and Maginn was appointed its junior editor, under the present able conductor, Dr. Lees Giffard. It was an ultra Tory Journal, and advocated the political principles which Maginn always held. At this time his time was greatly and profitably occupied. He produced a political novel, called "Whitehall, or the Days of George IV.," which is now forgotten, but is as singular a work of fiction as I have ever perused. It would not be understood, in this country, with the personalities which are to be found on nearly every page, without careful annotation. Maginn also wrote largely for the Annuals—his stories called "A Vision of Purgatory," and "The City of the Demon," appeared in the Literary Souvenir, for 1828–1829, and were specimens of his "Tales of the Talmud," which was repeatedly announced as "nearly ready."

In the winter of 1829, the first number of "*Fraser's Magazine for Town and Country*" saw the light. It was projected by Maginn and his friend Hugh Fraser. They wrote nearly the whole of the first three numbers. Very soon, a great deal of the floating talent of London was employed on this periodical, which had the distinguishing points of fearlessness and power. The Gallery of Illustrious Literary Characters (which opened in June, 1830, with a pen-and-ink sketch of Jerdan, of the *Literary Gazette*, to accompany a very clever etching) was a feature so attractive that, ere *Fraser's Magazine* was a year old, its circulation was considerable.

The portraits in this "Gallery" were executed by Daniel Maclise, one of Maginn's townsmen, and now among the first historical painters in London. The series was not completed until April, 1838, when No. LXXXI. exhibited no less a personage than the Rev. Sydney Smith. A prose description, occupying not more than a page, accompanied each portrait, and, with one or two exceptions, all these were written by Maginn. I have been told that he would dash these off, as readily as another man would write a letter. They are more or less personal,—lively, witty, sarcastic. The series included nearly all the principal male and female British authors of the day.

The editorship of *Fraser* naturally tended to draw Maginn away from *Blackwood's Magazine*. In 1834, however, he resumed his connection with Ebony, his "Story without a Tail," and "Bob Burke's Duel with Ensign Brady," being among his new contributions. The "Tobias Correspondence," which satirically exposes how newspapers are conducted in England, was published in Maga in July and August, 1840.

An article in *Fraser* for August, 1836, severely personal on a novel written by the Hon. Grantley Berkeley, led to a duel between that person and Maginn. Berkeley, a large and powerful man, went to Fraser's shop, met the publisher there, closed the door, and, while Craven Berkeley (his brother) kept watch, beat the unfortunate bibliopole (a small and infirm man, in bad health) with the butt end of a loaded whip, planting the blows upon the head and neck. On this, Maginn informed Berkeley that it was *he* who had written the offensive critique, and in the duel which ensued, each party fired three shots, quitting the ground without exchanging a word. For the assault upon Fraser, a jury made Berkeley pay £100 damages.

"The Shakspeare Papers" were begun in 1837, and the Homeric Ballads, of which he published sixteen, in 1838:—the very last was dictated on his death-bed, to his tried and faithful friend, Edward Kenealy.*

But the evil days had arrived. As Mr. Kenealy truly says, "The rock upon which Steele and Burns split, the sole blot upon Addison, the only stigma upon Charles Lamb, that which exiled Fox from the Cabinet of England, and reduced Sheridan to poverty and shame, was the ruin, too, of the late Willian Maginn." Irregularities caused by such indulgences led to the cessation of his connection with *The Standard*, and, to a great extent, now excluded his articles from *Fraser*. Imprudence accompanied the other evil. He was beset by duns, pursued by sheriff's officers, and passed his time between imprisonment for his debts and concealment, in obscure and mean retreats, from his creditors.

In 1839, he was induced—partly by the promise of a good salary, and partly from the hope that he would by distance escape persecution from the myrmidons of the law—to go to Liverpool, as editor of a weekly paper called the *Lancashire Herald*. Uufortunately, the proprietor of this paper was hospitable, with an excellent cellar. Maginn became his guest and—the result may be imagined: he wrote as little and enjoyed himself as much as he could. His articles, chiefly political, were only occasionally good. The end speedily came. The proprietor had not money enough to maintain the newspaper until its pecuniary outlay was returned. He failed. Maginn returned to London, at the close of 1839, bringing with him some half-dozen

* Edward Vaughan Hyde Kenealy, a native of Cork, born in 1819, entered Trinity College, Dublin, while yet in his school-boy's jacket and cap. He has acquired a remarkable knowledge of languages, having translated a variety of songs and ballads from and into the Greek, Latin, French, Italian, Portuguese, Dutch, German, Spanish, Swedish, Danish, Romaic, Magyar, and Irish. In this respect he merits a place between Dr. Maginn and the authors of "The Prout Papers." When Francis Mahony ceased to write for *Fraser*, his place was taken by Kenealy, whose Brallagan Correspondence made it very attractive. He has contributed to the leading periodicals of the day—including a curious "Polyglot Paper," in half-a-dozen languages, in the *Dublin University Magazine*. His last work is "Goethe; a new Pantomime,"—a sort of Faust-ish drama, in poetry, full of learning, strange fancies, and severe, but not unmerited, reproof of Goethe's worldliness. Mr. Kenealy is a barrister, on the Oxford Circuit, in England, and in such good and increasing practice as to render it likely that he will not soon woo the Muse again. Of all Maginn's many friends, he was the only one to tend him in his dying days, and record the incidents of his life.—M.

chapters of a romance, the scene of which was in Liverpool, which he had called "John Manesty, the Liverpool Merchant." After his death, Mr. Charles Ollier, gleaning from Miss Maginn her ideas of what her father had intended to write, completed the work, which was published, in two volumes, with illustrations by Cruikshank, for the benefit of the family.

In 1840, Maginn commenced the publication, in weekly numbers, of "Magazine Miscellanies, by Doctor Maginn." They were badly got up and brought out. In his palmy days, such a selection of his best articles would have sold extensively. Now, only a few numbers were issued. The only complete copy (containing ten numbers, and extending to 160 pages, small folio) is in the possession of Mr. Kenealy, who has favored me with a list of the contents for my forthcoming edition of Maginn's works.

After suffering imprisonment for debt early in 1842, and obtaining his liberty by passing through the Insolvency Court, Maginn partly resumed his connection with *Fraser*, and chiefly depended upon a very inadequate salary for writing for a paper called *The Age*. His health was quite broken. He had been the able and consistent champion of Toryism for a quarter of a century, and had some reason to expect to be remembered and rewarded, when his party came into power. They obtained office—hopes were held out that he should have a minor diplomatic appointment at Vienna. He was forgotten. Sir Robert Peel personally remembered him, and, hearing of his failing health, delicately sent him £100 from his private purse. Maginn retired to Walton-on-Thames, (a rural suburb of London,) whither, in July, 1842, Mr. Kenealy, almost his only remaining friend—and a brother in affection—was summoned to his bedside. He was penniless, but very confident that a sea-voyage or a few months at Cheltenham, neither of which he could afford, would restore his health.

In this extremity, Mr. Kenealy wrote a letter to Peel, simply stating the facts. Immediate relief, from his own purse, as before, was largely given by Sir Robert Peel. Maginn's family, probably from dread of exciting him, did not apprise him of this gift, and he died, of consumption, on August 21, 1842, ignorant of the Premier's humane liberality. He was only forty-nine years old.

Maginn left a widow, a son, and two daughters, wholly unprovided for. Sir Robert Peel presented the son with a cadetship in the East Indies. A public subscription was raised, if I recollect rightly, for Mrs. Maginn and her daughters, of whom only one now survives.

Maginn's Magazine articles were not confined to *Blackwood* and *Fraser*. There are some papers of his in the *Quarterly*, and many in *Bentley's Miscellany*, and in the first and second volumes of *Punch*. Most of the flash songs, and nearly the whole of Turpin's Ride to York, in "Rookwood," were written by Maginn. Like most literary men of active mind, he was full of projects. One of these was the production of "Tales of the Talmud"—another was a work on the subject of "Jason"—a third was a tragedy to be called "Queen Anne." He told Mr. Croker that he intended to write a serious work on the Greek Drama. In 1824–5, he certainly wrote an original work of fiction, the scene of which was laid in Paris, the hero being a student who passes to the last resting-place of the Morgue, through a variety of powerfully-drawn incidents of riotous living. The manuscript of this work was in Blackwood's hands in 1827, was duly returned to Maginn, and has not since been heard of.

In person, Dr. Maginn was rather under the middle stature, slight in figure, active in motion, and very natural in manners. He was gray at the age of 26, and, during his last ten years, was almost white—exhibiting the peculiarity of bright, keen eyes and youthful features with the hoary locks of age. Of the two portraits which have been published—by Maclise, in *Fraser*, and by Skillin, in the *Dublin University Magazine*—I think the latter is the better likeness. It forms the frontispiece to this volume.

It would be gross injustice to a most able and amiable man to conclude this notice without referring to the affecting narrative of Maginn's life and death which appeared in the *Dublin University Magazine* for January, 1844:—a truthful narrative, in which I know not whether most to admire the scholarly intelligence which pervades it, the labor lovingly bestowed in the collection of facts, or the truly Christian spirit of humanity with which it speaks of such of the errors of mortality as "profaned the spirit, sank the brow" of William Maginn, as gentle a creature, in all the relations of society, as ever breathed the breath of life.

Whoever has to learn or to write any thing about Maginn, cannot do either, satisfactorily, without studying this biography by Kenealy. In this rapid sketch I have drawn largely upon that memoir, and shall have to use it, yet more extensively, perhaps, in the Life of Maginn which will be prefixed to the Collective Edition of his Miscellaneous Writings, which I have undertaken to select, superintend, and annotate.* Of all men living, Mr. Kenealy is best fitted to execute this duty. He writes to me, "Seeing no hope of a republication of his writings in this conntry, [England,] I dismissed the matter wholly from my thought, but not without regret that no such monument should be raised to his fame and memory. I am delighted that it has fallen into such competent hands as your own to collect his works, for the great American people, and I have no doubt it will far exceed any thing of the kind I could do."

He adds, "You have a glorious opportunity to edit a rare work, where you have no fear of libel law before your eyes. Maginn's best things can never be republished here, until all his victims have passed from the scene."

* In concluding this outline of a memoir, (for the full biography, with personal anecdotes and traits of character, properly belongs to the forthcoming edition of Maginn's writings,) I have to acknowledge a supply of personal recollections, kindly furnished me by Mr. Kenealy, by Mr. Richard Martin, barrister, (of the Middle Temple, London,) and by my brother, J. Campbell Mackenzie, of *Galignani's Messenger*, Paris. All of these I shall make use of in the extended Memoir, to be prefixed to Dr. Maginn's collected Writings.—M.

Noctes Ambrosianae.

No. LX.—FEBRUARY, 1832.

SCENE—*The Snuggery*—NORTH *at his Dessert*—*Time, seven o'clock*—AMBROSE *the lord in waiting.*

North. Wretched raisins—paltry prunes—infamous filberts!

Ambrose. Sir! sir! sir! sir! sir!

North. Walnuts!!!

Ambrose. Yes—sir.

North. (*cracking one between forefinger and thumb*). Another devil's snuff-box!

Ambrose. Most misfortunate. Depend on it, gracious sir, that I shall institute the most rigid inquiry into this affair!

North (*Starting wildly*). What affair?

Ambrose. How, sir, (pardon, I beseech you, for my presumption,) that pluffy imposter found his way into a picked peck of walnuts, purchased but yesterday, for the enjoyment of my best—

North (*with spluttering noise rejected*). Curse all apples! what call you the infernals?

Ambrose. The basket on your right, sir, is Ribstone—on your left, sir, Golden Pippin—in front, sir, New York—the row beyond you are chiefly Clyderdales—and in the distance you perceive, sir, the products of France.

North. France! Citizen-King! Louis Philippe! Baroness de la Feucheres! Last of the Condès!* Suicide! Strangulation! Murder! Murder! Murder!

* This refers to a sad tragedy. The Prince of Condè, an aged man, and father of the Duc d'Enghein, shot by Napoleon in 1804, was the near and wealthy relative of Louis Philippe. He had an English mistress named Sophy Dawes. To conciliate *him*, Miss Dawes was created Baroness de la Feucheres. To conciliate *her*, "the Baroness" was actually received by Louis Philippe and his wife. The result was, Madame de la Feucheres induced the Prince to bequeath his vast estates (except a large slice for herself) to the Duc d'Aumale, Louis Philippe's third son, and, shortly after, the Prince of Condè was found hanging in one of his own apartments August 27, 1830. It was given out that he had committed suicide owing to the distraction of his mind on account of the recent revolution, but the counter-belief, all through Europe, was that he had been murdered—as, from the position of his corpse, suicide was impossible. In December, 1831, the Princes de Rohan brought a suit-at-law, in Paris, to set aside this will, on the grounds that it had been obtained by improper means and that the Prince de Condè (to whom they were heirs-at-law) had not come fairly to his death. After a long trial, the will was confirmed.—M.

Enter in consternation MON. CADET, SIR DAVID, KING PEPIN, TAPPITOURY, *the* PECH, *and "the rest."*

The Pech. Loshy-days! loshy-days! loshy-days! Is Mr. North and master fechtin! Hech! if they're no in grupps!

Ambrose (shaking his black brows). Avaunt, vermin!—(*They evaporate.*)

North. How considerate in the creatures!

Ambrose. Don't try to cough it up, my dear sir, don't try to cough it up.

North (gulping gaspingly). Can't swallow it.

Ambrose. Heavens, sir! Cough it up, my dear sir, cough it up! It's only one of the seeds. May I dare, my lord, to give you a slight —— on the shoulder? Yet the very idea is impious—

North. Asthma—Ambrose—asthma!

Ambrose. No, no, no, no, no, no, no—sir! No, no, no, no, no, no, no—my dearest Mr. North—not asthma—not asthma—'tis but a seed—a damned seed.

North. Hush. Perhaps the hooping-cough. My childhood was not like that of other——(*Severe fit.*)

Ambrose. I'm sure, sir, it was not. I know you had none of the diseases incident to common— Oh, dear! oh, dear! cough it up, sir! do cough it up!

North. Ach! ach! ach! That shoe pinches.

Ambrose. This must indeed be the kinkcough. Oh, sir! do not grow so black in the face, if you can help it, my dear sir; for I fear to look on it—but I do trust you are not angry, sir—

North (crowing like a cock). I feel somewhat relieved now, Ambrose.

Ambrose. How happy would I be could I believe that were a voluntary imitation; but alas! I fear it was the wild work of the cruel complaint—

North (crowing again). Did ye hear that, Ambrose! If—I am—to be—cut off—you—will—at—least—al—low—that I die—game. (*With a languid smile.*)

Ambrose. Be cheery, sir—be cheery. After the kinkcough, you will have to go through the measles, and the scarlet fever, and the—

North. O mother! mother! why was your little Kit never inoculated?

Ambrose. Not too late yet, sir, for vacillation. Many public characters—

North. At my time of life, Am—brose! 'twould be fatal.

(*Severest fit.*)

Ambrose. Let me venture to volunteer holding your honored

head on my breast. There, sir—there, my dear sir—oh! say that you re easier now, sir! Don't speak, sir!

North. "Murder most foul, as at the best it is,
But this most foul and most unnatural."

Ambrose. I would fain hope, honored sir, that you are not waxing delirious.

North. Not much. She devil!

Ambrose. Ha! now you begin to look like yourself again, sir. Thank heaven, the worst is over.

North. Thank you, Mr. Ambrose. My lungs, that even now did crow like chanticleer, are comfortably clacking like a hen at brood. But my head has left a white stain on your black velvet vest, mine host. Let me wipe it off.

(NORTH *dusts away the hair-powder from* AMBROSE'S *black velvet vest—the same which Picardy first sported on being presented to George the IV. in Holyrood, by Southside.*)

Ambrose (*bowing with blushes*). Prouder of that badge, sir, than were it a star.

North. I suspect, my good Ambrose, that I have got the jaundice.

Ambrose (*smiling*). The jaundice, sir? No—no—no. That disease dare not attack a man of genius. Nature, sir, will not suffer such eyes to look distemperedly on her works.

North. Finest of flattery, conveyed in the noblest of sentiments!

Ambrose. In the jaundice, sir, a man sees all things yellow. The patient would think those pale pink panels *ochre*—nay, the snows of his mistress's bosom would seem to him a bunch of dandelions——

North. I have got the jaundice. All the fruits on the table are of one hue—that of the forsaken—nuts, apples, pears, oranges, all of the same green and yellow melancholy—and you yourself, Ambrose, *a glower of gamboge!*

Ambrose. In all humility, sir, I trust not. No hint of the kind has dropped from any of the household——

North. Because I alone have got the jaundice. (*Pulling a few shillings from his purse.*) Look there! If I did not know them to be shillings, I should swear they were guineas.

Ambrose. But are you sick, sir?

North. Very very sick—sick of you—sick of the world—sick of life—sick of myself! For what are we—one and all—but so much animated brickdust?

Ambrose. "Eureka! Eureka!" I have discovered the cause of your disease!—(*Laughing joyfully.*)

North. I fear, sir, you are becoming somewhat too familiar——

Ambrose. If I am, then banish me from Snuggery and Saloon *in sæcula sæculorum.* Forgive me, sir; but if my gracious master will but doff these specs——

North (loosening the pressure of the elastic silver). Creation has recovered its character—the whole world of nature and of art.

Ambrose. These spectacles, sir, belong to a queer creature of an optician, at present one of our lodgers, who has a craze for staining glass of all colors—but how they got here is a mystery——

North. How potent imagination! I was as sick as a dog. But are you sure, Ambrose, that my face is not like one of these oranges —in color, I mean?—for in shape, I believe firmly, that it is much longer.

Ambrose. Why, the rose on your cheek, sir, is brightening like the daybreak.

North. Ambrose, you are a poet.

Ambrose (like one of those down-looking busts). Why, sir, I do sometimes indulge in a little——

North. Flirtation with the Muses, when Missus is at market, eh?

Ambrose. Just so, sir.

North. Publish no new poem, Ambrose, till after the burial of the Reform Bill.

Ambrose. Just so, sir. You may depend upon it, sir. Politics and poetry cannot live in the same atmosphere. The one thrives on the foul smoke of cities, the other breathes empyrean air remote from the hum of man, in rural—or mountain—solitude.

North. Whew!

Ambrose (enthusiastically). For poetical inspiration, sir, nothing like a jaunt in a gig to Peebles.

North. With a sleety wind in your face, on the first of June, as you jog through that loveliest pastoral scenery encircling that "cynosure of neighboring eyes," the Wellington Arms.

Ambrose. A friend of mine is taking in arable land there from the moss——

North. That is rational! He must be a sensible man. To attempt improving a poor soil, seems to me the last stretch of patriotism—of the love of the *natale solum.*

Ambrose. I much fear you won't pay, sir.

North. Oh, yes! Wages, profit, and rent.

Ambrose. Are you serious, sir?

North. Marked you never, Ambrose, the potatoe crop on those lazy beds? None of your big busy green shaws, plum-clustering yellow: but they "are lean, and lank, and brown, as is the ribbed sea-sand." Woe-begone, they look as if some misbegotten abortion, the untimely produce of a conjunction between an old docken and a middle-aged nettle.

Ambrose. A bad cross.

North. Very. Pull them up, and lo! a parcel of poteightytoes, like marrowfats, or the waxen cells of the humble bee, that "bigs its byke" in the mossy greensward, or among the roots of a thorn, on which the magpie stills her chatter within her round prickly nest, even by the roadside unafraid of the heedless traveller.

Ambrose. Boil them, and, sir, how scabby!

North. Then the barley-patch, pining in green sickness on the bosom of the cold, wet, black moss——

Ambrose. Fuzionless and plashy—in which the unherded stirk sinks up to his knees, for the scanty braird, yellowing long before it is shot, imprudently forsaking the more nutritious heather. Pardon me, sir.

North. There goes a snipe.

Ambrose. Living by suction, it contrives to keep soul and body together, sir; but 'tis a mere bunch of feathers, sir, for the very slugs are slender in such poor mud; and shallow water, crisp with ice nine months of the year, is fatal to the race of worms.

North. Does nothing ripen?

Ambrose. Nothing, sir—not even powheads. Few grow into froggies—and of these last, scarce six in a summer become full-sized spangers; yet spangers they must not be called—for they again are so weak, sir, that they cannot hop, and but crawl like toads.

North. Never saw I such stirks. It is wonderful to see such atomies walk. I presume they are bred merely for the skins.

Ambrose. I understand, sir, the tanner gets the bones into the bargain.

North. They are kept in countenance by the sheep. Never saw I such a spectacle of human misery as that old ram. His body is partially clothed with an extraordinary commodity, neither wool nor hair; but bare, bare, bare, poor fellow, are his hips; and what years of hunger and starvation are wreathed round his indurated horns!

Ambrose. All unfit, sir, for snuff-mulls.

North. Such a seraglio! Ilk ewie but a pound o' tawty woo'—here and there one with a four-legged something staggering at her side, which may be conjectured to be her lamb!

Ambrose. Did you ever notice, sir (pardon me for being so bold), the bees in that region?

North. The foggies?

Ambrose. Yes, sir. Or the red-dowps?

North. Less than bummers. The foggies are of a dirty yellow, instead of a bright brown; red-dowp is a misnomer, for the black wretches terminate suddenly in a spot of mud—and what a feeble bizz!

Ambrose. And think you, sir, they have stings?

North. Something of the sort—but they have not power to use them—and the impotents are angrier in their wretchedness than wasps. But in the midst of all this misery, the Wellington Arms is by no means an uncomfortable howf in a sleet-squash. Seldom have I tasted better cheese. They import their own meal—on her girdle the gudewife heats into crumpiness a fair farl*—and she is famous for her hams. 'Tis a house of call for carriers, you know, Mr. Ambrose; and unpromising as is that bare exterior that knows no other shelter from the storm than sometimes a row of wagons to windward with every inch of canvass set, yet within burns a cheerful fire, and there may be heard the gurgle in which the heart of the weary wayfarer rejoices, the music of the big-bellied bottle vomiting from its short throat the liquid lapse of the clear barley-bree, whose smack reminds you of Glenlivet, "alike, but, oh! how different"—and awakes a passing sigh for the far-off Highlands, whose mountain-tops rise before you in a visionary dream. You know the Wellington Arms, Ambrose?

Ambrose. Yes, sir. I bate alternately there, and at Leadburntoll. I have generally found, sir, that in the absence of interesting external objects the fancy is more fertile——

North. Do you understand, Ambrose, the distinction between fancy and imagination, as drawn by Coleridge in his Biographia Literaria, and Wordsworth in one of his philosophical prefaces, in which he labors to tell us what poetry is, in despair, I presume, of being able to effect that purpose by his verses?

Ambrose. I read no philosophical criticism, but in the magazine. As far as I have been able to master the occasional hints thrown out in that immortal work, it seems to me, sir, that fancy is the faculty by which the human mind collects round any object of thought a certain conglomeration of corresponding and congenial images, united rather by some accidental and capricious associations, which consequently are, in comparison, feeble and evanescent, inasmuch as they are obedient, as well in their going as in their coming, to moods moving along the surface of the mind, than by those everlasting links of feeling or of passion, sir, which, though oftentimes invisible, are nevertheless always felt, when the capacity of emotion is brought into power, and the creative functions of the soul is at work to reproduce, and in the reproduction beautifies the essential and primordial elements of emotion, one of these being, beyond all doubt, intellectual perception, and another intellectual conception, thus gradually growing into new and original forms, which, when intensified into life by the true Promethean fire, are universally confessed to be, even while the mystery of their generation remains a

* *Farl*—a cake.—M.

secret to the minds of those affected by them to very transport, forms of the imagination.

North. Ambrose, we must have you appointed Professor of Poetry in the University of Dumfries.*

Ambrose (*drawing himself up proudly*). Pardon me, sir, my glory in all future ages will be, that beneath my roof were celebrated the famous NOCTES AMBROSIANÆ—more poetry in them, my venerated sir, and more of the philosophy of poetry, than in the Dialogues of Plato, the Περι Ποιητικης of Aristotle, Blair's Lectures, La Harpe's Course of Literature, and all the lucubrations of both the Schlegels, with those of Göethe and Tiecke to boot. A thousand thanks, sir, for your offer—but no, I must not—cannot—will not go—Professor of Poetry—to Dumfries. Appoint the editor of the Dumfries Courier.

North. He is to be Professor of Natural History.†

Ambrose. I fear, sir, that I have been allowing my tongue unwarrantable license; but your condescending affability——

North. No man is a hero, Ambrose, to his valet-de-chambre.

Ambrose. But a philosopher is a philosopher, venerated, sir, at all times—yea, even to the humblest of his admirers—to him who now glories in the name of "mine host."

North. "I think like a sage, but I feel as a man."

Sit down, my good Ambrose, sit down; and let me pour forth my confessions into your honest heart.

Ambrose. I obey. (*Mr. Ambrose sits down in Southside's curule chair.*)

North. The best bred man in Europe since the time of Lord Stair. Take an orange. Yes—suck it—and scorn silver blade. Sour?‡

Ambrose. Honey-sugar sweet, sir.

North (*lying back with shut eyes on Auchie's patent Sloping-Easy*). I am the most miserable of men.

Ambrose. Oh! say not so, sir. You who make all the world happy by delight and instruction.

North. Remember, Ambrose, that this confidence is sacred—that

* Which does not exist.—M.

† The *Dumfries Courier*, under the editorship of John M'Diarmid, was one of the best provincial papers in Scotland. It was distinguished, above all other papers, for its incredible accounts of eggs hatched with penny pieces in the centre, miraculous anecdotes of instinct, the growth of mammoth turnips and gigantic cow cabbages, two-headed calves, and six-legged lambs. What a man would M'Diarmid have been to conduct a newspaper on the borders of that part of the Atlantic which the sea-serpent doth most frequent! He might live for a century, but the sea-serpent would be certain of some mention in every publication.—M.

‡ The Earl of Stair was Ambassador to one of the French kings, and bore a high name for politeness. To try him, the king one day asked him to take a ride in the royal carriage, and when they reached it, motioned his lordship to enter it first. This was done with merely a simple bow of assent, and the king afterward said, "Lord Stair *is* a very well-bred man. Any other would have delayed me with apologies for preceding me, but my lord went in at once."—M.

not a word of what I am now about to reveal must ever murmur from your lips—or glimpse from your eyes—or pass in shadow along that capacious forehead. You must be mum as the grave.

Ambrose. But then, Mr. Gurney, sir?

North. Fear not Gurney. He is *hocussed.* List! Don't you hear him snore?

Ambrose. For some time past, sir, have I heard that sound, but I thought it was the water beginning to run again into the water-pipe from the roof after the thaw.

North. No—'tis fancy. I have drugged his drink—have given him a potent posset. After life's fitful fever he sleeps well—he will extend not his short hand to tell our secret. He awakes not till midnight.

Ambrose. A strange awe comes over me, sir. Remember, sir, that I have a wife and children, and that anything very dreadful——

North. Ambrose! If you have any tears to shed, prepare to weep them now—Blackwood's Magazine is the curse of my existence.

Ambrose. Alas, and alack-a-day!

North. "I am acquainted with sad misery,
As the tanned galley-slave is with his oar!"

Ambrose. Then is the sun miserable, while man and nature bless his orb, as he sheds the seasons over all the variegated earth, from his rolling car in heaven.

North. Seek not, my Ambrose, to veil from my soul, in such dazzling imagery, the sense of its own doom! 'Tis the great and gracious law of nature, that old age should have rest. Like some mighty mountain seemingly made of snow, deeper far its hush than of any cloud-range that ever breathed the spirit of its stillness far and wide over the cerulean sky, and beautified by sunset that seems to look with love on its stainless sleep, to my imagination, world-wearied, and now sore averse to all passion's strife, rises up the fair idea of repose!

Ambrose (*apparently much relieved*). I too, sir, sometimes delight in indulging myself in a dream of retiring from public into private life—of purchasing a small——

North. As Wordsworth sublimely says—"To be laid asleep in body, and become a living soul!" Quietism, fathomless as the sea, and as the sea transparent, when it is one with heaven, and ships from clouds you know not, so motionless hang they, single or in fleets, with shade and sunshine alternately revisiting their idle sails!

Ambrose. I have seen such a sight between Leith pier-head and Inchkeith, a hundred times, sir; but then I could not have *said that,* sir, had I lived a thousand years. Were I struck blind, I should *see* again listening to your words. They would be to me, sir, like sunbeams.

North. For such spiritual quietude, nature yearns "with love and longings infinite," as in the evening of life, longer fall the shadows from the mountains.

Ambrose. Sir?

North. Nay, the soul seeks not—she demands release from the bonds of this world's day-darg life; and, like waves agitated no more, she expects all her thoughts to be at least settled down into a tideless calm, even like that sweet line of watery light that strews with stars the summer shores of the Mediterranean sea.

Ambrose. I could go to sleep, and dream of the ocean.

North. "O blessed retirement! Friend of life's decline!"

Ambrose. What more beautiful place about all the suburbs, sir, than Buchanan Lodge.

North. Oh! the wisdom of old age, serene as simplicity of childhood! the light wandering in the west ere yet it fade in darkness! —as gentle and as gorgeous, too, as in the east the day-spring about to run his race in heaven!

Ambrose. Pardon me, sir, for not speaking when you stop; but I hope you will allow me to listen——

North. Instead of all this, there is that INFERNAL MAGAZINE, THE CURSE OF MY EXISTENCE, idiotically called monthly, but, in truth, an annual, a perennial, a perpetual, an everlasting, an eternal CURSE!

Ambrose. You make me shudder, sir—indeed, sir, you make me shudder. O, sir, say not another such sentence; or if you must, I beseech you to say it quickly, for this state of fearful excitation is worse than being in a shower-bath with the string in one's hand.

North. With a long pull, a strong pull, and a pull altogether—I began in sadness, but I proceed in rage. Maga holds her head too high, Mr. Ambrose; and, would you believe it, has more than once had the audacity to *cut* Christopher.

Ambrose. Oh! no, no, no, no, no, no, no, no!

North. Yes, yes, yes, yes, yes, yes! I, her own dearly beloved editor—so, in her wheedling fits of hypocritical fondness, she delights to call me—her Kit—her Kit-cat—her Norry Norry——have been—grasp firm hold of the elbows of your seat, Ambrose—A REJECTED CONTRIBUTOR!!!

Ambrose. I am sick at heart. (*Sinks into a comatose state, between a swoon and a dwawm.*)

North. The slut solicited me for an opening article to Part Second of this very month, and there she had it—in two sheets—The Hindu Drama; as powerful an opening article as ever did honor to the Cock of the North; when, whew! she shoves me and my article aside, for sake of an Irishman, who, with all his blarney, can not love her as I have loved her—and (*here the old man absolutely shed tears*) as I will continue to love her, in spite of all her ungrateful cruelty, to the last hour of my life. (*He sobs.*)

Ambrose (*in a state of somnolency*). Whruhu—whruhu—whruhu—whruhu!

North. I see—I hear that I have your sympathy, Ambrose. May then this right hand, laden as it is with chalk-stones formed by toils in her service—the ingrate; yes, may this right hand wither like a shrivelled leaf—these lack-lustre eyes, bedimmed for her sake by many a wakeful midnight, the little vision lose that still is left within their faded orbs—if e'er again—(oh! hear me now, ye spirits that delight in just revenge!)—if e'er again I waste ink in her cause—if e'er——

Ambrose (*with astonishing energy*). Whruhu—whruhu—whruhu—whruhu!

North. Was that a trumpet? Such air-born warnings are not to be rashly despised by the soul of man, when, troubled by passion, it trembles on the verge of some—perhaps fatal—vow—and may be about to sell itself to perdition—to the ENEMY! It may have been the voice of my GENIUS.

Ambrose. Whruhu—whruhu—whruhu—whruhu!

North. Well—it matters not, if a man's soul be saved—by what instrument—whether by a snore or a clap of thunder.

Ambrose (*waking, and turning a sleep-drenched pair of poppey'd eyes on* NORTH). Whawawharawbraw—brr—ach!

North. A bit of Miss Kissirving's unknown tongue.* I said *waste* ink in Maga's service. Now I shelter myself under the double sense of that word. I may write—Madam—an occasional article for your miscellany—but, mind what I now say—*the first rejected article shall be the last*—and I will go over *in a body* to the Edinburgh Review.

Ambrose (*starting up*). Beg pardon for not answering the bell sooner, sir; but I have this instant returned with Leezy Lightfoot, who is preparing such a board of oysters, sir, as has not been witnessed in modern Athens since the erection of the pillars of the Parthenon.

North. "Sleep hath her separate world as wide as dreams."

Ambrose (*apparently disabused of his dwawming dream*). I fear that I have sinned beyond hope of forgiveness.

North. I never *dreampt an oyster*. Seems it, in sleep, more spiritual in the shell?

* At this time, there were various exhibitions of "the unknown tongues" in the Rev. Edward Irving's Chapel, in London.—M.

Ambrose. Prodigious Pandores all! Meet for the mouths of giants.

North. Most melancholy must it be to the entranced spirit as it relapses into waking, to see the magnificent spiritual oyster of a dream dwindling down into the mean material conch, half opening its lips on the way up from Prestonpans!

Ambrose. My dream was twofold, sir. But I shudder to tell its other vision. Methought I heard you vow never more to waste ink—

North. Hush. What an inconsistent and contradictory creature is man! To have my addresses to Maga rejected once in a twelvemonth, sends wrath boiling, like a lava-flood, through my whole frame, from head to heel—and yet—thinking of the contributions she levies—exacts from me—almost in the same breath have I called her the curse of my existence!

Ambrose. She is your lawful wedded wife, sir, and you must stick to her, tooth and nail—I quote your own words, sir—to the last.

North. O these printer's devils! Like urchins on an ice-slide, *keeping the pie warm*, from cock-crow till owl-hoot do they continue in unintermitting succession to pour from the far-off office down upon Moray Place or Buchanan Lodge, one imp almost on the very shoulders of another—without a minute devil-free—crying "Copy! Copy!" in every variety of intonation possible in gruff or shrill; and should I chance to drop asleep over an article, worn down by protracted sufferings to mere skin and bone as you see, till the wick of my candle—one to the pound—hangs drooping down by the side of the melting mutton—the two sunk stories are swarming with them—all a-hum! Many, doubtless, die during the year; but from such immense numbers they are never missed, any more than the midges you massacre on a sultry summer eve of being eaten alive. Then the face and figure of one devil are so like another's—though people who have time to pay particular attention to their personal appearance—which I have not—say they are different as sheep—that tipsy Thammuz is to me all one with Bowzy Beelzebub; so that, bewildered by that infinite series of small satans,

> "At the close of the day when the hamlet is still,
> And mortals the sweets of forgetfulness prove,
> When nought but the torrent is heard on the hill,
> And nought but the nightingale's voice in the grove;"

I am haunted by the mysterious thought of "one-in-many," and the still more mysterious thought of "many-in-one," each individual devil having the might of a million, and the million having the intensity of each individual devil,—a state of mind, I assure you, Mr

Ambrose, which it is not easy for a rational man like you to imagine, difficult to describe, and impossible to envy.

Ambrose. Reverend sir—

North (*eyeing the door with a raised expression*). Look—look—look—there they come—through the key-hole!

Ambrose (*in superstitious fear*). In spite of the key! Nay—you are frighting me—sir. (*Trying to smile.*)

North. One day in the seven—even they—and I too—are at peace.

Ambrose. And one night in every month—

North. The Noctes Ambrosianæ!—"and thus the year spins round."

Ambrose. Self-tormenting genius loves often to darken its lot by the shadow of a thunder-cloud of its own wilful gathering; but then how it exults in the illumination of the lightning!

North. Why you electrify me, Ambrose!

Ambrose. Any power of expression I have, sir—and of course any power of feeling or of thought—I owe to THE MAGAZINE. Till Maga mounted the throne, Ambrose may be said to have vegetated;—since that era—he has flourished—green all the year round—and brightest of all in winter—like the laurel.

North. Ambrose! I envy the equable current—the calm flow—of your existence. Then 'tis much for happiness to be an universal favorite.

Ambrose. On that principle, sir, as on every other, I venture again to say, that you must be the happiest of men.

North. The world—the poor ignorant deluded world—thinks me *happy!* Happy, forsooth, because I live "in the blaze of my fame!" Pitch-black all the while to me is meridian day as the noon of night. And hideously haunted by phantoms!

Ambrose. Oh, dear! Oh, dear! Oh, dear! That I should live to hear this, my beloved benefactor!

North. Hideously haunted—because lovely beyond all endurance are the pale, silent, beckoning phantoms! Trackless do they come and go in soul-subduing succession, each with its face of sunshine soon overcast with clouds, and then dissolving in strange showers of tears! They are the friends of my boyhood—of my youth—of my manhood—and sheeted and shrouded all, as if rising from far-off and long-forgotten graves! Gliding away, they disappear; and leave behind them but the troubled memory of the names they once bore among the living—names overgrown by white moss on the sunken grave-stones—haply in churchyards that are now burial-places no more—the very kirk evanished, whose small bell tinkled the joyous school-boy to worship on sunny Sabbaths sleeping stilly over the green gowany braes!

Ambrose (*much affected*). We have all of us lost friends, sir; and, if the truth were known, sweethearts too—

North. Ambrose! To me the living seem the dead—the dead the living! The sole realities are ghosts. What, in my eyes, can any human being appear, whose birth has been within these last forty years? Nothing—less—worse than nothing! What can they know of Christopher North, now a puny, peevish, bent, decrepit, old gray-headed man? Once—bear witness ye bold, ye bright, and ye beauteous dead—once strong, joyful, straight, as the sea-bathed eagle, shooting skyward through the rainbow-fragment that gave the calm of beauty to the bosom of the storm!

Ambrose. We have all heard, sir, and we all believe, that you were once the handsomest young man in Britain—

North. Seeing is believing—but believing is not seeing; and the eyes that beheld me in my prime, they are all extinguished in death. Their orbs dust! FUIMUS TROES! In these two words is comprehended a power of pathos that makes existence a burden heavier than I can bear. Best—as said the melancholy Euripides—never to have been born!

Ambrose. Surely, sir, you would not have had a world without any inhabitants; or, if the world had had its other inhabitants, and yet been obliged to whirl round the sun, without hope of ever having YOU; why then, indeed, sir, I agree with you, that better it had never been created; but as it is, I confess, for my own part, I look cheerfully upon the universe.

North. Over them I poured the whole power of passion resident in my soul. I hoped—I feared—I loved—I hated—I blessed—I cursed—I—

Ambrose. No—no—no—sir. You never cursed any mould of clay, however mean, that was shapen by the hand of God.

North. Mean! Mighty—Ambrose—and magnificent. There were giants in those days—and then the daughters of earth were like denizens of Heaven. With them

> "I strove with weapons made of clay,
> And conquer'd in the world's own way;"

with them my soul blended in bliss ineffable—while Hate, in its grandeur, was dear to my spirit as in its gentleness was Love. But now-a-days, the things called women are but as dolls flung scornfully by adolescents into a corner, discovering them to be but smeared wood; and as for those other moveables, men, they seem to me all Cockneys, so far below contempt, as to be safe from that crutch which owes it to itself to smite no perishable body uninhabited by an immortal spirit.

Ambrose. Sumphs say, sir, you are not sufficiently severe this season.

North. Wait. You have read Homer, Mr. Ambrose? The Iliad?

Ambrose. The Critiques on Sotheby in the Magazine, sir, which I feel assured are superior to the original.*

North. To me there is nothing in all the Iliad so affecting as the character of Nestor.

Ambrose. Till I was set right by your matchless critiques, sir, I had always imagined that Nestor was a heathen god; whereas now, I find that he was, what is far better, a wise old man like yourself, sir, whom the chiefs of his country consulted on all state affairs.

North. What made you think him a god?

Ambrose. Because my grandfather, who was a schoolmaster in Yorkshire, called our parrot Nestor—our parrot, sir, that you may now hear——

North. I have lost a link, surely, Ambrose, in the chain of your reasoning; for why should that have convinced you that Nestor was a heathen god?

Ambrose. My grandfather, sir, was a learned man, and had a mastiff, sir, whom he called Jupiter.

North. Oh. But what is the wretch screeching? "List! O list! if ever thou didst thy grandfather love!" I ask you again, sir, what is the wretch screeching?

Ambrose (*in great confusion and alarm*). 'Pon honor—sir—'pon conscience—as I hope to be—

North. O Ambrose! Ambrose! The enemy is within the gates! But if the Apostle Poll preached such politics, he must be plucked, nor one feather left to cover his nakedness. The wretch has grown a radical within sound of the Snuggery. With his thick, dry, Indian-rubber-like scoop of a tongue, the green goose gutturalizes, "Reform! Reform! Reform!" "The Bill! the whole Bill, and nothing but the Bill!" I am sorry to find that there is a reaction in favor of the measure. How is this, sir? Mr. Ambrose, how is this?

Ambrose. Availing themselves, sir, of my occasional absence from home, as a member of various committees on affairs of police, some members of the Political Union have insinuated themselves through the folding-doors, and sometimes succeeded in establishing themselves unsuspected in the parrot-parlor, Of course, the first thing they did was to set all their wits at work to corrupt the principles of the creature in the cage, who, I grieve to say it, has committed to memory a number of expressions, which, according to the doctrine of constructive treason, might, were he brought to trial at the instance of the Right Honorable Francis Jeffrey, Lord

* William Sotheby, author of Homeric translations, on which Wilson wrote several eloquent articles.—He was glanced at by Byron, who said, speaking of the Turkish women—

"No bustling Botherbys have they to show 'em—
That charming passage in the last new Poem."—M.

Advocate for Scotland, and convicted, subject him to capital punishment.*

North. Not the first parrot that has thus *suffered*, while his teachers have escaped. Ludicrous were it, but that 'twould be most lamentable, to see the Apostle Poll, as you facetiously call him, executed for high-treason. Only think of the hangman holding up his dissevered development over the edge of the scaffold, and crying, "This is the head of a traitor."

Ambrose (*smiling shudderingly*). At once funny and fearsome, sir.

North. But you must contrive to exclude the Political Unionists.† The prosperity depends on the respectability of the house.

Ambrose. One of my waiters, sir, was so infatuated as, unknown of course to me, to become a member of the Union—bribed by the offer of an office-bearership.

North. What! Sir David?

Ambrose. Oh! no, no, no, no, sir!

North. King Pepin?

Ambrose. Oh! no, no, no, no, no, sir!

North. Tappitoury?

Ambrose. Oh! no, no, no, no, no, no, sir; oh no, no!

North. The Pech?

Ambrose. Oh! oh! oh! no, no, no, no, no, no, no, no, sir! Oh! no, no, no!

North. Who the devil then? Mon. Cadet?

Ambrose. Heaven forbid! You might as soon suspect me, your devoted servant, sir, till death, of being President. 'Twas an idle fellow you never saw—a sort of boots—

North. Just so. But I was directing your attention, Ambrose, to the character of Nestor in the Iliad. To *me* his long speech to Achilles, on receiving from that most courteous of all heroes a prize due to his former exploits in war and in the Games, is more pathetic than the last interview between Hector and Andromache.

Ambrose. May I be permitted to say, since you have deigned, not only to let me be seated, but even to converse with you, sir—a privilege which I humbly hope I have not abused; and which, were I ever to abuse, might my head shake, and my limbs dwine away in a general palsy—may I venture on the strength of that gracious smile to say, "That in the whole range of inspiration," to borrow a beautiful phrase from the Magazine, as far as I have travelled within it, there is not another passage so pathetic as that interview;

* Jeffrey was promoted to the office of Lord Advocate for Scotland by the Grey ministry, got into Parliament, where he introduced the Scottish Reform Bill, and failed as a speaker. He was promoted to the bench on the first vacancy.—M.

† In 1830, Thomas Attwood, who was a banker, in Birmingham, founded the Political Unions, their avowed design being to obtain Parliamentary Reform. In a short time, most of the working classes entered this fraternity, and in 1831–2, seriously threatened and contemplated marching upon London to compel Parliament to pass the Reform Bill.—M.

that is to say, sir, as you have brought it out into more mournful light, in your immortal critique on Southey——

North. Sotheby.

Ambrose. Pardon the *lapsus linguæ*, sir. As a proof how true to nature that picture is, as drawn by yourself, sir, and Homer, not forgetting Mr. Sotheby, whom I do not remember ever having seen here——

North. You will see him here, Brosey, before we all die.

Ambrose. I shall be proud indeed, sir. As a proof, sir, I may mention that it came across me, affecting me even to tears, last time I parted with Missus in front of the Black Bull, when about to set off for Yorkshire, on the top of the mail-coach. There was Missus, with our youngest bairn in her arms.

North. Astyanax.

Ambrose. The child's name, sir, is Daniel.

North. The strength of the city.

Ambrose. I had a fur-cap on my head, sir—

North. I know it. Fox-skin, with the brush brought over; like a helmet with a waving crest. Ambrose in the character of Κορυθαιολος Ἑκτωρ.

Ambrose. The bairn, sir, frightened at the fur, gave such a squall——

North.

"He spoke, and stretched his arms, and onward prest
To clasp the child, and fold him to his breast;
The while the child, on whose o'er-dazzled sight
The cap's bright splendor flash'd too fierce a light,
And the thick fox-hair, as it wavy play'd,
From the high bonnet cast its sweeping shade;
Scared at his father's sight, bent back distress'd,
And, shrieking, sank upon his mother's breast.
The child's vain fear their bitter wo beguiled,
And o'er the boy each parent sweetly smiled:
Then Ambrose slow the brushy cap unbraced,
And gently on the ground its terror placed;
Then kiss'd, and dandling with his infant play'd,
And to the gods and Jove devoutly pray'd—
'Jove! and ye gods! vouchsafe that Ambrose' boy,
Another Ambrose, all surpass in Troy (Edinburgh),
Like me in strength pre-eminently tower,
And guard the nation with his father's power!
Heard be a voice, whene'er the landlord bends,
Behold the landlord who his sire transcends;
And grant, that home returning, charged with oil,
His mother's smile repay the hero's toil.'"

Ambrose. What a memory, sir!

North. "*Mutato nomine, de te
Fabula narratur.*"

Ambrose. "One touch of nature makes the whole world kin."

North. Shakspere.

Ambrose. 'Tis a line I often see in the Magazine, sir, and I always read it with additional delight. I thought it had been your own.

North. The truth is, that my style is so like Shakspere's, that 'tis often impossible to know whether some of the fine lines in Maga belong to the Swan of Avon or the Blackbird of Buchanan Lodge.

Ambrose. I fear, sir, that I am sitting too long here—but such is the witchcraft—pardon me if there be any abuse of that word—of your conversation, my honored master, that several times, when I have attempted within the last quarter of an hour to rise, it has been as if my coat-tails were fastened to the wood of the chair with nails, and my breeches glued——

North. Don't crowd too many images together, Ambrose. 'Tis the crying sin alike of my own written and oral discourse. The same *splendida vitia* are often apparent in your style; yet prodigality is better than poverty, and the most lavish profusion preferable to a niggardly prudence.

Ambrose (*making violent but fruitless efforts to rise*). If I do go, I must carry the chair along with me, sir.

North. You must on no account do that, Ambrose, for I expect Mr. Tickler this evening, and he will rage if he miss his free-and-easy. You have done me much good, my dear Mr. Ambrose; and that mild pleasant face of yours,

"The soul, the music breathing from that face,"

charms away the blue devils into their native limbo.

Ambrose. Should Mr. Tickler see me sitting in his chair, he will certainly put me to death.

North. Shallow critics, Ambrose, have seen in Nestor but the personification of garrulous old age—old age wise indeed from experience, back-thought being fore-thought—but still interesting, chiefly because his garrulity is true to nature, yielding unconsciously to the prosiness of dotage. True that he avails himself, of course, of his privileges of uninterrupted and endless discourse. But what colors it all with an air of melancholy? That not one is alive who witnessed his doings in the days of old! With him now all is but sayings; and though surrounding heroes, in their youth or their prime, hear his words, how languidly must they listen! The images of his triumphs pass before his own eyes alone—and visit not theirs, occupied with all their orbs by the glorious pageant. The aged hero, no doubt, desires that the living should be persuaded by his tales of triumph, that he too was great in his day, greater than any of themselves—only less than Achilles. But the impulse that bears him along on the stream of silver speech, is the imagined sympathy of the men of might whom his emotion re-embodies and reanimates from the dust. He forgets the world on which he stands a hoary orator, soothing many asleep. Across the chasm in which lie buried two generations, he is borne on the wings of desire and regret, and believes himself in his golden prime, victorious in battle against chiefs whose sons fell afterward before the gates of Thebes. Speaking of them, he feels as if speaking in their hearing; as if the life, and the world, in whose brightness his youth rejoiced, had undergone no change, were not rolled away from all memories but his into oblivion. But the sadness of the decay—of the change—of the revolution—comes ever and anon across the old man's soul, and brings upon the dream of the past, in which he was all, the melancholy reality of the present, in which he is nothing. For to be eloquent and wise, and reverenced for eloquence and wisdom, is nothing to him, whose glory was in war, and who had been numbered among the heroes. His speech, therefore, is often addressed—not directly, indeed, but in an indescribable earnestness that can only be accounted for by its holding communion with the spirit of the times gone by—to the heroes coeval with his prime; sometimes it seems to be almost a soliloquy—and in soliloquies, how strangely are we separated by passionate imagination into two selves!—and then again, it is so shaped as to gain credence from the living, whose sympathies, faint and dull as they must needs be, are yearned for, because they are human, and because their expression, though but in the silence of the *listening eye*—and the eye does listen along with the ear—reminds him of the flashes and of the shouts that hailed his victories of old, when Nestor was as young and as invincible as now is the son of Thetis.

Ambrose. Very fine—very fine, sir. I remember, sir, once being in a mist on the moor, a kind of glimmering golden mist, sir, that kept opening and shutting, showing me now bright breadths of rocky heather, now the blue glimpses of sky; and more frequently what at first I knew not to be the tops of mountains—for at first they scarcely seemed to be stationary, but became, as I gazed, fixed as fate. Sir, you will pardon me, sir.

North. My conversation likened by Ambrose to a Scotch mist. My tablets! (*Writes in his note-book.*)

Ambrose. It is impossible, sir, for me to express my delight in seeing you restored to your wonted cheerfulness, my honored patron. These clouds will—

North. Sometimes they blot the sun from the day, till life is like death, and then comes despair. Sometimes they but deform the sky, and then I see sights of pain or sorrow. Often do they melt over the atmosphere, till it is all an obscure dim haze to my old eyes, Ambrose, and Christopher then is Il Penseroso—you might take him for the author of Burton's Anatomy of Melancholy*—nor are such moods undelightful—for then it is that he is most musical, and chirps, at least, like a sparrow, plaintive in the night-eves, if he singeth not like a very nightingale. But on those bold bright breezy days, when the sun burns like a globe of fire, yet consumes not the asbestos clouds that go sailing unharmed across the furnace—then it is, O! St. Ambrose, that, stretched beneath "the umbrageous multitude of boughs," and eyeing through the "loop-holes of retreat," the far-withdrawing vale bedropt with cottages, single although not solitary, and round the knoll the parish church hanging, roof over roof, in one harmonious cluster—then it is that through these shrivelled veins of ours, the glad pulsations again begin to play, that, fifty years ago, were familiar to all our frame, and so inspired it with conscious energy, that matter was felt one with spirit, and the delightful union to be indeed life—then, as if born again—Ambrose—ay, even like a serpent shedding the scurf, and glorying in the burnished beauty of a new skin, that startles the meek-eyed flowrets that pass their days in shady places, far within the woods—ay! then it is—"the aged harper's soul awakes," and gives vent on the spot to a leading article.

"Wherewith all Europe rings from side to side!"

(*Loud clanking noise heard coming along the corridor.*)

Ambrose (*starting up*). Mr. Tickler! Mr. Tickler! These are Southside's cuddy-heels—beg pardon, sir—the iron crescents of his Wellingtons. I must be off. First, Timothy, you know, is proud as Lucifer. What am I saying—what am I saying?—God bless you, my dear friend, my—my—forgive me—but your honor's condescension this night shall never be erased from my memory—*Spiritus dum hos regit artus.*

North. Poo—poo—bad prosody, Picardy. Vanish.

(*Exit* PICARDY, *with a napkin in his hand, crestfallen into his customary manner as "mine host," and re-enters, bowing.*)

Tickler. Suaviter in modo, fortiter in re. That's the motto of St. Ambrose's, isn't it, my boy?

Ambrose. Yes, Mr. Tickler—just so, sir—of our branch—Southside (*Susurrans*).

Tickler. Ah! thou courtier. Have you provided relays of waiters for the oysters?

Ambrose. All harnessed, sir.

Tickler. Listen to me, Ambrose, with all the faculties of your soul. *Imprimis.* Let there be relays for—stews.

* Byron repeatedly said that Burton's Anatomy of Melancholy was the book out of which a man might easily pass off for an excellent scholar, so rich is it in classic lore.—M.

Ambrose. How many, sir?

Tickler. Six. *In rebus secundis*—scallops.

Ambrose. Six relays?

Tickler. Six relays, and let missus—my love to her—"be nothing if not critical" in her collection of shells.

Ambrose. How would you wish, sir, to have the——raws?

Tickler. You must establish the raws all at once on the board of boards. I forget its dimensions.

Ambrose. Nine feet by nine, sir.

Tickler. Eighty-one. Leave a moderate fringe of unoystered timber, which strew with rizzars,* interspersed at intervals, yet not 'like angels visits, few and far between," chiefly indeed for effect, for 'tis rarely indeed that either North (ha! North! how are you, my old cock?) or I eat much fin after shell-fish.

North. Rarely, indeed. How are you, Timothy?

Tickler. Rarely, indeed. Just come from hearing the Bohemian Chatterers.

North. They have been accused of being Whitechapel Jews.

Tickler. I did not, to my knowledge, deliver their mothers, nor have I even seen the certificates of their baptism in Bohemia. Perhaps they are natives of that Bohemia celebrated by Shakspere—and come from one of its seaports. Jews or Gentiles, Christians or Heathens, they are extraordinary singers, Kit—and all the four have admirable voices. They chirp and chant in perfect unison—bird or bard-like—and he who says they do not keep both tune and time must be no harmonist. Some of their native airs are beautiful—and they sing them like natives——

North. Not oysters.

Tickler. Don't be silly. There is no humor in mere nonsense.

North. I'm told the Basso Relievo roars like a Bull of Bashan.

Tickler. Don't be silly. I tell you again there is no humor in mere nonsense. The Basso Relievo, as you idiotically call him, does not roar like a Bull of Bashan. Next to my own he has the profoundest bass heard in public since Bartleman.†

North. How low can he reach?

Tickler. O. I go to Z. You will be amazed, North, with what I am now going to tell you, my old buck. By a *douceur* I induced the Bohemians to let me join them in a quintette—the finale.

North. *Coram Pop?*

Tickler. *Pro bono Pub.* Of course I put on the national dress.

North. The kilt?

* *Rizzars*—half-dried and half-salted fish.—M.

† The Bohemian singers were by no means entitled to the praise here given them. Their chief merit was their natural simplicity of style.—James Bartleman, abovementioned, was, in his day, the first bass-singer in England. Either by natural construction of his vocal organs, or by assiduous practice, he had obtained the power (most unusual for a bass) of singing, and even of holding the G of the second line of the treble clef in his chest voice. He died in 1821.—M

Tickler. Don't be silly, you old dolt. The Bohemian garb—green—like sharpshooter's uniform—belted round the waist—and broad-brimmed hat with plume of feathers. I gave my face a touch of varnish——

North. Which Ambrose uses for his top-boots——

Tickler. No—for his mahogany tables. It brought out the brown most outlandishly, and I frowned like Pharaoh. I pulled a pair of whiskers, and ditto of mustaches out of an old chair in the vestibule, whose bottom was rather ragged; and thus equipped I advanced to the rail, and bowing gracefully, with my hand on my heart, I addressed the audience in choice Bohemian, to the effect that I was the fifth brother of the most musical family in the universe, that I sang with "most miraculous organ," and had that morning arrived from Madeira, at which I had touched on my voyage from the metropolitan port of Bohemia, on account of a galloping consumption, by the air of that climate reduced to a walk, or rather a stand-still, originally, I believed, brought on by endeavoring to go below zero. This address, you may easily believe, was received with the most uproarious applause, and I took my place at the right of——

North. The Bull of Bashan.

Tickler. My brother was evidently jealous—indeed he bore me an old grudge—so at least the people seemed to think, who were inclined at one point of our contest to hiss him, but by putting my finger to my nose, I prevented that ungentlemanlike and unladylike mode of disapprobation.

North. By that most gentlemanly and ladylike mode of prevention—Hookey Walker!

Tickler. Well, my dear North—he drops down along the gamut, just as you may have seen in a gymnasium a strong-armed scholar descending a ladder by his hands, till he comes to K, where he thought he had me fast as in a vice. Poo—whoo! I came down waveringly, careeringly, and flourishingly, just as you have seen a lark from sky to furrow, without expanding my breast, or starting a single vein in my throat that towered white as snow from my shirt-collar, well flung back over my gawcy shoulders, from A to K; and dwelling upon the note with that proud reliance on my powers which gives assurance to the most timid of auditors that they are listening to a mighty master, without growing in the slightest degree black in the face, but simply showing such slight flush, or tinge on my cheek as the rose reveals within its inner leaf, while the zephyr turns it up to the light with the loss of its dew-drops, I challenged my brother with the tail of my eye, to L, M, N, O, successively, and successively; but there, my dear North, there he stuck fast in O, as a "pig in a gate," *at his last grunt.* I then began, like a wise man, to mind my P's and Q's; and one peal, or rather succession of peals, after another, had they been understood, would have told the crowds of people on the street, in front of the Assembly-Rooms, listening in wonder, as they thought, to the mysterious voice of the building, that the best of all Bohemians was on my way down from A to Z, which no sooner had my voice reached, that is to say, as soon as I thought it no longer safe for the audience to be kept at zero, then up went my voice in retrograde exultation—the expression is hardly accurate—till it reached the point A, where we—my brother and I—had started; at which point, what could satisfy the inspiration of my soul but to challenge the contr'alto, to terrify the treble, North, and to leave even tenor on his way, panting far behind like a broken-winded bogtrotter? Suffice it to say, that I did so—I ran up in that direction even higher, proportionally, than I had run down in the other; and if, in my first triumph, the power of my voice was like that of a lion laying his jaws to the dust, to disturb the desert quaking through Sahara to the roar-growl that silences the hum of the caravan, even as it first catches sight of the wheels beneath the palmy shade; so, in my second, 'twas in its silver chiming, clear as that of the bell-bird at morning or evening gloaming, listened to with delight by Waterton the Wanderer, in the wilds of Demarara,* while miles distant from the magician singing his roundelay from the top of living tower heaved over some cathedral-wood.

North. I give in—and shall speak truth during the rest of the evening.

Tickler. If so, I am off. I did not come here to hear you speak truth during the rest of the evening. You do not speak truth well, North; at the same time, I do not deny that you may possess very considerable natural powers of veracity—of truth-telling; but then, you have not cultivated them, having been too much occupied with the ordinary affairs of life. Truthiness is a habit, like every other virtue. There I hold by the Peripatetics. How unreasonable then—how presumptuous in you, to announce an intention of speaking truth during the rest of an evening scarcely yet begun—for 'tis but ten o'clock—you who have retired from practice, I may say, for nearly half a century? For shame, North—for shame!

North (chuckling—as is his wont, when hard pressed with geggery). Southside, by study of which of the fine arts, thinkest thou, the amateur is most speedily reduced to an idiot?

Tickler. Not easy to decide. I am tempted to say—music.

North. So am I. Your true musician is a jewel—your pretender paste. But among amateurs—and of these alone I now speak—how few true musicians—how many pretenders!

* Charles Waterton, traveller and naturalist, whose great exploit was riding a cayman in the West Indies!—M.

Tickler. Pretenders, but not impostors. Pretence is easy—imposition difficult—in music it requires at least—an ear. By the by, North, do you know the cause of what is called the want of a musical ear?

North. No.

Tickler. Then I'll tell you. Every man has two ears——

North. Indeed!

Tickler. And if it should so happen—which it not unfrequently does—that the one ear is finer—or coarser let me rather say—than the other—the two together make sad work of it—and on their tympanums there can be no concord.

North. Ay? But supposing the wretch in question has a musical ear, so far as to be in that respect on the ordinary level of humanity, and becomes an amateur. By the time he plays upon the fiddle with half the taste and quarter the execution of the common run of blind cat-gut-scrapers at penny-weddings, he presumes to find fault with Finlay Dun! He leads a concerto, perpetrated by a gang of murderous amateurs in a private parlor—and thenceforth expresses a poor opinion of Paganini!

Tickler. Catalani squalled—Pasta yelled—Sontag shrieked—and Wood squeals.* He lays down the law——

North. The Fa La.

Tickler. And while a vast audience entranced in delight, are still as death, he purses up his small disgusting round hole of a mouth, wrinkles his hairless eyebrows, perks his captious ears contemptuously towards the orchestra, and at the close of the strain divine, from lip or string, cheeps "Poor! poor! poor!" though St. Cecilia herself seemed to sing, and to harp Apollo.

North. Equally loathsome is your amateur in painting and in sculpture. Nothing makes even the most distant approach to his *beau ideal*. He is discontented with even Wilkie's portrait of our late noble King. Yet 'tis equal to the best of Vandyke's——

Tickler. Though nothing similar—either in conception or execution. No more glorious Highland chieftain ever trod the heather. Gazing on him, you feel the lines of Campbell,

> "Where the hunter of deer and the warrior trod,
> To his hills that encircle the sea."

The harmony of the coloring is perfect—so is the drawing—and the attitude is regal. There he stands,

> "All plaided and plumed in his tartan array;"

"every inch a king." The amateur lisps "'Tis too effeminate"—

* Finlay Dun, the best violinist of his time in Edinburgh.—Nicolo Paganini, who made the instrument all but speak.—Catalani and Pasta, successively Queens of Song.—Sontag, who sings almost as well in 1854 as I have heard her in 1828.—Joseph Wood, the tenor, and husband to Mary Anne Paton.—M.

having no idea of a hand but a bunch of brawn, or of a foot but a brogueful of muscle. Graceful, elegant, magnificent!

North. Chantrey's statue is distinguished by dignity and grandeur. With what natural and habitual grace the King holds his left arm across his breast, supporting the folds of drapery—and on the right how lightly leans the sceptre! The advanced right leg and thigh is majestic and commanding, and the whole figure that of a monarch standing proudly before the gaze of his loyal subjects in the metropolis of his happy dominions. The head crowns that bold broad bust with an air of empire—and from shoulder to heel, the robes have that wavy flow well becoming the princely wearer, easy in his state, and unencumbered by its pomp, as if 'twere the garb of his daily life.

Tickler. Chantrey in a bumper.* (*Looks all over the Circular in amazement.*) Where's the wine?

North. I am a member of the Temperance Society.

Tickler. So am I—but not of the Abstinence. A man, surely, may drink a few glasses, without running the risk of swallowing a couple of bottles?

North. Not without running the risk. At least you will allow Timothy, that there is less danger of swallowing a couple of bottles if you have no bottles to swallow.

Tickler (*ringing the bell violently*). *Enter,* AMBROSE.

North. The Raws! (*Exit* AMBROSE.)

Tickler. Ambrose—Ambrose—hollo—you deaf devil—a riddle of claret!

North. You may as well shout upon the wind, in a calm night. You may have a pot of porter, or two—but neither wine nor spirits shall wet your wizen this night, Tickler. Remember, I am—by agreement—Lord Paramount of this Noctes—there—read the RECORD.†

Tickler. I wonder what this wicked world will come to at last! The Noctes Ambrosianæ converted into a monthly meeting of the Temperance—the Abstinence Society!

(*Enter* PICARDY, MON. CADET, KING PEPIN, SIR DAVID GAM, TAPPYTOURY, *the* PECH, *and the* NOVICE, *bearing on their heads the Board of boards.*)

North. Behold the Procession introductory to the Feast of Shells!

Tickler. They stagger not, neither do they faint in their courses.

Ambrose. Halt! Make ready! Lower! Deposit!

(*The household deposit the Board of boards on the Circular. It creaks.*)

* Wilkie's own biographer admits that the full-length of George IV., in Highland costume, was not successful. Chantrey, who was the best bust-maker in England, was more successful with the king's statue, erected in Edinburgh.—M.

† A religious paper, edited with ability, on the Low Church side, and published in London.—M.

North. "Flowers of all hues, and without thorn the rose!"

Tickler. Have you numbered the city?

Ambrose. A gross and a half, sir; Mr. North bid me leave a broad border, sir.

(*Exit* PICARDY, *swinging his tail like a lion rampant.*)

Tickler. O you sucking turkey! Yes—sweet are the shells. How sappy, Kit, the sea-juice!

North. Mm—Mm—Mm—Mm—Mm!

Tickler. Intense power of palate.

North. Verra.

Tickler. Two dozen in two minutes. One—every five seconds—or thereabouts. Twelve minutes—at that rate—to the gross!

North. Don't—Mm—Mm—mind—me—Tickler—eat—Mm—Mm Mm—Mm—away—Tim.

Tickler. Mm—Mm—Mm—(*he lays down his watch on the Board of boards.*)

North. The porter. Hark you, my dear Tickler—(*drains the junior silver tankard.*) Did you hear my ears crack? Now I'll sing you an appropriate song—

STANZAS TO MUSIC.

WHERE are thy fountains, music, where the deep mysterious tide
That rolls through all creation's bounds its restless waters wide?
Though art may wake its dulcet strains, and bid the soul rejoice,
They're but the feeble mimicry of Nature's mightier voice.

There is a spell of harmony that reigns o'er earth and sky,
And tunes to one accordant strain the universe on high;
With songs the glittering host of Heaven awake the dawning light,
And pour their choral melody on the listening ear of night.

Oh! Nature hath a thousand songs—a thousand varied lays,
That send to Heaven's eternal throne the harmonious strain of praise;
The murmuring streams—the whispering woods—have each their own bright song,
And the mighty ocean proudly rolls in melody along.

There's music on the breath of eve, when, fading in the west,
The summer sun adorns the skies with bright and gorgeous vest—
The rustling boughs—the dying breeze—the soft and whispering rill,
And the voice of plaintive nightingales that echoes from the hill!

There's music in the glorious morn, when, waking from repose,
All nature starts to light and life, and earth all brightly glows;
Oh! sweetly on the gentle breeze those cheerful murmurs flow—
The lark's sweet main song above—the waterfall below!

Nor less when all is dark, and clouds the angry skies deform—
There is a tone of music in the wildness of the storm,
The thunder's diapason voice, the wind's tumultuous song,
And ocean waves, that, with deep bass, the choral strain prolong!

But yet, oh! sweeter far than these—kind feelings power can call
A music from the heart of man more lovely yet than all;

Though Nature sings her thousand songs on earth and Heaven above,
There's nought like that sweet voice within—the harmonious strain of Love!

Yes, minstrel, wake the impassion'd lyre, invoke the heavenly Nine,
The heart can tune its passions yet to sweeter lays than thine.
Thy notes are but the semblance faint—that speak, with mimic art,
Affection, friendship, love, and all the concord of the heart!

Tickler. "A childish treble!"

North. I am not one of the Bohemian chatterers. Yet at a simple lilt——

Tickler. You do trill like the lintie on the thorn. Allow me, sir, to repay the pleasure you have now imparted, with—the last oysters. Open your gab.

(NORTH *opens his gab, and* TICKLER *plops in the last of all his race.*)

North. These civilities touch!

Tickler. 'Twas but a—beard. Such is the selfishness of the most generous, that the last oyster is little more than a name.

North. Tip us a stave, Tim.

Tickler. I will. You know Beranger's Roger Bontemps.

North. I do well.

Tickler. *Mutatis mutandis.*

ROGER GOODFELLOW.

A SONG.

To be sung to all sorry rascals.

1.

Small sirs, so melancholy
  In patriotic wo,—
To cure your carking folly
  Comes Roger Goodfellow;
To live as best it list him,
  To scorn who does not so—
Ha, ha, this is the system
  Of Roger Goodfellow.

2.

At field the earliest whistling;
  At kirk the doucest seen;
On holidays a-wrestling
  The stoutest on the green;
Thus on in frank enjoyment
  And grateful glee to go—
Ha, ha, 'tis the employment
  Of Roger Goodfellow.

3.

Round Roger's cabin dangle,
  From curious carved pins,
All wonders of the angle,
  All mysteries of gins;
While in his cupboard niche, is
  A pewter pot or so—
Ha, ha, these are the riches
  Of Roger Goodfellow.

4.

To know the wind and weather
  Will make the salmon spring;
To know the spot of heather
  That hides the strongest wing;
To tell the moon's compliance
  With hail, rain, wind, and snow—
Ha, ha, this is the science
  Of Roger Goodfellow.

5.

For wine to think nought of it,
  With jolly good ale when lined;
Nor ma'am my lady covet,
  So housewife Joan be kind;
While of each old state-housewife, he
  Doth nothing ask to know—
Ha, ha, 'tis the philosophy
  Of Roger Goodfellow

6.

To say, "O mighty Maker,
  I bless thee, that thou here
Hast made me thus partaker
  Of love and lusty cheer:
As older still, oh, gayer,
  And jollier may I grow"—
Ha, 'tis a worthy prayer
  Of Roger Goodfellow.

7.

Ho, ho, ye wheezing whiners;
  Ye kill-joys of the land!
State-malady-diviners;
  Yarn-spinners out of sand!
On common-sense who'd trample,
  And lay religion low;
For God's sake take example
  By Roger Goodfellow.*

North. Thank you, sir, you have outdone the Frenchman! Heavens! Tickler, what a burst of literature there will be after the burial of the Reform Bill!† All the genius of the land has been bottled up for a year and more—and must be in a state of strong fermentation. Soon as the pressure has been removed by the purification of the atmosphere, the corks will fly up into the clouds, and the pent-up spirit effervesce in brilliant aspiration.

Tickler. Not poetry. "The wine of life is on the lees," in that department. We must wait for the vintage.

North. All the great schools seem effete. In the mystery of nature, the number of births by each mind is limited—and we must wait for fresh producers, Scott, Wordsworth, Southey, Coleridge—all the sacred band—have done their best—their all—but on the horizon I see not the far-off coming light of the foreheads of a new generation of poets. That dawn will rise over our graves—perhaps not till the forlorn "*hic jacet*" on our tombstones is in green obliteration. The era has been glorious—that includes Cowper and Wordsworth, Burns and Byron. From what region of man's spirit shall break a new day-spring of song? The poetry of that long era is instinct with passion—and, above all, with the love of nature. I know not from what fresh fountains the waters may now flow—nor can I imagine what hand may unlock them, and lead them on their mazy wanderings over the still beautified flowers and herbage of the dædal earth—the world of sense and of soul. The future is all darkness.

Tickler. Mighty fine. But how should you! In that case you were the very poet whose advent has not yet been predicted—and which may not be haply for a hundred years. Are there no younkers?

North. A few—but equivocal. I have good hopes of Alfred Tennyson. But the Cockneys are doing what they may to spoil him—and if he suffers them to put their birdlime on his feet, he will stick all the days of his life on hedgerows, or leap fluttering about the bushes. I should be sorry for it—for though his wings are far from being full-fledged, they promise now well in the pinions

* This translation was by Dr. Maginn.—M.
† There was a birth, not a burial; a few months later the three Reform Bills became the law of the land.—M.

—and I should not be surprised to see him yet a sky-soarer. His "Golden Days of good Haroun Alraschid" are extremely beautiful. There is feeling—and fancy—in his Oriana. He has a fine ear for melody and harmony too—and rare and rich glimpses of imagination, He has—*genius.*

Tickler. Affectations.

North. Too many. But I admire Alfred—and hope—nay trust—that one day he will prove himself a poet. If he do not—then am I no prophet.*

Tickler. I love L. E. L.

North. So do I—and being old gentlemen, we may blamelessly make the public our confidante. There is a *passionate purity* in all her feelings that endears to me both her human and poetical character. She is a true enthusiast. Her affections overflow the imagery her fancy lavishes on all the subjects of her song, and color it all with a rich and tender light which makes even confusion beautiful, gives a glowing charm even to indistinct conception, and when the thoughts themselves are full-formed and substantial, which they often are, brings them prominently out upon the eye of the soul in flashes that startle us into sudden admiration. The originality of her genius, methinks, is conspicuous in the choice of its subjects—they are unborrowed—and in her least successful poems—as wholes—there is no dearth of poetry. Her execution has not the consummate elegance and grace of Felicia Hemans—but she is very young, and becoming every year she lives more mistress of her art—and has chiefly to learn now how to use her treasures, which, profuse as she has been, are in abundant store; and, in good truth, the fair and happy being has a fertile imagination,—the soil of her soul, if allowed to lie fallow for one sunny summer, would, I predict, yield a still richer and more glorious harvest. I love Miss Landon—for in her genius does the work of duty—the union of the two is "beautiful exceedingly"—and virtue is its own reward; far beyond the highest meed of praise ever bestowed by critic—though round her fair forehead is already wreathed the immortal laurel.

Tickler. Her novel is brilliant.

North. Throughout.

"This morning gives us promise of a glorious day."

You admire good Latin verses, Tickler! Here are some—by that accomplished scholar, the Rev. G. J. A. Drake, who is willing they

* Alfred Tennyson, now Poet Laureate, has fulfilled the prediction.—Of the others named here, L. E. L. (Miss Landon, afterwards Mrs. M'Lean), died in Africa, in 1838, just as her poetry was acquiring a depth and power it had not possessed before. L. E. L.'s first novel was "Romance and Reality." Mrs. Hemans, too (who died in 1835), showed the poetic strength more truly in her latter days of illness than when she enjoyed health and the capacity for enjoying life.—M.

should appear in our pages, in which are sometimes set a few rare classical gems. 'Tis thus he does honor to the Hemans. Let me recite the lovely original—

THE FREE'D BIRD.

BY MRS. HEMANS.

Return, return, my bird!
  I have dress'd thy cage with flowers,
'Tis lovely as a violet bank
  In the heart of forest bowers.

"I am free, I am free, I return no more!
The weary time of the cage is o'er!
Through the rolling clouds I can soar on high,
The sky is around me, the blue, bright sky!

"The hills lie beneath me, spread far and clear,
With their glowing heath-flowers and bounding deer;
I see the waves flush on the sunny shore—
I am free, I am free—I return no more!"

Alas, alas, my bird!
  Why seek'st thou to be free?
Wer't thou not blest in thy little bower,
  When thy song breathed nought but glee?

"Did my song of the summer breathe nought but glee?
Did the voice of the captive seem sweet to thee?
—O! hadst thou known its deep meaning well,
It had tales of a burning heart to tell!

"From a dream of the forest that music sprang,
Through its notes the peal of a torrent rang;
And its dying fall, when it sooth'd thee best,
Sigh'd for wild flowers and a leafy nest."

Was it with thee thus, my bird?
  Yet thine eye flash'd clear and bright!
I have seen the glance of sudden joy
  In its quick and dewy light.

"It flash'd with the fire of a tameless race,
With the soul of the wild wood, my native place!
With the spirit that panted through heaven to soar—
Woo me not back—I return no more!

"My home is high, amidst rocking trees,
My kindred things are the star and the breeze
And the fount uncheck'd in its lonely play.
And the odors that wander afar away!"

Farewell, farewell, then, bird!
  I have call'd on spirits gone,
And it may be they joy'd like *thee* to part,
  Like thee, that wert all my own!

"If they were captives, and pined like me,
Though love may guard them, they joy'd to be free!
They sprang from the earth with a burst of power,
To the strength of their wings, to their triumph's hour

"Call them not back when the chain is riven,
When the way of the pinion is all through heaven!
Farewell!—With my song through the clouds I soar,
I pierce the blue skies—I am earth's no more!"

CARMEN LATINE REDDITUM.

Jam redi, dilecta Avis, ad puellam
Flore quæ multo decoravit aulam
Dulcè frondosæ ut violis olentem
Abdita silvæ.

Libera ego! non unquam ad te captiva redibo?*
Fessaque præteriit carceris hora mihi.
Nubila per liquidi sublimis deferor alâ—
Æthere cingor ovans—æthere cæruleo!

Despiciam longè subsparsa cacumina, gaudet
Cervus ubi croceis luxuriare jugis:
Despiciam apricâ quàm candet fluctus arenâ:
Libera sum! reditûs immemor astra peto!

Hei mihi! dilecta Avis, ah! vagari
Quis tibi suasit? fuerat cubile
Nonne pergratum, melos ut dedîsti
Nil nisi lætum?

Lætum ego visa tibi perfundere tempore carmen
Æstivo? aut captæ vox tibi læta fuit?
Si tantùm audieras, etiam graviora referri,
Quantus inest cordi carminibusque dolor!

Ingemuêre modis absentis somnia silvæ;
Et melos irrueret more ruentis aquæ;
Te quoque cùm mulcens, leni expiraverat aurâ,
Fronde torum cecini floriferumque nemus.

Me fefellisti, mea Avis? nitore
Usque perclaros oculos repentè
Gaudii, rore ut liquido, micare
Lumine vidi!

Indomitæ micuêre superbo lumine gentis—
Silvæ animâ indomitæ, silvæ ubi nata fui!
Per spatia ampla poli cupidissima solvere pennas—
Carpere, non unquam restituenda, viam!

* The fault of nearly all Latin translations of English verse is their giving only the *idea* and neglecting the peculiar turn of expression. Thus, in the first verse here, "Jam redi" does not convey the plaintive iteration of "Return, return;" and in the second, the "Libera ego" is but a weak reflection of the joyous "I am free, I am free," of the original. Archdeacon Wrangham, Dr. Maginn, and Father Prout (Francis Mahoney), have endeavored, and usually with success, to give an equivalent for every word of the original.—M.

Est domus arboreæ nutanti in vertice frondis,
Sunt germana animæ sidus et aura meæ;
Fonsque procul solâ qui ludere gaudet arenâ—
Undique qui circà dulcè vagatur odor.

Jam vale, dilecta Avis! evocavi
Forsitan lætos comites abire,
Te velut, sperans retinere amoris
Vincula cordi.

Languida si mecum membra et captiva trahebant
Quamvis Amor custos—desit Amoris opus.
Lætitiâ exiliunt vinclis, terrasque relinquunt,
Viribus alatis, Io triumphe! canunt.

Nec revoca sublata—novam nec finge catenam
Per spatium cœli carpit ut ala viam.
Jamque vale—ascendo per nubila carmine gaudens,
Ætheris hic subeo cœrula—Terra, vale!

Tickler. Worthy of Tibullus, or—Vincent Bourne.*

North. Great things remain to be said and sung, Timothy, of the sea.

Tickler. Before the reading public be sea-sick.

North. A mighty Marine Poem is a desideratum in the literature of the world.

Tickler. Do you mean a long poem by a marine? and if so, foot or horse marine?

North. Don't be silly, Tickler. There is no humor in mere nonsense.

Tickler. Plagiary!

North. Falconer's Shipwreck is a most ingenious performance—and affecting, not only in itself, there being in it not a few passages of the simplest human pathetic, but for the sake of the seaman who composed it on many a midnight watch, and perished in the Apollo frigate, when she went down with all her crew, "far, far at sea." Yet 'tis little read, I suspect; and has inspired no kindred but superior strain, though more than half a century——

Tickler. Seamen have seldom time to write long poems, Kit; and then their education is what it ought to be, *practical*, not poetical——

North. Their whole life is poetry, Timothy——

Tickler. Interspersed with some severe prose, Kit, as you would know, my man, had you ever been at the mast-head on a look-out for a lee-shore in a squally day when the master had lost his reckoning—and——

North. Hold your tongue. You are murdering the King's Eng-

* The Latin poetry of Vincent Bourne (who was sub-master of Westminster school, more than a century ago,) is remarkable for its singular purity and elegance.—M.

lish. If our William were to overhear you, or Basil Hall, or Marryat, or Glascock,* you would get "a dozen," you land-lubber, for your lingo, which is about as like the true sea-tongue, Timothy, as the paw of a tortoise-shell cat like that of a white bear.

Tickler. The technical language of no art should ever be admitted into poetry.

North. Sumph! How else could a poet show a ship sailing on whitey-brown paper, as on the blue-green sea?

Tickler. By flashing her into life and motion by the creative energy of general terms.

North. Good, my dear Tickler. Much may be so done—witness Campbell's glorious Mariners of England. And indeed a ship is, in the imagination of the merest squab, a thing so majestical, that she is like the devil himself—only speak of her and she appears.

Tickler. Good, my dear Kit. I owe you one.

North. But what then? Can not she bear being spoken of, aye, in the loftiest flights of song, in the language sailors love, the language dear to Britannia as she sits enthroned on the cliffs of Albion, and, who, long as tides obey the moon, shall rule the waves?

Tickler. Hear! hear! hear!

North. Dryden has been jeered by surly Sam for the use of some technical nautical terms in one of his poems—and justly; for never was there such *abuse*, such laughable ignorance, as therein exhibited by that illustrious Cockney. Mr. Place, the tailor, might as well call a marlinspike a needle. Now, sheer ignorance, on whatever subject, by sea or land, but especially by sea, assuming uncalled-for the office of rarest knowledge, is disgusting even in a great poet like "glorious John." Besides, even had he employed such terms aright, they had been absurd, bolting out suddenly in a single stanza, and never more seen or heard of, in a poem stinking of shore, instead of smelling of sea. But let a poet who knows and feels the grandeur of the character, and occupation, and appearance of the ocean-roamers, speak of them in calm or storm, in battle or on the blocks, in language ennobled and consecrated to every patriot's soul by the naval triumphs of England—let him speak of a man-of-war in a style that shows he knows a frigate from a three-decker, a cutter from a schooner, a brig from a ship, and the captain's gig from a Quaker's whisky—and Neptune shall be to him Apollo, the Nereids the Muses, and every line shall be a line of light—all a-dazzle with appropriate words, surcharged with the imagery of the great deep.

* "Our William" was then King of England.—Captain Basil Hall, author of "Travels in North America," and a variety of other works, died, insane, in 1844. His sea-narratives are bold and faithful.—Captain Marryat, the best naval novelist England has yet produced, was founder of the admiralty code of signals which bears his name. He visited the United States in 1837, and died in 1848.—Captain Glascock, though a lively writer, is much inferior to Hall and Marryat.—M.

Tickler. Hear! hear! hear!

North. No "technical terms of art in poetry." O sumph of sumphs! why sayest thou so? What! not of the art that lays its hand on the ocean's mane, and emboldens man to scorn the monster in his foamy wrath, as if he were a lamb lying asleep on the sunny bræ! But I speak of the science of the sea; and its language is in itself magnificent, many of its words are like winds and waves—imitative harmony of sound and motion, and light and gloom—

Tickler. Stop—stop—stop—harmony of light and gloom!

North. Yes—you blockhead. But—

Tickler. What do you mean, sir, by—BUT?

North. Would you weigh anchor in a poem, with a ship before your eyes, as if you were putting the mail-coach in motion from the inn at Torsonce! Is starboard a mean word? or larboard? or beating to windward? or drifting to leeward? or eating ye out of the wind?

Tickler. The wild ass is said, finely, to devour the wind—

North. Well, gulp away. Or the wind's eye?—or—but—

Tickler. What the devil, sir, do you, can you mean, sir, by eternally using the word BUT? Do you mean to be personal?

North. My dear Timothy—lend me your ears—here are some verses that give all such shallow and senseless critics the squabash.

THE FORGING OF THE ANCHOR.*

Come, see the Dolphin's anchor forged; 'tis at a white heat now:
The bellows ceased, the flames decreased; though on the forge's brow,
The little flames still fitfully play through the sable mound;
And fitfully you still may see the grim smiths ranking round;
All clad in leathern panoply, their broad hands only bare;
Some rest upon their sledges here, some work the windlass there,

The windlass strains the tackle chains, the black mould heaves below;
And red and deep, a hundred veins burst out at every throe:
It rises, roars, rends all outright—O, Vulcan, what a glow!
'Tis blinding white, 'tis blasting bright; the high sun shines not so!
The high sun sees not, on the earth, such fiery fearful show;
The roof-ribs swarth, the candent hearth, the ruddy lurid row
Of smiths, that stand, an ardent band, like men before the foe;
As, quivering through his fleece of flame, the sailing monster, slow
Sinks on the anvil—all about, the faces fiery grow—
"Hurrah!" they shout, "leap out—leap out;" bang, bang, the sledges go;
Hurrah! the jetted lightnings are hissing high and low;
A hailing fount of fire is struck at every squashing blow;
The leathern mail rebounds the hail; the rattling cinders strow
The ground around; at every bound the sweltering fountains flow;
And thick and loud, the swinking crowd, at every stroke, pant "ho!"

* Samuel Fergusson, author of this glorious lay, is yet alive, in Ireland, and has written much and well—but nothing to equal this, which beats Schiller's Casting of the Bell.—M.

Leap out, leap out, my masters; leap out and lay on load!
Let's forge a goodly anchor: a bower, thick and broad:
For a heart of oak is hanging on every blow, I bode;
And I see the good ship riding, all in a perilous road,
The low reef roaring on her lee; the roll of ocean pour'd
From stem to stern, sea after sea; the mainmast by the board;
The bulwarks down; the rudder gone; the boats stove at the chains;
But courage still, brave mariners—the bower yet remains,
And not an inch to flinch he deigns save when ye pitch sky high,
Then moves his head, as though he said, "Fear nothing—here am I!"

Swing in your strokes in order; let foot and hand keep time,
Your blows make music sweeter far than any steeple's chime;
But while ye swing your sledges, sing; and let the burthen be,
The anchor is the anvil king, and royal craftsmen we!
Strike in, strike in—the sparks begin to dull their rustling red;
Our hammers ring with sharper din, our work will soon be sped:
Our anchor soon must change his bed of fiery rich array,
For a hammock at the roaring bows, or an oozy couch of clay;
Our anchor soon must change the lay of merry craftsmen here,
For the yeo-heave-o, and the heave-away, and the sighing seaman's cheer,
When, weighing slow, at eve they go, far, far from love and home;
And sobbing sweethearts, in a row, wail o'er the ocean foam.

In livid and obdurate gloom he darkens down at last;
A shapely one he is, and strong, as e'er from cat was cast—
O trusted and trustworthy guard, if thou hadst life like me,
What pleasures would thy toils reward beneath the deep green sea!
O deep sea-diver, who might then behold such sights as thou?
The hoary monster's palaces! methinks what joy 'twere now
To go plumb plunging down amid the assembly of the whales,
And feel the churn'd sea round me boil beneath their scourging tails!
Then deep in tangle-woods to fight the fierce sea unicorn,
And send him foiled and bellowing back, for all his ivory horn;
To leave the subtle sworder-fish of bony blade forlorn;
And for the ghastly-grinning shark to laugh his jaws to scorn;
To leap down on the kraken's back, where 'mid Norwegian isles
He lies, a lubber anchorage for sudden shallow'd miles;
Till snorting, like an under-sea volcano, off he rolls;
Meanwhile to swing, a-buffeting the far astonished shoals
Of his back-browsing ocean-calves; or, haply in a cove,
Shell-strown, and consecrate of old to some Undinè's love,
To find the long-hair'd mermaidens; or, hard by icy lands,
To wrestle with the sea-serpent, upon cerulean sands.

O broad-armed fisher of the deep, whose sports can equal thine?
The Dolphin weighs a thousand tons, that tugs thy cable line;
And night by night, 'tis thy delight, thy glory day by day,
Through sable sea and breaker white, the giant game to play—
But shamer of our little sports! forgive the name I gave—
A fisher's joy is to destroy—thine office is to save.
O lodger in the sea-kings' halls, couldst thou but understand
Whose be the white bones by thy side, or who that dripping band,
Slow swaying in the heaving wave, that round about thee bend,
With sounds like breakers in a dream blessing their ancient friend—
Oh, couldst thou know what heroes glide with larger steps round thee
Thine iron side would swell with pride; thou'dst leap within the sea

Give honor to their memories who left the pleasant strand,
To shed their blood so freely for the love of father-land—
Who left their chance of quiet age and grassy churchyard grave,
So freely, for a restless bed amid the tossing wave—
Oh, though our anchor may not be all I have fondly sung,
Honor him for their memory, whose bones he goes among!

Tickler. That will do. Three cheers—my old boy—for the Wooden Walls! (*Hurra! hurra! hurra!*)

North. Had I kept to the navy, Tim, 'tis needless to say who had won Trafalgar.

Tickler. Kept to the navy! So you were once a Middy!

North. I served before the mast—a volunteer.

Tickler. Pressed at Portsmouth, while sowing your wild oats. Poor Poll! But is the "Forging of the Anchor" your own—Kit?

North. I wish it were. But the world will yet hear of the writer. Belfast gave him birth—I believe—and he bears the same name with the true poet of our own Scotland—Fergusson. Maga will be proud of introducing him to the world. There are not such a noble race of men in the wide world as our sailors and soldiers—and I rejoice to see that they have their own organ now to record and to emblazon the deeds of the brave—to defend their rights and privileges—and vindicate, against all shabby civilians, the character of their order—the United Service Journal.*

Tickler. A spirit-stirring work, full of useful instruction in these troubled times—North.

North. Contributed—edited—read by men—and gentlemen—and I will add—Christians. For, war there must be in this world, for some centuries to come; and therefore let us fight with as much humanity as is consistent with the end in view, the overthrow or destruction of all our enemies.

Tickler. What is the meaning of all this savage slang in the Radical newspapers against some article or other in the last number of that admirable Journal?

North. Some say there's a secret under it; it seems to my simple and unsuspecting mind, the pure spite of baffled sedition and rebellion. Some excellent soldier, whose countenance would get as red as his coat at the thought of shame befalling a brother in arms, when called upon to preserve property or life from the wicked madness of an infuriated rabble, has therein explained the plan that the military ought to pursue with mobs whose immediate object is fire, robbery, rape, and murder, and their ultimate object the same as that of the demagogues who drive them to such desperate crimes—the destruction, namely, of all social order, and the overthrow of the state.

* The *United Service Journal*, a monthly magazine, published in London, and edited, for many years past, by Sir John Philipart.—M.

Tickler. Proper—and patriotic.

North. Most considerate and humane. But—then death to the hopes of traitors. Hence gnashing of teeth among the cowards of the press-gang, and vomitings of fetid bile upon the brave, who would fain save, by forewarning, the "swinish multitude."

Tickler. Burke got abused for that epithet—

North. As he did for many others as eternally truthful; and therefore I say "swinish." Let the ruffian stand forth from the rabble, who dares to insult us for that word "swinish," step into the ring, and strip, and in one round, Old North will give him his quietus. I appeal to two hundred numbers, nearly, of this Magazine, in proof of our love for the people. Their virtues we have eulogized—as have all our contributors; their sufferings we—the Tories have sympathized with—and done our best—(what pauper patriot, bankrupt alike in fortune and in honor, dare deny it?)—by pen and purse to relieve; are we, therefore, to abstain from the use of the most appropriate word in the English language, when we see, with our very bodily eyes, a whole legion of devils entering into a raging rabble, and transforming them, with a sudden change beyond the power of all the sorcerers of sedition, into a herd of swine, that, instead of rushing into the sea and grunting out bells and bubbles till their carcasses float filthily together like one multifarious carcass in a drowned death, have gathered themselves, under that demoniac possession, from the lanes and alleys, where they had their styes, of a great city, into the streets and squares, and obedient to their now *brutal* nature, making use of the *human* faculties still left them, to set the city on fire, scampering up and down the lines of burning houses, while the cry of the Radicals is sent up with the sparks that kindle the night-sky, "Reform! reform! tyrants! Behold and tremble at the MAJESTY OF THE PEOPLE!"

Tickler. Good—strong—true.

North. Would I hang the rioters? Not if I could help it. But if such incendiaries be pardoned—there is no law any longer in this land.*

Tickler. Unless their lives be spared, that punishment may fall on the—instigators.

North. Who are they? The MINISTRY AND THE PRESS. Not every member, perhaps, of the revolutionary Ministry—not every member, certainly, of the revolutionary Press; but those who

* This refers to the riots, in the autumn of 1831, during the Reform excitement, when the city of Bristol was for two days at the mercy of a mob (who were at once incendiaries, thieves, and drink-maddened sots), the castle of Nottingham was burned down, and the town of Derby was invaded by armed delegates from Nottingham. Trials, convictions, executions, and banishments, were the result. Colonel Brereton, on whom a court-martial was held, for not having acted, in the Bristol riots, as commander of the troops, with requisite firmness and decision, committed suicide before the trial was over.—M.

preached to the populace such sermons that the sole practical conclusion ignorant congregations could draw from them was—"Let us break their bonds and cut their cords asunder—let us terrify our tyrants—and fire set us free."

Tickler. The Morning Herald itself, a reforming paper, but conducted in an honorable and a *humane* spirit, has admitted almost all that you have now said—has proclaimed it; and the charge is proved against the guilty in high and in low places, unless indeed words be but empty air, and sinless, therefore, the mere syllablings of sedition. Poor Brereton!

North. Peace to his ashes. He saw not the "coming events," even when they "flung," not only their "shadows before," but their own grimness black on his very face; and if he had not his secret instructions from the government, which I do not believe, he had his open instructions from the press it patronizes, and obeying them, but with no congenial spirit, he delivered himself up to shame, sorrow, and death.

Tickler. The unfortunate man believed that it was his *duty* to behave as he did to the mob. The belief showed weakness of understanding, and caused conduct, in which the honor of the soldier was sacrificed to a vain desire and hope of conciliating the base and brutal mob, by treating them as friends and brothers embarked in the same cause. "I, too, am a reformer!" Alas! alas! And so saying, as a smith indignantly testified, he shook hands with the "lowest of the low"—and that, too, after he had declared his *fears* that they would *murder* the dragoons! For his own life, Colonel Brereton had no fears. Doubtless, he was personally brave. But—

North. And yet there are public writers who have proposed paying marks of honor to his memory, as a soldier on service—that the conduct, which his sensibility to shame drove him to expiate so lamentably, might be held up to the admiration and imitation of the British army!

Tickler. Incredible baseness!—if any baseness were incredible in the sulky, sullen, and savage soul of a revolutionist.

North. Yet had Colonel Brereton acted with ordinary energy, my Lord Althorp might—would have spoken with disgust and indignation—little accustomed though he be to "speak eloquently"—of the "Bristol massacre."

Tickler. Ay! Ministers, who are not only the courteous correspondents, but the humble, obliged, and grateful servants of Political Unions, by themselves denounced as illegal, and which passed seditious resolutions in their very teeth, are the likeliest men in the world to have desired to break a military officer for dispersing by the edge of the sword one of their own mobs. You remember the 7th Epod. of Horace?

HORATIAN VERSION (EPODON VII.)

ON MEETING THE BIRMINGHAM MOB, DECEMBER, 1831

Whither away, ye dirty devils?
Why have ye drawn your fire-shovels,
Shouldered your pokers, and left your hovels?
Not enough yet of your Bristol revels?

Not, I'll warrant, like lusty fellows,
Going to save us from Whiggery's malice;
Handsomely handcuffing down from the palace,
Old Touch-me-not to a goodly gallows.

No; but fulfilling the infidel's cravings—
Lending yourselves to your own enslavings—
Where are the Whigs, so rank in their ravings;
Asses so mad in their misbehavings?

Snooks, I say, is it cold or hunger?
What ails Snivel and Snake, I wonder—
All run mad after rape and plunder,
Bit by a Revolution-Monger?

Scabs of the Legion-leper? are ye!
Why do I ask, when your faces carry
Lechery, treachery, gluttony—Marry,
God send you a merciful adversary!

So stands England's penal charter;
Even so, in every quarter,
Shall a red atonement smart her
For the sacred blood of a Royal Martyr!

North. Ay! that's right—let's be cheery—I challenge you to a contest of alternate song. I give the subject.

A NEW SONG TO BE SUNG BY ALL LOYAL AND TRUE SUBJECTS

North.
Ye good honest Englishmen, loyal and true,
That, born in Old England, look not for a New,
And your fathers' old principles love to pursue,
Join, join in our chorus, while yet we may sing,
Spite of treason and blasphemy—"God save the King!"

Tickler.
Priests, Prelates, and Churchmen, who honor the creed
For which martyrs have bled, for which martyrs may bleed,
When Atheists and Papists your flocks shall mislead;
Join, join in our chorus, and loyally sing,
From fiendish conspiracy—"God save the King!"

North.
Ye that mean to stand firm by a Protestant throne,
Nor would see Church or King be deprived of their own;
Nor for bread to the poor would but give them a stone;
Join, join in our chorus, and resolute sing,
With the true voice of loyalty—"God save the King!"

Tickler.

Ye that know well the plots of fool, knave, and profane,
That the very first act of the Devil's own reign
Would episcopize Cobbett, and canonize Paine;
Join, join in our chorus defiance to fling
At their blasphemous rage, and cry—"God save the King!"

North.

Ye that know when Whig Radical Orators shine
And bewilder the mobs whom they urge to combine,
What mischievous devils get into the swine;
Join, join in our chorus, and give them a ring,
To keep them from delving—so, "God save the King!"

Tickler.

Ye that honor the laws that our forefathers made,
And would not see the laurels they twined for us fade,
Nor would yield up your wealth to the cant of "free trade;"
Join, join in our chorus, and let the world ring
With our commerce and glory—and "God save the King!"

North.

All ye that are foes to mean quibbles and quirks,
And twopenny statesmen, well known by their works,
That have used the poor Greeks ten times worse than the Turks;
Join, join in our chorus, and manfully sing,
With good English honesty—"God save the King!"

Tickler.

Defend us from hypocrites, save us from quacks,
From saintly Macaulays,* and some other Macs,
And from white sugar said to be made by free blacks;
Join, join in our chorus, and still let us cling
To our ships and our colonies—"God save the King!"

North.

From, of all the vile humbugs that ever was known,
That vilest and direst, Sierra Leone,
That makes savages howl, and poor Englishmen groan;†
Join, join in our chorus, the downfall to sing
Of malice and slander—and "God save the King!"

Tickler.

Ye nobles, stand forth, and defend us, ye great,
From political sophists, their jargon and prate,
Defend Church and King, and keep both in their state;
Join, join in our chorus, a blessing to bring
On the land of our fathers—and "God save the King!"

North.

Defend us once more from the Regicide Bill,
And the Bedlamite Whigs, that have caused so much ill,
And would bind our bold King to their absolute will;

* Zachary Macaulay, father of the orator and historian, was a warm friend of Wilberforce (who was head of the Anti-Slavery and *serious* party in England), and died May, 1838, aged seventy-nine.—M.

† *Blackwood's Magazine* always contended that the British settlement, at Sierra-Leone, was a mere job, to benefit Macaulay, by opening a new market for his mercantile house of Macaulay and Babington.—M.

Join, join in our chorus, and still let us cling
To the laws of Old England—and "God save the King!"

Tickler.

From Lord Chancellors save us, who flop on their knees,*
And pretend to give up, while they bargain for fees,
And sneer about Bishops, and envy their sees;
Join, join in our chorus, and loyally sing,
From scheming hypocrisy—"God save the King!"

North.

That give friendly advice to the Lords they should shun,
That keep the King's conscience, and let him have none,
And strip him of all his tried friends one by one;
Join, join in our chorus and faithfully sing,
From evil advisers all—"God save the King!"

Tickler.

From a new House of Peers, that shall pull the old down,
And recruit from the Tinkers of Brummagem town,
And set a *mob*ility over the Crown;
Join, join in the chorus, and let the rogues swing,
And thus be exalted—so "God save the King!"

North.

From national robbers, call'd "National Guards,"
That for pike and for gun quit their thimbles and yards,
To hunt down the gentry, proscribed in placards;
Join, join in our chorus, and roar as we sing,
From Frenchified villainy—"God save the King!"

Tickler.

From a Citizen King, and a new La Fayette,
With his sword in the scales to weigh down a just debt,
And beggar the world for the whims of Burdett;
Join, join in our chorus—all ready to spring
To the rescue from tyranny—"God save the King!"

North.

From a dastardly Ministry, cringing and mean
To their sovereign mob, and reserving their spleen
To insult and to bully—a woman—a Queen!
Join, join in our chorus—true homage we bring
To the wife of our Monarch†—and "God save the King!"

Tickler.

Emancipate Ireland once more from the thirst
Of rapine and murder, with which she is cursed,
From Prime-Minister Sheil, and O'Connell the First;

* The allusion is to Brougham, who was then Lord Chancellor, and concluded his speech on the Reform Bill, when it came before the Lords, by entreating them, "Yea, even on bended knee," to pause before they rejected a measure which the British nation were resolved to have. He also recommended the Bishops, if they meant to vote against the Bill, "to set their house in order."—M.

† Queen Adelaide, wife of William IV., was what is called "a red-hot tory," and very much opposed to the Reform Bill. In November, 1834, when the Melbourne Cabinet was dismissed a notice appeared in the *Times* to this effect, "The Ministry are turned out—the Queen has done it all." This notice was attributed to Brougham.—William IV. died in 1837, and Adelaide (who had a dowry of £100,000 a year, besides other emoluments and rent-free palaces in and near London), survived him more than twelve years.—M.

Join, join in our chorus, and spurn all who wring
From the beggar his pittance—here's "God save the King!"

North.

From defiance of law, and from Catholic rent,
On open sedition by demagogues spent,
And from Parliaments held without England's consent;
Join, join in our chorus—a downfall we sing
To all turbulent scoundrels—so "God save the King!"

Tickler.

Brave William, stand forth from your Radical rout,
And trust your old Peers, that will stand you about;
And, oh! above all, kick your Ministers out!
And hark to our chorus—for that's the true thing,
Hurrah for our country—and "God save the King!"

North.

And if they cling fast, wrest them off like a winch,
Though they bully and storm with their mobs, never flinch,
Be the King of Old England, ay, every inch;
And fear not your people will thankfully sing
With true hearts and harmony—"God save the King!"

(*Left sitting.*)

No. LXI.—APRIL, 1832.

SCENE—*The Blue Parlor—Time, Six o'clock—Occupation, Wine, Dessert, &c., &c.—Present,* NORTH, TICKLER, YOUNG GENTLEMAN.

North. German literature, Hal, is all very well in its way, and Maga was the first periodical work in this country that did any thing like justice to it. She confined not herself to mere criticism, but gave specimens—translations of many of the finest things executed in the finest style by Lockhart, De Quincey, Gillies, Blair, Mrs. Smythe, Mrs. Busk, and other ladies and gentlemen of genius and erudition, who in general improved upon their originals, often changing geese into swans, and barn-door fowls into birds of Paradise.

Tickler. Some years having elapsed since the last of those articles, I begin to breathe more freely now, North, in reliance on your promise to afflict the world no more with such visitations.

North. They were indeed severe.

Tickler. Yet such is the natural buoyancy of my spirit, that, even during those dismal days, when no man could assure himself for a month against the black vomit, a burst of sunshine would occasionally make me happy in the midst of the misery of all your readers; or if happy be too strong a word, pleased with life, in spite of the liability of my existence to the embitterment breathed from the conviction, too often recurring, that Goethe was not yet dead, but growing more grievously garrulous as he continued to write his way to the grave.

Y. G. I beseech you, Mr. Tickler, not to be so sarcastic on "The Master."

Tickler. Ay, there is an appellation sufficient to sicken a horse. He has little credit in his scholars, for, with two or three brilliant exceptions, they are sumphs.

North. It is indeed laughable to hear obscure and muddy dunces acknowledge in jargon that would have seemed queer even among the builders of the Tower of Babel on the day of the confusion of tongues, the obligations their intellects, forsooth, ay, their intellects, labor under to the "Illustrious Sage."

Tickler. Old Humbug, Such jargon is not so laughable, Kit, as loathsome. The intellect of a fungus. Thomas Carlyle I excuse—he is entitled to be crazy—being a man of genius.*

North. And of virtue—as Cowper said of his brother—"a man of morals and of manners too!"

Tickler. But oh! sir, the impudent stupidity of some of the subscribers to that Signet-Seal!

North. Hopeless of achieving mediocrity in any of the humbler walks of their native literature, the creatures expect to acquire character by acquaintance with the drivel of German dotage; and, going at once to the fountain-head, gabble about Goethe. "The Master!" Yes—and I beseech you, Hal, look at the flunkies.

Y. G. In the soul of every "British man," delight in his own country's genius ought, I grant, to be paramount; nor can I comprehend how idolatry of Goethe could from any enlightened mind banish worship of Shakspere.

North. Superstition sometimes steals into consecrated shrines, Hal, putting to flight religion.

Tickler. Oh! the old Humbug!

North. Thomas Carlyle, my lads, has a soul that sees all that is good and great, beautiful and sublime, in the works of inspiration. And old Humbug, as you rightly call him, Tickler,—Goethe,—is, you know, a man of extraordinary genius.

Tickler. I know no such thing, North. Millions of men have some genius—thousands much—hundreds more—scores great—dozens extraordinary—"the stars are out by twos and threes" "in the highest heaven of invention"—and one only—need I name his name—by night the moon—by day the sun—SHAK—

North. SPERE!

Tickler. Now, why, pray, should any "British man," with the devotion of a disciple, prefer making mental pilgrimages to Weimar, rather than to Stratford-upon-Avon?

North. With Thomas Carlyle obvious is the reason. Shakspere has been long enthroned in installation. The glory of Goethe is yet—

Tickler. Won't do—won't do—

North. Carlyle's eloquent eulogiums on the Man of many Medals—for he is bedizened, I have heard, with paltry orders, and proud as a Punch of knots of ribands†—show that his fine mind is more possessed by the author of Faust than of Hamlet, of Charlotte and Werter than of Cordelia and Lear. He always writes as if 'twere impossible to be ignorant of Goethe and to know nature.

* Unquestionably a man of genius—but voluntarily yielding too much to its eccentricities, as shown by his peculiarly Germanized language.—A lady was asked, in Carlyle's presence, whether she had read his latest work? With a very sweet smile, she answered that she had not, as she waited for the new edition, which, she hoped, would contain a glossary to the Carlylean dialect.—M.

† Goethe was said to have been as proud of having been ennobled and decorated by the Duke of Saxe Weimar, as of having written Faust!—M.

Tickler. In that sphere alone will his mind deign to move—nor can you deny, North, with all your admiration of a friend so admirable, that he can not conceal his pity, perhaps his contempt, for all whose vision is confined within the limits of the horizon of England's poetry.

North. Enough. No man need be melancholy whose spiritual eyes have swept that range. Germany cannot bear comparison —for a moment—in greatness—with England. Set Shakspere aside—

Tickler. Suppose that he had never been born! Then had human nature not known "how divine a thing a woman may be made."

Y. G. "Two will I mention dearer than the rest,
The gentle lady married to the Moor."

North. "And heavenly Una with her milk-white lamb!"

Y. G. Bless Wordsworth for the exquisite beauty of these immortal lines! They link him with the poets whose divinest creations they memorize—Shakspere, Spenser, Wordsworth. Knowing well their works, I can reconcile myself to an imperfect knowledge of Goethe——

North. "The Master"——

Tickler. Oh! the old Humbug!

North. Setting Shakspere aside, think of the old English Drama. What has Germany to show in competition with that glory of the golden days of good Queen Bess.

Tickler. Golden days, indeed—before and after the rise of the virgin Queen of the West, whom none but dolts despise, because she was not so fair as that beautiful murderess——

Y. G. Whom she beheaded.

North. Show me the German Spenser——

Tickler. The High Dutch Fairy Queen.

North. The German Milton.

Y. G. Klopstock.

North. As Coleridge said, "a *very* German Milton, indeed!"

Tickler. A German Dryden, or Pope. All the fire of human passion that ever burned in all German bards, concentrated into one focus, would be extinguished by one flash from the Fables of glorious John; and indulge me so far as to imagine for a moment their misty metaphysics glimmering beside the clear common sense, and ethereal brightness, that pervades, like cloudless daylight, the noble Essay on Man!

North. Germany has never had, nor ever will have—her Ramsay, her Burns, her Bloomfield, her Hogg, her Cunningham, her Clare.

Tickler. Such flowers spring not from her sluggish soil.

Y. G. "Igneus est ollis vigor et cœlestis origo."

North. These are the representatives of the genius of our people. The "schoolmaster is abroad" but he made not these men. They are Nature's children—and she gave them an education such as Saxon never had by the Rhine.

Tickler. Much they say and much they sing of that river. Its water seems to induce a drowsiness unfavorable to poetic dreams—and I should be slow to suffer any considerable quantity of it to get into a jug of toddy intended for my own tipple. In great quantities it would kill unchristened Glenlivet.

North. Germany has no Crabbe. There is not sufficient passion in all her lower orders to furnish subject matter for one such tale as those in which that good old man delighted, so full at times, in their homeliness, of strong or simple pathos. Of what variegated texture, rough and tough, and fitted for the wear and tear of this weary work-day world, is the web of life in England, that it could furnish such patterns to such a poet! The hero of one of his most touching tales is absolutely a tailor, who, I believe, served his time with Mr. Place.

Tickler. No dung, but a flint.

North. The Germans admire Byron.

Tickler. And Scott.

North. All right. But do they understand those prevailing poets? Not they. Byron they imagine mystical—which he never is; and of all his works they least esteem the noblest far, Childe Harold. But where is the German Byron. That is the question. Such a "child of strength and state"—they cannot show among all their nobles. Yet probably Puckler Muskaw* conceits that he is like Don Juan.

Tickler. There's a vulgar beast.

North. Very.

Tickler. Begotten—one might conjecture—by some grovelling Irish bogtrotter on the body of some burgomaster's frow, who had shifted in her wanton widowhood from Amsterdam to Vienna.

North. The Baron de la Motte Fouquet† and his wife—I mention their names with the utmost kindness—are all that Germany has got to show by way of Sir Walter Scott—they are her "mighty magician."

Tickler. Like a big boy and a grown girl riding on sticks—equally astride—in imitation of knights at a tourney.

North. And no bad imitation either—the cane worthy of the cavalier—and the mop a palfrey suitable to his lady-love, who scorneth a side-saddle.

*Prince Puckler-Muskaw, whose pleasant and self-opinionated Tour of a German Prince, had just been translated and published in London.—M.

† The Baron wrote the beautiful and fanciful story of Undine, which has been translated into many languages, and was greatly admired by Walter Scott.—M.

Tickler. Of all German poets Schiller is the best. His Wallenstein is a fine drama.

North. It is; but rather the work of a great mind than of a great genius. His soul was familiar with exalted sentiments, and beheld the grandeur of the character of him he chose to be his hero. But Schiller had not a creative imagination. If he had, it at least gave forth few products; his muse had to follow the muse of history; and even then had power given to her over no wide range of events or variety of characters. He was no Shakspere.

Tickler. With more philosophy, he was in other respects not superior, perhaps, to Otway or Rowe. And in many respects inferior to both those best dramatists of our middle tragic school.

North. If the Germans really were what their most enthusiastic admirers imagine them to be, they would worship Wordsworth, the most philosophic of poets. But they do not. Some of his lyrical ballads are esteemed for their simplicity, and not for the beautiful pathos in which they are steeped, like violets in dew, "by the mossy stone, half hidden to the eye;" but few have read more than extracts from the Excursion. His poetry is too true to universal nature, to be understood by the disciples of "the Master." He is a magician—but has no dealings with the devil. He confines himself to earth and heaven.

Tickler. And leaves the Gentleman in Black to George Cruikshank.

North. His angels and fiends are human thoughts and feelings, and he can awake them at will from the umbrage of the old Rydal woods.

Tickler. Young Gentleman! are you dumb?

Y. G. No, sir—nor deaf. But my knowledge of German literature, poetry, and philosophy, is but slight—and through the medium chiefly of translation—and I hope that I know when it is my duty to be silent. To listen to such speakers, is to learn.

North. We have a host of illustrious living poets besides the few I have alluded to, to whom Germany can show no equals—Southey, Coleridge, Campbell——

Tickler. We are their superiors out and out in Criticism, and in the Philosophy of Taste.

North. And in all the fine arts, except Music. There they excel—why or wherefore I know not—but music, though celestial, is sensuous rather than intellectual or moral, and is a mystery, from Handel and the organ, to the black servant of the late Sir Michael Flemming and the jews-harp.

Tickler. The Germans are dabs in Divinity.

North. Yes—dabs.

Tickler. Michaelis and Eichhorn and——

North. Whish! Jeremy Taylor, Isaac Barrow, and old South, knew more "of man and nature and of human life," and of the BIBLE, WHICH IS THE BOOK, than all the German theologians——

Tickler. That ever grunted.

North. I call upon Thomas Carlyle to contradict Christopher North and Timothy Tickler.

Tickler. He can't. And then, O mercy! what shoals of silly, shallow, shilly-shallyers in all the inferior grades of the subordinate departments of the lowest walks of literature overflow all the land; flocking annually to the great fair of Leipsic to deposit their spawn upon the stalls!

North. A flitter of spawn that, unvivified by genial spirit, seems to give for a time a sort of ineffectual crawl, and then subsides into stinking stillness, unproductive of so much as the scriggle of a single tadpole. I shall take a sweeping survey soon, in a series of articles——

Tickler. Oh! not a series!

North. Of the German mind. In natural history they have done a good deal—a good deal, too, in illustration of the classics——

Tickler. I back Bentley, Porson, and Parr,* against Wolfe, Heyne, and Herman. But what will you make of their metaphysicians, Kit,—Schelling, Kant——

North. Show that they are as mice to men, when compared with Bacon, Berkeley, Locke, Hume, and Reid,† whom they plunder, rob, murder, and in vain try to bury in mud——

Tickler. Come, come, we must loosen the tongue of this younker. Yet it may be perilous to set it going; for good listeners are sometimes, when solicited to open, interminable talkers—and we sup at ten.

North. I love the society of young people. What is your age, Hal?

Y. G. Twenty-one.

North. Youth's glorious prime. Child—boy—lad—youth—man—all in one. Passions keen but unpolluted—sensibility sound but delicate—imagination bright and bold as an angel's wing—reason strong in intuition—the light of the soul tender as dawn, clear as morn, and shining more and more unto the meridian lustre of the perfect day. Twenty-one! and you and I, Timothy, both entering on our——

Tickler. Whish! Curse chronology when it becomes personal.

North. Thine, O Hal, is the world of Hope—ours of Memory—the dazzling lights of nature are all thine—ours, alas! but the pensive shadows!

* "Scholars, and ripe ones," such as England once could boast of.—M.

† These distinguished philosophers and metaphysicians had one surpassing merit—however closely they reason, or to what depth or extent, they are intelligible, and do not lose ideas in mere wordiness.—M.

Y. G. I am ambitious, sir, to attempt an Essay on Hope for Maga——

Tickler. Oh! oh! oh! Sink the shop.

North. An Essay on Hope? First, perhaps, of a series—No. I., on the Passions? In verse or prose?

Y. G. In prose, sir.

Tickler. In the true Blackwoodian style—full of the *splendida vitia* of the author——

North. Silence, Tim.

Tickler. Of——

North. Silence, you sinner.

Tickler. L——

North. Whish! Let me suggest a few hints, Hal, which you can expand and work up into a regular philosophical disquisition.

Tickler. Alas! alas! poor young gentleman! and is thine—with its fine, free, bold sunny smile—the face of a wretch doomed to be ——a contributor! I pity your poor mother.

North. Yes, my good boy, Hope is, as David Hume I believe says, though I forget perhaps his precise words, joy alternating with and overpowering mistrust. The joy which is produced by the possession of the good, by the immediate foresight of its possession, and by the trusting expectation, is essentially the same joy. Is it not so, my son?

Y. G. I cannot doubt it, sir. Your explanations of all states of mind are equally perspicuous and profound. I——

Tickler. Socrates and Alcibiades!

North. Silence, sir. It has been commonly and truly said, my dear boy, that Hope attends us through life. It may be likened in this respect to that supposed good genius, or guardian angel, which has been thought to be attached to every human being at his birth, and faithfully to accompany him till he drops into the grave.

Y. G. And then, sir,

> Hope, with uplifted foot, set free from earth,
> Pants for the place of her ethereal birth;
> On steady wings sails through the immense abyss,
> Plucks amaranthine flowers from bowers of bliss,
> And crowns the soul, while yet a mourner here,
> With wreaths like those triumphant spirits wear.

Tickler. Well recited, Hal, though with somewhat of a sing-song after the lilting elocution of the Lakers.

North. So should such poetry be said and sung—elevated in musical modulation, in which the harmony of the verse flows sweetly and strongly along, like the composite voice of a river that loses not the undertone of still streams and murmuring shallows even in the mellowed thunder of its waterfalls.

Tickler. Pretty enough image, and not unillustrative—yet if sifted, probably nonsense. What are you glowering at, you young gawpus?

Y. G. Beg your pardon, sir. But to hear such a word applied, even in jest, to——

Tickler. Downright, absolute nonsense. Have you the vanity to believe, lad, that you spout like the Tweed? I would have you to know, boy, that he is no Methodist preacher.

Y. G. (*smiling through a blush*). I—I—I—

Tickler. No farther apology, child. Your style of recitation, though peculiar, is not unpleasant—like the drone of the bagpipe. But remember that there are other kinds of music besides the Coronach. The lays, though solemn, were not lugubrious—liker a hymn than a dirge—yet you wailed them as if at a funeral.

North. He recited the lines like a poet—"most musical, most melancholy"—like a nightingale singing to the stars.

Tickler. Meanwhile I shall replenish the jug.

North. Hope is often spoken of, my dear Henry, as the chief good of life, without which it would be miserable, since there is so little of actual good given to it; so little in possession; but Hope, the promiser of good never or seldom realized, beguiles us of our real cares, and blesses us, it is said, with a delusive happiness.

Tickler. The sugar.

North. But believe, on the word of an old man, that this is false and ungrateful doctrine. This life is full of enjoyment, Hal, to those who do not destroy enjoyment by restless and intense desires. But it is true that Hope covers from us much of the calamity of life—sometimes by a golden mist——

Tickler (*bruising the lumps*). Which is anything but a Scotch one.

North. Yet this is not so much by nursing in us fallacious expectations, as by true anticipations, speaking generally, of the longed-for future.

Tickler. True it is, and of verity, that Hope meddles not with the past.

North. She does. She brightens her to-morrows with the sunrises of yesterdays——

Tickler. A commonplace truth in queer apparel—like a sumph at a masquerade in the character of a sage.

North. Some minds perhaps there are, my son, but yours I know is not among the number, that are fed chiefly on fallacious hope. They are bent with eager and passionate desire on some object which is hardly within their reach, and make it the chief or sole purpose of their life. Their pleasure, perhaps, is more in desire than enjoyment, and the hopes which lead them on they do not attain. They pursue a preternatural chase, in which phantoms dance before their eyes, and elude their grasp. This chase is rightly compared to the race of a child pursuing the rainbow.

Tickler. I remember having more than once catched a rainbow; one, in particular, that appeared to arch half the Highlands. By a dexterous countermarch, I cut it off from the sea, and turned it, toward the evening, into Glenco. I caught it on the cliff, and by the clutch disturbed a sleeping eagle, who, with a crash of wings, had nearly driven me into that black pool—before, with a calm sugh majestically oversailing the woods of Ballehulish, he vanished in the sunset beyond the rim of the sea.

North. Tim!—But these surely are a small portion of human kind. And even to these, if the whole play and power of their minds could be discovered and analyzed, it would appear that though brighter objects which have captivated their imagination, are of this nature, unrealized, and leading them on with all illusion of hope, yet that to them too, in subordinate forms, and in the continual process of life, hope serves as a spring of energy, not by its delusive and distant allurements, but by constant anticipations constantly realized. For in the vain pursuit of one great unattainable object, how many thousand subordinate objects, my dear boy, are attained! each of them inspiring the spirit with its own delight! Is it not so?

Y. G. I am sure it is so, sir.

North. It is of importance, Henry, to know this—that you may not regard this glorious principle in one of its aspects only, as the child of imagination and passion, when it shows to the soul dazzling possibilities, and calls on the human being with all his powers along his destined path in the world, and forget its daily and assiduous service, when it urges on and sustains the heart at every moment with immediate expectations justified by reason in their joy. I speak this to you, young man, for I see, nor am I sad to see it, that thou art an enthusiast.

Tickler (*emptying his tumbler*). Nay—that old proser must not have all the talk. Is it not hope, my boy, that commits the seed to the earth, that rejoices in the sun and shower, and watches over the growing harvest!—that sees the braird in the seed—the sheaf in the braird—and in the sheaf the quartern loaf surrounded in his sovereignty by his tributary rolls?

North. Is it not hope that freights the vessel, and long afterwards looks into the sky for the winds that are to fill its homeward sails?

Tickler. 'Tis your turn soon, Harry—tip us a touch.

Y. G. (*bashfully*). Is it not hope that plies the humblest trade which earns bread for human lips?

Tickler. Good.

Y. G. (*more boldly*). Not hope distant and fallacious, but present and sustaining, still fulfilled and rarely deceived—the calm, rational, solacing forethought of prosperous success, of good speed granted to present toil, the vital spirit of homely industry—the—the——

Tickler. Stop—don't stutter.

Y. G. The song of the heart which beguiles the hours of labor, and like the lays of the lark, more joyful the nearer heaven.

Tickler. North—my old boy? Eh?

North. Well—Harry?

Y. G. The poor man sees his wife's and child's face before him in his solitary toils—in the silent thoughts of his unrelaxing employment—while they are preparing his meal for him in his cottage, and the little one is about to take it to her father in the field during the midday hour of rest—and—and—hope——

North. Yes—my dear boy——

Y. G. Is religion, as, with the pretty child sitting beside him with the basket on her lap, he blesses ere he breaks the bread, and includes her and her mother in his prayer.

Tickler. Aye, there is something very touching, my laddie, in the thought of the children of poor people, sons and daughters, separated from their parents in very early life, and working far off, perhaps on very small wages, laying by a little pose, even out of such earnings, to help them in their old age——

North. What an exquisite line that is, in the "Cottar's Saturday Night," and how the heart of Burns must have burned within him, as the feeling was parent to the thought, and beautified the vision of the cottage-girl, that will live for ever in that simple strain,

"And deposit her sair-won penny fee!"

Tickler. Hope trims the student's midnight lamp.

Y. G. Rocks the cradle.

North. Digs the grave.

Tickler. And into each successive tumbler drops the sugar—plump after plump—just so. (*Mingles.*)

North. In this view of human life, the nature of hope may be said to be this—that man is dependent for all issues, partly on himself, and partly on uncommanded events; he has, therefore, in his own true and good ground of trust, and in the uncertainty of all human events, a ground of fear; hence his always fluctuating, yet still rising hope—like the flow of the tide, where every wave that advances falls back, and yet the waters still swell on the shore.

Y. G. Sometimes, sir, the soul seems to itself like the sea-sand, cold, bleak, and desolate; but in a few hours it overflows with joy, just as does that bay, when the tide has again reached the shell-wreaths on the silvery shore,—and on the merry music of the breaking billows the sunny sails of long-absent ships are seen coming homewards from the main.

North. Yes—just so, my young poet. And as thou art a young poet, though I have seen none of thy verses, what sayest thou of that hope which is more airy and illusive; that visionary hope which adorns the distance of life, filling the mind with bright imagery of unattainable good, promising gratification to desires which cannot be realized?

Y. G. I fear to speak—I love to listen.

North. And I, Hal, am on the verge—I know—I feel it—of garrulous old age.

Tickler. Which verge?

North. The mind, my son, cannot rest, for it was not made to rest, in realities. It lives on the future even more than the present. It lives by hope even more than enjoyment. How then shall reason confine that spirit which is to live in the future, the unknown realities even of the future? It cannot—we must hope beyond the truth.

Tickler. Don't puzzle the boy, North.

North. I am not puzzling the boy, Tickler. Am I, Hal?

Y. G. Not yet, sir.

North. Why flies the mind into the future! Because it is an escape from the present. The mind is thereby relieved from the immediate consciousness of all bitterness, restraint, irksomeness, disappointment, sorrow, fear, which may be in the present. And that is one reason, strong as a storm, to drive the mind, on the wings of hope, soft as a dove's, bold as an eagle's, into the future.

Tickler. Speak plain, Christopher. Remember you are not a young poet, but an old proser.

North. Another reason is, my dear boy, that the whole of life which is yet unacted and uncertain, lies in the future. Man looks on that part of his life which is yet before him, as a gamester looks on the remaining throws of his game.

Tickler. Ay—what shall the hours bring forth? From the bosom of futurity fortune throws her black and white lots.

Y. G. How throbbed my heart with hopes and fears,
To learn the color of my future years!

Tickler. There again—why you drawled that like a Presbyterian precentor giving out the lines of a psalm.

North. The past is over, and has less than imagination and desire; but the future is yet undetermined, and is equal to their largest measure. With whatever passion, therefore, Oh! Hal! thy soul hangs upon this life, with that passion will it hang on the yet undecided future.

Tickler. So must it be with all men—to their grand climacteric.

North. Does he long for those pleasures which fortune may give? Then he looks into that future which is still under the dominion of fortune.

Tickler. Does he desire that good which depends upon himself—his own achievements, his own virtues? He will look into that future which he can fill with his powers, because, Hal, and Kit, there is no reality there to give him the lie. But in the present he meets with many things to make him sing small—and for my single self, gents, I confess, that though six feet four on my worsteds, on looking back on the Timothy of the past, he seems diminished to his head, a Pech among the pigmies.

North. Then, think, my excellent young friend, that all present action tends to the future. It springs up and ripens in the future. In itself the present is nothing; it is subservient only to the years to come.

Tickler. Alas! alas! North—methinks—me feels—that my whole life has been but a disconnected series of broken fragments.

North. So oft do I. But in the presence of this eaglet here, my youth is momentarily restored, and like a swan, whose plumage, though tempest-proof, is yet softer than the snow, I seem to have alighted from some far-off clime on the bosom of a pellucid stream, winding away from its source among the mountains, till the region around grows magnificent with forest-woods.

Tickler. Said you, sir, a swan?

North. No sneers, sir; original sin never seems so baleful as in a sneer. Adam did not sneer till long after the fall. Not till he had outlived both remorse and penitence, did the old sinner grow satirical.

Tickler. I meant no offence, and ask your pardon.

North. Granted. We speak of man, my dear Timothy, as discontented, and revile him, because, when the time of enjoyment is come, he still looks, as before, into the future. Why, I say to you, Hal, that is the nobleness of his nature. He is a being of action; and every step of his progress only discovers to him wider and farther regions of his action lying outstretched before him, still or stormy as the sea.

Tickler. I wonder how many thousand times, during our innumerable Noctes, you have taken in vain the name of Neptune.

North. It don't matter. Yes, my fine young fellow, man can measure the present, but he always feels that on the present the unmeasured future rests. To him, a being of powerful and ever-enlarging action, the hour ministers to the years. In the moment he thinks for eternity!

Tickler. You have proved your point, Kit. Man's *real* action, you have shown, and well too, even eloquently, by its own necessary tendency and nature, carries the mind into *unreal* futurity. What say you to all this, younker?

Y. G. I listen with delight.

North. Once carried into the future, are there not reasons enow why the mind should believe in impossibilities? What shall bind down its belief? It seeks enlargement. Here, in this waking work-day world of ours, we are humbled in our will. It is subjected—not predominant. But from that thraldom we take refuge in the free unbounded future. There we can feel our virtues without our frailties; there we can exert our powers unfettered by our weaknesses; there we can mould even the capriciousness of fortune and the course of events to our will; there we can act and command success; there we can wish, and sure is the consummation; there are we lords indeed of our own life and our own destiny; and there may we sit on gorgeous thrones of state, overshadowed by immortal laurels.

Tickler (*To Hal aside*). Cut.

North. Thus the mind for its own wilful gratification, my dear young friend, overleaps impossibility; it has power given to it over the future—it useth it lavishly for its own delight—and in the intoxication of——

Tickler (*sotto voce*). Yes—cut to a moral.

North. What? what if this be carried to excess? Yet is it to a certain degree unavoidable—and I fear not to say to you, Hal, necessary; for the knowledge of that which will be, would often crush the heart with its own worthlessness and impotence. The knowledge of that which is possible, would be premature, and blighting wisdom.

Tickler. Dangerous doctrine, North, thus infused into the ardent spirit of an enthusiastic youth.

North. No—safe and salutary. Let the young heart, I say, strive awhile with impossibilities; and do the utmost for itself that nature will permit. It is only by hoping beyond nature, that it can ever reach at last to the utmost grandeur of nature.

Y. G. Yes, sir; thus may it be said that the soul's first reason for hoping beyond possibility is the force of its own great desires.

Tickler. As the old cock crows, the young chick——

North. Ay, Hal; and the second, my dear lad, is its—Ignorance. For how should it know these limits? That is what it has yet to learn. It may err as much in anticipating as in overlooking them; it may imagine impossibilities where they do not exist. It may yield to difficulties which it might have overcome. The future, oh! thou enlightened lad! is, in the truest sense of the word, uncertain;

for not only are the events which may be dealt to us unknown, but, Hal, the measure of our powers is undetermined, till we exert them; they are greater or less by our own act; and by that mystery of mysteries, our own free will.

Y. G. It makes me happy, sir, to hear you own that creed.

North. It makes me happy, Hal—for I loved your father—to see that thy soul, my dear boy, is alive to—Admiration.

Tickler. What do you mean, old man?

North. Admiration, Timotheus, is an act of the understanding; but of the understanding acting in concert with various emotions.

Tickler. Umph.

Y. G. I do indeed devoutly trust that my mind will never be induced to think and feel on the principle of "Nil admirari."

North. It does my heart good to look on the open and glowing countenance of a youth with thy endowments, Hal, about to start on the career of rejoicing life. Vividly dost thou feel now, my son, that man is a being placed in the midst of a system ordained by divine wisdom and goodness, inhabiting a world full of wonder and beauty, which in every part is indeed but a manifestation to human sense of the wisdom and goodness in which it was made. When, therefore, he opens the eye of his understanding to receive the impression that will flow in upon him from all surrounding things, from works so framed it is that all these impressions come.

Tickler. Beware of preaching, Kit.

North. But to fit him for such contemplations, Hal, are given him, not only senses to perceive, and intellect to comprehend, but the faculties of delight and admiration, without which sense and intellect were vain.

Tickler. Are you, sir, the author of the Natural History of Enthusiasm?*

North. I wish I were. This is the source from which the nobler delight of knowledge springs—admiration blending in all unpolluted, unperverted minds, with the impressions of sense, and the workings of intellectual power—a spirit, my son, which may it live vivid and inviolate in thy bosom to thy dying day!

Y. G. As I am sure, sir, it will in yours—and glorify to your closing eyes the last setting sun.

North. Good lad. He, Hal, who resolves by powerful agencies the combinations of bodies, and forces their elements to discover themselves to his sight; he who lays bare with delicate anatomy the structure of an insect's wing; and he who compasses and scans in thought the motion of worlds; he, too, who surveys the soul of man with all its passions and powers, and learns to observe the laws of the moral world, all are led on by the same wonder blending with

* It was written by Isaac Taylor.—M.

their knowledge; the admiration of beauty and of wisdom exalts their intelligence, and science, poetry, and piety, become one, in that mood which makes us feel our connexion with our native heaven.

Tickler. You must be the author of the Natural History of Enthusiasm.

North. Well—I am—and of the Saturday Evening—two noble productions. Who, Hal, has heard the deeds of his country's heroes told in the rudest simplest phrase? Who has ever read the tale of some gallant crew sailing on bold discovery through unknown seas, or of humble good men, cheerfully bearing a hard lot, contented while they could impart wisdom, virtue, or succor under hard necessity to the wants of others? Who has ever contemplated high qualities of any kind in the mind of his fellow-men, and not known—as you have, my bright boy, many million times—that emotion of admiration with which the mere conception of excellence is formed, and that transport of sympathy and love which attends it?

Y. G. 'Tis kindled now, sir, by your noble words.

North. Yes, Hal, with no other spirit leading you along but your mind's generous admiration, you feel, I know you do, the transport of affection toward one and then toward another of those great creatures whose works have guarded their memory from oblivion. Now toward some sage who forsook the splendors of this world to devote his soul to the meditative discovery of truth, and his life to imparting it in his precepts for the instruction of dark and bewildered men; now toward some warrior, whose great soul sustained the fortunes of his country on his single arm, and whose courage and achievements were equal to the weight laid upon them; now to him whose genius reared temples and statues ennobling the land, or whose voice sung the deeds to which the land had given birth; now to some mighty ruler, who swayed the spirits of a fierce intractable nation by the wisdom of his controlling will; now to some lawgiver, who left the impress of his own mind on that of his people; now to some sufferer in a righteous cause, who counted his life nothing in comparison with that pure good for which he cheerfully resigned it; to all these, thou, O Hal, dost give, by turns, thy love and the transport of thy desire, because to all does thy soul give its passionate admiration.

Tickler. Now, draw your breath, and permit me to attempt a slight sentiment. It is by this principle, North, that examples have their power. They are pictures that speak to admiration, and, through admiration, call upon all the powers of the awakened and uproused spirit.

Y. G. "Ecquid in antiquam virtutem, animosque viriles,
Et Pater Æneas, et avunculus excitat Hector."

Tickler. "Tu longe sequere, et vestigia semper adora."

Y. G. Poets are the guardians of admiration in the spirits of the people.

North. Good.

Y. G. Their songs, sir, emblazoning heroic achievements, and memorizing the spirit of lofty thoughts, make virtue a perpetual possession to the race.

Tickler. Good.

Y. G. Thus such actions can never die. They continue to shine brighter and brighter through the golden mist of years.

Tickler. Bad—and borrowed.

Y. G. The power of this spirit, to whatever influences a nation may be subject, still survives to it, through all changes; the spirit of the greatness of departed time living in its perpetual admiration.

Tickler. I am beginning to get sick of the word.

Y. G. See what wealth, sir, we possess at this hour, gathered from all ages, nations, and tongues, of the greatness that has ennobled our race! What should we be without it? It is now lifted up above the region of passion, purified by Death and Time, even as the heroes of the old world were changed into stars.

(*Silver-timepiece smites eight—Enter* PICARDY, *switching his Tail.—Tea Tea, and Coffee Tea, with mountains of Muffin.—*NORTH *reclines on his Tirocliniun—*TICKLER *takes the Chair—and* YOUNG GENTLEMAN *is promoted to* TIMOTHY'S *small settee.*)

North. You have thrown much "green light," as Ossian says, Hal, on those two powerful principles of human nature, hope and admiration. What have you to say, my imaginative moralist, on desire and aversion?

Y. G. I scarcely feel prepared, sir, to speak on such themes.

Tickler. How should you? North has lugged them in by head and shoulders, having crammed himself with Seneca and Cicero, and being desirous to show off—so, with permission, I shall don my nightcap.

(TICKLER *mounts his Kilmarnock, and lies back composing himself for sleep.*)

Pray waken me, my boy, should I snore so as to render you two mutually inaudible.

North. Pull the cap over his face.

Tickler. And, for goodness sake, release Gurney. I would not that you should expose yourself, before the public. But to be sure nobody now reads the Noctes.

North. Nor the Waverley Novels.

Tickler. Well, proceed, old proser. I am prepared.

North. Desire and aversion, Hal, are the two most general affections of the mind toward good and evil, and are the proper opposites to each other. Desire being the inclination of the mind toward any good, which is not absolutely possessed; and aversion the disinclination of the mind toward any evil, with which it is in any degree menaced.

Tickler. Who ever doubted that?

North. Not you; for you never knew it till this moment—nor wiser men.

Tickler. Indeed!

North. In deed you have always exemplified it; but you have never been conscious of it in thought—for, Tickler, you are no metaphysician.

Tickler. Are you?

North. Yes. The habitual use of the term, desire, in our metaphysical language, to describe certain principles of our nature, as the desire of power, the desire of esteem, the desire of knowledge, and so on, has led, my dear Harry, in some degree, to a partial conception of its true character.

Y. G. Has it, sir?

North. Dr. Brown, in his Moral Philosophy,* ranks all these principles as prospective emotions, and calls their opposite, fears. But as principles of feeling, they may be affected toward the past, the present, or the future. I do not know why the pain with which an ambitious man looks back upon his disappointment, is to be separated in speculation upon the mind, from the desire which accompanies his expectation. Both belong equally to one pain, to which time is indifferent; and therefore all these principles, such as ambition, love of glory, &c., ought to be considered under some title which is generic as to time, and includes past, present, and future.

Y. G. Dr. Brown proceeds, I believe, sir, on a theory that the desire is first, and that the pleasure is only felt because there has been desire, and it is a gratification of it, sir.

North. You say well—he does. But can you imagine a desire that is independent of the pleasure felt?

Y. G. I can not, sir. But I can easily conceive that a very slight degree of pleasure felt may give occasion to very strong desire, from the capacity of the soul, sir, to bring infinite multiplications of a small pleasure into its imagination, and so to frame desire without end. Prodigious, indeed, seems to be the soul's capacity of desire; but I humbly think, sir, that it must always begin from pleasure or pain actually experienced.

* Dr. Thomas Brown, who had been Professor of Moral Philosophy, in Edinburgh University, immediately before Wilson. His greatest work "On the Philosophy of the Human Mind" shows him to have been at once a profound and a clear thinker.—An article on the philosophy of Kant, the German metaphysician, which appeared in the second number of the Edinburgh Review, and attracted attention and admiration, was written by Dr. Brown.—M.

Tickler. Are you positive, young gentleman, that you know the meaning of what you have now said?

Y. G. No, Mr. Tickler, I am not positive—I said "I humbly think."

North. Therefore, Hal, in good metaphysics, the sensibility to such pleasure or pain ought to be first characterized, and the desire to be afterward superadded.

Y. G. I wished to have said so, sir.

North. To consider desire in its most ordinary sense, as the inclination of the mind to that which is to be obtained, and therefore as prospective merely, as Dr. Brown has done, is to give a most imperfect description of those principles he analyzes, which are principles of enjoyment and regret, as well as of desire, affected, all of them, by the present and past as well as the future. But, farther—please attend to this, Henry—desire itself, as thus represented by Dr. Brown, a prospective emotion merely, is imperfectly described, for to speak absolutely and truly of this emotion, time is not that which it regards; it is incidentally only that it has respect to time by which, therefore, it is not to be characterized.

Tickler. You have repeated that dogma a dozen times.

North. Not once. What then, Hal, is the circumstance truly essential to desire?

Y. G. I wait, sir, for your elucidation.

North. Simply—the state of separation of the soul from its object.

Y. G. It can be nothing else, I believe, sir.

North. Now, it is true that our mind and life are such, that our desire does, for the most part, look into futurity; both from the active nature of the mind, which chiefly fixes its desire on those objects which by exerted power it can obtain, and because all such attainment necessarily lies in the future. But this, though it happens for the most part, is incidental, and not essential to the nature of desire.

Y. G. I see clearly that it is not, sir. The separation of the soul from the good which is *lost*, may be the subject of desire; hence all those bitter and miserable yearnings toward irrecoverable good—bitter and miserable, because, alas! sir, useless. "We weep the more, because we weep in vain!"

North. Ay, ay, my dear boy, with fond and impotent longings looks back our desiring soul, as if that which time had swept away into its abysses might yet be restored. So too, with hopeless and idle desire, doth she look remorselessly on lost innocence, cleaving in imagination to that which has passed away for ever.

Y. G. Scenes and faces arise, and lofty thoughts and pure feelings return, for one moment of illusion. Is this not desire?

"She looks! and her heart is in heaven; but they fade,
The mist and the river, the hill and the shade;
The stream will not flow, and the mist will not rise,
And the colors have all passed away from her eyes!"

North. Poor outcast! And what is it, my son, but vain desire, which throws its longing arms round an illusive phantom that slips from its embrace? Does it not knock at the gates of death, and demand back the dead? or leave the living to live with the dead, till they too die of passion unrequited in the dust?

Y. G. This meaning of the word, sir, which you have so beautifully illustrated, is preserved in its original the exquisite Latin word *desiderium*, which pre-eminently expresses this desire to the past—to the lost. "Quis desiderio sit pudor aut modus tam cari capitis?" This idea of desire, in simple separation, not looking to the past or the future, but centred in the present moment, has also a beautiful Latin exemplification in the words of Tacitus, describing Agricola dying, and looking round as it were to find those who were not present, "*desideravêre* aliquid oculi tui?"

North. Thank ye, my good boy. Now mark, Harry, that this longing which arises in the soul by separation from the object of its love, is one of the great principles by which the soul is moved in all its action and passion. Very sublime views accordingly have been entertained of this principle by which sages saw it is capable of carrying itself out of that by which it is surrounded, and to conceive of good from which it is absent. Desire has been, therefore, called the wings of the soul. So may it be detached from the senses, and flying upwards, draw empyrean air.

Y. G. In love, the soul unites itself to its object; in desire it seeks that union.

North. It is indeed essential to all greatness, enlargement, and strength in the soul. For here we must live among many objects, which are not of a nature to satisfy our highest powers; but objects which are, do exist in heaven or earth, or have existed, or may exist. If it were necessarily wedded to those objects which are present with it, it would soon be sunk and lost. But having power, under all circumstances, to lift itself up to its just and natural elevation, it forsakes this dim spot which men call earth, and sojourns, for short seasons of perfect felicity, in its native heaven.

Y. G. The influence of desire, then, sir, seems in some respects akin to that of hope?

North. The two principles are allied in nature. By desire the soul is enabled to hope. By desire the soul is faithful to its object in separation. Nay, by desire it can pursue through many even hopeless years one aim, and reach it at last. By desire the mother hopes her son's return, when all others have given him to the deep or the grave.

Y. G. By desire the unconquered patriot hopes his country's deliverance.

North. By desire the good man hopes that his just purpose shall succeed against the opposition and division of the world. Finally, my dear Hall, this is the principle which distinguishes all minds that attain pre-eminent success. Each is capable of its own good, and may attain it if it has desire; but filled as the world is with thwartings and impediments, not else—that is the law.

Y. G. Sir, your noble and exalted sentiments inspire me with highest hopes of the whole human race. The world is yet young—for what to the mind seem sixty centuries in that mood, which, as Wordsworth sublimely says, "makes our noisy years seem moments in the being of the eternal silence!"

North. No—no—no—my dear Hal, the doctrine of the perfectibility of man is but an empty dream.

Y. G. Not scriptural.

North. Antiscriptural.

Y. G. Yet I hope, sir, that you believe there is decreed for man some mighty amelioration of his life, even on this earth?

North. No, my dear boy. I have no such belief. I see, indeed, some scattered gleams of a "redeeming happiness," but melancholy clouds hang over and envelop our life that is visited with such irradiations. The spirit of earth has seized on a celestial visitant, and bound him with itself in the chains of strong inexorable necessity.

Tickler. Don't pitch the tone of your talk, North, to too high a key. Yet I am willing that we should be serious—nay solemn—for 'tis Saturday evening—and we are both fast ageing; and I am aware we have got among us a young philosopher. Let us have, then, a grave, but, for Heaven's sake, not a melancholy Noctes.

North. Who but must be melancholy, my friend, contemplating the lot of man! By the bondage of mortal pain he is linked with all his powers to this material nature, to render bitter service for bitter hire. Hunted and scourged by an inclement sky, shaken back from the cold breast that yields to his aching desire a painful and scanted nourishment, he sees himself the thrall of a heavy law, and in the midst of a subjection from which there is no escape or deliverance; looking around and above in vain for help, he knows that there is no succor for him but in his own strength. And those proud powers, that high capacious intelligence, that burning spirit of desire, that will which was made only for heavenly obedience, that form which was framed for a heavenly spirit to dwell in, he bows down to the task of his mortal servitude. He turns their strength on the breast of this unyielding earth, and rends from it the sustenance and the safeguards of his life. In the sweat of his brow he eats his bread. He toils that he may live in toil. He reaps the fruit of his service, protracted years, which shall yield the same service, till the hand that gave him to this bondage release him from its chains.

Y. G. It is some solace, sir, to the kind who thus range the walks of the earth in their pain, that some portion of the nations have earned a brighter lot; that generation upon generation accumulating their labor, have built up out of the pain of their mortal condition a wealth that nature had not given, and releasing a few from the burthen of the common lot, have reared and guarded, in the heart of their civilized strength, a sovereignty of intellect, a little world of peaceful happiness, where thoughtful virtue may yet walk on earth in love!

North. Alas! let us look back upon the ages of the world, and know what man has done for man. Time that has swept away the works of the generations from their place of remembrance, has yet guarded the splendid shadows of their recollections for instruction to the successive ages. We can unroll the memory of the world of old—we can behold the cities that are fallen—and hear the hum of the mingling multitudes that swarm in all their gates. The glory of their empire, the pride of their unimaginable might rises up in its dreamlike pomp from the night of the past—and we are spectators of the works and the destinies of men whom thousands of years have buried in the dust. We read the annals of human glory. We ask what those happier brothers of mankind, whose enviable lot lifted them above the condition of the race, were moved to do for their toil-bowed brethren? To what service of the race they gave their unmeasured power? We know too well the answer. They were the desolating conquerors of the world, Hal, enslaving their people, through them to enslave the nations.

Y. G. Better, perhaps, for the species, had there been no such empires.

North. The release from the servitude of life could never release the will from the bondage which it renews for ever within itself. The lords of the earth were slaves within their own corrupted spirit—they were servants to a direr necessity than that which bowed the heart of the least among their innumerable multitudes; for the lawless will of the slave is tamed by the yoke that bows him down—but the will of the lord of the nations is mad with power, and the source of human evils swells ever in his bosom unceasingly and uncontrollably.

Y. G. Yes—my dear sir—we look on them, and the frailty of our own nature draws us for a moment to believe that the bright ease of their lives was a happiness won to them from the severity of our mortal condition; but we look again, and we know that the bitter evil of our nature was there; and that while they seemed to roll off on others their own part of the burden of human calamity, the invisible chain of suffering which binds down together all the brotherhood of mankind, had wound its fatal links around their hearts.

North. But it may be said that I am giving a false representation of the glory of mankind.

Y. G. Alas! I fear too true.

North. It is not, it may be said, to wealth and empire, once stately and flourishing, and now passing away, that our imagination turns with desire to discover the pride of our race, and to honor the recovered glory of the human spirit amidst the light and guarded peace of happy civilization. There *have* been nations on the earth, whose name brightens the story of mankind—nations in whose bosoms genius sprang up and worshipped wisdom—where liberty guarded the pride of life within her invincible arms. But if we indeed desire to see in the sad and serious light of truth the condition of our kind as they have lived upon this earth—it is in vain that we delight our imagination in these bright remembrances. Did the earth, indeed, see her children rejoicing and free? No; SLAVES tilled the soil of liberty—the deliverer of his country dashed cities of men into the dust, and scattered their inhabitants through the slavery of the world.

Y. G. But look again, sir, over the earth; and under the shadow of the cloud that broods over it, there is seen a still small light which hangs its lamp in every human heart—LOVE. Within the circling walls of every human dwelling, beneath its sheltering roof, is guarded a little world which love has knit together. Within the circuit which that presence hallows, pleasure springs up with innocence. Peace is there—and the light which sin had shut out, breaks again upon the spirit.

North. Mingled brightness and blackness—therein lies the mystery. What is it that huddles them all together—the high and the low—and gives them over to a common doom—almost to a common grave—while the sun of life yet shines brightly on them all? There is a capacity of good confessed by all, and none realize it. We seem to bring one destination into the world with us, and to accept another. We seem to be the fools of life. Ask the philosopher who has spent his life within his own mind,—ask the man of power who has spent it in moulding the will of others to his own,—ask the poet who has lived in the beauty of dreams,—ask the soldier of life who has lived in the warfare of realities,—what have they made of it—what had they made of themselves—what have they done with that good which they brought with them into the world—and which has vanished from them altogether, or floats like an unembodied spirit in the breath of imagination, still?—Is it that we have not power to bring down good among men?—No, we have the power; but we do not use it; we do not know where to find it. There have been those who have found the power, and have used it. Men simple in their spirit;—not radiant with genius nor strong in power; not pouring out the dazzling and exuberant wealth of their own minds before men's eyes; but pouring out their spirit through their hearts. Men unconscious of themselves—and of their destination—but who have brought down good into the life of men, by bringing it first into their own. Christians, Hal—Christians—but how few in this wicked and weary world deserve that holy name?

Tickler. Come, come, my dear friend, though it be Saturday night, let's be a leetle more lively—and surely, surely, North, it is not for us to say that there is no happiness in this world of ours—

North. No, it would be false to say so—yet what I have said is true. If great suffering and heavy duties are taken out of the lot, and the mind is left free to seek its own enjoyment, it is impossible to say how many modes of pleasure it will discover.

Tickler. True, Kit. Why, pursuits and gratifications so unimportant, that they have scarce a name in our greater estimates of the human condition, do yet, by continual supplies of small pleasure, contribute largely to the active state of happiness. For, do they not bring with them renovation and refreshment, keeping up the alacrity of the spirit, and protecting it from that languor which often turns it against itself. Endless are they as fancy!

North. It might be said, from the contemplation of a great part of mankind, that action of some kind, pressing forward continually to an aim, was an essential constituent of the state of happiness. Yet, what thousands are satisfied in perfect tranquillity of enjoyment, one day flowing after another in mere repetition—the peaceful sameness, like some sweet monotone in music, stilling all uneasy passion, and keeping all thought and feeling within the quiet domain of contentment!

Y. G. Some I seem to see satisfied in the love they feel for others, and that is felt for them, and happy without desire.

North. It might be said, that hope could not be dispensed with; yet there are those without hope, whose happiness is altogether in remembrance.

Y. G. Others—not few—but many—who, without hope, are happy in resignation.

Tickler. We all see how much of the richest joys of humankind are given them in their strong affections. We can imagine nothing, indeed, that should leave the lot of man more desolate than if these were taken away! Yet shall we say that the human being without them cannot know happiness? That the philosopher, with a soul dwelling apart from human loves, and entranced in the research and contemplation of nature, has not a happiness all his own,

> "Because not of this noisy world, but silent and divine!"

North. For are not beauty, and wisdom, and truth, and power, all poured in for ever into one soul, sufficient for entire bliss!

Tickler. Ay, my bold bright-eyed boy. *We* look on the light of day, we hear the voice of love, and it appears to us as if it must be miserable to bear night on the eyes, and silence on the ear. Yet the blind and the deaf have their own full and unstinted joy, that does not forsake their spirits.

Y. G. When oppression plunges her persecuted victim in the dungeon's depth, she seems, indeed, sir, in cutting him off from air, and light, and liberty, from the condition of living nature, to heap on him, in part, by mere privation, the misery she calls the wretch to endure. She seems, sir, in severing him from human faces, to break off his human ties; and inhumed in the prisons of her wrath, he may be said to dwell already with the dead, and to house in the grave. But is there no spirit that can descend into that buried and gloomy cell, to visit with her illumination that uncompanioned heart?

North. Yes, my noble Hal, conscience may sit there an angel of light at his side, whispering peace and hope and lofty consolation.

Y. G. The patriot who has raised his voice or his hand too soon, in redress of his country's wrongs; the martyr who bears with him in his bosom the faith on which he will pour out his blood; the just man who has offended by his virtue high-seated crime—all these, in that woeful and dreary seclusion can find their own happiness not less calm and self-consoled in that long dark expectation, than when the last act of unjust power sets them free from the bonds of life, and they feel on the brink of death that they have a foretaste of immortal happiness.

Tickler. The lad is an eloquent lad—and will one day be an orator.

North. Events nor condition are in our power, but the mind, with which we all receive them, is, Hal.

Y. G. "Fallen cherub! to be weak is miserable,
Doing, or suffering."

North. Suffering! Our lot may be such that we can do nothing —that we have to be merely passive. In that case all depends on our will. If we receive pain with a shrinking and impatient mind, we give it its full power over us.

Tickler. True, Kit. But though any body may triumph over the toothache, what man of woman born but must shriek at the *tic doloreux.*

North. The Indian undergoing torture, in which he sings war-sings, and laughs to scorn his tormentors, horrible to nature as his condition is, is surely not to be judged of by the mere imagination of what we ourselves should suffer in his place. That spirit which has been inured to pain, and which, in utmost agony, can feel its accustomed pride rise unconquerably above it all, must be regarded as, by the power of its own will, casting off from itself great part of natural suffering. It is a spirit no longer penetrable to suffering —invulnerable; pride, or whatever other feeling, truly

> "*Arms* th' obdured breast
> With stubborn patience, *as with triple steel.*"

Tickler. My temper is none of the best; yet I acknowledge that almost at any hour of one's life, there is opportunity given of determining for oneself what the tenor of his feelings shall be, whether for pleasure or for pain.

North. Neither is mine; yet I see, sometimes not without self-upbraiding, that those who cannot command themselves, draw from the continual stream of the incidents of life, uneasiness and vexation, while it would have been easier to draw from them cheerfulness and satisfaction.

Tickler. The common remark, Kit, that great part of the happiness and unhappiness of life depends upon its petty occurrences, a remark which, when simply stated, appears degrading to the pride of our mind, acquires a more reasonable meaning when we consider that the mind exercising itself, as it must do, on these little events, finds in them the occasion of yielding to the temper of pain and dissatisfaction, or of sharing the temper of pleasure and contentment.

North. True, Timothy. The mind is not subject, as the remark would intimate, to such events. They are not of magnitude to force on it either pleasure or pain. But because the ordinary state in which it exists must be either of the one character or the other, and as, in the absence of great and constraining occurrences, that ordinary state must be derived from its own disposition, therefore those slight and petty circumstances appear thus important, when in truth the mind does no more than exercise its faculty of throwing itself into the pain, or of sustaining in itself its natural spirit of joy and vigor.

Tickler. 'Tis but a shallow apologue, that of the Caliph who on his deathbed declared that in his long reign of prosperity and glory he had known but three days of happiness.

North. He must indeed have been a poor devil.

Tickler. He has not told us—has he—what constituted the hap piness of the three days? What do you conjecture was the busi ness of the blockhead? Sensual?

North. No. But our Alfred, I warrant him, knew many hundreds of happy days. For though subjected to horrid convulsion-fits, that often all at once made him fall down on the floor of his palace, like a beggar in the street-mire, he was happy in genius and virtue. But who ever supposed that a miserable despot could enjoy one hour's true happiness? Yet the Caliph ought not to have been ungrateful for his pleasures. For the joys of the harem, the slavery of bended knees, and of faces sweeping the floor in humiliation, the insidious flatterer and the deadly mute—all these may have been, during their hour, instruments of base, luxurious, or cruel pleasure —but such remembrances could bring no peace to a dying bed, and therefore he became at last a querulous moralist.

Tickler. Do you ever envy the condition of any man, North?

North. Not often now. Yet, 'tis not unnatural to do so, for we always look on the lot from which we are removed, my friend, with imagination; and sometimes the sense of the real disadvantages of our own lot turns our thoughts with something of envy, with a regretful comparison at least, toward those whose lot by its nature, whatever else may be its disadvantages, is exempt from that particular disturbance under which we may suffer.

Y. G. Who is there, sir, that, till he has read again and again the history of Genius, does not believe that the mind in which such beautiful creations were born, and which dwelt among them, was happy?

North. Alas! alas! Burns, Byron, Cowper.* I think of writing the lives of these three in one volume.

Tickler. Do. In like manner, Master Henry, we imagine the wealthy and the powerful to be happy, not merely because they are visibly exempted from many troubles, but because we know that there are principles in our nature to which superiority over our fellow-men is grateful, and that such possessions seem to enlarge the domain of the will. Does he wish for knowledge? The learning of ages lies open before his mind. Will he have luxury? A thousand hands are ready to minister to his delight. But he may be a coward—a scrub—or a dolt—and ends, perhaps, a life of slavery to some slut, by suicide.

North. I purpose writing a volume to be entitled, Compensation.

Tickler. Do. Ay, Kit, the sword hung by a single hair over the

* Burns, unquestionably, led rather a happy than an unhappy life. Byron's was an alternation of storm and sunshine, but gives the idea of a vast quantity of enjoyment, mental and bodily. Cowper was sometimes insane, and composition, by occupying his mind, prevented his falling into hopeless lunacy.—M.

royal banquet is much in point. That was the hidden ill of the heart which the courtier could not have divined.

Y. G. Methinks no man can be miserable who loves his country, I become happy in a moment when I think on Scotland.

Tickler. Why?

Y. G. Because of the—the——

Tickler. North—help him out.

North. The love of our country, my good boy, is not so much an attachment to any assignable object, as it is our participation in that whole spirit which has breathed in the heart of the whole race of men of which we are sprung; and therefore, without strong and fine sympathies, no man can be a patriot. That is our country, not where we have breathed alone—not the land which we have loved, because it has shown to our opening eyes the brightness of heaven and the gladness of earth—but the land for which we have hoped and feared—for which our bosoms have beat with the consenting hopes and fears of thousands of heroic hearts—that land, of which we have loved the mighty living and the mighty dead.

Y. G. That land, sir, the Roman or the Greek would say, where the boy had sung in the pomp that led the sacrifice to the altars of the ancient deities of the soil.

Tickler. Very fine. You are a brace of incomparable orators. But if declamation is still to be the order of the night, I beg to be heard, for I can harangue, if I have a mind, like one of the Lake poets. Why, the Campus Martius, and the Palæstra, where the youth exercised heroic games, what were they, gentlemen, but the schools of patriotism? For were not the youth taking part, then and there, in the passions, the power, the hope, the glory, that flowed through all the spirit of the nation?

North. True, Tim. Old warriors, and gowned statesmen, that frowned in brass or in marble, in public places, and in the porches of noble houses—trophied monuments and towers, riven with the scars of ancient battles—the temple raised where Jove had stayed the flight—or the victory, that with suspended wings still seemed to hover over the conquering bands—what were all these to the eyes and the fancy of the young citizen, but characters speaking to him of his hope and desire, in which he read the union of his own heart to the heart of the heroic nation of which he was one?

Tickler. True, Kit. And what if less noble passions must hereafter take their place in his mind—what if he must learn to share in the rivalries and hates of his house or of his order—these far deeper and greater feelings had been sunk into his spirit in the years when it is most susceptible, unsullied, and pure; and afterward, in great contests, in peril of life and death, in those moments of agitation, or profound emotion, in which the higher soul again rises up, those high and solemn affections of boyhood and youth would return upon him, and consecrate his warlike deeds with the noblest name that was known to those ancient states.

North. Therefore, Timothy, how was the oaken crown prized, which was given to him who had saved the life of a citizen. Yet perhaps he loved not the man whom he had preserved; but he had remembered in the battle, that it was a son of his country that had fallen, and over whom he had spread his shield. He knew, that the breath he guarded was part of his country's being.

Tickler. Wo to the citizen of the world! The man can have neither heart nor imagination. The *natale solum* is not on its own account dear; but dear as that by which the present and the past generations are all bound together.

Y. G. And hence the exiles carry with them the names of the mother-country.* The fugitives from Troy had formed a little Ilium, and named a little Xanthus—"et arentem Xanthi cognomine rivum."

North. The character of the mind of this country, Hal, is not to be spoken of lightly—yet 'twould be unsafe to say that it is sound at the core. It presents to our eyes a spectacle of energy and ardor in all the ordinary pursuits of life.

Y. G. Indeed, the life of no order, sir, is that of repose.

North. So far, well. Repose is stagnation. But the agitations of the late eventful years have occupied the minds of all men, with interests which, though of the utmost importance and magnitude, were nevertheless, in one respect, temporary. For every new event that arose, or was in preparation, seemed as if the fate of a nation, or, I might almost say, of mankind, were involved in its issue, and therefore no excess of passionate expectation which could be fixed on it could appear misplaced. Thus have we been accustomed to live in a succession of vivid emotions which were all but the birth of the times, and could only have the duration of the events with which they had arisen. The events passed away, and with them our thoughts took wing into oblivion.

Y. G. I can indeed understand, sir, from your pregnant words, that the strong and pervading sympathies with the fortunes of nations and humanity, however ennobling to the minds which it filled—

North. Ay, Hal, and accompanied with lessons of the highest instruction—

Y. G. May have been injurious to the highest faculties of thought.

Tickler. How the deuce may that be?

* So, as we know, the emigrants, who left Scotland singing the melancholy Gaelic song of which the translated refrain is "We return, we return, we return no more," have given to their new homes in Canada, the beloved and familiar names of the old scenes.—M.

North. Tell him, Hal.

Y. G. Because they may have withdrawn the imaginations of men, sir, from the great objects which to the self-collected mind, wrapt in meditation, have always appeared of paramount importance—

Tickler. And what, pray, are they?

Y. G. They are the—they are the—the——

North. It seemed, indeed, Tickler, as if the more thoughtful mind turning itself to those remote objects—

Tickler. Confound ye, Kit, what objects?

North. Those remote objects and their shadowy speculations, were deserting the great hazards of mankind to busy itself with the dreams of a fantastic and indolent philosophy.

Tickler. Very fine indeed, sir, very fine.

North. We have found, Timothy, almost ever since the great French Revolution—

Tickler. The small one was a shabby concern.*

North. We have found, Timothy, in the occurrences and scenes of a shifting world, the full scope for all our capacity of hope and desire: and hence it may be difficult for the soul of the nation to turn itself to higher and more lasting contemplations; and if it were to do so, impossible perhaps to recover that zeal and those devout convictions of their eternal worth, which belonged to them of old, and have been easy and habitual to men who lived in calmer times of the world.

Tickler. I am where Moses was when the candle went out.

North. No high philosophy, Hal, pervades our literature; and I fear none is in——

Tickler. The nation's soul, as you call it, Kit. Yet the nation is a decent body enough.

Y. G. Surely, sir, the arts of imagination——

North. Can not supply, Hal, that kind of continued strength which the mind now requires——

Tickler. The soul of the nation.

North. For in the luxury of a people, their arts, Hal, take the tone of the times. Imagination is too much in sympathy with pleasure! it yields itself too easily to the enchantment from which the mind itself seeks deliverance.

Tickler. Now let him alone, Hal, and you shall hear the inconsistent old sophist contradicting all he has said to-night.

North. No. All the arts to which imagination gives birth have greatly changed their character, Tickler, with the changing genius of a people. Strong, masculine, and rude in older times, and bearing the stamp of the bold spirit which created them, they have

* The glorious Three Days of July, 1830.—M.

at a later period become enervated and effeminate, and tainted with the weakness of a luxurious age—breathing back on the soul of the people——

Tickler. There again: for people, say nation.

North. The indolent softness they had already received from it.

Tickler. Oh dear! oh dear!

Y. G. Yet, in their power and beauty, how they exalt——

Tickler. The national soul.

North. In the work of the painter or sculptor, Hal, you see finely exemplified the process by which conception, imagination, and intellect kindle, "even at the *forms* themselves have made."

Y. G. Yes—sir?

Tickler. What?

North. Think—feel—*do;* think—feel—and *do* again; and how glories the spirit in beholding of what itself creates! The painter begins to work—his hand performs the bidding of his thought, and the forms of beauty which arise in his mind dawn on the tablet before his eyes.

Y. G. Now he sees what he has conceived; and his imagination takes fire from its own product.

North. Yes. And no sooner does he behold the forms in palpable representation, than his conception itself changes; for his feelings, Hal, are warmed by that beauty as by "touch ethereal of Heaven's fiery rod;" his thoughts glow as in a spiritual furnace——

Tickler. A spiritual furnace!

North. And that first imperfect conception is invested with purer brightness, and moulded to shape divine. From unknown dwelling-places in his genius the fair ideas come flocking——

Tickler. All birds of a feather.

North. And then indeed, Tickler, his mind teeming with a thousand unembodied conceptions, all ready to burst into life, he understands in his joy what creative mind itself may owe to the works it would frame for others' delight, and perceives that his own art is the only muse he must invoke to inspire his genius.

Y. G. How much, sir, have the best, the most sacred conceptions of men's souls, been affected by edifices reared at their own bidding! How vast the power of a Gothic cathedral! There, all is subjected under its one use of a house of religious worship. There are found all that serves to the many ministrations of religion; and there too is another important use, not necessarily connected with them, it is a repository of the dead. Its natural sanctity, as a house of worship, has made it a fit mansion of expecting rest, a dormitory of the living dead!

Tickler. Be intelligible, sir.

Y. G. And again, sir, all these uses, and all that appears extrinsic to them, in the elaborate and prodigal beauty of its forms, are subjected to the one great purpose, the one imagination of the whole structure, religious awe. It is thus, sir, that the human being gives his own spirit to the insensate stone, till it breathe back again upon him a still loftier and more divine inspiration.

North. Well said, my good lad. That which the works of the fine arts effect partially, speech may be said to effect to the human species. Suppose us from the creation all dumb!

Tickler. Well for us had it been so with women.

North. Savage! We should have lived in an obscure dream haunted by shapeless phantoms. Silent people often get insane. It is not safe to have too many dealings with wordless thoughts. You can not discover what they would be at—they are at the best suspicious characters—and sometimes vagrants that would not scruple to murder you at midnight in your bed.

Tickler. The thought uttered in speech (don't keep staring at North) is embodied, young gentleman, in a sort of distinct reality, and is thus made apparent to the mind itself in a palpable form, just as its beautiful conception of visible things become defined and strong in the colors and lineaments of the growing picture.

Y. G. And hence it is, sir, that the orator, as the torrent of his speech rushes on, kindles in his eloquence, just like the painter in his works of creation.

North. You are thinking, I perceive, Hal, of one of those great men, who, inspired with the zeal of their holy cause, have stood up to speak fearlessly before the face of kings and in the presence of corrupted courts, those truths which bow down courts and kings to the level of the peasant and the beggar.

Tickler. That race is extinct.

Y. G. He heard himself the voice that thundered in the ears of his audience; the fervor of passion which was pouring forth in the sound, urged on and bore along his own spirit—the—

Tickler. Stop—pull up—hold fast. All that and much more applies to the extemporaneous eloquence—but not to MSS., much less to printed sermons—or to discourses got by heart and spouted forth by a hypocrite, not ashamed by assumed fervor to swindle you into a belief that all his sedulously got up paragraphs are sudden inspiration.

North. I would have the great minds among us, and there must be many, study more profoundly the laws of thought and feeling.

Y. G. Of all studies, sir, surely the most ennobling! Higher far such science than those that deal with mere matter—but, alas! more difficult far, as is seen in the result, sir. The mind is as great a mystery now as it was to Plato.

Tickler. Or Pythagoras.

North. To the observer of physical science, it may be said truly, the subject is uniform and constant. Gold, iron, are the same metals now and heretofore—here and in every place. The races of living nature have continued unchanged. The growth of every plant is a constant process. Every spring brings the same blossoms—every autumn the same fruit. The same air breathes—the same showers fall—the same ocean rolls to all nations through all time. The stars keep their place, and the planets their motion, and Astronomy, from the sun's latest eclipse, can read back the heavens to the moment when his orb was first darkened in the sky.

Tickler. North—I am not given to compliments—but douse my daylights, if that be not spoken like a poet and a philosopher.

North. It is evident what is the result to science of this unchangeableness in the subject of observation. Every inquirer knows that the same matter is before him which was before the eyes, or under the hands, of all his predecessors in inquiry; he knows that he has but exactly to follow definite methods of observation which they have pursued and prescribed, and all the means of which are as constant and unchangeable as the matter itself, and the results which they found must discover themselves too to his sight. All that has been gained is possessed; every province that is won is at the same time secured; and the empire of science, continually enlarging, descends an unimpaired inheritance to each new generation of inquirers.

Y. G. The only chance, perhaps I may be permitted to say, sir, that is possible, is improvement; because the methods of physical science, which are too definite in their nature to be lost when they are recorded, are yet susceptible of endless amelioration; and by those only erring knowledge set aside.

Tickler. Nothing in this world, therefore, so easy as to be a chemist.

Y. G. And more so to be a mathematician.

North. Compare with this the condition of moral science. To it there is but one subject—assuming endless modifications. One dart of it is—the passions. Love, ambition, revenge! We give, indeed, one name to a passion, supposed to be one in different minds. But examine that one passion in different minds, and see where is its unity.

Tickler. O'er the hills far away. What say you, Hal?

Y. G. Nothing, sir.

North. We see love in one mind a fierce, self-willed, devouring passion, that seeks nothing but its own gratification at all consequences. In another we see it pure, generous, and heroic, in its every height of strength sacrificing itself to its object, or to solemn duties, and enabled by its own intense strength to make that sacrifice. In another we see it humble and meek, the sorrow and the solace of a gentle, patient, uncomplaining life. Is this the same passion to which we have given the same name?

Y. G. Vain delusion, indeed!

North. We read the story of two men who have signalized them selves by their giant usurpation of power over the obedience and destinies of their kind. We call both ambitious. Yet I find Julius Cæsar shedding no blood but as a soldier in the field, dropping tears to see the pale mangled head of his mightiest foe, and taking those, in the frankness of generous affection, to his unmistrusting confidence, who were ere long to whet their daggers against his life.

Tickler. He was a tyrant.

North. We may live—nay, not we—but Hal here—to see worse. We find another to whom ambition supplies a very different heart; whose spirit it steels against remorse; to whom it makes the paths of peace and of blood alike on the way to empire, from whose own heart it shuts out peace, sowing fear, suspicion, and hate in its place; to whom it makes the happiness and life of one man and those of millions a matter of like indifference, in the calculations of that sole arbiter of will and destiny. Can we think that in the two men we have understood the passion of their ambition, because we have given it one name in both? The truth is, Hal, that the poets have done great and glorious things with the passions—the philosophers little—and the metaphysicians nothing.

Y. G. In that field, revered sir, as in others, you are born to work wonders that shall make the name of North immortal.

North. Turn to those with whom you live, Hal, and see how the same affection toward yourself is different in different breasts. Is intellect, is judgment, is memory the same? The entire mind is different by the complex difference of the thousandfold variety in all its faculties and powers.

Y. G. "A mighty maze, but not without a plan."

North. Nay, it is different to itself. Every new passion—that enters, each successive year's longer experience of life, changes all that was before—the whole mind, through all its feeling and all its thoughts.

Tickler. Ay—every mind undergoes metamorphoses more miraculous than any sung by Naso.*

(*Silver Timepiece smites Ten—Enter* AMBROSE *with roasted Goose, Turkey ditto, and the accustomed etceteras.*)

(*Curtain drops.*)

* Publius Naso Ovidius, contemporary with Virgil, Horace, Tibullus, and Propertius, and author of "De Arte Amandi," "Heroic Epistles," the "Fasti," and "Metamorphosis."—M.

No. LXII.—SEPTEMBER, 1832.

SCENE—*Southside*—*Time, nine P.M. August 6th.*

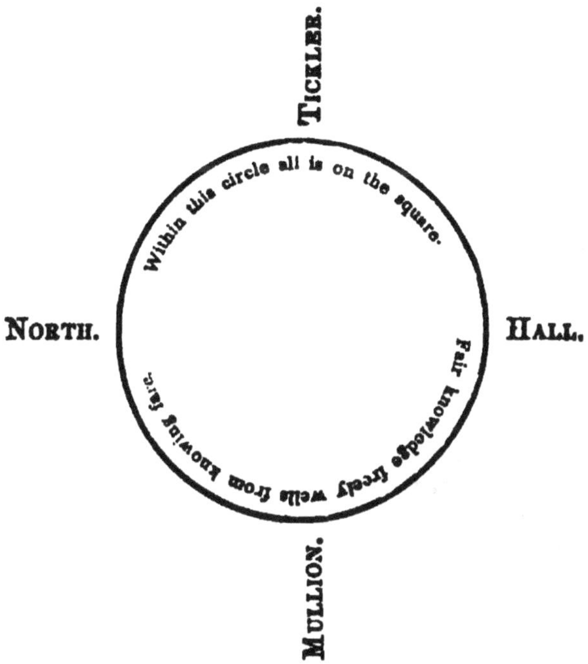

Tickler. I hope the souchong's to your mind, Captain?* Come, North, another magnum or a bowl—what say you? I've got some fresh limes to-day from our friend of Dunoon.

North. O, a bowl, then, by all means! What, Skipper, do you

* Captain Basil Hall, author of a variety of works, among which the best known are the account of his Voyage of Discovery to the Western Coast of Corea and the great Loo-Choo Island in the Japan sea (which is full of interest and went through several edition). Travels in North America, Fragments of a Voyage and Travels, Schloss Heinfeld, and Patchwork. He was intimate with Sir Walter Scott, and his account of a Christmas visit to Abbotsford, in 1824, enriches Lockhart's admirable life of that great man. There is also his graphic account of Scott in lodgings (June, 1836) after Constable's failure had ruined him. Captain Maitland's narrative of the reception of Napoleon on board the Bellerophon, after Waterloo, had the advantage of Hall's revision. In 1631, when a visit to a foreign climate was recommended, it was on Hall's suggestion that the British government placed a ship of war at Scott's disposal, and he it was, also, who personally assisted in his embarkation at Portsmouth. Afflicted with insanity, he became an inmate of Haslar Hospital, Portsmouth, where he died in 1844, aged fifty-six.—M.

mean to cleave all night to that wish wash? For shame, man, such doings were never heard of in the "Grand House."

Hall. Never mind me—I'll back Canton against Kingston all the world over—the cup "that cheers but not inebriates" for me!—(*Sings.*)

> "Barnaby, Barnaby, thou'st been drinking,
> I can tell by thy nose, and thine eyes winking.
> Drunk at Richmond, drunk at Dover,
> Drunk at Newcastle, and drunk all over,
> Hey, Barnaby! Take't for a warning,
> Be no more drunk at night, dry i' the morning.'

Mullion. Very well, Captain. I'faith you are a gallant commander, to make head against us with such a woful inferiority of *materiel.* Shall I play maker, Laird?

Tickler. Surely. In the absence of the Teeger,* who but yourself? Create away. *Esto* punch!

Mullion (*rings*). I stepped into the bayonet-room a few minutes before last bottle but one. Punch *est.* Bring in the china, Mrs. Marjoribanks. That's a kind body.

Tickler. Bonum est quod fecisti. I scarcely desiderate the Arns. O, Captain, Captain!—and you that touch off scenes of jollification with such a true Barnabesque gusto. Why, they're the best things in your book†—worth fifty lectures on naval discipline—the Ship-Church—the theory of the trade winds—and passenger St. Paul off La Valetta. But no matter, fill fair any how.

North. I should like to hear Sam Coleridge's commentary on the undoubted, but to me inexplicable fact, that our friend was a hearty toper in the days of his Whiggery, but no sooner turned one of the tautest of Tories, than he took to the tea-pot. It seems a thing against nature.

Tickler. A cyathological curiosity.

Hall. Quite out. As long as that cold, sour curd lay on my stomach, not all the brandy in Bordeaux could ever make me feel truly comfortably—but now that it's gone, I need no artificial stimulants. A Tory conscience is its own sufficient *vade-mecum.*

North. Nay, nay. We Tories, from my friend Eldon downwards don't drink port by the pipe, and punch by the puncheon, to keep our own hearts up—not at all; but merely to enable us to look at the wicked part of the world without an intolerable degree of disgust.‡ Flowing cups are the sunshine of humanity. But for them

* Doctor Dunlop, an early and able contributor to *Blackwood.* He was commonly called "Tiger Dunlop." His portrait appeared in the Literary Gallery published in *Fraser's Magazine.* He emigrated to Canada, became a member of the legislature there, and died a few years ago.—M.

† Hall's Fragments of Voyages and Travels.—M.

‡ However economical Lord Eldon might be in other matters, he never stinted himself in port-wine—called *Blackstrap* in days departed.—M.

there would be nothing to break the black shadow of prevailing villany, and one would be apt to get sick of life. They cast some redeeming halos round even the ugliest objects; and to speak for myself, when, as Moore says of Byron, "under the full influence of Bacchus," I can contemplate with passable equanimity even a Whig in pride of place, and a King in duresse vile.

Hall. Avast, there! Haven't I for these two years been preaching up faith, hope, and even charity, *totis viribus*, while you and all the rest of your set have been keeping the world ringing with the doleful changes of your eternal toll, toll, toll?

Tickler. Tol de rol—(*sings.*)

> "Toll for the brave!
> Brave Kempenfelt is gone!
> His last sea-fight is fought,
> His race of glory run!"*

Mullion. Well, if you mean Mr. North, you will at least allow that

> "When Kempenfelt went down,
> His fingers held the pen."

Hall. Down? Out upon your downs! The cause was never in a more thriving case than at this moment; but I maintain that it has never been in bad case at all—never. If I were allowed to play what pranks I pleased in politics, I honestly tell you I don't think I should be inclined to alter one, even the minutest, movement that has taken place, from the 27th of July, 1830, down to this blessed 6th of August, 1832. Capital! excellent! nothing could have been better! affairs have been conducted abroad and at home, by ourselves and by our enemies of all sorts, precisely as in my steadfast opinion a truly wise, deep, foreseeing Tory, or patriot, would have desired to see them. Oh! the game has been beautifully played. In fact, my only doubt is whether we have not been too fortunate all through.

Tickler. That's your distress, is it? So with your own self, after all,

> "Surgit amari *aliquid* medio de fonte leporum."

North. Unmixed happiness would have been too much even for a tea-drinking Tory. I condole with you, dear Pangloss—I commiserate your case—not one glass?

Hall. Neither glasses nor groans for me, old cock o' the roost. I've long since put the mulligrubs as well as the parrot-palate in Schedule A. But I'll give you a toast if you like, and drink it my-

* From Cowper's spirited ballad on the loss of the Royal George, an English first-class man-of-war, which went down at Spithead, 29th August, 1782, while under repairs at Spithead, when Admiral Kempenfelt, with several other officers, and more than 900 men, women, and children, were drowned. At the moment of this sudden casualty, Kempenfelt was writing in the cabin.—M.

self in what Dr. Johnson called "an effusion as red as blood;"—here's CHURCH AND KING!!!—They were never more flourishing—long may they flourish!—Hip—hip—

Tickler. Hip and thigh you mean.

Hall. ——Hip-hurrah! hurrah!! hurrah!!! (*conhipeure omnes.*) That's the thing! Strong, fixed, immovable, eternally glorious and growing in glory, the Church and the Monarchy have outlived already and will outlive hereafter, storms a thousand times fiercer than any our times have witnessed—or shall witness—

> "Moor'd in the rifted rock,
> Proof to the tempest's shock,
> Firmer they root them, the ruder it blow."

Their only danger, if it were possible for them to be really in danger, would consist in the felonious faintheartedness of their, if they would but see and feel it, invincible friends. One chirp of despondency among you, gentlemen, is more damaging than all the brazen-trumpetfuls of foul breath that ever Treason charged or will charge with; but even your chirping won't help them to their ends. No, no, sirs; it was only the Philistines that succumbed, in the long run, to the jaw of an ass. We are the true believers, and we must succeed——

Tickler. If we choose?

Hall. Whether we choose or no. As my friend Bonaparte used to say, "Quod scriptum, scriptum." When I was in Holland, during the peace of Amiens, there came a horrible roar of surge and billow and howling Boreas one evening, so horrible that the worthy Dutchers of the place were inclined to give all up, and in fact many of them sent wife and bairns, goods and plenishing a-packing God knows how far into the interior, never doubting, in short, that the dike must give way, and their whole town be swamped into annihilation. Next morning, however, the sun rose clear and bright, and when I among others took courage to go down and examine the site of the anticipated breach, we found the concern stronger a million times than all the labor of half-a-dozen plodding centuries had ever been able to make it—by Jupiter!

North. By Neptune, if you please.

Hall. Yes, μα τον Ποσειδωνα—The raging ocean, in fact, had hurled before him such a mass of sturdy solid stuff, that every heave it gave only added a new line of bulwark to the deserted barrier of trembling Mynheer, who, in consequence of that fortunate hurricane, has ever since rejoiced in a circumvallation that would defy a deluge. That's the way to look at things. Depend on't, this brutal Bill,*

* The Reform Bill, which had received the royal assent on the 7th June, 1832, after a struggle of unexampled excitement, perseverance, and duration, in and out of Parliament.—M.

whatever the designs of its framers, and the fears of its enemies, will turn out our breakwater after all.

North. I back your Nic Frog against Mother Partington.*

Tickler. I have no objection to back Basil Hall against Sydney Smith, as to the article of apt illustration, any day in the prophetical week—which, you know, consists of seventy years. But wit and argument are both out of date *now;* and as to this beastly business——

Hall. Nil desperandum de RepublicA!

North. Why, *we* never doubted that it would come to a Republic.

Hall. Pooh! and if it does, what's the harm? 'Twon't last five summers, man. Heavens! what a day will be the Restoration!

North. Why, old Urquhart, super-exquisite Rabelaisian Sir Thomas, the quaint descendant of Ουριχαρτος King of Thessaly, lawful representative, in the three hundred and thirteenth generation, of Japhet Emperor of Europe, and *facile princeps* of all translators that ever Europe nurtured, except only Sotheby—that dear old worthy royalist who domesticated Panurge among us, on hearing of rascal Monk's message to Breda, as he was sitting over a black mutton-chop and a thimbleful of Cape Madeira in a dining parlor sunk seven feet odd inches beneath the level of Fleetditch—ordered in a whole bottle of the best port the beggarly place could afford—tossed it off in an ecstacy of two rummers, and died on the spot of sheer joy;—a touching termination of a queerly mixed life!† Perhaps you, dear Basil, may live to treat yourself to a basin of prime gunpowder, after several weary winters of saloop, on being certiorated that some future Buffer Jones, in anticipation

> "Of a right honorable name
> To call his vixen by,"

has thought it meet, fit, and becoming to invite Queen Victoria from Herrenhausen—and may have the glory of an equally sublime though more sober exit from this visible diurnal sphere,—as we may well call an age of the world in which journals rule the roast over all things. Well, so be it! What came of the surviving Urquharts then? And what would be the fate ten years hence of those Tory champions, who, having nerves strung after the fashion of Timothy's or mine, were never-meant to die either of grief for a revolution, or of joy for a restoration—tough, even-pulsed, whip-cord codgers born to sit unmoved, whether among the crack of corks or of crowns?

* Sidney Smith's account of Mrs. Partington's endeavor to resist the Atlantic with a besom was recent at this time.—M.

† This may be true. Sir Thomas Urquhart, who translated Rabelais, was a Cavalier, and fought at the battle of Worcester. Of his own works, his favorite was "Logopandecteision, or an introduction to the Universal Language."—M.

My dear fellow, the treatment of the Cavaliers will sit by-and-by a deuced heavy lump on the spirits of the Tories. If good Sir Thomas had weathered Oporto, he must have gone back to the Cape. "Gratitude," as Clarendon said, and lived to prove in his own person,* "is a flower that seldom blossometh in the breast either of a Bourbon or a Stuart." The time is like to come for showing whether the Guelph soil be a more congenial one.

Hall. I doubt the fact;—but all this is to little purpose. I hope at least we shall escape the reproach of having in any stage of the drama acted, or declined to act, from motives or dissuasives of the kidney you point to.

North. In one sense I admit what I was talking of is little to the purpose. You and I, Timotheus, may crack with commendable composure about what is likely to turn up in the land, after such a period as the Skipper probably looks to—you and I, my hearty, or any one else

> "Cui *bis* octavum trepidavit Ætas
> Claudere lustrum."

But what say you to the case of the juvenals?—the rising chicks of the cause?—mine ancient favorite's staunch and able descendant, for example, or his historian, worthy to indite goodly matter of all Scottish worthies? Would you table this pack at The Stove? —*vix.*

Hall. I should like to have a good round swinging bet on your both being visible—Nestors as ye are—at the first drawing-room after the proclamation of George and Victoria—for I'm clear against allowing Hanover to part company.†

North. I am more interested to hear your views about Ireland. That cable begins to creak in good earnest, however.

Hall. Just as it ought to do. If you will read, as I have lately done, for the first time, I blush to say, Spenser's Dialogue, on what he calls at its outset "that rich unhappy island," and so downward through Temple, Swift, and the rest of them, to the Moores and Sheils of our own day, you will be thoroughly impressed with one great fact, namely, that Ireland has never yet been properly conquered—and another not less important—to wit, that the sooner she is so conquered the better; and then, I apprehend, you will agree with me that the main question is how to find or fix on the best time and pretence for beginning the real subjugation, and that that question is now likely to be settled in precisely the way most desi-

* The great Clarendon, after all his devoted loyalty to Charles II., was disgraced through the intrigues of the Duchess of Portsmouth (one of the many mistresses of the King), and went into voluntary exile to escape the consequences of impeachment. He died at Rouen, in 1674.—M.

† The marriage of Prince George of Cumberland (now King of Hanover) with the Princess Victoria, quite a child in 1832, was a favorite speculation of the high-Tory party.—M.

rable for us Tories—I mean by some horrid outbreak of the Catholics—consequent on the concession *by*, or *for*, the Protestants, of the last of the demands which they, the scamps, could possibly bring forward, *quâ* Catholics.

North. Halt, friend; I thought you had tipped us something like a speech in favor of the passing of the Duke's "Relief Bill?"

Hall. Peccavi. There was still one little drop of dirty Whig blood in my body, and it was then that it got squeezed out of me. I admit that *I* was quite in the wrong as to the view I then took of the working of his Grace's measure;* and I have no doubt the glorious old fellow would say as much himself if he were here among us, which I am sure he would much enjoy being—but as to the measure itself, I maintain it was a most fortunate thing that it passed. But for that we should never have known how the ship was to right again. What you call, and always called a blunder, and which no doubt was a blunder, *quoad* the persons that moved in it, was, nevertheless, in itself, the cleverest thing that could have been hit on for the safe and easy attainment of our ultimate objects. It was, in short, necessary to bring matters to a point. We had got both internally here in Britain, and more so still as to Ireland, and our whole system of Irish connexion, into a false state—but how *revocare gradum?* That was the difficulty—and this has solved it—evidently—quite evidently.

North. In short, the coachman had got on the wrong track, and when that sort of thing occurs, the best way is always to drive on *slick*, as your friends the Yankees say, till you near the precipice, and not to haul up even then, but to go the whole hog, as the same classical vocabulary expresseth it, and make a clean Sam Patch job of it—at it, my tits, 'ware bolting—down you go; when once we're snug at the bottom, we can easily move round to the other extremity, and avoid accidents in future.

Tickler. Phaeton never sketched a shrewder programme.

Hall. Why, I hope, after all, I am not among a conventicle of heathen infidels. Surely, people can't outlive the *sextum decimum lustrum*, on even (my own case, heigho!) the *octavum*, without being pretty well convinced that matters don't go on either for good or for evil in this world of ours, merely according as the human movers-apparent thereof happen to be dull or shrewd in their own personal guesses as to the working of this as yet untried thing, or that. I am not more satisfied of my own existence, than of the continual superintendence and efficacious control of Providence over all the springs and evolutions of the political system; and the creed you seem so well disposed to smile at, amounts, after all, to nothing more

* The Catholic Relief Bill of 1829, brought in and passed by Wellington and Peel, in the teeth of their former political principles and pledges.—M.

than a conscientious application to public affairs of the old maxim, "whatever is, is right"—a maxim for which I beg leave to claim quite as high a descent as the poet does for Γνωθι Σεαυτον.

Tickler. Hang it, are ye up to Greek too?

Hall. Ay, ay, and I suppose I need not remind you that old Homer himself has left the whole essence of Toryism compressed for eternal use, in three sounding hexameters, that might be printed on the rim of a halfpenny.

Tickler. Repeat your credo.

Hall. υκ αγαθον πολυκοιρανιη· 'Εις κοιρανος ἐςω:
'Εις Βασιλευς—ᾡ ἐδωκε Κρονυ ϖαις αγκυλομητεω
Σκηῶτρον τ' ηδε Θεμιςας ινα σφισιν εμβασιλευῃ.

Mullion. A right dulcet triplet for the ear of Mein Metternich.

Tickler. Well, and I for one am by no means ashamed to confess, that I feel myself waxing more and more Austrian, every winter of our discontent that rolls over my bald pate.

North. Come, Captain—I'm a country gentleman—translate.

Hall. In the absence of Sotheby, here goes:

Whene'er the Whig impostors have their swing,
They rob the people, and oppress the King;
But King and people soon detect their jobs,
And pluck the plunder from their bursting fobs;
Scorn rises in an universal shout,
And sees them trundled to the right about.

North. Very good doctrine. Thanks!

Mullion. Perhaps the Captain could favor us with a Hebrew edition also.

Hall. To be sure. Do you think a right-minded officer would ever have the brass to preach a sermon, even in the Ship-Church, without having made himself a bit of a dab in both of the original tongues? Tell that to the marines!—

לא־הסור מעליו אולתו אם תכתוש את האויל במכתש בתוך הריפות בצלי

North. You must review my friend Wrangham's edition of Walton's Prolegomena for my next double number.*

Hall. I wonder you have the face to talk to me of reviewing. Why, you have never yet had a single article on my Fragments—and here, I think, is the fifteenth or so on Sotheby's Homer.

North. A great work, sir, a solid addition to English literature. Tickler, I know, calls it merely bad Pope, but he's no more fit to appreciate such a writer, than I am to criticise yours, Captain.

Tickler. Smoke the editor! Come Basileutate Basil, if you want your autobiography to be recorded in Maga, you must e'en pocket

* Archdeacon Wrangham, one of the most elegant scholars of modern times, and especially eminent for the classic beauty of his translations into Latin.—M.

humbug, and do the job yourself. That, after all is generally much the most satisfactory plan—and I'm sure if I were so far left to myself as to turn bookmaker, I should never dream of any other. Stick to the old Spanish adage, and never ask another man to do for you that which you can do for yourself.

Hall. But what if the thing spunks out?

Mullion. Laugh, of course, and there's an end; but he's a green hand who ever does let any thing of that kind spunk out. Here's Mr. Tickler, now, I warrant you he has not allowed a single line of his autograph to appear in any printing-office since the beginning of this century; and indeed, if I were worth any body's detecting or suspecting, I believe I should follow his example. See what an ugly scrape Brougham has just got into, in consequence of the MS. of his infamous critique on the Hours of Idleness casting up in some d—d corner of one of old Willison's drawers, after the lapse of four-and-twenty years!

Hall. Why, I doubt if the Chancellor would have given three coppers to avoid the grand discovery. What, after all, does it signify? Who was to detect a future Nelson of song in these middy mumblings about Pollys and Lucys, and Cambridge Choristers, and Sympathetic Oaklings? Stuff. The review does Brougham credit It was the making of Byron.*

North. Upon the same principle that the Reform Bill is to be the making of the Tories.

Hall. Exactly. Neither the poet nor the party wanted any thing in this world but to be put upon their mettle. You'll see what you'll see by-and-by. No more "Hours of Idleness," I promise you; no more weak imitations of false models; but sturdy self-reliance—real substantial spleen and venom—indefatigable thorough-going industry—an universal uproar of applause—and Brougham himself only too happy to lift his trumpet in the van of our triumph.

Tickler. In the meantime, we certainly seem to have set out on a pretty considerable pilgrimage from the regions of Downing Street. We sha'n't show our noses there again for some while, I opine.

Hall. I hope in God not. We had been much too long in office, and have picked up, I must own, not a few scurvy tricks and propensities, which must be got rid of effectually, before we have any chance of reappearing to real advantage in that part of the world.

North. Come, I'm glad to hear these little admissions, however. I can remember the day when honest Maga was in rather baddish

* Byron's "Hours of Idleness," whoever wrote the critique in the *Edinburgh Review*, are scarcely above mediocrity. Byron believed Brougham to be the critic, and has repeatedly sneered at him—commencing in the English Bards, and concluding in Don Juan.—M.

odor up stairs, for being the only one of all the Wise Virgins that ventured to whisper any thing of this sort. *We* were all along against the whiggification of the Tory System; whereas—but what were you saying only this blessed minute? I thought your theory was, that we had never done any thing but what was exactly right and proper in the circumstances.

Hall. Not at all. I admit a thousand sins, and, what's worse, blunders—which must be repented of and atoned for, no doubt about that. What I asserted was, that we had done just what we ought to have done throughout that particular stage of the affair that refers to this Reform Question—ever, in short, since we were turned out in the end of 1830, by that brutal combination between your Ultra-Tories,—God forgive ye!—and the Whigs. O, ye old sinners, do you think I've forgot your trumpetings of Grey and Brougham just before that epoch—your constant sneering at Peel, and your savage abuse of the immortal Duke himself?

North. Not being a prophet, which I freely confess your Quarterly article on Charles X. and Polignac has proved you to be, Captain Hall, how could I judge of people except from what they said or did about that time? Had we not good reason for it, if in sorrow and sadness we did say of the Duke and Peel what the fellows that were greediest to lick their spittle *then*, are saying loud enough and bitterly enough *now?* and, on the other hand, hadn't we heard this dirty griping body Grey bellowing in the House of Lords, in apparently the most genuine tone of Toryism, on the subjects of the Currency and Free Trade, and I know not how many more of the Whig conundrums? and hadn't we seen Brougham himself, as Cobbett elegantly expressed it, sticking his knees in Canning's back, lending all his gigantic energies to the support of a government, the very first acts of which were to throw the Papist Question overboard, denounce all plans of Parliamentary Reform whatever as pernicious humbug, and form a strict alliance with a whole legion of the cidevant most obstreperous Whigs, on the express condition of their putting all their Whiggery into one breeches pocket, and a decent *quantulum* of place and pension into the other? How could a mere mortal observer pretend to doubt that these folks were likely to be at least as sound and constitutional ministers of the crown, as those soi-disant *Tories*, who had for a series of sessions done little but outrage in every way then thought possible, every feeling and principle dear to the great Tory heart of Old England!

Hall. Well, I'm sorry I touched that string. At all events, the people you blame have seen the errors of their former ways now, and the Tory party in Parliament and in the country have once more rallied in hearty union round the only efficient chiefs the times afford us.

Tickler. That's exactly the thing I doubt. During a certain recent, not unimportant handful of days, when *Who's to be in? Who out?* was once more the question on every lip, I fancied I could perceive ugly symptoms of the old sores being very likely to break out again, in case a certain bold throwster had swept the pool. Indeed, the more I reflect on all that happened then, the more am I satisfied that there is at this moment no real, hearty, sincere union among the Dons of the different parliamentary cliques of Toryism. How do you account for the non-appearance of Peel, or any of his coterie, at the Pitt dinner?*

Hall. Peel had not been to any Pitt dinner since 1829, and did not, I suppose, choose to run the risk of being supposed to have stayed away on grounds of mere temporary convenience.

Tickler. Temporary fiddlestick! If he had gone there, and made one stout Protestant speech, confessing past mistakes, and promising staunchness in all time coming, 'tis my belief, the real fellows would almost have cracked the roof over him with their cheers. 'Twas an opportunity lost, and the like mayn't turn up in a hurry again for Peel.

Hall. It was a glorious scene. I wish you, North, had been there, it would have warmed your heart for six months. Though I stuck all the evening to toast-and-water, I confess I felt as if I had swallowed a vat of champagne.

Tickler. Shall I tell you exactly what I suspect to have been the *dessous des cartes?* You fine folks about St. James's parish may think and whisper what you please, but the simple and the consolatory truth is, that the gentry you smile at as the Ultras, have more sterling solid power with the mass of Tory population throughout England, Scotland, Ireland, and the colonies, dominions, and dependencies thereunto pertaining—ay, about a thousand times more power than the big wigs you speak of as the only efficient chiefs the times affords us. I may be mistaken, but it is my firm belief, that if Sir Robert Peel were to plant himself in one corner of any given county to-morrow, and Sir Richard Vyvyan or Sir Robert Inglis in another,† and each cry, *hoop, halloo!* for one pretty man that would rally round the ex-secretary, five hundred with broader shoulders, though not perhaps so well-polished boots, would swell τυς αμφι THE Protestant. In other words, the Parliamentary

* Annually held in London, on the anniversary of William Pitt's birthday. The Whigs have a like celebration in honor of Charles James Fox. Both have dwindled down into mere social festivals.—M.

† When the Catholic Relief Bill was proposed, in 1829, two of its most bitter opponents, in the House of Commons, were Sir Richard Vyvyan (then a young Cornish baronet and member for Bristol), and Sir Robert Harry Inglis, who was elected for Oxford University, when Peel resigned on announcing his abandonment of anti-Catholic politics. Vyvyan settled down into calm Conservatism, in which he continues. Inglis, who remained M. P. for Oxford, until the beginning of 1854, has never once (even by accident) given a liberal vote. From first to last, he was intolerant.—M.

chieftainship has unfortunately been dissevered from the popular. There was but one principle, broad and deep, to which Tories could appeal as a counterpoise—and more than that—to all the mob-flattering nonsenses habitually in these latter days promulgated from the Cathedra of Whiggism. Down to 1829, the real Parliamentary captains of our array leant surely and firmly upon this gallant spear, and none could shake their steps—they then, in evil hour, snapped and spurned it, and took to a reed which presently pierced their sides. A considerable section of the host followed their error and their fortunes; but the allegiance, the true, hearty, soulfelt faith of the party at large, was at once transferred to other hitherto less distinguished persons. By-and-by, the party itself was reduced to such a situation, that every one saw nothing could give it even a chance of salvation, except a general recognition, once again, of some compact knot of leaders; and I, for one, entertained considerable hopes, that at the earliest opportunity steps would be taken to present the country with such a band, composed, in just and equal proportion, of men belonging to the two unfortunately dissevered sets—the ex-ministerial "*Waverers*" of 1829, and the unflinching champions of Protestantism of the same epoch. But what was the upshot? At the very first crisis that occurred in which it might have been possible to hold forth this saving banner of concord, at the first moment when the ex-ministers seemed to have it in their power once more to arrange a cabinet, among fifty various whisperings about who was and who was not to have a place in the said cabinet, it so happened, that nobody ever appeared even to dream that a fair share was to be tendered to the Tories proper.

North. Why, I doubt if even one of all their gallant array, with the exception of a lawyer, whose professional position made his a distinct case, was ever seriously talked of for cabinet-office on that occasion.

Tickler. No, sir, no,—not even within the walls of the Carlton Club House,* an institution then about three weeks old, and which had claimed, at starting, the support and adhesion of the *party*, on the express footing that thenceforth there was to be an end of all *clique*-rendezvouses whatsoever.

Hall. I believe you were in London at the time. I was not, and therefore can't speak with certainty as to some of these matters. But surely, surely, you never fancied it possible that an efficient government could be formed mainly of the Ultras? I know, esteem, and even admire some of them; but I can't suppose any one of themselves ever to have entertained an idea so extravagant.

Tickler. I know several of them pretty well, and esteem them deeply, and admire the talents of some almost as highly as I do

* In London. It admits no members who are not Conservative in politics.—M.

the principles that hold them together; but it never, most assuredly, entered my noddle to conceive that they could make the real working pith of an administration. They could as soon fly. But no more could the others do without them than—they by themselves; and my complaint is, that one heard of no sort of attempt toward some decent amalgamation of the two, singly powerless, but if united, invincible elements.

North. In short, you think, out of a dozen cabinet places, the half, or nearly so, ought, in order to give us any chance, to have been tendered, *in limine*, to our friends of the Oxford Blues?

Tickler. That's it. No doing without it.

Mullion. Rem acu tetigisti. But what signifies dwelling on this one little feature of the case? It has been, from beginning to end, a series of miserable blunders. The Captain himself gives up the real points when he limits his defence to the affairs of the last two years.

Tickler. 'Tis the last drop that makes the cup run over; and few are accustomed to look further. The truth is, that from the hour of Lord Londonderry's death the doom of our party was sealed for our time. The division between the Wellingtons and the Cannings began from the moment when my brilliant friend took his place in the Cabinet of 1822. That division it was which rendered the Duke's government weak, *ab initio;* and if there ever had been a chance of its being got over, the absurd, idle, ridiculous quarrel with Huskisson riveted *that* mischief.* The Duke's sense of weakness, separated as he was from the Canningites, ought to have made him throw himself with the most open cordiality on the Protestants; on the contrary, he followed poor Canning's own fatal example, and strove to invigorate himself by tampering with Whig measures first, and afterward with Whig men. He thus contrived to lose his hold of the only party whom he ever in prudence ought to have trusted; while another small, but then influential, detachment regarded him every day with growing personal fierceness of dislike; and, meantime, the gross mass of enemies in principle laughed at the notion of their being disarmed either by his borrowing half-leaves (all *Errata*) from their book, or bribing over a few subalterns from their ranks. The Whigs lay by for a promising opportunity of an assault-general, and, at the moment when that opened on them, they found also the means to mask it by a side attack, in which those who, though not the Duke's friends, ought to have been their most

* On the contrary, Wellington's turning Huskisson out of the Cabinet was a step as judicious as bold. Huskisson, who had actually been a member of the Jacobin Club at Paris (and had there worn their *bonnet rouge*) had crept up, through a variety of offices, into the Wellington Cabinet, which was essentially Tory. He endeavored to make the public believe that *he* had obtained the Duke's pledge that it should become Liberal, and lost office by playing the double game. When the Duke saw what he was manœuvring for, he dismissed him.—M.

resolute enemies, were so infatuated as to lend them a hand. Down went the Duke, and up came Whiggery in all its glory.

North. The consequences ought to have reconsolidated every shaken link on the other side; and I was in hopes such had been the case—now at least. But Timothy, it appears, has his reasons for considering the old rent as even at this hour only slurred over with filigree. If it be so, more's the pity.

Tickler. If it be so? Why, you have not yet said a syllable of one wee bit chink, that, unless I be sorely mistaken, has as much to answer for as to the last of our tribulations as any that yawns in all men's view.

Hall. What may this be? Do you allude to Lady ——?

Tickler. Not I; petticoats be hang'd. I allude to a not uncommon suspicion, in which I am sorry to tell you I have for some time partaken, that there is a crack within a crack, and that while the Ex-Ministers are far enough from having really reconciled themselves to the Ultras, they are not even completely at one *inter se*. In short, I fear there is but too much ground for questioning the solidity of the tie that seems to unite his Grace of Wellington and the Right Honorable of Tamworth.*

Hall. What a chimera! (begging your pardon.) How could any jealousy spring up between two such persons so situated with regard to each other, their party, their country, the world? *Credat Judæus!*

Tickler. I have hardly the honor of being personally acquainted either with the Duke or Sir Robert Peel—perhaps they are the only two very eminent men of my own times with whom I have never happened to find myself at the same round dinner-table—but that, among other consequences of provincial life, must be put up withal. My notions of them can, therefore, have been formed from little better than the usual sources of information patent to all the lieges; and they will, of course, pass for what notions so formed may be worth. It is, however, an opinion I have long ago taken up, that when a really able, and active, and self-relying peer happens to be Prime Minister of this country, it is next to impossible that he should not presently begin to regard with no very friendly eye that cabinet-colleague who has the lead of the House of Commons. Among the many heavy blows that, partly with and partly without design, Mr. Pitt inflicted, during his long career, on the aristocracy, not the least important was that which resulted, perhaps unavoidably, from the mere circumstances of the length of his sway supreme,—I mean the fact that, during his day, a generation had sprung up to whom the very idea of any but a commoner

* Sir Robert Peel represented Tamworth (where he had large property) from 1830 till his death, in July, 1852.—M.

being Premier, seemed a something which *abolevit ætas*. The chief business of the state had occasionally, before his reign, been transacted in the Lower House during limited periods; but his almost lifelong tenure of office accustomed the public generally to think of that as the natural, the fit, in fact the only fit place for it to be dealt with *pro virili*. The unfortunate notion has never since been seriously shaken, and every member of the House of Lords, who has in the intervening period, tried the thing, has found himself sorely hampered accordingly. In all such cases the Premier has found himself somewhat in a false position. But the embarrassments that must have surrounded the Duke of Wellington, probably far surpassed those that any of his noble predecessors within the last century had had to encounter.

Hall. Very well; and you'll allow him nerves proportionate, I calculate.

Tickler. Sans doute—nobody questions the glorious Duke's nerves—*triplex illi circum corda robur!* But observe the absolute novelty of his case. He was the first English Prime Minister, since the Duke of Newcastle, that could not speak.*

Hall. Not speak! Why, I once heard Lord Brougham himself characterize one of his grace's speeches in the House of Lords as *sublime*.

Tickler. I am glad to hear that, or anything else, to Lord Brougham's credit; but I certainly never heard of it before. Let me guess—could it have been a personal explanation?

Hall. Hum—yes, I believe you have guessed right enough there.

North. Nobody doubts that every great man must occasionally be eloquent.

Tickler. No—no—nobody. Strong feelings of assaulted honor, or outraged pride, can, I doubt not, stir a Wellington for a few seconds into a Demosthenes; and I can easily believe that he may have flung out, on some great occasion, in which his heart, more than his head, was concerned, a score or so of sentences worthy of being written in gold. But what signifies all this, if a man be under ordinary circumstances a dry, cold, hesitating, maniac, abrupt, confused mouthpiece of his own government? When I talked of *speaking*, I did not allude to anything so lofty as bursts of passion, which in a man like Wellington, high fed with thirty years of universal applause and veneration, a personal explanation is most likely to consist of. For the jogtrot rhetorical round-round-round-

* There was a vast difference between the men. Wellington had acquired great knowledge of men and things, during his wars in various parts of the world, and had also acted in a diplomatic capacity on several occasions. Newcastle was profoundly ignorant, though a prime minister. As a speaker, he was verbose, but not intelligible. He was so timid that he was afraid to sleep in a room alone. Wellington, who had no pretensions to the title of orator, spoke with plain simplicity, which, added to the weight his public services gave him, was highly impressive.—M.

about of a popular assembly, depend upon it, he was never born; and I am apt to conceive (for I say nothing positively) that the conscious want of a qualification which he probably in his heart despised, and despises, and ever will despise, may have had no trivial share—not only in the quarrel which we now know to have sprung up, almost at the outset, between the Duke and Canning as co-members of Lord Liverpool's cabinet—but eke, if it does exist, which our friend in the cloth shoes seems to persist in doubting, in that quieter grudge which I have fancied I could smell out between him and the *ore-rotundo*-est of the moderns.

Hall. Well, I wonder to hear you ascribe sentiments of so petty a cast to minds of such calibre.

Tickler. My dear Basil, this is an age of vigorous intellects, but not of great minds.

Hall. I have come in contact with some such, however. I have breakfasted with Bolivar—I have lunched with Napoleon*—I have dined with Wellington—and now, blessed be the stars above, here am I drinking tea with North and Tickler.

North. *By* them, with your leave.

Hall. Oho! This is bringing us back to the old controversy again.

North. Under favor, I am entirely in order. The concern we have been chattering over during our last bowl, and your six last basins, resolves itself into a mere *umbra* of the much more interesting one we started with.

Hall. I don't take you, for once.

Tickler. What Kit means, is, that both the Duke and Peel are of your own d——d heretical sect of the Hydorites. From all I have ever heard, it is, I am sorry to say, extremely doubtful to me, whether any Prime Minister of this country, as Prime Minister, has been on any one occasion gloriously drunk, since the exit of William Pitt.

Mullion. Tell it not in Gath. Did you not observe what the Standard said, the other day, against the sin of traducing one's party?

Tickler. And when did I ever do anything else but extol them to the seventh heaven, in black and white? But is a man never to spirit out a single mouthful of the raw *truth*, even *viva voce* under the impenetrable sanctity of one's own rooftree? Mr. Secretary Mullion, the chain is on the door, and not a bonnie lassie in the village has the slightest suspicion but that I am, at this moment—

"Wasting what poets call the midnight taper,"

over Hume or Du Bos.

* Simon Bolivar, the celebrated liberator of South America, first President of Colombia, and Dictator of Peru; born in 1783, died in 1830.—Napoleon was much pleased with Captain Basil Hall, with whom he held a long conversation at St. Helena.—M.

North. All right, that. But, Captain Hall, though our friend is fond of putting things in a broad, and therefore sometimes, peradventure, in a coarse light, I suspect you must allow there is some homely truth at the bottom of what called out my worthy secretary's admonitory reclamation. Is it, or is it not, a fact that the days of what is vulgarly called good fellowship were, after all, more favorable to the maintenance of lively, lovely brotherhood of feeling among the politicians, than this new, dandified era of milk-sopism? Come, now, speak honestly—could any of the worst misfortunes of late years have befallen our party, had our chiefs been real hearty bowsing lads of the old three-bottle school?

Tickler (*sings*).

Vixi regulis majorum,
Dicens jocum, miscens jorum.
In pistrinis, in popinis,
In coquinis, in culinis,
Huc et illuc, istic, ibi,
Empsi potus plus quam cibi.
Huc et illuc, &c.

Puer, senex, mundum totum
Tanti esse quanti potum
Semper duxi: mallem mori
Quam vitare vitam Tori;
Sobrius est jungendus agno,
Ebrius Alexandro Magno.
Sobrius est, &c.

Mores *hic* muntantur nondum,
Hodie idem sum qui quondam;
Haurio mixtum, haurio merum,
Neque Whiggior sum quam eram—
Plenus mixto, plenus mero,
Qualis nunc sepultus ero!
Plenus mixto, &c.

Mullion. The archdeacon never jingled more charmingly!

Hall. I yield—I yield—give me a bumper! The Immortal Memory of William Pitt!!! (*Three times three.*)

North. That's a good lad at last.

Mullion. O that we could make similar converts in the high places!

Tickler. Utinam! Oh, sir, if—when Wellington and Peel really made up their minds to pass the Catholic Bill, which we now know they had done months and months before any body but themselves suspected it—they had, in place of locking up the secret, and allowing all their best friends to go down into the country in utter ignorance of what was intended, there to commit themselves to their allies and constituents by a thousand new speeches and pledges—if, instead of this, they had, the moment the resolution was taken, called together some twelve or twenty good fellows I could name, Sir Robert Inglis, Sir Charles Wetherell, and Lord Winchilsea among the rest,* and after a capital dinner, say at the Ship at Greenwich, or the Star and Garter on Richmond Hill, and a few rounds of the blackstrap, one or other of the two had risen, and in a short, plain, unvarnished oratiuncle, told the company that the thing *must* be done, and *why*—or—or else they must give up the government; that to attempt to carry such a measure without the conscientious, however sorrowful concurrence, and the sincere and hearty united countenance and support of *them*, and such as them, would be alike irreconcilable to their personal feelings as fatal to the party; and, in short, that it rested entirely with the worthy compotators either to assist the cabinet *totis viribus*, or to speak the word, and see it break up on the instant. If this had been done, who can well doubt, after what has since occurred, that the Duke and Sir Robert would have received the support they asked, and strong in that support, been able to pass their measure in some much less offensive form than it ultimately assumed? I do not, for one.

North. Why, if such a dinner had been to take place, I myself should no doubt have been invited to be present, and I think I can safely say that my voice would have been theirs, *absque morâ.*

Tickler. To be sure, it would. But, granting the aid requested had been refused, and the Government had on that account gone out, what would then have been the result? Who doubts that, with the great Tory party heartily united on the Opposition benches, the Whigs, coming in under such circumstances, would have been well content to yield conditions such as might have rendered *their* bill comparatively a safe one; or that, *their* said bill once carried, and the confidence of the Tory union remaining undisturbed, they must, very speedily after doing the deed, have retired once more, and been replaced by a Tory cabinet, capable of holding its ground for perhaps an indefinite period?

Hall. The thing might have had a great effect—I admit all that.

Mullion. Effect! I'd lay Charlotte Square to the Cowgate that every thing would have gone smooth, *Falerni exigui jactu!*

Tickler. And now, again, on this late almost as melancholy occasion, suppose, in place of three or four days of stealthy messages, and timid roundabout whisperings, and catlike pokings and purrings in the dark, the Duke, immediately on receiving his Majesty's commands from Lord Lyndhurst, had convened the chief men of all the

* Sir Charles Wetherell, who was the Duke's first law officer (Attorney-General) complained, in parliament, that the Catholic Relief Bill, which he should have drawn up, *ex officio*, had never been seen by him until a copy of it was laid on the table of the House of Commons.—While the Bill was *in transitu*, the Duke fought a duel with the Earl of Winchilsea, a Tory peer, for having published a letter imputing to him a desire to introduce popery into every department of the state.—M.

different Tory sections over a friendly board,—say, in that grand dining-room of his own, that has Canova's statue of Napoleon over the sideboard—and put it to them, *inter pocula*, to consider the actual circumstances of the King's case and the country's, and decide, *they*, the Tory party at large, not *he*, nor his own particular section of adherents, what ought to be done—had such a frank course been adopted even then, can any body question that, while no evil could possibly have come of it, a very great deal of substantial good might?*

Hull. Why, the King was so committed, that I don't see, really, how any good could have come of any course of procedure that might have been substituted for that which the Duke adopted.

North. Begging your pardon—had the Duke of Wellington been in a situation to announce to the King, not his own views, but those of the assembled representatives of one of the great parties in the state, I can, after all, though without going Tickler's lengths, easily fancy that even the King's position might have been essentially altered and improved.

Mullion. Yes—certainly; you are quite right, Mr. North—

Tickler. As it appears to me, the course, under such circumstances, would have been a short and plain one. Having ascertained to what extent the Sovereign had really pledged himself, the Tories must have seen that there remained only two lines to choose between. They might have spoken to his Majesty in a tone such as no individual, however exalted, nor even any mere clique or section of individuals, however distinguished, could have been expected to assume, or perhaps justifiable in assuming. They might with perfect propriety have said to the King—"Your Majesty is in a sad scrape; we are most deeply afflicted to find that it is so; but there can be no doubt that, acting from the best of motives, but through a real misapprehension of what your constitutional duty demanded, you have permitted these mad or malignant Ministers of yours to use your name and authority in a manner most injurious to the interests not only of your royal person, but of the house of which you are the head, and the country of which you are the anointed chief and sworn guardian. We find this abuse of your name has been

* In 1832, though the second reading of the Reform Bill had been carried by a majority of nine in the House of Lords, it was so cut up in committee that (a majority of thirty-five giving a vote by which all control over the measure would be taken out of its proposers' hands) Lord Grey and his colleague told the King that eighty new peers must be created, so as to ensure a ministerial majority. William IV., who had been persuaded by his wife (Queen Adelaide) that the Bill was revolutionary, refused his consent to what he called "swamping the House of Lords." The Grey Cabinet resigned. The King sent for Lord Lyndhurst, ex-Chancellor, who recommended him to call in the Duke of Wellington. This was done, but with a hostile House of Commons, the feeling of the nation against him, and the dead-weight of his own party, who foolishly stuck out against *all* Reform, the Duke was unable to form a government. Lord Grey was recalled. A compromise took place:—Ministers consented not to create peers, and the Opposition peers seceded from the House of Lords (on the King's earnest entreaty, communicated through Sir Herbert Taylor, his private Secretary), until the Reform Bill became the law of the land.—M.

apparently so sanctioned and enforced by some of your own words, and even actions, that to convince the nation, by any ordinary means, that it has been *an abuse* at all, is now hopeless. What, then, is to be done? Is your Majesty prepared to adopt the only course by which it is, in our solemn opinion, possible *yet* to arrest the tide of popular delusion, and put a bar to the progress of what, calling itself reform, is, or at least must inevitably and speedily lead to, revolution? Is the Monarch prepared to sacrifice himself, in order that he may yet save the Monarchy? Your Majesty well remembers that when a measure less dangerous than the present was urged on the high-spirited Prince, whose blood flows in your veins, he answered in these words, *I will go to Hanover first!*"

Hall. I suspect there would have been something cousin-german to misprision of treason in such a suggestion.

North. Perhaps there would—but what if substantial high-treason not only against the individual *King*, but the hereditary *Crown*, were conscientiously felt to be involved in advising his Majesty to adopt the only alternative at the time within his power?

Mullion. You have him there, Mr. North!

Tickler. And, after all, is it not clear—est ce qu'il ne saute aux yeux—that his Majesty would have run very little risk of any sort, by taking his stand on old George's dictum? Why, 'tis my opinion that a confession of error, so gallantly, so heroically put forth—tabled in a form so unimpeachably and admirably sincere, noble, unselfish, and patriotic, would have had the effect of rallying the whole nation round William IV., personally, in a style never equalled in the history of the last three centuries.

North. Not a doubt of it. If he had gone to Hanover he would have been called back by acclamation within a fortnight.

Tickler. Yes, yes—but even granting that had not happened, where was the wonderful sacrifice to be encountered? I know Hanover well, and a right pleasant place it is. Ample are the halls of Herrenhausen, and grand are the ancestral woods of the Hartzgebirgen! As Wordsworth singeth,

> "Fair scenes for childhood's careless days—
> For sportive youth to stray in;
> For manhood to enjoy his strength,
> For age to wear away in."

Come, fill the glass, Mordecai.

Mullion. Obey the tinkle of the devil-dreadness long shaft—(*Sings.*)

> "O send Lewie Gordon hame,
> And the lad I darena name;
> Though his back be at the wa',
> Here's to him that's far awa'.

Hey hone! my honest man,
My firm, heroic, honest man,
Weel wad I my true King ken
Amang ten thousand modern men!

"O to see his face again,
Back restored to lawful reign—
A freeman worthy of the free—
That's the lad we'd a' gang wi'.
Hey hone, &c.

"O to see this princely one,
Safe reseated on his throne!—
Then a' our Whigs wad disappear,
And Tories hail the jubilee year!
Hey hone," &c.

Hall. Very well sung—but our host's notion never occurred, I venture to say, to any human mortal but himself. However, my good fellow, what if your assembled Tories had *not* felt themselves entitled or inclined to offer any such precious advice as you have been suggesting?

Tickler. Why, if they had not done so, sir, it must have been—I conceive we may take that for granted—only because of their feeling that even compliance with advice of that antique cut could no longer arrest the flood of mischief—in short, that even if the King went out, the bill must go down.

Hall. Well, what then?

Tickler. What then?—why, the Tory party in both Houses of Parliament should have openly declared their feeling that such was the case—allowed the Government, without further ado, to carry the bill *in statu quo*—and, in short, seceding for a time *in a body*, left the unmixed responsibility on the ministers, and avoided needless delay, vexatious to a large proportion of their fellow-subjects—to say nothing of a bundle of Londonderryisms and Ellenboroughisms, offensive to all the world.

Hall. I don't see that what has been done leaves the case much different. The secession, such as it was, has been sufficient to let the whole bill pass, nay, to pass with some rather democratical additions, and the creation of peers has been avoided—quite as well as it could have been by your tactics.

North. I set much store by that feature of the case! The creation has been avoided.

Tickler. The idea of such a thing has been thoroughly familiarized to us all; and no man can doubt that it will be reduced to practice, *sans phrase*, IF the existing peers should ever again pluck up courage enough to place themselves in the way of the tyrant-demagogues—which I don't believe they ever will do—not I.

Hall. A fig for such wire-drawing! They will rally again—and that right early—on some occasion when more support from without may be looked for. At all events, here they are as yet intact, and we ought to *hope.* "As I said in my synod sermon," *Cheerfulness is a duty.*

Tickler. Intact! I had much rather have seen their dignity openly violated *brevi manu,* than giving way to a mixture of threat and bribe. I say *bribe*—for the importance they have at least *seemed* to attach to the mere preservation (*pro tempore,* too) of the outward gauds of their order, when they felt and knew that its authority was set at nought, but too well, I fear, entitles me to use a mean word on a melancholy occasion. Much better for them would it have been, that a hundred blackguards should have been forced among them, than that they should have, by conceding all that was really wanted, made themselves parties to the perpetration of the crime. As some Roman says, RAPTU INFELICIUS STUPRUM!

North. The intruders would have received forthwith some sticking soubriquet. They would have been felt by themselves, as well as by the rest of the community, to form a class apart.

Tickler. To be sure—they would, in case of the public mind coming right by-and-by, have been found drawn up themselves in their own dirty corner, ready-made victims for a new Schedule A*—and there an end of *them!*

Mullion (*sings*).

Schedule A!—Schedule A!
Spite of Althorp and Grey,
We shall hear of thee, darling, this many a day!
Neither Boroughs nor Peers
Will take edge from thy shears—
Which must clip yet some selvedges richer than they.

If the fact be so clear,
That' 'tis insolence sheer,
When the Peers with elections at all interfere—
Is't not plain as a pike,
Riper reason must strike
At the Midwife election—whose product's a Peer?

Then, what prop shall we bring
For so monstrous a thing
As a peerless, and, maybe, unpopular King?
Schedule A!—Schedule A!—
'Tis not once and away;
I feel certain, *dear* Schedule, you'll sweep all the ring.

When you've done with the Blacks—
And the tithes—and the tax
That vile corn-growers piled on poor corn-eaters' backs—
Where, I ask, are the *rents*
Of the Pittish per cents?
Shall Cornhill be more safe than Mark-Lane or Almack's?

* In the Reform Bill, all the rotten boroughs intended to be disfranchised, were named in Schedule A.—As many of the Whig nomination boroughs as the Whig Minister could find or make an excuse for, were ~~not~~ so scheduled.—M.

Borough, Peerage, and Crown,
Each we see must go down,
As they chance to encounter the Schedular frown;
And, for certain, sweet Jews,
You may shake in your shoes,
Since the Adjective is but the beard of the Noun.

Hall. Capital! Why, we must have you up to town in the spring. You come nearer to Theodore than any body I have met with in the line.

North. Don't seduce Mordecai. He's a useful lad; you would only spoil him. Timothy, the bowl's as dry as Macculloch.*

Tickler. 'Tis now high time for a flask of champagne. Mullion, you'll find him up to his chin in ice behind that large paper copy of the last volume of Lodge. Untwist the wire, like a hero, and set about another *creation*.

Mullion. To hear is to obey!—(*fit.*)—Well, there's no denying that a caulker of Aix makes a prettyish parenthesis, here and there, in a Clarendonian three-page-sentence-paragraph of the Broth. Now, taste that.

Hall. Excellent!—well, almost thou persuadest me!—I begin to think it very possible that a more liberal infusion of the old-fashioned principle of jollity might really have had a considerable effect in soothing and sweetening the inevitable asperities of conflicting and rival interests and ambitions in the upper sphere of life. John Bull, after all, is none the worse for his grog any more than his prodigal son, poor Jack.

Mullion. I thought in your last series you had spun a yarn to the praise and glory of the Cocoa-system.

Hall. Wait till Easter, and you shall have a hearty palinode.

North. That's right—and pray don't forget to give us a chapter on sea-songs—I mean the real homespun staves—none of your Dibdinisms about "sweet little cherubs that sit up aloft," and such Cockney flams—but the true, original outgushings of the warm heart that beats beneath the pea.

Hall. I shall take a note of your suggestion. Depend on't, the whole of my next *livraison* shall be redolent of the spirit.

Tickler. Do you recollect, North, a conversation on subjects something akin to what we have been handling, that occurred one of the evenings that you and I dined with George the Fourth (God rest him!) at Dalkeith?†—heigho! much about ten years ago, I think!

North. I never heard his Majesty more entertaining—you allude, of course, to his dissertation on the decline of British loyalty,

* The political economist.—M.
† Dalkeith Palace, the seat of the Duke of Buccleuch, near Edinburgh, occupied by George IV. in 1822, when he visited Scotland.—M.

which he was inclined to attribute in the main to the long series of non-convivial reigns between Charles the Second's time and his own. Faith, it was a rare scene of royal high-jinks, to be sure. Honest David Stewart of Garth was present, if you remember. Gads! how he snorted with glee—and then the Laird of Cockpen, and the closing threesome reel of those hairy madmen in the fillibegs!

Tickler. Glengarry was great—Lord Huntly sublime*—indeed, almost every body shone in some way or other; but the King himself certainly played the first fiddle. He was charming that night—I never remember to have seen him more so—and came out, *inter alia,* as the very Horace Walpole of the secret antiquities and private history of the royal wine-bibbery.

North. Ay, and a sound, shrewd theory of his own, too, which he expounded, and to dear Garth's mind, established.

Hall. Let's have it.

North. Speak, Tickler. I've just lighted my cigar.

Tickler. Why, he said the Revolution of 1688 was chiefly owing to the abstemious habits of James the Second, which gradually drew him out of the sympathies of the High Church party; and showed, I think, very clearly, that the monarchical principle was never at all reinvigorated among us, until the ultra-jovial propensities of Sir Robert Walpole came to the support of it, wavering and waning as it had been through the unsocial period of William III., who only snoozed over a nipperkin of Schiedam with a few Dutch favorites, and the still weaker one of Anne, who, though well disposed to the bottle, could only, being a queen, indulge alone, and being a woman, of course, in cherry-bounce.† George I., as his descendant admitted, was a heavy boor, who had no idea of the refined and humanizing luxuries of a festive board, but merely swilled occasionally a quart of black mum, with the brute eagerness of a thirsty horse over a pail of ditch water. His son was not only as dry a bear as himself, but a petulant prig to boot, and must have upset every thing, had not his Prime Minister been the man he was. Then passing on to the beginning of his own father's reign, his Majesty explained how clearly the American affair must have been quite fatal, but for the intensely convivial predilections and potatory prowess of bland Lord North; and again, how the Constitution was preserved amidst all the hurricane fury of the first French Revolution, simply through the never-sufficiently to be extolled Bacchanalianism of Billy Pitt and Harry Dundas, and their

* Colonel Ranaldson Macdonnell of Glengarry, who died in 1828, was a true Highland Chieftain—hot, impetuous, easily angered, quickly forgiving, bold, and generous.—The Lord Huntly of 1822, eventually succeeded to the honors and estates of the Duke of Gordon, and was so popular, that a monument erected in his honor, at Fochabers, in Aberdeenshire, bears an inscription, in which he is described as "The Cock of the North."—M.

† In her life-time, the populace usually spoke of Queen Anne, as "Brandy Nan."—M.

principal assistants in the good work. Lord Sidmouth's love of port carried us over the dismal epoch of Pitt's retirement at the peace of Amiens, and then the great man came back to Downing Street, like a giant refreshed, to push the decanter with a triumphant hand down to the last moment of his invaluable career. His Majesty freely admitted that he himself was not at all sensible to these great truths, until his eyes were opened by the results, in Parliament, of the thin potations patronised by that smart little body, Perceval, and after him by good solemn Lord Liverpool—a state of things which, as he observed, must have been absolutely ruinous, had its influence not been counteracted by the contemporary carousing of Carlton House. Thus, providentially, as it were, he said, whenever we had had a water-drinking King, we had been provided with a bowsy Premier; and *vice versâ*, when the Premier was a milksop, the Prince had rarely failed to be a jolly companion.

North. It was a luculent diatribe; and if a Bozzy had been present, would have much gratified posterity.

Tickler. He summed up, if you recollect, with some rather gloomy anticipations. My brother Frederick,* he said, is a true fellow, but wo to England if a time shall ever come, when the tinkle of the crystal shall be a rare sound both in Windsor Castle and the righthand corner of Downing Street!† I can never forget the tone in which his Majesty spoke these words.

North. Peel was present, and, though he said nothing on the subject, I hoped at the time he would have laid them to heart.

Mullion. From Mr. Tickler's account of things up yonder, I suspect the lesson was nearly thrown away.

Tickler. Entirely. When at college, I have heard, he gave considerable promise, but from his first entrance on public life he began to fall off, and has not, it is currently said, been known to take his dose decently during several Parliaments past. And hence, I presume, the want of a hearty following among the younger hands. Indeed they have, on many recent occasions, shown strong symptoms of revolt, and there has been even open enough talk of electing some statesman more imbued with the ancient time-hallowed veneration for the worship of

"The barrel-strider, ivy-garlanded."

North. What a pity! As for the Duke, he has been a two-glass-of-sherry man, I believe, ever since the battle of Assaye.

Tickler. Eheu! I fear it is but owre true a tale. And this sort of nonsense to be persisted in, in front of such a prince of merry

* Frederick, Duke of York and Albany, second son of George III.—M.
† The principal Government offices in London are located in Downing-street.—M.

after-dinner darlings as Brougham! *Quos Jupiter vult perdere!*—and then our present King, God bless him, seems to be by no means aware of the doctrine so ably enforced by his august predecessor! These grand "banquets" of half a hundred Christians at a time—mere mobs of Jockey Clubs, or Nulli Secundus Clubs, or Tory Clubs, or mixed messes of outlandish mountebanks, harnessed with cordons—these, sirs, are no substitutes for the snug little circles of five to eight, in which our late lamented Sovereign felt it his duty to delight. 'Tis a horrid business; and what darkens our prospects still more is the likelihood of a lady reign to succeed. Heavens! if a new race of statesmen don't spring up, what have we before us!

North. I was much cheered by the announcement of this Carlton Club, the very name seemed to have been chosen with an eye to the drooping condition of post-prandial business; and I pleased myself with anticipating a long series of industrious, persevering, unflinching hilarities—all the repentant chieftains of our host striving who should most zealously and successfully enforce the immortal resolution—

"If any pain or care remain,
Let's drown it in the bowl."

Tickler. Alas! even there we have had a disappointment. The thing's next door, I fear, to a failure. Once or twice I had the satfaction to overhear, as I thumbed the Standard, or Albion, in the long corridor, the agreeable tenor of Wetherell warbling, "Ale, good ale! thou art my darling!" or Sadler's magnificent rich bass, rolling out "Sally in our Alley," but with a few such exceptions, all ascribable to the innate, unconquerable rightmindedness of the Ultra Section, there was little to cheer my heart in that quarter.

North. I thought you seemed to insinuate that the younger hands generally were inclined to be orthodox.

Tickler. Yes, I believe they are; but they are sorely tied down, those of them that don't adhere out and out to the Episcopal purple, by the example of their seniors. There is, however, much to be hoped for; and I rejoice indeed to say so, among the juveniles. I am persuaded that such fellows as Ashley, Mahon, Porchester, Pusey, Walsh, Wrangham, Praed,* and many others worthy to be

* Tories, to a man.—Lord Ashley, who has held office under Wellington and Peel, and sat in the House of Commons from 1826 to 1851, when he became Earl of Shaftesbury, on his father's death. He is lay-leader of the Low-Church party, and may almost be named as having taken up the business of public philanthropist.—Lord Mahon is eldest son of the Earl of Stanhope, held office under Peel in 1835, and is one of his literary executors. He is author of several important historical works.—Lord Porchester, author of "The Moor," and several other poems, succeeded to the Earldom of Carnarvon in 1833, on his father's death.—Sir John Walsh, a good parliamentary debater, entered the House of Commons in 1830.—Mr. Philip Pusey, M. P. for Berkshire, for many years, editor of the *English Agricultural Journal.* His brother, Dr. Pusey, Canon of Christ Church, Oxford, has given his name to the High Church schism there.—Praed (whose Lillian and other poems, edited by Dr. Griswold, have first been published in this country in a collected form) held office under Peel, in 1834–5, and died, prematurely, in 1839, in the prime of life, and with reputation, as an orator and a lyrist, which was high indeed.—M.

classed even with them, want nothing but a little encouragement to turn out genuine jollifiers; and it is pleasing to know that the hopes of the Irish and Scotch youth, with whom they commingle, appear every way disposed to set them a right example. Our own trusty friends, Robert Adam Dundas, Charles Cumming Bruce, his brother Sir William, Sir John Hay, Whytbank, your cousin Lord Selkirk, Captain, young Hope, Lord Stormont, and. above all, the Duke of Buccleuch, are sound shoots of the tough old Caledonian tree, and likely, *Deo volente*, to work a world of good in this line as well as in others.*

North. Ay, and I believe we may count against next session on a stout and stalwart addition to your muster-roll in the person of the princely Buccleuch's brother. Lord John, by all accounts, has taken the field at Teviotdale, backed by Willie Ogilvie of Chesters, and other true lads, in a style that would have rejoiced the heart-strings of glorious old Earl Walter, or dear lamented Duke Charles, to behold.† This is as it should be. Thank God, the Queen of the Border is safe.

Hall. Glad to hear that, however. Come, you're all veering round to my own point of the compass, after all. Hope for ever, say I.

Tickler. There's another good symptom up *yonder*. For many years past the chief rendezvouses of what they call fashion, had certainly been so many hot-beds of Whiggery; but the tables are turning in that walk also—indeed, old Grey himself has been heard to grunt something about the women being against him.

Hall. To be sure they are—but don't blame our Tory dames of high degree, that it is only now, on a really immediately pressing emergency, they have begun to bestir themselves in the line you point to. It's in fact a deuced difficult thing for a woman to be what's called a leader of fashion, unless she brings with her at least a demi-equivocal reputation; and in that sort of article our market has, it must be admitted, been always, comparatively speaking, very much understocked. In times like these we can get on without that species of stimulant and you will now, I am persuaded, see the swing of dandyism run faster and faster to our side.

Mullion. A fig for Almack's! Let's look nearer home—what's to be the upshot here in our own good town and county? Who stands for Lanarkshire? How does Sir George Murray get on in Perth? —Colonel Lyndsay in Fife? Are you really sure that Elliot is to be defeated in Roxburghshire? How do the subscriptions progress? Is there to be plenty of the ginger?

* Of these budding Scottish worthies, Hope, who became a Judge, was the only one who fulfilled Tickler's expectation.—M.

† Lord John Scott (brother of the Duke of Buccleuch, owner of most of the Border-land) was pretty sure of being elected, for the tenants must vote for him, or—turn out.—M.

North. Perth seems all but safe—Fife and Roxburgh are quite so—I am extremely happy to hear, that though the young marquis of Douglas may, if he choose, walk the course in the west country, he can do so only because he distinctly forswears that line of politics of which the Duke his father is at heart sick—as how could the first blood in Britain be otherwise? In Mid-Lothian, Sir George Clerk is as snug as possible—and last of all, I believe, Mr. Blair may now be considered as landed, in Auld Reekie. I much regretted that Sir John Forbes would not stand; I have loved that house through three generations, and feel almost a paternal pride in the rich promise of this young gentleman's talents and virtues, which all his modesty won't prevent the world's doing justice to *belyve*. But since he would not come out on this occasion, a more honorable substitute certainly could not have been found than Blair; and the party owe him a deep debt of gratitude for the frank hearty zeal he met their call with. He, as I said, is now safe. Even in Leith, Aitcheson appears to be driving the Clerk of the Pipe before him like a bundle of chaff.* Come, Mordecai, you have had some hand in these domestic triumphs. Tip the Captain one of your broadsides. He'll smoke enough of the allusions to enjoy the Musa Trivialis.

Mullion. Captain Hall, you've heard, no doubt, of the Right Honorable James Abercrombie—and Sir John Dalrymple, baronet—and John Archibald Murray, Esq.—and Francis Jeffrey, Lord Advocate for Scotland—and *eesome* Aytoun, President of the Cowgate Union—and so forth?

Hall. Everybody knows Sir John, and the Advocate, and the worthy and amiable, though Whiggish, John Murray; but who the mischief is Squire Aytoun?†

Mullion. A younger brother of some Fifeish lairdie, and a hitherto neither famous nor followed perambulator of the outer-house boards, who, having stepped into that bewildered roundhead Geordie Brodie's shoes, as tribune of the rascality in these regions, has of late shot up into a quasi-personage, and really bids fair, if only one Tory stands, to share with him the representation of the capital of old mother Scotia, to the sore and bitter humiliation of the Lord Chief Baron that is or was, commonly called Grieve Abercrombie, Sir James Gibson Craig of Riccarton, Bart. (whom you may remember as long Jamie Gibson the W. S.)—this eminent cavalier's clever underlings, Jeffrey and Murray, Adam Black, bookseller there, Peter Brown, Jamie Spittal, Sandy Craig, and *tutti quanti*.

* The reader will not complain, I think, of my not entering into explanatory details of the Scottish elections of 1832.—M.

† This Mr. Aytoun must not be confounded with William Edmonstone Aytoun, author of "Lays of the Scottish Cavaliers," Professor of Literature in the University of Edinburgh, son-in-law of the late John Wilson, and present Editor of *Blackwood*. The Radical candidate of 1832 is not the strong Conservative of 1854.—M.

Hall. A pure radical, in short, giving gallant battle to the mealy-mouthed.

Mullion. Just so—although Aytoun, to do him justice, was no always a radical, but, on the contrary, did yeoman's service the last time that spirit was up in these quarters, having, in fact, lost several inches of hide at the trot of Airdrie, the canter of Kilmarnock, and various others of those illustrious scenes which stamped deathless renown on our own *Sour Milks* of Attica, in the year of grace 1821, and have been duly commemorated in the Tyrtæan strains of John Lockhart and Peter Tytler, co-laureates in those days to the well-booted myrmidons of Elcho, Hay, and Donald Horne the reaver.

Hall. Pooh! pooh! What signifies looking so far back as the twenty-one? Let's have your stave, however, Mr. Secretary.

Mullion. On the Conservative principle of upholding rank and station, I suppose I must begin with the gentlefolks. Well, here goes—

A NEW SONG.

FOR THE ELECTORS OF THE COUNTY OF MID-LOTHIAN.

Tune—"The Young Lochinvar."

"Oh! the gallant Sir John is a knight of renown,
And from London post-haste he has lately come down,
Having fairly got out of that innocent scrape
Of the Banners, and Mottoes, and bits of Black Crape;
So that trumpery story may pass and begone,
Nor stain the fair fame of the gallant Sir John!

"To be sure there are some, who, in *their* simple way,
Still give an account of "that glorious day."
Which, were it believed, it were awkward to tell
When a Knight has *explain'd* his own story so well;
But of these foolish people there surely are none
Whom you'd weigh in the scale with the gallant Sir John!

"Though half of our townsfolk the TREASON might see,
Or *think* that they saw it—'tis nothing to me—
They were only *spectators*—and can you suppose,
That they either could see, or describe it like those
Who were part of the mob, or perhaps led it on—
Or harangued on the hustings like the gallant Sir John!

"Nay, though AYTOUN himself, the *disclaimer* disclaim,
That would rob *him* of half of his merited fame—
If 'twere hard to condemn him, 'twere surely more hard
To question the faith of THE SCOTTISH BAYARD—
For a bard must recur to the days that are gone
To find a compeer for our *tache*-less Sir John!"

Hall. Very fair, Mr. Mullion. Well, all this sort of thing is quite new here away. Streets placarded—ballads a-bellowing—pothouses opened—hustings, harangues—banners and processions, and "a' the lave o't." I must say, I wish you joy.

Tickler. Why, the ballads swarm out every morning by the skep-full. Mullion's are the best, but there are twenty besides him at it late and early. Come, Mordecai, fill the glasses, and clear your pipes for another touch of the treble.

Mullion. Most of these productions are, I must own, disfigured with horrid coarsenesses. I hardly know how to choose a decently cleanly stave among the bunch. There's one begins well—A Parody on Byron's Sennacherib; but it runs off into fearful filth. I can give you but the opening verse.

North (aside). Lord! how delicate my secretary's becoming! he'll be fit for Campbell or Bulwer by-and-by!*

Mullion (sings).

"Abercrombie came down like a wolf on the fold,
And his pockets were furnish'd with Devonshire gold;
And his pale senseless face was as fearful to see,
As the dark troubled wave on the deep Galilee.

"Like the leaves of the forest, when summer is green,
The Whigs in the morn with their banners seen;
Like the leaves of the forest, when autumn hath blown,
That host on the morrow lay wither'd and strewn.

"For the breath of the Union came strong on the blast,
And bung'd up the Chief Baron's eye as it pass'd;
And the hopes of the Whigglings are gloomy and drear,
When they think of the 'Pipe' and 'Two Thousand a-year.'"

That's all that's producible. But these things, even the worst of them, seem to go down, and may therefore teach the Whigs a lesson.

Tickler. I grudge Abercrombie nothing. His appointment was perhaps the most flagrant outrage on Tory feeling that the Duke of Wellington was wild enough to perpetrate during the worst era of his staggering statesmanship.† The man was offensive—the motive

* At this time Bulwer was Editor of the *New Monthly Magazine*, Thomas Campbell having seceded from it to establish *The Metropolitan* for himself.—M.

† What was called "The Abercrombie Job," was a scandalous concern; nearly as bad as the Duke of Wellington's placing Mrs. Arbuthnot, his handsome friend, on the Pension List, for £700 a-year, on the plea that she had assisted him—in reading his French letters! James Abercromby, a younger son of Sir Ralph Abercromby (killed at the battle of Alexandria, in Egypt), was a heavy plodding barrister without practice. He became a sort of steward, or rent-receiver to the Duke of Devonshire, who put him into Parliament and paid him £2,000 a-year. When Wellington became Premier in 1828, he wished to conciliate Devonshire, and therefore made his man, Abercromby, Chief Baron of the Exchequer in Scotland, with a salary of £4,000 a-year. So much of a sinecure was this judgeship that, in the thirty months it was held by Abercromby, he only tried four cases, for which he was paid £10,000. So notorious was this, that Ministers, for very shame-sake, had to abolish it—but Mr. Abercromby, who had received £10,000 for doing nothing, was granted £2,000 a-year, for life, to console him! In 1832, Jeffrey and himself were returned to represent Edinburgh city in the first Reformed Parliament. Some time after, he declined an official situation—on the plea that he had his £2,000 a-year for doing nothing, and must be paid extra if he did any work. When the new Parliament called by Peel assembled in February, 1835, Abercromby was put up as Whig candidate against Manners Sutton, the late Speaker, and was elected by a majority of ten. This gave him the position of the "first commoner in England" (there was little of the gentleman in his boorish manners, clownish appearance, or selfish feelings) with £6,000 a-year salary, £1,000 more for house-rent, and some patronage. He occupied this post for four years, and then pleading ill-health (though this was

could not have been other than small—a poor, silly dream of neutralizing a solitary great Whig interest in England, at the expense of trampling in open visible contempt, upon the whole of the most influential class of men in Scotland. But let byganes be byganes. I think I'll venture on a ditty mine ain sel, noo. What for no? And what for should it no be on Johnny Murray, braw worthy fallow though he be? Them that comes to the fish-market maun mak up their minds for creeshy creels. Captain Hall must understand that this Whig lawyer comes of a Tory household, and received, when yet in his cradle, a valuable sinecure in the Scotch Exchequer, from his good old father's friend and coeval, the late Lord Melville. He has been, in short, all his life what they call "Clerk of the Pipe." What the *name* means I can't say; but the *thing* runs, I have heard, to the tune of something like £600 a-year, which, considering that John must now have held the office for at least half a century, would seem to point to not a bad tottle of the whole.

Mullion. Exactly thirty thousand pounds of public money received for doing nothing, by a staunch and consistent friend of the people—that's all.

Tickler. Well, well—he's a capital, good, gentlemanlike fellow, for all that;—but here's the strain which now delighteth, at his expense, the worthy burghers of Leith's unromantic town.—(*Sings*).

"The Clerk of the Pipe is a man of some weight,
And nothing will serve him but serving the State;
And the State being rebuilt on a broad-bottom'd plan,
He has fairly set up for a Parliament-man.
Sing down down, down derry down.

"He's a gallant Reformer, and ever has been,
And abhors sinecurists and all things unclean;
Being bravely resolved as he often has shown,
To make war on all sinecures—saving his own.
Sing down down, down derry down.

"He's an orator too,—though a copy, they say,
Of leather-lung'd Jacky, the member for Bray;
And he'd fain be a wit—though by some odd mischance
It reminds one of Jacky just learning to dance.
Sing down down, down derry down.

"But though dull to the eye, and more dull to the ear,
Though heavy in front, and most heavy in rear,
The path of ambition he still must pursue,
And exhibit his parts, Oh! my country, to you!
Sing down down, down derry down.

"So with two or three speeches got up with due care
And two or three jokes somewhat worse for the wear;

fifteen years ago, and he is as hale as pensioners usually are) retired with the title of Lord Dunfermline, and £4,000 a-year for his own life and the life of his eldest son.—These details are necessary to understand the disparaging mention of him throughout this "Noctes."—M.

And two or three friends, such as one might suppose,
In the good town of Leith he his nakedness shows,
Singing down down, down derry down.

"In Leith, then, behold him, discoursing at large,
Of all that has never been laid to his charge;
His contempt for the rich—his regard for the poor—
But as to the fact of his own sinecure,
Singing down down, down derry down.

"'Then,' quoth he, 'I not only must make my appeal,
In behoof of myself, but of all that's genteel,
For a mercantile town you will never degrade,
By choosing a member that's risen by trade.'
Sing down down, down derry down.

"Says a Voter—'All this may be good in its way,
But will you, my good sir, have the kindness to say,
How among the Reformers you thus should appear,
With your sinecure place of six hundred a-year?'
Singing down down, down derry down.

"His Clerkship to this answer'd never a word,
But look'd round in a way that was very absurd;
And I merely will add, since his own mouth is shut,
If he went as The Pipe, he came back as the Butt.
Sing down down, down derry down."

Mullion. I think I can cap that, howsomdever; though, how to make the Captain comprehend anything about the *soubriquet* he is to hear so often repeated, I can't guess. As to the rest, you must know that Murray is proud, though a friend of the people, of his gentle descent—which is all right enough in itself, for he comes of the Tullibardine blood—and indulged himself in some sneers at the mercantile pedigree of his antagonist, Mr. Aitchison, which were very unworthy of his own good taste in the first place, and wofully ill calculated to conciliate the loons he was haranguing in the second.*

North. The truth is, Aitchison's a well-connected man, and in appearance and manners, as well as character, quite a gentleman; much more so than one can lay a finger on in every corner of the Parliament House—but all that signifies nothing—so to your chant

Mullion (*sings*).

Air—"The Lammie."

"Whar hae ye been a' day,
My puir Bottom?
Whar hae ye been a' day,
My witless, weary Bottom?
I've been the voters for to woo,
In Leith and Musselburgh too;
The carles they leuch, and crook'd their mou',
And cried—Awa wi' Bottom!

* This John A. Murray was returned for Leith, and became a Scottish Judge, which he now continues to be.—M.

"But did ye fleech and speak them fair
In truth did I, quo' Bottom!
Say, did ye fleech and speak them fair?
Adeed did I, quo' Bottom!
I spoke them fair, as fair might be,
And roosed their wit and honesty—
Then we're the mair unlike to thee,
My voters said—Od rot 'em!

"I took my *pipe* and play'd a spring,
Quo' feckless, silly Bottom,
A dull newfangled Whiggish thing,
Quo' heavy, hopeless Bottom:
I swoor that pensions were a shame,
And sinecures were sair to blame—
This put the people a' in flame—
Sic clash frae PENSION'D Bottom!

"They said, Ye maun your *Pipe* resign—
I'll no resign, quo' Bottom;
They said, Ye maun your *Pipe* resign—
I canna do't, quo' Bottom:
It's been my meat, it's been my claes,
It's been my comfort a' my days:
The voters said, Then gang your ways,
Ye fause and greedy Bottom!

"O Aitchison's o' low degree,
Quo' mighty Bully Bottom;
There's no a *Peer* upo' his tree,
Quo' vain and senseless Bottom.
But frank and hearty, kind and leal,
He kens our wants and wishes weel;—
We'll send all lawyers to the deil—
Sae down wi' windy Bottom!"

North. Very well; but I think we've had almost enough of these local Fescennines. Can't you start something a little more general? You'll weary the Skipper, I fear.

Hall. Quite the reverse. Come, Mullion, give us something on the Aytoun fellow you mentioned.

Mullion. With pleasure—and I'll take a tune that you can all join in at the chorus—to wit, *Carle an the King come.*—(*Sings.*)

"Here's a health to Aytoun,
Health and wealth to Aytoun;
He's the man we understan'—
Here's success to Aytoun!

"The Tories they have had their day,
The lang-tongued Whigs have had their say;
But Freedom now comes into play,
And cries 'Huzzah for Aytoun!'
Here's a health to Aytoun, &c.

"Nae doubt the Whigs were for the Bill,
But yet to us they're nae gude-will,

But are the same Whig tyrants still,
And hate baith us and Aytoun!

"Nor was it them that gain'd our cause,
But us ourselves, who, clause for clause,
Aye keepit at them wi' the tawse,
Laid on by men like Aytoun!

"And noo already may be seen
The unco difference between
What they've professed, and what they mean,
Which isna lost on Aytoun!

"The path, they say, to all is clear—
How do they mak the fact appear?
They ask—three hundred pounds a-year,
From members sich as Aytoun!!!

"And though that clause withdrawn may be,
Wi' mony a base and Whig-like lee,
A moudewart itsell micht see
'Twas aim'd at us and Aytoun!

"Then how they show their shameless face,
Dealing themselves in jobs so base,
And yet abusing power and place.
To humbug us and Aytoun!

"There's Abercrombie, who would rob
The country by a vile Whig job,
And ca's the people 'Aytoun's mob'—
Yet he'd contend wi' Aytoun!

"But mob or no, we're no to toil
To mak a placeman's kettle boil,
And he maun e'en gie up the spoil,
If he wad stan' with Aytoun.

"There's Murray too, who's known to clear
A guid sax hundred pund a-year,
For doing—what doth not appear—
Must be shown up by Aytoun!

"At Leith he's had the face to say,
'If I've the Pipe, yet I've to play'—
And that, in short, he *earns* his pay,
Like us or honest Aytoun!

"But this he'd best have let alone,
For in due time it shall be shown,
His PIPE, like others, has its DRONE,
A joke I got from Aytoun!

"Jeffrey himsell, o' Whigs the wale,
Is feckless, fushionless, and frail,
And through the reek he'll hae his kail,
Gin he appear 'gainst Aytoun.

"Weel do we ken, in time o' need,
Up yonder he cam little speed,
And this last clause has dune the deed,
As he shall hear frae Aytoun.

"Then, brave Reformers, stainch an' true,
The path o' honor still pursue,
The sacred cause depends on you,
Of freedom and of Aytoun.

"And you, Auld Reekie's dochters fair,
See that the RIBBON GREEN you wear,
For look around and tell me where
You'll find anither Aytoun.

"CHORUS. Then here's a health to Aytoun,
Health and wealth to Aytoun;
I'll blythely gie my last baubee,
To drink success to Aytoun."

Hall. Eh bien! No great symptoms of the doleful dumps in these effusions of the Tory spirit in your hyperborean climes, however. That's the plan—sing on, laugh on;—the mob is, after all, good-humored at bottom; and, hang me, if I expect, when all is done, that we shall see half as many raffs in the next house as in the present.

Tickler. Let's be thankful for mercies. We are already plenteously provided, to be sure. 'Tis certainly a comfort to observe, that though Scotland will probably return more Whigs than heretofore, her pride is still too much awake to permit a radical scamp to have any chance, except in a few stinking corners, where nothing sweeter could ever have been looked for. But I fear this is far from being the case so generally in England; and 'tis but too plain that exactly the reverse is to be the rule across the water.

Hall. Why, what would you have? Here's my boy Hobbio, confessing, that in place of 18,000 electors for Westminster, there won't be above 4,000 registered for the next turn-up. Here's De Lacy Evans howling about the same sort of phenomenon appearing in a dozen dirty corners he chooses to be informed about.* By the great Plutus, God of Battles! I don't mind offering two to one that we shall have a Tory majority. I betted, when Lord John Russell tabled the original Bill, that *not one borough* would be practically disfranchised—and what would you say now, if I ultimately re-pocketed my ten shiners? What, if the very first scene of the new Parliament should be ten thousand petitions from THE PEOPLE to undo this humbug, and replace every thing precisely on its old footing? Depend on it, there is nothing, *in rerum naturâ*, more impossible than to really revolutionize this country. We may be disturbed, but 'tis only to rouse our mettle. The moment there's a lull, all comes right again *somehow*. We shall either have it in our power to cancel the Whig schedules *in toto*—or be convinced, of what we ought never perhaps to have doubted, that schedulize to

* Sir John Hobhouse now (Lord Broughton) was re-elected for Westminster in 1832. De Lacy Evans was an unsuccessful candidate on that occasion.—M.

the end of the chapter, the national heart is Tory, and that, under whatever scheme the M. P.'s may be elected, the majority will never be long enough on the enemy's side to permit of any solid substantial mischief being inflicted on the constitution.*

"They sin who tell us *that* can die,
For *that* is indestructible."

North. I have forsworn London town; but I shall certainly make a push to be present at the opening of the Reformed Parliament. It will afford me consolation, in the midst of all our sorrows, to be ocular witness of the out-turning of this Grey gang—for *that* at least, I augur, is pretty sure to be the Neophyte's first performance.

Tickler. You may give the long odds on that. I defy them to stand a week. As sure as a gun, we shall have Joseph Hume Chancellor of the Exchequer, and leader of the House of Commons; Joseph's late avowal of voting against his conscience, with the reason why,† was, of course, meant to show the world that he *could* play the part of a lavish Minister just as ably, need occurring, as he filled, before Lord Melville (I think it was) refused him something, that of a Ministerial Mute, or, as he has since done, that of a radical cheese-parer. A man, though "most noble," not unworthy to be named in the same breath with the most ignoble, I mean Lord Clanricarde, that yelping numskull, who disgraces the chivalrous name of De Burghe, and in whom I am sorry to see the son-in-law of Canning—he will be Lieutenant of Ireland‡—and O'Connell, (Heaven bless his fat sides!) will be Secretary over the Spoon; and, in short, with one grand exception, we shall see a complete change of the *dramatis personæ.*

Hall. And what's your exception?

Tickler. Brougham will of course be Premier. Every Chancery lawyer says that the style of his behaviour in Court, of late, can leave no doubt that he has made up his mind for one or other of the two following alternatives,—either to have the judicial part of the Chancellor's office separated from the political,|| and retaining

* The popular complaint was, not of the great extent but the limited action of the Reform Bill.—M.

† Hume had openly declared in Parliament that he would vote black to be white, if his doing so would keep the Whigs in office.—Hume sat for Weymouth from January to November, 181[illegible] as a Tory. So far from his becoming Chancellor of the Exchequer, as Tickler anticipated, the complaint of the Liberals is, that Hume has never been offered even a minor office under any Whig administration.—M.

‡ Another unfulfilled prediction. O'Connell was not made Irish Secretary, and Lord Clanricarde, though Ambassador to Russia for a time, never was Irish Viceroy. He was in the Russel Cabinet, 1846–52, as Postmaster-General. In 1854, he opposes the Aberdeen Ministry,—as Byron says—

"Here and there, some stern, high patriot stood—
Who could not get the place for which he sued."—M.

|| Not only Brougham, but other Chancellors have endeavored to separate the political from the judicial functions of the first equity Judge, which will be done, no doubt.—M.

the latter, yield a former to somebody that understands something of the business, and can maintain a decentish appearance on the bench, without being obviously, at every turn, at the tender mercies of Sugden—or to cut the woolsack altogether, and take the post for which, by all men's confession—and women's and children's too—poor doting, drivelling Grey is as deplorably unfitted in respect of temper and manners, as of mind and language——

> The mumping phantom of incarnate spite,
> Loath'd, but not fear'd, for rage that cannot bite;

the object, at best, of pity to the Christian bishops, whom alone he has the pluck to bully.

Mullion. You forget the Chancellor's late attack on Sir Edward.*

Tickler. No—nor do I forget he has crept out of the scrape. All's right.

North. Why should Brougham not play Wolsey over again, and be at once Lord Treasurer, and Lord High-Chancellor?

Tickler. I know of no serious objection, except Sugden, and that one of the devices I alluded to, might get over at a leap. Lord Dundonald would, of course, be a fair Lord High-Admiral under him; and for want of a better, perhaps Mullion's Bayard, Sir John Dalrymple, might be accepted for the Horse-Guards. Then, I think, he would admit things altogether to be in comfortable train.

Mullion. Come, Mr. North, the bowl's nearly out again and Captain Hall has heard us all sing, except yourself. Is that the fair thing, reverend senior?

North. Me sing! I'm as hoarse as a raven, and as gloomy to boot; but come, if you won't let me off without something, I can at least sport you a small specimen of heroics. Give me a subject, Skipper.

Hall. A subject? What, Christopher among the improvvisatori? Well, then, take H. B.'s sketch of the Vision of the Head.†

North. With all my heart—*incipe nunc, musa!*

> The unequal conference and the vex'd debate
> Of England's duty, and of Poland's fate,
> Thank God! are o'er: with faint and feverish lips
> His opiate draught the pensive Premier sips—

* Sir Edward Sugden, Irish Chancellor in 1834–5, and from 1841 to 1846. He was made Chancellor of England, by Lord Derby, in 1852, with the title of Lord St. Leonards. He and Brougham have long been on friendly terms. When he was only a year at the Bar, he published his Practical Treatise on Powers, a subject which he has simplified down to the capacity of every student. When in practice, he was the best equity lawyer in England, and his income varied from £20,000 to £25,000 a-year.—M.

† John Doyle, an Irish gentleman, was the artist of the celebrated H. B. Sketches, which, oddly enough, were beaten out of the field by "Punch," in which the rival political caricatures were by Richard Doyle, the son. From 1830 to 1850 about a thousand of the H. Bs. were published. They were popular all over Europe, and were remarkable for accurate likenesses of public characters. Some were first-rate portraits—such as the full-length sketches of Charles Buller, Sir William Follet, Railway Hudson, Lord Melbourne, Sir R. Peel, "The Duke," O'Connell, and the Napiers.—M.

Revolves what Eldon look'd, what Mansfield said,
And creeps in languor to no rosy bed.

Deep sleep at length has smooth'd the *lofty* brow,
Nor protocols nor pledges knit it now;
Far from the care-beat bounds of Downing Street,
The "erring spirit" swims in visions sweet,
Amidst ancestral Deira's upland roves,
And high-built Howick's sea-o'erhanging groves,
Where blest Content, but yesterday it seems,
Was not the glow-worm spark of dear-bought dreams,
But the fixed sunshine of a sober'd breast,
Whose sins had been repented, and confest—
And pitied and forgiven. For man is kind
To the wept past, and to the future blind.

How long the flattering demon of the night
'Mid these soft scenes indulged his fancy's flight,
Ask not the muse. The July moon shone clear,
When whispers low and stern disturb'd his ear.
Upsprung the chief, in agony of awe,
And, steadfast in the lambent splendor, saw
(While darkness veils the garment of the dead,)
With melancholy eyes great Canning's head.
Still as the icy ray upon his cheek,
The godlike shadow stood, in act to speak;
Still—save what spirits pure may taste of pain—
Scorn without anger, calm serene disdain.

"And thus," he cries, "thy penitentials end!
Thine Order's champion thou!*—thy Prince's friend!
Alas! must England's law and England's crown,
By Dulness' dastard spleen, be both struck down?
Greece's first spirit gave the wound of Greece;
The star of Athens paled to Pericles—
To her own firmest arm and brightest mind,
Rome, weeping blood, her ark of pride resign'd;
Even France, when she her air-born hopes must yield,
Receiv'd the judgment on Marengo's field.
But we?—what fond illusion waits for us,
If, blest beyond them all, we perish thus—
More wise our liberty, more rich our sway,
Our ruin unredeem'd—our fate a Grey!"

He spoke, and vanish'd in the fading beam,
The impostor woke—and lo! it was a dream.

Hall. Admirable old buck! Well, Conscript Fathers, now that I have once penetrated the *sanctum sanctorum*, may I hope to be considered as a regular member?

North. Come back next month, young gentleman, and we'll let you hear the result of the ballot. One black ball, you know, excludes—and certain princes of Israel, which be not now with us in

* Earl Grey had declared, in Parliament, that, come what might, *he* would "stand by his order."—M.

the flesh, must be present. Order a call of the house, Mordecai, for the 20th of September. Good night.

Mullion. Must we part so soon? But, Mr. North, you have forgot one thing. The Captain has not been told that he must send in a probationary article.

North. Very true. Thank ye for minding that. You must let us have a first-rate paper, friend, and that within this fortnight at latest.

Hall. What sort of paper?—Political?—Nautical?—Scientifical?—Literary?—I'm a jack of all trades, you know.

North. Ay, and a master of most. Sink politics—leave them to Tickler and other rabidly carnivorous animals—you're too smooth for us in *that* line. Keep your nauticals for your book; and as for science, rot it. Can't you wait for the next convention of The Watchmakers, as poor Davy used to call them, whether at York, or Cambridge, or Banff, or Belfast?—for I trust old Oxford is not to be pestered with another visitation of the beasts in our time.*

Tickler. An abominable humbug! And the more shame to Sedgewick and Sam, that two men of genius could be found so far forgetful of their own place as to countenance the weary, dismal bleatings of such a pack of one-idea'd nincompoops. And the fun! and the wit! and the ladies! and the lectures! and the dinners! and the breakfasts! and the horsemanship of the Mammothites! O ye gods! No, no, Hall; sport us an elegant touch of the belles-lettres. Your last series contains some of the neatest, tersest, and most unpretendingly original criticism, I have lately met with. Don't you agree, Christopher?

North. Cordially. The fact is, Captain Hall, that you have a very delicate discrimination, a very pretty tact indeed, for this department. I saw it long ago, too; but how, or when, or where, I don't at this moment think fit to tell you.

Hall. One syllable of your approbation is, I need not say, more valuable than all the elaborate compliments I have received of late years. Well, I'll at all events do my best, Mr. Mullion; for who would not rather be dubbed a knight of the Noctes, than receive all the grand crosses between Cadiz and Kamtschatka?

North. You were well acquainted with Lord Byron, poor fellow—and you have travelled over most of the ground of his masterpiece. Why not take up this new edition of "The Childe!" It is certainly the most interesting volume that has come out of late; and a good vigorous paper, with copious extracts from the notes and so forth, if produced in time, could not fail to answer. I wish Murray had asked me to give him a lift in the way of *notulæ*, for I

* The British Association for the Advancement of Science held its initiatory meeting at York, in 1831.—M.

think I could have supplied him with something not unworthy of a place among the rest, and I own I should rather have liked to see myself figuring here and there, as well as Jeffrey and John Wilson, and others who are mere boys to me. Come, Captain, will this do?

Hall. Peut-être.

Tickler. Capitally, Hall. But don't forget to ask what's come of some magnificent stanzas on Vathek Beckford, which I once heard repeated, with infinite gusto, by an Irish bishop (who shall be nameless), and which must of course have meant for canto first of Childe Harold. They were superb—quite in Byron's highest flight, and would have been prime *kitchen* unto our kail.*

North. The new verses on the Dilettanti—I mean their humbugging *London* Dilettanti—should be quoted—and don't omit that charming ditty on the Girl of Cadiz, which Byron originally designed to fill the place now occupied by a dismal concern. The lines on Sir William Gell, too, must come in—they are very clever, though quite unjust—for Gell is one of the most learned of the virtuosi, the prince of the sect, indeed, to my mind—and a capital good fellow into the bargain, and many the merry day he and I have had together in this weary world, I can tell ye.

Tickler. I wonder, by-the-by, that the editor of the English Bards, in his new series, has omitted to mention one of the best specimens of Byron's lightness to a puffing or pasquinading people—his alternations of the epithet on Gell in that lampoon. In the first edition, he said,

"I leave topography to coxcomb Gell,"

In the second, this was turned to "*delving* Gell;" and in the third, unless I be dreaming, the Satirist, having in the interim made Sir William's acquaintance, wrote "classic Gell." The last epithet, I presume, is the only right one—though I don't know why a man should not be both *classical* and *coxcombical*, if he has a mind—I mean a young man—which Gell was in those days, and a very handsome one to boot, as you would wish to see on a summer's day, or any lady in Naples on a winter's night.† Heigho!

North. Take in the volume before Harold, by all means. I never read the half of the little poems there given until this came out, and I must say they much surprised me. Some of them I can't believe to have been written, as we see them, at the dates affixed to them. He must have polished them up in after years—if not, 'tis a wonderful case, for they are worthy of his best period, and quite

* The reason why they were not published was simply this—they were too indelicate, alluding to certain rumors respecting Mr. Beckford, which Byron affected to believe. The sly inuendo, "by an *Irish Bishop*," [of Clogher?] suggests what the rumors were.—M.

† *Coxcomb* was changed to *classic*, because in the interval between the writing and publishing of the Satire, Byron had made Gell's acquaintance, and did not like to hit him.—M.

unlike the real "Hours of Idleness." The notes to that volume, too, especially to the English Bards, are terse and piquant, and will look well in an article.

Mullion. The sight of Byron thus handled makes a reader of my standing begin almost to wish the time were come, when a body might expect to have others of the great cycle of our age dealt with in the same fashion. I don't wish Wordsworth dead, God knows, nor Coleridge neither, but what curious things would be editions of their early lyrics, illustrated with notes *a la Byron!*

North. Ay, very true, and you may live to be gratified with them. I hope I shan't, for they're both much my juniors. Crabbe, however, dear old fellow, is gone—and I do hope we may see his *opera omnia* rendered thoroughly intelligible ere many more months go over our heads.* I know of no body of poetry so likely to rise in popularity, from this kind of clearing up of allusions—and if I may judge from the few letters he favored me with, his own correspondence would go far to furnish the wherewithal.

Tickler. There's a braw time coming for all of them. Meantime, I have interleaved Don Juan, and mean to tender the Emperor† my own illuminations of the only work of Lord Byron that I ever could bring myself to care very much about.

North. Ah! hang your *care!* Well, odd things will turn up. It is now, I believe, certain that they have laid their hands somewhere on Byron's often-talked of Letter to the Editor of Blackwood's Magazine, and that we are to have that by-and-by, as an appendix to the production it is chiefly connected with.‡

Hall. Yes, I heard of that in London, and was heartily amused to understand that Byron never doubted the writer who used to lash him in Maga, in her wild frolicsome days, under the name, style, and title of Presbyter Anglicanus, was—— But guess.

North. Presbyter Anglicanus? I quite forget all about him.

Hall. Well, then, Lord Byron had quite made up his mind that Presbyter Anglicanus meant—the Rev. Dr. Chalmers!—ha!—ha!—ha!

Tickler. Capital. Well, I think I must e'en mount a shovel-hat upon this.

North. I'm glad the Letter's turned up, however; and hope we shall have it unmutilated,

"With all its horrors bristling on its brow,"

even though my own noble self should chance to come in for a skelp or so. How could such a man be taken in, as he was, about such

* Crabbe's Life and Words did so appear, soon after.—M.

† John Murray, having changed his place of business from Fleet street, in the city, to Albermarle, in the fashionable part of London, was facetiously called "Emperor of the West."—M.

‡ It was so appended to the collected and annotated edition of Byron's Life and Works.—M.

things? Only to think of his confounding the style of a Tickler with that of a Chalmers!

Hall. Probably he was not so well versed in the Doctor's works, as he seems to have been in our landlord's.

North. The more's the pity. Few works of any time, and none of ours, would have had so fair a chance of turning his thoughts in the right direction. But really it will be rare fun to hear Byron blackguarding Chalmers for having called Don Juan a blackguard, for that, I think, was about the substance of the Pseudo-Presbyter's sermon.

Tickler. Perhaps, now that I rank with Dr. Chalmers, a volume of Practical Discourses for a certain quarter might toddle off pretty briskly.

North. No doubt, especially if opened with a life of the venerable author, and garnished with foot-notes, explaining the various moods of his mind when he penned the grave effusions, the individuals whose cases he felt it right to be glancing at, &c., &c., &c. 'Twill be a valuable tome. Give us your head too, bands and all.

Tickler. Nay, nay—no bands—at best I'm but a stibbler. Well, then, Basil, you will yoke on Byron in the mean time.

Mullion. By-the-by, I believe I can repeat an epigram of Byron's that has never yet been in print. It's only a versification of a *fact*, but you may like to stick it into your article.

Hall. Let's hear it. But Murray's sure to have laid his paw on it for his next volume, for he's been beating the bush in all directions.

Mullion. Very likely—'tis no great matter.* Here it is, however, in the meantime.

LEATHER BREECHES *versus* LANTHORN JAWS.

Sir Thomas Lothbridge, fresh from Somerset,
Hot stalking down Whitehall Macculloch met.
"Where now, Professor?"—"I'm to Horton bent—
I've just discover'd the true sense of RENT."
"Ay!" chuckles cheerily the Lord of Land,
On lateral doe-skin slaps a brawny hand,
And, his purse jingling in the Scarecrow's ear,
Cries "RENT!!! More RENT than e'er you finger'd '*s here!*"

Tickler. Not bad—but why the skit at Wilmot Horton?

Hall. O! Horton sided with the lady, I believe.

North. Make a copy, Mordecai, and send it up in case of accidents to Joannes de Moravia—and ask him to let's have the sheets of the next volume of his Byron *quam primum*. By the advertisement of the contents it will be even a richer one than the last—and, by-the-by, write to Finden too, and tell him I'm much obliged to

* Very true—"it *is* no great matter," and not at all like Byron.—M.

him for his Illustrations. He has got upon the right track at last; real localities and real portraits are worth all the imaginery fiddle-dees we used to be humbugged with, under the name of *Illustrations*—and nothing can be more exquisite than his execution—and I hope the sales will be upsides with the annotated poetry itself?

Mullion. I don't know if you have seen the last brochure. It has a charming head of Lady Byron, who has, it seems, sat on purpose;* and that's very agreeable to hear of, for it shows that her ladyship has got over any little soreness that Moore's life occasioned; and is now willing to contribute any thing in her power to the real monument of Byron's genius—I mean a really intelligible edition of his *opera omnia.*

North. I'm delighted to hear of this—'tis really very noble in the unfortunate lady. I never saw her—is the face a striking one?

Mullion. Eminently so—a most calm, pensive, melancholy style of native beauty—and a most touching contrast to the maids of Athens, and Annesley, and all the rest of them. I'm sure you'll have the proof Finden has sent you framed for the Boudoir at the Lodge.

North. By all means—I mean to do that for all the Byron Beauties. But come, lads, do you mean to sit all night?

Tickler. Eheu! must you really go then? Never sorrier to part wi' you all—

Hall. Au revoir then, gents. But pray let *mum* be the word; for if Tom Hill should hear of it, I'm sure to see myself in the Chronicle.†

* Murray earnestly solicited Lady Byron to sit for a portrait to be engraved among the Byron Illustrations, and met with a cold and peremptory refusal. Thomas Wright, who was editing and annotating Byron (the seventeen-volume edition of 1832–4), went down to Ealing, near London, where Lady Byron was residing, placed his artist in a position where she could be sketched, and had her portrait taken in that sitting. In the afternoon they again went to church, and her ladyship was again an involuntary sitter. This was repeated on the next Sunday, and, as was then intended, Lady Byron saw the artist at work. After prayers, Wright and his friend were visited by an ambassador from her ladyship to inquire the meaning of what she had seen. The reply was, that Mr. Murray *must* have her portrait, and was compelled to take what she refused to give. The result was, Wright was requested to visit her, which he did, taking with him—not *the* sketch, which was very good, but another in which there was a strong touch of caricature. Rather than allow *that* to appear as her likeness (a very natural and womanly feeling, by the way), she consented to sit to W. J. Newton for the portrait, which was engraved, and is here alluded to.—M.

† "Little Tom Hill," as everybody called him, was quite a character. When he died (December, 1840), he was aged eighty. He did not look sixty, but—to hear him talk about them—seemed as if he had intimately known every personal notoriety for a century before. When his likeness appeared, in *Fraser's Magazine*, Maginn said, in the accompanying description, that, though he was not one of the *little Hills* whose skipping propensities are celebrated in the Psalms, he must at least have been one hundred and sixty years old. James Smith, of the Rejected Addresses, said he was born in the reign of Elizabeth, on the same day with Shakspere (April 23, 1564), but that the parish-register was lost in the Great Fire of London, in 1666. He had originally been a merchant, but so fond of literature, that his library, when he failed, was valued at £5000. He then took to the pen, as an author, and for over forty years had confidential connection with authors, actors, artists, and publishers. He was extremely inquisitive, and was the original of Poole's humorous Paul Pry. He was put into Gilbert Gurney, as Tom Hull, by his friend Theodore Hook. He "happened to know" everything and everybody, and *did* know much more about individuals and incidents, than was generally believed. His library and curiosities, sold after his death, brought great prices. His collection of autographs was large

North. So much the better, Captain. It would act as a puff for "SERIES THE THIRD"—but as you please. Mullion, do you canter on, and see that the old woman has the devil ready, by the time the Captain and I reach the Lodge. And by-the-by, it will be sharpish work driving three miles in this moonlight—so, Mordecai, my boy, you may as well brew a bishop.

Voices (*without*). Mr. North's carriage stops the way.

(*Exeunt Omnes.*)

and valuable. Garrick's famous cup, formed from the mulberry-tree planted by Shakspere, sold for a guinea. In his later years, Hill was a sort of news-collector and paragraph-maker for the *Morning Chronicle*, in London. In his prosperity, Hill edited the *Monthly Mirror*, which brought him into communication and acquaintance with men of the pen and the pencil. In stature he was short, in figure rotund, in complexion rubicund, in motion rapid, in laughter loud, in curiosity unbounded. He was sagacious withal, and piqued himself on being able to ferret out any secret, state or private, "at the shortest notice, with accuracy and dispatch." He appeared almost ubiquitous also. At twelve o'clock he might be reported as having been spoken to at Charing Cross, and somebody would affirm that he had also been encountered, about the same time, in the Royal Exchange, fully three miles distant. He happened to know the title of every author's forthcoming work, and the subject of every artist's forthcoming picture—and this before the book had been named, or the canvas purchased for the painting! In a word, there was only one Tom Hill in the world, as there was only one Falstaff.—M.

No. LXIII.—OCTOBER, 1832.

SCENE— *The Boudoir at Buchanan Lodge—beautiful moonlight chequering the influence of a couple of Argands*—NORTH *and* MULLION *at work—the Round Table covered with MSS., Proof-Sheets, new Pamphlets, &c. &c. &c. The large Ebony inkstand, and a Tappit-Hen, with her Chicks, occupy a central position. The melodious warbling of Nightingales in the Medora Shrubbery is distinctly audible.*

North. Well, I think I've pretty well combed out this fellow's tangled sentences, however. 'Tis wonderful how few people can write grammar. Not one man in a thousand seems to have the slightest notion that it may signify just *every thing* whether he puts *but* in a particular place, or *for*, or *and*, or *since*, or *however*, or *notwithstanding*. Confound their puzzled pates!—and half of all this would be avoided, if they would only be contented to write as they talk. Oh!—a curse of all curses on the ambition of fine writing! What lots of good sense have been strangled in the birth for the sake of rounding a paragraph! My dear, your progress in the art has been remarkable, but you have still much to learn, or rather, I should say, to unlearn.

Mullion. Most sensible of that am I, my dear sir. The great rule I *try* to keep before me is Voltaire's—Always be sure, before you write any thing, that you have a perfectly clear idea of what you want to say.

North. A good rule—but by no means of universal application. There are many moods of the mind in which one appears to compose, and in fact does compose capitally, without having any thing like distinct notions beforehand of what one's about. After walking up and down my room for half an hour, with my cigar in my mouth, thinking all sorts of things in the heavens and the earth, and the waters under the earth—friends long since dead and buried—places once familiar, that I shall never put mortal eyes on again—books *in posse*—bores *in esse*—last summer's butterflies—Chateaux en Espagne, no matter how high or how low—suddenly the cigar's out, and by a natural instinct, as it were, I place myself at the table and begin writing. What suggests the first sentence? Probably the title-page of a book lying uncut on the desk. What the next? Of course some turn in the first sentence which suggested itself during the operation of penning that—and so on—a long series of little minute dovetailings, in fact quite spontaneously evolving and enlinking each other, down to the end of the sheet. By this time the mouth begins to feel uneasy—I pick another cheroot from Cotton's last box, and walk up and down *reverie-ing* as before. Presently I take the sheet I had covered with my fine Roman hand from the table, and read it over. What the devil is this? I never meant to say any of these things when I sat down to write. Here are observations which, if I had heard them from *your* lip half an hour ago, I should have pronounced *new*—thoughts of which, if they had ever entered *my* sensorium, pineal gland, or whatever the bit is, half an hour ago, I remained entirely unconscious, until the very moment they were oozing in ink from my finger's ends? Where did they come from? What brought them out? What are they worth, now that they are there? Here, now, is my own lucubration of this morning.

Mullion. For God's sake don't tear the paper, Mr. North.

North. Not I—I'll wait and look at the thing after breakfast first. Meantime, you may take my word for it, that one-half of the books in this world, or, at all events, of the *articles*, compose themselves. Come, have you polished your pebble, Mordecai? Heigho! let's bundle all into the Balaam-box for the present, and finish our *Magnum* quietly. The laborer is worthy of his hire. Come, put away the dirty linen.

Mullion. Très volontiers. I'm sick of the very name of this coxcomb, Babbage. Such a cold, dry, prig it is! So intensely ignorant, too; hang me, if I don't think his calculating machine could have turned out something quite as edifying.

North. The man seems to be not a bad calculating machine himself—Babbage rhymes to cabbage, to be sure. Here's the same rubbish ejected first as Lectures at Cambridge, then as articles in an Encyclopædia—and now, forsooth, a book, a treatise—with a head of Friar Bacon (could he find no Brazen Head nearer home?) on the title-page, and the paragraphs numbered, for the sake of ease to the unborn *citator*, I presume—yes, numbered, I see, to the very last page of the blarney, as pompously as the Pandects.*

* Charles Babbage, Lucasian Professor of Mathematics in the University of Cambridge, for several years, had recently put forth the work here referred to, called Economy of Manufactures. In 1821, he commenced the construction for the British Government, of a machine by which logarithmic tables might be calculated without error. In 1833, part of this mechanism was put together, and found to work with precision. It calculated the sums given to it, and also delivered the result, printed. It would compute with 4,000 figures, and "calculate the numerical value of any algebraic functions: and would, also, at any period previously fixed upon, contingent upon certain events, cease to tabulate that function, and commence the calculation of a different one. By its aid," adds the biographer from whom I quote, "he prepared his Table of Logarithms of the Natural Numbers, from 1 to 108 000, a work whose facile arrangement and unparalleled accuracy were received with gratitude throughout Europe, into the languages of which it was speedily translated." The machine has not been completed, though £17,000 has

Mullion. You had better take him in hand yourself, or ask Tickler to revive his Series of Letters to Eminent Literary Characters—the job is not for me—the figures disgust me so consumedly, that I can't muster merriment, which is all it deserves, for his augmentation.

North. How much more agreeable a subject of contemplation is this fine old boy of a cobbler! Hand me the last Bull again. Ay, here it is—(*Reads.*) "Died lately at Bradfield, near Manningtree, aged 82, PAUL LITTLE, of that place, shoemaker. The deceased was a man of eccentric manners—a dabbler in politics—and a staunch adherent of the Blue Party. He always prided himself on his unflinching Toryism and loyalty to his King; and although Bradfield is thickly studded with Tory and High Church partisans, none were more zealous in the cause. Some of the opposite party were to be found who would argue politics with, but it was ineffectual to attempt to turn, the village cobbler. He was a strict observer of the birthday of his late Majesty George the Third, and the 4th of June always found him sitting in his parlor, in an old arm-chair, dressed up fancifully with laurels and other evergreens, with a brown jug of mild ale before him, out of which he had, for nearly half a century, quaffed his Sovereign's health. Like most True Blues (or at least like what most True Blues would like to do) he had saved a little money, and accordingly he left a will, in which, among other directions for his funeral, he ordered that his coffin should be painted blue, which his executors complied with. He also left behind him the following epitaph, written by himself, to be placed at the head of his grave, leaving a space for the insertion of his age:—

'Here lies Paul Little, to give him his due,
When he was alive he was a True Blue,
And loved a moderate drop:
His age was eighty-two, and no more;
Of shoes he made in *one shop*
Fourteen hundred score!'"

Here now was a cock of the right feather. Fill your glass! THE MEMORY OF PAUL LITTLE!

Mullion. The memory of LITTLE! The "moderate drop" of mild ale finishes the picture. I would have gone fifty miles to take a pipe and pot with this worthy, Mr. North. A great moral lesson, sir.

North. Anything good in this month's Magazines, Mullion? How does Thomas the Rhymer get on?

Mullion. Exceedingly well—much better than when he was with

been expended on it. The idea was not new, Pascal and other mathematicians having previously suggested it. Mr. Babbage has written several works on Science and Scientific Societies.—M.

Colburn. The eternal puffing of quackery enjoined on Campbell in those days, had evidently weighed down his spirits. Now he's drawing in couples with such a dashing fellow as Marryat, 'tis another affair; and with Moore, he'll carry almost everything before him in his own way.* But Marryat himself is enough almost to bear the concern through. A capital writer, sir—beats the American, Cooper, to shivers—he's only second, in fact, to Tom Cringle.

North. That's high praise, I promise you, sir. Cringle, indeed, is a giant.†

Mullion. By-the-by, I haven't read his new MS.

North. Would it be a bore for you to let me hear it while I smoke a cigar?

Mullion. With all my heart. I'll look for it immediately—but, sure, I hear something—hark! isn't that a carriage?

North. Hum—I believe it is. Who the deuce can be coming to bother us at this time o' night? Come, Mullion, jump out, and see that nobody's let in, unless it should be Timothy or some of the elect. (*Exit* MULLION.) I wonder what sets Tickler in motion at such hours. By eight o'clock I thought his long legs were pretty sure to be folded for the evening—but he's one of the indescribables, and ever was, and ever will be, as unintelligible to himself as to other folks.

Enter MULLION.

Mullion. Gadso! Mr. North—this beats cockfighting. Here's the Advocate come in full fig to canvass you for your second vote in Auld Reekie.‡ John had the sense to tell him you were particularly engaged, but should be immediately informed of his arrival. He's in the library—do you wish to see the spark?

North. Who's with him?

Mullion. He came alone in his chariot—but there's a Jarvie chokefull of his little Parliament-house jackalls in the rear. They have been beating up all the outlying voters between this and Preston-Pans, it seems. I suppose we need not have in those animals?—they seem rather fuddled, too, John says.

North. I'm extremely happy to receive his visit; but the state of my health is so delicate I can't possibly see much company;—in short, he may come in, and welcome, if he will shake off his tail. (*Exit* MULLION.) Well, this is an odd fancy! Can the callant really suppose it possible? No—no—it can't be—'tis of course a

* Thomas Moore, Thomas Campbell, and Captain Marryat, were the editors of *The Metropolitan Magazine*, at first, in 1831–2. Some of Moore's poems therein are not included in his works. Marryat eventually became sole editor and proprietor.—M.

† Michael Scott, of Glasgow, was author of Tom Cringle's Log and the Cruise of the Midge, both of which first appeared in Maga. Even Blackwood did not know who Scott was until after his death in 1835, so close was his incognito.—M.

‡ At this time, Jeffrey was Lord Advocate of Scotland, and a candidate, with Abercrombie, for the representation of Edinburgh, in the first Parliament after the Reform Bill was passed.—M.

mere form—a piece of civil routine. And yet some people have such a——*Nous verrons.* Here he comes.

Enter JOHN MACKAY—

Mackay. The Lord Advocate!

North. Some more glasses, John. (*Exit* MACKAY—*enter* JEFFREY.) My Lord Advocate!!!—delighted to see you. I thought you had quite forgot the way to the old Lodge—come (*they embrace*), how well you look after all those cursed stories about sinking health and so forth in the blasted newspapers! Why—save a little sprinkle of the grizzle—you're not altered a whit, I protest. I wish I had your receipt, man. Sit down—sit down.

Jeffrey. 'Pon my word, Mr. North, you appear to me to carry your years as bravely as any man. Here you are, at the old work, I see—the Bramahs and the bottle always in requisition!

(*Enter* MACKAY *with glasses, and exit.*

North. My dear Lord, be seated; my secretary won't come back—take his chair. I had been scribbling all the afternoon, and was just about to compose myself with a little of Johnny Brougham's *fifteen.** Will you let me help you, for auld langsyne, to the maidenhead o' a Tappit Hen? You are now entitled, you know, to claim the *droit du Seigneur.*†

Jeffrey. Ha! ha! *merci.* I have the honor to wish health, and wealth, and length of days, to the Redoubtable. Capital stuff! a perfect *bouquet!*

North. And here's health, wealth, and length of days, to your father's son, and every good thing besides that's really for your good. Ay, this is the right sort—and a bin that had been quite overlooked—so much the better for us both this blessed day! Fill again, my dear Lord!

Jeffrey. Superb! exquisite! nonpareil! Ay, ay, 'tis your quiet way of life, and keeping good hours, and sanctifying them with such libations as these, that has preserved you so marvellously. Why, you scarcely look older to me than you did when I was a boy at your knee.

North. Aha! No flattery! There spoke the candidate! Ha, ha, ha!

Jeffrey. Why certainly, my dear sir, it is in that capacity I have taken the liberty of calling on you at such an unseasonable hour as this. There has been a good deal of literary sparring in certain

* John Brougham, brother to the Lord Chancellor, was a wine-merchant in Edinburgh, some time before this, and unfortunate in business.—M.

† A singular custom in some parts of England and Scotland, in olden days, by which the Lord of the Manor was allowed the privilege of sleeping with a bride on her marriage night. Beaumont and Fletcher wrote a play called "The Custom of the Country" on this *droit du Seigneur.* What is called Borough English arose out of this. I am freeman of a Scottish burgh, as second son—the local law presuming that the elder son was the child of the Seigneur. The right was usually commuted for some money-payment, and long since ceased altogether.—M.

quarters for some years back, but I hope no personal hostility on either side; and as things now stand, I really thought you would have every right to be offended if I did not take the opportunity of requesting a little of your support and countenance on this occasion. I know very well, of course, that you signed the requisition to Mr. Forbes Blair; but as his seat is now safe enough, I presume I may ask you to split your vote in my favor, with at least as much chance of success as any of the other Liberals in the field?

North. Meaning Mr. Abercrombie and Mr. Aytoun?

Jeffrey. I have heard of no other; and your own party seem to have dropped all notion of starting a second competitor.

North. My dear Lord Advocate, I have no sort of acquaintance either with the umwhile Chief Baron, or this Mr. Aytoun; and if no other Tory offers, and I split my suffrage at all, you may certainly depend on its being in your Lordship's favor. And that's as much, I think, as you could expect me to say, *hoc statu.*

Jeffrey. Why, I don't exactly know what to say to that, Mr. North. But perhaps ere we finish our claret we may understand each other a little better. 'Pon honor, I believe there is no man whose views have been more misrepresented than mine. 'Tis my belief, that if you could read me aright, you would not refuse me a fair claim to this very epithet you so hug and cherish as your own peculiar property. I feel and know that if any man living be in heart and mind a *Conservative*, 'tis your humble servant, Francis Jeffrey.

North. Ex-editor of the Edinburgh Review, author of a Bill for amending the Representation of that part of the United Kingdom, called Scotland, and principal law-officer in these parts, under Charles Earl Grey, Henry Lord Brougham and Vaux, and Sir James Gibson Craig of Riccarton, Baronet?

Jeffrey. Adsum. But why the Sir James? Come, a truce to your fun, my good friend, for once.

North. O, if he really be not the viceroy over you, my lord, I beg your pardon. Men in the quiet walks of life are like enough, no doubt, to be misinformed.

Jeffrey. Yes, indeed, Mr. North; there is a vast mass of misinformation and misrepresentation too now afloat, and I have suffered from it during this canvass more than I could ever have permitted myself to anticipate.

North. Is it possible?

Jeffrey. Hang it! yes. Byron says, in his sarcastic vein, that what the Romans called the *Bellua multorum capitum* has fortunately, in this country, no head at all; but I am taught by severe experience, that it has a fair allowance both of ear and tongue, notwithstanding. I have been an ill-used man, North—I have indeed.

North. Ill-used, Jeffrey?

Jeffrey. A continued succession of annoyances—a perpetual running fire of the disagreeables! As your friend, the archlaker, sings:—

> "Beyond participation lie
> My troubles, and beyond relief!"

North. Well, I am sorry to hear you say so—fill another bumper, however; and take an old man's word for it, that this world is a very good world, as worlds go, nevertheless, and I sincerely wish neither you nor I may ever have any experience of a worse one.

Jeffrey. Oh, you old quiz!

North. Quite serious, my dear. Ups and downs, no doubt, there will be in every man's course of life; but by the time one reaches middle age, as far as I have observed, our contemporaries settle into something wonderfully like a just notion of us in the main; and I'm sure I may say, without flattery, that few persons of his class and station have had more reason, on the whole, to be satisfied with the ultimate impression than the present Lord Advocate of Scotland.

Jeffrey. I can't suppose you speak one way and think another; but seriously, my good sir, I don't find myself at all situated as you seem to fancy. I have many kind personal friends—without that, what would life be worth to any man? and there is a considerable class of the middling order that appear to regard me warmly enough; but, somehow, there it stops. I can't feel that I stand, either with Parliament or with the public at large, in any very enviable position, and there are whole divisions of the body politic that decidedly scout me *in toto.*

North. The mass rarely comprehend real merit of any kind; that I admit.

Jeffrey. That's not all. You can't, now, imagine it to be a very agreeable thing for a man of my tastes, attainments, habits, and pursuits, to discover, in the course of such a business as this, that in my own native city, to whose European celebrity I have so largely contributed, I am considered with about equal hostility by the bulk of the upper orders—the wealth, the talent, the accomplishment, the good society of the place, and by all but a ludicrously trifling fraction of the people.

North. My dear Advocate, folk of your persuasion deal wholesale in misnomers. How often have I warned you all that no good could come in the long run, even to yourselves, of this confounded nonsense, begging your pardon, of dropping out of your vocabulary the good English word *populace?* The *people* of Edinburgh are among the *elite* of the earth—her *populace* have always been what you now begin to suspect them of being; and I, for one, knew them just as well when you were in your first corduroys, man, as you are likely to do by the time of Aytoun's chairing.

Jeffrey. They really seem disposed to cut both Abercrombie and myself for this noisy spouter, of whom no human being ever heard good, bad, or indifferent, until now, and considering what both Abercrombie and I had done for the public—

North. Eh? What?

Jeffrey. What we had done for the public, I say—

North. I should like a *précis* of *that*, before I strengthen my pledge.

Jeffrey. Come now, my dear Mr. North, 'tis all very well to turn out a bigoted Monthly Magazine, if that sort of thing suits the swallow of the Tory *Bellua*—but here, talking as a private gentleman over a bottle of Lafitte, can you positively mean to insinuate that neither Abercrombie nor your humble servant have established any substantial claims on the general favor and confidence of our contemporaries?

North. I by no means wish to insinuate any thing, my dear Lord Advocate, only I'm an old man, and memory begins to shake a little sometimes, even while the other faculties of mind, as well as body, continue steadyish.

Jeffrey. Come now, North, drop gammon!

North. *Sans persiflage*, then, Jeffrey, if you ask me what Squire Abercrombie has done in the sort you allude to, my answer must be *non mi ricordo*.

Jeffrey. Why, is it possible you should have forgot that James Abercrombie was for twenty years on end the great Parliamentary advocate of a Reform in the Scotch borough representation?

North. No; but if I recollect rightly, during all those twenty years the Edinburgh Review was the steady, unflinching, and, I must add, the very able and effective opponent, and merciless vituperator, and cruel derider, of the whole scheme of Parliamentary Reform; and I am, therefore, at a loss to comprehend why Mr. Abercrombie by advocating, and my Lord Brougham and you by denouncing, the same thing, at the same period, should all three of you have been founding equal claims to the gratitude of the same set of persons.

Jeffrey. Poh! Brougham and I knew very well what we were about.

North. The devil you did!

Jeffrey. Yes! yes! It was our object to prepare the public mind at large for liberal ideas in general, and in the meantime to discountenance so sweeping a thing as Parliamentary Reform, until we should feel that our doctrinal seed had had leisure to spring up, and its fruits were white unto the harvest. Abercrombie, perhaps, differed from us as to thinking the time *was come*, while we only in our mind's eye saw it, and *sotto voce* hailed it, *a-coming*. And why might not he have been well employed in keeping what could be said in favor of the thing before people's view, although Brougham and I were still better employed in refreshing the old armament of doubts as to the same subject, in the hope and expectation of a sure hour for drawing up in right earnest the curtain of a new scene political?

North. Pleasant, but wrong, I fear, my dear lord. But to keep to Mr. James Abercrombie. Didn't he go to Canning in 1827, one of the very first of your congregation, and give in his adhesion to that Government, on the express conditions, 1mo, that he, Abercrombie, should thenceforth throw Reform overboard *in secula seculorum;* and 2do, that he, Abercrombie, should receive, first opportunity, a good fat place from George Canning?

Jeffrey. Non mi ricordo. There were a number of oddish things done on all sides about that time—I certainly gave in no adhesion to Canning's Government myself.

North. Why, as neither Advocate's nor Solicitor's gown were just then vacated, I don't exactly see in what way you could have been called for to signify either your personal adhesion, or the contrary. I believe the Whigs of the Parliament House, generally, were more cock-a-hoop for the first day or two after hearing of the break-up, than they appeared to be when the extent of the changes was ascertained. But your Review sided with Canning, if I remember, pretty distinctly—quite as much so, indeed, as could well have been expected to do him any good; for, of course, if you had been to wheel right-about at once, you must have lost a part of your influence with your readers; and, in short, poor Canning's Reform-Reprobating, and Catholic-Claim-Cushioning Government would have been openly detected in the fact of—buying Punch. Meantime, I suspect, I must consider you as admitting, substantially, what I suggested as to this Mr. Abercrombie's proceedings at that crisis.

Jeffrey. Why, he might be tied up a little through his connection with Devonshire House. It was, you know, a great object with George IV. that the Duke should play Chamberlain under Canning.

North. No doubt—and because the King (God rest him!) who detested Reform, wanted Canning, who despised and abhorred Reform, to be supported by the rotten borough votes of the Duke of Devonshire,* who was never, I'm told, capable of comprehending

* The Duke of Devonshire, for a man of wealth and rank, has been singularly unambitious of distinction in public life, but his literary acquirements are respectable, his taste in the fine arts refined, and it is to his appreciation of the man, whom he found a rough lad from the Scottish

what Reform meant, the great and consistent advocate in Parliament of Scotch Reform, was bound, in duty to the Scotch people, whose suffrages he on that ground alone now claims, to put his principles as to Reform into his pocket, rather than—hum!—

Jeffrey. Rather than embarrass, by individual pertinacity, as to a particular detached question, the general objects and views of the great party to which he belonged.

North. With submission, my dear Lord, let me finish my own sentence,—rather than give up a rotten borough seat in the House of Commons, and 2000*l.* a-year of lawful money of these realms, both of which the said patriotic gentleman then held, *durante bene placito*, of the Solomon of Chatsworth.

Jeffrey. You forget yourself, dear Mr. North, when you use language like this. But—to pass my amiable, and really not altogether unintelligent friend, the Duke—James Abercrombie is a younger brother; and, somehow, he has never got on at the bar. And, really, when a man has a wife and a rising family, Mr. North, it is only *humanum* that he should occasionally act as to money matters in a manner not *ex facie* reconcilable with the most stoical theory of independence. But this I merely throw out as a hint, which, in candor, I know you will admit the possible weight of. What my friend Mr. Abercrombie's conduct and motives at that delicate juncture actually were, I can't by any means pretend to say.

North. You can't? that's something!

Jeffrey. No—but I have an intimate conviction that he is a worthy, honorable Whig, who, with whatever temporary errors of judgment he may be chargeable, has through life had the objects and interests of the party sincerely at heart. This suffices for me, personally; and if you desire more explicit information, you will of course have a public opportunity of catechising the culprit himself at the hustings.

North. Not so fast, my dear Lord. Why should you feel anywise nervous about my scrupulosities touching this fortunate political adventurer? You approve, also, of his *acceding* to the Duke of Wellington, and receiving, from the great Titan of unholy Anti-Reform, the high and lucrative sinecure, as it is now, I see, called, of the Chief Baronship of the Scotch Exchequer? Upon what grounds did the hero of Scotch Reform take that 4000*l.* a-year?

Jeffrey. I believe the bottle's with me. My dear sir, we are conversing as men of sense and candor, capable of transposing in our fancy's eye the relative position not only of individuals, but of parties.

North. To be sure—to be sure—

border, that the world is indebted for the practical knowledge of Sir Joseph Paxton, architect of the Crystal Palace, in 1851.—M.

Jeffrey. Now, suppose it had been generally felt at Brookes's that the chances of a complete subversion of the Tory Government were tremendously endangered by the fact, that more of the influential places in the internal as well as colonial administration of authority, were in the hands of the steadfast out-and-out adherents of the dominant sect; and that, with the view of gradually relieving the Whig party of a portion of this particular species of obstacle, it had been resolved that certain individual members of that body should, to a certain extent, modify the external show of their personal procedure, to the end of getting themselves fixed in influential posts of the order alluded to, thereby immediately and permanently providing for themselves and the families for whose welfare it was their first and most sacred duty to provide, and at the same time securing, in the end, the attainment of a general object judged important to the interests of a great party, who desired power, mark me, not from any dirty hankering after pelf, not at all, but from really and truly the purest and most patriotic motives——

North. Hah! hah! hah! ha! ha! Pass the claret.

Jeffrey. Beg pardon. Supposing all this to have been the case, will you, my dear Mr. North, just have the directness to imagine the whole position of the two parties reversed at the time in question, and say honestly, that if TORIES had acted as in my hypothesis WHIGS did act, you would have felt disgusted with your own corporation, as over-lax and ultra-Machiavelitish in its course of tactics, or permitted yourself to hold in any hopeless abyss of suspicion the individuals who had so devoted themselves to a specific branch of their party's service?

North. The heroic Curtii of the horrid gulf of Sinecure!

Jeffrey. Pooh, pooh!—Come, answer fairly.

North. You began as a poet, my Lord Advocate, and will always have a lively fancy. I'm a plain prosaic, if not dull man; and must freely confess myself altogether incapable of following the airy flight you have so ingeniously traced for my earth-bound wing. Thank God, however, there's one subject we are sure to agree about—to wit, that, as our bottle's out, it is most meet, fit, and necessary, that we, penitent sinners, should have another of the same.—(*Rings, &c.*)

Jeffrey. Amen! I should be concerned to offer any opposition to so orthodox a motion. What, must I have this pucellage too? Well, well.

North. HONEST MEN AND BONNY LASSES! It's a gude auld toast.

Jeffrey. HONEST MEN AND BONNY LASSES! So you're still the same man in all things?

North (*sings*).

Air—Je ne veux la mort de personne.

Grands yeux bien noirs et bien piquans,
 Oreille ou poitrine rôtie,
Petite bouche, belles dents,
 Cervelle grasse et bien farcie,
Taille légère, bons gigots,
 Sein de lis, langue délectable,
Jambe de mignonne, pieds de veaux.
 Voilà ma maitresse, et ma table.

Jeffrey. What a pipe! One stanza more!

North. Why the devil didn't ye come in time for dinner? (*Sings.*)

A table on compose, on ecrit,
 A table une affaire s'engage;
A table on joue, on gagne, on rit;
 A table on fait une mariage;
A table on discute, on résout;
 A table on aime, on est amiable.
Puisqu'à table on peut faire tout,
 Pourquoi, mon cher, quitter la table?

Jeffrey. You are the most incomprehensible of mankind! Years are as nothing upon ye! Out or *in*, all's one with you! Well, I can't but honor the genuine old Tory, ever true to his friends and his flask, in hopeless heresy good-humored, in hottest hostility humane, whose worst brickbat is a bottle of Bordeaux, his only *practical* tyranny no skylights! But there's no denying it—you were meant to be one of us.

North. Not I.

Jeffrey. Yes, but you were; and if you had joined, we should have known how to appreciate you.

North (*sings*).

There was a jolly miller once
 Lived on the river Dee,
He worked and sung from morn till night
 No lark more blithe than he.

And this the burthen of his song
 For ever used to be—
I care for nobody,—no, not I,
 If nobody cares for me.

Jeffrey. But we should have cared for the jolly miller, man. Don't ye see what we do for our friends, now we have the wherewithal?

North. Oh! that's it! I should have had ere now the honor and glory of a riband of the Guelph, and Sir Christopher North might have walked out of a room, perhaps, before Sir John the Leslie. Why the mischief, then, have none of the dons among ye taken the watch-riband yourselves? Why did Brougham not get Mackintosh, or Rogers, or Hallam, or Moore, or Shee, or Sheil, to hansel it?—or why, in God's name, did he not sport it himself? Why is Lord

Holland—or why are *you*, or Sidney Smith, or even Milad̃i's Atheist, at this hour without it? By avoiding the concern yourselves, have not you, the prime Quacksalvers, done your best to mark it as a miserable sign of menialism for your *Merrymen?**

Jeffrey. Pooh! pooh! I wasn't thinking of such fifth-rate trumpery for you.

North. Nor I for myself, my dear. The late King, God bless his bones, asked me more than once to be a Grand Cross of the old Bath—and once to be a Privy Counsellor—and I declined both offers. If I had had a son to inherit Strath-North, and had been in those days tempted with a revival of the peerage we so foolishly forfeited in the Fifteen, I don't know what I might have said; but certainly any thing under that sort of touch would never have flattered me—and most certainly *that* would not flatter me or any sane Christian *now*.

Jeffrey. God bless me! You talk as if the Peerage were not worth the having. Are you serious?

North. Never more so in my life, talking of this present moment. Why, you don't mean to hum me at my own fireside as to that matter?

Jeffrey. I protest I don't understand you the least in the world. In what possible shade or degree has the dignity of the Peerage been diminished in our hands?

North. In *your* hands! The question answers itself! Fill your glass, my Lord.

Jeffrey. The question answers itself! What, in the name of wonder, can you mean?

North. Every thing that's mean.

Jeffrey. The bottle's with you again. Come, speak plainly, old boy; no riddles *inter pocula!*

North. Well, of all faults in the world, I never expected to be charged with a want of plain-speaking! If you will have it *a la Readingmadeasy*, every fool sees that Brougham and the rest of your clique have humbugged the Devonshires and Lansdownes,† and so forth, most illustriously, and made them, the ninnies, the instruments of roturier spleen to knock down the noblesse, which, 'tis my belief, will not rally again in my time, or even in yours. Why, you have not used one *serious* argument all through this affair, that, if pursued to its legitimate conclusion, is not as fatal to the peerage, as an independent branch of the legislature, as it has already proved, by your own story, to their influence in St. Stephens.

* In the earlier years of King William's reign, the Grey ministry very freely gave the order of the Guelph to men of letters and science. But, as if to mark its inferior value, as a distinction, not one member of that Ministry asked for it for himself.—M.

† The Marquis of Lansdowne (Lord Henry Petty, of All-the-Talents Cabinet in 1806), the staunch friend of Thomas Moore.—M.

Jeffrey. Not at all. You have quite mistaken us. We have made that part of the peerage which entertains rational views of what is due to the people, far more powerful in every respect than it ever was before. Between ourselves, my friend, the manipulation of the schedules was magnificent; and besides, it was not our fault that the King would not let a Whig majority be created in the Upper House itself this year, and there is every reason to hope that that may still be managed.

North. And *that* would strengthen the peerage?

Jeffrey. Yes. There's nothing can strengthen such a body, in the midst of an enlightened age like the present, but making it sensible that its only legitimate part is to watch the signs of the times, and ratify the decisions of the public at large.

North. Strengthen indeed! Do you mean merely strengthening their tenure of the domains of their ancestors, *your grace* and *your lordship*, and the right of walking out of a drawing-room before you and me, and being seated at dinner high up among the dull feathered and flounced dowagers, while plain esquires have the felicity of flirting lower down with the bonny blooming skelpy-limmers,

> "Sweet as the dewy milk-white thorn,
> Dear as the raptured thrill of joy?"

If this be all, I understand you—but even so I think you wrong, and that those boobies have been bamboozled still, for depend upon it what's sauce for a goose will do well enough for a gander, and the latter end of Grosvenor Square will be even as the latter end of the Faubourg St. Germain, as indeed has often been distinctly predicted in your Review. Do you remember Brougham's speech about the peers, at the dinner you, his cronies, gave him here in Edinburgh, when he came down after the Queen's trial?

Jeffrey. Ah! he was much excited at that time, and no doubt said some rather broad things; but the fact is, Brougham never seriously disliked the institution, and, now he is a peer himself, seems, if I must say so, to attach indeed rather more importance to the concern than one would have expected of him.

North. Ay, I liked his getting himself hooked on to the old Barons of Triermain! Very well, Brougham is a man of ancient and respectable pedigree, as we all know, and now he's a lord, very likely he'll forget his Brandenburg House theories, and do all he can for the order;* but my opinion is, that it is no longer in his or

* His title is Baron Brougham and Vaux, and he traces his descent to Saxon ancestors, long before the Norman Conquest, and took his second appellation to mark his relationship with the house of Vaux, Lords of Triermain. He was Attorney-General to Queen Caroline, who resided in 1820-'21, at Brandenburgh House, near London, and, as the majority of the peers were opposed to her, the replies she made to public addresses were not over complimentary to the peerage.—M.

anybody's power to undo the mischief that the sect he originally belonged to had among them managed to do—before he was belorded, or even dreamt of being so.

Jeffrey. It will last our time.

North. There's the old story. Recollect how Segur describes the liberal *Grand Seigneurs* of 1786. "We were lost," he says, "in a dream extremely flattering to our personal vanities. We fancied that by clever management we might reconcile the expression of *philosophical* opinions with the maintenance of our own dear *privileges*, which the real *philosophes*, of all things, abhorred, and had sworn to exterminate. At all events, we made sure of being able, by appearing to join the new sect, to mitigate the rapidity of its movements, and if we could not ultimately avert the downfall of our *order*, create at least such a diversion in its favor, as might prolong its existence in ease and splendor for the period of our own generation." I have so often read the passage, that I think I can repeat it pretty exactly. Well for your fine friends, under their gilded canopies, if they had weighed that same in August, 1830!

Jeffrey. After all, institutions of every kind must be altered and modified according to the wants and wishes of successive ages. Your Grand Seigneur of the present time carries the same title that his ancestor did in the days of Elizabeth or James, but no more fills the same sort of place in our social system, than a modern half-crown will buy what a half-crown did in the days of "King Stephen, worthy Peer." Perhaps fifty years hence there will be dukes, marquisses, and so forth, as unlike in essentials even to our contemporary magnates, as the present Earl of Warwick is to Guy of the iron kettle, or his grace of Norfolk to

"High-souled Surrey, darling of the muse,"

and yet extremely comfortable personages, and discharging many important functions with considerable benefit to the community. Thank God! the principle of property is very sacred in the eyes of our countrymen of all classes.

North. Of all classes that have a tolerable share of it, I admit; but are you serious in thinking that you and your friends have not given it a confounded shake in the opinion of certain other classes?

Jeffrey. Why, if I must speak *latiné*, the idea of gravely discussing the question of Parliamentary Reform, with men who could describe the boroughmongers as about to be deprived of *property*, in the proper sense of that term, always appeared to me absolutely ridiculous.

North. Perhaps. But it had not done so to either the English or the Scotch judges of any preceding twelvemonths in our history, and the long unbroken series of their decisions on the subject had, however absurd, so completely settled the matter in the opinion of individuals and corporations, that nobody hesitated about investing what you will admit was *property*, *i. e.* money, in the purchase of that which you will not allow to have any right to be called *property*.

Jeffrey. Why, it was *their* business to consider the nature of the affair, before they took any such steps.

North. Yes, and I believe they gave it what they considered the best possible sort of consideration. That is, they considered the Sages of the Long Robe, before they risked their cash. For example, I am informed that Sir Thomas Denman* happened to be one of the lawyers that examined the title-deeds of Gatton, when that estate, two thirds of whose value in the market consisted in the borough, was purchased but three or four years ago by the guardians of a minor peer, Lord Monson, as a better thing for his tiny lordship, when he should come of age, than £160,000 in the three per cents. He has now the house and park—and a copy of Schedule A. Again, it is said—whether correctly or not, you can answer—that when the trustees of one of our Scotch hospitals wanted to invest in real property, even more recently I believe, the amount of a legacy bequeathed to them for the maintenance and education of an additional score or two of orphan children, they took the advice of counsel learned in the law on the concern, and bought a handful of *superiorities*, under the professional sanction of a gentleman now holding a very distinguished station among the crown officers of this part of his Majesty's dominions.

Jeffrey. I have no recollection of being consulted in that affair; it may have been so, however; and, at all events, there can be no doubt I have been engaged in hundreds of cases, where we argued for superiorities as *property* INTER CAIUM ET TITUM. No doubt as to that. But 'tis another affair when the question comes to be one INTER CAIUM ET QUIRITES: this sort of property, if you must call it so, was vested in the individual, to be used not for his own advantage, but *pro bono publico*. The condition failing, the tenure drops; and the moment the injured party, the Public, comes into court, the law, silent as long as that party did not appear, speaks out—and things are restored to the *status quo ante pactum*.

North. I should like to hear L'Amy† on all this. Meantime, just apply your doctrine. King Henry VIII., after robbing the monasteries, on the ground that they had not used *their* properties *pro bono publico*, gave, of course with the view of securing its being held in all time coming for the benefit of the *Quirites*, a certain

* Attorney-General in 1832, and subsequently Chief-Justice of England, with a peerage.—M.
† James L'Amy, then Sheriff-Depute of Forfar-shire, and one of the ablest members of the Scottish Bar.—M.

ex-monastic manor to the reformed ancestor of a certain reforming Duke now *in rerum naturâ*. He at the same time created a borough on the same manor, at the express request of the same ancestor, but no doubt with the same liberal view as to the use to be made in all time coming of the votes in the House of Commons thus initiated. Now, it having been discovered that the said votes had sundry times been employed for the mere personal advantage and worldly lucre of the heirs of the said ancestor, his liberal successor, of course, has nothing to object when the public comes into court, and demands the abolition of the said borough. "Quite right!" he says; "I give it up with great satisfaction to myself—I was, in fact, always of opinion that I had no sort of right to keep such a borough."

Jeffrey. Sir, posterity will do justice to the noble persons you sneer at.

North. To be sure—to be sure. But let me go on. Now, suppose a time to come, when our friend, Mr. Public, may choose to walk into court again, and call another suit—alleging that the manor had been perverted even more egregiously than the thereto appended franchise—that whereas, when Henry VIII. of blessed memory gave the soil, he understood the owner and his successors were to live constantly or habitually thereupon, spending its produce among its inhabitants, and superintending their physical and intellectual condition, under a solemn sense not only of moral duty, but of legal obligation; nevertheless these personages had entirely neglected this duty and obligation, scarcely ever seeing the said manor, dwelling hundreds of miles off, consuming its rental in voluptuous pleasures, in cities the very names of which were new and strange to the said poor husbandmen of the said manor; and that therefore the manor could not, either by a Brougham, a Shadwell, a Lyndhurst, or a Tenterden,* be considered as the *property* of its existing lord, but that his tenure thereof ought to be *absque morâ* pronounced cass, null, and determined for ever—and the annual proceeds in all time coming of the said manor, applied for the purposes originally contemplated by the most religious and gracious King, Henry VIII. Suppose all this to happen, and to happen not in the case of one hereditament, but of many thousands, say *of all beyond a certain yearly value*,—what, I ask, is the court to do? Will the Denmans and Abercrombies of that not impossible time, be minded *anent* that question, as they have been as to the recent one *inter Caium et Quirites?* and will the Duke of that day be as hearty a reformer as he of the day that now is?

Jeffrey. I beg your pardon—I really believe I've filled twice.

* Sir Lancelot Shadwell was then Vice-Chancellor of England and Lord Tenterden Chief Justice of the King's Bench from 1818 to 1832.—M.

Why, Mr. North, you certainly put a—a—a rather puzzling case, that is, I mean to say, a case that might seem puzzling to a person of limited information. But the fact is, you assume throughout that it is for the public advantage that landlords should be resident on their estates; whereas, my worthy friend, it has already been over and over again demonstrated by Professor Macculloch, in the Review, that it signifies not one straw to the tenantry and husbandmen of any manor on the face of the earth, whether the proprietor thereof ever sets a foot on its soil or no: that, for example, whether the Duke of Devonshire spends the rental of the Blackwater at Lismore, or in Naples, is of no more importance to the farmers and cotters of that beautiful valley, than whether the same Duke dines in a white neckcloth, or, as he at present chooses to do, in a black one.* It is only on the supposition that you never read, or have entirely forgotten, the capital and conclusive arguments of my friend Macculloch on this subject, that I can at all account for your presenting such a case as this as a *pendant* to the borough one.

North. Very well. You admit, then, that if ever the public were to be so brutally negligent of Professor Macculloch and the Edinburgh Review, as to hold generally the doctrine on this point so triumphantly demolished by these authorities, the said public might be very likely "to come into court" with such a case as I ventured to suggest for your consideration?

Jeffrey. But to suppose such a time—such a public! I wonder you never speculate on the decline of the cotton manufacture, when we take back to the tattooing.

North. I suppose you also admit, that if ever such a Pictish public should disgrace such a tattooing time, and bring such a case into court, the court would be bound, however, to entertain it—to hear the pleadings of the parties?

Jeffrey. Considerable deference should always be shown to public opinion. A fair discussion of the question would very soon settle it on its right footing, and the ignorant plaintiff, being enlightened, would bundle up his papers, and withdraw, with a suitable apology for having occupied the time of the bench.

North. Your professional phraseology may perhaps embarrass you on this occasion. For *Bench* read a House of Commons elected by universal suffrage and by ballot; and for *Plaintiff* realize to your lively imagination all that heterodox part of the population, who do not believe in the inspiration of Macculloch—*in arms.* Happy defendant, whose only demurrer shall be a Lord Chamberlain's wand in one hand, and a number of the Edinburgh Review in the other.

* This absurd theory of Absenteeism was long since exploded as untenable.—M.

Jeffrey. You make no allowance for the progressive, and now rapidly progressive, march of intellect 'Tis this indeed that lies at the bottom of all the Tory pseudo-arguments on the great questions of the present time.

North. Come, now, are we to understand, that when the march of intellect has progressed for a few years of *Sessions* more, the result will be, that if you were to shut up Craigcrook, Sir Alexander Keith to shut up Ravelstone, John Hope to shut up Granton, Tom Allen to shut up Lauriston, and so forth for two miles round, the poor old bodies about Muttonhole would be either quite as sure of a flannel petticoat, or a glass of blackstrap in case of need, as all the world knows they are at present—or in that exalted state of illumination that they would be, in case of a six weeks' black frost or a cholera, more anxious about the Scotsman's last extract from Macculloch's last article, than about any such dirty material objects as their backs or their bellies?

Jeffrey. You always run into personalities, my dear sir. Why should you fix now on my own particular neighborhood!

North. Simply, my dear lord, because I presume you know better about it than Macculloch did about Ireland, which he had never set his ugly pins upon, when he served up the crambe recocta of his absenteeism *demonstrations* before the Committee of the House of Commons on the Condition of the Irish Poor.

Jeffrey. Personal again! Fie! fie! Why, you're as bad as your Magazine.

North. Like man, like Mag. But I'm sure I meant nothing uncivil. Come, you know in your heart now, that I had always a sincere liking for you. I think your system all wrong, rump and stump, that's certain; but I know you are a good-hearted, well-disposed man, and only led astray in your public doings by submitting to the dictation of a parcel of animals utterly inferior to you in every sort of intellectual grace, but unhappily as much superior in brass and impudence, and all the coarse qualities that carry people best through the tug and tussle of actual sublunar humbug. You were grossly imposed upon when you suffered your Review to be the vehicle of the dull, dismal nonsense of that porridge-brained botherer, which, if it had produced any effect on the public, except getting him scorned, and yourself laughed at, must have gone near to drive the Irish people to actual despair. No wonder your Review never got over that beastly blunder, in which cruelty and stupidity were equally mixed, and that you, my dear Lord, were well pleased to get out of the concern at the first convenient opportunity thereafter ensuing. Fill your glass!

Jeffrey. You and I will never agree as to Political Economy, I see. 'Tis at best a dry subject, and, perhaps, you may never have bestowed much time thereupon. Let's stick to politics proper, where we are both at home—'faith this bottle's near out too. As for Macculloch, I perceive you have a strong personal prejudice against the man; so it's no use telling you, that whatever you and your ultra coteries may think or say, he is at this moment one of the most influential persons in the empire, and likely to have more hand in settling the great questions now afloat, than all the Tories in England Scotland, Ireland, and Berwick-upon-Tweed.

North (*rings*). Another bottle, John.—O yes, I know all that. 'Tis no secret that Political Economy is no longer to be considered as a separate mystery, lying apart from what you say we had better stick to, Politics proper. The real politics, henceforth will be all Political Economy; and the real politicians, the doctors of that science. Blessing on them! The Tithe Question, the Poor-Law Question, the Corn Question, the Indian Question, and the West Indian one—they are all to be settled, for our sins, according to the sage saws of Poulett Thomson,* and Peter Macculloch, and Java Crawfurd, and half-a-dozen young lordlings whom you have stuck down in Downing Street, to transfer from eighteenpenny pamphlets to official foolscap, gilt-edged and skewered down with green ribbon at the corners, the *verga magistrorum*. Yes, yes, *cuique in suâ arte credendum est!* But you've lost one great card of this pack, I hear. 'Tis said Whateley has come over to us AS TO CHURCH PROPERTY, since Lord Grey transmogrified him into an Archbishop, in reward of his demonstration of the non-divine origin of the Christian Sabbath.†

Jeffrey. You have been naming some of what I used to consider my best hands; and really now, are you not, you Tories, a sadly unreasonable set of people? Why, you had every thing your own way for half a century on end nearly; and having, as you must admit, failed to make this country what such a country ought ere now to have been, here are you, man and mother's son of you, grumbling at the notion of any thing so out of the course of nature as that we poor Whigs, Economists, and so forth, should have, if it were but for a matter of two short twelvemonths, the opportunity of manufacturing laws and archbishops after our own fancy! Your system ended, all the world acknowledge, in a cruel bad state of things. Why not possess your souls in patience for a little, and see what's to be the upshot of ours? In equity, in honor, in charity,

* At this time Charles Poulett Thomson was Vice-President of the Board of Trade, but not a member of Lord Grey's Cabinet. In 1834 he was President of the Board of Trade, and entered the Ministry. In 1839, he succeeded Lord Durham, as Governor-General of Canada, and in 1840, was raised to the peerage as Baron Sydenham of Toronto. He died, in Canada, from the effects of a fall from his horse, in September, 1841.—M.

† Dr. Richard Whateley, appointed Principal of St. Alban's Hall, Oxford, and Professor of Political Economy in 1830, and made Archbishop of Dublin in 1832. He is author of a standard work "On Logic," and the celebrated "Historic Doubts of the Existence of Napoleon Bonaparte."—M.

by every sanction to which enlarged minds owe respect, you are bound to be quiescent witnesses of the grand series of experiments, on which we have as yet barely entered.

North. I know very well that I have no claim to the title of Philosopher. I am, I must confess, altogether unable to shake off many prejudices, which younger, and of course wiser, men have long since discarded *in toto*. Age, they say, is naturally a coward; and maybe that's the whole secret. But, in truth, I—damn it!—I do, my Lord. I do abhor experimental cuttings and carvings upon the body politic—ay, although the knife were a Weiss's, and the hand that directed it a Liston's.* But here's a junto of jolter-headed empirics, and they have found instruments as coarse, as they themselves are rash—as the *subject* is sensitive.

Jeffrey. Come, your own government was far more liberal than you as to some things. Several of these same empirics were not a little in request in Downing Street, even before your head-quarters were shifted to another part of the town.

North. Our head-quarters! Ah! my dear Lord, you have me there. 'Tis indeed but owre true a tale, that we had taken enemies within our lines. Had it not been so, our Turres Veteres might have cost you as much trouble as ever the Torres Vedras did Massena.

Jeffrey. Well, what would ye be at? Tory pleases you not, no, nor Whig neither, though by your smiling you seem to say so.

North. I don't like a Whig, *quâ* a Whig, but I must own I have even less affection for a Whiggizing Tory. What signifies it to me what set of individuals are in the enjoyment of salary, pension, patronage? Some set must have them, and, considered merely as individuals, it is very likely yours are every whit as amiable as their predecessors. What I have seen, and would fain hope to see again, is a government, no matter for the name it may bear, acting in calm contempt of cold-hearted theorists on one hand, and hot-headed riotists on the other, upon the principles to which England owed her

* Weiss, a well known surgical instrument maker in London.—Robert Liston was a Scotch surgeon of great celebrity. He resided at Edinburgh. In March, 1822, a duel was fought, in Fife, between Sir Alexander Boswell, the son of Dr. Johnson's biographer, and James Stuart, of Duncarn, who had been lampooned by Sir Alexander in some contemptible rhymes, and the knight was known to be so noted a shot that no surgeon would consent to attend the meeting. Liston went, however, and, contrary to expectation, the unfailing marksman was mortally struck down by a casual random bullet from a man who seldom handled a pistol. The seconds, of course, ran away, and the surviving duellist as prudently absented himself; Mr. Liston alone remaining to chronicle the particulars of a transaction which, such is the perversity of fashion, was the means of his introduction to several of the first families in North Britain. From this period his reputation was well established as a *surgeon*. He dissected and gave lectures, and ultimately attained the summit of his then ambition—he was appointed one of the surgeons of the hospital in Edinburgh, and there obtained his eminence as lecturer and operator. In 1834, he was appointed surgeon to one of the hospitals in London, and subsequently Professor of clinical surgery in University College, where he reached the utmost height of reputation for his extensive and accurate anatomical knowledge and the facility and rapidity of his operations. In 1847, he was snatched away by the influenza—which aggravated a slight attack of bronchitis to a fatal disease. His chief work was his Principles of Surgery.—M.

greatness, and to the violation of which, from August, 1822, down to this present jollification, we have owed nothing but a regular series of declension in everything that goes to constitute the true health, as well as wealth, of a great naval, and commercial, and agricultural, and, let me add, Christian empire.

Jeffrey. You seriously wish to see us recurring to the old system of Navigation Laws, and Prohibitory Duties—re-establishing the Protestant Ascendency in Ireland—upholding the East India Company in the China Trade, and the West India Planters in the Slave Trade—re-enacting Castlereagh's Six Acts at home—re-adhering to the Holy Alliance abroad—a fresh crusade to re-re-re-restore the Bourbons—and the indefinite prolongation of corn from the tight little islands, and timber and sugar from Sir Howard Douglas's own dear American colonies?*

North. 'Tis true 'tis pity, and 'tis pity but 'tis true. I am even the old-world animal you scarcely allow a place in the collected catalogue of Mammalia! Shall I tip you a chaunt?

Jeffrey. Any thing more agreeable could not have been suggested.

North. You shall judge. (*Sings.*)

Air—Come bother their buttons, quoth Tom o' the Goose.

There were times, my Lord Jeffrey, between you and me,
Rather blither than those we are likely to see;
When plain folks went to church, loved and honor'd their king,
And our hard-working farmers heard nothing of SWING.

No groans then were given for Tithes, Taxes, or Rent,
The rich man look'd kindness, the poor man content,
And though war raged without we were deaf to its din,
Midst the heart-cheering hum of our treddles within.

There was work on the shore, there was wealth on the sea,
Abroad there was glory, at home there was glee;
Men stuck to the counter, the shop, and the loom,
And laugh'd at the ravings of Cobbett and Hume.†

But our Solons in place have found out, it would seem,
All this wealth was a burden, this comfort a dream;
Our homes must be left for the hustings—God wot!
And Happiness turns on a franchise or not.

Look after your Till was the rule till of late,
But now 'tis, look after the Till of the State;
Even our Schoolmaster's ta'en such a fancy to roam,
You will never by chance find him flogging AT HOME!

* Sir Howard Douglas, a schoolfellow of Sir Walter Scott (who gave a review in the Quarterly, of his work on Military Bridges) and had held military command in British North America. He was subsequently Commissioner of the Ionian Islands.—M.

† Joseph Hume would probably have been very indignant at finding himself thus placed *côte à côte* with William Cobbett, though there was more in the latter's little finger (to use a familiar phrase) than in Hume's whole body. Hume has been a useful public man—in his day. In Parliament he never asserted any great principle, never viewed any question in a broad basis. He was an indifferent speaker, and could not reason. But he crept over the Public Accounts, figure by figure, arriving at what, in his broad Scotch accent, he called "the tottle of the whole," and let no extravagance escape exposure and blame.—M.

Time was when we drank to the health of our King,
But now we've discovered that isn't *the thing*—
That our rulers henceforth should have nothing to do—
And the mob should be monarch and ministry too!

Time was when the Mace or the Sword of the Law
Kept the good man in safety, the scoundrel in awe:
Now law must to brickbats and bludgeons give place,
And burning a town throws new light on the case!

Are we richer, or better, or happier now?
Sits life with its troubles more light on our brow?
Does plenty flow in with the "Minister's Plan?"—
Does Man look more kind or more loving on Man?

Is the Hum of our Engines more loud? Do we see
More ships in the harbor, more ploughs on the lea?
Will flags and processions pay weavers their hire,
Or a vote lay a log on the laborer's fire?

Oh! not—till the spirit of change shall be laid,
Till the limbs reacknowledge the rule of the head;
Till each honest Reformer shall stoop to the art
Of reforming his own rotten borough—THE HEART;—

Till banish'd Religion and Faith shall return,
And bright in our bosoms old Loyalty burn,
Till Labor and Confidence walk side by side,
And Reverence sit in the place of Whig Pride;—

Will the clouds of distress that o'ershadow our sky,
Like mists of the morning, break up and blow by;
Our tumults, our terrors, our sufferings cease,
And Plenty come smiling, sweet daughter of Peace!

(*Lights a cigar.*)

Jeffrey. Superbly sung! inimitable! But am I to take all this for the *bona fide* sentiments of my venerable bass?

North. In prose or in verse (though these fairish stanzas are none of mine, my Lord), in sobriety or in civilization—I am the same Kit, and these are my dogmata. Put them in your pipe and smoke them.

Jeffrey. Well, 'tis amusing, however. (*Lights a cigar.*) To speak fairly, my worthy old friend, I should almost as soon have expected to find myself discussing a third bottle of claret with the Homo Caudatus of Monboddo!

North. Well, I don't despair of having a tolerable tail yet. There's Lord Grey himself now—why, before the French rascals made this row of theirs, and the Duke was turned out, he himself had shown pregnant symptoms of an inclination to join me.* He made a capital speech in the House of Lords upon the currency and another on the Corn Laws—for both of which, if I remember, your Review

* In 1827, Lord Grey was so vexed at Canning's having been made Premier, instead of himself, that he went into bitter opposition, voting and speaking with the Tories against him. This he called—Patriotism.—M.

skelped him soundly, and perhaps, although he has been obliged to cushion his orthodox notions as to some points, until he began to feel himself warm in his seat, now that he has carried his Reform Bill he may find leisure and courage to deserve another of your jobations—or rather, I cry ye mercy, of Macvey's.*

Jeffrey. Impossible, my dear sir, impossible. The Government are just as much pledged *now* to emancipate blacky and wheat, and tea and timber, as they were a couple of years ago to demolish Old Sarum, and enfranchise Wapping. You must e'en make up your mind to what's inevitable.

North. 'Tis a Christian duty, my Lord. You begin, then, with the Corn?

Jeffrey. You throw out a Vesuvian whiff! Macculloch is clear for that.

North. Ay, and he's a Galloway laird too, I've heard—no doubt.

"A fair domain,
If purple heath were golden grain."

Jeffrey. Poh! Lord Milton,† who has better things to look after than a moor farm in Galloway, is just as clear for the change as the Professor.

North. I can better understand a man with a fifty thousand a year estate being willing to see such an experiment tried, than the same conundrum finding its way into the deep brain of your moderate landholder—and I take it for granted you're not going to work without carrying your own portion of the Squirearchy along with you. I wonder what *they* expect.

Jeffrey. As far as I have observed, there's a very general impression both among our country gentlemen and their farmers, that if the tithe were got rid of, the Corn Laws might be abolished without any very serious risk either for rents or profits.

North. If that's the view in favor with your agricultural supporters, we may expect, I presume, to see the Church Reform run neck and shoulder with the corn affairs?

Jeffrey. Have you read Lord Henley? See what Peel's brother-in-law, and a judge of the land,‡ and an earnest disciple of the godly, says on this subject.

North. Ay, I've seen all that, and perpended it too. He means well, no man better, I dare say, and his pamphlet is written with extraordinary ability. You may well plume yourselves on having got such an ally. If he sees you safe to Hounslow, you'll reach Windsor without much trouble. But don't flatter yourself that

* Macvey Napier was then Editor of the Edinburgh Review.—M.

† Lord Milton, now Earl of Fitzwilliam, and owner of vast landed estates in Yorkshire, Northamptonshire, and Ireland.—M.

‡ Lord Henley, an Irish Peer, was scarcely a Judge; he was only a master in Chancery.—M.

Lord Henley speaks his brother-in-law's creed as to this business. I can tell you, if you calculate on that, you are a good league out of your reckoning. Peel knows he made one mistake—and he's not the man to err twice in the same direction.

Jeffrey. I wonder that you, a staunch Presbyterian as you call yourself, should be so much concerned for the possible rending of the rochet!

North. Presbyterian as I am in Scotland, I should have been a sterling Episcopalian, I warrant you, had the lines fallen to me on t'other side of the silver Tweed. We have got our own system here, and no wise man would wish to see it tampered with *now*. They have theirs, and so far from wishing to see it changed to be nearer our pattern, I confess, if I were to countenance any change in such things at all, it would be in the contrary line, my Lord.

Jeffrey. What! patronise the shovel-hat here! Are you in earnest?

North. Not I—but I'm free to say I had rather, if I must choose between two changes, see a sprinkling of mitre here, than an abolition, or even a humiliation of it yonder.

Jeffrey. Don't be alarmed. We sha'n't go to work quite so sweepingly as you seem to anticipate. Modification, not abolition, is our motto both in church and state.

North. Doubtless—but at that rate it will be some time before the squires and the farmers have the full enjoyment of that grand innovation, which is to enable the latter to compete on equal terms with the serfs of Pomerania, and the former to be as sure of the chariot and pair as an Earl Fitzwilliam, if you leave him his land at all, is of his coach and six.

Jeffrey. I have understood the Pomeranians are a very comfortable peasantry.

North. Not a doubt of it—I know them and their country well—and the English farmer will learn by-and-by to be very comfortable too, with a pig-stye for a house, a sheepskin for a jacket, and sour cabbage for a dinner. To walk barelegged in wooden shoes hardens the muscular system, and, in point of fact, a man with the *Plica Polonica* may be considered as independent of a hat.

Jeffrey. Ha! ha! 'tis very possible that both squires and farmers may be obliged to come down a peg or two. I admit all that, though there's no use telling them so just at present. But what can be done? The manufacturing towns are the repositories of the intelligence, the activity, and above all, of the physical strength of the nation; and we must do what those places consider necessary for their comfort. We have no choice.

North. That's honest, however. The agricultural population, nevertheless, still outnumbers the operative, three to one, at the least—and I have yet to learn that the manufacturer is, generally speaking, of more importance in the scale of intellect than the squire, or even the laird; or that the activity of the most strenuous weaver exceeds that of his cousin,

> "Albeit his name be Roger,
> That drives the groaning cart,"—

or that, if you come to physical strength, one

> "Brawny, bainie, ploughman chiel"

of the old cut, would think he had earned another cog for his supper, by having adorned the pericranium of the President and Committee of any Mechanics' Institute that ever the Gorbals rejoiced in, with as many bumps of osity and isitiveness as ever delighted a turnipologist in a tour through Sweden.

Jeffrey. The agriculturists are a scattered generation—the upper ranks of them proud as Lucifer, on their little dunghills; and the lower, I mean in England, in a brutal state of mental obfuscity. They read little that can tend to enlighten them either as to the theory of government, or the true doctrine of wages and profits. They have more pleasure in some old ballad, now, of Robin Hood and Little John, than in the most elaborate demonstration of an economical problem. They have more respect for a crumbling cathedral than the neatest factory that ever diffused population and occupation through a district lying within the oolitic range. They spend their winter evenings over Fox's Martyrs, and such like trumpery, well calculated to nurse and keep warm their great grandmother's horror of Lord Peter; crazy high-flying lumber about the Grand Rebellion—for so, in spite of Nugent and Macaulay, they still will call it; the Hymns of Bishop Ken, the homilies of Jeremy Taylor, Bunyan's Pilgrim's Progress, Buchan's Domestic Medicine, the Lamentable Tragedy of Arden of Feversham, Histories of the Peninsular War drawn from English sources, and the annual prophecies of Francis Moore, physician;—are these the people you compare, as to intellectual rank and condition, with the liberal and well-informed mechanics of our great marts of industry and ingenuity——

North. Who abominate a cathedral, or even a parish church, discuss in debating clubs, much *a la* speculative, whether Cromwell or Bonaparte was the purer patriot, take in the twopenny numbers of the Philosophical Dictionary, consider the Corn Law Rhymes as better poetry than the Cottar's Saturday Night—have been used to reverence no Book of books quite so highly as that which gladdens human optics, according to Byron's profane description—

> "In healing wings of saffron and of blue."

Jeffrey. Personal again, North. But I protest I can scarcely hear what you say, for these scoundrels under the window. That infernal hurdy-gurdy!—how come you to let the ragtag and bobtail into your pleasure ground?

North. We seldom steek our yetts here—'tis a pleasure to me to see the bit weans puin' gowans on the green. But these, I suppose, are some of the gentry that have been drawing your lordship's carriage through the village.

Jeffrey. Devil a bit did any of them drag my carriage, I can tell ye. For God's sake, turn out the ragamuffins. They'll split my head with their squawling. There again!

Ballad-Singers (*without*).

"The Whigs think they are grand and great,
But O! they're proud and idly gaudy,
How much unlike the manly gait
Of Aytoun, our dear Union laddie!"

Chorus of Ten-Pounders.

"O my charming Union laddie,
Our meet and graceful Union laddie:
What man would e'er a Whig compare
With Aytoun, our dear Union laddie!"

North. There's a good tenor among them—hark again.

Ballad-Singers.

"The Whigs humbug and speak ye fine,
Though in their hearts they scorn and hate ye,
But Aytoun is the genuine,
'Tis he's the proper clean potaty."

Chorus of Ten-Pounders.

"O my charming Union laddie,
My sweet delightful Union laddie;
No paltry sham, but the real yam,
Is Aytoun, our dear Union laddie."

Jeffrey. This is really too bad—why—Mr. North, I say—

Ballad-Singers.

"Then when the Parliament's dissolved,
Which it's said 'twill be before November,
With heart and soul we've all resolved
Aytoun he *shall be* the people's member."

Chorus of Ten-Pounders.

"O my charming Union laddie,
My darling comely Union laddie;
A plumper vote we'll each allot
To Aytoun, our dear Union laddie."

Jeffrey. Was ever such ingratitude! Confound this canaille!

Mullion (*from the window above*). I say, you honest carle with the hurdy-gurdy—and you, my fine fellow in the leathern apron, the old gentleman of the house is in a very feeble way, and you'll clean worry him if you go on at this rate. Come now, my good lads, here's a gold sovereign to drink Mr. North's health at Lucky MacLearie's, and so be off with you all, bag and baggage.

Ballad-Singers. God bless your honor—God bless his worship! we wadna hae inconvenienced him for the saul o' us, if we had kenned he was onywise wailkly.

First Ten-Pounder. We'll drink the auld gentleman's health wi' all the heart i' the waurld. Tell him, wi' oor best coampliments, we war only serenauding "the unfortunit clause."

Second Ten-Pounder. We hae nae objections till a Tory, gif he be's a gude landlord, and a friend to the puir. Maister North's character's weel kenned, and we houp he'll see mony a blithe day yet.

Third Ten-Pounder. What! is this CHRISTOPHER's policy? he's a grand auld cock. Can he aye tak his horn at the Noctes yet?

Mullion. Ay, my braw chiel, it will be ill indeed wi' him when he canna do that—wheesht—(*Sings*).

> Mynheer Van Dunk,
> Though he never is drunk,
> Sips his brandy and water gaily;
> He quenches his thirst
> With two quarts of the first,
> To a pint of the latter daily—
> Singing, Oh! that a Dutchman's draught could be
> As deep as the rolling Zuyder Zee. (*Bis.*)

There now, I've given you stave for stave—good-night, and joy be wi' ye a'—now, don't meddle with the Lord Advocate's carriage, you little tinkler!—

Hurdy-Gurdy. Come awa, ye ne'er-do-weels! Huzzah! huzzah! huzzah! North and Noctes for ever—hurrah!

Jeffrey. Had I not reason to say that I am an ill-used man?

North. Thus it is, you see, my friend. Modification's your motto —but Abolition outbids you. Hear glorious John!

> "O hadst thou been content to serve the crown
> With virtues only proper to the gown!
> O had the rankness of the soil been freed
> From cockle, that oppress'd the noble seed!
> But wild Ambition loves to slide, not stand,
> And Fortune's ice prefers to Virtue's land;
> Disdain'd the golden fruit to gather free,
> And lent the crowd his arm to shake the tree.
> Almighty crowd! that shortens all dispute,
> Power is its essence, wit its attribute;
> But thou, nor those thy faction's arts engage,
> Shall reap the harvest of rebellious rage.
> Insatiate as the barren womb or grave,
> When flattery pauses, shall *that* cease to crave?"

Jeffrey. So you are willing to identify yourselves with the Tories of Charles the Second's time?—thank ye.

North. No more than you to identify yourself with Achitophel—but human nature's human nature still, and, as sure as Cromwell plucked the bauble from before Lenthal, we shall, ere long, see some out-and-outer union-man replace even on the Woolsack your illustrious friend, who now

> "Bends the black brows that keep the Peers in awe,
> Shakes the full-bottomed wig, and gives the nod of law."

Hang me if this Aytoun carries his election, I see no reason why he should despair of being Advocate as well. 'Tis all on the cards.

Jeffrey. Psha! The Radicals could never make a government. They are well enough in their own place; but, depend upon it, we shall know how to keep them there. Now we've bought off Hobhouse, there's scarcely a man of any talent left among them.

North. Of talent? Can you sincerely dispute the extraordinary talents of Daniel O'Connell, or Richard Sheil, or Joseph Hume, or—for you need not limit your glance to those already in the House—of such people as the Editor of the Examiner,* or your old antagonist and victim the bone-grubber†?

Jeffrey. Why, as there's no doubt the Church goes bodily in Ireland, I'm not in the least afraid of Sheil, who is a gentleman in all respects, and will, that job over, gradually melt into our own temperature. O'Connell, if he goes on at this rate, will get his neck into a noose, and there's an end of him! Joseph Hume is a wealthy man, and besides wants a baronetcy, and perhaps we may think of office in his case, which he would no more refuse than did "my boy Hobbio." Fonblanque I admit to be a very able fellow, and much regret I didn't find him out a few years ago, to nail him to the Edinburgh Review, where he would have been more useful than even Tom Macaulay, I suspect. He too is a gentleman, and therefore, however he may foam away just now, I don't despair of seeing him veer round on a seat at the Board of Control, or the like, some pretty morning. As to Cobbett, his influence is no longer what it was. He never recovered, though I say it, the lashing I gave him in the Review. His Register no longer brings him £60 a-week, which I think it was at one time proved to do on the King's Bench; he is not in any very formidable degree of credit *hodie*—and Cobbett's aging now.

North. As to the matter of age, I believe he may be half-way or thereabouts between yourself, my dear Lord, and your humble ser-

* Albany Fonblanque, for many years Editor of the Examiner; a very brilliant political writer. He now holds office under the crown, at the Board of Trade, and has relinquished journalism.—M.

† Cobbett, who brought to England, from America, Tom Paine's bones.—M.

vant—who has not yet lost all his teeth. Whether his Register has fallen off in the article of sale, within the last twenty years, more or less than other periodical works of eminence, the Edinburgh Review for example, I can't tell—all such concerns are subject to fluctuation. But, without at all disputing that your capital article, which you have so much reason to remember with pride and satisfaction—perhaps, indeed, the very ablest out of mere literature that ever dropped from your goosequill—without disputing that that most admirable paper did its work at the time, and for years kept Cobbet at low-water, in quarters where he had, before it appeared, begun to make considerable demonstrations—allow me to ask your lordship, whether you preserve any very exact recollection of what the principal practical *giste*, bearing, purpose, substance, tendency, and so forth, of that highly important, truly patriotic, eminently satisfactory, and splendidly eloquent exposé in the Edinburgh Review, then dominant, really was?

Jeffrey. I preserve but a slight reminiscence of the course I adopted in my new show-up of the old scoundrel. The object generally was neither more nor less than to convince the people of England that William Cobbett was, though a vigorous sort of lampooner, an inconsistent politician, and, in the midst of noisy pretences to patriotism, almost to exclusive patriotism, the advocate of doctrines in essence diametrically hostile to the true interests of the mass of the community. I believe I established my points too, and that you do me merely justice in saying, that I severely damaged the ragamuffin in many quarters where he had begun with his cursed blarney to make something like an impression.

North. All great authors are modest, and their modesty is in nothing more conspicuous than in the imperfect recollection which, after the lapse of a few years, they occasionally retain even of their own chefs-d'œuvre. You really don't remember, then, the prime argument, I mean material, of your Philippic *in Cobbettum?*

Jeffrey. Not I, my dear North. I'm not like the old quiz in the play, who was always reading "Uncle's own works."

North. The last man in the world that anybody would suspect of it. Come, now, fill a huge Homeric bumper of red wine, rich and blameless—that's the thing, thankye—and know that your immortal article, all but the head-piece, which was flourish, and the tail-piece, which was ferocious abuse, consisted of a clear, logical, analytical examination, and triumphant, philosophical, unanswerable refutation of the then current arguments for Parliamentary Reform; of which same identical arguments your Lordship's speech in the House of Commons, in seconding Lord Johnny Russell's great motion of the first of March, 1831, was, whether well or ill received in St. Stephen's, a really, brilliant, compact, and nervous resumé, rifacciamento, and hash.*

Jeffrey. This cigar is impracticable—*Peut-être*—but you'll admit that what might be absurd THEN, might possibly be, notwithstanding, a very fair argument NOW!

North. Of course—*tempora mutantur et nos mutamur in illis.* Here's the box—please yourself. I am not recalling this fact with the slightest intention of disparaging the arguments which you proved to be worthless when you were a man of forty, and proved to be golden gospel at the riper age of fifty-nine—no idea so preposterous could ever have entered my brain. No—I was not thinking of any trashy *argumentum ad hominem*—a thing I despise, though you, by-the-by, did not, when you, on that very occasion, reproached Cobbett with having been at an earlier period of his life a protegé of Windham, and a trumpeter of Pitt.† No—I was not adverting *in invidiam* to your Lordship, but only *in terrorem* to the public—the populace—what you call the people—in short, these same huzzaing Ten-pounders—or rather the nine-pounders, and the seven-pounders, and the five, and the three, and the two, and the one, and the *no*-pounders, who being all in their opinion as wise men, and as valuable citizens as any Ten Thousand-pounder within the four seas, must, of course, be presumed to have studied the Edinburgh Review *ab initio*, and not unlikely to be now comparing the articles of its golden age with your Lordship's Parliamentary speeches of 1831, quite as unceremoniously as your Lordship did Cobbett's Registers of 1807, with Cobbett's Porcupines of 1794.

Jeffrey. Why, the public of the time you allude to approved of my article, and the public of last year took a much more favorable view of my speech than the House of Commons seemed to do—so that I am somewhat at a loss to follow you.

North. Have patience, my dear Lord Advocate. Tell me now, however, what is your real opinion of Cobbett as a writer?

Jeffrey. Poh! extremely clever, but unconscionably coarse—terse, but tautological—great nerve, but no variety—occasionally humorous, but never witty—with not one glimpse of power over either the gentler or the loftier passions of our nature, possessing certainly a brutal, coal-hammer energy for stirring up the slumbering ferocity of the clodhopper—the Swift of the Chaw-bacons—perhaps the Tyrtæus of the Rick-gang—the worthy champion of the Ballot-Box and the Sponge.

* Lord John Russell, though not then a member of the Grey Cabinet, and a very bad orator (owing to a natural hesitation in his speech) was selected, because he was a Duke's son, to introduce the Reform Bill into Parliament, on March 1, 1831.—M.

† Cobbett's change from Tory to liberal politics, is said with some show of probability, to be owing to his having received some personal slight from Pitt, whom he often met at the table of Mr. Windham, then Secretary at War.—M.

North The Ballot-Box and the Sponge!! Cobbett or no Cobbett, these twain will go together.

Jeffrey. What, do you tremble even for the per cents? My dear Mr. North, we've not finished our third bottle!

North. I believe your Lordship holds a good deal of stock?

Jeffrey. Why, yes; I believe I may have somewhere about £60,000 in the three per cents; but, to be sure, *you* won't consider that as a heavy stake. You're Crœsus, I know.

North. Sixty thousand's a sum not to be sneezed at as times go. I had about as much in that book two years ago, but I thought it as well to sell out, and have now invested it, one half in Russian debentures, and t'other in American canal shares. I am now endeavoring to get rid of my land in Kilkenny, and mean, if I can find a purchaser, which I doubt, to put the proceeds into the Bank of Amsterdam. 'Tis an old rule not to have all one's pullet-sperm in one basket. I have a fair estate, you know, in Rosshire, and that, with this little *rus in Urbe* here, my old pew in the Grey-friars, and so forth, I think quite enough to retain in that particular creel which your Lordship will, ere long, have to defend, *totis viribus*, against rather more egg-fanciers than Mr. William Cobbett.

Jeffrey. Psha! Haven't I told you already that Gridiron's quite gone by? He's not the old Hector now, man: as I said before, we did his business in the Edinburgh.

North. Most certainly—to my mind nothing could be more conclusive: but wasn't it of the Ten and No-pounders we were talking?

Jeffrey. Well, and what if it were so? Confound Cobbett! *He's* in the valley of Jehoshaphat.

North. Not a bad location for a lover of dry bones, Lord Advocate. But to be serious—the severest thrashing ever Cobbett had was, it is admitted on all sides, your article against his Reforming Registers. Now, if one puts oneself into the position of a No-pounder, and considers that your Lordship's best speech in Parliament was neither more nor less than a translation of those same Registers out of the old-fashioned *English* of Daniel Defoe and Dean Tucker, into the more elegant *British* of the Speculative Society of Edinburgh, how is it possible not to suspect that the No-pounder may be inclined to say to himself, "Come, old Cobbett's now allowed to have been in the right o't for once?"

Jeffrey. My dear Mr. North, must I again remind you that the times were totally changed?

North. My dear Lord, 'tis not me you're to deal with—'tis the No-pounder—the very patriot that has just been splitting our ears with this Aytoun, who, I humbly presume, will be worthy to tie Cobbett's shoe-latch on the same day that his predecessor George

Brodie draws a character fit to be printed on the same page with one of Clarendon's.

Jeffrey. You quite forget the Bill, North—your No-pounder's *no go*, man.

North. I'm not sure that he'll turn out to be *no come*, though.

Jeffrey. Well, well, make your best of your beast. Hallo! another magnum scheduled!

North. One more, then?—or shall we have a cheerer?

Jeffrey. You were always celebrated for your whiskey. I don't mind trying a tumbler, ere I start.

North (*rings*). That's right. I have some prime stuff from Mull at present on the tap, and I'm glad to see you have not been Englified out of this at least. (*Enter* MACKAY, *with tray, &c.*) Put your thumb where I'm to stop. Another lump of sugar? I've lemons in the house, if you would like a touch of the acid, my lord.

Jeffrey. No, thank ye—my stomach won't stand that sort of thing now-a-days. This is a superb elixir, my friend.

North. And now I'll mix another for myself. (*Sings.*)

Foin de ces gens que tout depite,
Qui veulent singer Héraclite!
Leur système n'est pas le mien,
Car je ne m'attriste de rien.

Dans son inevitable trappe
Si bientôt la mort nous attrappe,—
Si nous devons mourir demain,
Mettons-nous gaîment en chemin.

Jeffrey. Euge! Euge! Here's true High Church Philosophy for you!

North. High Church or Laigh Kirk—let's have naething against John Barleycorn. But *revenons a nos moutons.* What were we upon? Ay, ay, Cobbett.

Jeffrey. Sink the old monster—finish your song, my hero.

North. By-and-by. What I wanted to ask you was, whether it never struck you as a possible case, that, Cobbett being now ascertained to have been in the right in the main as to *the* great question of our time, the fact of his doctrine on that head having ultimately obtained so signal a triumph over that which, down to the eleventh hour, was yours, might have a tendency to buttress him up as to other points? He has, after all, a confoundedly pithy style of urging his heresies on the vulgar ear; and I'm sorry to say, I can fancy him turning this *rattery* of your lordship's to some account, when the ballot and the sponge come to be on the table as prominently as we have of late seen Lord Durham's blessed schedules. As to the Corn question, he will work you the devil's own delights, I calculate.

Jeffrey. I have given up reading his trash for years past. What's his plan as to the Corn?

North. Why, he's not of the opinion of the squires and farmers you spoke of, that our agriculture could stand its ground fairly against Poland, if the tithes were but put on a diminishing regimen. He has a deeper notion of the difficulties of the case, and suggests a bolder course.

Jeffrey. Would he kick out the actual incumbents? What a savage!

North. Rather more than that. He says to the Chaw-bacons, Here's a little island containing a thousand acres, on each of which acres more or less, a sturdy clodhopper can easily raise as much as clothes himself, his wife, and five children, in comfortable drugget, and fills their bellies three times a-day with whacking rashers, and huge slices of wheaten bread, and deep draughts of milk and beer. They, however, take it into their heads that it would be a fine thing to turn one of their number, his Joan, and little Jacky, and so forth, into a gentleman, a lady, and so on. They, therefore, squeeze themselves into a narrower compass each family of them, in order that a hundred acres may be at their command whereupon to build an elegant house for the future Squire, enclose a park, a garden, &c., &c., &c., and establish him there *en Seigneur*. They then bind themselves to give him thenceforth at Ladyday and Lammas, each man of them, a certain proportion of the product of his own industry —say one-half.

Jeffrey. What a theory of the Origin of Rent!

North. Most absurd—but hear him out. Presently the Squire's second lad, Jem, grows up, and the Squire makes a scholar of him, and these excellent clodhoppers are seized with a strong desire to have Jem planted among them as a Parson. 'Tis a shame that so fine an island should be the only one that has not a shovel-hat upon it, and Parson Jem they will have. So they pare off another fifty acres for a rectory glebe, and 'tis agreed that over and above the moneys paid at Lammas and Ladyday to the old Squire, the value of every tenth sheaf, pig, and so forth, shall be in all time coming paid with like regularity to Jem; and the Squire is delighted, and Jem is overjoyed, and sits down in the rectory fully determined to remain all his days among these good clodhoppers, unless he is offered a glebe of sixty acres, and more sheaves and pigs, in some other island. Now mark, quoth Cobbett, the result. Before these doings, it had been an old custom for a great man called a King to send every year into the island, and claim of the people a certain number of *sheaves*, which they freely admitted he had a good right to, because he kept a ship with armed men on board expressly for the purpose of guarding their island, and preventing any blackguard fellows from other islands coming and pillaging their fields and barns for them. But presently when the King's messenger comes, it begins to be found a matter of some difficulty to get the sheaves together for him; and by-and-by, after much consideration, it occurs to the poor people, that perhaps this difficulty may be connected in some way with their indulging themselves in such expensive luxuries as a Squire and a Parson, and from less to more, it gets to be generally the opinion about the place, that the only plan will be to turn the Squire into a clodhopper like themselves again, and send Jem away to some island where the folks can afford better to keep up the shovel-hat. This, concludes the patriarch, is the whole secret. England is this little island. The Squire is the whole body of lords and gentlemen, and Jem's shovel-hat stands for every thing from what they call the Bishop or Archbishop of Canterbury down to Parson Trulliber, my next door neighbor at the Barn-Elms, Surry.*

Jeffrey. And you think so meanly of our countrymen as to fancy that stuff like this can go down with them? What! reduce the whole population to a base level of mere animal wants and wishes? Banish all the grace of manners, the elegance of leisure, the stimulus of ambition, the humanizing influences of Religion, Morality, Science and Literature? My dear sir, this is a sort of Utopia that will never find many to covet it!

North. I hope not; but only when you write THE ARTICLE smashing it to pieces, and abusing Cobbett up hill and down dale, for inventing such a pestilent bundle of trash, and wondering that he should be able to sell even a weekly dozen of pamphlets filled with such beastlinesses, what will his answer be? You railed at me just as bitterly a few years ago for saying that there was no good came of boroughmongering, and that to call that sort of thing *property*, was an insult to common sense, and yet you have lived to get yourself turned from Archy Constable's paragraph-nibber into a learned lord, with five thousand a-year, public money, simply and entirely by coming round to my opinion, and shouting out that boroughmongering was as bad as Babylon in the Revelation, and that a man might as well pretend to property in the moon as in the tree of Sarum or the mound of Gatton.† Wait a little, good clodhoppers, this fine fellow has turned once—do you continue to show a fixed resolution to get rid both of Parson Jem and the Squire—and he'll turn again. He's a clever gemman at bottom, and can see how the wind sits as well as another.

* Where Cobbett was then residing, and whence he dated his Political Registers.—M.

† Two rotten boroughs, disfranchised by the Reform Bill of 1832.—M.

Jeffrey. Come, you'll admit that if old Cobbett sports such nonsense as you have been talking about, he is quite alone in doing so. The liberal press is all right, as to the necessity of guarding sacredly the Rights of Property.

North. Begging your Lordship's pardon—the two honestest and perhaps ablest of your own sect's newspapers are much nearer Cobbett's way of thinking than your Lordship's. The Morning Chronicle sees no property in Tithes, and is clearly of opinion that the little island would do very well without the Squire too. The Examiner openly proclaims war against both Jem and his papa—and not very covertly against a higher incumbent still. The Westminster Review is written by the same people, I perceive, and preaches the same doctrines.

Jeffrey. None of these, I am sure, ever talk of the sponge!

North. No—not yet—at least not very distinctly—but when Jem and the Squire begin to be alarmed, perhaps *they* may suggest that the sponge would answer the clodhopper's purpose quite as well as what these folk do now talk of—at all events they might be ready to lend a hand, in case they were deprived of their present situations, in making your sixty thousand pounds in the three per cents look blue, with as little ceremony as you have already exhibited in turning my ancestral parchments *in comitatu de Ross* into the sere and yellow leaf.

Jeffrey. If this sort of thing goes on, the country's done for. But at all events, you will never blame me for what I never anticipated —do not now anticipate—and if it ever should happen, would have as much reason as yourself to deplore?

North. I'm close on eighty—and shan't see probably even *your* play out, far less the afterpiece. But if my ghost should chance in those days to revisit the glimpses of the moon, I'm sure it could be with no disposition to blame any person of your Lordship's excellent natural character, and sincere, however mistaken zeal, for the service of your country and your kind. I might perhaps laugh a little at the ex-Duke of Devonshire—but really, really, I should be much concerned about your Three per Cents.

Jeffrey. Come now, North, 'tis easy for you to stand by and laugh or groan, as the mood suggests, at what's going on—but what would you do if you were in my position? What in God's name can I do?

North. I don't just see why I, that gave you so many warnings not to get into this scrape, should be called upon to help you out of it, either by tongue, or pen, or poker; but one thing I should imagine is plain enough—namely, that you should no longer neglect wholly and entirely your personal duties as chief law-officer for Scotland.

Jeffrey. What? prosecute citizens for the over free expression of honestly maintained political opinions?

North. I don't say that—but surely, if you really lament, and would fain arrest, the progress of sayings and doings directly hostile to the very principle and essence of social order, you ought not to suffer the Scotch newspapers to revel week after week in the luxury of coupling the Government you make a part of with the cause of Anarchy.

Jeffrey. What is it you're looking for?

North. O, I've got it. 'Tis only the last Dundee newspaper. Will you do me the favor to put on your spectacles and read this report of a public dinner held last week in that fine city? There—begin with the Chairman's speech on proposing the healths of his Majesty's Ministers.

Jeffrey. The Chairman? Who is he?

North. Just the same most respectable Mr. Christie, citizen and banker! that was chairman to your Lordship's committee in Bonny Dundee, at the time when you stood against Donald Ogilvie. Read, my Lord, read.

Jeffrey (reads). "THE CHAIRMAN. 'The next toast is, Earl Grey and his Majesty's Ministers.' May they never forget or undervalue the power of the millions by whom their patriotic exertions have been rendered effectual. May they never forget that the measure of reform they have accomplished, is only the first of a series of inroads which the people of Great Britain and Ireland are determined to make on institutions dictated by the spirit of feudalism, despotism, or *aristocracy.* In order to save time, and not to trench on the liberty of speech and special privileges of the gentlemen who are to follow, I shall merely hint *at certain inroads, which I have no doubt the British people are determined to make on existing institutions.* We all know that the declaration of Wellington against Reform hurled him from power. Earl Grey's administration succeeded; and being based on public opinion—being supported by the good-will of the millions—he has withstood the fiercest assaults of a desperate faction. On a late occasion, the enemy enjoyed a momentary triumph, which made them almost frantic with joy; but their joy was short-lived. (Cheers.) Although the King would have bestowed his confidence on Wellington, he found out that the people were differently minded. Yes, the majesty of the people never appeared to more advantage than on that occasion. When the King said ay, the people said no. (Cheers.) The British lion was roused and shook his mane. *The voice of the people had no equivocal meaning;* it was this—*restore Lord Grey's administration, or a Republic may be the speedy result*—(Hear! hear!)—A CONSUMMATION WHICH WE ARE DESTINED TO SEE AT NO DISTANT DATE! (Great cheering.) The very significant hint was timeously taken. Earl Grey and his colleagues were brought back to power upon the shoulders of the people, and with their support and assistance carried the Reform measure. But what is Reform? Why it is *only and simply the means to an end.* It is only an instrument put into *our hands* wherewith to work out our political salvation. I trust, by means of it, we shall operate a cure for many evils; for be it remembered, our just grounds of complaint are neither few nor small. And it is only by comparing our vicious and wasteful government with a good and a cheap one, that the enormous disparity will appear. *Does the measure of Reform give us that which we want?* I say, NO—the Union responds in the negative. (Hear, and cheers.) Compare the allowance to the chief magistrate of the United States of America, of £5000 a-year, for performing efficient services—(cheers) with the allowance given to ours of £500,000 a-year, I shall not say for what! (Hear, hear.) The divine rights of kings, the privileges of aristocracy, and other fine things, are now well understood; and, along with *his Grace of this,* and *my Lord of that,* must soon come to an end (hear, hear), as must also the law of Entail and the law of Primogeniture. They must soon cease, and these little alterations will work wonders. (Loud cheers.) It is only the Radicals who will bring about a radical remedy of all these and other grievances. (Loud cheers.) There are no such things on the other side of the Atlantic. The profitable laborers in the national vineyard, the thews and sinews of the empire, who have too long been the victims of misrule, will by-and-by triumph over the unprofitable, the useless, the unproductive laborers, the illustrious, the noble, the reverend, and right reverend, military, civil, and diplomatic tax-eaters of these kingdoms, who will soon be called to account. (Loud cheers.) I beg to propose Earl Grey, and the rest of his Majesty's Ministers."

North. A magniloquent money-changer, my Lord!

Jeffrey. This will never do!

North. Why, nothing the better, my friend, for coming from the very gentleman whom, when you wanted to sit for those boroughs, you were but too happy to have for your own chief *presidium et dulce decus.*

Jeffrey. Oh! Christie, Christie! Wherefore art thou Christie?

North. This it is, my dear Lord, that gives treble authority to what this banker, this would-be Lafitte of Dundee, thinks fit to say on such subjects, upon such an occasion; and this it is also which perplexes your Lordship's present position, ties up your mighty hand, and stands between the Guardian of Law and Order and the prompt and vigorous discharge of the most important duties of his high, responsible, and not ill-paid office!

Jeffrey. I certainly must consult with my deputies on this subject!

North. Your Deputies!—Why, you know very well that the most intelligent and active of the set was employed diligently on your Dundee canvass—lived all the while under this seditious, if not treasonable, spouter's roof—and probably got joyous with him every evening for a week on end, in the most hearty intercommunication of political sentiments.

Jeffrey. That's an old affair, now.

North. Yes; but would it not be rather awakened if the banker, being hauled before our friends Mackenzie and Meadowbank,* to answer for his insurrectionary diatribes, were to defend himself by sticking into the witness-box half a score of worthy fellow-citizens who had all partaken, in the course of that memorable canvass, of the patriotic punch-bibbery of the panel and the prosecutor?—who, not being very much accustomed to share the confidential intercourse of the powers that be, might perhaps have retained, with Boswellian accuracy, every grave saw and *modern instance* that chanced to drop, then and there, from the oracular lip of your Lordship's bailie-bamming, and, peradventure, bowsyish depute?

Jeffrey. Hang the banker!—I wonder what he wants.

North. Ay, find that out; and if he has a son at the bar, be sure you make him your next depute—and probably that will be chemistry sufficient to decompose his bile. And don't be afraid of people's saying this is truckling. You will only be walking in the steps of your betters. The two first very good things that Brougham had to dispose of, after attending to family duty, were given to Daniel Whittle Harvey,† the ablest, perhaps, and till then the most indefatigably ferocious of the hip-and-thigh heroes in the House of Commons, and a brother of Mr. Barnes of the Times. Disdain not the example of your "guide, philosopher, and friend."

Jeffrey. Oh! North, North! If you knew but the miseries of patronage, you would not rub me in this line. What with would-be deputies, and would-be sheriffs, and would-be judges, and—could you believe it?—would-be lord-advocates, the Lord have mercy upon us! I'm bothered entirely—life's a burden.

North (sings).

"Oh! what had my youth with ambition to do?
Why left I Amynta, why broke I my vow?
O give me my sheep, and my sheep-hook restore,
And I'll wander from love and Amynta no more!"

* Lord Mackenzie, a Scottish judge, was the eldest son of the author of the Man of Feeling. Lord Meadowbank, also on the Scottish bench, sat next to Sir Walter Scott, who was in the chair, at the Edinburgh Theatrical Fund Dinner, on February 23, 1827, and, in proposing Scott's health gave the first public notification of the actual and undivided authorship of the Waverley Novels. This brought out Scott who "owned the soft impeachment."—M.

† Then M. P. for the town of Colchester, and one of the most eloquent men in Parliament. For several years past, Commissioner at the head of the Police of the city of London.—M.

You regret, in short, the old easy days of Craigcrook and the Blue and Yellow!

Jeffrey. Ex profundis. O, North, I was never meant for this sort of thing. I really can't tell you whether the Edinburgh part of the job, or the London one, be the worst. *Here*, nothing but the eternal claim-claim-claiming of hungry on-hangers, old, young, and middle-aged, God knows which of the three the most horse-leechy, relieved by mad ebullitions of mobbery, which I can not, dare not, meddle with! *There*, that weary House, with its diabolical outwatchings of the bear, and that Peel, and that Croker, and that Sugden,—and that O'Connell, and that Hume, and that—

North. Sadler, for sixpence! He's blowing Macaulay to atoms, I see, in Leeds.

Jeffrey. Where the mischief did that fellow learn to speak? He's an orator, sir—a real orator—and is doing us more damage among the new constituencies than all the Radicals put together.*

North. That's your sort. Stay you a little longer, and you'll see who will be *the friends of the people!* So the Tories, for all their sins and stupidities, do contrive to give you a little trouble, both in and out of Parliament, after all?

Jeffrey. It was a sad misfortune that we had nothing for it but setting Brougham on the woolsack.

North. Why, if I remember, the Times and Chronicle both predicted, at that juncture, that the Lord Advocate of Scotland would fill Brougham's place in the Commons. But I suppose it takes some training to be a master of any sort of mountebankery?

Jeffrey. Had I gone up twenty or thirty years ago, my friend, I feel that I should have done something—but now—now—'tis out of the question. If you were to take Peel or Croker, and bid them tilt with Peter Robertson or me in the Jury-Court, they could not look more like fish out of water, than I feel myself when I glance my eye across that box-built table, and see their calm smiling visages.

North. If the Tories Ultra, and the Tories Moderate, bring their now pending negotiations to a really satisfactory conclusion, and Peel raises the banner blue next Spring at the head of a firmly compacted band, whose line has been distinctly traced beforehand, as to every important question likely to be started—if Field-Marshal Peel, I say, opens the campaign in this style, with such a second

* Michael Thomas Sadler was in business, as a merchant, in Leeds, when (the repute of his Toryism and talents having reached the Duke of Newcastle, owner of the borough) he was invited, in 1828, to oppose Mr. Sergeant Wilde, now Lord Truro, at the parliamentary election for Newark. He was returned, and spoke very ably, in 1829, against Peel's Catholic Relief Bill. In 1830 he was again elected for Newark, and in 1831 for a Yorkshire borough. He strongly opposed the Reform Bill. He suggested that Ireland should have Corn Laws and have her waste lands reclaimed and cultivated. He died in 1831, aged only forty-one. There was no politician more sincere or less of a mere partisan. His reputation will rest on his very able work, The Law of Population, directed against Malthus, whose theory he declared to be inconsistent with Christianity, and even with the purest forms of Deism.—M.

in command as Croker, such generals of division as Chandos Hardinge, Vyvyan, and Murray—such quartermasters as Inglis and Sadler, and such a provost-marshal as Sugden*—and such an army as, even the Ministerial prints now admit, we are like to take the field with—and such a confounded enemy in *your* rear as the Radicals proper will then assuredly be—it is to be confessed that you may have some call to pick your marches.

Jeffrey. Our only hope, to speak frankly, is now in your disunion. If that continues, we shall play one section of you against the other this day, and both sections against the radicality the next, and thus get through. And, thank God! such is still the general anticipation, as far as I could observe, at Brookes's.†

North. Well, we've got our Brookes's too, it seems, now—better late than never; and as to our continuing (if we are so now) *disunited*, I can only say, that if we do, we deserve to be damned, and had better make up our minds at once for Tophet and Gehenna.

Jeffrey. The Ultras don't like Peel—that's the hitch; that will be our salvation.

North. Why, the Ultras, not being idiots, can probably see, just as well as you Whigs and Radicals have already done, that there is but one man fitted by talents, acquirements, station, and temper, to lead our troops with perfect certainty of success; and that one man being, I presume, quite capable of understanding that the most ingenious of generals is little without a willing army in the day of battle—is it very unnatural to conclude that two parties, each so necessary to the other's efficiency, and each equally zealous, mind, to trample the common enemy into perdition, may, somehow or other, bring disputed specialities to a rational compromise, *inter se*, and act thereupon, until, at all events, *you* evacuate the citadel? I guess not, my good Lord Advocate; and I think, to all appearance, the only man in the Cabinet, whose brains would be much worth out of it, guesses pretty nearly as I do. Well, with £5,000 a-year to play with, to say nothing of James and William so snugly placed ‡ and the House of Lords for an occasional canter, Harry Brougham might contrive to pass a pleasant enough evening of life's troubled day.

Jeffrey. Ay, and Brougham Hall is such a charming thing. You've no notion how he's been improving. 'Tis a perfect paradise.

North. A sweet situation; and, as your favorite poet says,

"Those pleasant walks on Emont's side!"

* Croker had greatly distinguished himself by the eloquence and tact with which he opposed the details of the Reform Bill, but has not sat in Parliament since 1832. The rest named here, though able debaters, did not give Peel the great assistance here anticipated.—M.

† The Whig club in St. James's street, London, to counterbalance which, the Carlton club was established by the Tories.—M.

‡ James Brougham received a good official appointment, and William Brougham was made Master-in-Chancery, salary £4000 a year.—M.

But I'm thinking of yourself, man. 'Tis a pity that Chief Baronship's dished—it would just have suited you. Charles Hope seems as fresh as a daisy. Boyle puts out his leg yet like a fugleman!* Well, if a double gown drops between and Christmas, you had better just put your pride in your pocket.

Jeffrey. I need that hint, I suppose. Oh, North! however we may be progressing as an entire nation, there's no doubt you Tories of the old Belhaven breed have too much reason for saying that our mother Caledonia is getting her sails sadly out of the wind. I confess, I myself can't help sometimes regretting that this should be so; but 'tis probably a lingering prejudice of boyhood—perhaps I ought to say at once, a provincial hallucination.

North. Don't be ashamed of it, my dear Jeffrey; while I at least am your father confessor, dread no heavy penance on that score.

Jeffrey. We've knocked up the Excise-board, and the Customs-board, and the Court of Exchequer; and the Parliament House itself is losing every year some more of those prizes that used to attract the upper orders. I wish to God these things could have been gone about less rapidly and sweepingly; but the upshot will no doubt be good in the main.

North. Whether the upshot be mainly good, or, as I expect, entirely evil, there can be no doubt we owe these mutations purely to the doctors of the Whig *Sapientia;* and I am sometimes tempted to think that some of them may already be beginning to repent of having on certain occasions permitted themselves to forget that they were Scotchmen before they were Whigs. The tone of society in Edinburgh has been sinking damnably since you first knew it.

Jeffrey. No doubt of that. None of the nobility have houses here now. Every laird, indeed, that can stand the expense of three months in London, thinks it quite necessary to cut Auld Reekie. But how to help this? One can't say "thus far and no farther" to London.

North. But London will by-and-by say "thus far and no farther" to England. As for Scotland, good-by to that auld sang. The only things that at all counteracted the natural influence of the change of the seat of government are now disappearing *a vue d'œil,* and your children, for I have none, will see Auld Reekie rank below Manchester in all other respects—as much as she already does in the two articles of population and wealth.

Jeffrey. What do you anticipate for us?

North. A confounded Babylon of what Sir John Sinclair calls "Educating Individuals," and their respective knots of sucking economists; a capital, in short, no longer heard of, except as a sort

* In 1832, Charles Hope was Lord President of the first division of the Scottish Court of Session, and David Boyle was the Lord Justice Clerk, in the second division of that Court. In 1834, Jeffrey was promoted to the Bench.—M.

of overgrown academy; a bar, to which nobody that can afford a gentleman's education will ever dream of bringing up his son; a bench of poor fifth-rates, only fit to record the *rules* of Westminster Hall; and a new order of Lord Advocates, not unworthy to begin with Bobby Thompson, Sheriff as yet of Air, or Jemmy Ivory, now depute to your Lordship.*

Jeffrey. You must have some young Stover† about you, that crams you with outer-house tittle-tattle. I wonder you listen to such stuff, North.

North. My dear Jeffrey, I care as much about the whole concern—as you do who are to be the corporals in Don Pedro's seventh regiment of Caçadores.‡

"Suave mari magno turbantibus æquora ventis,
E terrâ magnum alterius spectare laborem;
Non quia vexari quemquam est jucunda voluptas,
Sed quibus ipse malis careas quia cernere suave est:
Suave etiam belli certamina magna tueri
Per campos instructa, tuâ sine parte pericli.
Sed nil dulcius est, bene quàm munita tenere
Edita doctrinâ Sapientum templa serenâ,
Despicere unde queas alios, passimque videre
Errare atque viam palantes quærere vitæ,
Certare ingenio, contendere nobilitate,
Noctes atque dies niti præstante labore
Ad summas emergere opes, rerumque potiri.
O miseras hominum mentes! ô pectora cæca!"

Come, my dear Advocate, another tumbler? Do!

(*The clock strikes twelve.*)

Jeffrey. Think of those poor posters—well, one small eke—but no more of the thorny places. Come, North, you promised me a song—you're in sweet voice to-night.

North (*sings.*)

Air—The Ploughboy.

When I was a mere schoolboy, ere yet I'd learned my book,
I felt an itch for angling in every little brook;
An osier rod, some thread for twine, a crooked pin for hook,
And thus equipped I wandered by many a bubbling brook,
Where prickle-backs and minnows each day I caught in store,
With stone-loaches and miller's-thumbs, such brooks afford no more.

Twas thus the tiny angler
With crooked pin for hook,
Would shun each noisy wrangler
To fish the murmuring brook.

Jeffrey. Sweet and simple—do go on, my dear North, you awaken a thousand long-forgotten dreams of innocence.

* Robert Thompson is now Sheriff-Depute of Caithness, and "Jemmy Ivory" is on the Scottish Bench, as Lord Ivory.—M.

† The idle and briefless lawyers who used to lounge around the stove, which warmed the outer hall of the Law-Court in Edinburgh, were called *stovers.*—M.

‡ Don Pedro, ex-Emperor of the Brazils, and father of Queen Donna Maria of Portugal.—M.

North (*sings.*)

Then next I bought some farthing hooks, and eke a horse-hair line,
An hazel rod, with whalebone top, my playmates to outshine,
With which I soon aspired to angle with a float,
And when I could not fish from shore, I tossed it from a boat;
Thus roach, and dace, and bleak I took, and gudgeons without end,
And now and then a perch would hook, which caused my rod to bend:

Come, join in chorus.

And thus the little angler,
Pleased with his line and hook,
Would shun each noisy wrangler
To fish the murmuring brook.

Very well, dear Advocate, you've a pretty treble.

Bream, chub, and barbel, next I sought, their various haunts I plied
With scowered worms, and cheese, and paste, and twenty baits beside;
With hooks of *Kirby-bent* well chose, and gut so round and fine;
By slow gradations thus I rose, to fish with running line:
A multiplying *Winch* I bought, wherewith my skill to try
And so expert myself I thought, few with me now could vie.

CHORUS.—Thus still the little angler,
With rod, and line, and hook,
Would shun each noisy wrangler
To fish the murmuring brook.

My mind on trolling now intent, with live and dead snap-hook,
I seldom to the rivers went, but pike or jack I took;
Near banks of bullrush, sedge, and reed, (a dark and windy day,)
And if the fish were on the feed, I rarely missed my prey.
If baits be fresh and proper size, no matter what's the sort,
At gudgeon, roach, or dace, they rise, with each by turns we've sport

So now a dexterous angler,
With rod, and line, and hook,
I shunned each noisy wrangler,
To fish the murmuring brook.

Is that enough, now?—well, well—

And now to cast a fly-line well, became my earnest wish,
I strove each sportsman to excel, and cheat the nimble fish.
Now, trout and grayling I could kill, if gloomy was the day;
The salmon, too, against his will, beside my basket lay.
Now, fly and palmer could I dress, aquatic insects too;
Their various seasons I could guess—their uses well I knew.

Yet still, a master angler,
With rod, and line, and hook,
I shunned each noisy wrangler,
To fish the murmuring brook.

Now, the finale!

So, now to close the charming scene, which none but sportsmen feel,
Be sure you keep the golden mean, nor arm your heart with steel;
The fish with moderation take, and to the fair be kind,
And ne'er with them your promise break, but virtue keep in mind.
So, wives and sweethearts now let's drink, let each man fill his glass;
And may we never speak or think, to disconcert our lass!

Then when our lines are all worn out,
And feeble bends the hook,
They'll ne'er forget the angler
That angled in the brook.

Jeffrey (*sings.*)

"They'll ne'er forget the angler
That angled in the brook!"—

Perfect! I wonder if my hand has quite forgot its cunning. Jove! how I should like to stroll somewhere about the Highlands with you for a week, having vowed with oaths sublime, North, ere starting, never to talk politics, and no books with us but a Don Juan in your pocket, and Wordsworth's Ballads in mine.

North. How charming!—I'm afraid you won't go with me just my first excursus, though, for you must know I've made everything right and tight in the way of business, and proceed to-morrow morning for the best of all fishing districts, to my fancy, in Braid Scotland—but our lines would be apt to get entangled just at present in that quarter.

Jeffrey. To-morrow morning?—Why, 'tis now near one, I swear!

North. Ay, ay—but no day dawns on me before I've had a round o' the clock, I can tell you.—(*Sings.*)

And I'm off with the morn
At thy call, Donald Horne,
To give NOVAR a lift 'gainst that dangerous man:
Dear in private to North
Is the courteous SEAFORTH,
But in public we'll powder his wig if we can!

Jeffrey. Come, come, no Ross-shire politics! Well, I must leave you at last—you'll split your Auld Reekie vote, now, this time? Come do, that's a brave old buck! Show an example of liberality for once to your disciples.

North. The Lord *Ordinary* takes that *ad avisandum.* Good night, my dear Lord Advocate—good night. *Au revoir*—vale! (*Exit* JEFFREY.) Why, the evening has slipped away like a knotless thread—(*Rings—Enter* MACKAY.) John, carry Ben the cold sheep's head—and, hear'st me, bid Bauby scollop some oysters—and, I'm saying, let Mr. Mullion know the coast's clear—and be sure you have the plotty ready. (*Exit* JOHN.) Poor Mordecai has been cheated o' his liquor. The laddie will be starved.—(*Sings.*)

After which I make sail,
For the regions of Traill,
If again, as a Whig, he for Orkney contend;
Though I love him of old,
It shall never be told,
I deserted a Tory to pleasure a friend.

Enter MULLION.

Mullion. Monsieur, est servi! (*Exeunt.*)

No. LXIV.—NOVEMBER, 1832.

Library in the Lodge—Time, Seven o'clock—Present NORTH *and* TICKLER.

North. No—I have not left the Lodge for ten miles, or two hours, during the whole summer.

Tickler. Domestic Devil!

North. Say rather, bird in a cage, that keeps perpetually hopping about, up and down, from turf to twig, now and then with loving bill nibbling the wires of its beloved imprisonment, occasionally picking a little seed, and not seldom on the spur of the moment drawing up its tiny bucket, and sipping a drop of the mountain dew, to clear its song and brighten its plumage.

Tickler. Liker a cock on his own——

North. Hush! or Bird of Paradise, who——

Tickler. Whew! or Bubbly-Jock erecting his tail in proud persuasion of his being a Peacock; or——

North. Woodlark, Scotia's Nightingale, who, unfatigued by day-songs poured around the grassy nest, where sits his mate assiduous o'er callow brood or chirping shells, prolongs his ditties far into the night, and by the homeward shepherd on the hill is heard, not seen, sweet-singing midst the stars.

Tickler. Blanks! by all that is musical! But "say, sweet warbling woodlark, say," what mysterious meaning lies enveloped in the image of "mate assiduous" sitting on eggs? I devoutly trust Mrs. Gentle is not in the fam——

North (*rising up in great indignation*). Sir, the honor of that lady is dearer to me than a million lives, nor shall the villain who dares to insinuate the remotest hint——

Tickler. Be not so furious, my dear sir; I insinuated no remote hint——

North. She has been in Switzerland, sir, for more than nine months—

Tickler. Not another word, North. Your explanation is perfectly satisfactory; but why did you not accompany her and her lovely daughter to Lake Constance?

North. For fear of a censorious world, that will not suffer old age to escape its slanders, with one foot in the grave.

Tickler. She is indeed a sad gossip, old Madam Public; yet there are some good points about her; and let me whisper in your ear, North, you are a prodigious favorite with the Frow—in her eyes a perfect Dutchman.

North. Her affection for me, Tickler, is, I assure you, of the most spiritual sort.

Tickler. And yours for her, as becomes a philosopher, Platonic. Yet human nature is weak; and be advised by me, North, to trust yourself alone with her as seldom as possible; for what, were you some day to declare with the Public a private marriage.

North. The *reading* Public! I well remember the days when she could spell with difficulty a simple dissyllable—when she lost herself in a complicated Polly, like a benighted nymph wandering through a wood.

Tickler. A complicated Polly! What is that?

North. Nebuchadnezzar.

Tickler. Chrononhotonthologos.

North. Methinks I see her, Tickler, in her Little Primer!

Tickler. Conning her "Reading made easy."

North. Leaning her rosy cheek on a rosier arm with elbow rosier still——

Tickler. Peony of Peonies!

North. Now, alas! like a yellow lily that seems, in lieu of dew, to be fed with lamp-oil!

Tickler. And she has become the *writing* Public too?

North. That is the melancholy part of the concern, Tickler. She is now—to her shame and sorrow—a confirmed scribble.

Tickler. And appears, without a blush on her brazen face, in print.

North. Yes—with my own eyes have I seen her absolutely in capitals.

Tickler. Worse than in kilts.

North. Kilts! Kilts are but petticoats of a smaller size; but it goes well nigh to the breaking of my heart to see the reading, writing, ranting Public (an old woman too) in wire-wove hot-pressed paper printed breeches—*in shorts*, Tickler.

Tickler. Nay, *in tights*, which show her shapes to the worst advantage; for, as you observed, she is well stricken in years, and time tells on the figure even of a Diana.

North. Let's be serious. 'Twould seem as if reading and writing were the chief occupation now, in this once happy island, of human life. The constant cry or croak is—Education, Education. The People will sink under this eternal tuition—the next race will be a generation of Idiots. The invention of printing is a blessing which, by "busy Meddling Intellect," has been abused into a curse.

Tickler. Among the lower orders reading has grown into a dull disease, that dries up the sap, and slackens the sinews of life.

North. Ay, Tickler—the poor man's fireside was, I verily believe, in general, far happier in former times than now—with himself resting, after his day's darg, in an elbow-chair—if the house happened to hold one—his wife *fistling* about in eager preparation of supper—and the brats on stools forming perhaps an octagon, each with a horn spoon in its hand expectant of the coming crowdy——

Tickler. A pleasant picture. No boy or girl, from four to fourteen years of age, knows the extent of his or her mouth's capaciousness, till it gradually opens to its utmost width, in order to admit with unruffled surface, a huge horn spoonful——

North. Of crowdy. True. Now, crowdy is crowdy still, though with more difficulty procured than in the days I speak of; and poor people are still happy in supping it, for sacred hunger is the solace of life.

Tickler. Ay—the Pigot Diamond would be a poor price for a good appetite from a palate-palsied king to a *yawp* beggar.

North. But, now-a-days, reading it placed on the list of necessaries before eating.

Tickler. A greasy——

North. Say creeshy.

Tickler. A creeshy periodical, price a penny, takes precedence of a black pudding of strong bull's blood and the generous suet—

North. The age of Haggis is gone! And Journeymen Tailors having discovered that "Knowledge is Power," starve on half-commons of this earth's cabbage, that they may feed on celestial custocks from a circulating library.

Tickler. Yes, North, Knowledge *is* Power. He who knows to cut out, and stitch, and sew, and with unbaffled art, in defiance of nature's spite, to make a fit of it even on my amiable and most ingenious friend Sheridan Knowles's Hunchback—he—tailor though he be—is a MAN of Power, and is entitled to a Jubilee to unfold, emblazoned with that illustrious motto, the Standard of the Snips, to all the winds of of heaven.

North. It is *leze majestie* now to speak of the "*lower* orders." But that is their right name, and they hold it from heaven. The "*laboring* classes" is a foolish form of speech. All that live labor.

Tickler. The Mite—the Mouse—and the Monarch.

North. The very Drone labors—in his own vocation—for soon as the Queen Bee is impregnated in the sunny air—all her stingless paramours are put to death.

Tickler. The Bee is a most inexplicable creature.

North. Who labors harder than I?

Tickler. I.

North. You—you Dragon-Fly?

Tickler. Yes—I—you Midge.

North. Whereas "lower" expresses the everlasting position of the classes to which it is in all honor applied; and he who pales or reddens at the epithet is a radical and a slave.

Tickler. Bravo!

North. And to them what knowledge is power? Of themselves and their duties, and where shall they find it?

Tickler. Why, in our farthing—and if our more ambitious modern circulating medium did not disdain that coin diminutive—in our *doit* political literature, that through lanes and alleys flutters its ephemeral life away on wings of whitey-brown.

North. Such are the means which sage philosophy doth now employ for the regeneration of fallen man! The *lower* classes—I love the word—for it carries with it a calm humble meaning that speaks of Christian contentment—may still read the Bible if they will—Heaven forbid that the philosophers should prevent or dissuade them from so doing as often as they choose!—for the philosophers are occasionally of opinion that the Bible should be included in the School of Useful and Entertaining Knowledge.

Tickler. Are they?

North. But the Bible, according to their creed, is not in itself an all-in-all. The poor creature that reads but it, or even it chiefly, must be miserably ignorant—and all unfit to walk with any thing like the dignity of a Reformer in a processional Jubilee.

Tickler. Nor must he ever hope to rise into a Ten-Pounder.*

North. And millions on millions never can—nor could though all the rags of all the beggars in Ireland were manufactured into paper, and when printed, strewed over the entire earth as thick as leaves in Vallambrosa.

Tickler. The forced—pumped waters will subside.

North. And leave the soul unenriched by any deposit.

Tickler. But not unencumbered with sand, gravel, and stones.

North. Which, however, will in good time be cleared away; and flowers and herbage, under a better system of culture, will be reinduced over the land.

Tickler. The people of Scotland—I leave you to speak of the English—are not more intelligent, and they certainly are less moral and religious, than they were even a quarter of a century ago.

North. I would fain hope that education with us is in much improved, though I fear in not a little deteriorated; but the people

* The Reform-Bill of 1832 gave the elective franchise to householders paying ten pounds a year in rent, provided they had also paid their government taxes. - M.

themselves, except in our large towns, or our small manufacturing ones, are still deeply impressed with a belief of the paramount importance of moral and religious instruction over every other kind; and while this is the case, let every other kind be encouraged in due subordination to that, without which no man's soul is safe, and the heart within him, overcome by this world's troubles, pines and dies.

Tickler. The object of almost all the paltry preaching about the education of the "laboring" classes is avowedly political; and despicable as in itself it is, most of the instruction diffused is at this crisis perilous; for wiser and better men than were ever found among the Apostles of Infidelity——

North. Now,

> "See the deep fermenting tempest brew'd
> In the grim evening sky."

Tickler. Knowledge! Oh, dear! Listen for two minutes to a political pauper, who at the Chequers runs up a score for the sponge, the best-informed and the most acute of the coterie, that chuckles as he crows, and, in what nook of Cimmeria gabbles a naked wretch, that lives in an earth-hole, and in Nature's destitution, almost "wants discourse of reason," such a hideous hubbub of disordered savageness, which, as it foams or slavers from the lips of the truculent drunkard, is deemed "knowledge" by his long-eared audience, whose shallow brains are obfuscated by the fumes of ignorance and gin!

North. And there are thousands of such bestial. But more lamentable far than such brutalities, are to me the miserable mistakings of minds by no means depraved, on subjects that lie far beyond their comprehension, and with which, were they allowed to obey the dictates of their own reason and their own conscience, they would know and feel they had nothing to do—nothing but to follow the guidance and perform the mandates of those whose business it is to understand, to direct, to rule, and to govern—their own duty being not to scrutinize but to serve, not to expound but to obey.

Tickler. Truth and Toryism.

North. Yes—doctrine, which, when wisely acted on by rulers and by subjects, has saved those from becoming tyrants and these from being slaves.

Tickler. And the "miserable mistakings" you speak of are part and parcel of that "knowledge which is power!"

North. They talk of a state of transition. From what to what? From helotism to freedom? I ask you, Timothy, were the companions of our boyhood, among the rural villages and farms, the children of Helots? No—bold-faced boys and meek-eyed girls were they—with whom—

Tickler. Especially the girls—

North. You and I loved

"Round stacks at the gloaming at bogles to play!"

Tickler. Sweet creatures—many of them—even

"The lass with the gowden hair."

North. Would you or I, and we were no windlestraes then, Tim, but two young oaks, have dared to insult, had the devil entered us, the sister before her brother's face——

Tickler. Thank Heaven, no such devil ever entered into either of us—no, no, Kit, fair play's a jewel, and honor bright was the pole-star of our youthful days.

North. It was. But would not the callant whose home was a hovel, and his Saturday's and Sunday's breeches one and the same, have smashed his fist in the nose of any Aristocrat (Heaven bless the mark!) who dared to dishonor the pretty flower that grew beside his father's humble door? Had he not pride in his sister's innocence, and is such pride the virtue of a helot, is such innocence a jewel worn on the forehead of a slave?

Tickler. Your loquacity borders on eloquence. Fire away.

North. Did we find ignorance in "the huts where poor men lay?" No—the "auld clay biggins," dim as they were with peatreek, were illuminated with knowledge—

Tickler. Illuminated! somewhat too fine a word—but I must not be too critical on the extemporaneous orator of the human race. Fire away, Kit.

North. You and I have stood at the ELDER'S DEATHBED.*

Tickler. We have—some threescore years ago—and yet there were a hundred good as he in the same wild moorland parish.

North. We could remind one another of many a high history of humble worth, were we to stroll for an hour or two over that kirkyard!

Tickler. Ay—that we could, Kit. Let us go next summer, and meditate among the tombs.

North. That parish was, as it were, an epitome—

Tickler. No—not an epitome, a fair specimen—

North. Of Scottish rural life. And is there at this hour a single parish in braid Scotland, more virtuous than was the beautiful wilderness in which thou and I, Tim, learned poetry and religion, to understand and to venerate the liberty of Nature, as it breathed and broke forth from the peasant's heart?

Tickler. Not one. Its own dear self, I fear, is not what it was in that refulgent time—

* The name of a story in Wilson's Lights and Shadows of Scottish Life.—M.

North. Refulgent! Somewhat too strong a word, Timothy; but I must not be too critical—

Tickler. Yes—refulgent. And it is by far too weak a word.

North. God bless you—it is. Many of its black bright mosses are drained now, they say; and I cannot well deny that no rational objection can be made to the change of heather-moor into clover-meadow; thorn-hedges, in pretty circles, and squares, and oblongs, are green and bright now, I am told, where of old not so such as a crumbling gray stone wall enclosed the naked common; nor in spite of the natural tears shed from the poor widow's eyes, can I for more than a minute at a time seriously lament that deep-uddered kine should now lazily low and browse where ragged sheep did once perseveringly bleat and nibble;—single trees, that seem to have dropped from the sky, so quick their growth, now here and there hang their shadows, I have heard, over the band of reapers at their mid-day meal, where, when our "auld cloak was new," one single sickle sufficed for the sma' barley-rig, and the "solitary *lowland* lass" had to look for shelter from the sunshine beneath some rock in the desert; and to that change, too, can I conform the feelings of my somewhat saddened heart;—nay, groves and woods, the story goes, have girdled the stony hills where we two used to admire, all brightening by itself, the glorious Rowan-Tree, independent of the sun in its own native lustre; and may never the swinging axe be heard in that sylvan silence, for I confess the superior beauty, too, of the vesture that now decks the sides of those pastoral pyramids;—the shielings that we used to come upon, like bird's nests, far up near the heads of the glens where the curlew bred among the rushes, have "been a' red awa';" nor is their place, if sought for, to be found in the solitude; and farmhouses, slated too I hear—for thatch, wae's me! is fast falling out of fashion—now stand where no smoke was then seen but the morning mist; and God forbid I should grieve that such like spots as these should have their permanent human dwellings;—mansions, in which rich men live, from upland swells overlook the low country far as the dim-seen spires of towns and cities that divide without diminishing the extent of the Great Plain through which rivers roll; and of a surety pleasant 'tis to think of honest industry finding its reward in well-used wealth, that builds up the stately structure on the site of the cottage where its possessor was born in poverty;—gone, I know, is the old House of God, walls, roof, spire, and all—spire not so tall as its contemporary Pine-Tree—and the heritors have done well in erecting in its stead another larger kirk—with a tower—since they preferred a tower to a spire—nor could they be wrong in widening the burial-ground, that had become crowded with graves—though methinks they might have preserved, for sake of the memorials sunk far within it, some sacred stones of the south wall;—oh, friend of my soul! though all these changes seem to have been from good to better, and some of them such as in the course of time must almost of themselves have taken place, men only letting the laws of Nature have "their own sweet will," yet such is the profound affection I bear to the past, and such the tenderness with which my heart regards all that appertained to the scenes where it first enjoyed all its best emotions, that I could almost weep to think that my beloved parish is not now, even to the knoll of broom and the rill of hazels, in all the selfsame place which it was of old, when we walked in it up and down, through all seasons of the year to us equally delightful, as perfectly happy as spirits in Paradise!

Tickler. North, your picturesque is always pathetic; but now for the practical application.

North. I hate practical applications, except in cases of tetanus, a cataplasm to the soles of the feet, of—

Tickler. Mustard and so forth.

North. The virtues which we loved and admired during those happy days, were rooted ineradicably in the characters which sometimes they somewhat severely graced, by the power of causes which had not any alliance, however remote, with those which are now thought, by too many persons, to be of such wondrous efficacy in the formation of right principles and feelings, which, by-the-by, always grow together, and maintain through life their due proportion. Some of the means which are now so pompously set at apparent work to enlighten the minds of the people, and to emollify their manners (*mores*), were then never dreamt of, even by the most visionary; and yet their minds were as full of light, and their manners were as full of rurality, or sylvanity, or urbanity, as they will be found to be now with the dwellers in grassy fields, leafy woods, or stony towns.

Tickler. And much more so.

North. Then it will be found in the long run, that the attempt to elevate the character of a people by cheap publications, is very expensive.

Tickler. Very.

North. A penny a-week is not, for a poor and industrious man, much to pay to a friendly society; for his condition is always, from within and from without, exceedingly precarious; and 'tis well to guard, at such sacrifices, sometimes no inconsiderable one, against the day in which no man can work.

Tickler. Good.

North. A penny paper fills the empty stomach with wind—or lies in it, in the shape of a ball; and 'tis hard to say which is the worser, flatulence or indigestion.

Tickler. Sometimes, no doubt, the small swallow is harmless, and sometimes even salutary; but, at the best, it cannot give much strength; and, at the end of a year, the money would have been far better bestowed in purchasing some pecks of meal, or half a boll of potatoes.

North. Or, ere the winter sets in, linsey-woolsey petticoats for the ditchers' daughters.

Tickler. I doubt if any man, earning wages by ordinary handwork, ever continued such subscription through a twelvemonth.

North. Never. They almost all give in within the quarter; for they either get angry with themselves, on finding that they are not one whit the wiser from studying the Tatterdemalion—or, growing conceited, they aspire to write for it—and a rejected contributor will not condescend to be an accepted subscriber.

Tickler. The word "cheap" is never out of some poor creatures' mouths—cheap bread, cheap law, cheap government, cheap religion.

North. Ay, above all things else, they must have cheap religion. They grudge a fair price for heaven.

Tickler. Charity, too, must be cheap. Give such *relief* to the poor as will just hold soul and body together—and when they part company, let the dissection of the pauper's carcass pay for its burial.

North. "Why go to any unnecessary expense" on the birth, baptism, death, or funeral of any lump of clay? The most illustrious man-howdie would be munificently rewarded by a guinea, for ushering into existence any man-child that it is possible to conceive; and, for a mere lassie, there ought assuredly to be a drawback. There is something absolutely shocking in the idea of fees to the gentleman in black for making a baby a Christian. If any one thing on this earth ought to be cheap, it should be the marriage ceremony, for marriage itself, in the long run, is apt to prove a most expensive business; and, as interment consists mainly in digging a hole and filling it up again, that surely may be done for a mere nothing, in a country that has been so long overflowed by a ceaseless influx of Irishmen, the best diggers that ever handled spade or shovel. A plain coffin may be made of four rough deals, with a few second-hand nails to hold them together till the box reaches the bottom, and none but a madman would dream of studding it with extravagant brass knobs, bedecking it with a profuse plate of the same metal, and that again with a ruinous inscription, which no eye may read in the dark, so soon to be bedimmed with dark mould and the slime of worms. As for a hearse and six horses, large enough to contain, and strong enough to draw, ten tons of coals, or twenty butts of porter, caparisoned with plumage—and few things are dearer for their weight than feathers—all to convey an emaciated corpse that probably does not ride six stone, though the man might have once walked twenty—why, the custom is at once so preposterous, and so expensive, that the philosopher is at a loss to know whether he ought to laugh at the folly, or to weep at the waste—for his maxim on such matters is, "if it be done at all, let it be done cheaply."

(*Enter* PETER *with rizzars and cigars—he wheels his venerable Master's easy-chair to the accustomed nook, and then places* SOUTHSIDE *so as to face the good old man—sets before each worthy his own little circular table, with its own Argand lamp—rakes and stirs the fire into a roaring glow—and stumps out, noiselessly closing behind him the double door, that looks like one of the numerous oak panels of the wall.*)

North. Affectionate and faithful creature!

Tickler. Ha! what worthies have we got here over the chimney piece?

North (*smiling*). Who do you think?

Tickler (*with a peculiar face*). Wordsworth, with Jeffrey on the one side, and Brougham on the other!

North. How placid and profound the expression of the whole bard! The face is Miltonic—even to the very eyes; for though, thank Heaven, they are not blind, there is a dimness about the orbs. The temples I remember shaded with thin hair of an indescribable color, that in the sunlight seemed a kind of mild auburn—but now they are bare—and—nothing to break it—the height is majestic. No furrows—no wrinkles on that contemplative forehead—the sky is without a cloud—

> "The image of a poet's soul,
> How calm! how tranquil! how serene!"

It faintly smiles. There is light and motion round the lips, as if they were about to discourse "most eloquent music." In my imagination, that mouth is never mute—I hear it—

> "Murmuring by the living brooks,
> A music sweeter than their own."

Tickler. Is he wont so to sit with folded arms?

North. 'Twas not his habit of old, but it may be now—there seems to my mind much dignity in that repose. He is privileged to sit with folded arms, for all his life long those hands have ministered religiously at the shrine of nature and nature's God, and the Priest, as age advances, may take his rest in the sanctuary, a voiceless worshipper. There is goodness in the great man's aspect—and while I look love blends with reverence. How bland! The features in themselves are almost stern—but most the humane spirit of the grand assemblage—

> "Not harsh, nor grating, but of amplest power
> To soften and subdue!"

Tickler. Jeffrey has a fine face. Mere animation is common; but those large dark eyes beam with intellect and sensibility—*naturally* finest both—alive perpetually and at work—yet never weary as if that work were play—and needed not the restoration of sleep. Wit, in its full acceptation, is a weighty word—and by it I designate the mind of the Man! Taste in him is exalted into Imagination—Ingenuity brightens into Genius. He hath also Wisdom. But *nemo omnibus horis sapit;* and he made an unfortunate stumble over the Lyrical Ballads. He has had the magnanimity, however, I am told, to repent that great mistake, which to his fame was a misfortune—and, knowing the error of his ways, has returned to the broad path of Nature and Truth. How nobly has he written of Crabbe and Campbell, and Scott and Byron! Incomprehensible contradiction—the worst critic of the age is also the best—but the weeds of his mind are dead—the flowers are immortal. He is no orator, they say, in St. Stephen's; but that mouth, even on the silent paper, gives them the lie; and I have heard him a hundred times the most eloquent of speakers.* His is a brilliant name in the literature of Scotland.

North. It is—Francis Jeffrey.

Tickler. Brougham in his robes! Lord High Chancellor of England! Stern face, and stalwart frame—and his mind, people say, is gigantic. They name him with Bacon. Be it so; the minister he and interpreter of Nature! Henry Brougham, in the eyes of his idolators, is also an Edmund Burke. Be it so; at once the most imaginative and most philosophical of orators that ever sounded lament over the decline and fall of empires, while wisdom, listening to his lips, exclaimed,

> "Was ne'er prophetic sound so full of wo!"

North. Come—come, Tickler—none of your invidious eulogies on the Man of the People.

Tickler. There he sits—a strong man—not about to run a race——

North. But who has run it, and distanced all competitors. There is something great, Tickler, in unconquerable and victorious energy——

Tickler. A man of many talents he—some of them seeming almost to be of the highest order. Swordlike acuteness—sunlike perspicacity——

* He failed as a Parliamentary speaker.—M.

North. And sledge-hammer-like power.

Tickler. There is a wicked trouble in his keen gray eyes——

North. No. Restless, but not unhappy.

Tickler. Scorn has settled on that wide-nostrilled probo——

North. No. It comes and goes—the nose is benevolent.

Tickler. Do you say there is no brass on that hard forehead?

North. I see but bone—and though the brain within is of intellect "all compact," the heart that feeds it burns with passions not unheroic.

Tickler. King of them all—ambition.

North. "The last infirmity of noble minds."

Tickler. No—you misunderstand—you misrepresent Milton. He spoke of the love of fame.

North. So do I. In Brougham—do him justice—the two passions are one—and under its perpetual inspiration he has

"Scorned delights, and lived laborious days,"

till with all his sins, by friend and foe, he is held to be, in his character of Statesman, the first man in England.

Tickler. Are you fuddled?

North. Not to my knowledge; yet that champagne does effervesce in an old man's brain——

Tickler. And makes him utter confounded nonsense.

North. No—no—no—my dear friend, I am in sober sadness—and therefore I do not fear to ask you to look on—yonder picture.

Tickler. Where?

North. There!

Tickler. Ay—ay—ay—I can not look on it—without a throb within my heart—a mist before my eyes—Sir Walter to the very life!

North. Allan's.

Tickler. Most admirable.

North. The Minstrel—the Magician—the Man.

Tickler. At times I cannot believe that he is dead.

North. Nor I. He once showed me the place where he hoped his bones would lie.

Tickler. And do they?

North. They do.* The people of Scotland could not have endured to lose them—no—not if he had died in the most distant land; nor would his bones have rested in any sepulchre, though consecrated by a nation's tears, out of that dear region of the earth which his genius has glorified for ever.

Tickler. All's well.

North. How affectingly our friend Allan has strewn the silver

* In Dryburgh Abbey, near his own Abbotsford, where he died on the 21st September, 1832.—M.

hair along his magnificent forehead! The face is somewhat aged —and it had begun to look so a few years ago—before that, so healthful that it promised to filial eyes a long, long life. But there is a young expression of gladness in the eyes—unbedimm'd as yet by any mortal trouble—the light of genius there being all one with that of gracious humanity—two words which, I feel, contain his character.

Tickler. Surrounded with relics of the olden time!

North. Ay—as he looked on them how his imagination kindled! At the sight of that Scottish spear, Flodden was before him—or Bannockburn.

Tickler. These deer-hounds have missed their master. Come—North. The picture is beautifully painted—no man who looks at it needs be sorrowful.

North. All Scotland is sorrowful.

Tickler. No—her hills and valleys are rejoicing in the sunshine. Scotland is not sorrowful—though she has interred her greatest son. He will live for ever in the nation's heart.

North. You remember Milton's lines on Shakspere—

"What needs my Shakspere for his honor'd bones,
The labor of an age in piled stones;
Or that his hallowed relics should be hid
Under a star-y-pointing pyramid?
Dear Son of Memory! Great Heir of fame!
What needst thou such weak witness of thy fame!
Thou, in our wonder and astonishment,
Hast built thyself a living monument."

That high feeling was natural in such a soul as Milton's; but it would pass away, and the Poet of Paradise would have reverently regarded in his mind's eye a star-y-pointing-Pyramid over the Swan of Avon. A national monument is a depository of many thoughts—the gathered tribute of millions raises it—yet every man sees in it his individual feelings—and therefore the work is blest. "It is an expression of gratitude—an act of reverence."

Tickler. The nation will do what is right.

North. Homer represents Greece—Virgil, Italy—Cervantes, Spain—Voltaire, France—Goethe, Germany—Shakspere, England —and Scotland, he in whom we exult—he whom we deplore. I hope you admire the arrangement of my Martins?

Tickler. Eh?

North. The noblest of all his works is Belshazzar's Feast.

Tickler. They are all noble. I do admire the arrangement of your Martins; for so should the prodigious shadowing of Sin, Wrath, Judgment, and Doom, be all gathered together in their own region that expands and extends far, wide, and high into the pomp and grandeur—

North. Don't mouth so. Martin is the KING OF THE VAST.

Tickler. Nineveh—Babylon—in our ears heretofore but names—now before our eyes cities—

North. With all their temples renovated from the dust—unshorn their towery diadems—

Tickler. Or settling down in the "gloom of the earthquake and eclipse."

North. This great painter is said to repeat himself—and I am glad of it; so does the rising and the setting sun.

Tickler. Have you seen his Illustrations of the Bible?

North. They are lying on that table. Martin has shown in them that he has the finest feelings of beauty both in nature and in human life. "The fairest of her daughters, Eve," stands before us in the only painted Paradise that ever reminded me of Eden.

Tickler. What! You have been there?

North. In sleep.

Tickler. I would rather be in the Highlands. Have you Colonel Murray's Outlines?

North. No. What Colonel Murray?

Tickler. Son of Sir Peter—nephew of Sir George.

North. What's their style of character?

Tickler. Why, that outline style of drawing and engraving, the adaptation of which to the faithful delineation of scenery of a bold and picturesque character, was so well exemplified a few years since by Mr. Robson.*

North. One of the best landscape-painters of the age.

Tickler. The Colonel is an admirable artist. He has given us Loch Maree, the Scuir of Egg, Loch Alsh, with Castle Donnan, Kilchurn Castle, and Loch Awe—

North. "Child of loud-throated War!
Now silent!"

Tickler. Ben Venue and the Trosacs, Basaltic Scenery near Ra-na-haddon, Skye, the Red Head, Angus, Dunottar Castle, Coir-Urchran on the Tay, Killiekrankie, and Shehallion—

North. You pronounce those glorious names like a true Gael, like a Son of the Mist.

Tickler. It is published in numbers—and deserves encouragement from all Scotland. The history and literature of the country are

* George Fenney Robson, a fine draughtsman and eminent painter in water-colors, devoted the profits of his first publication (a view of his native city of Durham) to a pedestrian journey over the most romantic scenery of Scotland. With Scott's Lady of the Lake in his wallet, he wandered over the mountains in summer and winter, sketching wherever a fine view caught his attention. His "Outlines of the Grampian Hills" were the fruits of these studies, as well as his "Landscape Illustrations of the Waverley Novels." He died in 1833.—M.

identified with the scenes represented, not by casual or incidental allusions, but by a mode of illustration calculated to give a deeper and more lasting interest to the subjects and places. Each leaf of the descriptive letter-press being made applicable to the sketch which accompanies it—each subject is thus kept distinct—every number is complete in itself, and any person may select, at wonderfully small expense, faithful likenesses and illustrations of those places which are endeared to him by early recollections, or from the impressions they have produced on his mind in riper years. At present the work will be confined, I perceive, to all the remarkable places in Scotland *north of Edinburgh*. That division of it will be comprised in Twenty Numbers, but *two shillings* each—forming one volume, accompanied by copious references, indices, and a map, and will form the Illustrated Record of the North of Scotland.

North. A MAGNUM OPUS, *quod felix faustumque sit*. The Murrays are a noble family. And yonder lie eight Numbers of a work, in different style indeed, but illustrative of many of the same scenes,—"Select Views of the Lakes of Scotland from Original Paintings, by John Fleming, engraved by Joseph Swan, with Historical and Descriptive Illustrations, by John Leighton." It is published at Glasgow, a city of late years becoming as distinguished for genius and talent in the fine arts, as it has long been for integrity and enterprise in the pursuits of commerce.

Tickler. I know it—I have it; and the two works together bring the lakes and seas of Scotland, its woods, glens, and mountains, more vividly before my eyes, than any other works of art that I now remember.

North. I have often admired Fleming's water-color landscapes in our annual exhibition here; and Mr. Swan has by his burin done them ample justice. None of our southern neighbors should visit the Highlands without being possessed of both works.

Tickler. Pray, what are the two green-board vols. perched pertly near your lug on the surbas?

North. "Wild Sports of the West." They contain many picturesque descriptions of the wildest scenery in Connaught, many amusing and interesting tales and legends, much good painting of Irish character, and the author is a true sportsman.*

Tickler. That branch of our literature is in full leaf.

North. It flourishes. Lloyd, Hawker, and Mundy, are accomplished gentlemen—and as for Nimrod, he is "*The* Great Historian of the Field." But I shall have an article on the vols. at my lug, probably in our next number†—so I need not—

* William Henry Maxwell, once an officer in the British army and then a beneficed clergyman in Ireland. His Stories of Waterloo, and other works of fiction, as well as his Life of Wellington, have been very popular.—M.

† No such article appeared. Lloyd's Northern Sports, Colonel Hawker's work on Wild-duck

Tickler. Toss them over to me, and I shall put them into my pocket.

North. Not so fast. I never lend books now—for, like Scotchmen who cross the Tweed, they never return home again.

Tickler. And these others?

North. Two truly delightful volumes—Characteristics of Women, Moral, Poetical, and Historical, with fifty Vignette Etchings, by Mrs. Jameson. Shakspere's Women!

Tickler. It used to be said by the critics of a former age, that he could not draw female characters.

North. The critics of a former age were a pack of fools.

Tickler. So are too many of the present.

North. And will be of the future. All the ancient dramatists drew female characters well—especially Massinger. But Shakspere has beautified the sex—

Tickler. "Given perfume to the violets."

North. Mrs. Jameson arranges all Shakspere's women into classes:—Characters of intellect—Portia, Isabella, Beatrice, Rosalind; characters of passion and imagination—Juliet, Helena, Perdita, Viola, Ophelia, Miranda; characters of the affections—Hermione, Desdemona, Imogen, Cordelia; historical characters—Cleopatra, Octavia, Volumnia, Constance of Bretagne, Elinor of Guienne, Blanche of Castile, Margaret of Anjou, Katherine of Arragon, Lady Macbeth.

Tickler. What a galaxy! In every name a charm. In imagination a man might marry nine tenths of them—a spiritual seraglio.

North. My critiques on Sotheby's Homer seem to have been pretty well liked, though dashed off hurriedly, and I suppose they were not without a certain enthusiasm. I purpose haranguing away in a similar style, for a few articles, on Mrs. Jameson's Shakspere.

Tickler. Do. You are extravagant—not seldom absurd; but still there is, I grant, a certain enthusiasm—

North. Don't come over me with the Mocking-Bird. I have frequently observed, that whatever disparaging character a man carelessly sports of himself or writings, his common-place people forthwith adopt it as gospel; and thus a modest person like myself, being taken at his own word, is estimated far below his great genius—

Tickler. Hem!

North. This most charming of all the works of a charming writer has revived in me my old love of the Acted Drama. I shall again be a Play-goer.

Tickler. Here?

Shooting, Mundy's Adventures in India, and Nimrod's [Apperley] Contributions to the Literature of the Turf and the Hunting-field, are well known.—M.

North. Yes—here and in London, which I shall visit next spring—if alive; and I am engaged, indeed, to dine on the 1st of May with my friend Allan Cunningham.

Tickler. I shall be of the party.

North. It is false and most unjust to living genius to say that there are now on the stage few or no great actors. There are as many as ever there were at any one era. Young has just retired; but I trust to see him once or twice again ere I make my final exit—Macready is first-rate—Kean, in some characters, greater than Garrick.

Tickler. But the actresses?

North. A few—and there never were more than a few at any one time—are admirable.

Tickler. Miss Tree I saw lately in Julia in the Hunchback, and she is a charming performer.*

North. She is—but there are—THE THREE FANNYS.

Tickler. Eh?

North. Miss Fanny Kelly—a woman of original genius—fine taste—strong intellect—and exquisite sensibility—equal to any part of passion.†

Tickler. She is.

North. Miss Fanny Kemble acts nobly, like a Poetess as she is—and equal to either of them in all things, and in some superior to both, is—our own Miss Fanny Jarman. Equal to either in power and pathos, and superior to both in grace, elegance, and beauty.‡ The Three are all as much respected for their virtues in private life, as they are admired for their genius on the stage. And that lends a charm to their impersonations of such characters as Imogen, Desdemona, Ophelia, and Cordelia, which is felt by every audience, and for the want of which no accomplishments can compensate.

Enter LOUISA, HARRIET, *and* HELEN, *with the tea-tray, &c. &c.*

Tickler. Angels and ministers of grace!

North. One or other of you, my good girls, look in upon us now

* Ellen Tree, now Mrs. Charles Kean, born in 1805, and for many years a leading actress in the lines of genteel comedy and youthful tragedy.—M.

† Miss Francis Maria Kelly, born in 1790, of whom (when in her prime) it was said "in genteel comedy she is more than respectable; in domestic tragedy, unrivalled; and in opera, capable of sustaining a first-rate part, though not with first-rate powers." Charles Lamb complimented her, in a sonnet, which concludes thus,

"Your tears have passion in them, and a grace,
A genuine freshness, which our hearts avow;
Your smiles are winds, whose ways we cannot trace,
That vanish and return we know not how—
And please the better from a pensive face,
A thoughtful eye, and a reflecting brow."

Miss Kelly was niece to Michael Kelly, of whom, in his double capacity, of wine-merchant and opera-maker, Sheridan said that he was "composer of wine and importer of music."—There was another Miss Kelly (Frances H.) whose Juliet, some six-and-twenty years ago, was considered one of the most charming representations of that character.—M.

‡ Miss Jarman, now Mrs. Ternan.—M.

and then, during the hour, to see if we require any of your services. God bless you. (*They curtsy and retire.*)

Tickler. Eh?

North. Sisters three—and daughters of the Grieve on my little property in Tweddale, on a visit at present to an uncle, gardener to our friend in Trinity Tower. My worthy housekeeper has a young party in her own room this evening, and these obliging creatures requested permission to be attendant nymphs on the old gentleman——

Tickler. They did not call you so?

North. Not to my face, Tim; but depend on't, middle-aged men like us are thought as old as the hills by Miss in her Teens; and as for these pretty creatures, I look on them as mere children. Such a sight as that is good for the eyesight. But pray, what were we talking about?

Tickler. Confound me if I remember. These witches have—

North. You see that blue folio? 'Tis the report from the Select Committee on Dramatic Literature, with Minutes of Evidence. I glanced over it this afternoon, along with Mr. Bulwer's excellent speech on moving the appointment of the said Select Committee.* Have you studied the Question?

Tickler. What Question?

North. That of the patents granted to the Two Great Theatres for the performance of the Drama.

Tickler. Not I—but let us study while we discuss it. I know no better method of mastering any subject. I forget what you were going to say?

North. How would you define or describe the "regular drama?"

Tickler. The regular drama is—is—the regular drama is—that drama which comprehends—or say rather which excludes all dramatic perform—performances—that is compo—stop, I must correct myself—the regular drama may, I think, be defined to be that—no—described—as that which—nay, let me perpend—why, after you—if you please, Kit—for you have been ruminating on the subject. Pray, North, let me ask you—my good fellow—before we go any farther, how would you define or describe the regular drama?

North. I see nothing that can be either added or taken away from the truly Aristotelian definition which you have now given of it; and everything democratic not included within the terms thereof, may be philosophically pronounced to belong to the irregular drama.

Tickler. Having settled that point, which is at once nice and

* It was Bulwer who obtained a parliamentary committee, to inquire into the laws affecting the drama, and broke down the monopoly of the patent theatres, and who afterwards carried a Bill to grant stage copyright to written and published dramas.—M.

knotty, we may proceed to overhaul the minutes of evidence, and judge of its bearing on the general question of the patents.

North. Would that worthy Mr. Winston* had had the benefit of hearing your admirable definition before he was badgered by the Select. "What do you consider is meant by the regular Drama?" asked one of the inquisitors. And the veteran Ex-Manager of the Haymarket replied, "The regular Drama I consider to be Tragedy and Comedy, *and every thing on the stage.*"—"What! Burletta?" —"Yes; because TOM THUMB *was played in the regular theatres,* and is printed and called a Burletta."—"What do you consider a Burletta to be?"—"Recitative and singing; no speaking whatever; THE GOLDEN PIPPIN is a *strong specimen* of it—and OLYMPUS IN AN UPROAR."—"Is OLYMPUS IN AN UPROAR the regular Drama?"—"Yes; for it is played at the regular theatres, and played under license."—"Do I understand you to include every stage representation?"—"Yes—the regular Drama *includes everything.*"

Tickler. Very sensible.

North. One of the Select then asks Mr. Winston what he "considers to be *not* the regular drama?" At that he shakes his head, and says, "I do not know; that is a very difficult thing to ascertain;" but plucking up courage, he adds, "if they can play every thing, *then every thing is the regular drama.*"

Tickler. So in a regular drama there is no need for the performers, unless they like it, to utter a single word.

North. None in the world.

Tickler. And Tom Thumb, the Golden Pippin, and Olympus in an Uproar, are all *strong* specimens of the regular drama?

North. Samsons. Mr. Winston is then asked if "tumbling be the regular drama?" and his silence speaks consent. So, of course, must be dancing and swinging on the rope.

Tickler. Why go into particulars? Did he not say the regular drama included "*every thing?*"

North. But he qualifies that somewhat sweeping assertion; for, on being asked, "Are lions the regular drama?" he answers promptly and firmly, "No, I should consider not; not lions, certainly."

Tickler. Well, well—though there may perhaps be some slight difference between Mr. Winston's definition and mine of the regular drama, they seem to agree on the main points; so let's to the general question of the patents.

North. It is well stated by Mr. Bulwer to be this—"How far is it expedient for the public, that privileges and enactments of this monopolizing description should be continued?"

* Mr. Winston who once had managed the Haymarket, and was Treasurer of Drury Lane Theatre, for several years. He finally became Secretary of the Garrick Club in London.—M.

Tickler. What privileges and enactments?

North. Why—to use the words of Mr. Bulwer—by a late decision of the Lord Chancellor, it seems that all performances worthy the attendance of persons pretending to a reasonable degree of education—all performances, except those of the most mountebank and trumpery description, fit only for the players of Bartholomew Fair, are to be considered as infringements of the law, and as subjecting those who assist in them to serious penalties.

Tickler. Pray, what, generally speaking, is the character of the Minor Theatres?

North. More or less respectable.

Tickler. Clear and explicit.

North. And can there be a doubt that their character would be elevated by lawful liberty to enact the regular drama?

Tickler. "To be or not to be—that is the question."

North. There is much difference of opinion among the witnesses as to the comparative adaptation of large and small theatres for general dramatic effect. Charles Kemble (one of the proprietors of Covent Garden Theatre) argues with much ability in favor of very large ones, such as Covent Garden and Drury Lane. The same plays, acted by the same performers on alternate nights, at the Haymarket and the Opera House, paid better by £200 or £300 at the larger than at the smaller.

Tickler. That proves nothing.

North. Mind, the smaller was not half full.

Tickler. Ho—Ho—then it would seem to prove a great deal.

North. Mathews the Admirable, whose amusing and ingenious evidence, however, is far from convincing on the general merits, treated the Select with John Kemble's opinion, delivered as if by John himself; for, quoth Charles, "I can never repeat a conversation, unless I do it in the style of the person who gave it."

Tickler. O rare Charles Mathews! He becomes the original with such intensity, that the original seems to dwindle into an imperfect and ineffectual imitation of his own self. You cannot allow the original original, after you have seen and heard Charles in him, to perform himself; he looks so very tame; he wants that brilliance, which burns round and about his creative doubleganger; and the wisest thing he can do is to become, in the critic's row in the pit, an ecstactic admirer of his own perfections.*

North. "It is a common complaint," quoth Charles as John, "to speak about the size of the Theatres; the Public will tell you they

* This is a very accurate description of the extraordinary ability with which the late Charles Mathews threw himself, as it were, into whatever personal imitation he chose to give. Among the personations which he sometimes gave in private circles, but never, I believe, on the stage, were Tate Wilkinson, the eccentric Manager of the York theatre, and Charles Macklin, who first showed how the part of Shylock should be played.—M.

like small Theatres; *sir, they lie!* they like large Theatres. They go to the Opera, because it is a large Theatre; and when my sister and myself, and Mr. Cooke, acted in Henry the Eighth, when we acted at the King's Theatre, we played to £600; and when we went over to the Theatre opposite, we never got £200 to the same play."

Tickler. "Sir, they lie!" Christopher North in Charles Mathews in John Kemble in Samuel Johnson.

North. One of the Select says, that he can perfectly well understand that there are certain sorts of representations which can only be represented in large Theatres, such as pantomimes, melodramas, and spectacles, and things of that sort; but Charles Kemble rather sharply replies—"Excuse me; I think, with respect to melodramas and pantomimes, it is a mistake to suppose they can be better acted at large than at small Theatres. Indeed, I think a pantomime may be better acted in a small Theatre than in a large one; because those changes which are necessary for the great success of a pantomime, are much more easily effected in a small Theatre than in a large one. With respect to melodramas, they do not depend for success entirely on splendor. On the contrary, I should say the most successful melodramas have been those which depend on strong excitement in the story or incidents of the piece; for without these, all the splendor in the world will do nothing, either in a large or in a small Theatre. Splendor alone does nothing, or next to nothing, to the success of a piece."

Tickler. Well said, Charles Kemble. One of the most delightful sights in this world, North, is a fine melodrama. Wiseacres, prigs, sumphs, and your general blockheads, abuse such beautiful spectacles; yet even they are not insensible to their fascination, as may be seen in the glaring stare of their great goggle eyes devouring the stage. That the Public loves the melodrama, is a proof that she is not so prosaic a Public as she seems to be when in the act of reading through the advertisements in a morning newspaper.

North. Worthy soul! she has some poetry in her after all—some imagination—some perception of moving grace or skill—an eye and a heart—a soul—for the fairy of world-enchanted Cloudland and its floating inhabitants. I too, Tim, do dearly love the melodrama.

Tickler. What farther sayeth the deponent?

North. That there are certain plays which require enlarged space—for example, Coriolanus, Julius Cæsar, and Macbeth.

Tickler. All tragedies that involve magnificence in the grouping of the characters, in the incidence of the events, in the scenic shows.

North. Just so; whereas dramas of a humbler, of a domestic, of a more familiar kind, such as the Hunchback——

Tickler. A beautiful play.

North. Very—may be as effectively performed, or perhaps more so, in a theatre of very moderate size.

Tickler. Plain as a pikestaff.

North. Mr. Macready's opinion coincides with Mr. Kemble's. He tells us that he finds it much easier to act in a small theatre than in a large one, and that for merely domestic scenes and simple dialogue, when there is nothing of pomp and circumstance attending it, he should prefer a small theatre; but as for Shakspere's Plays, that very few of them can be found which can have due effect given them in a small theatre. Even the Haymarket he thinks hardly large enough to allow a fair acting of Shakspere's Plays. In scenes where only two persons have been on the stage—and one of these Kean—he thought nothing about the size of the house; but when a great number occupied the stage, he felt the want of space and too great proximity of the performers.

Tickler. What say Young and Kean?

North. Mr. Young does not appear at all.*

Tickler. Extraordinary! The finest actor on the stage—*Ultimus Romanorum.* So must all have felt who ever saw him in Brutus.

North. Mr. Kean prefers a large stage—Drury-Lane. He thinks the intellect becomes confined by the size of the theatre—that in a larger one the illusion is better preserved—that the illusion is heightened by the somewhat diminished appearance of the performers—and that any actor, with a good enunciation, may be heard as well at Drury-Lane as any theatre in the world—even in the one-shilling gallery—if the gods will but be silent——

Tickler. And not keep perpetually performing "Olympus in an Uproar."

North. That an eye of average power can perfectly well distinguish the play of the countenance at that distance—and that there is this other very material consideration, that the faults of the actor are less observable——

Tickler. Pray, how is that? Beauties all distinct, defects all hidden—how is that, pray?

North. Ask Mr. Kean. You know Dowton?

Tickler. Well—a first-rater of the Old School.† How deponeth Dowton?

North. "I am astonished," quoth Mister William, "at Mr. Kean's opinion; because, when I am told that actors can be as well seen in Drury-Lane Theatre as in a smaller one, I can as well believe you can hang a cabinet picture on the top of that tower, and say,

* Charles Young, who made his *debut* in 1798, and is yet in vigorous old age, was superior, in the part of Rienzi (in Miss Mitford's play), to any actor who has played it. He was one of the best of the second rate actors—always relying on his judgment, never trusting to his feelings; acting from the head rather than the heart.—M.

† William Dowton's Falstaff and Sir Anthony Absolute were never equalled. He visited America, in his decline, too late to show more than the reflection of what he had been.—M.

'Do you observe those beautiful touches—do you observe its lights and shadows? No—I cannot see it at all.' This is my opinion as to the stage. Give me a theatre of moderate size, *where you can be natural.*"

Tickler. That "must give us pause."

North. Mr. Dowton is then asked whether Mr. Kean's acting is the more effective at Drury-Lane or Covent-Garden, or in a small theatre in the country? And he says, "much more to my satisfaction in a small theatre in the country." He thinks that even a play like Julius Cæsar could be much better performed in a theatre of the size of the Haymarket, than in one of far greater dimensions —not only as regards the merit of one actor, but the whole body of performers, if they have any pretensions to acting at all. It was said by John Kemble, that about two-thirds of the audience at Covent-Garden could see and hear well, and Mr. Dowton is much of his opinion with regard to that; hear they may, for the actor knows he must be heard, and will bawl.

Tickler. And if he bawl, that third who could not otherwise have heard him, must be wonderfully delighted with his bawl, softened ere it reach their ears into a sound not a little extraordinary, but still a bawl; for believe me, a bawl will be a bawl to doomsday, to whatever distance it may be projected by the action of mortal lungs, and of the organs of inhuman speech.

North. Then the two-thirds who would have heard the unfortunate man, or still more wretched woman, had he or she spoke naturally, must be placed immediately under the unbated bawl, and thence an inevitable universal headache.

Tickler. Yet, North, I love a large theatre. My friend Beazley, an architect of the first eminence,* asserts that a very large theatre may be so scientifically constructed, that articulate sounds shall most audibly circle its entire extent; and how far off was heard the whisper of the Siddons!

North. Could we imagine one of Shakspere's greatest tragedies performed, in all its great parts, by consummate actors, in an immense overflowing house, so finely constructed, that every auditor felt possessed of the ear of Dionysius, then, Tickler, would the manager "give the world assurance of a *play.*"

Tickler. But performers, with feeblish faces that must frown, punyish figures that must strut, and squeakyish voices that must crack, before they can be at all tragical, on a large stage, may act very naturally and effectively in one of a corresponding size, and prove their popularity by bumper benefits.

* Samuel Beazley was a London architect, who had built several theatres, and written a good many plays. A novel called "The Roue," in which there are many luxurious descriptions, several warm scenes, and a great deal of doubtful morality, was written by Mr. Beazley.—M.

North. The truth is, that genius will achieve its highest triumphs alike, on stages of all sizes, from that of Covent-Garden, down even to the mud floor of a barn.

Tickler. Illusion! Did not Garrick, in his every-day clothes, in a small parlor, with such terrible transformation assume the sudden insanity of a mother, out of whose arms her child had fallen from a window, and been dashed to pieces before her eyes, that women fainted in horror at his feet, on "acting of that dreadful thing?"

North. Good. And had he come on a stage, wide as a wilderness, hearts far remote in the galleries as in the clouds, would have beat

> "At every flash of his far-beaming eye."

Tickler. Good.

North. Mr. Mathews and I are at one when he says, that the magnificence of the style of John Kemble and his sister were seen to as great effect in a large theatre as in a small one; but there are a great number of persons whose countenance alone carries them to small theatres, for they cannot be seen to the same advantage in a large one. But Charles adds wisely, "I never heard that objection stated during a fashion to run after every thing attractive; I never heard any people say they could not see Miss O'Neil; she was a beautiful actress, and every body admired her"——

Tickler. All the world, and his wife.

North. My esteemed friend then observes, that he finds "all the people *who go in with orders*, say the theatres are far too large, but those *who pay for their admission* are good-tempered."

Tickler. Our provincial theatres, compared with the great London ones, are all small—yet——

North. Except that in Glasgow. It is of the same class as Covent-Garden but of peculiar construction. It may be divided into three parts; in one you cannot hear, in another you cannot see, and in the third you can neither see nor hear. I remember once sitting alone in the third division—and never before or since have I had such a profound feeling of the power of solitude.

Tickler. I say, our provincial theatres are all of moderate size; yet when stars appear, are they not worshipped? All our great performers have trod the Edinburgh stage; and there has been "hush as deep as death," followed by peals of thunder.

North. And where else than on provincial boards have great performers been bred?

Tickler. Has this discussion any drift?

North. Oh, yes. Without joining the cry against the size of the great London theatres, I for one am clear for putting an end to their monopoly of the regular drama. In theatres of a smaller size, it may be, and has been, acted as effectively as in them; and experience alone can decide whether with Freedom of Trade it will flourish or decay.

Tickler. It has not flourished under Patents—without them it may.

North. Sir Charles Wetherell would not listen with patience to any proposed change in the Close System, nor agree to Mr. Bulwer's motion, unless he could prove to him that the multiplication of theatres will "give us another Shakspere and Ben Jonson, and restore the golden age of Dramatic Literature."

Tickler. That was rather a little unreasonable in our most excellent friend.

North. Rather. Another Ben Jonson may be imagined—though one is quite enough; but Mr. Bulwer expressed no hope of being able, by any efforts of his in Parliament, to produce another Shakspere.

Tickler. Nor yet so far as I have heard, to restore the Golden Age.

North. Not he; but seeing the regular drama in a languishing condition at the Great Houses, and, as Sir Charles himself says, "Lions and Tigers, and Cameleopards, and, in fact, the whole of Noah's Ark trotted up and down the stage," he thinks, that were there several moderate-sized theatres judiciously set down in the Mighty Metropolis, such would be the resort to them of respectable and well-educated people, that they would always be able to engage, and would sometimes probably produce, excellent actors; and that thus a permanent love of the regular drama (along with an occasional passion for the irregular) would be created, and more encouragement given than at present to men of genius to write for the stage.

Tickler. I should have voted for Mr. Bulwer's motion.

North. Charles Kemble has no doubt, that along with the patents would go the very life of the Two Great Theatres.

Tickler. I should be sorry for that—but they could be vanquished only by better houses—and the public would in that case gain by the death.

North. His arguments are ably put, but to me they appear inconclusive. He says "that the new theatres would bribe away certain individuals of acknowledged talent and celebrity," (and he adds, parenthetically and pathetically, "God knows they are too few!") "but those few would be scattered then in half a dozen different theatres, instead of being collected in one or two; and the perfection of a play depends extremely on the talent you get into it."

Tickler. No doubt it does.

North. The conclusion he draws from these premises is, that the Great Theatres would be ruined, and at the same time the smaller ones good for nothing.

Tickler. Whew!

North. If one first-rate actor could not support a small theatre, and if, as Mr. Kemble thinks, only one at the most could be got, then, in a very short time indeed, the small theatres would be changed into conventicles—and Covent-Garden and Drury-Lane, after transient obscuration, effulge, like suns, brighter from eclipse. He says that a long time would elapse before the legitimate drama could be adequately represented in one of those theatres; and I say, that, if so, the public could not wait a long time, and the actors of genius and celebrity, that had been bribed away, would return to their former spheres.

Tickler. I have the highest esteem for Charles Kemble, but I fear you are right.

North. Neither will he admit that the competition of the new theatres would bring forward new actors of talent or genius. "If," says he, "you divide the little talent there is among us into a *great number* of theatres, you will be worse served."

Tickler. Whew!

North. There would not be a great number of theatres; nor does any body suppose, that, by dividing a given quantity of talent, and that quantity little, you will make it great. It is to talent not yet displayed, not yet born, that the stimulus of competition will be applied——

Tickler. Don't dwell longer on that point, or you will get prosier than you may suspect. Keep moving.

North. "It is not the increase of theatres," cries Charles, with great animation, "that will give you an increase of fine actors. The qualifications of a fine actor are a gift that God gives, and they are not to be multiplied as theatres may be."

Tickler. That is very spunky—but whence arise fine actors but from theatres? John Kemble—Sarah Siddons——

North. Don't get prosy, Tim. Mr. Kemble then says that many of the smaller London theatres have acted the legitimate drama in *defiance of all law;* but that we do not see those results which the advocates for minor theatres seem to calculate on—we have not seen that great actors have arisen in them.

Tickler. A manifest sophism. Those theatres have indeed occasionally acted the legitimate drama (some of them never have), but *in defiance of law;* and is it to be expected, that, under such uncertainty and peril, and even discredit, great or good actors are to arise?

North. Mr. Kemble even goes the length of denying that there is any demand for any other theatres. If the public call for them, there is good reason he allows, for answering the public; but the present demands are got up, he asserts, by a set of interested adventurers and speculators, who have nothing to lose, and think the best course they can pursue is to ruin those whom they think have. Some have already become bankrupt.

Tickler. In that case then he has little to fear. But great theatres, alas! become bankrupt too—

"The paths of glory lead to the Gazette."

North. Mr. Charles Kemble, however, though arguing throughout under a strong bias, is a man of honor; and on this question being forcibly pressed upon him, "Do you not think that the cultivation of a taste for the drama, which would be favored by the increased number of theatres having the power to exercise the legitimate Drama, would more than make up for any loss you might sustain by competition?" He answers with laudable candor, "If I speak conscientiously, which I wish to do, I should think they might prove a nursery; that it is probable that in a length of years, if the number of theatres were restricted to a reasonable number, and those theatres were only allowed to act the legitimate Drama, and that there might be none of those spurious entertainments given"—(no, no, my dear Charles, that would be a most unfair restriction, while spurious entertainments were allowed in the great theatres)—"then I agree that the Drama might be improved, and in course of years we might expect to have eléves, who would fully replace the good actors we have now."

Tickler. What says Mathews?

North. To my utter astonishment and dismay, that permission to perform the legitimate drama at other theatres besides the two patent ones, and the Haymarket, "would in the course of a very short time *brutalize the drama*."

Tickler. I am dumbfounded. How feel you at that discharge?

North. As if a bullet had gone through my head.

Tickler. In at one ear, and out at the other, without touching the brain.

North. Nevertheless, I would fain try a fall with this Charles; but I feel fatigued with my tussle with the other strong man, so must retire from the ring; though it forces me to eat my heart to see the castor of such a customer flunk up without my pitching in after it my vernon.

Tickler. I take.

North. The Drama, I fear, is in a bad way, Tim, in London; and if so, it can not be very flourishing in the provinces. Mr. Mathews acknowledges that fashion is fatal to it. "I meet young gentlemen now," he says, "who formerly used to think it almost a crime not to go to the theatre; but they now ask, 'whereabouts is Covent-Garden Theatre?' although the same people would faint away, if they thought they had not been to the Italian Opera. If they are asked whether they have seen Kean or not lately, they will say, 'Kean? Kean? No. Where does he act? I have not been there these three years.' Formerly, it was the fashion to go to the theatre; but now a lady can not show her face at table next day, and say she has been at the theatre. If they are asked whether they have been at Covent-Garden or Drury Lane, they say, 'Oh, dear, no! I never go there—it is too low!' "

Tickler. Taglioni, I am told, is a seducing Sylph—Heberlé a dangerous Dryad. They dance you into a delirium.

North. And the German Opera is divine.

Tickler. Those morning, forenoon, afternoon, evening, and midnight concerts, private and public, are sadly against play-going. To say nothing of déjeunés prolonged from meridian to twilight, and dinners of countless courses—

North. Gaming tables in drawing-rooms, parlors, boudoirs, *bedrooms*.

Tickler. O Lord! not in bedrooms—

North. Yes, even so. There is nothing too good or too bad, too beautiful or too ugly—

Tickler. Ugsome.

North. That Fashion and Folly will not fix on with a mad desire, till all at once the passion sickens and dies, and "off to some other game they both together fly!"

Tickler. Mathews is right here—if wrong there.

North. "I remember the time," saith the green and glorious veteran (he has been nearly forty years on the stage), "when it was no shame to go to see the legitimate drama; but it is now." "But," asks one of the Select, "do you not think that may be the result of the acting not being sufficiently good?" "I want to know when the actors *have not been sufficiently good* FOR THEM?"

Tickler. Spoken like a man.

North. "It was the fashion," he adds, "to go and see Miss O'Neil *for a season;* and Mr. Kean *for a season;* if they were real and sincere admirers of those actors, they would have followed them; but we found that theatres at which they acted, dropt down from £600 to £200."

Tickler. There are lamentably few sincere admirers of any thing admirable in this world.

North. You know old George Colman?

Tickler. No.

North. You have read his "Broad Grins?"

Tickler. No. Eye and nose shrunk from the dunghill in disgust.

North. He holds under the Lord Chamberlain the office of Examiner of all theatrical entertainments.

Tickler. That is sufficient of itself to damn the drama.

North. He was sworn, he gravely tells us, in February, 1824, "to take care that nothing should be introduced into plays which is profane or indecent, or morally or politically improper for the stage."

Tickler. I see no use, in his case, of such an oath.* I presume were he to suffer any thing of the sort to defile a play—profanity or indecency I mean—he would be dismissed and lose his salary; and that fear, being of this world, would be likely to be as operative on the hoary-headed perpetrator of the filth of "Broad Grins," as the reverence of any oath regarding merely the life to come. 'Twas a needless profanation of the Prayer-book or Bible.

North. The dotard has become intolerantly decent in his old age; so pious, that he shudders at the word "angel" in a play! "The Committee have heard of your cutting out of a play the epithet 'angel' as applied to a woman?"

Tickler. Nay—that must be calumny on Colman.

North. No. George, as Mawworm, cantingly, and yet, I doubt not, leeringly replies, "Yes, because it is *a woman*, I grant, but it is a *celestial woman*. It is an allusion to the scriptural angels, which are celestial bodies. Every man who has read his Bible understands what they are; or if he has not, I will refer him to Milton."

Tickler. Well, I did not know till now that there is a man in England who denies that a human woman—a female woman, as the sailors say—is an angel. Is the old sinner—

North. We are all old sinners.

Tickler. True. Is the old sinner serious when he insinuates, that a human female is not a celestial creature?

North. He seems so—stupidly and doggedly serious.

Tickler. Does the aged docken deny that she is a "celestial body?"

North. He does.

Tickler. Fie on the old Eunuch.

North. He utters a falsehood when he says that every man who has read his Bible understands what the scriptural angels are; no man understands what they are; they are a mystery. But note the impudence of the hypocrite. "*If he has not*, I will refer him to Milton." That is, "if he has not read his Bible;" and this language is used sarcastically to the member of the Select Committee who was courteously interrogating the Broad Grinner.

Tickler. I trust not courteously.

North. His impudence is only less than his ignorance, in referring his questioner to Milton, in proof of the scriptural angels being celestial women. That gentleman mildly remarks, "Milton's angels are not Ladies. Instead of blushing, he brazens it out, and replies,

* No man has introduced more swearing and expletives, into actor's mouths, than this same Colman did—in his own plays!—M.

"No—but *some* scriptural angels are Ladies—*I believe*"—showing that he is as ignorant of his Bible as of Milton. Then how his profanity breaks out pettishly in the word "*Ladies!*" That word was quite right in the mouth of his questioner, for he was a gentleman and a Christian, and in his mind the ideas of angels and ladies have always been united as the beings themselves are in nature. But with his awful and reverential feelings with regard to all "scriptural angels," it was shocking in the author of Broad Grins to call them in the same breath "*Ladies*"—in his mouth an equivocal term—even when provoked to do so by the exposure of his shameful ignorance of the Book on which he had sworn. Ladies! he must have been thinking of the Saloons.

Tickler. You are too severe, Kit.

North. Not a whit.—He also says insolently, and with his religious belief, impiously, "I do not recollect that *I struck out an angel or two*, but most probably I have at some time or other." This affectation of a profound religious spirit in such a man, and on such an occasion, is at first ludicrous, and then loathsome—and I have thought it worthy of castigation, my good Timothy, for it is a nauseous habit of hypocrisy now-a-days to pretend to discern evil in the use of the most harmless and amiable expressions which a fine spirit of humanity may not only have justified, but consecrated; and of them all, not one is there more delightful in the dreams it awakens of brightness, beauty, goodness, innocence, and bliss, than "angel," when applied, as it is, by the whole Christian male population of the earth to all the unpolluted daughters of Eve.

Tickler. Why, Kit, you have given me an absolute sermon—but your doctrine, though sweet, is, I fear, scarcely sound. You are not orthodox.

North. I am orthodox. But let me give grinning Geordie another punch. He says, "an angel is, I grant, a woman, but it is a celestial woman." Now here again he shows that he has not read his Bible. "*Some* Scriptural angels," he also admits, "are ladies". They are not only women, but ladies. Now, he mistakes the matter most entirely; they may be said, in the Bible, to be females, but certainly not *women*. In short, women are angels, but angels are not women. A woman, though human, being universally admitted all over the world, with the single exception of George Colman, to be an angel, is, *in rerum naturâ*, by participation celestial, too; but an angel, though celestial, being universally admitted all over the world, with the exception of George Colman, to be no woman, is not, *in rerum naturâ*, by participation human; so that woman has the superiority over angel—only the one dwells on earth, and the other in heaven.

Tickler. What must George the Grinner think of the famous

debate among the doctors of the dark ages on the theological question, "How many angels could dance on the point of a needle?"

North. He would faint like a young lady suspected of having been at Covent-Garden Theatre.

Tickler. In what play is it said, or is it said in any play, that a person "played the fiddle like an angel?"

North. I forget—but it is very wicked. "Supposing," asks the committee-man, "you were to leave the word 'angel' in a play or farce, will you state your opinion as to the *effect it would have on the public mind?*" Colman—"It is impossible for me to say what effect it would have! I am not able to enter into the breasts of every body who might be in the gallery, pit, or boxes.

Tickler. Poor devil!

North. Mr. Moncrieff, in his examination, says, "Mr. Colman has been rather particular—very capricious—he would not let one mention the word 'thighs' in the Bashful Man—he said *those were indecent.*"

Tickler. "Drawn from the thighs of mighty cherubim."
Milton. Are "those indecent?"

North. "His cuisses on his thighs."
Shakspere. Are "those indecent!"

Tickler. Are hips indecent?

North. No—nor haws.

Tickler. The man's mind, we shall hope, is rather diseased than depraved.

North. The Queens of Spain, you know, have no legs. 'Tis high treason to say they have. And were a poet in that kingdom to praise the ankles of his young female sovereign, he would be broken on the wheel.

Tickler. I wonder what old Colman thinks of Madam Vestris's legs?

North. He would not license them——

Tickler. But grin like a satyr.

North. He is horrified at the word *damme*—and it is at the least a silly sound—but then he is asked, "how do you reconcile that opinion with your making use of *damme,* or any of those small oaths, which you say are immoral and improper, to say nothing of the vulgarity, in some of your own compositions?" His answer to that question is a cool curiosity of its kind—"If I had been the examiner, I should have scratched them out, and would do so now; but I was in *a different position then*—I was a careless, *immoral author*—I am now the examiner of plays. *I did my business as an author at that time,* and I do my business as an examiner now!"

Tickler. Ha! Ha! Ha!

North. But George gives us the reason of his dislike of *damme*. "Sir Simon Rochdale in John Bull* says, '*Damme*, if it isn't the Brazier!' Now, *putting a gentleman in that position* is wrong; in the first instance morally so; if he *happened to make a mistake, and it was not the Brazier*, HE WOULD BE DAMNED!' Now, if he said, '*hang me*,' if it isn't the Brazier—would not that do *as well*?"

Tickler. Good.

North. It seems to me very unmerciful religion to hold that Sir Simon Rochdale "would be damned" if it was not the Brazier.

Tickler. Why, if it was a deadly sin to say *damme*, Sir Simon would be damned, I humbly presume, according to Mr. George's creed, whether it was the Brazier or not.

North. And if he said "*hang me*," then on the same principle he would be hanged, whether the Baronet was a brazier or a butcher, or even a retired tallow-chandler visiting his old establishment on melting-days.

Tickler. Hanged—not the position of a gentleman.

North. It seems in Colman's comedy, John Bull, there is what his examiner in the Select is pleased to call "a very good joke about Eve." One of the characters is said to have no more idea of something, "than Eve had of pin-money." This "very good joke" Colman now thinks improper, and would fain it were omitted in representation. It sounds to my ears silly in the extreme—and shows what was the strength of this person's wit in the prime of manhood; but "the audience are always struck with it!"

Tickler. And the pretty mantua-maker in the middle of the pit hangs down her head, and with lily hand hides the burning blushes that kindle beneath the knowing gaze of the gallant man-milliner by her betrothed side.

North. It appears that this once most base and licentious (writer), but now most stanch and strait-laced licenser, had given in a paper to the Committee, stating that a piece had been brought forward in Paris, in which incest, adultery, murder, parricide, &c., formed the groundwork; and he is asked if he considers that he could be justified in refusing to license a piece in which those crimes were introduced. He answers, "No, *not precisely that;* let me see how the plot thickens. I should not refuse to license the murder of Richard III., *and so on;* but when it comes to such things as human nature and morality shudder at and revolt against." They do not, it seems, shudder at and revolt against incest, murder, and parricide.

Tickler. He is muddle-headed.

North. Yet his brains are not mere mire; for, when asked if

* "John Bull" was written by Colman.—M.

human nature and morality do not shudder at Macbeth, he says, "Yes; but it is matter of history."

Tickler. And what does that signify? The tragedy would have been equally great had it not been matter of history.

North. The reason he gives is childish; but he adds rightly that he would withhold the license from those plays which seem to have justified such acts.

Tickler. Are there any such?

North. None that I ever heard of. Odd notions are always floating about, but I do not remember ever having heard, either in prose or verse, any elaborate eulogy on parricide.

Tickler. He seems to show more indulgence to foul and questionable deeds than a few venial words—such as "angel," "thighs," "damme," and the like; but what could the committee mean by asking the opinion of such a person on so profound a question, as whether the crimes now mentioned are or are not fit subjects for the Tragic Muse?

North. They should have examined the author of the celebrated Essay on Murder, considered as one of the Fine Arts.* Charles Kemble himself is here very absurd. Speaking of the general noisiness of our theatres, he says, "When you see Macbeth, John Bull is perfectly quiet, as he always is, when the representation of murder is going on." Very natural. But immediately afterward, Charles says to another question, "*I am afraid* the representation of a murder is very attractive." Why afraid?

Tickler. He may think, since John Bull enjoys the representation so intensely, he may have no great objection to the reality—to lending a helping hand in a *bonâ fide* flesh and blood murder.

North. I can't say; but he continues, "*I am sorry it is so*—it was tried in the case of Thurtell, and was very attractive; but they added to the attraction by introducing the gig that had carried the murderer down to the scene;† *a most atrocious thing.*" There is great confusion of ideas in that statement of good Master Charles. The murder by Macbeth of the gracious Duncan was, in a moral and religious point of view, far worse than the murder by Thurtell of the black-leg Weare. But, nathless, it was a grand subject for the most dreadful of all dramas. The murder, and the remorse, and the expiation, are all sublime. The murder by Thurtell of Weare, again, not so wicked, was a mean subject for a drama, but not without the strong interest that belongs to the vulgar horrible; and, therefore, any theatrical representation of it could not fail to administer a strong purge of coarse pity and terror to vulgar minds. The persons who flocked to see it had, for the most part, minds of

* This celebrated Essay, which appeared in Blackwood, was written by De Quincey.—M.
† This was at the Surrey Theatre, in 1824.—M.

that nature; but in almost all, say at once in all minds, there is something of this vulgar disposition to get drunk on the worst of common British gin. Now, I ask, was it one whit more disgraceful for a Cockney public to gloat over, on the stage of an illegitimate theatre, "the acting of a dreadful thing," like the murder of a raff by a ruffian, than to do so in the columns of a newspaper? The newspapers for weeks were filled with nothing else but all the details of the throat-cutting and corpse-bundling, and pond-dragging and grave-digging, by the song-singing pork-shop-gormandizing assassins of both sexes, who "assisted at the deep damnation of that taking off." The proprietors of the daily press lived on it. The finding of the body was meat and drink to them; and they fared sumptuously on the scattered brains. They got up in Printing-House Square the famous Herefordshire Tragedy before it was enacted across the water; and yet the rich proprietor of the newspapers howled at the enormity of the poor Manager, and the penny-a-liners over that of the farthing-a-speechifiers turned up the whites of their eyes and tipt.

Tickler. It was by no means a bad subject for the drama.

North. Why, it was not. Such a man as Lillo* would have made rather a fearful thing of it—would have brought it fairly within the range of the lower regular and legitimate drama. He has done so with other murders as bad and more hideous. I dare say the affair over the water was a most miserable one; but Mr. Kemble speaks nonsense when he says, that the introduction of the very gig that carried the murderer down *was a most atrocious thing.* There can be nothing atrocious in a green gig and an iron-gray horse. It "was a bit of good truth," that struck the imagination through the most powerful of all the senses; and though there might not be great genius shown in the introduction of such machinery, it showed perfect knowledge of the portion of humanity that constituted that audience of spectators, and the effect, I have been told, was prodigious among the apprentices. Charles seems to have forgotten the crime of the exhibition—to wit, that it was got up before the trial of the murderer, and assumed his guilt. Had he been hanged or condemned, the green gig and iron-gray horse—a fast trotter—might have stood on the boards of the painted Gill's Hill Lane a most blameless set-out; and all that had then needed to be said, would have been, that vulgar folks like to sup full of vulgar horrors—and that there are at all times, in London, multitudes of men, women, and children, who have a strong "pawpensity for the bastard dwama."

* George Lillo's best plays are founded on circumstances of domestic horror:—viz. George Barnwell, Fatal Curiosity, and Arden of Feversham.—M.

Tickler. Hush! I hear girls giggling!

Enter Louisa, Harriet, and Helen, each with a silver salver glittering with tiny crystals of various-hued liqueurs. NORTH *and* TICKLER *take each a small celestial caulker in either hand, and drink to the maidens, who curtsy and retire with the salvers, tea-trays, &c.*

North. Silent Sirens!

Tickler. Delightful Damsels!

North. I wish they had been but two.

Tickler. Ay, Kit. It would have been impious to have let the third go away with untasted lips; yet worse than impious, indelicate for both of us to kiss the same mouth—so, "like considerate gentlemen of the good olden time," we suffered all three to go as they came. Hush! I hear them giggling! I hope they won't tell. If they do, they shan't go unpunished next time. We shall have our revenge at supper.

North. Och hone aree!

Tickler. Savourna deligh! Shighan, oh!

No. LXV.—MAY, 1834.

SCENE—*Tent in the Fairy's Cleugh*—NORTH *and the* REGISTRAR *lying on the brae.* (*In attendance,* AMBROSE *and his Tail.*)

*Registrar.**

> "The day is placid in its going,
> To a lingering stillness bound;
> Like a river in its flowing—
> Can there be a softer sound?"

What, my dear North! Can't I waken you from your reverie even by a stanza of your own bard—Wordsworth? Hallo! are you asleep, you old somnolent sinner? (*Shouting through the hollow of his hands into North's ear.*) Nay, you must be dead. That posture grows every hour more alarming, and if this be not death, why then I pronounce it an admirable imitation. Laid out! Limb and body stiff and stark as a winter clod—mouth open—eyes ditto, and glazed like a window-pane in frost. How white his lips! And is there no breath? (*Puts his pocket-mirror to North's mouth.*) Thank Heaven, it dims—he lives! North, I say again, you old somnolent sinner, "awake, arise, or be for ever fallen!"

North. (*Motionlessly soliloquizing in a dream.*) Never in this well-wooded world, not even in the days of the Druids, could there have been such another Tree! It would be easier to suppose two Shaksperes.

Registrar. Sleeping or waking, always original. I must let the bald-headed bard enjoy a little longer his delusion, (*Pats North on the forehead.*) What a pile!

North. Yet have I heard people say it is far from being a large Tree. A small one it can not be with a house in its shadow. An unawakened house that looks as if it were dreaming! True, 'tis but a cottage—a Westmoreland cottage—

Registrar. The buck is at the Lakes.

North. But then it has several roofs shelving away there in the lustre of loveliest lichens—

Registrar. "And apt alliteration's artful aid." Yet methinks

* Samuel Anderson, once wine merchant in Edinburgh, whom Lord Chancellor Brougham had appointed Registrar of the Court of Chancery.—M.

such affectations are beneath the dignity of his genius. Kit, you're a conceited callant.

North. Each roof with its own assortment of doves and pigeons pruning their plumage in the morning pleasance.

Registrar. Again? Poo—poo—on such prettinesses, North.

North. The sun is not only a great genius, but, what is far better, a good Christian.

Registrar. That's not so much amiss by way of an obs.

North. Now is he rising to illuminate all nature; yet in his universal mission, so far from despiting this our little humble dwelling, God bless his gracious countenance! he looks as if for it and for us he were bringing back the beautiful day from the sea.

Registrar. The habits and customs of our walking life we carry along with us into dream-land. The Unit calls himself Us.

North. O sweetest and shadiest of all sycamores—

Registrar. Incurable.

North. —we love thee beyond all other trees—*because thou art here!* May we be buried below thee, and our coffin clasped by thy roots—"and curst be he who stirs our bones!"

Registrar. Again—*our* bones. Indeed there is little else of him now. The *anatomie vivante* would find it difficult to be much more of a skeleton were he a corpse. Yet he is a true Scotchman—for his bones are raw. Could it be—as tradition reports—that he was once inclining to corpulency—"like two single gentlemen rolled into one!" All the fat has melted in the fire of his genius—gone "like snaw aff a dyke," and the dyke itself "a rickle o' stanes!"

North. Yet have we lived, all our lives, in the best sylvan society—we have the entrée of the soirées of the Pines, the Elms, the Ashes, and the Oaks, the oldest and highest families in Britain.

Registrar. The old Tory! Aristocratical in his dwawms.

North. Nor have they disdained to receive us with open arms, when, after having been "absent long and distant far," we have found them again on our return to park or chase, as stately as ever among the groups of deer!

Registrar. In Mar-Forest—with the Thane.

North. But with this one single Tree—this sole sweet Sycamore—are we in love. Yet so spiritual is our passion, that we care not even if it be unreturned.

Registrar. In the Platonics.

North. Self-sufficient for its own happiness is our almost life-long affection, pure as it is profound—no jealousy ever disturbs its assured repose. SHE may hold dalliance with all the airs and lights and shadows of heaven—may open her bosom to the thunder-glooms—take to her inmost heart, in its delirious madness, the shivering storm.

Registrar. Who could have thought there was so much imagination left within those temples—

"His lyart haffets wearing thin and bare?"

North. Oh! blessed is the calm that breathes over all emotions inspired by the beauty of lifeless things! Love creates delight that dies not till *she* dies; and then, indeed, dead seems all the earth. But wherever Love journeys—ay, be it through the Great Desert —before her feet "Beauty pitches her tents." And oh! how divine their slumber—of Love in the arms of Beauty—by the Palmtree Well!

Registrar. What a pity the creature never wrote in verse!

North. Alas! not so with Love—when Love, a male spirit—

Registrar. That's heterodox, old boy—seraphs are of no sex.

North. —is in love with the fairness of a Thing with life—

Registrar. A thing with life!

North. —how often is the imagination alarmed, as by the tolling of a bell in the air for some unknown funeral; and while it knows not why, the whole region, even but now bathed in day, grows night-like! and the heart is troubled.

Registrar. Ay—ay—my dear friend, I too have felt that, for, gay as I am, North, to the public eye, you know, Kit, that I have had my sorrows.

North. That virgin, Heaven may have decreed, shall be the wife of your dearest foe! O! the cruel selfishness of Love's religion! The fear is worse than the thought even of her death! Rather than see her walking all in white, and with white roses in her hair, into the church, leaning on *that* arm, her fair face crimsoning with blushes at the altar, as if breathed from the shadow of a rosy cloud, Love would see her carried, all in white, with white roses in her hair then too, towards that hole in the churchyard—a hole into which distraction has crowded and heaped all that is most dismal on this side of hell—her pale face—though that he dares not dream of —yellowing within her coffin.

Registrar. Nay, that's too much—hang me if I can stand that— *ne quid nimis*, North—and for having made me blubber, you shall have your face freshened, my lad, with the Woodburn.

(*Runs down to the Woodburn, fills his hat to the brim, and dashes the contents into the face of the Dormant.*)

North (*starting up in a splutter*). Whew! a water-spout! a water-spout. Sam! Sam! Sam! Where are you, First Samuel.

Registrar. What's all this?

North. A mystery, Sam. Not a cloud in the sky—yet, look here—

Registrar. A mystery indeed! Never till this day beheld I the beau-ideal of a drowned rat.

North (*musing*). There are more things in heaven and earth than are dreamt of in your philosophy, Samuel.

Registrar. My philosophy! I make no pretensions to philosophy —but won't you walk into the Tent, and change yourself, sir.

North. A Scotticism, Sam, a palpable Scotticism. No—I will never change myself; but to the last be Christopher North. Ah, Sam! I am quite up to your tricks; but was it kind—was it fair, to steal upon my slumbers so, and take advantage of my sleeping innocence? "I had a dream, yet 'twas not all a dream." I thought I was at Windermere, beneath the shadow of the sycamore, and that for me, and for me alone,

"Jocund morn
Stood tiptoe on you rosy mountain's head."

Registrar. And here we are in the Fairy's Cleugh, among the mountains of——

North. Peebles-shire, Dumfries-shire, Lanarkshire, for here all three counties get inextricably entangled; yet in their pastoral peace they quarrel not for the dominion of this nook, central in the hill-heart, and haunted by the silent people.

Registrar. You do not call us silent people! Why, you out-talk a spinning-jenny, and the mill-clapper stops in despair at the volubility of your speech.

North. Elves—Sam—Elves. Is it not the Fairy's Cleugh!

Registrar. And here have been "little feet that print the ground." But I took them for those of hares——

North. These, Sam, are not worm-holes—nor did Mole the miner upheave these pretty little pyramids of primroses—for these, Sam, are all Fairy palaces—and yonder edifice that towers above the Lady-Fern—therein now sleeps—let us speak low, and disturb her not—the Fairy Queen, waiting for the moonlight—and soon as the orb shows her rim rising from behind Birk-fell—away to the ring will she be gliding with all the ladies of her Court——

Registrar. And we will join the dance—Kit——

North. Remember—then—that I am engaged to——

Registrar. So am I—three-deep.

North. Do you know, Sam, that I dreamed a dream?

Registrar. You cannot keep a secret, for you blab in your sleep.

North. Ay—both talk and walk. But I dreamed that I saw a Fairy's funeral, and that I was myself a fairy.

Registrar. A warlock.

North. No—a pretty little female fairy, not a span long.

Registrar. Ha! ha! ha!

North. And they asked me to sing her dirge, and then I sang—for sorrow in sleep, Sam, is sometimes sweeter than any joy—ineffably sweet—and thus comes back wavering into my memory the elegiac strain.

THE FAIRY'S BURIAL.

Where shall our sister rest?
  Where shall we bury her?
To the grave's silent breast
  Soon we must hurry her!
Gone is the beauty now
  From her cold bosom!
Down droops her livid brow,
  Like a wan blossom!

Not to those white lips cling
  Smiles or caresses!
Dull is the rainbow wing,
  Dim the bright tresses!
Death now hath claimed his spoil—
  Fling the pall over her!
Lap we earth's lightest soil!
  Wherewith to cover her!

Where down in yonder vale
  Lilies are growing,
Mourners the pure and pale,
  Sweet tears bestowing!
Morning and evening dews
  Will they shed o'er her;
Each night their task renews
  How to deplore her!

Here let the fern grass grow,
  With its green drooping!
Let the narcissus blow,
  O'er the wave stooping!
Let the brook wander by,
  Mournfully singing!
Let the wind murmur nigh,
  Sad echoes bringing!

And when the moonbeams shower,
  Tender and holy,
Light on the haunted hour
  Which is ours solely,
Then will we seek the spot
  Where thou art sleeping,
Holding thee unforgot
  With our long weeping!

Ambrose (*rushing out of the Tent*). Mr. Tickler, sirs, Mr. Tickler! Yonder's his head and shoulders rising over the knoll—in continuation of his herald the rod.

North (*savagely*). Go to the devil, sir.

Ambrose (*petrified*). Ah! ha! ha! ha! si—sir—pa—pa—pard—

North (*unmollified*). Go to the devil, I say, sir. Are you deaf?

Ambrose (*going, going, gone*). I beseech you—Mr. Registrar—

North (*grimly*). "How like a fawning publican he looks!"

Registrar. A most melancholy example of a truth I never believed before, that poetical and human sensibility are altogether distinct—nay, perhaps incompatible! North, forgive me (*North grasps the Crutch*); but you should be ashamed of yourself—nay, *strike, but hear me!*

North (*smiling after a sort*). Well—Themistocles.

Registrar. You awaken out of a dream-dirge of Faery Land—where you, by force of strong imagination, were a female fairy, not a span long—mild as a musical violet, if one might suppose one, "by a mossy stone half-hidden to the eye," inspired with speech.

North. I feel the delicacy of the compliment.

Registrar. Then you feel something very different, sir, I assure you, from what I intended, and still intend, you shall feel; for your treatment of my friend Mr. Ambrose was shocking.

North. I declare on my conscience, I never saw Ambrose!

Registrar. What! aggravate your folly by falsehood! Then are you a lost man—and——

North. I thought it a stirk staggering in upon me at the close of a stanza that——

Registrar. And why did you say "sir"? Nay—nay—that won't pass. From a female fairy, not a span long, "and even the gentlest of all gentle things," you suffer yourself to transform you into a Fury six feet high! and wantonly insult a man who would not hurt the feelings of a wasp.

North (*humbly*). I hope I am not a wasp.

Registrar. I hope not, sir; but permit me, who am not one of your youngest friends, to say to you confidentially, that you were just now very unlike a bee.

North (*hiding his face with both his hands*). All sting—and no honey. Spare me, Sam.

Registrar. I will. But the world would not have credited it, had she heard it with her own ears. Are you aware, sir, that you told Mr. Ambrose "to go to the devil"?

North (*agitated*). And has he gone?

Registrar (*beckoning on Ambrose, who advances*). Well, Ambrose?

North. Ambrose! do you forgive me?

Ambrose (*falling on one knee*). No—no—no—my dear sir—my honored master——

North. Alas! Ambrose—I am not even master of myself.

Ambrose. It was all my fault, sir. I ought to have looked first to see if you were in the poetics. Such intrusion was most unpardonable—for (*smiling and looking down*) shall mere man obtrude on the hour of inspiration—when

> "The poet's eye in a fine frenzy rolling,
> Glances from heaven to earth, from earth to heaven,
> And as imagination bodies forth
> The forms of things unknown, turns them to shape,
> And gives to airy nothing
> A local habitation and a name!"

Registrar. Who suffers, Ambrose?

Ambrose. Shakspere, sir. Mr. Tickler! Mr. Tickler! Mr. Tickler! (*catching up his voice*) Mr. Tick——

Registrar. Yes—verily—and 'tis no other!

Tickler (*stalking up the brae—rod in hand—and creel on his shoulder—with his head well laid back—and his nose pretty perpendicular with earth and sky*). Well—boys—what's the news? And how are you off for soap? How long here? Ho! ho! The Tent.

North. Since Monday evening—and if my memory serves me right, this is either Thursday or Friday. Whence, Tim?

Tickler. From the West. But is there any porter?

Ambrose (*striving to draw*). Ay—ay—sir.

Tickler. You may as well try to uproot that birk. Give it me. (*Puts the bottle between his feet—stoops—and lays on his strength.*)

Registrar (*jogging* NORTH). Oh! for George Cruikshank!

Tickler (*loud explosion and much smoke*). The jug.

Ambrose. Here, sir.

Tickler (*teeming*). Brown stout. The porter's in spate.* THE QUEEN.

Omnes. Hurra! hurra! hurra! hurra! hurra! hurra! hurra! hurra! hurra!

Ambrose. Hip—hip—hip—

Registrar. Hush!

Tickler. Hech! That draught made my lugs crack. Oh! Kit—there was a grand ploy at Paisley.

North. Since Gordon was not to be the man, I rejoice in Sandford.†

Tickler. Dan dang the Radicals all into the dirt. The lad has spunk, Kit—is eloquent—and will do. He did not leave Crawfurd the likeness o' a dowg.

North. I hope he left Douglas the likeness of a gander.

Tickler. Scarcely. John waddled away, with his disconsolate dowp (Anglice, dolp) sweeping the dust from the plainstones so clean, that he left behind him no print of his splay web-feet. He could not so much as cry quack. His plight was so piteous, that the brown-duffled damsels at the mouths of closes absolutely shed tears. The *clique* accompanied him across the Abercorn Arms—I speak of what I saw—for I was leaning over some pretty dears who filled the bow-window—and he did his best to look *magnifique*, the gander at the head of his goslings—but it would not do. Once he paused before a pretty large mob of small ragamuffins, as if he would address them in his native lingo—but his opened bill gave but a gasp, as if the iron hand of adversity clutched his neck—and all he uttered was a hiss.

North. Poor payment to his supporters.

Registrar. His bill—at sight.

Ambrose (*laughing*). Very good, Mr. Registrar—very good. The wittiest of the witty are you, sir—but, pardon me—nature gave Ambrose a quick sense of the ludicrous——

Registrar. And of the pathetic.

* *Spate*—a flood, in foam.—M.

† Sir Daniel Kyte Sandford, who had greatly distinguished himself at the University of Oxford, was appointed to the chair of Greek, at Glasgow University, at an unusually early age. As a teacher, he was most successful, bringing great enthusiasm in cooperation with extensive learning. Among other works of his, an Introduction to the Writing of Greek has long been a class book in Scotland. When the Grey Ministry brought in their Reform Bill, Sir Daniel used his eloquence, which was great, in advocacy of popular rights. When the Bill passed, he was sent to Parliament by the Scottish borough of Paisley, which he represented for some time, but did not take the position there which his friends and the public expected he could attain. He died in 1838, in the prime of life. Dr. Sandford the episcopal Bishop of Edinburgh, was his father.—M.

North. Waddled he, think ye, Tickler, all the way from Cross to Cross?

Tickler. The story ran that he took rest and refuge of the top of the Cheap-and-Nasty.

North. On the road are there no pools?

Tickler. But one; and in he went. 'Twas thick and slab—and he came out green mud.

North. After dinner I shall dedicate to him a voluntary and extemporaneous song.

Tickler. No. Now's the time. I shall save you the trouble, Kit—for I have an elegy in my pocket. You know Burns's fine lines, written among the ruins of Lincluden Abbey. My genius is original, and I scorn to imitate even rare Rab—but taking a solitary stroll the evening after the election, through a scene that used to be a favorite haunt of mine of old, I know not how it happened, but Rab's lines came into my mind—and sitting down on a tombstone, I saw a vision.

Ambrose (*pale*). A ghost, sir?

Tickler. Ay—Brosey—a ghost. You are a topping elocutionist, Ambrose, and I would gladly request you to recite. But my MS. is very cat-paw-ish—and, besides, poets like to tip off their verses trippingly from their own tongue; so here goes—

THE GHOST OF THE GANDER.

"Alas, poor ghost!"

Through Glasgow's fair town, in the dead of the night,
  As homeward I went on my way,
Each star in the heavens shone beauteous and bright,
And the goddess in mantle of silvery light
  Held her gentle and ladylike sway.

By the church of St. Mungo I silently pass'd,
  And thought on the days that are gone,
And how long *any* church might be likely to last
In the new Reformation that's coming so fast—
  When the bell of the steeple toll'd ONE!

And the sound of that dismal and deafening bell
  Was hardly yet out of mine ear,
When there suddenly rose a strange, ominous smell,
And 'twas fearful to think, but too easy to tell,
  That THE GHOST OF THE GANDER was near!

And lo! the fat Phantom—the spectre was there!
  My nerves they are none of the best—
But I mutter'd my shortest and readiest prayer
And, holding my nose with particular care
  I gazed on the Goose of the West.

Oh! how changed, since the day when he carried the prize,
  Was his carcass, all blister'd and bare!

Yet, changed as he was, you might still recognise
Some features of more than unnatural size,
  And THE BADGE he continues to wear.

'Twas a sad and a sorrowful thing to behold
  The featherless spirit of wo,
As standing before me he shiver'd with cold,
Yet thought with affright of his roasting of old,
  When by Ambrose he first was laid low!

And while all now was hush'd in a stillness profound,
  'Twas dismal and doleful to hear
The Phantom, with voice of a tremulous sound,
As he pour'd forth his griefs to the echoes around,
  Uuconscious that mortal was near.

"Oh! hard is my lot," did the Gander exclaim,
  "Cut off in my prowess and pride,
While Glasgow, fair Glasgow, the scene of my fame,
Makes a jest of my fate—and my well-earned name
  Is the sport both of CART and of CLYDE!

"I might have my frailties—but oh! was it meet
  That my merits should thus be forgot?
And that here I should *stand*—for alas for my *seat!*—
An example of honest ambition's defeat
  By a foul and unnatural plot!

"My place in our National Council of Geese
  I almost had reckon'd secure;
And oft did I think how my fame would increase,
And inferior gabbling all suddenly cease—
  When the Gander advanced on the floor!

"But, visions of grandeur and glory, farewell!
  My spirit, disturb'd and distrest,
To the owls and the echoes the story must tell—
How formerly flourish'd and recently fell
  The unfortunate Goose of the West."

It ceased; and surprised, as I surely well might,
  I thought, as I went on my way,
That the very next morning to HIBBERT I'd write
How thus I had learnt from a spirit of night
  That "every Goose has his day!"

Omnes. Alas, poor ghost!

Ambrose. He! he! he! he!

Registrar. I wonder, sir, you do not pitch your tent—take up house—all the summer months among the hills or mountains.

North. For an old man, Sam, fondish of literature, nothing like a suburban summer residence like the Lodge. I confess I cannot be now without a glance at the new publications—and you cannot get that in rural retirement. A well-chosen library, consisting of the same everlasting books, aggravates the wretchedness of a wet day in the country—and it is desirable that the key of the room be lost, or something incurably wrong with the lock. The man who reads only all the best authors is sure to have a most unmeaning face.

Registrar. I would rather read all the worst.

Tickler. That you might have a countenance beaming with intelligence. Members of Parliament seem to read no books at all. I know no jabber so sickening as jabber about "the House." A puppy of a Representative conceives all human knowledge confined to "a Committee of the whole house"—to which he believes all things under the sun have been "referred"—or made the subject of a "motion." He loses his seat, sings small, and for the rest of his life—*

Registrar. Is a sumph. For a year or two he is occasionally heard intimidating one of the Seven young men with "when I was in Parliament;" but people above the salt look incredulous or contemptuous, and the *quandam* statesman restricts himself on "Divisions" to his poor wife.

North. No politics, Sam. Pray, did either of you ever read the Solitary, a Poem, in Three Parts, by Charles Whitehead!†

Both. No.

North. It is full of fine thoughts and feelings, and contains some noble descriptions. Some of the stanzas committed themselves to my memory—and I think I can recite three, suggested by the quiet of this scene—for they are pregnant with tempest.

"As when, of amorous night uncertain birth,
The giant of still noontide, weary grown,
Crawls sultrily along the steaming earth,
And basks him in the meadows sunbeam-strown,
Anon, his brow collapses to a frown,
Unto his feet he springs, and bellows loud,
With uncouth rage pulls the rude tempest down,
Shatters the woods, beneath his fury bow'd,
And hunts the frighted winds, and huddles cloud on cloud.

"Nor rests, but by the heat to madness stung,
With headlong speed tramples the golden grain,
And, at a bound, over the mountains flung,
Grasps the reluctant thunder by the name,
And drags it back, girt with a sudden chain
Of thrice-braced lightning; now, more fiercely dire,
Slipt from its holds, flies down the hissing rain;
The laboring welkin teems with leaping fire
That strikes the straining oak, and smites the glimmering spire.

"And yet at length appeas'd he sinks, and spent,
Gibbers far off over the misty hills,
And the stain'd sun, through a cloud's jagged rent,

* He usually makes an epoch of the great event of his life, and thenceforth, for ever, dates every event, private or public, with "When I sat in Parliament for the Borough of So-and-So.'—M.

† Mr. Whitehead subsequently wrote a romance called "Richard Savage," founded on the life of Johnson's friend.—M.

> Goes down and all the west with glory fills;
> A fresher bloom the odorous earth distils,
> A richer green reviving nature spreads,
> The water-braided rainbow melting, spills
> Her liquid light into the air, and sheds
> Her lovely hues upon the flowers' dejected heads."

Registrar. You have a miraculous memory, sir.

North. I have indeed. I can remember nothing that does not interest me—and months of my existence in every year now, Sam, are a blank. That faculty called Recollection, in me is weak. When I try to exert it, I seem to "hunt half a day for a forgotten dream." But the past comes upon me in sudden flashes—without active will of my own—and sometimes one flash illuminates the whole mental horizon, and lo! lying outspread below what was once a whole present world. No idea of past time distinguishes it as a dream—I am, as it were, born again—heaven and earth recreated—and with the beautiful vision, believed to be a reality, is blended the burning spirit of youth.

Registrar. That is Imagination, sir—Genius—not Memory.

North. No, Sam, it is neither Memory, nor Imagination, nor Genius, but a mysterious re-revelation—made not *by* but *to* my soul—the same as happens to all men in sleep.

Registrar. Is it true, sir, that you have by heart all Spenser's Faery Queen?

North. As great a lie as ever was uttered. But thousands and tens of thousands of small poems lie buried alive in my mind; and when I am in a perfectly peaceful mood, there is a resurrection of the beautiful, like flocks of flowers issuing out of the ground, at touch of Spring. I am in a perfectly peaceful mood now. And since you like to hear me recite poetry, my dear Registrar, I will murmur you a few stanzas, that must have committed themselves to my memory, for I feel assured I did not write them, yet I have no recollection of them—mind that word—and perhaps they will take their flight now, like a troop of doves that on a sudden are seen wheeling in the sunshine, and then melt away from the eye to be seen nevermore.

> Come forth, come forth! it were a sin
> To stay at home to-day!
> Stay no more loitering within,
> Come to the woods away!
>
> The long green grass is filled with flowers,
> The clover's deep dim red
> Is brighten'd with the morning showers,
> That on the winds have fled.
>
> Scatter'd about the deep blue sky,
> In white and flying clouds,

Some bright brief rains are all that lie
  Within those snowy shrouds.

Now, look!—our weather-glass is spread—
  The pimpernel, whose flower
Closes its leaves of spotted red
  Against a rainy hour.

That first pale green is on the trees;
  That verdure more like bloom;
Yon elm-bough hath a horde of bees,
  Lured by the faint perfume.

The cherry orchard flings on high
  Its branches, whence are strown
Blossoms like snow, but with an eye
  Dark, maiden, as thine own!

As yet our flowers are chiefly those
  Which fill the sun-touch'd bough,
Within the sleeping soil repose
  Those of the radiant brow.

But we have daisies, which, like love
  Or hope, spring every where;
And primroses, which droop above
  Some self-consuming care.

So sad, so spiritual, so pale,
  Born all too near the snow,
They pine for that sweet southern gale,
  Which they will never know,

It is too soon for deeper shade;
  But let us skirt the wood,
The blackbird there, whose nest is made
  Sits singing to her brood.

These pleasant hours will soon be flown;
  Love! make no more delay—
I am too glad to be alone,
  Come forth with me to-day!

Ambrose. Dinner on the table, sir.

North. As my old friend Crewe—the University Orator at Oxford—concludes his fine poem of Lewesdon Hill—

"To-morrow for severer thought, but now
To dinner, and keep festival to-day."

SCENE II.—*Time four o'clock. Scene changes to the interior of the tent.* DINNER,—*Salmon—Turbot—Trout—Cod—Haddocks—Whitings—Turkey—Goose—Veal-pie—Beefsteak ditto—Chicken—Ham*—THE ROUND,—*Damson, Cherry, Currant, Grozet* (this year's) *Tarts, &c. &c. &c. &c. &c. &c.*

SCENE III.—*Time, five o'clock. Without change of place.* DESSERT,—*Melons—Grapes—Grozets—Pine-Apples—Golden Pippins—New-Yorkers—Filberts—Hazels.* WINES,—*Champagne—Claret—Port—Madeira—Cold Punch in the Dolphin*—GLENLIVET IN THE TOWER OF BABEL—*Water in the Well.*

North. Ambrose, tuck up the tent door. Fling it wide open.

(AMBROSE *lets in heaven.*)

Registrar. "Beautiful exceedingly!"

North. Ne'er before was tent pitched in the Fairy's Cleugh! I selected the spot, gents, from a memory, where lie many thousand worlds—great and small—and of the tiny not one sweeter, sure, than this before our eyes!

Registrar. I wonder how—by what fine process—you chose! Yet, why, might I ask my own heart—why now do I fix on one face—one form—and see but them—haunted as my imagination might be with the images of all the loveliest in the land!

Tickler. Sam, you look as fresh as a daisy.

North. That is truly a vista. Those hills—for we must not call them mountains—how gently they come gliding down from the sky, on each side of the valelike glen!——

Registrar. Vale-like glen! Thank you, North—that is the very word.

North. —separated but by no wide level of broomy greensward—if that be a level, broken as you see it with frequent knolls—most of them rounded softly off into pastures, some wooded, and here and there, one with but a single tree, the white-stemmed, sweet-scented birk—

Registrar. Always ladylike with her delicate tresses, however humble her birth!

North. Should ye say that the "spirit of the scene" is sylvan or pastoral?

Registrar. Both.

North. Sam! how is it I see no sheep?

Registrar. Sheep and lambs there must be many—latent somewhere; and I have often noticed, sir, a whole green region without a symptom of life, though I knew that it was not a store-farm, and that there must be some hundred scores of the woolly people within startling of the same low mutter of the thunder-cloud.

North. How soon a rill becomes a river!

Registrar. A boy a man!

North. That is the source of the Woodburn, Sam, that well within five yards of our tent.

Registrar. How the Naiad must be enjoying the wine-cooler! Imbibing—inhaling the aroma, yet returning more than she receives, and tinging the taste of that incomparable claret—vintage 1811—with her own sweet breath! Whose?

North. Albert Cay's.*

Registrar. Listen, lads—all around, and above,

> "Sounds that are silence to the ear."

I see no insects, yet the air lowly hums—that ground-breath must be that of the grass growing—of the soft unfolding of many millions of flowers—bees utter not a word at their work, but murmur as they fly, for the music is in their wings—yet coming and going, the wilderness can scarcely hear them, for 'tis only when careering round and round some strange object that the creatures make much noise. Seldom have I seen so far and high up, so soon in the season, such splendid moths. But of all life, theirs is the most entirely divested of sound. Fine-ear himself could not have heard that lovely one alight on the stone—still and steady the living speck as a weather-stain, yet shut your eyes a few moments—look, and it is gone!

North.

> "O many are the poets that are sown
> By Nature."

and thou, dear Sam, art of the number; but "wanting the accomplishment of verse."

Registrar. I occasionally amuse myself with a metrical version from the Greek; and I hope to send you a trifle or two for your next Anthology. We scholars in England liked those articles very much indeed;—you should resume the series. Here is a silly thought from Eubulus.†

Tickler. Eubulus! Give us the Greek, Sam.

Registrar.

> Τρεῖς γάρ μόνους κρατῆρας ἐγκεραννύω
> Τοῖς εὖ φρονοῦσι· τὸν μὲν ὑγιείας ἕνα,
> Ὃν πρῶτον ἐκπίνουσι· τὸν δε δεύτερον
> Ἔρωτος ἡδονῆς τε· τὸν δὲ τρίτον δ' ὕπνου,
> Ὃν εἰς πίοντες ὁι σοφοὶ κεκλκημένοι
> Ὄικαδε βαδιζουσ'. ὁ δὲ τέταρτος ὀυκέτι
> Ἡμέτερός ἐστ', ἀλλ' ὕβρεως. ὁ δὲ πέμπτος, βοῆς.
> Ἔκτος δὲ μανίας, ὥστε καὶ βάλλειν ποιεῖν.
> Πολὺς γὰρ εἰς ἓν μικρὸν ἀγγεῖον χυθεὶς
> Ὑποσκελίζει ῥᾶστα τοὺς πεπωκότας.

* Wine merchant in Edinburgh, famous for his claret—as Sneyd was in Dublin.—M.

† Eubulides of Miletus, the preceptor of Demosthenes.—M.

Tickler (*in amazement*). Πολυφλοισβοιο θαλασσης!

Registrar. Genitive case for the vocative! Oh, soul of Sir John Cheek! Now, Tim, you smile at my scholarship; but here is old Eubulus in the English tongue.—(*Sings.*)

1.

Three goblets of wine
  Alone should comprise
The extent of the tipple
  Of those that are wise.

2.

The first is for health;
  And the second I measure,
To be quaffed for the sake
  Of love, and of pleasure.

3.

The third is for sleep;
  And, while it is ending,
The prudent will homeward
  Be thinking of wending.

4.

The fourth, not our own,
  Makes insolence glorious;
And the fifth ends in shouting,
  And clamor uproarious.

5.

And those who a sixth
  Down their weasands are pouring,
Already are bruising,
  And fighting, and flooring.

6.

Oh! the tight little vessel,
  If often we fill it,
How it trips up the heels
  Of those who may swill it!

Tickler. Registrar, thou warblest well!—and Eubulus was a trump.

North. Cuckoo! cuckoo! cuckoo! Yonder she goes!—see, see, Sam!—flitting along the faint blue haze on the hill-side, across the burn. In boyhood, never could I catch a glimpse of the bird any more than Wordsworth.

"For thou wert still a hope!—a joy!
Still longed for, never seen!"

But so 'tis with us in our old age. All the mysteries that held our youth in wonderment, and made life poetry, dissolve—and we are sensible that they were all illusions: while other mysteries grow more awful; and what we sometimes hoped, in the hour of passion, might be illusions, are seen to be God's own truths, terrible to sinners, and wearing a ghastly aspect in the gloom of the grave!

Tickler. Cuckoo! cuckoo! cuckoo!

North. She has settled again on some spray—for she is always mute, gents, as she flies! And I have stood right below her, within three yards of her anomalous ladyship, as, down head and up tail, with wings slightly opening from her sides, and her feathers shivering, she took far and wide possession of the stillness with her voice, mellow as if she lived on honey; and indeed I suspect, Sam—though the bridegroom eluded my ken—that with them two 'twas the honey-moon. Have you seen Mudie's British Birds, Tickler? 'Tis a delightful work—and I must have an article on it in a month or two—for Mr. Mudie is one of the naturalists I love best—he has studied nature in the fields and woods, and by the banks and braes of streams, all up to the highest waterfall, beyond which there are neither trouts—

Registrar. Nor minnows.

North. My dear Registrar, those were charming lines you repeated to me last night. Even Tickler would be moved by them.

Tickler. I have a thorough contempt for all poetry; and I beg leave to say now, before going farther, that if we are to be bothered with any more lines, and absurd——

North. I fear, Mr. Tickler, there has been some mistake. Pray, have you got in your pocket my card of invitation to the Tent?

Tickler. Um!

North. Not that Sam and I had any objections to your joining us; but as your presence was quite an unexpected pleasure, perhaps, on reconsideration, you will permit the Registrar to grant my request.

(TICKLER *scrapes caddis from his cotton jacket and stuffs his ears.*)

Registrar.

Do you see our vessel riding
  At her anchor in yon bay,
Like a sleeping sea-bird biding
  For the morrow's onward way?
See her white wings folded round her
  Rocked upon the lulling deep—
Hath the silent moonlight bound her
  With a chain of peace and sleep?

Seems she not, as if enchanted
  To that lone and lovely place,
Henceforth ever to be haunted
  By that fair ship's shadowy grace?
Yet come here again to-morrow,
  Not a vestige will remain;
Though those sweet eyes strain in sorrow,
  They will watch the waves in vain.

'Twas for this I bade thee meet me;
  For one parting word and tear;
Other lands and lips may greet me,
  None will ever seem so dear.
Other lands—I may say other!
  Mine again I shall not see!
I have left my aged mother—
  She has other sons than me.

Where my father's bones are lying,
  There mine own will never lie;
Where the pale wild-flowers are sighing
  Sweet beneath a summer-sky.
Mine will be less hallow'd ending,
  Mine will be a wilder grave;
When the shriek and shout are blending,
  Or the tempest sweeps the wave.

Or, perhaps, a fate more lonely,
In some sick and foreign ward,
When my weary eyes meet only
Hired nurses or sullen guard.
Be it wound or be it fever,
When my soul's death-doom is cast,
One remembrance will not leave her,
Thine will linger to the last.

Dearest maiden! thou art weeping!
Must I from those eyes remove?
Hath thy heart no soft pulse sleeping,
Which might waken into love?
No! I see thy brow is frozen,
And thy look is cold and strange;
Oh! when once the heart is chosen,
Well I know it cannot change!

And I know thy heart has spoken
That another's it must be;
Scarce I wish that pure faith broken,
Though the falsehood were for me.
No! be still that guileless creature
Who upon my boyhood shone;
Couldst thou change thy angel nature,
Half my trust in Heaven were gone.

With these parting words I sever
All my ties of youth and home,
Kindred, friends, good-by for ever!
See! my boat cuts through the foam!
Wind, tide, time, alike are pressing,
I must leave my native shore;
One first kiss, and one last blessing—
Farewell, love, we meet no more!

Tickler (*taking the cotton from his ears*). I wish, North, you would either fine me in a bumper, or force me to sing a song.

North. I will do both. Up with your little finger—no heel-taps, sirrah—good—now, Tim, your stave.

Tickler.

Tune—The Brown Jug.

Though I can't make a speech, yet a bumper I crave,
And I'll give you my toast in an old-fashioned stave—
It is not the King, nor our good Tory Queen,
Nor Army, nor Navy, nor Church, that I mean—
No toast such as these down your throats will I cram—
I'll give you the health of the Registrar Sam!

The Registrar Sam! it's a big-sounding name,
And yet let us hope that he still is the same—
The same honest Sam that we knew him of yore
When honors, still higher, so meekly he bore,
That all men allowed that the Lion and Lamb
Were too feeble a type of the Grand Warden Sam.

Then amidst former greatness, what frolic and fun!
What a lack of all "weariness under the sun!"
What flashes of glee from that eloquent face,
The planet, the pole-star, the moon of the Place!*
They may talk of big Peter—but he's all a sham—
Mere pinchbeck, compared to the sterling of Sam!

Oh! how oft has it gladden'd each true Tory heart
To witness his feats in the thirst-slaking art;
I call it not *drinking*, for that were a word,
In speaking of Sam, altogether absurd—
Let us rather declare that no mortal e'er swam
On the spring-tide of Bacchus so buoyant as Sam.

Yet it was not in wit, nor yet was it in wine,
That alone he held sway—for Sam woo'd the whole Nine—
It's now an old story, yet many a tongue
Still rejoices to tell of the days of Bill Young,
When Baxter's fine speeches (which some thought *Balaam*)
Were sure to call forth something finer from Sam.

And then, though the Muses his youth might engage,
Still science severe fix'd his more mature age;
And Oxford shall glory for many a day
In "Sedgwick and Sam" 'mong her learned array,†
For long may you wander by Isis or Cam,
Ere you chance to fall in with a fellow like Sam!

Such has Sam ever been, and long, long may he be
Precisely the Sam he has still been to me!
The Thistle we now must entwine with the Rose, (*Affetuoso.*)
But our hearts still are with him wherever he goes,
So now, in conclusion, I make my salaam,
By proposing the toast of the evening—SAM!

Registrar (*rising*). Mr. Chairman (*bowing, with his hand on his heart.*) Mr. Vice (*bowing*). On rising, gentlemen——

Ambrose (*rushing into the Tent, stark naked, except his flannel drawers.*) Hurra! hurra! hurra!—hurra! hurra! hurra!—hurra! hurra! hurra! Who'll dance—who'll dance with me—waltz—jig—Lowland reel—Highland fling—gallopade? Hurra! hurra! hurra! (*Keeps dancing round the Tent table, yelling, and snapping his fingers.*)

North. Be seated, gentlemen—I see how it is—he has been drinking of the elf-well, up among the rocks behind the Tent, and human lip never touched that cold stream, but, man or woman, lost his or her seven senses, and was insane for life.

Registrar. A pleasant prospect.

Tickler. That may be—but, confound me if Ambrose be the man to be caught in that kind of trap. Where's the Tower of Babel!

* Picardy Place, where Ambrose's Hotel is. The Peter here named was Patrick Robertson, now one of the Lords of Session in Edinburgh—a large man, full of wit and frolic.—M.

† It is Cambridge, not Oxford, which can boast of Dr. Adam Sedgwick, the geologist, as her Woodwardian Professor.—M.

North. There!

Ambrose (*pirouetting*). Look yonder, mine honored master, through those rocks.

North. Nay, Brose, I can see as far through a millstone, or a milestone either, as most men; but as for looking through rocks——

Ambrose. I saw him, with these blessed eyes of mine, I saw him—on horseback, sir, driving down the hill, yonder, sir, at full gallop——

North. Whom? ye saw whom?

Ambrose. Himself, sir—his very own self, sir—as I hope to be saved.

Registrar. I fear his case is hopeless. Those sudden accesses are fatal.

Tickler. Why, his drawers will be at his heels if——

Ambrose (*somewhat subsiding*). I had gone in to the dookin', gentlemen, as you say in Scotland, and was ploutering about in the pool, when, just as I had squeezed the water out of my eyes, after a plunge, I chanced to look up the hillside, and there I saw him—with these blessed eyes I saw him—his own very self.—(*Horses' hoofs heard at full gallop, nearing the Tent.*)

Tickler. The Wild Huntsman!

(*Horse and rider charge the Tent—horse all of a sudden halts—thrown back on his haunches—and rider flying over his head, alights on his feet—while his foraging cap spins over the Lion's fiery mane, now drooping in the afternoon calm from the mast-head.*)

Omnes. THE SHEPHERD! THE SHEPHERD! THE SHEPHERD! hurra! hurra! hurra! hurra! hurra! hurra! hurra! hurra! hurra!

Shepherd. Hurraw! hurraw! hurraw!

North (*white as a sheet, and seeming about to swoon*). Water!

Shepherd. Whare's the strange auld tyke? Whare's the queer auld fallow? Where's the canty auld chiel? Whare's the dear auld deevil? Oh! North—North—North—North—ma freen—ma brither—ma father—lat's tak anither intil ane anither's arms—let's kiss ane anither's cheek—as the guid cheevalry knichts used to do—when, haen fa'en oot about some leddy-luve, or some disputed laun', or some king's changefu' favor, or aiblins aboot naething ava but the stupit lees o' some evil tongues, they happened to forgather when riding opposite ways through a wood, and flingin' themsells, wi' ae feelin' and ae thocht, aff their twa horses, cam' clashin' thegither wi' their mailed breists, and began sobbin' in the silence o' the auncient aiks that were touched to their verra cores to see sic forgiveness and sic affection atween thae twa stalwart champions, wha, tho' baith noo weeping' like weans or women, had aften ridden, side by side thegither, wi' shields on their briests and lang lances shootin' far oot fearsomely afore them, intil the press o' battle, while their chargers, red-wat-shod, gaed gallopin' wi' their hoofs that never ance touched the grun' for men's faces bash'd bluidy, and their sodden corpses squelchin' at every spang o' the flyin' dragons. But what do I mean by a' this talkin' to mysell? Pity me—Mr. North—but you're white's a ghaist! Let me bear ye in my airms intil the Tent. (SHEPHERD *carries* NORTH *into the Tent.*)

North. I was much to blame, James—but——

Shepherd. I was muckle mair to blame mysell nor you, sir—and——

North. Why, James, it is by no means improbable that you were——

Shepherd. O ye auld Autocrat! But will ye promise me—gin I promise ye——

North. Any thing, James, in the power of mortal man to perform.

Shepherd. Gie's your haun! Noo repeat the words after me—(NORTH *keeps earnestly repeating the words*)—I swear, in this Tent pitched in the Fairy's Cleugh, in presence of Timothy Tickler and Sam An——

North. They are not in the Tent.

Shepherd. I wasna observin'. That's delicate. That I wull never breathe a whusper even to my ain heart—at the laneliest hour o' midnight—except it be when I am sayin' my prayers—dinna sab, sir—o' ony misunderstaundin' that ever happened atween us twa—either about Mawga, or ony ither toppic—as lang's I leeve—an' am no deserted by my senses—but am left in fu' possession o' the gift o' reason—an' I noo dicht aff the tablets o' my memory ilka letter o' ony ugly record, that the enemy, takin' advantage o' the corruption o' oor fallen natur'—contreeved to scarify there, wi' the pint o' an airn pen—red-hot frae yon wicked place—I noo dicht them a' aff, just as I dicht aff frae this table thae wine-draps wi' ma sleeve—and I forgie ye frae the verra bottom o' ma sowl—wi' as perfeck forgiveness—as if you ware my ain brither, deein' at hame in his father's house—shune after his return frae a lang voyage out-owre the sea!

(NORTH *and the* SHEPHERD *again embrace—their faces wax exceedingly cheerful—and they sit for a little while without saying a word.*)

North. My dear James, have you dined?

Shepherd. Dined? Why man, I've had ma fowre-oors.* But I maun tell ye a' about it. A bit lassie, you see, that had cum to your frien' Scottie's to pay a visit to a sister o' hers—a servant in the family—that was rather dwinin'—frae the kintrie down about Annandale-wise, past by the Tent in the gray o' the morning, yes-

* *Fowre-oors*—luncheon, taken four hours after breakfast.—M.

terday, afore ony ane o' you were out o' the blankets, except a cretur that, frae the description, maun hae been Tappytourie, and she learned frae him that the Tent belanged to a great lord they ca'd North—Lord North—and that he had come out on a shootin' and a fishin' ploy, and forbye, to tak a plan o' a' the hills, in order to mak a moddle o' them in cork, wi' quicksiller for the lochs and rinnin' waters, and sheets o' beaten siller for the waterfa's, and o' beaten gold for the elements at sunset—and that twa ither shinin' characters were in his reteenue—wham Tammy ca'd to her—as she threep'd—Sir Teemothy Tickleham Bart. o' Southside, and the Lord High Registrar o' Lunnon. Ma heart lap to ma mouth, and then after some flutterin' became as heavy's a lump o' cauld lead. The wife gied me sic a smile! And then wee Jamie was a' the while, in his affeetionat way, leanin' again' ma knee. I took a walk by mysell; and a' was licht. Forthwith I despatched some gillies to wauken the Forest. I never steekit an ee, and by skreigh o' day was aff on the beast. But I couldna ken how ye micht be fennin' in the Tent for fish, sae I thocht I micht as weel tak a whup at the Meggat. How they lap! I filled ma creel afore the dew-melt; and as it's out o' the poor o' ony mortal man wi' a heart to gie owre fishin' in the Meggat durin' a tak, I kent by the sun it was nine-hours, and by that time I had a' my pouches, the braid o' the tail o' some o' them whappin' again' ma elbows. You'll no be surprised, Mr. North—for though you're far from bein' sic a gude angler as you suppose, and as you cry yoursell up in Maga, oh! but you're mad fond o't—that I had clean forgotten the beast! After a lang search, I found him a mile doon the water, and ma certes, for the next twa hours the grass did na grow aneath his heels. I took a hantle o' short cutts, for I ken the kintra better than ony fox. But I forgot I was na on foot—the beast got blawn, and comin' up the Fruid, rested wi' me on Garlet-Dod. The girth burst—aff fell the saddle, and he fairly laid himsalf doon! I feared he had brak his heart, and couldna think o' leavin' him, for, in his extremity, I kent the raven o' Gameshope wad be picked out his een. Sae I just thocht I wad try the Fruid wi' the flee, and put on a professor. The Fruid's fu' o' sma' troots, and I sune had a string. I couldna hae had about me, at this time, ae way and ither, in ma several repositories, string and a', less than thretty dizzen o' troots. I heard the yaud necherin', and kent he had gotten second wun', sae having hidden the saddle among the brakens, munted, and lettin' him tak it easy for the first half hour, as I skirted Earlshaugh holms I got him on the haun gallop, and I needna tell you o' the Arab-like style in which I feenally brought him in, for, considering that I carried wecht, you'll alloo he wad be cheap at a hunder guineas, and for that soom, sir, the beast's your ain! Rax me owre the jug. But didna I see a naked man?

(*Re-enter* TICKLER *and the* REGISTRAR.)

Tickler. O King of the Shepherds, may'st thou live for ever!

Shepherd (*looking inquisitively to* NORTH). Wha's he, that? (*turning to* TICKLER)—Sir, you've the advantage of me; for I really can not say that I ever had the pleasure o' seein' you atween the een afore; but you're welcome to our Tent—sit doun, and gin ye be dry tak' a drink.

Registrar. James?

Shepherd. Ma name's no Jeems. But what though it was? Folk shouldna be sae familiar at first sight. (*To* NORTH *in an under tone.*) A man o' your renown, sir, shou'd really be mair seleck.

Tickler. I beg pardon, sir, but I mistook you for that half-witted body the Ettrick Shepherd.

Shepherd. Ane can pardon ony degree o' stoopidity in a fallow that has sunk sae laigh in his ain esteem, as weel's in that o' the waurld, as to think o' retreevin' his character by pretendin' to pass himself aff, on the mere strength o' the length o' his legs, for sic an incorrigible ne'er-do-weel as Timothy Tickler. But let me tell you, you had better keep a gude tongue in your head, or I'll maybe tak' you by the cuff o' the neck, and turn ye out o' the Tent.

North (*to the* SHEPHERD *in an under tone*). Trot him, James—trot him—he's sensitive.

Shepherd. You maybe ken him? Is't true that he's gotten intil debt, and that Southside's adverteezed?

Tickler (*coloring*). It's a lie.

Shepherd. That proves it to be true. Nay, it amaist, too, pruves you to be Tickler. Oh! nae mair nonsense—nae mair nonsense, sir—Southside, Southside—but I'm happier to see you, sir, than tongue can tell—but as the heart knoweth its ain bitterness, sae knoweth it its ain sweetness too; and noo that I'm sittin' again atween you twa—(*putting one arm over* CHRISTOPHER'S *shoulder, and one over* TIMOTHY'S, *starting up and rushing round the circular* —"guid faith, I'm like to greet." Sam! Sam! Sam!

Registrar. God bless you, James.

Shepherd. And hae ye cum a' the way from Lunnon to the Fairy's Cleugh? And werena ye intendin' to come out to Altrive to see the auld Shepherd? Oh! but we were a' glad, man, to hear o' your appointment, though nane o' us ken very distinctly the natur' o't, some sayin' they had made you a Bishop only without a seat among the Lords, some a Judge o' the Pleas; and there was a sugh for a while—but frae you're bein' here the noo, during the sittin' o' Parliament, that canna weel be true—that the King, by the recommendation o' Lord Broom and Vox, had appointed you his Premier, on the death o' Yearl Grey; but tell me, was the lassie right after a' in denominatin' ye, on the authority o' Tapytourie, Lord High Registrar o' Lunnon, and is the post a sinecure, and a free gift of the Whigs?

Registrar. That, James, is my appointment—but 'tis no sinecure The duties are manifold, difficult, and important.

North. I wish somebody would knock me down for a song.

Shepherd. I'll do that—but recollect—nae fawsettoes—I canna thole fawsettoes—a verra tailor might be ashamed of fawsettoes,—for fawsettoes mak ye think o' something less than the ninety-ninth pairt o' a man—and that's ten times less than a tailor—and amaist naething ava'—sae that the man vanishes intil a pint. Nae fawsettoes.

North (sings).

Tune—John Anderson, my Joe.

Sam Anderson, my Joe Sam, when first I saw that face,
You then were quite a beau, Sam, a lad of life and grace,
But now you're turning grave, Sam, your speech is short and slow,
You've got a cursed official look, Sam Anderson, my Joe!

Sam Anderson, my Joe Sam, when Blackwood first began
To try his canny hand, Sam, at each and all he ran—
And you among the rest, Sam, the world was made to know,
A burning and a shining light, Sam Anderson, my Joe!

Sam Anderson, my Joe Sam, when in the claret trade,
A customer right good, Sam, unto yourself you made,
But sober as a judge, Sam, you now to bed must go—
Aye, sober as a Chancellor, Sam Anderson, my Joe!

Sam Anderson, my Joe Sam, how sportive were the tricks
That on the "general question," Sam, beat Peter all to sticks,
But Peter now will rise, Sam, upon your overthrow—
You're all on *affidavit* now,* Sam Anderson, my Joe!

Sam Anderson, my Joe Sam, in days of youthful glee,
You sported in the shade, Sam, beneath your mulberry-tree—
But strains of rural love, Sam, you must alas! forego,
Now "kiss the calf-skin's" all your song, Sam Anderson, my Joe.

Sam Anderson, my Joe Sam, you've been in many a scrape,
But still with wit or luck, Sam, you've managed to escape—
But now your friends, the Whigs, Sam, have taken you in tow—
They've got your head in Chancery, Sam Anderson, my Joe!

Tickler. That must be all Greek to you, James.

Registrar. The less you say, the better, Tim, about Greek. The Shepherd was not with us when I sung a scrap of old Eubulus—but——

Shepherd. I have been studyin' the Greek for twa wunters. Wunter afore last I made but sma' progress, and got but a short way

* In Chancery proceedings, in England, there is no *vivâ voce* evidence. All is written, sworn and signed.—M.

ayont the roots—for the curlin' came in the way—but this bygane wunter there was nae ice in the Forest—or at Dudinstane either—and I mastered, during the lang nichts at hame, an incalculable crood o'dereevative vocables, and a hantle o' the kittlest compounds.

Registrar. What grammars and lexicons do you use, Shepherd?

Shepherd. Nane but the maist common. I hae completed a version o' Theocritus, and Bion, and Moschus—no to mention Anacreon; and gin there's nae curlin' neist wunter either—and o' that there's but sma' chance, for a change has been gradually takin' place within these few years, in the ellipse o' the earth—I suspect about the ecliptic—I purpose putting a' ma strength upon Pindar. His Odds are dark—but some grand, as ane o' thae remarkable simmer nichts when a' below is loun, and yet there is storm in heaven, the moon glimpsing by fits thro' cluds, and then a' at ance a blue spat fu' o' stars.

North. The Theban Swan——

Shepherd. He was nae swan, but an eagle.

North. As H. N. Nelson said t'other day in that noble paper on Pindar, in the Quarterly.

Registrar. A noble paper, indeed, North.

Tickler. I have heard it attributed to you, Sam.

Registrar. No—you never did.

Shepherd. I'm owre happy to sing this afternoon, but I'm able, I think, to receet; and here's ane o' my attempts on an Eedle o' Bion—the third Eedle—got the teetle frae Tickler.

Tickler. Third Idyll of Bion.

Shepherd (*receets*).

Great Venus once appear'd to me, still slumbering in my bed,
And Cupid in her beauteous hand, a tottering child she led;
And thus with winning words she spake, "See, Cupid here I bring,
Oh, take him! shepherd dear to me, and teach him how to sing!"
She disappear'd, and I began, a baby in my turn,
To teach him all the shepherd's songs—as though he meant to learn,
How Pan the crooked pipe found out, Minerva made the flute,
How Hermes struck the tortoise-shell, and Phœbus form'd the lute.
All this I taught, but little heed gave Cupid to my speech;
Then he himself sweet carols sung, and me began to teach
The loves of gods and men, and all his mother did to each.
Then I forgot what I myself to Cupid taught before;
But all the songs he taught to me, I learnt them evermore;

North. Quite in the style of Trevor, who did such fine versions for my articles in the Greek Anthology. Are you sure, James, they are not Trevor's?

Shepherd. Trevor's. Is he an Englisher? Then dinna let him compete—nor that callant Price o' Hereford either—wi' the Ettrick Shepherd in Theocritus, or Bion, or Moschus, or any o' the Pastorals. Yet they're twa fine lads baith—and gin they were here—they shou'd be welcome to ony geeven number o' glasses o' Glenleevit. Here's their healths—Mr. Trevor and Mr. Rice.

North. I should like, my dear Shepherd, to hear some of your Anacreon.

Shepherd. Na. Wullie Hay beats me blin'. He's as gude, or better nor yoursell, sir. Gi'es some o' Hay.

North.

Come, thou best of painters,
Prince of the Rhodian art,
Paint, thou best of painters,
The mistress of my heart—
Though absent from the picture
Which I shall now impart.

First paint for me her ringlets
Of dark and glossy hue,
And fragrant odors breathing—
If this thine art can do.

Paint me an ivory forehead
That crowns a perfect cheek,
And rises under ringlets
Dark-colored, soft, and sleek.

The space between the eyebrows
Nor mingle nor dispart,
But blend them imperceptibly
And true will be thy art.

From under black-eye fringes
Let sunny flashes play—
Cythera's swimming glances,
Minerva's azure ray.

With milk commingle roses
To paint a nose and cheeks—
A lip like bland Persuasion's—
A lip that kissing seeks.

Within the chin luxurious
Let all the graces fair,
Round neck of alabaster
Be ever flitting there.

And now in robes invest her
Of palest purple dyes,
Betraying fair proportions
To our delighted eyes,

Cease, cease, I see before me
The picture of my choice!
And quickly wilt thou give me—
The music of thy voice.

Shepherd. I wunner hoo many thoosan' times that Odd has been dune intil verse. It's beyond a' dout an extraordinar veevid pictur' in poetry—a perfect *ut pictura poesis*—and the penter had mair sense nor to attempt her in iles after ink.

Registrar. I like better his Carrier Pigeon.

Shepherd. What for do ye like ane better nor the other? It's no like you, my Lord Registrar, to hurt the character o' ae bonny poem by sinkin't aneath another as bonny, but nae bonnier nor itsell. In a case o' that kind there's nae sic thing as the comparative degree—only the positive and the superlative—which, in fack, are the same—for the twa are baith equally positively superlative—and if at ae time you dereeve mair pleasure frae the advice to the penter, and at anither mair frae the address to the Dove, the reason o' the difference is in you, and no in Anawcreon—just as your pallet prefers at this hour a golden rennet apple, and at that a jargonel peer.

Registrar. You are right, James, and I am wrong.

North. (taking out his pocketbook). Why, here are some very pretty lines, James, by a young creature not fifteen—and I am sure you will say she is herself as innocent as any dove.

LINES ON A WHITE DOVE.

BY A GIRL.

Emblem of innocence! spotless and pure,
  Sweet bird of the snowy-white wing,
So gentle and meek, yet so lovely thou art,
Thy loveliness touches and gladdens my heart,
  Like the first early blossoms of Spring.

There are birds of a sunnier land, gentle dove,
  Whose plumage than thine is more bright;
The humming-bird there, and the gay parroquet,
But even than they thou art lovelier yet,
  Sweet bird with the plumage of white.

For purity rests on thy feathers of snow,
  Thy dark eye is sad, gentle dove;
And e'en in the varying tones of thy coo,
There's an accent of sadness and tenderness too,
  Like the soft farewell whisper of love.

The eagle is queen of the cliff and the wave,
  And she flaps her wild wing in the sky;
The song of the lark will enrapture, 'tis true,
When no one would list to my white dove's soft coo,
  No one—save her young ones—and I.

Farewell, then, sweet dove! if the winter is cold,
  May the Spring with her blossoms appear
In sunny-clad beauty, to waken the song
Of the sweet-throated warblers the forests among,
  And the nest of my fav'rite to cheer.

Shepherd. She maun be a dear sweet bonnie bit lassie—and I would like to ken her name.

North. A gracious name it is, James. (*Whispers it to him.*)

Shepherd. I canna mak out, Mr. North, the cause o' the effect o' novelty as a source o' pleasure. Some objects aye please, however common.

Tickler. Don't prose, Jamie.

Shepherd. Ass! There's the Daisy. Naebody cares muckle about the Daisy—till you ask them—and then they feel the hae aye liked it, and quot Burns. Noo naebody tires o' the Daisy. A' the warld would be sorry gin a' Daisies were dead.

Tickler. Puir auld silly body!

Shepherd. There again are Dockens. What for are they a by-word? They're saft, and smooth, and green, and hae nae bad smell. Yet a' the world would be indifferent were a Dockens dead.

Tickler. I would rather not.

Shepherd. What for? Would a Docken, think ye Mr. North, be "beauteous to see, a weed o' glorious feature," if it were scarce, and a hot-house plant? Would leddies and gentleman, gin it were ony ways an unique, pay to get a look at a Docken? But I fin' that I'm no thrawin' ae single particle o' licht on the soob-ject; and the perplexing question will aye recur, "Why is the Daisy, though sae common, never felt to be commonplace? and the Docken aye?"

Tickler. The reason undoubtedly is——

Shepherd. Haud your arrogant tongue, Southside, and never again, immediately after I hae said that ony metapheezical soobject's perplexing, hae the insolence and the silliness to say, "The reason, undoubtedly, is." If it's no coorse, it's rude—and a man had better be coorse nor rude ony day—but O, sirs, what'n a pity that in the Tent there are nae dowgs!

Tickler. I hate curs.

Shepherd. A man ca'in' himself a Christian, and hatin' poetry and dowgs!

Tickler. Hang the brutes.

Shepherd. There's nae sic perfeck happiness, I suspeck, sir, as that o' the brutes. No that I wuss I had been born a brute—yet aften hae I been tempted to envy a dowg. What gladness in the cretur's een, gin ye but speak a single word to him, when you and him's sittin' thegither by your twa sell's on the hill—Pat him on the head and say, "Hector, ma man!" and he whines wi' joy—snap your thoombs, and he gangs dancing round you like a whirl-wind—gie a whustlin' hiss, and he lowps frantic owre your head—cry halloo and he's aff like a shot, chasing naething, as if he were mad.

North. Alas! poor Bronte!

Shepherd. Whisht, dinna think o' him, but in general o' dowgs. Love is the element a dowg leeves in, and a' that's necessary for his enjoyment o' life is the presence o' his master.

Registrar. "With thee conversing he forgets all time."

Shepherd. Yet, wi' a' his sense, he has nae idea o' death. True, he will lie upon his master's grave, and even howk wi' his paws in an affeckin manner, but for all that, believe me, he has nae idea o' death. He snokes wi' his nose into the hole his pows are howkin', just as if he were after a moudie-warp.

North. God is the soul of the brute creatures.

Shepherd. Ay, sir—instinct wi' them's the same's reason wi' us—only we ken what we intend—they do not—we reflect in a mathematical problem, for example, how best to big a house; they reflect nane, but what a house they big! Sir Isaac Newton, o' himsell, without learnin' the lesson frae the bees, wud na hae contrived a hive o' hinney-combs, and biggen them up, cell by cell, hung the creation, like growing fruit, on the branch o' a tree!

North. I have read, my dearest James, "Lay Sermons, by the Ettrick Shepherd."*

Shepherd. And may I just ask, sir, your candid opinion?

North. The first few glances relieved my mind, James, from some painful fears; for I confess I was weak enough to lay my account with meeting, to use your own words in the Preface, "cases of unsound tenets and bad taste," though I know, my dearest Shepherd, that your whole life has borne witness to the sincerity and strength of your religion. But nothing of the sort has once offended my eye, during several continued perusals of the unpretending, but most valuable little volume.

Shepherd. I'm gladder ten times over to hear you say't, sir, than they had been a volumm o' Poms. "A maist valuable little volumm." Comin' frae sic a quarter, that's high praise; but it's no praise I'm wanting, though a' the warld kens I'm fond o' praise—ay, to my shame be it spoken—even the worthless praise o' it's ain hollowhearted wardly sell; it's no praise I'm wantin, and I ken, on this occasion, you'll believe me when I say it, sir; ma wush its to do good.

North. And he who takes "Lay Sermons by the Ettrick Shepherd" to bed with him, "a wiser and a better man will rise to-morrow's morn." It is a volume that may be read in bed without danger of setting fire to the curtains. Several successive houses of mine have been set on fire by sermons, and one, fortunately insured, was burnt to the ground.

* Scott had written Two Sermons for Huntley Gordon, which were published, and Hogg followed the example, with a serious, readable, entertaining, and characteristic volume of Lay Sermons.—M.

Shepherd. But did ye recover? For I aye thocht there was a savin' clouse in the insurance ack o' very Company, insurin' theirsells again' ony insurer at their office, who could be proved to hae had his house burned by bein' set on fire in that way by a sermon.

North. It has always puzzled me, James, to account, not for almost any sermon's almost always setting man or woman asleep in bed, not for almost any candle's almost always setting the bed on fire as soon as he or she has been fairly set asleep. These you perceive to be two separate problems; the solution of the first easy—of the second, perhaps not within the limits of the human understanding.

Shepherd. It's at least no within the leemits o' mine. But the problem itsell's an established fack.

North. I have tried to solve the problem, James, empirically.

Shepherd. It's lucky you've used that word the noo, sir; for though I see't in every serious wark, I canna say I attach to it ony particular meaning.

North. Experimentally, James, have I sometimes taken to bed with me a volume of that perilous class, and after reading a few paragraphs—perhaps as far as Firstly—have put it under my pillows, and pretended to fall asleep. But every now and then I kept looking out of the tail of my eye at the candle—a stout mutton-mould of four to the pound—resolved, the instant he so much as singed a particle of nap off my curtains—always cotton—to spring out of bed—seize the incendiary, and extinguish him on the spot in the very basin in which he blazed; but in justice to one and all of the luminaries that have ever cheered my solitary midnight hours, I now publicly—that is, privately—declare, that not only did I never discover in the behaviour of any one of them a single circumstance that could justify in me the slightest suspicion of such a nefarious design, but that in most cases he visibly began to get as drowsy as myself; and with wick the length of my little finger hanging mournfully by his side, have I more than once sorrowed to see a faithful mutton light expire by my bedside—not in the socket, James—oh! no, not in the socket—for the flicker and that evanishing are in the course of nature, and the soul of the survivor is soon reconciled to the loss—but with one side of the tallow continuing unmelted from head to heel—and the tallow a tall fellow, too, James—the spirit that animated him an hour ago, now mere snuff!

Shepherd. You've sae impersonated him, sir, intil a leevin' cretur, that I cou'd amaist greet—were it no for the thocht o' that intolerable stink. I can thole the stink o' a brock better than o' a caunnle that has dee'd a natural death. But I perceive I'm thinkin' o' death in the socket.

North. Nor will your sermons, my dear James, set the shepherds asleep on the hill—as they lie perusing them, wrapped up in their plaids—for you illustrate—and on the authority and example of Scripture—your doctrines by many a homely image, familiar to their eyes and heart—and that is the way to awaken the spirit to a keen sense of their truth. Thus is your Lay Sermon on Reason and Instinct—the very mystery you were alluding to so beautifully a few moments ago—(*taking the volume from the pocket of his sporting jacket*)—you say——

Shepherd (*affected*). Ma Sermons in his pouch!

North. ——"But the acuteness of the sheep's ear surpasses all things in nature that I know of. A ewe will distinguish her own lamb's bleat among a thousand, all braying at the same time, and making a noise a thousand times louder than the singing of psalms at a Cameronian sacrament in the fields, where thousands are congregated—and that is no joke neither. Besides, the distinguishment of voice is perfectly reciprocal between the ewe and the lamb, who, amid the deafening sound, run to meet one another. There are few things have ever amused me more than a sheep-shearing, and then the sport continues the whole day. We put the flock into a fold, set out all the lambs to the hill, and then set out the ewes to them as they are shorn. The moment that a lamb hears its dam's voice it rushes from the crowd to meet her, but instead of finding the rough, well-clad, comfortable mamma, which it left an hour, or a few hours ago, it meets a poor naked shrivelling—a most deplorable-looking creature. It wheels about, and uttering a loud tremulous bleat of perfect despair, flies from the frightful vision. The mother's voice arrests its flight—it returns—flies, and returns again, generally for ten or a dozen times before the reconcilement is fairly made up."

Shepherd. That's ane o' the mair hamely and familiar passages, sir; and some folk may think it souns better in a Tent at a Noctes than it would do from a tent at preachin', or frae a poopit. And perhaps, they're richt. But the very word LAY on the teetle tells they're no for the kirk, but for the study, the spence, the stream-side, or the hill. And waur religion noo-a-days may be learnet in mony a stane-and-lime chapel in Lunnon or Embro', than frae us twa Divines here in the Tent o' the Fairy's Cleugh.

North. You and I, my dearest Shepherd, must write a book or two together, in alternate chapters, or, if you please, volume about.

Shepherd. Oh! sir, what a series o' warks in three vollumms, couldna you and me in union write, to be enteetled "STORIES O' THE WAY-SIDE WELL!" The water peeryin' out amang the loose stanes o' an auld stane-wa—loose, that is to say, gin the ivy didna bind them a' fast thegither, bulgin' as if they were aye gaen to fa', and yet fa'en never, but firm, as the primrosy brae—the clear caud water peerin' out here, and oozing out there, and fillin', and aye keeping filled, in a' weathers, however sultry it may be, a freestane trough, or haply ane o' blue slate, or granite itsell—sae that, stoopin' down, wi' your hat at your feet, you see a face comin' up, as if frae a great depth, to meet yours, and as like yours as egg is to egg; but then, sune as your lips touch the blessed element, the shadow disappearing in the wrunkle dispersed roun' the mouth o' you, a sinful, nae doubt, but at that moment surely a grateful man!

Registrar. Painting, poetry, and piety!

Shepherd. Day, midsummer—sun, meridian—nae clouds—nae trees—twenty miles travelled sin' dawn—and twenty mair to travel afore gloamin'—feet-sair—in shoon little better than bauchles—stockings that are in fack huggars—breeks tattered—nae siller in his pouch but twa or three bawbees—pity ye na the poor wayfarer—and feels na he that man indeed is but dust?

North. James, you are a truly good man—a Christian.

Shepherd. But she sooks up strength fra that spring—strength, sir, believe me, that penetrates to the poor cretur's heart. I dinna mean to say, sir, that poverty directly thanks God every time it takes a drink o' water, or a mouthfu' o' bread. That's impossible; though it's a custom that should aye be countenanced among a' ranks, askin' a blessin' on every meal folk eat sittin'—if it be but shutting the een, muvin' the lips, or hauden' up a haun'. Custom's second nature, you ken, sir; and that apogthegm has mony a pathetic application in a poor man's life.

North. We shall set about the Series instanter, my dearest Shepherd.

Shepherd. There's a sodger wi' a wooden leg stechin' strecht out afore him, that gin he dinna tak' tent, 'll be in the way o' the wheels o' the mail cotch. I cou'd tell a story fu' o' strange facks about him—and as sure's I'm leevin' there is a female sittin' within two yards o' him—whom I didna see before—her dusty brown claes bein' sae like the road—a faded female, yet rather young than auld—but na babby at her breist, nae bit callant to toddle at her foot, when she and her husband again rises to go their ways. That face was ance a bonnie one—and it's no unbonnie yet—were ony justice done to it—and it wou'd na be sae waefu' had the heart not known the necessity o' buryin' an only bairn—and leevin' it far ahint her, never mair to see the grass on its grave.

North. We must.

Shepherd. I see a beautifu' cretur, na saxteen; I hear her sabbin' at the Wayside Well; but she has a babby at her breist, and the thocht o't brak her mither's heart, and the sicht o't drave her father mad—or waur than mad—for the vera nicht she was delivered—

(he had been out a' day at his wark—and, you see, he had been telt nathing o what was gaun to happen by her noo in her grave—for she had died suddenly—before she could bring herself to tell her husband—a stern man, and an elder o' the kirk)—twa hours after her time was over, he stood beside her bed, where the bit lassie, his dochter, lay wi' her wee sweet bonny new born life atween her breists—and wi' white lips, and a black face, and fiery een, commanded her to rise—some said the Evil Ane had put a knife into his haun', but if sae, something took it out, and hid it safe awa'—and, she did sae a trumlin', and hardly fit to put on her claes—but on, somehow or ither, they were put—and though unable to a' appearance to staun' by hersell, yet to the amazement o' folk at the doors and windows, she walked awa', without daurin' ance to look back—wi' baith arms and baith hauns folded across her breist—and whisperin' something wi' a sweet voice, no in to herself, but wi' her mouth breathing on that immortal jewel—sinfu' as she was—intrusted by the Almichty to the care o' her who last simmer used to drap a curtsy on entering the school—for said I na that, sittin' there at the Wayside Well, Helen Irvine will no be saxteen till the First Day o' May! And whare think ye she's gaun? I need na tell the reason—but the silly child—as she keeps sit sittin' there—for fear if she were to rise up that she micht fa' doon, and hurt the breathin' blessing o' God, that is drawin' life from her breist—the silly child is thinkin' o' takin' shippin' as some far off seaport, and sailin' awa'—I need na tell the reason—sailin' awa' to the wars in Spain!

North. James, spare the Registrar's feelings—

Shepherd. My Lord High Registrar, I didna think ony thing I could say would hae sae affecked you—but your heart's ane with the lowly Shepherd's; and, as Shakspere says,

"Ae touch o' natur' makes the hail warld kin!"

North. Ah! James! I wish you had seen Allan's new picture before it went to Somerset House—POLISH EXILES CONDUCTED BY BASHKIRS ON THEIR WAY TO SIBERIA.

Shepherd. What'n a fine and affeckin'—ay, sooblime, soobjeck for an ile-pentin', by a great maister like Wullie Allan! Twunty or thretty wild Tartars on lang-maned, lang-tailed horses gallopin' like mad in the middle distance—in the far-aff distance, a comin' storm o' Siberian thunder and lightning—in the fore-grun, disarmed troops o' Polish patriots, o' a' ages and sexes, that wad fain hae dee'd fechten for the laun' ance set free by John Sobewhiskey—noo loaded in chains, like gangs o' slaves in the soothern states o' American Virginia.

North. No, James, no—"When bonny Kilmeny gaed up the glen"—it was all by herself—and by a few simple touches you showed her to us in her spiritual beauty, going and coming from Fairy Land.

Shepherd. Sure aneuch I did sae.

North. Allan, James, has conceived, in the same spirit, his Polish Exiles. They are but one family, but in their sufferings, they represent those of all sent to Siberia, and cold and base would be that heart which melted not before such a picture. Towards evening, fatigue has weighed them down—one and all on the roadside; but there is no fainting, no hysterics. That man in fetters in Poland was a patriot—in the steppes of Siberia he is but a father! With humble—almost humiliated earnestness, he beseeches the Bashkirs to let his wife and daughter, and other children, and himself, rest but for an hour! The Bashkirs are three; and he who refuses, does so without cruelty, but, inexorable in his sense of duty, points toward the distance, a dim dreary way along the wilderness, not unoccupied by other wretches moving toward the mines! The other two Bashkirs are sitting without any emotion on their jaded horses, and if *they* be jaded, how low must be the pulses of that lovely girl and that matron, who, with the rest, have travelled on foot the same leagues—unaccustomed—for they are noble—to be thus trailed along the dust!

Shepherd. It maun, in good truth, be an affeckin' sicht.

North. To my mind 'tis Allan's best picture.

Shepherd. Say rather—"to ma heart." For though the mind, dootless, has something to do wi' a' our emotions, *frae* the heart they a' spring; and on feelin', which is the only infallible way o' judgin', a picture o' emotions, whether in poetry or pentin', *tae* the heart is made the feenal appeal. The feelin' i' the heart then sanctions and ratifies the decision o' the mind; and you hae, as in the case afore us, sae beautifully, and beyond a' question sae truly, touched aff by Christopher's pen, after Wullie's pencil, A JUDGMENT.

North. The poor Poles! I honor them for their patriotism and their valor. All brave men are my friends, Shepherd; and I was proud to have beneath my roof, and at my board, that old Polish patriotic poet, whom his countrymen call their Scott. Sczyrma, too, the brave and bright, thy name I love—to its sound mine ear is true—but to mine eye illusive are the letters—may happier days yet dawn on thee, and may the exile behold again the fair face that once beatified his household! France betrayed Poland, and if England were to speak at all, why was it not by the mouths of her cannon? With Thomas Campbell I would walk to death;* and I admire the bold British eloquence of Cutlar Fergusson. James, he is a MAN.

* "When Poland fell, unwept, without a crime:—
Hope for a season bade the world farewell,
And Freedom shrieked when Kosciusko fell."—*M.*

Registrar. Noble sentiments, North. I always thought you were, like myself, a Whig.

North. Never. Nor are you a Whig, Sam; but to me Liberty is the air I have ever breathed, and when I have it not, I *will* die. May all men be free!

Shepherd. "Wha sae base as be a slave!"

North. Some six months since, Sam, Achmet Pacha, the Intendant of the Palace, and the Sultan's especial favorite, set out from Constantinople for Odessa, in order to proceed to St. Petersburgh, there to conciliate the favor of the new master of Turkey—a title the Russians eagerly arrogate for their Czar. Achmet was laden with jewels and other costly presents, but that to which the vanity of the Russians attaches most value, was an old sword, selected from the ancient Turkish collection, of which the handle and scabbard, covered with precious stones, was sent to Nicholas as the weapon of CONSTANTINE PALEOLOGUS, who died, as you know, in the breach, when the capital was stormed by Mahomet the Second. So far the talented correspondent of the Times. Mr. Simmons, of Templemore, Tipperary (why not name a man of genius?) the writer—under the signature of Harold—of some noble lines in Maga, entitled "Napoleon's Dream," saw the letter in the Times, and "on that hint he spake." I have had his lines in my book for some moons—but such poetry outlives the politics of the day,* and its interest is as strong now as ever—even here in the Fairy's Cleugh. I may mention that Alp Arslan, or the Valiant Lion was one of the most powerful monarchs of the Seljukian (Turkish) dynasty. He was buried at Maru; and, according to Gibbon, had the words inscribed over his tomb: *O ye who have seen the glory of Alp Arslan exalted to the heavens, repair to Maru, and you will behold it buried in the dust!*" His son, Malek Shah (in the stately phraseology of the same historians), extended his astonishing conquests until Cashgar, a Tartar kingdom on the borders of China, submitted to his sway—which swept from the mountains of Georgia to the walls of Constantinople, the holy city of Jerusalem, and the spicy groves of Arabia Felix. Soliman, Sam, one of the princes of his family, was the immediate founder of the Ottoman Empire. Sam, you are the best reader of poetry I know, for a Scotchman. There—out, and up with them—*ore rotundo.*

* Bartholemew Simmons, a native of Kilworth, in the south of Ireland, was my schoolfellow, and gave no evidence, in boyhood, of the great ability—if it may not even deserve the name of genius—which made his maturer years honorable and distinguished. For several years after this, his second appearance as a contributor, he wrote largely for *Blackwood.* His poems were collected and had a considerable sale. Mr. Simmons, who had latterly been an inhabitant of London, where he was in the employment of the Government, died, a few years ago in the prime of life.—M.

Registrar.

O'er the golden-domed shrines of imperial Stamboul,
High rises the morning resplendently cool,
Till that proud double daylight is burning in smiles
On blue Marmora's waters and olive-hid isles.

All Stamboul is astir—the Imaum's minaret
Is scarce hush'd from the Hu of his godliness yet;
When—your brows to the dust! Achmet Pasha appears
'Mid the thunder of horse and the lightning of spears!

In a tempest of splendor—with banner and tromp,
By bazaar and atmeydan is winding his pomp,
Till it sparkleth away through yon gateway of gold,
Like a stream in the sunset triumphantly roll'd.

He doubtless goes forth the Vicegerent of Fate,
O'er some THEME of that despot dominion, whose state
Shot the arch of its empire's plenipotent span
From the summits of Zion to yellow Japan.

May the head of his Highness be lifted! Not so,
Achmet Pasha is bound for the Cities of Snow,
Where the glow of his grandeur will scarce be deemed meet
To warm him a way to their Autocrat's feet.

By the God-wielded brand of Red Beder! he bears
The high Heir-loom of Empire—the falchion that wears
The dark hues of that morning its terrors were humbled,
When the last sceptred Roman's last rampart was crumbled!

He transfers the free blade of unkinged Constantine—
Who died as can die but the deathless—divine—
To a son of rude Ruric, that Wasp of the Wave,
The Slavonian who lent us his epithet—Slave!

Oh thou, who though dead, from thy tomb at Maru
Yet speaketh, till tyranny pales in its hue—
Alp Arslan! crown'd Whelp of red Valor, awaken—
The strongholds of thy dwindled puissance are shaken!

Once more for the flap of thy flag, Malek Shah,
That shook wide over terrified Asia its awe!
Ruthless Soliman—west from the Euphrates' marge
Again let thine all-blasting cavalry charge!

For the Wolf of the North, the foul battener in blood,
Gutted hot from the marsh where a monarchy stood,
Is panting to couch in his pestilence, where
The lush grapes of Scutari are purpling the air:

And his hordes will descend like the bloom-killing gale,
And as crushingly cold as its hurricane-hail,
To thaw the dull ice from their veins in the zones
Of the breasts whose white billows are heaving on thrones.

Stern shades of the proud Paleologi, come,
And when midnight is stone through the broad Hippodrome,
There pledge to the shroudless Comneni the cup,
Which the moon-crown'd Sultana like ye, must drink up!

As for *thee*—the Mistitled—Frail Shadow of God—
On the Janizar's gore-dabbled turban who trod—
And who, casting thy Bigot-sires trammels behind,
Buckled round thy freed spirit the harness of MIND—

Where *now* is that spirit, lost Mahmoud the Last?
Like the Cross, is the Crescent's supremacy past?
Then up! and let echoing Christendom tell,
That a Moslem could fall as a Constantine fell!

Ho! Leopards of Albion, and Lilies of France—
Let your flags in the breeze of the Bosphorus dance—
Or, by Allah the Awful! if late by a sun,
The Carnatic will stable the steeds of the Don!

North. You that are a Greek scholar, James, do you remember an inscription for a wayside Pan, by Alcæus?

Shepherd. I remember the speerit o't, but I forget the words. Indeed, I'm no sure if I ever kent the words, but that's naething—at this moment I feel the inscription in the original Greek to be very beautiful! For sake o' Mr. Tickler perhaps you'll receet it in English?

North.

Wayfaring man, by heat and toil oppress'd,
Here lay thee down thy languid limbs to rest,
Upon this flowery meadow's fragrant breast.
Here the pine leaves, where whispering zephyrs stray,
Shall soothe thee listening to Cigala's lay,
And on yon mountain's brow the shepherd swain
Pipes by the gurgling fount his noontide strain,
Secure beneath the platane's leafy spray,
From the autumnal dog-star's sultry ray.
  To-morrow thou'lt get on, wayfaring man,
  So listen to the good advice of Pan.

Shepherd. Thae auncients, had they been moderns, would hae felt a' we feel oursells; and sometimes I'm tempted to confess, that in the matter o' expression o' a simple thocht, they rather excel us—for, however polished may be ony ane o' their maist carefu' compositions, it never look artificial, and the verra feenish o' the execution seems to be frae the fine finger o' Nature's ain inspired sell! O how I hate the artificial!

Registrar. Not worse than I.

Shepherd. Ca' a thing artificial that's no ony sic thing, and ye make me like it less and less till I absolutely dislike it; but then the sense o' injustice comes to ma relief, and I love it better than afore—as, for example, a leddy o' fine education, or a garden flower. For, I'll be shot, if either the ane or the ither be necessarily artificial, or no just as bonnie, regarded in a richt light, as a lass or a lily o' low degree. Ony ither touchin' trifle frae the Greek, sir?

North. We have had Pan—now for Priapus.

Shepherd. Ye maun heed what you say, sir, o' Priawpus.

North. Archias is always elegant, James.

Registrar. And often more than elegant, North—poetical. He had a fine eye, too, sir, for the picturesque.

North.

Near to the shore, upon this neck of land,
A poor Priapus, here I ever stand.
Carved in such guise, and forced such form to take,
As sons of toilsome fishermen could make,
My feetless legs, and cone-shaped, towering head,
Fill every cormorant with fear and dread.
But when for aid the fisher breathes a prayer,
I come more swiftly than the storms of air.
I also eye the ships that stem the flood:
'Tis deeds, not beauty, show the real God.

(*Loud hurras heard from the glen, and repeated by all the echoes.*)

North. Heavens! what's that?

Shepherd. Didna I tell ye I had wauken'd the Forest? What's twenty, thretty, or fifty miles to the lads and lassies o' the south o' Scotland? Auld woman and weans 'll walk that atween the twa gloamings—and hae na they gips, and carts, and pownies for the side-saddle, and lang bare-backed yads that can carry fowr easy, and at a pinch, by haudin' on by man and tail, five? Scores hae been paddin' the hoof since morn frae the head o' Clydesdale—Annanbanks has been roused as by the sound o' a trumpet—and the auld gray mare has been a' day whusking her tail wi' pleasure to see Moffatdale croudin' to the jubilee.

(*They all take their station outside on the brae, and hold up their hands.*)

North. I am lost in amazement!

Tickler. A thousand souls!

Registrar. I have been accustomed to calculate the numbers of great multitudes—and I fix them at fifteen hundred, men, women, and children.

Shepherd. Twa hunder collies, and asses and mules included, a hunder horse.

Registrar. Of each a turm.

Shepherd. Oh! sir, is na 't a bonny sicht? There's a Trades' Union for you, sir, that may weel mak your heart sing for joy—shepherds, and herdsmen, and ploughmen, and woodsmen, that wud, if need were, fecht for their kintra, wi' Christopher North at their head, against either foreign or domestic enemies; but they come noo to do him homage at the unviolated altar which Nature has erected to Peace.

Registrar. A band of maidens in the van—unbonnetted—silken-snooded all. And hark—they sing! Too distant for us to catch the words—but music has its own meanings—and only that it is somewhat more mirthful, we might think it was a hymn!

Shepherd, (*to* TICKLER *and the* REGISTRAR). Dinna look at him, he's greetin'. If that sound was sweet is na this silence sublime?

Tickler. What are they after now, James?

Shepherd. They hae gotten their general orders—and a' the leaders ken well hoo to carry them intil effeck. The phalanx is no' breakin' into pieces noo, like cumstrary cluds—ae speerit inspires and directs a' its muvements, and it is deploying, Mr. Tickler, round yon great hic-kirk-looking rocks, intil a wide level place that's a perfect circle, and which ye wha hae been here the best pairt o' a week, I'se warrant, ken naething aboot; for Natur', I think, maun hae made it for hersell; and such is the power o' its beauty, that sittin' there aften in youth, hae I clean forgotten that there was ony ither warld.

Registrar. "Shaded, with the branching palm, the sign of Peace."

Shepherd. Ay, mony o' them are carrying the boughs o' trees—and its wonnerfu' to see how leafy they are so early in the season. But Spring, prophetic o' North's visit, has festooned the woods.

Tickler. Not boughs and branches only——

Shepherd. But likewise furms. There's no a few mechanics among them, sir, house carpenters and the like, and seats 'll be sune raised a' round and round, and in an hour or less you'll see sic a congregation as you saw never afore, a' sittin' in an amphitheatre—and aneath a hanging rock a platform—and on the platform a throne wi' its regal chair—and in the chair wha but Christopher North—and on his head a crown o' Flowers—for lang as he has been King o' Scotland—this—this is his Coronation-Day. Hearken to the bawn!

Registrar. I fear it will soon be growing dark.

Shepherd. Growin' dark! O you sumph. This is no the day that will grow dark—and though this bold bricht day luves owre dearly the timid dim gloaming no to welcome her to sic a scene—and though the timid dim gloaming has promised to let come stealin' in by and by her sister, the cloud-haired and star-eyed Nicht, yet the ane will gang na awa' as the ither is making her appearance—for day is in love wi' baith o' them, and baith are in love wi' day—sae 'twill be beautifu' to see them a' three thegither by the licht o' the moon "a perfect chrysolite"—and the sky abune, and the glen aneath, and the hills between them a', will be felt to be but ae Earth!

END OF ACT FIRST.

No. LXVI.—JULY, 1834.

SCENE—*The leads of the Lodge—Present,* NORTH, TICKLER, *the* SHEPHERD, *and* BULLER. *Time—Evening.*

Shepherd. This fancy beats a', and pruves o' itsell, sir, that you're a poet. In fine weather leevin' on the leeds! And siccan an awnin'! No a threed o' cotton about it, or linen either, but dome, wa's, cornishes, and fringers—a' silk. Oh! but she's a tastefu' creatur that Mrs. Gentle—for I see the touch o' her haun in the hingins, the festoonins, the droopins o' the draperies—and it's a sair pity that ye twa, who are seen to be but ae speerit, are nae likewise ae flesh. Pardon the allusion, Mr. North, but you'll never be perfectly happy till she bears your name, or aiblins you'll tak' hers, my dear auld sir, and ca' yoursells Mr. and Mrs. North Gentle; or gin you like better to gie hers the precedence, Mr. and Mrs. Gentle Christopher North. But either o' the twa would be characteristic and euphonous—for you're humane, sir, by nature, though by habit rather savage, and a' you want to saften you back into your original constitution is to be a husband——

Tickler. And a father.

Shepherd. As likely to be that as yoursell, Mr. Tickler, and likelier too; and a' the warld would admire to see a bit canty callant or yelegant lassie trotting at his knee—

Tickler. "With all its mother's tenderness,
And all its father's fire!"

North. James, is it not a beautiful panorama?

Shepherd. A panorama! What? would ye wush to hae a panorama o' weans?

North. I mean the prospect, James.

Shepherd. A prospect o' a panorama o' weans!

North. Poo—poo—my dear Shepherd—you wilfully misapprehend my meaning—look round you over land and sea!

Shepherd. I canna look farrer than the leeds. Oh! but it's a beautiful Conservatory! I never afore saw an Orange-tree. And it's true what I had read o' them—blossom and fruit on the same plant—nae doot an evergreen—and in this caulder clime o' ours bricht wi' its gowden ba's as if we were in the Wast Indies!—What ca' ye thir?

North. These are mere myrtles.

Shepherd. Mere myrtles! Dinna say that again o' them—mere; an ungratefu' word, o' a flowery plant a' fu' o' bonny white starnies—and is that their scent that I smell?

North. The balm is from many breaths, my dear James. Nothing that grows is without fragrance——

Shepherd. Hooever fent. I fand that out when a toddler—for I used to fling awa' or drap whatever I pu'd that I thocht had nae smell—till ae day I began to suspect that the faute might lie in my ain nose, and no in the buds or leaves—and frae a thoosan' sma' experiments I was glad to learn it was sae—and that there was a scent—as ye well said the noo—in a' that grows. Wasna that kind in Nature! Hoo else could that real poet Tamson hae said, "the air is bawm!"

Tickler. I desiderate the smell of dinner.

Shepherd. What'n a sensual sentiment! The smell o' vittals is delicious whan the denner's a gettin' dished, and during the time o' eating, but for an hour or mair after the cloth has been drawn, the room to ma nose has a close het smell, like that o' ingons. It's no the custom o' the kintra to leave wi' the leddies—but nae drawin'-room like the leeds. What'n frutes!

North. Help yourself, James.

Shepherd. I'll thank ye, Mr. Tickler, to rax me owre thae oranges.

Tickler. They are suspiciously dark in the color—but perhaps you like the bitter?

Shepherd. They're na mair ceevil than yoursell—but genuine St. Michaelers—and as they're but sma', half-a-dizzen o' them will sharpen the pallet for some o' thae American aipples that never put ane's teeth on edge—which is mair than you can say for Scotch anes, that are noo seldom sweeter than scribes.

Buller. Scribes?

Shepherd. Crabs. Mr. North, we maun tak' tent what we're about, for it wou'd na answer weel to stoiter owre the edge o' the leeds; nor yet to tumble down the trapdoor-stairs.

North. The companion-ladder, if you please, James.

Shepherd. Companion ladder? I suppose because only ae person can climb up at a time—though there's room eneuch, that's true, for several to fa' doon at ance—but the term's nowtical, I ken—and you're a desperate cretur for thinkin' o' the sea.

North. Would that Tom Cringle were here—the best sketcher of sea-scenery that ever held a pen!

Buller. And painter too, sir.

Shepherd. I ken little mair, or aiblins less o' ships than Tam Cringle kens o' sheep—but in his pages I see them sailin' alang—

North. In calm, breeze, gale, or storm——

Shepherd. Dinna tak the words oot o' ma mouth, sir—in his pages I see them sailin' alang, in cawm, breeze, gale, or storm, as plain as if I was lookin' at them frae the shore, or——

Tickler. Scudding under bare poles like you and I, James, without our wigs.

Shepherd. Naething's mair intolerable to me than a constant attempt at wut. Besides, wha ever was seen—either men or ships—skuddin' under bare poles in a cawm?

Tickler. Or sailin'—James—in a cawm—as you said just now.

Shepherd. But I didna say a deed cawm; an' gin I had, does na the wund often drap a' at ance, and a' at ance get up again—and wasna the ship lying waitin' for the wun' wi' a' sail set—or maybe motion still in her? And therefore nane but an ignorawmus in nowticals would objeck to a Shepherd, wha is nae sailor, speakin' o' a ship sailing in a cawm. Are ye satisfied?

North. My friend Marryat finds fault with Tom Cringle for being too melodramatic.

Tickler. His volumes are indeed a mellow dram in two calkers.

Shepherd. Faith, for a pun, that's no so very far amiss; and in a few years, frae playin' on words, I shouldna be surprised to see you, sir, gettin' grupp o' an idea.

Buller. My friend Fonblanque characterized Captain Cringle truly by three words in the Examiner—the Salvator Rosa of the Sea.

North. The truth is that Tom is a poet.

Buller. And of a high order.

North. Marryat missed to remember that while he was penning his critique. Strike all the poetry out of Tom's prose——

Shepherd. I'll defy you.

North. And Marryat would have been right. Read his prose by the light of the poetry that illumines it, and Marryat is wrong.

Shepherd. Wha's he, that Marryyacht?

North. A captain in the navy, and an honor to it—an admirable sailor, and an admirable writer—and would that he too were with us on the leads, my lads, for a pleasanter fellow, *to those who know him*, never enlivened the social board.

Shepherd. I like the words you slipped in there, sir, wi' a marked vice, like italics in prent—"*to those who know him*"—for them that's gotten' the character o' bein' pleasant fellows on a' occasions, and to a' men, are seldom sound at the core—and oh! but they grow wearisome on ane's hauns when ane's no in the humor for diversion or daffin', but wish to be quate.

North. Right, James. I have no conceit of them "who are all things to all men." Why, I have seen John Schetky himself in the sulks with sumphs, though he is more tolerant of ninnies and noodles than almost any other man of genius I have ever known—but clap him down among a choice few of kindred spirits, and how his wild wit even yet, as in its prime, wantons! Playing at will its *virgin* fancies, till Care herself comes from her cell, and sitting by the side of Joy, loses her name, and forgets her nature, and joins in glee or catch, beneath the power of that magician, the merriest in the hall.

Shepherd. I houp I'll no gang to my grave without forgathering wi' John Schetky.

North. Marryat is often gruff.

Shepherd. Then you and him 'll agree like brithers, for you're aften no only gruff, but grim.

North. He would have stood in the first class of sea-scribes, had he written nothing but Peter Simple.

Shepherd. Did he—did Marryyacht write Peter Simple? Peter Simple in his ain way's as gude's Parson Adams.

Tickler. Parson Adams!

Shepherd. Ay, just Parson Adams. He that imagined Peter Simple's a Sea-Fieldin'. That's a better compoun' yepithet, Mr. North, nor your sea-scribe.

North. Methinks I see another son of Ocean sitting on that couch.

Shepherd. Wha?

North. Glascock.

Shepherd. Let me look intil his face. (*Rising up and going to the couch.*) Na—na—na, sir, I'm sorry to say this is no Man-Glascock—It's neither his fine bauld face, nor his firm springy figur'.

North. Dicky Phantom!

Shepherd. And nae mair.

North. Glascock had a difficult game to play, Buller, in the Douro, but he played it with a skill and a resolution that have gained him the praise of the whole service.

Buller. No man stands higher.

North. All his books have been excellent, but his last is best of all.

Shepherd. Shall I ca' him a Sea-Smollet?

Tickler. You may, if you choose to talk stuff.

Shepherd. I was speerin' at Mr. North—nane but a fule wou'd speer sic a question at you—for you was never in a ship but ance; and though she was in a dry dock, you was sae sea-sick that there was a want o' mops.

North. I call him what he is—a Sea-Glascock. No man alive can tell a galley-story with him—the language of the forecastle from his lips smacks indeed of the salt sea-foam—his crew must have loved such a captain—for he knows Jack's character far better than Jack does himself—and were there more such books as his circulating in the service—they would assist, along with all wise and humane and just regulations and provisions made by Government to increase and secure Jack's comfort at sea and Poll's on shore, in extinguishing all necessity for press-gangs.

Buller. Glascock, sir, can tell, too, a story as well as the best of them all—Hall, or Marryat, or Chamier—of the Gunroom and the Captain's cabin.

North. He can—and eke of the Admiral's. Marryat and Glascock in a bumper, with all the honors.

Shepherd. Na. I wunna drink't.

North. James!!!

Tickler. What the devil's the matter with you now?

Buller. Mr. Hogg!

Shepherd. If I drink't, may I be——

North. No cursing or swearing allowed on board this ship.

Tickler. Call the master-of-arms, and let him get a dozen.

Shepherd. If ony man says that ever I cursed or sweered, either in ship or shielin', then he's neither mair nor less than a confoonded leear. Fules! fules! fules! Sumphs! sumphs! sumphs! Sops! sops! sops! Saps! saps! saps! Wou'd you cram the healths of twa siccan men, wi' a' the honors, intil ae bumper? Let's drink them separate—and in tumblers.

North. Charge.

Tickler. Halt. "I wunna drink't."

Shepherd. I'll no be mocked, Tickler. Besides, that's no the least like ma vice.

Tickler. "I wunna drink't"—unless we all quaff, before sitting down, another to Basil Hall.

North. With all my heart.

Shepherd. And sowle.

Buller. And mind. "Stap—I wunna drink't."

Shepherd. That's real like me—for an Englisher.

Tickler. Craziness is catching.

North. Well said, Son of Isis.

Buller. Tom Cringle.

Omnes. Ay, ay, sir—ay, ay, sir—ay, ay, sir.

North. Instead of the rule *seniores priores*—to prove our equal regard—let us adopt an arithmetical order—and drink them in Round Robin.

(*Four—that is, sixteen—bumper tumblers—not of the higher ranks, but the middle orders—are emptied arithmetically, with all the honors, to the healths of Captains Cringle, Glascock, Hall, and*

Marryat. For a season there is silence on the leads, and you hear the thrush—near his second or third brood—at his evening song.)

Shepherd. Fowre tummlers, taken in instant sequence, o' strang drink, by each o' fowre men—a' fowre nae farder back than yestreen sworn in members o' the left haun' branch o' the Temperance Society! I howp siccan a decided exception, while it is pruvin', may no explode the general rule. The general rule wi' us fowre when we forgather, is to drink naething but milk and water—the general exception to drink naething but speerits o' wine—that was a lapsus lingy—speerits *and* wine. It's a pleasant sicht to see a good general rule reconciled wi' a good general exception; and it's my earnest desire to see a' the haill warld shakin' hauns.

North. Peter, place my pillows. (*Peter does so.*)

Shepherd. There's ane gaen weel shued up.

Tickler. St. Peter? I'm Pope. Kiss my toe, James.

Shepherd. Drink aye makes him clean daft.

Buller. 'Tis merry in the hall, when beards wag all. Then all took a smack—a smack, at the old black-jack—to the sound of the bugle-horn—to the sound of the bugle-horn. Such airs I hate, like a pig in a gate—give me the good old strain—and nought is heard on every side but signoras and signors—like a pig in a gate, to the sound of the bugle-horn.

Shepherd. Drink maks him musical—yet he seems to remember the words better nor the tune. North! nae snorin' alloo'd on the leeds. Tickler! do you hear? nae snorin' alloo'd on the leeds. Buller, pu' baith thair noses. Fa'en owre too! Noo, I ca' that a tolerable nawsal treeo. It's really weel snored. Tickler! you're no keepin' time. Kit, you're gettin' out o' the tune. Buller, nae fawsetto. Come here, Peter, I wush to speak to you. (*Peter goes to the Shepherd.*) Is na Mr. North gettin' rather short in the temper? Hae na ye observed, too, a fa'in' aff o' his faculties—sic as memory—and, I fear, judgment? And what's this I hear o' him (*whispering Peter*). I do indeed devoutly trust it'll no get wun'! (*Peter puts his finger to his nose, and looking toward North, winks the Shepherd to be mum.*) Ye needna clap your finger on your nose, and wunk, and screw your mouth in that gate, for he's in a safe snorin' sleep.

Peter (*indignantly*). Mr. Hogg, I trust I shall never be so far left to myself as to act in any manner unbecoming my love, gratitude, and veneration for the best and the noblest of men and masters.

Shepherd. You did put your forefinger to your nose—you did wunk—ye did screw your mooth—ye did gesticulate that ye suspecked his sleep wasna as real's his snore—and ye did nod yes when I asked you wi' a whisper in your lug if it was true that he had taken to tipplin' by himself in the forenoons.

North (starting up). You backbiting hog in armor—but I will break your bones—Peter, the crutch!

Shepherd. The crutch is safe under lock and key in its ain case—and the key's in ma pocket—for you're no in a condition to be trusted wi' the crutch. As for backbiting, what I said I said afore your face—and if you was pretendin' to be asleep, let what you overheard be a lesson till you never to act so meanly again, for be assured, accordin' to the auld apothegm, listeners never hear ony gude o' theirsells. Do they, Buller?

Buller. Seldom.

Shepherd. Do they ever, Tickler?

Tickler. Never.

Shepherd. Then I propose that we all get sober again. Peter—THE ANTIDOTE! It's time we a' took it—for I've seen the leeds mair stationary—half an hour back, I was looking eastward, but I'm sair mista'en if ma face be na noo due wast.

North. Yes—Peter. (*Peter administers the Antidote.*)

Shepherd. Wasna that a blessed discovery, Mr. Buller! Ae glass o' THE ANTIDOTE taken in time no only remedies the past, but ensures the future—we may each o' us toss aff ither fowre bumper-tummlers with the same impunity as we despatched their predecessors—and already what a difference in the steadiness o' the leeds!

Buller. Hermes' Molly!

Tickler. The Great Elixir!

North. O sweet oblivious ANTIDOTE indeed—for out of the grave of memory in bright resurrection rises hope—and on the wings of imagination the rekindled senses seem to hold command over earth and heaven!

Shepherd. O coofs—coofs—coofs! wha abuse the wine-bibbers o' the Noctes.

Buller. Coofs indeed!

Shepherd. Never, Mr. Buller, shall they breathe empyrean air.

Buller. Never.

Shepherd. For them never shall celestial dews distil from evening's roseate cloud—

Buller. Never.

Shepherd. Nor setting suns their fancy ever fill with visions born o' golden licht—when earth, sea, cloud, and sky, are a' interfused wi' ae speerit—and that speerit, sae beautifully hushed in high repose, tells o' something within us that is divine, and therefore that will leeve for ever! Luik! luik!

Buller. Such a sunset!

Shepherd. Let no man daur to word it. It's daurin' eneuch even to luik at it. For oh! ma freens! are na thae the gates o' glory—

wide open for departed speerits—that they may sail in on wings intil the heart o' eternal life! Let that sight no be lost on us.

North. It is melting away.

Shepherd. Changed—gane! Anither sun has set—surely a solemn thocht, sirs—yet, come, let's be cheerfu'—Mr. North, let me see a smile on your face, man—for, my dear sir, I canna thole noo bein' lang melancholy at ae time—for every year sic times are growin' mair frequent—and I hope the bonnie leddy moon will no be lang o' risin', nor do I care whether or no she brings wi' her ane, nane, or ten thousan' stars. Here comes the caffee.

Enter AMBROSE, *with tea and coffee silver service.*

Ambrose. Tea or coffee, sir?

Shepherd. Chaclat. Help the rest. Mr. North?

North. Sir?

Shepherd. Is that America, on the other side of the Firth?

North. Commonly called the kingdom of Fife.

Shepherd. Noo that steam's brought to perfection, aiblins I may mak' a voyage there before I dee. Can you assure me the natives are no cannibals?

North. They are cannibals, James, and will devour you—with kindness; for to be hospitable, free, affectionate, and friendly, is to be *Fifeish*.

Shepherd. I see through the blue haze touns and villages along the shores, the kintra seems cultivated, but no cleared—for yon maun be the woods o' bonnie Aberdour, atween whilk and the shore o' Scotland sleep the banes o' Sir Patrick Spens and a' his peers. We can write no sic ballant noo-a-days as,

"The king sat in Dunfermline tower,
Drinking the blood-red wine."

The simplest pawthos, sir, sinks deepest in the heart—and lies there —far doon aneath the fleeting storms o' life—just as that wreck itsell is lyin' noo, bits o' weed, and airn, and banes, lodged immovably amang other ruefu' matter at the bottom o' the restless sea.

Buller. Exquisite!

Shepherd. Eh? what said ye, sir? did ye apply that epithet to my sentiment, or to your sherry?

Buller. To both. United, "they sank like music in my heart."

Shepherd. Here's to you, Mr. Buller. Did ever I ask, sir, if you're ony relation to the Bullers o' Buchan?*

Buller. Cousins.

Shepherd. I thought sae, sir, frae the sound o' your vice. You're a fine bauld dashin' family, and fling the cares o' the wauld aff frae your sides like rocks.

* Caves, in Aberdeenshire.—M.

Buller. Scotland seems to me, if possible, improved since my last visit, even

"Stately Edinburgh, throned on crags,"

more magnificently wears her diadem.

Shepherd. Embro', as a town, taken't by itsell, 's no muckle amiss, but I canna help considerin't but a clachan' sin' my visit to Lunnon. Mercy on us, what a roar o' life! Ane would think the haill habitable yerth had spewed its haill population intil that whirlpool! or that that whirlpool had sook't it a' in—mair like a Maelstrom than a metropolis!

North. There's poetry for you!

Buller. It is.

Shepherd. Whales and mennows a' are yonner, sir, dwindled down or equaleezed intil the same size by the motion o' millions, and a' sense o' individuality lost. The vera first morning I walked out o' the hotel I clean forgot I was James Hogg.

Buller. Yet, a few mornings after, Mr. Hogg, allow me to say, that the object most thought of there was the Ettrick Shepherd.

Shepherd. Na—no on the streets. Folk keepit shoalin' past me —me in ae current o' flesh, and them in anither—without a single ee ever seemin' to see me—a' een lookin' stracht forrit—a' faces in full front—so that I coudna help askin' mysell—will a' this break up—is it a' but the maist wonderfu' o' dreams?

Buller. But in the Park?

Shepherd. Ay! that was a different story—I came to my seven senses on Sunday in the Park—and I had need o' them a'—for gif I glowered, they glowered—and wherever I went, I cou'dna but see that I was the centre——

Tickler. "The cynosure of neighboring eyes."

Shepherd. O man! wheesht. The centre—the navel o' the great wheel that keepit circumvolvin' round, while rays like spokes, innumerable frae leddies' een, shot towards me frae the circumference, and had na my heart been pierced, it wad hae been no o' wud but o' stane.

North. O thou Sabbath-breaker!

Shepherd. That thocht sadden'd me, but I shook it aff, and I houp I may be forgiven, for it wasna my ain fawte, but the fawte o' that Lord that munted me on his ain charger, and wou'd show me —whether I wou'd or no—in the Dress-Rings.

Tickler. And how were you dressed, James?

Shepherd. Wiser-like than you in your ordinar—just in the Sabbath claes I gang in to Yarrow kirk.

North. Simple son of genius! Buller, is he not a jewel?

Buller. He is.

Shepherd. Fie, lads—think shame o' yoursells--for I ken that ahint ma back you ca' me a rouch diamond.

North. But the setting, my dear James! How farther were you set?

Shepherd. I had na on the blue bannet—for I had nae wush to be singular, sir—but the plaid was atowre ma shoulders——

North. And across your manly breast, my Shepherd, which must have felt then and there, as here and now, entitled to beat with the pride of conscious genius and worth.

Shepherd. I shall na say that I was na proud, but I shall say I was happy; for the Englishers I hae ever held to be the noblest race o' leevin' men accept the Scotch—and forbye that, sir, a poet is nae mair a poet in his ain kintra than a prophet a prophet; but yonner my inspiration was acknowledged, and I thocht mair o' mysell as the owther o' the Queen's Wake, five hunder miles awa frae the Forest, than I ever had ony visible reason to do sae, in the city owre which Mary Stuart once rang, and in the very shadow o' Holyrood.

Tickler. How you must have eclipsed Count D'Orsay!*

Shepherd. I eclipsed nane. There's nae eclipse yonner—for the heaven was a' shinin' wi' many thousand stars. But the sugh went that the Ettrick Shepherd was in the Park—the Shepherd o' the Wake, and the Pilgrims, and Kilmeny——

North. And the Noctes—

Shepherd. Ay, o' the Noctes—and what were they ever, or wud they ever again hae been, withouten your ain auld Shepherd?

North. Dark—dark—irrecoverable dark?

Shepherd. Your haun. Thousans o' trees were there—but a' I kent o' them, as they gaed gliding greenly by, was that they were beautifu'—as for the equipages, they seemed a' ae equipage——

Tickler. Your cortège.

Shepherd. Wheesht—wheesht—O man, wunna ye wheesht! Representin'—containin' the wealth, health, rank, beauty, grace, genius, virtue o' England——

Tickler. Virtue!

Shepherd. Yes—Virtue. Their een were like the een o' angels, and if virtue was na smiling yonner, then 'twould be vain to look for her on this side o' heaven.

* For many years Count D'Orsay was "the glass of fashion and the mould of form," in London. A Frenchman by birth, he entered the army, in which his father was a General—met with the Countess of Blessington, then fair as well as frail—abandoned his sword, his prospects, his family, his country, to follow her—and remained by her side, enthralled by her beauty and converse, for nearly thirty years; reposing by her side, in death, in the churchyard of Chambourcey, near St. Germain. His whole career was ruined by that life-long infatuation. His talents, as a man of letters and an artist, were great and varied. What might he not have been? *Dis aliter visum.*—M.

North. I fear, my dearest Shepherd, that you forgot the Flowers of the Forest.

Shepherd. Clean. And what for no? Was na I a stranger in Lunnon? and wou'd I alloo fancy to flee awa' wi' me out the gates o' Paradise? Na—she cou'd na hae dune that, had she striven to harl me by the hair o' the head. Oh, sir! sufficient for the hour was the beauty thereof—sowle and senses were a' absorbed in what I saw—and I became——

Tickler. The Paragon of the Park.

Shepherd. Wull you no fine him, sir, in sawte and water?

North. Silence, Tim!

Shepherd. He disturbs ane like the Death-Tick.

North. Well, James?

Shepherd. Oh, sir! the leddies yonner—it maun be confessed—stoops their heads mair elegantly—mair gracefully—mair royally far—than the leddies in Embro!

Tickler. Indeed! I should have thought that impossible.

Shepherd. Wi' a mair enchantin' wave o' their arms do they bless ye, as they pass by, wi' a kiss o' licht frae the white saft pawms o' their hauns, that micht amaist mak the sad lily herself begin to grow ashamed o' her leaves! Can it be possible, sir, think ye, that yon gleams are a' o' the real bare skin, and no kid gloves? Yet kids they could na be—for I observed them drawin' them off, as I cam near—and snawy as they were, the slichtest tinge o' pink served to show what pure blood was in their veins; but 'twas on their faces you could see the circulation frae their hearts, for there danced the sunshine on roses, and Beauty in its perfection was Joy and Love.

North. Twenty years ago, my dear Shepherd, and what would have become of your heart?

Shepherd. Mr. North, you dinna need to be tauld that the heart o' every human—ay, o' every leevin thing's a mystery—and a great and afttimes a sair mystery to me has been mine; but at nae time o' life wou'd I hae felt muckle itherwise amang a' that fascination than I did then—for the sense o' my ain condition—o'my ain lot—has aye lain upon me—and held ma speerit doun, true to the cares and duties o' the sphere in which it pleased Providence I should be born.

North. You know, my dear James, that I was not serious.

Shepherd. I kent that, my dear sir,—for ye hae the insicht. No that seldom the sense o' what I said the noo, has been sae heavy that I was like to fent in the weary wilderness; at ither times, and aftener far, though it was like a pack on my shouthers on a hilly road, I hae carried it not only without complainin', but contented, and wi' a supporting gratitude; while aftenest o' a'—and you'll, sir, no think that strange—it has been to me even like wings on which I walked alang the green braes in the dewy mornin' wi' steps o' air, and envied not leevin cretur in a' the wide warld. And when something within me whuspered that I had genie, then the wings o' themselves unfaulded, and I thocht, without leavin' or losin' sicht altogether o' the Forest, that I sailed awa into still lovelier launs—intil Fairylaun itself—sir—for 'twas there I met Kilmeny—and asked the bonny doo where she had cum frae, and where she was gaun—and if she were to return ever mair—and she confided a' her secrets to the Shepherd—and——

North. The Shepherd sung of her "one song that will not die."

Shepherd. That was kind in you, my revered sir, to help me out. Gin conversation had nae ither interruptions than o' that sort, frinds micht keep talkin' on a' nicht without ever noticin' the sinkin' o' the cawnles or the risin' o' the stars.

Tickler. Hem!

Shepherd. The Forest for me after a'! Sae would it hae been, sir, even had I been ca'd up to Lunnon in my youth or prime. Out o' utter but no lang forgetfulness it would hae risen up, stretchin' itsell out in a' its length and breadth wi' a' its lochs and mountains, and hills and streams—St. Mary's and the Yarrow, the dearest o' them a'—and wafted me alang wi' it, far aff and awa' frae Lunnon, like a man in a warld o' his ain, swoomin' northward through the air, wi' motion true to that ae airt, and no deviatin' for sake o' the brichtest southern star.

Buller. Most beautiful.

Shepherd. If it wou'd hae been sae even then, Mr. Buller, hoo much mair maun it hae been sae, but some three simmers back, when my hair though a gae dour broon, was yieldin' to the gray? You was never at Mount-Benger, sir, nor Altrive, and the mair's the pity, for happy should we a' be to see sic a fine, freenly fallow—and o' sic bricht pairts—though the weans micht na just at first follow your English——

Buller. For their sakes, my dear Shepherd, forgive my familiarity—I should learn their own Doric in a day.

Shepherd. That you wud, my dear Mr. Buller; and think na ye, gin if I ever, for a flaff, in the Park, forgot my ain cozy beild, that the thocht on't cam na back on my heart—ay, the verra sicht o't afore my een—dearer than ever for sake o' the wee bodies speerin' at their mother when father was comin' hame—and for sake o' her who, for my sake, micht at that moment be lettin' drap a kiss on their heads.

Tickler. Now that we have seen the Shepherd in the Park, pray, James, exhibit yourself at the play.

Shepherd. The last exhibition you made o' yoursell, Mr. Tickler, at the play, as you ca't—meanin', I presume, in the playhouse—was no quite sae creditable as your freens wud hae wished—sittin' in ane o' the upper boxes wi' a pented wax-doll—no to ca' them waur—on ilka haun——

North. Is that a true bill, Tickler?

Tickler. A lie.

Shepherd. I never answer that monosyllable—but canna help followin' it up, on the present occasion, wi' an apogthegm; to wit, that a man's morals may be judged by his mainners. But I tell you, Mr. North, and you, Mr. Buller, that I was in ane of the houses—ance, and but ance; I gaed there out o' regard to some freens, and I ever after staid awa' out o' regard to mysell—for o' a' the sichts that ever met my een, there never was the like o' you; and I wonder hoo men-folk and women-folk, sittin' side by side, could thole't in a public theatre. The performance was queer by name, and queer by nature—the first I wasna able to remember, and the second I shall never be able to forget. But will ye believe me when I tell you, that on the verra middle o' the stage, gaen well back to be sure, but only sae as to saften them in the distance, visible to the haill audience were a bevy o' naked lasses, a' plowterin' in a bath, wi' the water no up to their waists!

Omnes. Shocking! shocking! shocking!

Shepherd. Dinna ye believe't? I grant it's a gay lee-like story, but it's as sure's death. They micht hae some sort o' cleedin on, but gin they had, it was no visible to the naked ee, and I cou'd na for shame ask the len' o' an opera-glass fra an auld gentleman ahint me, who was kecklin' like a gouty gander across a burn to a gang o' goslings. I perceived mysel' getting red in the face—for though no blate, I houp I hae a' life-lang had a sense o' decency; and the young leddy at my side began fannin' me wi' her fan. But I pretended to be readin' the bill o' the play—only noo and then takin' a peep wi' the tail o' my ee—but oh, sirs! yon was a great shame; and though I'm again' a' sorts o' tyranny, or intermeddling wi' the liberty o' the soobject, I am clear for mainteening, were it even by force o' law, the decency of a' public entertainments. I cou'd na help lookin' roun' for some member o' the Society for the Suppression o' Vice.

Tickler. Some folks are so very inflammable.

Shepherd. I turned roun' upon the fourscore-and-twa fule ahint me, and ask't the odious dotard if it was na maist laithsome to see him hotchin' on his seat, and to hear him mumplin in the mouth at sic a sicht, in the same box wi' a grown lassie that maun hae been at least his great granddaughter? But the auld toothless satyr was awre deaf to hear me, although wi' help o' ever so mony lenses—baith clarifiers. and multipliers—he had sic vision o' the hawrem as made a monster o' him' sufficient—but for the perversion o' public taste and feeling—to hae brought on his bald head the derision, disgust, and horror o' a full house.

Tickler. Poo—poo—whew!

Shepherd. That's the way o't. To the pure a' things are pure—and on the faith o' a sayin' in scriptur'—ane o' the haliest ever inspired—do people justify indecency after indecency—till—where, may I ask you, Mr. Tickler, is it proposed there shall be a stop?

Tickler. I have been at Peebles.

Shepherd. I ken what you mean. You hae seen a dizzen hizzies on the banks o' the Tweed trampin' claes in boynes, wi' their ain weel tucked up, and frae ane o' the pleasantest sichts o' the usefullest o' employments, in the pure air and sunshine—pursued wi' "weel-timed daffin," and the industrious merriment o' happy hearts—you wou'd reason by a fawse analogy in favor o' the exposure o' weelnigh a' they hae got to expose, o' a gang o' meretrishus limmers—for they're no respectable actresses yon—like them that it's a delicht to see in Rosalind or Beatrice or Perditta—sic as Miss Jarman and Miss Tree—female characters that micht be witnessed even by ministers—but hired at laigh wages—sae might it seem—the grand feck o' them aff the verra streets—to pander to the diseased appeteets o' a luxurious or worn-out generation—or would Lord Grey, think ye, sirs, ca't—the Speerit o' the Age?

North and Buller. Bravo—bravo—bravo!

North. Yet in the same city, and at the same season, were represented to agitated or deeply interested audiences such Fair Humanities as my friend Sheridan Knowles's heart awakens before his fancy, and his genius gives ideal being, to be realized before our delighted eyes by such sweet representatives as those you have now named, and who carry into their characters on the stage the same qualities that make them all that is good and amiable in private life!

Buller. Perhaps, Mr. Hogg, you have somewhat overdrawn—though not over-colored the picture. Yet knowing to what pitch public representations were brought in Rome——

Shepherd. To what pitch!

Buller. Read Juvenal.

Shepherd. But I canna—and sae muckle the better—for nae man, I suspeck, was ever improved by satire that painted the vices it denounced; but many have been corrupted by the physical display, who wanted wisdom or will to draw the moral. Mind ye, sirs, my indignation was not prurient—and were ony coof to ca' it coorse, he wou'd only shew that he kent na the difference atween hypocritical sympathy with grossness affectin' cynical contempt, and genuine disgust giving vent in plain language to the feelings o' a man.

Tickler. James—your hand.

Shepherd. There. Dog on't, you'll bring bluid!

Tickler. These boys flatter you, James—but that I never do—

Shepherd. You err, sir, rather in the opposite direction—but atween the twa it'll be feenally found about richt. Oranges, aipples, grapes, and ither frute, are dootless unco refreshin'; but in their case "increase o' appeteet grows on what it feeds on" far mair surely than in Mrs. Hamlet's—sae may I ask you, sir, to ring the siller bell for anither desert?

North. You will find one behind that stand of Japonicas, James.

(*The Shepherd wheels round the reserve from behind the Japonica stand—and at the same time enter Peter with chasse-caffee.*)

What is your opinion, my dear Shepherd, o' these bills for the better observance of the Sabbath?

Shepherd. What'n bills?

North. Sir Andrew Agnew's and Lord Wynford's.*

Shepherd. I'm ashamed, sir, to say that I never heard tell o' them afore; yet taken by surprise and on the sudden, I shall not pronounce that sic an object lies out o' the sphere o' legal legislation. Stap. I recolleck noo, thinkin' Sir Andrew's motion no very weel matured—and that Lord Winefort's speech was real sensible—but what'n a daft protest was yon o' Lord Vox's? It had a queer sound, yon sentence beginning, "Whereas any attempt to restrain drunkenness"—I canna quot the precise words—but frae his speech it seemed something shocking to the Chancellor to shackle intoxication—and something absurd in the Chancellor to assert, that it was next to impossible to ken when anither man was fou.† Perhaps he mayna stoiter—but tak' tent o' his een—and you'll see he's no sober. Gin he shut them, that's in itsell suspicious; but wait till you hear him tryin' to speak—and unless he's sae far gaen that there's nae mistakin', and, therefore, nae need o' ony particular index to his contents—ye can tell to a trifle, gin he be a freen, the

* Sir Andrew Agnew, a Scottish Baronet of much wealth, was in Parliament at this time, and made it a practice, year after year, to bring forward a Bill for the Better Observance of the Sabbath. The penal provisions of this proposed statute were so severe that the Legislature always declined sanctioning them. Sir Andrew who was not a little puritanical (what Burns calls "unco righteous"), was generally known by the appellation of—Sir Andrew Aguecheek. Lord Wynford had been Chief Justice of the Common Pleas, which he resigned in 1825. He also had an anti-Sabbath-breaking Bill, one provision of which was that no public bakery should be open during any part of Sunday. Considering that one third of all the Sunday dinners in London are cooked at public bakeries, the proposition was admitted to be untenable and the Bill did not pass.—M.

† This refers to a rumor, originating with one of the London newspapers, that the Lord Chancellor (Lord Brougham and Vaux) was of intemperate habits. There was no foundation for such a statement or insinuation. The quantity of headwork which his Lordship was getting through, then and since, was such as none but a person of moderate habits, in eating and drinking, could have transacted.—M.

nummer o' tummlers, or gin an ordinary man o' a stranger, within half-a-dizzen. A' his Lordship's specifications o' the different taps a man may visit who is on the rove, and his argumentations thence deduced as to the diffeeculty, or rather impossibility, o' ony ae landlord's catchin' him at the pint atween the drunk and sober, which, if he passes, he belongs, as the logicians say, to another category, are no sae solid as they may be ingenious, and comin frae ane less acquented wi' the ways o' the world than Hairy Broom, might have been thocht to show that the speaker was sae fond o' theory, as to ken naething about the practice o' the matter in haun; to say naething o' bein' sae uncommon funny in sae grave a place as the House o' Lords. Dinna he gang the length, sir, o' hintin' that they werena "an assembly o' rational beings?"

North. No, no—James—he merely said in his protest that some of the provisions of the intended measure were such as had never before been offered to the consideration "of an assembly of rational beings."

Shepherd. You'll find, sir, that rational and irrational are a' ane by implication. But if you canna see that, why then, as his lordship said to the Yearl o' Wicklow, "I am not bound to find you understaundin'," nor yet, as he said to the Marquis o' Londonderry, to gi'e you "the smallest glimmer" o' insight into the recondite meanin' o' my remark.

Buller. Why, my dear sir, you seem to have all the most remarkable passages of the Parliamentary eloquence of the day at your finger's end.

Shepherd. Stale sourocks.

Buller. Sir?

Shepherd. Naething. As for the Sabbath—"keep it holy." But in Lunnon hoo can that be brocht aboot? Oh! gin it cou'd, wouldna a' Protestant Christians be glad indeed! But if religion cannot guard frae profanation her ain especial day, my heart misgies me as to the power o' ony ither law. Yet may the magistrate, commissioned with salutary authority by mere human wisdom, enforce obedience to the mandate of the King of kings. Outward obedience may come to foster inward; for submission becomes habit—and habit inclination—and inclination love—and love piety—and thus, though of mean origin, may grow up a sentiment that shall be high —no less, sirs, than a sacred sentiment inspiring a man's speerit with all that is holy—on the holy day. For a day set apart from secular concerns—and, as far as may be from the worldly feelings that cling to them even in thought—has a prodigious power, sirs, ower all that is divine in our human—and lang before the close o' life—or the beginning o' its decline—ay, even in youth—boyhood—childhood—yea, we have a' read and believed o' sic effects wrought even in the heart o' verra infancy—becomes like a law o' nature. Ay, as if the sun rose more solemnly—yet not less sweetly—on the Sabbath morning—and a profounder stillness pervaded not the earth only, but the sky.

North. My dear James.

Shepherd. I'm no meanin' to deceive either you or me, sir, with the belief that much o' this is no the wark o' imagination. For mony a stormy Sabbath has sunk mony a ship on the sea. But still, for the main o' human life, in a true Christian kintra, sic as Scotland,* the Sabbath is a day o' rest—first to men's bodies, and then to men's souls; and gin the Sabbath be lown, which, far oftener than itherwise, a thousand memories tell me it has been in the Forest—the peacefu' and gratefu' heart collects all the lang-gane cawms intil the thoughtfu' feelin' o' ae endurin' cawm—and *it* hangs owre the idea o' the Sabbath, making it, even when the elements are at strife, still in the soul as the heart o' a kirk, when the minister is rising to pray, or a sweet serene sound at intervals rises upon our ear, like the psalm the congregation sings, when even some amang the three-year-auld infants are not wholly mute!

North. How unlike the Sundays I have seen, James, in many Roman Catholic countries! Yet I dared not there to condemn the happiness with which I could not sympathize so entirely as I would fain have done—for though creed and custom had deeply engraved all the impressions of which you have so beautifully spoken, not on the tablets of my memory, but of my conscience—yet what was I that I should see sin where the eyes of far better and wiser men saw no sin, but looked on well-pleased with faces now bright with mirthful smiles, that an hour ago at the altar were drenched in tears?

Shepherd. David danced before the Ark. But what if the Moderator were to do sae on his way up the High Street to hear the sermon preached before the Commissioner!

North. In England, Mr. Buller—I speak of the places I best know—the Sabbath is so well observed, that I know not if it could be better—yet its spirit is not either to my eye or my heart the same as in Scotland. Should I say rightly, were I to say that the Sabbath-spirit in England is serene—in Scotland austere? Hardly so. For—let no lightness, or frivolity, or indifference, or torpor, be seen any where around him; and neither in the kirk—nor walking to or from the kirk—nor in his own house or garden—should I say the countenance of THE ELDER or of any of one of his family was

* The *outward* show of Sabbath-keeping is great indeed, in Scotland. I have known an Elder of the Church, in one of the principal cities, threaten a man (who, on the Sabbath, "whistled as he went, for want of thought") with imprisonment, as a Sabbath-breaker. Whether said Elder closed that day with his accustomed three or four glasses of hot toddy is "nothing to nobody."—M.

austere, though he and they be true, in faith and in works, to their forefathers of the Covenant.

Shepherd. I canna bring mysell to doubt—though without a grain o' dogmatism—that o' a' the ways o' observin' the Seventh Day, that which has prevailed in Scotland—if no ever sin' the Reformation, sin' the establishment o' the Presbyterian kirk—is the best; and for this ae reason—that wi' us the Sabbath is Itself. The common use of the term Sabbath-breakin' conveys a' that is shockin'—and I'm no speakin' o' that; but the Sabbath may be broken, surely, sir, in anither sense, and perhaps without ony sin—for there can be nae sin without evil intention, and nae evil intentions in the hearts o' thae Roman Catholic lads and lasses—be they Italians or Germans—or what not—wha break down and fritter awa the Sabbath—dancin' aneath poplar or linden tree. Na—for a' that I ken—that may be the best kind o' Sabbath for them—seein' that to judge what is best requires a knowledge o' their character and o' their condition the ither days o' the week. Perhaps they cou'dna bear a different Sabbath—though it were as a Sabbath far superior spiritually to that o' theirs —but fit only for a people leevin' under a clearer and a fuller light. The mair Christian the people, the mair Christian the Sabbath; and though I'm no unacquainted wi' the controversy about the change thought by some divines to hae been wrought in the law regarding the Jewish Sabbath—yet hae I nae mair doubts than o' my ain existence, that the events recorded in the New Testament have made the Sabbath holier—if that might be—even than in the days o' Moses—therefore let it be kept holy; and if—as I believe—it be kept so in Scotland—then the blessing of God will be upon her—and as she is good, so shall she wax great.

North. Alas! James—alas!

Shepherd. I ken Scotland's no what she ance was—but I believe that instead o' continuin' to get waur, she'll get better—for that cant aboot the decent observance o' this, and the decent observance o' that, and the rational view o' this soobject, and the leeberal view o' that ither soobject, will no much langer stand the test o' reason—for reason enlightened to the height kens that the cause o' a' good resides, as Cowper says, in that heavenly word—Religion; and that Faith re-established, what's ca'd Philosophy—that's waur nor superstition—will die—then men will feel, that, to leeve as they ought to do, ither instruction and ither support are necessary than they can get frae a' the books that ever were or will be prented—and which seeking, they shall find in One.

Buller. All the highest minds in Europe now see and declare the immortal truth, that all education must be based and built on the Christian religion.

Shepherd. Owre lang were they blin', and owre lang hae they been dumb. For all the humblest have seen and declared it a' their lives lang—though their declaration was confined to a sma' sphere—includin' chiefly twa homesteads—that in which they live and die—and that in which they are buried!

North. The difficulty in London—in England—and in Scotland too—is to all that may be done for the Sabbath, without interfering with the comforts—may I say the amusements, of the lower orders—the working classes—the poor.

Tickler. The million.

Buller. The great multitude of mankind.

Shepherd. The majority o' the human race.

North. Let legislators look to themselves, and not to their individual selves alone, but to their order, in legislating for the Sabbath.

Buller. Let them begin with the rich and end with the poor.

Tickler. And the poor will then submit to the law, and, as the Shepherd admirably observed, love the law. Not else.

North. I have no holy horror of hot Sabbath-baked mutton pies.

Shepherd. Nor me—though on Sabbath there's no a het denner, if you except potawtoes, in a' the Forest.

North. Nor would I too much trammel the Thames.

Shepherd. "The boatie rows—the boatie rows." And after sermon I can see nae sin in a sail. No that ever ony body saw me on the Sabbath in a boot on the loch. But St. Mary's is a still sheet o' inland water, wi' but few inhabitants on its banks—and the Thames is a rinnin' river, wi' ebb and flaw o' tide, wi' magnificent brigs, and wharfs, and stairs, by which a michty city keeps up continual communication wi' the sea, and perhaps the Sabbath would be owre deathlike on that great water, were the law to hush the voice o' human life, and a nichtlike silence to settle doon there even on the Lord's day. But I canna tell. It's no for me to judge what's best, for I'm no the Bishop o' Lunnon, but only the Ettrick Shepherd.

North. The Sabbath day has been so long kept holy in Scotland, that Sabbath-breaking here—as you well said, James—is justly considered to be a shocking sin. Should it be thought right to strengthen by law such observance of the Sabbath as has become a national characteristic, here it may be comparatively easy to do so; for such law can affect only a small minority of offenders, with whom there is no sympathy among the good of any class or any creed—and reform will be restoration.

Shepherd. Burns sang the Cotter's Saturday Night, and James Grahame the Sabbath—and Poetry is indeed a heaven-taucht art when it sanctifies Religion.

North. The spirit of the age in Scotland is religious, and the people, in spite of all this noise, love its simple Church. Great cause have they for their love—for that simple Church has cared for them—and they owe all that is best in their character to its ministrations. Philosophy has not made our people what they are —neither moral nor natural philosophy—though both are excellent; human science cannot control the will—but in the will lies all good and all evil—and to know how to gain dominion over them, search the Scriptures.

Shepherd. Alas for the people who will not! Then, indeed, may they be ca'd "the lower orders"—below the beasts that perish. Men ca' the wee sleek mole blin' because he has na een they can see, and leeves darklin' in the moul—but he has een fitted for his condition as well as the eagle's—and travels along his earth-galleries aneath the soil as surely as the royal bird alang his air-paths on the sky. But we that ca' him blin' are far blinner oursells; for we forget we hae speeritual as weel as corporeal een—that they see by a different licht—far ither objects—and that the ae set may be gleg and bricht, while the ither's blunt and opake—the corporeal farkeekers indeed, that wi' the aid o' telescopes can look into the heart o' the fixed stars—the speeritual sae narrow-ranged, that a's black before them as a wa', though God-given to gaze into the verra gates o' heaven.

North. My beloved Shepherd, after that I shall say nothing.

Buller. Yes! I will see you in your own house in the Forest—my dear—

Shepherd. I'll drive you oot, Mr. Buller, in the morn in the gig. Gie's your haun on't. That's settled.

North. Thinking on human life in humble households, my heart sums up all the holiest sights I have so often seen there in two words carrying with them the profoundest pathos—Contentment and Resignation.

Shepherd. Mr. North, hearken till me, and I'll gi'e you, in as few words as I can, an illustration o' your true and wise remark. I ken a howe amang the hills where staun three houses—apairt frae ane anither about a quarter o' a mile—a rather unusual occurrence for three houses to be sae near in sic a sitiation—yet they are there noo, as they hae been for mair nor a hunder years, and, though auld like, are cozey, and care na either for wund or snaw.

North. Why, James, you have already painted a picture.

Shepherd. I didna mean to be descriptive—but I canna help it. In the house at the fell-fit, where the burn is a spring, the family consists o' fourteen sowls—pawrents and childer—no that they are a' leevin' at hame—for some o' baith lads and lasses are at service —but last time I was there I coonted seven growin' anes, twa three o' them bein' weans, and ane a babby. The couple hae been man and wife twunty year, and death has never ance knocked at their door; no ane o' them a' ever had a fivver. Then they hae a' turned out weel—without vice or folly—what'n a blessin' in sic a large family!—are a' weel-manner'd and weel-faured—indeed, far mair nor that—for the twa twuns are the maist beautifu' creturs ever seen, and like as lilies.

Tickler. I should like to go a Maying to the Howe.

Shepherd. You wud get gran' curds and ream—and the lassies nae lack o' lauchin'. The twa twuns wud get prime fun wi' Lang-legs—passin' themselves aff on him for ane anither—and first the ane and then the ither declarin' it was na her that had gotten the ribands.

Tickler. The fairies!

Shepherd. In the neist house—laigher doon beside the linn—I remember there bein' born first a bairn and then anither—lad and lassie time about—till there were nae fewer than ten. You cou'd na say, when you luikt at them as they were waxin', that they were ony way unhealthy—though rather slennerer and mair delicat than you might hae wushed your ain bairns. But, waes me! sirs, no ae single ane o' a' the ten ever saw the sun o' their twuntieth simmer—few reached saxteen—the rest dwined awa' earlier—and noo they are a' dead!

North. And the parents!

Shepherd. Wait a wee and I'll tell you aboot the pawrents. In the house laighest o' the three—and that you can see peepin' by itsell—as if the ither twa were na near it—leeve a pair noo wearin' awa'—wha married when I was a herd—and they had never ony bairns ava: sae that the freens in the twa ither houses sometimes used to fear the sicht o' their families micht wauken envy in the hearts o' them wha sleepit in a barren bed. Nor wou'd it hae been unnatural if it had; but na—God, they kent, gied—and God withheld—and God took awa'—and through a' their lang life childless, yet through a' their lang life hae they been cheerfu' as birds, and industrious as bees. In troth they hae been just a meeracle o' contentment—and though they liked best the cawm o' their ain house, yet they were merry as grigs among ither folks' weans—wha aften ca'd her mammy as weel's their ain mither.

North. God bless you, James.

Shepherd. And you, sir. Noo, sir, I dinna fear to say—for I know it to be a truth and a great truth—that thae three couple are at this hour a' equally—but oh! how differently happy! Them that has never kent the blessings o' bairns—them that has enjoyed it in overflowing measure, and without ae drap o' what can be ca'd bitter in the cup—and them that saw a' their bairntime meltin' awa' till they had to kneel doon by their ain twa sells in prayer. Ae word—or twa words—and the twa, though ane and the same, soun' sweet and awfu' thegither—explain the mystery. The Bible —Religion.

(*There is silence for a time. North rings the silver bell, and appear Peter and Ambrose with the cold round, ham and fowls, and tongues, and the unassuming but not the unsubstantial etceteras of such a small snug Mid-summer supper as you may suppose suitable at a Noctes on the Leads of the Lodge. North nods, and Peter lets on the gas.*)

Shepherd. Farewell to the moon and stars.

North. What will you eat, James?

Shepherd. I'll take some hen. Mr. Buller, gie me the twa legs and the twa wings and the breast—and then haun the hen owre to Mr. Tickler.

(*They settle down into serious eating. The Shepherd taking the lead pressed by Mr. North.*)

Tickler. How are you getting on, James?

Shepherd. But slawly. Canna ye sook that back without your jaw-banes clunkin'? Soopin' on the leeds o' the Lodge aneath a silk yawnin' in a conservatory lichted up with gas! Buller, what are ye aboot?

Buller. Tucking in a trifle of brawn.

Shepherd. Mr. North, I've seen naething frae your pen, for years by, comparable to "Christopher on Colonsay." I howpe we're to hae anither Fytte.*

North. I believe Fytte Second opens the Number.

Shepherd. That's richt—and had Gurney no been in the Heelans, you might hae concluded the Nummer wi' this Noctes.

A still small voice. I'm here.

Shepherd. Gude safe us!

North. Here's a tribute from an admirer near Cirencester.

Say, who is this with crutch so strong!
With beard so grizzled and so long,
Riding o'er mountain and o'er dell,
Rushing thro' forest and thro' fell,
As tho' he were an imp from hell,
Who is that thus scours away?
'Tis Christopher on Colonsay.

Look! look upon that Tory steed!
With eye and snort that mark his breed;
Shod too is he with hoofs of brass,
That gleam like lightning as they pass
To tread down every Whig and ass,
Is it a horse or Demon? Say—
'Tis Christopher on Colonsay.

* Christopher on Colonsay, Fytte I., appeared in *Blackwood* of June, 1834: the second part was the opening or leading article of the succeeding July number.—M.

Tremble, ye traitors, fight or fly;
But if ye fight, then look to die.
No weapon can ye wield that e'er
The weight of that dread crutch can bear,
Which those who feel must ever fear.
When question'd why ye run, then say—
Here's Christopher on Colonsay.

Tho' Lords and Commons marshall'd stand,
Tho' Brougham may jeer, or Grey command,
Should little Johnny stop the way,
Or Durham mingle in the fray,
Or Althorp mount a bull at bay,
They'll have no time to fight or pray*—
Here's Christopher on Colonsay.

No power can check him or his steed,
A centaur of celestial seed,
Smack thro' the frighten'd host he flies,
Prostrate each smitten Whigling lies.
They who escape may bless their eyes
That they could scamper from the way
Of Christopher on Colonsay.

Low sprawling in the dust and mire,
And well besmuch't he leaves the quire.
Io! triumphe! on he goes
O'er kicking Lords and prostrate foes;
Graham and Stanley shake their clothes,
And swear they'll never more essay
Dread Christopher on Colonsay.

On, man and steed! On! ride your round
While Radicals or Whigs are found,
Lay on the crutch with heart and hand,
Go, scatter and confound the band,
And prove them but a rope of sand,
That rogues may ever run and say—
Here's Christopher on Colonsay.

Shepherd. Never heard I a man receet his ain praises wi' sic an emphasis!

North. You would not have had me mumble such spirited lines, like an old woman without a tooth in her gums, James?

Shepherd. I could mention an old man that has na mony teeth in his ain gums, though for a' that, his receetation's no that o' a mumbler, Kit. Vanity! vanity! a' is vanity!

North. Vanity is one of the most amiable of the large Family of Human Frailties.

Shepherd. I never said ye was no amiable, sir.

North. Nobody at least can justly accuse me of being proud.

Shepherd. Lucifer's a Moses to you, sir, in pride. You're a sin

* Earl Grey's reign as Premier had terminated when this Noctes was published. He was driven from office by intrigues which made Lord Melbourne his successor. Brougham was Lord Chancellor, Lord John Russell, the Earl of Durham, and Lord Althorpe (the last named being a great cattle breeder) were Cabinet Ministers.—M.

gular instance o' pride and vanity—till your time thocht incompatible—meetin' in equal proportions in the same character. For an hour I've seen you sae vain that I couldna help pitying ye—during the neist sae proud that I couldna help hatin' ye—and yet sae strange a thing is human nature, that at the eend o' the third hour, the only feelings I had for the anomaly were admiration and love.

North. It is with you as with the rest of mankind, James—I bring you all round to unite in admiration and love of me at last.

Shepherd. Heard ye ever the likes o' that, Mr. Buller? Luik at the cretur. Vanity in his left ee and pride in his richt! and yet it maun be confessed, diffused owre the ither features o' his face something verra delightfu', and a halo round the head o' him, as if, instead o' sinner, he were a saint.

Tickler. I have seldom seen you, James, brighter than you have been to-night—you have felt yourself at home on the leads—on ground-flats I have seen you somewhat dullish—like a luminary in damp.

Shepherd. There's naething in the warld I like waur than to be drawn oot by a sumph.

Buller. I beg pardon.

Tickler. Or sumphess.

Shepherd. The she's ill, but no sae ill's the he. Dinna you agree wi' me, Mr. Buller?

Buller. In what?

Shepherd. In thinkin' the she sumph's no sae ill's the he.

Buller. I hope the he will soon get better—but I am in outer darkness—pray, what is a sumph?

Shepherd. Anither instance o' that extraordinary ignorance that no that seldom breaks out unexpectedly in weel-educated Englishmen, and seems sae surprising to us on this side o' the Tweed! But leavin' you to construe sumph, I shall simplify the question, sir, by askin' ye just "hoo like ye to be drawn oot ava?"

Buller. I very much doubt if I should like it. What is the nature of that process?

Shepherd. He's in the dark aboot that limb o' the query, too. The sumph, you see, sir, sits himsell doon richt opposite to ye at denner, and afore you hae had time to cool the first spoonfu' o' cocky-leeky, or potawtoe soup, by blawin' upon't, he selecks ane frae some twa three dizzen o' toppics, that are a' lyin' arranged, cut and dry, in separate raws on the floor o' that lumber-room, his head.

Buller. Good, good—I have you now, Mr. Hogg.

Shepherd. And in which he conceives you to take sic an enthusiastic interest, as to amount on't to the half-mad, whereas the soobjects are lyin' so laigh doon amang the dubs o' obscurest dirt, that even in your meaner moments you would despise yoursell for condescending to honor't wi' your contempt.

North. What think you, James, of being *pitted?*

Shepherd. O bein' what?

North. Asked to dinner, that you may be pitted by your host against a cock, fed, clipped out, and heeled to slay you on the sod.

Shepherd. It's weel kent I never argue none—therefore I'm never asked to denner to be pitted—only drawn out.

North. I can spar and fight a bit too, James—but 'tis teasing to be tackled to by a Bantam. Onwards he comes sidelong with his wing down, comb and wattles glowing like fiery furnace, and picking up straws in his pride of place—then drawing himself up to his whole extent, he crows to cow your heart, and without farther ceremony flies at you like a fury to tear you into pieces. With one cuff you make him spin out of sight—and if any one hopes to find him, he must look below the table.

Shepherd. That's makin a short business wi' the bit bantam.

North. Or perhaps you have been invited to single combat with a Dunghill. Sole monarch of all he has been habituated to survey on the stercoraceous heap, he has come to think himself invincible —but at the first tussle of

> "The sportive fury of the fencer's steel,"

with one insane scraugh he bolts, and hides his head in a hole in the wall, unashamed of the exposure of his enormous bottom.

Shepherd. Pootry shou'd never be pitted wi' ggemm.

North. I have known the master of a house entice you to dinner that he might see a set-to between you and a mastiff.

Shepherd. Surely no wi' the conneevance o' the mistress?

North. The surly brute, with black muzzle and swarthy eyes, has kept grimly watching you till the cloth be drawn—and then curling up his lips to show you his fangs, without any provocation on your part, began to growl—

Shepherd. Afore the leddies?

North. And then, in spite of your submission, leapt at your throat, with his paws over your shoulder, with a view to the jugular.

Shepherd. What a pictur o' a great big brindled outrageous Radical, insistin' on the separation o' Church and State!

North. It requires some strength, James, I assure you, to shake off such a monster.

Shepherd. But his bark's waur than his bite.

North. The best way is to seize him with both hands and then throttle him, till his tongue is bitten through and through by his teeth, his eyes goggled, and he drops. I call that the *argumentem ad canem.*

Shepherd. It's conclusive.

North. Or what think you, James, of a pack of young Whig curs—

Shepherd. Pups.

North. Yelping at you all round the table—

Shepherd. And Christopher North the whupper-in! I pity the puir pups.

North. I have suffered all that, and more, James. Yet perhaps worse than them all is it, on a three weeks' invitation to go, as an especial favor, and to confer an obligation which will never be forgotten—to meet an ass.

Shepherd. Or a mool.

North. A downright positive ass.

Shepherd. As a' the asses are o' ma acquaintance—but I'm speakin' the noo o' oor own native breed, an' aiblins you're alludin' to ane frae foreign parts—where they grow to a far greater size—as in Spain.

North. No, James—your continental cuddy coming over to this country is mostly mute.

Shepherd. Has na learned the language.

North. The one I last met—for upwards of four hours—never for a moment ceased to bray.

Shepherd. And did ye cudgel him sair?

North. I did. But I am bound in candor to confess that he was little or none the better of it—and for the first time in my life, I am ashamed to say, I was fairly brayed off the field.

Shepherd. And the neist day, a' the town would nae doot be ringin' wi' your defeat.

North. Ichabod! Ichabod! the glory of our conversational powers was gone for ever, and the victorious donkey kept braying his way over the border, communicating tidings of our discomfiture all over merry England.

Shepherd. Swearin' he had swallowed the Thane o' the Scotch Thristles at a single chow!—I had a delicat compliment paid me yestreen, sir. I was asked to soop wi' a family that said they had inveeted a pairty to meet me just after my ain mind. And there they were a' sittin' on chairs roun' the room, as I entered, accordin' to agreement, wi' my plaid, staff in haun, and dowg at fit, a great grandson o' Hector's. What he thocht I canna say, but I cou'd hae sworn, sir, that they were sheep. The same large, licht, mild, rather unmeanin' een—the same lang, white smooth faces as the cheviots—and the same lip-like noses—formin' in fact atween the twa but ae fetur, overhanging their mouths, without in ony way interferin' wi' the feedin'—and then a' at ance the same baa—baa—baa—maa—maa—maa—for rams, and ewes, and wethers, and gimmers, and hoggs, and lambs, had been a' gathered thegether frae mony pastures into ae hirsel—a' to do honor to the Ettrick Shepherd.

Tickler. Not by any means an unoriginal idea.

Shepherd. Were it no' a pure maitter o' fack, it micht pass for wut—for wut is a sayin' at ance felt by the auditor to be baith apt and new—givin' rise in his mind to wonner that he hadna thocht o' sayin't himsell, sorrow that he didna say't, and generally conviction that to hae said it was ayont his power.

North. James, what is your opinion of the state of public affairs?

Shepherd. O, sir! but yon was like to be a great national calamity!

North. Probably it was, James. Pray, what was it?

Shepherd. The horizon was black indeed—the tempests were about to break lowse frae their slumbers—and we heard a mutterin' sound as o' the angry sea.

North. I hae no sort of doubt of it whatever—but I forget the particulars.

Shepherd. There were nae particulars—and it was the want o' them that made it sae awfu'—at least I saw nane deservin' the name o' particulars in the newspapers—a' wore a general look o' danger—the fear was universal—and therefore I was justified in sayin'. as I did the noo, "O, sir! but yon was like to be a great national calamity!"

North. I devoutly trust, James, the storm's blown over.

Shepherd. Wha can say—wha can say? The stocks fell doon a' at ance, like quicksiller in a barometer, ever sae mony degrees—thretty or thereabouts in the twunty-four hours—for folk feared a national bankruptcy, and in sic panic wha wou'd buy in?

North. The national credit must have received a shock. But how? Do relieve my anxiety, James.

Shepherd. The greatest pairt o' the poppilation o' the island—an overwhelmin' majority—were on the eve o' emigratin' to America. They had secured their fright and passage, and were only waitin' for a change o' wun'—as a freen wrott me frae Portsmouth—to rin through the Needles. What that meant I knaw not—but that the British navy was hired for the simmer frae the Admiralty for the purpose aforesaid, I ken to be a fack—and Sir James Graham* fand securities that it was to mak twa trips. O, sir! but yon was like to be a great national calamity!

Tickler. The Plague?

Shepherd. Far waur than the Plague—'cause threatenin' to be mair universal—though, like the Plague, it was in London—thank Heaven—where it first brak out—The Tailors' Strike!

* Sir James Graham was First Lord of the Admiralty in 1834.—M.

North. 'Twas an appalling event—and, like the great earthquake at Lisbon, was, no doubt, felt all over Europe.

Shepherd. Ay—at the great earthquake o' Lisbon, sir, I've heard tell that the waters o' Loch Lomond ran sky-high as in storm, and at the great Tailor-strike o' Lunnon, I daur to say that the kilts alang its shores flew up as in whirlwinds, exposing the hurdies o' a thoosan' John Heelandmans.

North. Buller, how picturesque! The Shepherd is the most poetical of political economists.

Shepherd. For dinna tell me that kilts are ae thing and breeks anither—they baith alike appertain to the person, and the same pairt o' the person. A' the causes that affeck the tredd in breeks, affeck, nearly or remotely, immediately or after a lang lapse o' years, the tredd in kilts—a' the usefu' arts, and the fine anes too—and *à fortiori*, them that's at ance usefu' and fine, and aboon a' tailorin'—bein' a' connecket by inveesible threeds—ony feck o' which being cut or run, or runkled or ravelled, the rest feel it like a speeder's wab—and shrink up till the haill commercial system is disordered and deranged, and the social system too—and the political likewise—and the moral also—and if sae, hoo can the religious escape—till the universe itsell seems to be rushin' intil ruins, and it requires na seer to predick that there is speedily about to be an eend o' a' things—and the heavens and the earth reduced back by a grand convulsion o' nature to their original chawos.

North. Let us hope there may be some little exaggeration——

Shepherd. No a grain. Did you no listen to the overpoorin' eloquence o' the Maisters? I hae been only usin' some o' their language, subdued doon to Noctes pitch. The een o' a Britain, Stultz* said, was upon them——

North. "They read their history in a nation's eyes."

Shepherd. And they were a' fu' o' tears! The nation grat while it glowered——

Buller. And significantly smote its thigh.

Tickler. Methought I met Sir Henry Hardinge† in Bond Street without his coat—arm in arm with a member who had dispensed with his breeches; in the rear I saw a flaming patriot, not unlike Lord Nugent,‡ with nothing but his shirt—while

* Stultz, a native of Germany, was the fashionable tailor in London for many years before and after 1834. His family have returned to their father-land since his death, with a large fortune, earned by this fortunate Snip, who purchased the title of Baron a long time before his death.—M.

† Sir Henry Hardinge, who was Irish Secretary under Wellington's administration, in 1830, and 1834, and again under Peel in 1841, lost his left hand at Ligny, in 1815. In 1844, he was sent out as Governor-General of India, took part in the first war of the Punjaub, concluded the treaty of Lahore, and obtained a Peerage from the Queen, with £5000 pension from the East India Company. In 1852, on the death of the Duke of Wellington, he was placed in Chief Command of the British Army.—M.

‡ Lord Nugent who died in 1850, was Lord-Commissioner of the Ionian Islands from 1832 to 1835. He was very liberal in politics, very stout in person.—M.

"A painted vest Prince Vortigern had on,
Which from a naked Pict his grandsire won."

Shepherd. Haw! haw! haw!

Tickler. Funerals were no more black-jobs.*

Shepherd. Gude again.

Tickler. See that chief mourner in red breeches—yellow vest, with long flapping lappets—and coat bright with the purple light of love—a superb dress got up by his great-great-great-grandsire, in honor of the Restoration—and in 1834 worn by a disconsolate son, but determined anti-Trades-Unionist, strong in filial love and patriotism, following, like the fragment of a weeping rainbow, a Conservative father to the grave!

Shepherd. What o' deed he? What deed he o'?

Tickler. Of Tailor-strike.

Shepherd. In the midst o' a great national calamity, hoo indifferent, alas! grows the heart to individual distress! At ony other time the thocht o' sic a funeral wou'd hae been affectin'—but noo I can hear o't without a tear.

North. The misery was confined to the metropolis. The rural districts at least providentially escaped the infection——

Shepherd. Yet the complaint was fearsomely contawgious—and rinnin' like wild-fire through the streets o' Lunnon.

Tickler. Where did it first break out?

Shepherd. Beneath a skylicht. It raged awfully in the attics afore it got doon to the other flats—and howp grew sick and dee'd on seein' and hearin't roarin' oot o' the wundows o' the grund-flat.

North. A fine subject for an Epic.

Buller. Better fitted, perhaps, sir, for the drama. Yet the nation, I fear, has lost its love for the highest and deepest tragedy—and to rouse it even by such a theme, would require more than the genius of another Shakspere.

Tickler. The Flints flash fire, and the day of the Dungs is gone.†

Shepherd. The rural districts, as you ca' them, Mr. North, hae na

* The Earl of Portsmouth, who died in July, 1853, had been brought before a Commission *de lunatico inquirendo*, and (as the half-witted hero of "The Entail' says) was "found guilty of being *daft*"—or out of his senses. It was proved in evidence that his favorite amusement—amounting, indeed, to a passion—was attendance on funerals, which he called "black jobs." It may be added, as curious, that one of his remarks was quoted by one lawyer as evidencing his folly, by another as showing his wit. Some large boxes had arrived at Hurtsbourne Park, his seat in Hampshire, and his servants were not able to raise the lids without calling in the aid of a carpenter. While they were pausing, an Irishman who was the Earl's personal attendant, said, "Faith, one would think 'tis oysters they were, they're so hard to open." Lord Portsmouth replied, "If they are oysters, put them on the fire, and the heat will open them soon enough."—M.

† "The Tailors, a Tragedy for Warm Weather," in which the terms *flints* and *dungs* are first applied, was produced in London, in July, 1767, when there had been great disturbances between the master tailors, and their journeymen about wages. Those who held out for the advance were honored with the name of Flints, while those who continued to work at the former prices, were called Dungs.—M.

always escaped sic a calamity. I weel remember, in the year wan, a like visitation in the Forest. It wasna on sae big a scale—for the boonds wou'dna admit o' its bein' sae—but the meesery was nae less—though contrackit within a narrower circle.

Tickler. Diffused over a wider sphere.

North. When?

Tickler. And how?

Shepherd. The tailor at Yarrow-ford, without havin' shown ony symptoms o' the phoby the nicht afore, ae morning at sax o'clock—*strack!*

North. How dreadful!

Shepherd. You may weel say that, sir. 'Twas just at the dawn o the Season o' Tailors, when a' owre the Forest there begins the makin' o' new claes and the repairin' o' auld——

North. Making—as Bobby says—

"The auld claes look amaist as weel's the new."

Shepherd. The maist critical time o' the haill year!

North. Weel, James?

Shepherd. At sax he strack—and by nine it was kent frae Selkirk to the Gray-Mare's Tail. A' at ance—no ordinar claes only—but marriage-shoots and murnins were at a deed staun. A' the fo'k in the Forest saw at ance that it was impossible decently to get either married or buried. For wou'd ye believe't, the mad body was aff owre the hills, and bat Watty o' Ettrick Pen! Of coorse he strack—and in his turn aff by a short cut to the Lochs, and bat Bauldy o' Bourhope, who lowpt frae the boord like a puddock, and flung the guse in the fire, swearin' by the shears, as he flourished them round his head, and then sent them into the awse-hole, that a' mankind micht thenceforth gang naket for him up to the airmpits in snaw!

North. We are all listening to you, James, with the most intense interest.

Shepherd. The Three Tailors formed themsells intil a union*—and boond themsells by an aith—the words o' which hae never transpired—but nae doot they were fearsome—and they ratified it—it has been said—wi' three draps each o' their ain bluid, let oot wi' the prick o' a needle—no to shue anither stitch gin the Forest were to fa' doon afore them on its knees!

North. Impious!

Shepherd. But the Forest had nae sic intention—and bauldly stood up again' the rebellion. Auld Mr. Laidlaw—the father o

* This allusion to the trinity of tailors, was caused, no doubt, by a recent joke of Peel's. Some petition was presented, as from a large body, with very few signatures, and Peel said that it reminded him of three tailors in Tooley street, who met in the Reform Bill excitement, and drew up a solemn League and Covenant, commencing "We, the People of England!"—M.

your freens, Watty, George, and James—took the lead—and there was a gatherin' on Mount Benger—the same farm that, by a wonnerfu' coincidence, I afterwards came to hauld—at which resolutions were sworn by the Forest no to yield, while there was breath in its body, though back and side micht gang bare. I there made ma maiden speech; for it was na ma maiden speech—though it passed for such, as often happens—the ane ye heard, sir—ma first in the Forum.*

North. I confess I had my suspicions at the time, James. I thought I saw the arts of the sophist in those affected hesitations—and that I frequently heard, breaking through the skilful pauses, the powers, omnipotent in self-possession, of the practised orator.

Shepherd. Never was there sic a terrible treeo as them o' Yarrowford, Ettrick Pen, and Bourhope! Three decenter tailor lads, a week afore, ye micht hae searched for in vain owre the wide warld. The streck changed them into demons. They cursed, they swore, they drank, they danced, they fought—first wi' whatever folk happened to fa' in wi' them on the stravaig—and then, castin' out amang theirsells, wi' ane anither, till they had a' three black een—and siccan noses!

Tickler. 'Tis difficult for an impartial, because unconcerned spectator, to divine the drift of the different parties in a fight of three.

Shepherd. They cou'dna hae divined it theirsells—for there was nae drift amang them to divine. There they were a' three lounderin' at hap-hazard, and then gawn heed oure heels on the tap o' ane anither, or collecket in a knot in the glaur; and I cou'dna help sayin' to Mr. Bryden—father o' your favorite Watty Bryden, to whom ye gied the tortoise-shell mull—"Saw ye ever, sir, a *Tredd's Union like that?*"

Tickler. Why not import?

Shepherd. As they hae dune since in Lunnon frae Germany? Just because naebody thocht o't. Importin' tailors to insure free tredd!!

Tickler. And how fared the Forest?

Shepherd. No weel. Some folk began tailorin' for theirsells—but there was a strong prejudice against it—and to them that made the attempp the result was baith ridiculous and painfu' and in ae case, indeed, had nearly proved fatal.

Tickler. James, how was that?

Shepherd. Imagine yoursell, Mr. Tickler, in a pair o' breeks,

* The Forum a debating society in Edinborough, of which Hogg was a member; during the time when he was fluctuating between

"Obscurity and Fame
The glory and the nothing of a Name."—M.

wi' the back pairt afore—the seat o' honor transferred to the front——

North. Let us all so imagine, Tickler.

Shepherd. They shaped them sae, without bein' able to help it, for it's a kittle art cuttin' oot.

Tickler. But how fatal?

Shepherd. Dandy o' Dryhope, in breeks o' his ain gettin' up, rashly daured to ford the Yarrow—but they grupped him sae tight atween the fork, that he could mak nae head gain the water comin' doon gay strang, and he was swoopit aff his feet, and ta'en out mair like a bundle o' claes than a man.

Tickler. How?

Shepherd. We lister'd him like a fish.

North. "Time and the hour run through the roughest day!"

Shepherd. And a' things yerthly hae an end. Sae had the streck. To mak a lang story short—the Forest stood it oot—the tailors gied in—and the Tredd's Union fell to pieces. But no before the Season o' Tailors was lang owre, and pairt o' the simmer too—for they didna return to their wark till the langest day. It was years afore the rebels recovered frae the want o' wages and the waste o' pose; but atween 1804 and 8, a' three married, and a' three, as you ken, Mr. North—for I hae been direckin' myself to Mr. Tickler and Mr. Buller—hae been ever sin' syne weel-behaved and weel-to-do—and I never see ony o' them without their tellin' me to gie you their compliments, mair especially the tailor o' Yarrow Ford—for Watty o' the Pen—him, Mr. Buller, that used to be ca'd the Flyin' Tailor o' Ettrick*—sometimes fears that Christopher North hasna got owre yet the beatin' he gied him in the ninety-odd—the year Louis the Sixteenth was guillotined—at hap-stap-and-lowp.

North. He never beat me, Mr. Buller.

Buller. From what I have heard of you in youth, sir, indeed I can hardly credit it. Pardon my scepticism, Mr. Hogg.

Shepherd. You may be as great a sceptic as you choose—but Watty bate Kitty a' till sticks.

North. You have most unkindly persisted, Hogg, during all these forty years, in refusing to take into account my corns——

Shepherd. Corns or nae corns, Watty bate you a' till sticks.

North. Then I had been fishing all day up to the middle in the water, with a creel forty pound weight on my back—

Shepherd. Creel or nae creel, Watty bate you a' to sticks.

North. And I had a hole in my heel you might have put your hand into——

* The flying tailor of Ettrick was the subject of, and gave a title to, one of Hogg's imitations in his Poetic Mirror.—M.

Shepherd. Sound heels or sair heels, Watty bate you a' to sticks.

North. And I sprained one of my ankles at the first rise.

Shepherd. Though you had sprained baith, Watty wou'd hae bate you a' till sticks.

North. And those accursed corduroys cut me——

Shepherd. Dinna curse the corduroys—for in breeks or oot o' breeks, Watty bate ye a' till sticks.

North. I will beat him yet for a——

Shepherd. You shanna be alloo'd to make sic a fule o' yoursell. You were ance the best lowper I ever saw—accepp ane—and that ane was wee Watty o' the Pen—the Flyin' Tailor o' Ettrick—and he bate ye a' till sticks.

North. Well—I have done, sir. All people are mad on some one point or other—and your insanity——

Shepherd. Mad or no mad, Watty bate you a' till sticks.

North. Peter, let off the gas. (*Rising with marked displeasure.*)

Shepherd. O man! but that's puir spite! Biddin' Peter let aff the gas, merely 'cause I tauld Mr. Buller what a' the Forest kens to be true, that him the bairns noo ca'd the AULD HIRPLIN' HURCHEON, half-a-century sin', at hap-stap-and-lowp, bate Christopher North a' till sticks!

North (*with great vehemence*). Let off the gas, you stone!

Shepherd. That's pitifu'! Ca'in' a man a stane! a man that has been sae lang too in his service—and that has gien him nae provocation—for it wasna Peter but me that was obleegd to keep threepin' that Watty o' the Pen—by folk o' my time o' life never ca'd ony thing less than the Flying Tailor o' Ettrick, though by bairns never ca'd ony thing mair but the Auld Hirplin' Hurcheon, at hap-stap-and-lowp—on fair level mossy grun'—bate him a' till sticks.

North (*in a voice of thunder*). You son of a sea-gun, let off the gas!

Shepherd. Passion's aften figurative, and aye forgetfu'. But I fear, he'll be breakin' a bluid-veshel—sae I'll remind him o' the siller bell. Peter has orders never to shaw his neb but at soun o' the siller bell. Sir, you've forgotten the siller bell. Please tingle—tingle—ting.

North (*ringing the silver bell*). Too bad, James. Peter, let off the gas. (*Peter lets off the gas.*)

Shepherd. Ha! the bleeze o' Morn! Amazin'! 'Twas shortly after sunset when the gas was let on—and noo that the gas is let aff, lo! shortly after sunrise!

Buller. With us there has been no night.

Shepherd. Yesterday was the Twenty-First o' June—the Langest Day. We could hae dune—without artificial licht—for the few hours o' midnicht were but a gloamin'—and we could hae seen to read prent.

Buller. A deep dew.

North. As may be seen by the dry lairs in the wet grass of those cows up at pasture.

Shepherd. Naebody else stirrin'. Luik, there's a hare washin' her face like a cat wi' her paw. Eh man! luik at her three leverets, like as mony wee bit bears.

Buller. I had no idea there were so many singing birds so near the suburbs of a great city.

Shepherd. Had na ye? In Scotland we ca' that the skreich o' day.

North. What has become of the sea?

Shepherd. The sea! somebody has opened the sluice, and let aff the water. Na—there it's—fasten your een upon yon great green shadow—for that's Inchkeith—and you'll sune come to discern the sea waverin' round it, as if the air grew glass, and the glass water, while the water widens out intil the Firth, and the Firth awa' intil the main. Is yon North Berwick Law or the Bass—or baith—or neither—or a cape o' cloodlaun, or a thocht?

North. "Under the opening eyelids of the morn."

Shepherd. See! Specks—like black water-flees. The boats o' the Newhaven fishermen. Their wives are snorin' yet wi' their heads in mutches—but wull sune be risin' to fill their creels. Mr. Buller, was you ever in our Embro' Fish-Market?

Buller. No. Where is it, sir?

Shepherd. In the Parliament Hoose.

Buller. In the Parliament House?

Shepherd. Are you daft? Aneath the North Brigg.

Buller. You said just now the Parliament House.

Shepherd. Either you or me has been dreamin'. But, Mr. North, I'm desperate hungry—are ye no intending to gie us any breakfast?

North (*ringing the silver bell*). Lo! and behold!

(*Enter* PETER, AMBROSE, KING PEPIN, SIR DAVID GAM, *and* TAPPIETOURIE, *with trays.*)

Shepherd. Rows het frae the oven! Wheat scones! Barley scones! Wat and dry tost! Cookies! Baps! Muffins! Loaves and fishes! Rizzars! Finnans! Kipper! Speldrins! Herring! Marmlet! Jeely! Jam! Ham! Lamb! Tongue! Beef hung! Chickens! Fry! Pigeon pie! Crust and broon aside the roon' —but sit ye doon—no—freens, let's staun—had up your haun—bless your face—North, gie's a grace—(NORTH *says grace.*) Noo let's fa' too—but hooly—hooly—hooly—what vision this! What vision this! An Apparition or a Christian Leddy! I ken, I ken her by her curtshy—did that face no tell her name and her nature. O deign, Mem, to sit doon beside the Shepherd. Pardon me—tak the head o' the table, ma honor'd Mem—and let the Shepherd sit doon aside YOU—and may I mak sae bauld as to introduce Mr. Buller to you, Mem? Mr. Buller, clear your een—for on the Leads o' the Lodge, in face o' heaven, and the risin' sun, I noo introduce you till MRS. GENTLE.

North (*starting and looking wildly round*). Ha!

Shepherd. She's gane!

North (*recovering some of his composure*). Too bad, James.

Shepherd. Saw you nocht? Saw naebody ocht?

Omnes. Nothing.

Shepherd. A cretur o' the element! Like a' the ither loveliest sichts that veesit the een o' us mortals—but the dream o' a dream! But, thank heaven, a's no unsubstantial in this warld o' shadows. Were ony o' us to say sae, this breakfast wou'd gie him the lee! Noo, Gurney, mind hoo ye exten' your short haun.

Small Still Voice. Ay, ay, sir.

Buller.

> "O Gurney! shall I call thee bird, or but a wandering voice!

North.

> "O blessed bird! the world we pace
> Again appears to be
> An unsubstantial faery-place,
> That is fit home for Thee!"

No. LXVII.—AUGUST, 1834.

SCENE—*The Shepherd's Study, Altrive—The* SHEPHERD *seated at Dinner—Time Six o'clock*—AMBROSE *in waiting.*

Enter hurriedly, NORTH *and* TICKLER.

Shepherd. What for keep ye folk waitin' in this way, sirs, for denner? and it is past Sax! Sax is a daft-like hour for denner in the Forest, but I'm aye wullin' to humor fules that happen to be reseedin' in my ain house at hame. Whare war you—and what hae ye been about? No shavin' at least—for twa sic bairds I dinna remember haen witnessed sin' I was in Wales—towards the close o' the century—and they belanged to twa he-goats glowerin' owre at me frae the ruins o' Dolbaldron Castle. Tak your chairs—ye Jews. Moses! sit you on my richt haun—and, Aaron! sit you on my left. (NORTH *and* TICKLER *sit down as commanded.*)

North. 'Tis the first time in my life that I have been one moment behind the hour.

Shepherd. I believe't. For you can regulat your stammack, like a timepiece. It gangs as true's a chronometer—and on board a ship you cou'd tell by't to a nicety when she would reach ony particular port. I daursay it's correck the noo by the sun—but I aye mak Girrzzy bate the girdle twa three minutes afore the chap o' the knock.

Tickler. Bate the girdle?

Shepherd. Ay, just sae, sir—bate the girdle. I used to hae a bell hung on the bourtree at the gable-end—the auld Yarrow kirk-bell—but it got intil its dotage, its tongue had the palsy, its cheeks were crackit—and pu' the rape as you wou'd, its vice was as puir's a pan's. Then the lichtning, that maun hae had little to do that day, melted it intil the shape o' an airn icicle, and it grew perfeckly useless—sae I got a drum that aince belonged to the militia, and for some seasons it diverted the echoes that used to take it aff no amiss, whether braced or itherwise—but it too waxed old and impotent, and you micht as weel, for ony music that was in't hae bate the kitchen-dresser wi' the lint-beetle—sae I then got a gong sent owre frae India frae your freen' and mine, Dr. Gray—God bless him—and for a lang, deep, hollow, trummlin' sea-like, and thunderous soun', it beat a' that ever was heard in this kintra—but it created sic a disturbance far and wide, that, sair again' my wull, I had to shut it up in the garret.

North. Wherefore, James?

Shepherd. In the first place, it was sae like thunner that folk far aff couldna tell whether it was thunner or no; and I kent them yoke their carts in a hurry to carry in their hay afore it was dry for stacking, fearin' a plump. Ae Sunday the soun' keepit a' the folk frae the kirk, and aften they wou'dna ventur' on the fuirds, in dread o' a sudden spate frae a water-spoot. I learnt at last to bate it mair gently; but then it was sae like the soun' o' a bill afore he breaks out intil the bellow, that a' the kye in the forest grew red-wud-mad; sae then I had to tak' to batin' the girdle—an idea that was suggested to me ae day on the swarmin' o' a tap-swarm o' a skep o' bees in the garden—and I fin' that on a clear day sic as this, when the atmosphere's no' clogged, that it answers as weel's either the kirk-bell, the drum, or the gong. You wou'd hear't ayont the knowe, sirs; and was na't bonny music?

Arcades Ambo. Beautiful exceedingly.

Shepherd. If her I needna name had been at hame, there wou'd hae been a denner on the table wordier o' ma twa maist esteemed and dearest freens—but I howp wi' sic as we hae—without her mair immediate yet prospective care—you will be able to mak a fenn.

North. Bread and cheese would be a feast with the Shepherd.

Shepherd. Deed it wud be nae sic thing. It's easy to speak o' feastin' on cheese and breed, and butter and breed—and in our younger days they were truly a feast on the hill. But noo our pallets, if they dinna require coxin', deserve a goo; and I've seen a barer buird. Mr. Aumrose, lift the lids.

(*Mr. Ambrose smilingly lifts the lids.*)

North and Tickler (*in delighted wonder*). Bless us!

Shepherd. That's hotch-potch—and that's cocky-leeky—the twa best soops in natur'. Broon soop's moss-water—and white soup's like scalded milk wi' worms in't. But see, sirs, hoo the ladle stauns o' itsell in the potch—and I wush Mr. Tickler cou'd see himsell the noo in a glass, curlin' up his nose, wi' his een glistenin', and his mouth waterin', at the sight and smell o' the leeky. We kilt a lamb the day we got your letter, sir, and that's a hind-quarter twal pun' wecht. Ayont it's a beef-stake poy—for Geordy Scougal slaughtered a beast last market day at Innerleithen—and his meat's aye prime. Here are three fules*—and that ham's nae sham, sae

* *Fules*—fowls. The Duke of Bucclengh, while yet a lad, called at Hogg's house in Altrive, and noticed there a gun with a remarkably long barrel. He asked what it was for. Hogg (who pronounced the word Duck as if it were Duke), answered "Oh, we just keep that gun for shooting *dukes* and siccan sort o' *fools*."—M.

we call him Japhet. I needna tell ye yon's a roasted green-guse frae Crosslee—and neist it mutton-chaps—but the rest's a' ggemm. That's no cat, Tickler—but hare—as you may ken by her lugs and fud. That wee bit black beastie—I wuss she mayna be wizen'd in the roastin'—'s a water-hen; the twa aside her are pease-weeps—to the east you may observe a leash o' groose—wastwards ho! some dyeucks—a few pints to the south a barren pair o' patricks—and due north a whaup.

North (helping himself to a couple of flappers.)

"O' a' the airts the wun can blaw
I dearly loe the west,
For there the bonny dyeucky lies,
The dyeuck that I loo best."

Shepherd. But you maunna be expeckin' a second and third coorse. I hate to hae denner set afore me by instalments; and, frae my no havin' the gift o' prophecy, I've kent dish after dish slip through my fingers in a succession o' coorses, till I had feenally to assuage my hunger on gratins they ca' parmesan. Sir George Warrenner* will recolleck hoo I picket them aff the plate as if I had been famished, yet frae first to last there had been nae absolute want o' vittalls. I kept aye waitin' for the guse; but nae guse o' an edible kind made its appearance, and I had to dine owre again at sooper in my ain hottle. That's a sawmon.

Ambrose. There's somebody at the door, sir.

Shepherd. Let him in. (AMBROSE *opens the door, and enter Clavers, Giraffe, Rover, Guile, and Fang.*) It's the dowgs. Gentlemen, be seated. *(The Canine take their seats.)*

North. "We are seven."

Shepherd. A mystical nummer—

North. The Pleiades.

Tickler. "And lend the lyre of heaven another string."

Shepherd. I ken, Mr. Tickler, ye dinna like dowgs. But ye needna be feared, for nane o' them's got the hydrophoby—accepp it may be Fang. The cretur's been verra snappish sin' the barommator reached ninety—and bat a goslin' that began to bark—but though the goslin' bat him again, he hasna yet been heard to quack ony, sae he's no muckle mad. You're no mad, Fang?

Fang. Buy—wuy—wuy.

Shepherd. His speech's rathey affeckit. He used to say—bow—wow—wow.

Tickler (sidling away nearer the Shepherd). I don't much like his looks.

Shepherd. But, dear me! I've forgotten to help you—and hae been eatin' and talkin' awa' wi' a fu' mouth and trencher, while

* A celebrated dinner-giver in London, at this period.—M.

baith o' yours is staunin wide open and empty—and I fear, being oot a' day, you maun be fent.

Tickler. Say grace, James.

Shepherd. I said it, Timothy, afore I sat down; and though you twa wasna in, it included you, for I kent you wadna be far aff; sae it's a' richt baith in time and place. Fa' tae.

Tickler. If you have been addressing me, my dear sir, never was there more needless advice. A more delicious duckling—

North. Than Fatima I never devoured.

Shepherd. O, ye rabiautors! Twa wild dyeucks dune to the verra dowps! I intended to hae tasted them mysell—but the twa thegither wou'dna hae wechted wi' my whaup.

Tickler. Your whaup?

Shepherd. You a Scotchman and no ken a whaup! O, you gowk! The English ca't a curly.

Tickler. Oh! a curlew. I have seen it in Bewick.*

Shepherd. And never in the muirs? Then ye needna read Booick. For to be a naturalist you maun begin wi' natur', and then study her wi' the help o' her chosen sons.

North. After duckling I like leveret.

Shepherd. Sae I see.

Tickler. And I grouse.

Shepherd. Now, sirs, I beseech you, dinna 'peach. It's three weeks yet till the Twalt,† and if Finlay at Selkirk heard o' our haen ggemm to denner—and me, too, no haen yet taken oot the leesense—I sou'd be soommoned afore the Exchequer, and perhaps sent to jail. I'm no feared o' your 'peaching—but dinna blab—thank Heaven, Gurney's no here——

Small Voice. Sir?

Shepherd. Safe us! there he is—cheepin' like a moorse in the closet. Mum—mum—mum. It's miraculous the cretur bein' here—for when you druv' up yestreen there was only you twa in the fore pairt o' the gig—and Ambrose sittin' ahint.

North. 'Twas a dog-cart, my dear sir, and Short-hand was among the pointers.

Shepherd. I wush they had worried him—he haunts every house I visit like a ghaist.

Tickler. And a troublesome guest he is——

Shepherd. Haunin' doon a' oor sillinesses to immortality. But what think ye, sirs, o' thae pecks o' green peas?

* John Bewick was an English artist, residing at Newcastle, whose History of Quadrupeds, by the beauty and spirit of his illustrations, gave the first impulse to that improvement in the art of wood engraving which is now carried to most exquisite perfection. He died in 1795. His brother Thomas, who followed the same profession, died in 1828.—M.

† Under the British game laws, the shooting of grouse before the twelfth of August, is prohibited.—M.

North. By the flavor, I know them to be from Cacra-bank.

Shepherd. Never kent I a man o' sic great original genius, wi' sic a fine delicate taste. They're really sae. John Grieve kent ye was comin' to Altrive, and sent me owre baith them and the young potattoes. You'll be delichted to see him the morn in Ettrick-kirk —for I hae na kent him lookin' sae strang and fresh for a dizzen years—oh! there's naething for ane ony way invalidish like the air o' ane's native hills! And then sic a season! He's oot in the wee gig wi' Wallace, or the close carriage wi' Big Sam, every day; and on Tuesday, when he nodded to me wi' a lauch out o' the window, it did my heart gude to see his face amaist as bricht as it was the day we three first brak bread thegither in my lodgings, in the screw-staircase, as you used to ca't, aneath the North-brigg. Confoun' thae great big starin' New-Buildings—in spite o' our freen John Anderson's shop—for they hae soopit awa' Anne Street frae the face o' the earth.

North. But not into oblivion.

Shepherd. Na, na. Mony a spat exists in the memory—in the regions o' the heart—visible nae mair to man's unregardin' een; but hoo saft, hoo bricht, hoo lown they lie there, a' ready to rise up at the biddin' o' a thocht, and then to sink waveringly awa' back again intil their ain mysterious stillness, till frae our melancholy fancy they utterly melt into mist.

Tickler. Come, Mr. Hogg, do tell us how you got the game.

Shepherd. It was no my blame. Last Saturday, that's this-day-week, I gaed out to the fishin', and the dowgs gaed wi' me, for when they're left at hame they keep up siccan a yowlin' that folk passin' by might think Altrive a kennel for the Duke's jowlers. I paid nae attention to them, but left them to amuse theirsells—Claverse and Giraffe, that's the twa grews—Fang the terrier—and Guile and Rover, collies—at least they ca' Rover a colley, though he's gotten a cross o' some outlandish blood, and he belangs to the young gentlemen at Thirlstane, but he's a great frien' o' our Guile's, and aften pays him a visit.

Tickler. I thought there had been no friendship among dogs.

Shepherd. Then you thocht wrang—for they aften loe ane anither like brithers, especially when they're no like ane anither, being indeed in that respect just like us men; for nae twa human beings are mair unlike ither, physically, morally, and intellectually, than you and me, Mr. Tickler, and yet dinna we loe ane anither like brithers?

Tickler. We do, we do, my dear Shepherd. Well?

Shepherd. The troots wudna tak; whup the water as I wud, I cudna get a lowp. Flee, worm, mennow, a' useless—and the water, though laigh, was no laigh aneuch for guddlin'.

Tickler. Guddlin?

Shepherd. Nae mair o' your affeckit ignorance, Mr. Tickler. You think it fashionable to be ignorant o' every thing vulgar folk like me thinks worth knawin', but Mr. North's a genteeler man nor you ony day o' the week, and he kens brawly what's guddlin'; and what's mair, he was ance himsell the best guddler in the south o' Scotland, if you excepted Bandy Jock Gray o' Peebles. He cou'dna guddle wi' Bandy Jock ony mair than lowp wi' Watty o' the Pen, the Flyin' Tailor o' Ettrick.

North (laying down his knife and fork). I'll leap him to-morrow for love.

Shepherd. Wheesht—wheesht. The morn's the Sabbath.

North. On Monday then—running hop step and leap, or a running leap, on level ground—back or forward—with or without the crutch—let him use sticks if he will——

Shepherd. Wheesht. Watty's dead.

North. Dead!

Shepherd. And buried. I was at the funeral on Thursday. The folk are taukin' o' puttin' up a bit moniment to him—indeed hae asked me to indite an inscription. I said it should be as simple as possible—and merely record the chief act o' his life—"HIC JACET WALTER LAIDLAW OF THE PEN, THE CELEBRATED FLYING TAILOR OF ETTRICK, WHO BEAT CHRISTOPHER NORTH AT HOP STEP AND JUMP."

North (resuming his knife and fork). Well—fix your day, and though the Tweed should be in flood, I will guddle Bandy Jock.

Shepherd. Bandy Jock'll guddle nae mair in this warld. He dee'd o' the rheumatiz on May-day—and the same inscription wi' little variation—leavin' out "hop step and jump," and inserting "guddlin'"—will answer for him that will answer for Watty o' the Pen.

Tickler. 'Pon honor, my dear sir, I know not guddlin'.

Shepherd. In the wast they ca't ginnlin'.

Tickler. Whew! I'll ginnle Kit for a pair of ponies.

North (derisively). Ha, ha, ha!

Shepherd. I've seen Bandy Jock dook doon head and shouthers, sae that you saw but the dowp o' him facin' the sun, aneath a bank, and remain for the better part o' five minutes wi' his mouth and nostrils in the water—hoo he contrived to breathe I ken not—when he would draw them out, wi' his lang carrotty hair a poorin', wi' troot a fit lang in ilka haun, and ane aiblins aughteen inches atween his teeth.

Tickler. You belong, I believe, Mr. Hogg, to the Royal Company of Archers.

Shepherd. What connection has that? I do; and I'll shoot you ony day. Captain Colley ance backed Bandy Jock again' a famous tame otter o' Squire Lomax's frae Lancashire—somewhere about Preston—that the Squire aye carried wi' him in the carriage—a pool bein' made for its accommodation—in the floor wi' air-holes—and Jock bate the otter by fifteen poun'—though the otter gruppit a sawmon.

Tickler. But, mine host, the game?

Shepherd. Do you no like it? Is't no gude? It surely canna be stinkin'? And yet this het weather's sair compleened o' by the cynick, and flees will get intil the safe. I gie you my word for't, howsomever, that I saw her carefully wi' a knife scrapin' oot the mawks.

Tickler. I see nothing in the shape of maggots in this one.

Shepherd. Nor shall ye in this ane—(*forking it*)—for I see that though I'm in my ain house, I maun take care o' mysell wi' you Embro' chaps, or I'll be famished.

Tickler. But, mine host, the game?

Shepherd. That cretur Fang there—him wi' the slicht touch o' hydrophoby—'s the gleggest at a grupp o' ggemm sittin' in a' the Forest. As for Rover, he has the nose o' a Spanish pinter, and draws and backs as if he had been regularly brak in by a dowg-breaker, wi' a dog-whup on the muirs. On my way up the Yarrow—me wi' my fishin' rod in my haun—no put up—and no unlike the Crutch—only without the Cross—Rover begins smokin' and twinin' himsell in a serpentine styles, that aye denotes a strang scent—wi' his fan-like tail whaffin'—and Fang close at his heels—when Fang pounces on what I thocht micht pruve but a tuft o' heather, or perhaps a moudiewarp—but he kent better—for in trowth it was the Auld Cock—and then whurr—whurr—whurr—a covey o' what seemed no far short o' half a hunder—for they broon'd the lift; and in the impetus o' the moment, wi' the sudden inspiration o' an improvee-sistreecky, I let fly the rod amang them as if it had been a rung. It wounded many, but knocked down but three—and that's them, or at least was them—for I noo see but ane—Tickler haen taken to his share the Auld Cock.

North. And the ducklings?

Shepherd. Ca' them flappers. A maist ridiculous Ack o' Parliament has tried to mak them ggemm—though it's weel kent that tame dyeucks and wild dyeucks are a' ae breed—but a thoosan' acks o' Parliament 'll never gar me consider them ggemm, or treat them as ggemm, ony mair than if you were to turn out a score o' howtowddies on the heather, and ca' them ggemm.

Tickler. Pheasants.

Shepherd. I ken naethin' aboot feesants, accepp that they're no worth eatin'.

North. You are wrong there, James. The Duke sends me annually half-a-dozen, and they eat like Birds of Paradise.

Shepherd. Even the hen's no half sae gude's a hen. But for the flappers. A' the five dowgs fan theirsells a' at aince in amang a brood on a green level marshy spat, where escape was impossible for puir beasts that cudna yet flee—and therefore are ca'd flappers. It wud hae been vain for me to try to ca' the dowgs aff—sae I cried them on—and you never saw sic murder. The auld drake and dyeuck kept circling round—quack—quack—quacking out o' shot in the sky—and I pitied the puir pawrents lookin' doon on the death o' their promising progeny. By gude luck I had on the sawmon-creel—and lookin' round about—I crammed in a' the ten—doon wi' the lid—and awa' alang the holms o' Yarrow as if I was selecking a stream for beginnin' to try the fishin'—when, wha sud I meet but ane o' his Grace's keepers! Afore I kent whare I was, he put his haun aneath the basket, and tried to gie't a hoise—but providentially he never keekit intil the hole—and tellin' him I had gran trootin'—but maun be aff—for that a lassie had been sent to tell me twa gentlemen frae Embro had come oot to Altrive—I wushed him gude day—and tuke the fuird. But my heart was lowpin', and I felt as if I was gaun to fent. A sook o' Glenlivet, however, set me a' richt—and we shall hae the lave to sooper. I howp poossey's tasty, sir?

North. I have rarely ate a sweeter and richer leveret.

Shepherd. I'll thank ye, to ca' the cretur by her richt name—the name she gaed by, to my knowledge, for mony years—a Hare. She hasna been a leveret sin' the King's visit to Scotland. I hope you dinna fin' her tyeuch?

North. Not yet.

Shepherd. You maun lay your account wi' her legs bein' harder wark than her main body and wings. I'm glad to see Girzzy hasna spared the stuffin'—and you needna hain the jeel, for there's twa dozen pats o' new, red, black, and white, in that closet, wi' their mouths cozily covered wi' pages o' some auld lowse nummers o' Blackwood's Magazine—the feck o' them balangin' to twa articles, entitled "Streams" and "Cottages."

North (*wincing*). But to the story of the game.

Shepherd. The witch was sittin' in her ain kale-yard—the preceese house I dinna chuse to mention—when Giraffe, in lowping owre the dyke, lowped ower her, and she gied a sprang intil the road, turnin' roun' her fud within a yard o' Clavers—and then sic a brassle a' three thegether up the brae! And then back again—in a hairy whirlwind—twa miles in less than a minute. She made for the mouth o' the siver, but Rover, wha had happened to be examining it, in his inquisitive way, and kent naething o' the coorse, was comin' out just as she was gaen in, an' atween the twa there ensued, unseen in the siver, a desperate battle. Weel dune witch—weel dune warlock—and at ae time I feared frae his yelpin' and yowlin' that Rover was gettin' the warst o't, and micht lose his life. Auld poosies cuff sair wi' their forepaws—and theirs is a wicked bite. But the outlandish wolfishness in Rover brak forth in extremity, and he cam rushin' out o' the siver wi' her in his mouth, shakin' her savagely, as if she had been but a rattan, and I had to chock him aff. Forbye thrapplin' her, he had bit intil the jugular—and she lost sae meikle bluid, that you hae eaten her the noo roasted, instead o' her made intil soop. She would hae been the tennerer o' anither fortnicht o' this het wether—wi' the glass at 92 in the shade o' the Safe in the larder—yet you seem to be gettin' on—

North. Pretty well—were it not that a sinew—like a length of catgut—from the old dame's left hip, has got so entangled among my tusks that—

Shepherd. You are speakin' sae through your teeth as no to be verra untelligible. Let me cut the sinny wi' my knife.

(*The* SHEPHERD *operates with much surgical dexterity.*)

North. Thank you, James. I shall eat no more of the leveret now—but take it minced at supper.

Shepherd. Minshed! ma faith, you've minshed it wi' a vengeance. She's a skeleton noo, and nae mair—and let's send her in as a curiosity in a glass-case to James Wilson*—to meet him on his return frae the grand scientific expedition o' thae fearless philosophers into the remotest regions o' Sutherland, to ascertain whether par be par, or o' the seed o' sawmon. We'll swear that we fand it—embedded in a solid rock, and it'll pass for the young o' some specie o' antediluvian yelephant.

Tickler. Clap the skin upon it—and tell James that we all three saw it jump out of the heart of the trap.

Shepherd. A queer idea. Ambrose, bid Girrzzy gie the hareskin of that auld hare that's noo eaten intil a skeleton by Mr. North.

(*Exit* AMBROSE, *and enters with a hare-skin.*)

North. Allow me to put it on. (NORTH *seems much at a loss.*)

Shepherd. Hoot! man. The skin's inside oot! There—the lugs fit nicely—(*The* SHEPHERD *adroitly refurs Puss*)—and the head—but there's a sair fa'in aff everywhere else—and noo that it's on—this unreal mockery is mair shocking than the skeleton. Tak it awa—tak it awa, Mr, Awmrose—I canna thole to look at it.

North. Stop, Ambrose. Give it me a moment.

(NORTH *lends it a legerdemain touch after the style of the late celebrated Othello Devaynes of Liverpool, and the witch, in*

* Brother to Professor Wilson, and a great naturalist.—M.

point of activity, apparently not one whit the worse of having been eaten, jumps out of the window.)

Omnes. Halloo! halloo! halloo!

(*Clavers, Giraffe, Rover, Guile, and Fang, spring from their seats, and evanish—Fang clearing the sill as clean as a frog.*)

Tickler. Now, Ambrose, down with the window—for, though my nose is none of the most fastidious, we have really had in every way quite enough of dogs.

SCENE II.—*The Arbour in the Garden*—MR. AMBROSE, *assisted by* GIRRZZY, *arranging the Table and Seats.*

Enter MR. HOGG, MR. NORTH, *and* MR. TICKLER.

North. I have read, my dear Shepherd, of the melancholy life you have long led at Altrive, in a cold, damp, comfortless, empty house, hidden by gloomy hills from the sun, and with hardly enough of heaven's light to warm the lichens on the weather-stained walls.

Shepherd. Some that said sae meant well, as you ken, sir, but were sair mista'en—ithers meant ill, and merely lee'd; but whatever I may owe to my fellow-creturs—and amang them, mair especially to my kintramen—wicked should I be were I no humbly gratefu' to heaven for a' its mercies. O' this wald's gear I hae but little—but I hae a mine o' contentment within my ain breast, that's mair productive than a' the mines o' Potosi and Peru. There hae been times when I had to draw deep on the materials there, but I rejoiced to find that they were inexhaustible—

North. ——"transcending in their worth
The gems of India, nature's rarest birth."

Shepherd. True that I'm getting rather auld*—but I'm no frichtened at that thocht—only sometimes pensy aboot them that I shall ae day hae to leave behind me in a warld where my voice will be mute. But what's singular to my case in that? You needna look at me, my dear sir, wi' a wat ee—for mine ain are dry—and for ae tear I shed on wee Jamie's head I shower down ten thousan' smiles. The holiest affections o' natur' sir, as weel baith you and Mr. Tickler kens, may grow into habits. Noo it's no a maitter o' prudence wi' me,—nor yet o' feelosophy—for I hae little o' either—but it's a duty o' religion wi' me, sirs, to encourage a cheerfu' disposition throughout a' ordinar hours, and in a' the mair serious and solemn, which, though like angel-visits, are neither short nor far atween, hope, faith, and resignation—knowing that in His hands are the issues of life and death.

* This was in 1834. Hogg died in November, 1835, aged sixty-three. With his death closed the Noctes.—M.

North (*cheerfully*). THE WIFE AND WEANS.

Tickler (*with a glowing countenance*). God bless them all.

Shepherd (*laughing faintly*). They'll be tauld o' this toast. They're a' happy the noo in Embro—perhaps takin' a walk on the Calton Hill—na, they'll be drinkin' tea wi' that excellent man, Dr. Crichton, in Stockbrigg. You ken him, sir?

North. I do, my dear James, and he is an excellent man—and knows well his profession. Perhaps we had better be drinking tea too.

Shepherd. Sae I think we had. I see Mr. Awmrose, walkin' amang the flowers, and pu'in' a posy. I'll cry till him. Mr. Awmrose, tak' awa' a' thir things, and bring the tea-tray.

North. Stop—don't disturb Love among the roses.

Tickler. Nor yet has Molly put the kettle on.

Shepherd. Weel—weel—we can wait for an hour or twa—but I see Mysie milkin' the kye—wull ye ha'e a drink o' milk frae the pail?

Tickler. New milk sits ill on old porter.

North. I shall take a bowl before going to bed.

Shepherd. No you. Gin it were placed on a chair at the bedside you micht skim aff some o' the ream—but nane o' the milk wou'd wat your whuskers (safe us, whatna baird!) and there would be a midnicht feast for the rattans.

Tickler. What! are you infested with rats?

Shepherd. Sair. We ha'e the common house-rat—and the water-rat—and the last o' the Norways. Except theirsells, there's nae Norways in the Forest—perhaps in all Scotland.

Tickler. I request to have Fang for my bed-fellow.

Shepherd. What? and him wi' a touch o' the phoby?

Tickler. Well, then,—Clavers or Giraffe.

Shepherd. The grews? You're welcome to them baith—but, mind you, dinna meddle wi' them when they loup on the tester—for grews that are growin' gray about the muzzle are gay surly—I micht say savage—in their slumbers—and I ken this, that gin you offer to shove Clavers aff you, he'll no content himsell wi' a growl—sae tak' tent, afore you try to gather up your feet, to row yoursell weel up in the claes—for he can bite through three ply o' blankets.

Tickler. I shall get the sofa brought down here, and sleep in the arbour.

Shepherd. The arbour's a circle o' five feet in diameter—and you sax feet five inches lang even yet—I remember you nearer seven—and you shou'd hae considered, afore speaking o' the sofa, that your head is noo just touchin' the wicker-wark o' the croon o' the bower, and your feet on the gravel-walk in front o' the door. The sofa itsell's no abuve five feet and a half, and the best bed's no lang aneuch—but Girrzzy had the sense to tak' out the fit-brodd—only mind no to ding doon the wa' by streekin' yoursell ont in a dream at the dead o' nycht.

North. "The dowie holms o' Yarrow!"

Shepherd. In theirsells they're no dowie—but as cheerfu' as ony ever sang ower by the laverock—and many a linty is heard liltin' merrily in the broom. But Poetry and Passion changed their character at their ain wild wull—tauld the silver Yarrow to rin red wi' lovers' bluid—and ilky swellin' turf, fit for the Fairies' play, to look like a grave where a human flower was buried! Sic power has genie transfigurin' a' nature in its grief!

North. Write you no songs now, James?

Shepherd. Nane! Isna five hunder or mair sangs anew? I shanna say ony o' mine's are as gude as some sax or aught o' Burns's—for about that nummer o' Robbie's are o' inimitable perfection. It was Heaven's wull that in them he shou'd transcend a' the mennisingers o' this warld. But they're too perfeckly beautifu' to be envied by mortal man—therefore let his memory in them be hallowed for evermair.

North. A noble sentiment.

Shepherd. At least a natural ane, and flowin' frae a heart elevated at ance and purified by the sangs o' ane, let us trust, noo a seraph.

North. Peace to the soul of the Poet.

Shepherd. Peace and glory that fadeth not away! His sins were a' born o' his body—that is dust—and if they tainted his immortal soul—and oh! wae's me! mournfully and mysteriously I fear that sair did they sae—what's the mornin'-dew or the well on the mountain to what has washed out a' thae stains—and made it purer noo than even the innocent daisy that on this earth—ay, even when toilin' at his wark at ance like a slave and a king—his kindled heart changed into a flower o' heaven!

North. I wish Allan Cunningham were with us.

Shepherd. And sae maist fervently do I.

Tickler. And I.

North. Some of Allan's songs, too, James, will not die.

Shepherd. Mony a bonnie thing dees—some o' them, as it wou'd seem, o' theirsells, without onything hurtin' them, and as if even gracious natur', though loath, consented to allow them to fade awa' into forgetfulness; and that will happen, I fear, to no a few o' baith his breathin's and mine—but that ithers will surveeve, even though Time shou'd try to ding them doon wi' his heel into the yird, as sure am I as that the nicht-sky shall never lose a single star till the mornin' o' the Day o' Doom.

North. Ramsay, Fergusson, Bruce, Burns, Hogg, Cunningham*—

* Of the poets here named, all but two have been previously noticed. Robert Fergusson,

Shepherd. Pollok.*

North. Aye, Pollok, a gifted spirit. All born "in huts where poor men lie." Lift up, O Scotland! all thy hills to heaven! Let loose thy cataracts from all thy cliffs! Let dash all thy sea-lochs flowing and ebbing from thy heart—and in encircling thunder let the multitude of thy isles rejoice!

Shepherd. At this hour, sae sweet and solemn, my filial love prays for the eternity o' a' images o' peace. Pure be the sunshine as the snaw on the bonny breist o' Scotland, and may the ages, as they roll alang, multiply the number o' her honored graves! Still may she be the land o' freedom, and genius, and virtue, and religion! And see, sir, hoo the evenin' sun is bathin' a' the serene circle o' thae hills in a mair verdant licht—for there's a communion between the heart o' Nature and the hearts o' her worshippers, and if you want her face to look beautifu', you have but to let rise within you a gentle feeling or a noble thocht.

Tickler. I hear you, my dear Shepherd, even with my deaf ear—just as I hear music with it still—though along the streets mail-coaches, which I suppose are rattling, seem going at the rate of twelve miles an hour, even over the unmacadamized causeway, as noiselessly as if they were hearses moving slowly upon snow.

Shepherd. Nae man need be ashamed o' sic a compliment as that—and oh! sir, but I'm happy to hae you at least sittin' aside me in the arbour.

North. I think, my dear sir, you used the term *minnesinger*. Are you a German as well as a Greek scholar?

Shepherd. Much about it. I hae glanced owre Goth in the original—I mean his Fast—and read a' the English and what not translations o' him, baith in verse and prose—and o' the hale tot, I like far best Mr. Hayward's prose version. Yon's a poem!

North. I am no great German scholar myself, James—but the language is gradually lightening up before my eyes——

Shepherd. Like the *Mare Ignotum* before the een o' a navigator in a ship sailin' intil the dawn.

North. Good again. I would give the world my idea of Faust, were it not that about Goethe the world is mad.

Shepherd. The mair reason to set her richt—to bring her back to her senses. She's no in a state o' idiocy? That's hopeless.

North. Goethe's idolators—mind ye, I exclude Thomas Carlyle and Hayward, and all minds of that order and stamp—are of course

who died in a lunatic asylum in 1774, wrote several poems; those in the Scottish dialect possess considerable merit—those in the English are often below mediocrity.—Michael Bruce, whose parents were of the poorest class, died in 1767, aged twenty one. His poems are few in number, but singularly plaintive and elegant.—M.

* Robert Pollok, who died in 1827, aged twenty-eight was a Scottish clergyman. His principal work is "The Course of Time," in ten books, which has obtained more popularity in the United States than in Scotland.—M.

not Christians, and use a heathenish lingo worse than the unknown tongue.

Shepherd. There's nae harm in ony unknown tongue—sic as Tam Stoddart's—but nae punishment's owre severe for them that swear they're respeckin' their mither's, a' the while they're murderin't—and flout in your een a wab o' words, like gaudy patchwork shue'd for the bottom o' an easy arm-chair by an auld wife.

North. It is declared by all great and true German scholars, that the poem of Faust in execution is as perfect as in conception magnificent, and that Goethe has brought to bear on that wonderful work not only all the creative energy of a rare genius, and all the soul-searching wisdom of a high philosophy, but likewise all the skill of a consummate artist, and all possible knowledge and power over his native speech. His was the unconfined inspiration from above, that involuntarily moves harmonious numbers; and his the regulated enthusiasm from below, that enables the poet to interfuse with the forms of earth, the fire of heaven.

Shepherd. A noble panegyric.

North. Not pronounced by me, but by the voice of Europe.

Shepherd. But ye hae na borrowed the words?

North. Not that I know of—and they are too feeble for Faust. To show such a work an English Poem would require—whom? Not twenty boys—however clever, or better than clever—but one man of mature mind, and that mind of the highest order—a mind that "with sweepy sway" could travel through the shadowy into the illimitable—and distinguish and command the phantoms of beauty and of grandeur rising up from the "unapparent deep."

Shepherd. Micht Byron?

North. No.

Shepherd. Shelley?

North. No—imperfectly, and but in part.

Shepherd. Wordsworth?

North. No—no—no. Wordsworth's world is not Goethe's world—the Wordsworthian star, like that of Jove itself, "so beautiful and large," is not like the star of Goethe. Both are the brightest of the bright; but the breath of peace envelopes the one, with "an ampler ether, a diviner air"—at its height, the other often looks troubled, and seems to reel in his sphere, with a lurid but still celestial light.

Shepherd. Puir, puir lassie!

North. Ay, James, had Ophelia been in her place, she would have been Margaret.

Shepherd. And Hamlet Fowst?

North. Nay; in comparison with that Prince of the Melancholious, Faust is little better than a fantastic quack doctor.

Shepherd. Are ye no unsaying a' you've said—for is na he Getty's hero?

North. I said "in comparison." That comparisons are often odious, I know—but then only when made in a spirit of detraction from what shining by itself is glorious; the idolators of Goethe set him above Shakspere—not by declaration of faith—for they durst not—but virtually and insidiously—for they either name not the Swan of Avon, or let him sail away down the river of life, with some impatient flourish about the beauty of his plumage, and then falling on their foolish faces before Faust, break out into worship in the gabble of the unknown tongue. Shakspere!

"Creation's heir! the world is thine."

Shepherd. There's a tawk in Mr. Hayward's notes o' the hidden meanin' o' muckle or the maist o' Fowst; but for my ain pairt I hae nae misgivin' about either the general scop and tendency o' the wark, or the signification o' ony o' its details. It's a' as clear's mud.

North. Mr. Hayward is too rational a man—I use the epithet in its best sense—to believe that a great poet would purposely wrap up profound meanings in mysterious allusions to be guessed at in vain by the present purblind race, but to be deciphered and solved by a wiser generation not yet in embryo in the womb of time. What Goethe in his old age may have said or done, all who admired the great Poet in his perfect prime should forgive or forget; and vast though be the Edifice, the architect planned not "windows that exclude the light, and passages that lead to nothing." Deep the Gothic niches, and gloomy the long-withdrawing galleries, and dismally on their hinges grate some of the doors, and difficult may they be to open;—but self-fed lamps of "naphtha and asphatic yielding light" are pendent from roofs "by their own weight immovable and steadfast," and though he who wanders there will meet with ghosts, and witches, and misbegotten hell-cats, and imps, and fiends, and the devil himself, yet, without muttering *Ave Maria* or *Paternoster*, let him not fear but that, with no other guide or guardian but his own conscience, he will be able to find his way out into the open light of day, and more blessedly beautiful because of all those glimmering and shapeless terrors mingled with radiant tenderness ruefully wading through a perplexing mist of tears, he will again behold high over head the most unapproachable peace of heaven, which seems then descending half way to meet the holy seeking to soar homewards on a spirit's wings.

Shepherd. Are you hearkenin' till the sage, Mr. Tickler?

Tickler. I hear a murmur as of a hive of bees.

Shepherd. Soun' without sense—but pleasant withal, for sake o' the indefinite and vague hum o' happiness o' that countless nation a' convenin' and careerin' roun' their queen.

North. Articles have been sent to me on Goethe, chiefly on the Faust—some not without talent—but all, except one, leaving on my mind the unpleasant impression of their having been written by prigs.

Shepherd. What's a prig.

North. You might as well ask what's a sumph. There are nuisances in this sublunary world, almost as undefinable as unendurable, and to no class of them ought the eye of the literary police to be more rigorously directed than to that of prigs. They greatly infest our periodical literature, and are getting bolder and bolder every day. For their sakes should be revived the picturesque exposure of the pillory, and the grotesque imprisonment of the stocks.

Shepherd. Try the pump.

North. 'Twould be a pity, after Pindar's panegyric, so to use the element of water—nor could I find it in my heart, James, looking at his head and handle, so to humiliate the pump.

Shepherd. Oh, sir, but I would like fine to see a fule tarred and feathered—for though my imagination's no that unveevid, and can shape to itsell maist absurd and amusin' sichts, it has never been able to satisfy my mind wi' an adequate representation o' the first start frae the barrel o' an enormous human blockhead, changed intil a bird—nae wings, nae tail, neither a cock nor a guse, but an undescribable leevin' and lowpin' lump o' feathers frae Freezlan', in fear, pain, and shamefacedness, uttering strange screechs and scraughs, as down alang lang lanes o' hootin' spectators, the demented phenomenon, aye keepin' to the gutter, and after rinnin' foul o' the lamp-posts, faster far than a cur wi' a kettle till his tail scours squares and streets o' cities, and then terrifyin' the natives o' the kintra, bent on suicide, as if he were a drove o' swine possessed o' a legion o' deevils, rushes intil the sea.

Tickler. The Atlantic Ocean. I admire the Americans for the ingenious and humane invention.

Shepherd. Yet they're no sae original in their poetry as micht hae been expected, and predicted, frae their adoption o' sic a punishment.

North. Prigs are of opinion that the present age has not eyes to see into the heart of Goethe's poetry, which will lie hidden in its mysteries for a thousand years. Nay, 'tis pitiable to hear such cant even from critics of considerable and not undeserved reputation, who, at the same time, would pucker up the lines at the corner of their mouths and eyes——

Shepherd. Crawfeet.

North. ——were you to question their clear and full comprehension of the character and condition of Macbeth, Othello, Hamlet, and Lear. The worthy, weak, well-meaning, common-place, not ill-fed, and decently-dressed European and American publics and republics must wait for a few centuries before they can hope to gain sight of more than some glimmerings of the glory enshrined in the genius of a certain German charlatan, known by the name of Goethe, who used to strut about in his prime and in his decay all bedizened with gaudy gewgaws, given him by the prince of a petty principality, to mark his admiration of the manager of a provincial theatre, whom the Dog of Montargis drove from his box into private life—though a real living flesh-and-blood dog—a Newfoundlander or St. Benardine, as humane as sagacious—while the jealous and jewelled bard's own canine fancy was in comparison a cross-bred cur and a mangy mongrel, whom Charley Westropp of the Westminster pit would have despised, and his famous Billy the rat-killer worried till he could not have been brought in time to the scratch, nathless he were the dog of hell!

Tickler. Court and theatre of Weimar.

Shepherd. Ma heed's a' in confusion—and what is your real judgment o' Gutty, as you ca' him, is athegither ayont ma comprehension.

North. Of all schools of poetry and criticism, James, the most contemptible is the Oracular.

Shepherd. That's just what I was gaun to say. Naebody can wi' truth say that I hae a bad temper, though it's sometimes rather het and short——

Tickler. Like gingerbread not yet cool from the oven.

Shepherd. ——but the instant I discover that the owthor o' ony poem that I may happen to be tryin' to peruse, is either takin' pains to conceal his meanin' or his want o' meanin'—and the first is the warst, for weakness is naething to wickedness—than I fin' ma face growin' red, and a chokin' in ma thrott, as if I were threatened wi' a stroke o' the apoplex, and, risin' in a passion, I dash the half-witted or deceptious cretur's abortive concern wi' sic a daud on the floor, that I've kent it stot up again on till the table, and upset the jug.

Tickler. Hoo! hoo! hoo! My dear James, you're first-rate this evening.

Shepherd. If I werena, I wud hae a queer look in sic company—for a' Lunnon cou'dna produce three sic first-rate fallows as noo, unknawn to the hale warld, are sittin' in the Shepherd's Bower in the heart o' the Forest! What's that stirrin'? Gurney ahint the honeysuckles! I wush he was deed. But he's no ane o' your folk that dee. He'll see us a' oot, sirs, and then he'll publish the owtobiography of a' Us Three, first piecemeal in Maga, and then ilka ane by itsell, in three vols. crown octavo, gettin' a ransom for the copy-richts.

North. The greatest sinner of the oracular school was Shelley—because the only true poet. True poets admire his genius, but in spite of love and pity for the dead, they disdain the voluntary darkness in which he perversely dallied with things of light that should never have been so enshrouded, and according to the command and law of nature should have been wooed, won, wedded, and enjoyed in the face of heaven.

Shepherd. I consider mysell a man o' mair than ordinar genie, and of about an average understaunin', and haen paid sic attention to the principles o' poetry laid in the natur o' things, as ane canna weel avoid doin' wha engages with life-warm and life-deep and life-lang luve in the practice o' the maist heavenly delichtfu' o' a' the divine arts, I canna bring mysell to accuse mysell o' ony thing rash nor unreasonable-like in declarin' that to be doonright drivellin' nonsense, which, though expressed in words, and printed in gude teep, and on gude paper, in a byeuck, either bound or in buirds, by day or by nicht, by coal, cannle, lamp, or sunlight, continues to lie afore ma een in shoals o' unintelligible syllables o' which a' you can safely assert is, that they seem as if they belanged, however remotely, in some way or ither, to the English tongue.

North. Poor Shelley would turn on his face in his coffin——

Shepherd. Oh! remember—remember, sir, that his drowned body was burnt on the sea-shore!

North. I had forgot it.

> "Custom lies upon us with a weight
> Heavy as frost, and deep almost as death."

Buried in the grave! In the Christian world so disposed is the dust of the disembodied spirit, and I dreamed not of the dismal smoke of Shelley's funeral pyre.

Shepherd. But what was you gaun to say?

North. That the worst dishonor done to his memory is the admiration in which his genius is held by feebles, and fribbles, and coxcombs, and cockneys.

Tickler. And prigs.

Shepherd. And sumphs.

North. Their imitations of their oracle—who did indeed often utter glorious responses from a cloudy shrine, all at once, and not transiently, illuminated from within by irrepressible native light—are better nonsense-verses than I ever knew written by men of wit for a wager. For unconscious folly in its own peculiar walk can far surpass the wildest extravagance of wit—perfect no-meaning can be perpetrated only by a natural numskull, and is beyond the reach of art.

Shepherd. Leigh Hunt truly loved Shelley.

North. And Shelley truly loved Leigh Hunt. Their friendship was honorable to both, for it was as disinterested as sincere;* and I hope Gurney will let a certain person in the city understand that I treat his offer of a reviewal of Mr. Hunt's London Journal with disdain. If he has any thing to say against us or against that gentleman, either conjunctly or severally, let him out with it in some other channel, and I promise him a touch and a taste of the Crotch. He talks to me of Maga's desertion of the principle: but if he were a Christian—nay, a man—his heart and head too would tell him that the Animosities are mortal, but the Humanities live for ever—and that Leigh Hunt has more talent in his little finger than the puling prig, who has taken upon himself to lecture Christopher North in a scrawl crawling with forgotten falsehoods. Mr. Hunt's London Journal, my dear James, is not only beyond all comparison, but out of all sight, the most entertaining and instructive of all the cheap periodicals, (the nature of its plan and execution prevents it from all rivalry with the Penny Magazine edited by my amiable, ingenious, and honorable friend, Charles Knight;) and when laid, as it duly is once-a-week, on my breakfast table, it lies there—but is not permitted to lie long—like a spot of sunshine dazzling the snow.

Shepherd. I gied vent to what shall ever seem to me to be a truly Christian sentiment, at the last Noctes. It was something to this effect—that, for my pairt, I desire naething sae earnestly as to see the hale warld shaking hauns.—Hollo! hollo! hollo! Rover! Rover! Rover! Fang! Fang! Fang! Lend me the crutch, sir—lend me the crutch! For if there be na the twa striks brocken intil the garden, and scamperin' through the second crap o' green peas! O! the marrowfats!—the marrowfats are a' ruined—

Tickler. "Like ocean-weeds heap'd on the surf-beaten shore."

(*The Shepherd, armed with North's crutch, Tickler with his gold-headed cane, and Mysie with a rung, attack the stirks, and drive them out of the garden of Altrive.*)

Shepherd. Camstrairy deevils!

North. I could have thought them red deer.

Shepherd. And sae they are. I gied three pun' the pieces for them at St. Boswells, and they've done mair mischief in a fortnicht about the place, than thrice that soom wou'd repair. Ane o' them,

* Sincere on Shelley's part, no doubt. But, considering how Leigh Hunt, *more suo*, spunged upon him—acknowledging, in his Autobiography, to have accepted £1400 from him at one haul, besides large amounts at other times—one is forced, on reflection, to doubt whether his friendship for Shelley was *quite* "disinterested." The question might be referred to Harold Skimpole, Esq., of Bleak House.—M.

only yesterday, ate twa pair o' wursted stockins aff the hedge; and I shou'd na hae cared so muckle about that, had na the ither, at the same time, devoor'd a pair o' breeks.

North. Such accidents will happen in the best-regulated families. But we must not allow this sally of the stirks to put an end to our literary conversation.

Shepherd (*rubbing his face with his small red pocket-handkerchief.*) Heeh! I'm sweatin'.

Tickler. Goethe! Faust! Give me Pope and any one of his epistles.

"Search then the ruling passion; there alone
The wild are constant, and the cunning known;
The fool consistent, and the false sincere,
Priests, princes, women, all consistent here!
This clew once found, unravels all the rest,
The prospect clears, and phantom stands confest.
* * * * * *

And you, great Cobham! to the latest breath
Shall feel your ruling passion strong in death.
Such in those moments as in all the past—
'Oh! save my country, heaven!' shall be your last."

What truth, force, conciseness, correctness, grace, elegance and harmony! But Pope was no poet.

North. The passage is worthy of admiration, and is a fair specimen of the best style of the Nightingale of Twickenham. I suspect, Mr. Tickler, you have misquoted him—if not, "consistent" should not have been repeated. Pray, is it quite correct to say that "a clew unravels?" If it be—yet "the prospect clears" seems to me an image that has no connection with a labyrinth and a clew. I shall not quarrel with Wharton—but he is somewhat abruptly introduced—and since "he stands confessed," will you have the goodness—from Pope—to tell us what really was his character!

Tickler. Poo! verbal hypercriticism is my contempt, sir.

North. Well, then, let us dissect the doctrine. The idea here intended to be inculcated is, that the only way of understanding the character of any man is to discover his Ruling Passion, and that this will then serve as a key to explain all the peculiarities which have arisen under its influence.

Tickler. Just so.

Shepherd. Preceesely.

North. Now, Mr. Hogg, that the strong influence of any strong principle will extend itself through the mind, and discover itself in many unexpected results, is undoubted, and it is one important fact which has to be borne in mind, in the philosophy of human

ture.

Shepherd. That's grand soundin' language, the feelosophy o' human nature.

North. But it is a very small part of that philosophy, James; and when it is represented to us that the consideration of such a passion is to enable us to understand human character——

Shepherd. And a' its outs and ins——

North. ——a false and inadequate representation of the truth is made. Such a passion is not the essence of the character. It is a single part of it, that has grown to unnatural strength; and it would be much more true to say that by such a passion the character is disguised, than elucidated.

Shepherd. That's capital. Mr. Tickler, he can tawk you blin'.

North. In such cases, Mr. Hogg, it usually happens that the passion which is thus strong and overruling, exhibits only a temporary state, or disorder, if it may be so called, of the mind. It shows not its permanent character, but one which has been induced by casual circumstances fostering certain feelings to excess, and which altered circumstances might perhaps repress, reducing the whole mind to its natural and proper equipoise.

Shepherd. Mr. Tickler, do you hear that? That's a poser.

North. The true nature of men is to be understood by penetrating through their passions which appear, while we witness their operation, to absorb all other faculties, and by discovering what the powers are which lie concealed under them, and which, even though they should appear for a time to be dormant, are yet alive and ready to be awakened by a touch, and to leap forth.

Shepherd. Profoonder than Pope.

North. What can less resemble our actual experience of the world than this description of human character by single despotic passions?

Shepherd. Like sae mony rams at the head o' sae mony flocks o' sheep.

North. Why, there are great numbers o' mankind, in whom it would be absolutely impossible to point out any such governing and overpowering principle of action.

Shepherd. And deevilish clever chiels and gude Christians, too.

North. Men in whom the elements of nature are more balanced, and in whom natural feelings appear to arise to the occasion that requires them—but nothing is seen of one superior desire absorbing all other affections and interests.

Shepherd. The maist feck o' mankind—

North. A great part of men adopt for the time the passion of their profession.

Shepherd. And thus we a' smell o' the shop.

North. Now, Tickler, while to many men no ruling passion can be assigned, and many appear to be, for a time merely, strongly actuated by that with which their situation furnishes them, observe with respect to those in whom strong passion does arise from their own mind, and for a time does possess and rule over them, how even then different passions will hold alternate ascendency. As one in whom the passion of renown has great force, and has seemed alone to have the government of his life, may suddenly become absorbed in the passion of love, and forget entirely those purposes for which alone he seemed to live; showing in the most marked manner how little this notion of a permanent ruling passion is founded in nature. Joanna Baillie has exemplified this in Count Basil.

Shepherd. I never read no plays but Shakspere's—and them no aften—for there's no a copy o' him in the house.

North. Besides, where such a passion actually exists, and takes this constant lead of the mind through life, it is to be ascribed not to the mind alone, but to the situation concurring with the passion, and raising it to a degree of strength beyond nature. Passion itself would not be permanent.

Shepherd. I howp no.

North. But the situation to which a man is engaged may be so; and in that—believe me—is found the seeming permanence of the passion.

Shepherd. I'll believe ony thing. (*Yawning.*)

North. For it calls forth the same, day by day, nourishing it, and fixing it as habitual in the mind. Yet even in such cases it will appear at last, when some change of circumstances breaks up the bondage in which the mind has been held, that this permanent habit is broken up with it, and other strong natural principles reassume their native strength.

Shepherd. As it is richt they should do.

North. But there are arguments of a still more important kind, Mr. Hogg, connected with the refutation of this theory.

Shepherd. Theory! It's nae theory—it's but a bit of sophistical apothegm.

North. For the fact is, that such a ruling passion is incompatible with that state of mind which ought to be desired, with its sound and healthy condition. The vigor of the mind is supported and nourished by the alternation of its passions. When exhausted with one, it recovers its force and alacrity by giving itself up to the influence of another. Its thoughts, its understanding, its whole moral nature, are filled and replenished by the variety of affections with which it is thus made acquainted. But a single passion taking possession of it, binds it down, narrows it, confines it in ignorance, destroys its moral power, by substituting one usurping affection for that whole variety of feelings which are proper to the human soul, which are its excellence and its happiness.

Shepherd. Puir Pop! Puir bit Poppy! Why, sir, sic a ruling passion's a doonright disease.

North. Its effect upon the mind, if it is permanent, without vehemence, is to confine it within narrower and narrower limits, to withdraw it from the natural freedom and enlargement of its being, to make it partial, servile, destitute of knowledge of itself or others. If it is permanent, and at the same time vehement, it overpowers and deranges the other faculties, and in its ultimate excess, reaches that state of entire and utter derangement, which includes even physical disorder of the structure of the human being, and becomes either imbecility or madness.

Shepherd. I could select a dizzen cases in pint.

North (*with much animation*). Is it not evident, then, Mr. Tickler, that there cannot be a greater absurdity, in endeavoring to establish philosophical canons fit for the judgment of human character, than to propose as one of the fixed conditions and appearances of the mind, a state which, in all its degrees, is adverse to the proper excellence and strength of that mind, and in its utmost degree is its highest disorder, and finally its destruction?

Shepherd (*shaking* TICKLER *in vain*). This is real sleep—there's nae pretendin' here, sir—your eloquence overpoored him, and he has ta'en refuge frae discomfiture in the land o' nod.—(*Aside.*) Faith I'm getting rather droosy mysell.

North (*with increasing animation*). There have at times been men of great character who have devoted themselves wholly to some great object which has occupied their thoughts and purpose for their whole life; and in some sort this might be said to be a ruling passion, since their lot was so cast that that one great desire became justly the preponderant determination of their will while they lived —such as Clarkson and Howard.*

Shepherd. Wha?

North. But how unlike is this to the description of human nature by ruling passions! Even in these great men, high as their purpose was, it must be supposed that their full moral nature was in a certain degree warped by the exclusive desire with which they pursued these objects. These objects were in truth so great, that for them it was worth while to sustain, to a certain degree, such an injury of their moral nature. And it must be added, that if their minds were in some degree warped, they were in a much greater degree exalted by the dignity of their purpose.

* John Howard, the philanthropist, to whom is due that reform in Prison Discipline, which makes the condemned criminal better fed and every way more comfortable than the poor and honest laborer.—Thomas Clarkson, whose life was devoted to one purpose—the Extinction of the Slave trade.—M.

Shepherd. Wha were they? I wush you would tell me wha they were. An anecdote or twa wad relieve the pressure on the brain o' your fine feelosophy, and lichen the lids o' ma een.

North (with enthusiasm). But before we compare with these any of the ordinary pursuits and situations of men, let it be recollected how peculiar these situations were: that these men were contending singly against the abuses and crimes of a nation, or of the world. Less than the entire life and powers of an individual human being would have been unequal to such a contest. And other instances there are no doubt more obscure, though not less virtuous, in which single men have striven, and do yet strive, against the vice and corruption of a whole generation. In all such cases, this paramount object demands, and must have, all the powers of the mind. But only in such instances which are necessarily rare, can the mind justly be given up to a single purpose. It is evident that extraordinary strength of character, and intensity of desire, and faculties of great vigor, are necessary to the adoption of purposes of this description. How rare such a union.

Shepherd. Go on, sir.—(*Aside.*) O dear me! but I wush he was dune!

North. The ruling passion, then, my dear James, you see, so far from giving any insight into its deeper composition, does, in fact, express what lies at the mere surface of character.

Shepherd. That's just what I was sayin'.

North (with an air of triumph). What, I would ask, is the knowledge imparted of the real character of a man in public station, and of high rank in his country, such as Lord Cobham was, by telling us that he was a strenuous patriot? The place in which he stood, and not the urgency of his own peculiar feelings, required of him to take his part in the public affairs of his country. And who will pretend to say, that in knowing the simple fact that Lord Cobham was one of the distinguished patriots of his day, he can tell, whether that patriotism arose from that ardent zeal for the welfare of human beings, which is one principle of our nature—or from a proud imaginative attachment to the majestic land of which he was the son, which is another—or from the stern independence and inflexible integrity of an upright and honorable mind placed by circumstances in the midst of public life, and thus, in unavoidable opposition to what there might be of corruption and selfishness at that time in the administration of the affairs of his country?

Shepherd. Hear! hear! hear!

North (rising and resting on the crutch). These and other original grounds in the mind itself, may all, with equal probability, be supposed as the cause of the patriotism of such a man; as long as his patriotism is the only known fact of his character. In this instance, then, it is evident, that the objection I advanced is true, namely, that what is called a ruling passion, often shows merely an effect produced by the emergency of the situation in which a man is placed, rather than any thing of the original and characteristic constitution of his mind. The utmost we can be said to know in such a case is the spirit of his conduct, but nothing of that which, in speaking of character, it is our object to understand, namely, the peculiar form under which human nature was exhibited in that individual human being, or the source from which his conduct sprung.

Shepherd (*resigning himself without further trouble to sleep*). OH!

North (*with great self-complacency*). Upon this view of the subject I am induced to say, in conclusion, Mr. Hogg, that it appears to me that the theory or doctrine, by whatever name we may call it, which holds up the *ruling passion*, as that which explains and exhibits in its strongest light the individual character, does, while it undertakes to set before our observation what is deepest in the composition of the mind, in fact mark out only what is most superficial. It shows us not in what manner the mind is framed, it shows us not the great elements of power which are joined together in its composition, neither the peculiar character nor the principles of its strength; but it directs our attention exclusively, and as if the whole of character were comprised in this, to some seeming outward form and aspect, which, under the pressure of circumstances, external and accidental, the mind has been constrained to assume.

Tickler (*asleep opposite the* SHEPHERD). OH!

North (*exultingly on taking his seat*). So little of real truth and instruction may there sometimes be, gentlemen, in an opinion, which, under the name of philosophy, gains attention by the grace with which it is recommended to notice, and obtains something of sanction and currency, by that which is its essential falsehood, namely, the substitution it makes of what is obvious to sight for that which lies most hidden from observation, and the flattering facility which it therefore seems to afford to the commonest observers and slightest reasoners, for understanding those subjects which are more than sufficient for the efforts of the most searching sagacity and the profoundest thought.

Shepherd (*in his dreams*). Soho! Soho! Soho! I see her èen aneath the brent broo o' the knowe.

North (*in mixed anger and amazement*). Hogg!

Shepherd (*starting up*). Halloo! halloo! halloo! Weel dune Clavers! That's it, Giraffe! A wrench—a turn—he's moothin' her—he's gruppit her—but Clavers wunna carry—fetch her here, Giraffe—and I'll wear her fud in ma hat. But I'm sair blawn.

Tickler (*in his dreams*). Razor-strop not worth a curse—razor like a saw—water lukewarm—soap sandy from scrubbing the stair—blast the brush!

North. A madman on my right hand, and an idiot on my left!

Shepherd (*recovering his senses, and rubbing his eyes*). Sae, by your ain accoont, sir, you're something atween the twa. Our freen Dr. Macnish has speculated wi' great ingenuity on the cause o' dreams in his Philosophy o' Sleep. Wull he tell me what for I was haunted by that hare, and no Mr. Tickler, wha devour'd her stoop and roop? Hae dreams, then, nae connection wi' the stammack?

North (*drawing himself up proudly*). Really I did not know, gentlemen that my conversation had been so soporific.

Shepherd. Conversation! Ca' ye't conversation to deliver a treatise on the fawse theory o' the ruling passion, a' divided intil separate heeds, and argufied back and forrit again' twa peacefu' folk like me and Mr. Tickler, wha never open'd our mouths till we fell asleep? In place o' bein' angry, you shou'd gie us baith the maist unqualified praise. As for mysell, I stood it out langer nor ony ither man in the Forest. If you had but seen the faces I made to keep mysell wauken, you wou'd hae thocht me a demoniac. I keepit twitchin' my upper lip, nose, and cheeks, like the Lord Chancellor——

North. What shall the world say, my dear Shepherd, is his ruling passion?

Tickler (*broad awake*).

> "That clew once found unravels all the rest,
> The prospect clears, and Wharton stands confest!"

North. A Reform Ministry! The Lord High Chancellor of England giving himself the lie night after night on the woolsack—

Tickler. In presence of the Peers, whom he loads with insult—

Shepherd. And in hearing o' the whale kintra, who wonder that there is nae wisdom even in his wig.

North. I have always admired the man; and the world, I verily believe, will pardon in him almost any aberration—but that from the straight line of honor and truth. The name of Henry Brougham will be eminent in the history of England; and the great champion of the Education of the People is worthy to hear that name given by the gratitude of his compatriots to the first new-discovered star.

Shepherd. That's glorious.

North. Much—much—much—I repeat it—will be forgiven to one who so nobly aspired—and in sincerity—by the power of intellect to become a moral benefactor of the race.

Shepherd. But slichted he na religion!

North. No, James—no man with such a mind—in many of its qualities so grand—did ever yet slight religion. Into Natural Theology his various science must have shown him in strong streaming lights*—and let no one dare to say that, with a heart so accessible, he is not a Christian. I desire that he may live long—and that the nation may mourn in grateful sorrow over his grave. Almost all our great have been good men; and such epithets may—I devoutly hope—be duly inscribed in his monumental epitaph.

Tickler. Amen.

Shepherd. Amen.

North. But never—never may that be—if he pause not in his wild career—and recede not from the present paths of his reckless—shall I say, his unprincipled ambition.

Shepherd. I'm a simple shepherd, sir, and therefore shall be mute. If I hae said ony thing unbecoming, I'm sorry for't; but what maitters a few silly words frae a lowly son o' the forest?

North. A thousand times more matter the thoughts and feelings of lowly sons of the Forest, than all the flatteries that have been wafted to his footstool from the dark dwellers in city-lanes, on the breath of disease and corruption.

Tickler. Popularis auræ! how fetid the pestilential smell!

North. How unlike his bearing to that of the Red-Cross Knight! He would have died to save his silver shield from slightest stain—and if self-inflicted, how bitterly had it been rued! His lips *he* would have wished to wither in death ere touched by falsehood's mildew, breathed on them from his own wavering heart—*he* would have held his words holy as his thoughts—for what are words but thoughts embodied in air—and yet imperishable—for once uttered and heard, they are your only immortals—deny them, and they come flying against you on all the winds—*επεα πτεροεντα*—that will tear your liver like vultures—or, if you will it so, flying to and fro in the sunshine, will gather round your head when living, and when you are dead round your tomb, like doves, messengers of peace, and love, and glory, whose bright plumes time shall never touch with decay, nor all the storms of this world ruffle or bedim.

Shepherd. That's beautifu'—but methinks you're speakin', in sic eem: gery, no o' politicians, bnt o' poets.

North. Of statesmen. Their instruments may be mean—but their ends how mighty! In legislating for England now, they legislate for the whole world hereafter—and shall the Spirit of the Age suffer in her service, from the lips of her most eloquent minister, at once reckless, and systematic, and flagrant, in the face of day, a violation of truth?

Tickler. "Rest—rest, perturbed spirit!"

Shepherd. But he canna rest! Oh, that he would but tak Mr. North's advice!—for like a' the rest o' the warld, great and sma',

* Lord Brougham edited, and in some respects expanded (by illustrations) Paley's great work, on Natural Theology.—M.

nae dout Lord Chancellor Brougham reads the Noctes. Had we him sittin' here, for ae hour, we'd convert him—divert him—frae the path intil whilk he has by some evil demon been deflected frae the right line o' his natural career—and giein' him a shove, send him spinnin' awa' on his ain axis like a planet through the sky. But haw! haw! haw! haw! haw! haw!

Tickler. What the deuce now?

Shepherd. Lord Althropp—Lord Althropp—Lord Althropp! My sides are sair.

North. Laughable indeed, James.

Shepherd. Then dinna grin sae gruesomely—but join me in a guffaw.

Omnes. Ha! ha! haw! ha! ha! haw!

Shepherd. It's an hysterical creesis in a nation's calamity, when the King, and the Commons, and the People (but no the Peers), wou'd have a' resigned their situations—the King his throne, the Commons their seats, and the People their kintra, unless Lord Althropp had been persuawded to condescend to continue to remain Chancellor o' the Exchequer,* and yet him for a' that universally allow'd to be an Oxe!

Tickler. There has been no such political appointment since Caligula made his horse consul.

Shepherd. I'm nae great Roman historian—but I dinna see't mention'd in thae learned articles, "The Cæsars," that the consul either imposed or defended a tax on mawte. In ae thing, I hae nae doubt, he ackit like Lord Althropp.

Tickler. Eh?

Shepherd. He left open the Corn Question.

Tickler. The consulship was a sinecure.

Shepherd. And the Nag himsell on the Ceevil List.

Tickler. For past services.

Shepherd. O' various kinds to the State.

Tickler. As how?

Shepherd. Mair especially for workin' a great improvement on the Imperial Cavalry.

Tickler. His Lordship, more indirectly, has equally improved the breed of cattle—of long horns.

Shepherd. I think I see him—the Consul—stannin' in his stall, high-fed at rack and manger, and on mashes, forbye, wi' his mane

* Lord Althorp (afterwards Earl Spencer) was Chancellor of the Exchequer in the Grey Administration, in 1830–4. As no one Budget which he brought forward ever was adopted by Parliament, without such organic changes, as wholly altered its character and purpose, it may safely be said that his Lordship was one of the very worst Finance Ministers who ever threw "confusion worse confounded" into the British Treasury. He was misplaced in life. Nature meant him to be a grazier, bringing up his fatted cattle to Smithfield market, dining at the Pig and Whistle, and riding home in the cool of the evening, with a light heart and full purse. Instead of that, he was a wealthy Peer, attempting to be a Politician, breaking his shins against National Finance, and making all auditors smile at his miserable attempts at oratory.—M.

nicely platted, and ribands on his tail. But in a' his consular pomp, he's no sic a wonderfu' animal to the imagination as Lord Althropp.

Tickler. His Lordship is not without a certain share of small abilities.

Shepherd. Sae the newspapers say—but under a Lilliputian bushel he cou'd easily hide his licht.

Tickler. His Lordship owes a debt of endless gratitude to the press. Not that the gentlemen of the press flatter him on the score of talents—for with one voice they unanimously and harmoniously proclaim him the weakest Chancellor that ever got his head into Exchequer.

North. Yet in the Owl they see a Phœnix.

Tickler. And as if they were all knaves themselves, lift up their hands in admiration at the sight of an honest man.

North. Your severity, Tickler, is unjust; yet the editors, who have joined in that senseless cry, have indeed fairly subjected themselves to such imputation. There is not a more contemptible term in the language, in its vulgar colloquial misuse, than the term—honest; for it denotes a stupid man with a fat face—low brow—heavy eyes—lips that seem rather to have been afterwards sewed on to the mouth than an original feature—chubby cheeks—double chin—large ears—and voice——

Shepherd. "Timmer-tuned—tempered by the beetle." But ye dinna mean to say that's a pictur o' Lord Althropp?

North. No—I do not. I know better what is due to a nobleman and a gentleman. But I do mean to say that some such sort of application as the term "honest" has been unconsciously made in the case of his Lordship—to his political character—by many of his admirers. They extol his good-nature.

Shepherd. In the Forest a gude-natured man means a quate, useless boddy, henpeck'd at hame, and cheated abroad, and for whom every excuse is made when he's seen no verra weel cled at kirk or market, on the grun' o' his wife's no bein' contented wi' wearin' the breeks, unless she gets haud o' the best pair, in which she sits in velvet. That's a gude-natured man in the Forest, but he may be a different character in the House o' Commons, mair especially when the leader there, wi' a seat o' coorse in the Cabinet, and, to croon a', Chancellor o' the Exchequer!

North. In Smithfield his Lordship's character is without a stain. But, to speak plainly, as a minister of the Crown, he is the most dishonest that ever received, returned, reaccepted, and retained the seals of office.

Shepherd. The maist dishonest!

North. Yes! Steeped to the eyes in dishonor—yet all the while superstitiously believing himself "the noblest work of God."

Shepherd. Tak' time to cool, sir. Though I canna say your face is ony way distorted—which it aye is when you're in a passion—nor that your voice trummles—which it aye does when about to be left to yoursell—yet your words are viciously cuttin'—and the sharper the edge because a' the while you're sheerin' him doon, you're as cool, calm, and collecked in your manner as a cucumber.

North. The Chancellor of the Exchequer is often called candid, for stammering out the most blundering admissions to crafty querists, cunningly ensnaring him to commit himself on the most important points, which he, good easy man, has not the sense to think points of any importance at all—mumbling "Yes," when, in common prudence, to say nothing of pride, it should have been "No."

Shepherd. And "No" when it should hae been "Yes." Eh?

North. He afterwards sees his errors, that is, when he is insultingly told of them, and then he again falls back on his character for candor, and frankly, that is foolishly, confesses that he has said more than he meant, or the reverse of what he meant—and the crafty, having so far obtained their object as to make him ridiculous, and consequently powerless, cry hear! hear! hear! and the morning papers are next day filled with honest eulogiums on honest Lord Althorp, who looks next evening in his place as well pleased as a fozey turnip after a shower.

Shepherd. You'll please me, sir, by mentionin' shortly a few dizzen instances o' his dishonesty.

North. I could mention five hundred—but

"Lo! in the lake soft burns the star of eve,
And the night-hawk hath warn'd your guests to leave
Ere chilling shades descend our leafy tent."

Shepherd. Ae dizzen.

North. What has the entire system of Whig Government been from first to last, but a complicated and ravelled web of falsehood? Almost every clause in the Reform Bill, as it now stands, enacted a measure, which every man in power (Lord Grey excepted, and Lord Durham, when Mr. Lambton), who could wag a tongue or hold a pen, however impotently, had all their political lives resisted and scorned. The Reform we have now got they had continued for many years to denounce as revolution, in speeches, pamphlets, books, without beginning, middle, or end; and the Bill they at first proposed to bring in was founded on principles of conservatism, which almost all moderate men might have in much approved. Wellington and Peel themselves would not have objected to them, though they had too much sense to introduce, as Ministers, at such a crisis, any Reform at all. Whether they were wrong or right is not the question—the question is, were the Whigs honest men—and the answer has been given by the voice of the country, Radicals and all, that they were, politically speaking, knaves—and conspicuous among them, with his enthusiasm for the tricolor, was my Lord Althorp.

Shepherd. But will ye no alloo a man to eat in a few o' his words, sir?

North. No; a very few indeed, eat in, are sufficient to choke an honest man. But the Whigs re-ate all they had ever spewed on Reform—nor seemed, James, to scunner at the half-digested gobbets.

Shepherd. Coorse.

North. Does the Shepherd believe that Lord Althorp in his heart loved and admired—as he said he did—the Political Unions—composed, according to Lord Brougham, of the philosophical classes of Brummagem, and bright with the scientific splendor that holds all the great manufacturing towns of England in perpetual illumination?

Shepherd. Na.

North. He is not so simple.

Shepherd. And yet, to my cost, I'm simple eneuch.

North. Once seated in places of power, the Whigs were not slow to denounce Political Unions—which were good, they said—and constitutional for purposes of national agitation to carry the great measure, but bad and unconstitutional, they had the audacious ingratitude to declare, after Reform had established a liberal Government, for then it was time for the Philosophical and Political Unionists to resume their aprons—and that the smith must thenceforth be contented to "stand at his anvil—thus, with open mouth, swallowing a tailor's news."

Shepherd. I canna be angry for lauchin'.

North. Place himself was degraded into a newsmonger—the very tailor who had invited himself, at the head of a kindred deputation, to a conference with the Premier, to show him how he should cut his cloth—with what suit he should lead—what measures adopt for the use and ornament of the body politic—while a number of Jews remained at the bottom of the stair, with bags in which to carry off the State's old clothes.

Shepherd. You're real wutty, sir, the nicht.

North. But did my Lord Althorp, or any other of the time-serving, place-seeking Whigs, ever explain to the Political Unions on what principle they were either encouraged or denounced? The kind of crisis at which they were a blessing—and the kind of crisis at which they became a curse? To have done that even slovenly would have required an abler and an honester man. But his ability and his honesty were on a par, and far below par—and now stand at zero.

Shepherd. I never saw Mr. Tickler listenin' sae attentively be fore—and yet he's no asleep.

North. That no connection could be imagined to subsist between Political Unions and Trades' Unions, is even yet, James, the Whig cry. They have fed, do feed, and will feed one another; and thousands, and tens of thousands, and hundreds of thousands of poor men have rued, do rue, and will rue, the base arts of their betrayers, the Whigs, who, in the lust of power and place, seduced them to uplift the banners of sedition, misnamed of patriotism by tyrants who changed freemen into slaves, by first pretending to knock off from their limbs fetters that were never forged, and then grinding their very faces in the dust, and shipping some of the misguided wretches, now not only useless but dangerous, to expatriation and death.

Shepherd. A Psalm-singing Methody or twa wha had taken and administered unlawfu' oaths, and some half-dizzen ne'er-do-weels, wha might hae been stappin' doon aboot this time frae the tredd-mill.

North. All the reasonings of the Liberals against Combination Laws were false, foolish, and futile, as I proved a few months ago, in a paper which the impartial press declared conclusive and unanswerable; and the severities which the Government inflicted, legal as they were, were shocking to the sense of justice, seeing that they came from the hands of men who had selfishly laboured to spread wide the delusion under which those poor ignorant creatures sinned and suffered.

Shepherd. Wasna Lord Melbourne then Home-Minister?

North. He was, and the more shame to him; but my honest Lord Althorp had been a far more flaming reformer than he, and should have shown some bowels of compassion to the poor, who, I fear, are now the greatest part of the people. Such cruelties—tender mercies according to the Whig creed—soon cease to be remembered by the rich and noble—for though the revengeful Whigs have long memories for the slightest injuries done to themselves, the best among them have memories even shorter than their wits for the sufferings of others, and, with all their cant slang about secondary punishments, prefer them to the capital, because, barbarous as they often are, the nation does not shudder at their infliction—"out of sight out of mind,"—and hard-hearted philanthropists can thus transport for life as many wretches as they choose; nor have they left to themselves even the privileges of remission, so that hundreds are now annually separated for ever from all they hold dear, for crimes which used justly and humanely to be punished and expiated, and perhaps repented, by a year's imprisonment.

Shepherd. You're expawtiatin' ower a wide field. I wuss you wou'd be mair personal on Lord Althropp.

North. I am never personal. I have said enough to show you.

my dear James, that that Statesman cannot be honest, who leads the House of Commons as a Member of the Cabinet of such a Government.

Shepherd. Then they're a' dishonest thegether, and why single out his Lordship?

North. I never singled him out. I see him singled out to my hand as the only man among them who deserves the epithet, honest; and am, therefore, to presume that there is something peculiar in his character and conduct, distinguishing him from all the Ministers with whom he acts in concert—and pray, will you, who have a fertile fancy, favor me, who am a matter-of-fact man, with a conjecture what that peculiarity may be, made plausible by "a round unvarnished tale" of one honest deed he has performed, or one honest word he has uttered, since he began to draw his salary?

Shepherd. That's no fair—for he may hae dune and said a thousan', though I never happen'd to hear o' ane.

North. In not one instance, regarding taxation, has he acted a plain, open, straightforward, bold, and intelligent part. Either he has never once happened to know what he intended to do, or never once chosen unequivocally to declare it. Irresolution is bad enough,—but equivocation is insufferable; and our Chancellor of the Exchequer is the Equivocator of the Age. There are the Taxes on Knowledge, as they are called—*videlicet*, newspaper stamps. Did he not promise to modify, or reduce, or take them off entirely, or did he not? That the Equivocator hummed and hawed, and was unintelligible, I grant; but, as usual, he said enough to commit himself with the venders of that most useful of all commodities, knowledge; and it was mortifying, humiliating to them to find that they had been cajoled and deceived by Honesty personified. But that was a trifle—for no honest man could belong to the present Ministry after the prosecution of the *True Sun*, and pride himself at the same time on being not only a friend, but a champion of the press. "Might not a Government be justified in prosecuting for sedition the editor of a newspaper whose offence was the same that had been committed by a Peer and a Commoner in their places in Parliament?" Some such question was put lately to the Lord Chancellor by the Attorney-General, and the answer was "No!" The wily Attorney was outwitted by the bold Chancellor. In the well-known circumstances of the case he thought he had his Lordship on the hip; but the stalwart man of the people (alas! alas!) flung the rejected of Dudley, and the accepted of Edinburgh (we are a proud people, the Scotch) across his knee, and the head of "plain John Campbell" rebounded a yard from the sod.*

* William Brougham, the Lord Chancellor's brother, represented the borough of Southwark in Parliament, and declared, in the House of Commons, that, until the Reform Bill was pas[illegible],

Shepherd. I'm amazed, and yet I hae nae idea—no the least in the warld—o' what you're speaking aboot. Gang on.

North. Baron Smith is one of the best beloved men in all Ireland. The Protestants adore him——

Shepherd. That's wrang. They should leave that to the Catholics.

North. All the virtuous Catholics regard him as their friend—but O'Connell hates and fears him, and sought to sacrifice the character of the stainless sage on the altar of his unfeeling ambition.

Shepherd. Ambition's no the word.

North. It is not. Honest Lord Althorp good-naturedly joined the conspiracy against the venerable patriarch, and candidly instigated a reformed House of Commons to drive him with disgrace from the bench. Mainly by his influence—for he is all in all in that highminded assembly—a vote was passed for that useful, honorable, and upright purpose; and candid, conciliating, conscientious, highminded, and warm-hearted, true English nobleman, Lord Althorp, looked at the House with a blandness of physiognomy which must have been either more or less than human to resist, and received from her in return one of her most subduing and subservient smiles. But in this instance, his lordship had prevailed over the virtue of the House at what is called a weak moment—for, a few nights after, she rejected his addresses, and left him in the lurch, for one who was not troubling his head about her—the self-same aged gentleman whom she had meditated to unwig—verging on threescore and ten—even Baron Smith*—but though he treated her courteously, he declined having any thing to do with her—so she again returned to the embraces of the grazier.

Shepherd. That was far waur than his equivocation about stamps. The ither was a trifle.

North. His behaviour, and that of all his colleagues, to Mr. Sheil—a man of genius and virtue—all the world knows, was such as

he would not pay Government taxes. Lord King made the same declaration, in the Upper House. The *True Sun* newspaper, after Reform was carried, laid down, as a principle, that while the People were not done justice to, they were justified in refusing to pay taxes, and quoted Lord King and William Brougham, as authorities. The Government prosecuted the *True Sun*, for sedition, and were defeated. The Attorney General who prosecuted, was Sir John Campbell, who, at the Edinburgh Election, in 1832, uttered a strong diatribe against hereditary rank, boasting that he was "plain John Campbell." Soon after he accepted a peerage for his wife, who was created Baroness Stratheden, and, some years later a peerage for himself, when he assisted in the scandalous *job* which turned Plunket out of the Irish Chancellorship, to give it to "plain John Campbell" for a few weeks—an hour's occupancy of that office carrying with it, as it did to Campbell, a life-grant of £4000 a year, as a retiring pension.—M.

* Sir William Smith, one of the Barons of the Exchequer in Ireland, was accused, by Daniel O'Connell, in February, 1834, of introducing political subjects into his charges to grand-juries at the Assizes, of not coming into Court, to try prisoners, until the afternoon, and of having tried fourteen prisoners, at Armagh, between six o'clock in the evening and six in the morning. O'Connell's motion for inquiry into Baron Smith's conduct was carried by a majority of 167 to 74—the Whig Ministry supporting it. A week after, Peel took up the case, defended Smith, accused O'Connell of personal and vindictive motives, proposed that the vote for inquiry be rescinded, and succeeded, by a majority of 165 to 159.—M.

in private life would have shut against them the doors of all gentlemen's houses, even in Coventry. Still honest Lord Althorp not only held up his head and showed his face, but became, on that pitiable exposure, more candid than ever, and while he apologized, gloried in his gossip.* He was in reality, though not aware of it, about as dignified a personage and in as dignified a predicament, as a dowager in a small tea-drinking town, convicted, on her own reluctant confession, of having circulated a *fama clamosa* against a virgin spinstress, of being nearly nine months gone with child.

Shepherd. What'n a simile! It was rash in the dowager to say nine months, far had she said sax, the calumniated lassie would hae had to wait three afore she cu'd in ony way get a safe delivery—either o' the charge or the child. Wha was she? and what ca' they the sma' tea-drinking toun?

North. You know, Mr. Hogg, that the sin charged against Mr. Sheil was that of having thought one way and spoken another, on a question deeply affecting Ireland—the Coercion Bill. In Parliament he had been, as was to be expected, one of the most eloquent and indignant denouncers of the tyrannical, and unconstitutional, and insulting, and injurious, and unnecessary injustice of that measure.

Shepherd. Injurious injustice! Is that correct?

North. Quite correct in grammar. Out of the House he was accused of having declared it to be all right, and that the state of Ireland demanded it. So shocked and horrified was the moral sense of honest Lord Althorp by the idea of such ultra-Irish violation of all honor and all truth, that he lost his head, and avowed his inability to conceive a punishment adequate to such an unheard-of crime. In the event of the conviction of the accused, he hinted, that if the House was not found too hot for him, he would probably be found too hot for the House. Mr. Sheil seemed standing on the brink of expulsion—and it was supposed that he meditated going out with his evil conscience as an unsettled settler to Van Diemen's Land.

Shepherd. Was Mr. Sheil married?

North. Yes—not long before, to a very beautiful and accomplished woman, and that aggravated the hardship of his case—for to a bachelor a trip even to Botany Bay is a mere amusement.

Shepherd. I forget the result o' the inquiry—for I never recolleck ony thing noo I read o', unless it has had the gude luck to happen centuries ago.

* It was Lord Althorp who, in 1834, charged Sheil with having secretly and treacherously urged the Whig Ministry to carry an Irish Coercion Bill, which the Irish liberal members were publicly opposing. The investigation which took place, on Sheil's own requisition, established the falsehood of the accusation, and Lord Althorp had to withdraw it and make an humble apology.—M.

North. Lord Althorp prayed Mr. Sheil might have a safe deliverance—

Shepherd. O the hypocrite! Pretendin' that he didna credit a calumny o' his creatin', and invokin' heaven to show that he was a leear, in an eye-upturning prayer!

North. You misunderstand me—he did not create the calumny, my dear James.

Shepherd. Then wha did?

North. Nobody cares. The candid Chancellor of the Exchequer persisted in believing it to the last—clung to it after it stank like a dug-up cat—sulkily retracted his belief—said something for which Mr. Sheil would have shot him but for the Sergeant-at-Arms—looked big and small—bullied—explained again—apologized—begged pardon—and expressed what a relief it was to him to see Mr. Sheil honorably exculpated and acquitted of a charge, of which, had he been guilty, his lordship, laying his hand on his heart, and looking as impressively as nature would allow, was free to confess that he must have been lost for ever to that society—to that country of which he was now one of the brightest ornaments—brighter than ever, because of the passing away of the black cloud that had threatened to obscure or strangle its lustre.

Shepherd. I'll be hanged if Lord Althropp ever said ony sic word.

North. James?

Shepherd. Sic words never flowed frae a mouth like yon. But you've, nae doot, gien the sense, and made him speak as if he was wordy—which he never will be—o' sittin', and noo and then venturin' on a bit easy remark, at the Noctes.

North. Now, my dear James, mark—for I know you are no *quid nunc*—and read little about what is passing in London—else had I not spoken a single syllable of politics in the still air of this beautiful arbour. Honest Lord Althorp has been convicted—and has confessed it—of the same crime charged against Mr. Sheil—with circumstances of aggravation, that, were I to tell you of them, would, to your simple mind, be incredible.

Shepherd. My mind, sir, 's at ance simple and credulous—I can believe ony thing—a' the gude that tongue o' man cou'd tell o' a Tory, and a' the ill that the tongue o' deevil cou'd tell o' Whig—sae there's nae occasion to dwell on the incredible circumstances o' aggravation—they are a' true as gospel.

North. Mr. Sheil, I said, James, is a man of genius—a fine-eyed, fine-souled son of Erin. Had he been a hypocrite—a traitor—I would have bitterly lamented it, and blushed for the form I wore.

Shepherd. You would hae had nae need to do that, even though Mr. Sheil had been a black sheep. Considerin' your time o' life, the form ye wear's verra imposin'; as for your countenance it is comely—and I'm no surprised Mrs. Gentle considers you a captivatin' cretur.

North. We must not too coldly scan even the principles of patriotism. They may be such, carried to excess, or flying off oblique, as we cannot approve, even though we can apprehend them within our sympathies; but to fall away from them in faintness of heart is pitiable—to desert them is shameful—to fight openly against them execrable—but insidiously to betray them——

Shepherd. Is damnable—o' that honest Lord Althropp thoucht guilty Mr. Sheil—but you dinna say that he himsell has committed that very sin?

North. He could not commit that very sin—for he is not Mr. Sheil. But he committed it as far as nature would suffer Lord Althorp. That Coercion-Bill, which he thought *ought* not to be passed, he consented to make pass through Parliament!

Shepherd. That seems the converse o' the charge against Mr. Sheil—and if I ken the meanin' o' the word conscience, confoun' me gin' it's no a thoosan' times waur.

North. A million times worse.

Shepherd. I'm sorry for him—in what far-away hole, puir fallow, can he be noo hidin' his head? I howp in baith senses that he's resigned.

North. He has ousted Earl Grey—

Shepherd. What?

North. And honest Lord Althorp is the most popular man in England.

Shepherd. Then England may sink intil the bottom o' the Red Sea. Na—she maunna do that, for she wud drag Scotland alang with her—and then fareweel to the Forest?

North. You can have no notion, James, of the despicable intrigue by which honest Lord Althorp ousted the Premier.

Shepherd. He maun be desperate angry.

North. He does not appear so, but his son and son-in-law have resigned.*

Shepherd. Which was right, for even a Whig, setting selfish considerations aside, doesna like to hae advantage ta'en o' his ain father. Hoo O'Connell, frae what ye hae hinted, maun be crawin'!

North. Lord Althorp secretly commissioned Mr. Secretary Littleton to sound, consult, conciliate, and truckle to the Agitator. O'Connell and Littleton had a blow-up, and abused each other like pickpockets.† The cat was let out of the bag, and began not only

* Lord Howick (the present Earl Grey) and the late Earl of Durham.—M.

† Mr. Edward John Littleton (now Lord Hatherton) had been Chief Secretary for Ireland, and had arranged with Mr. O'Connell—with Lord Althorp's concurrence, but wholly without the knowledge of Lord Grey, head of the Government—that certain measures should be passed, to

to mew, but to hiss and puff and prepare her paws for serious scratching—there was a regular row in the Lower House, and a very irregular one in the Upper. Earl Grey declared his entire ignorance of the shameful and slavish submission of honest Lord Althorp to the Big Beggarman—and, would you believe it, James, a question has arisen, and has been debated with much acrimony, whether or not, by such proceedings, the Premier was betrayed?

Shepherd. He shou'd just hae gaen to his Majesty, and said, "Sire! Lord Althropp is a fule, or warse, and has been playing jookery-paukery wi' that chiel O'Connell, through ane o' your Majesty's understrappers, and the twa thegither hae brocht the Ministry intil a mess. I maist respectfully ask your Majesty what your Majesty wou'd wush me to do? Here are the Seals." His Majesty wou'd immediately hae said, "Yearl! kick Lord Althropp to the back-o'-beyond—carry ye on the Coercion-Bill—for it's necessary to the pacification o' Ireland—put the Seals in your pocket, alloo me to ring the bell for your cotch—and write me in the mornin' hoo things are lookin' in the Upper House." I ken that's what I wad hae dune mysell had I been King—and frae a' I hae heard o' his Majesty sin' he sat on the throne, and when he walked the quarter-deck, I'm as fairly convinced that he would hae supported Yearl Grey, as that, supposing me a proprietor o' laun', I wad hae discharged on the spat ony servant o' mine, whether lad or lass, that had been detected plottin' again' my head greave, which would, in fack, hae been plottin' again' his master, and therefore deserved to be punished by dismissal—whether wi' wages and board-wages up the term or no, wad hae been a question to be reserved for future consideration—but assuredly, without a character. (*Starting up.*) Mercy on us, whare's Tickler?

North. Who?

Shepherd. Didna Mr. Tickler come oot wi' ye frae Embro?

North. Mr. Tickler! I have not seen him for some months. There is a coolness between us, but it will wear off—and—

Shepherd. Only look at him, sir, only look at him—yonner he's helpin' Mysie to let out the kye! That's a bat

North. The gloaming—what a beautiful word—gives a magical character to the stillness of the Forest—and the few trees seem as if they were standing there in enchantment—human beings reconciled to the thrall of vegetable life—and breathing the dewy air through leaves, whose delicate fibres thrill to the core of their quiet hearts. One star! I ought to know where to find the Crescent.

carry out "an instalment" of that "justice for Ireland," which O'Connell was contending for:—it was part of the compact, also, that the Irish Coercion Bill should be dropped or modified. As related by North, a difference arose between O'Connell and Littleton. Lord Grey indignantly repudiated the idea of any bargain with O'Connell, and quitted office. By all rule of right, Lord Althorp should have gone out, and not Lord Grey.—M.

Not so bad a practical astronomer--for there is the Huntress of the silver bow, just where I expected her—and in all that region of heaven there is not a cloud.

Shepherd. Let's in to sooper. This is Saturday night—and you'll read the family a chapter. Lean on ma arm, or rather let me lean on yours, for you're the younger man o' the twa—no in years—but in constitution—and you'll be famous in history as the modern Methusalem. *(They enter the house.)*

No. LXVIII.—NOVEMBER, 1834.

SCENE I.—*Green in front of* TIBBIE'S—*Head of St. Mary's Loch —Time, Four afternoon*—SHEPHERD *standing alone, in a full suit of the Susalpine Tartan—Arrive* NORTH *and* TICKLER *on their Norwegians.*

Shepherd. True to time as the cuckoo and the swallow. Hail, Christopher! Hail, Timothy! Lords o' the ascendant, I bid ye hail!

Tickler. Hoo's a' wi' ye, Jeems?

Shepherd. Brawlies—brawlies, sir; but tak ma advice, Mr. Tickler, and never attempt what ma excellent freen, Downie o' Appin, ca's the Doric, you doug, for sic anither pronountiation was never heard on this side o' the north pole.

North. My beloved Broonie! lend a helping hand to your old accomplice while he endeavors to dismount.

Shepherd. My heart hotches, like a bird's nest wi' young anes, at the sound o' your vice. Ay—ay—I'll affectionately lend a helpin' haun to my auld accomplice while he endeavors to dismunt—my auld accomplice in a' kinds o' innicent wicketness—and Clootie shinna tak the ane o' us without the ither—I'm determined on that —yet Clootie's a great coward, and wull never hae courage to face the Crutch!

Tickler. And how am I to get off!

Shepherd. Your feet's within twa three inches o' the grun already —straught your knees—plant your soles on the sward—let gae the grupp, and the beast 'll walk out frae aneath you, as if he was passing through a triumphal airch. Cream-colored pownies! Are they a present frae the Royal Stud?

North. They are Norwegians, James, not Hanoverians. Lineally descended from the only brace of cavalry King Haco had on board at the battle of Largs.

Shepherd. His ain body-guard o' horse marines. Does he bite?

North. Sometimes. But please to observe that he is muzzled.

Shepherd. I thocht 'twas but a nettin' over his nose. Does he kick?

North. I have known him kick.

Shepherd. I canna say I like that layin' back o' his lugs—nor yet that twust o' his tail—and mercy on us, but he's gotten the eevil ee!

Tickler. Tibbie! a stool.

(TIBBIE *places a cutty-stool below* TICKLER'S *left foot—and describing half a circle with his right,* TIMOTHY *treads the sod—then facing about, leans with his right elbow on Harold's shoulder—while his left forms the apex of an isosceles triangle, as hand on hip he stands, like Hippolitus or Meleager.*

Shepherd (admiring Tickler). There's an equestrian statue worth a thoosan' o' that o' Lord Hopetoun and his horse in front o' the Royal Bank—though judges tell me that Cammel the sculptor's a modern Midas. Hoo granly the figures combine wi' the backgrun'! See hoo that rock relieves Tickler's head—and hoo that tree carries aff Haco's tail! The director-general was wrang in swearin' that sculptur' needs nae scenery to set it aff—for will ony body tell me that that groopp would be as magnificent within the four bare wa's o' an exhibition room, as where it noo stauns, in the heart o' licht encircled by hills, and overhung by heaven? Gin a magician cou'd by a touch o' his wand, convert it intil marble, it would be worth a ransom. But, alas! 'tis but transitory flesh and bluid!

Tickler. Why don't you speak, James?

Shepherd. Admiration has held me mute. I beseech ye, sir, dinna stir—for sic anither attitude for elegance, grace, and majesty's no within the possible combinations o' the particles o' maitter. Tibbie! tak aff your een—it's no safe for a widow woman to glower lang on sic a spectacle! Then the garb! what an advantage it has owre Lord Hopetoun's! His lordship looks as if he had lowped oot o' his bed on sae sudden an alarm, that he had time but to fling the blankets owre his shouthers, and the groom nae time to saddle the horse, which his master had to ride a' nicht bare back'd—altogether beneath the dignity o' a British general. But there the costume is a' in perfeck keepin'—purple plush jacket wi' great big white horn buttons—single breasted—cape hangin' easily owre the back o' the neck—hauncuffs fliped to gie the wrists room to play—and the flaps o' the mony-pouch'd reachin' amaist doon to the knee, frae which again the ee travels alang the tartan trews till it feenally rests on a braw brass buckle—or is it gowd?—bright on his instep as a cairngorum. But up wi' a swurl again flees imagination, and settles among the lights and shadows o' the picturesque scenery o' that mony-shaped straw hat—the rim o' its circumference a Sabbath-day's journey round—umbrageous umbrella, aneath which he stauns safe frae sun and rain—and might entertain a select pairty in the cool o' the air! which he cou'd keep in circulation by a shake o' his head!

Tickler. Now that I have stood for my statue, James, pray give us a pen and ink sketch of Christopher.

Shepherd. There he sits, turned half roon' on the saddle, wi' ae haun restin' on the mane, and the ither haudin' by the crupper—no that he's feared to fa' aff—for I've seldom seen him tummle at a staun-still—but that I may hae a front, a back, and a side view o' him a' at ance—for his finest pint is what I wou'd venture, wi' a happy audacity, to ca' the circular contour o' his full face and figure in profile—sae that the spectawtor has a comprehensive visey o' a' the characteristic attributes o' his outward man.

North. The circular contour of my full face and figure in profile! I should like to see it.

Shepherd. I fear I sha'na be able to feenish the figure at ae sittin', for it's no easy to get rid o' that face.

North. I am trying to look as mild as cheese.

Shepherd. Dinna fasten your twa gray, green een on mine like a wull-cat.

North. Verily, they are more like a sucking dove's.

Shepherd. Surely there's nae need to look sae cruel about the doon-drawn corners o' your mouth—for that neb's aneuch o' itsel'—every year liker and liker a ggemm-hawk's.

North. I am a soft-billed bird.

Shepherd. A multitude o' lang, braid, white, sharp teeth's fearsome in the mouth o' an auld man, and makes ane suspeck dealins wi' the enemy, and an unhallowed lease o' a lang life.

North. Would that I had not forgotten to bargain for exemption from the toothache!

Shepherd. I wuss there may na be mair meant than meets the ee in thae marks on the forehead. They tell na o' the touch o' time, but o' the Tempter.

North. I rub them off—so—and lo—the brow of a boy!

Shepherd. Answer me ae question—I adjure you—hae ye sel't your sowle to Satan?

North (*smiling*). James!

Shepherd. Heaven bless you, sir, for that smile—for it has scattered the dismal darkness o' doubt in which ye were beginning to wax intil a demon, and I behold Christopher North in his ain native light—a man—a gentleman—and a Christian. But whare's the crutch?

North. Crutch! The useless old sinecurist has been lying in velvet all autumn—henceforth I believe I shall dispense with his services—for the air of the Forest has proved fatal to gout, rheumatism, and lumbago—of which truth behold the pleasant proof—James—here goes!

(NORTH *springs up to his feet on the crupper, throws a somerset over Haco's rump, and bounds from the greensward as from a spring-board.)*

Tickler. Not amiss. Let's untackle our cattle—and make our toilet.

(NORTH *and* TICKLER *strip their steeds, and turn them loose into the meadow, green as emerald with a flush of after-grass, in which they sink to the fetlocks, as at full gallop they describe fairy-rings within fairy-rings, till in the centre of the field they subside into a trot, and after diversely careering a while with flowing mane and tail, and neighings that thrill the hills, settle to serious eating, and look as if they had been quietly pasturing there since morn.)*

North. That's right, my good Tibbie. Put my pail of water and my portmanteau into the arbour.

Tickler. That's right, my pretty Dolly, put my pail of water and my portmanteau into the shed.

(NORTH *retires into the arbour to make his toilet, and* TICKLER *into the opposite shed.* SHEPHERD *remains midway between—held there by the counteraction of two equal powers of animal magnetism.)*

Shepherd. Are ye gaun in to the dookin' in thae twa pails?

North. No—as rural lass adjusts her silken snood by reflection in such pellucid mirror—so am I about to shave.

Shepherd. Remember the fable o' the goat and the well.

North (*within the arbour*). How beautiful the fading year! A month ago, this arbour was all one dusky green—now it glows—it burns with gold, and orange, and purple, and crimson! How harmonious the many-colored glory! How delightfully are all the hues in tune!

Shepherd. Are na ye cauld staunin' there in your linen? For I see you through the thin umbrage, like a ghost in a dirty shirt.

North. Sweet are autumn's rustling bowers, but sweeter far her still—when dying leaf after dying leaf drops unreluctantly from the spray—all noiseless as snow-flakes—and like them ere long to melt away into the bosom of mother earth. It seems but yesterday when they were buds!

Shepherd. Tak tent ye dinna cut yoursel'—it's no safe to moraleeze when ane's shavin'. Are ye speakin' to me, or was that meant for a soliloquy?

North. In holt or shaw, in wood or grove, on bush or hedgerow, among broom or bracken, the merry minstrelsy is heard no more! Soon as they cease to sing, they seem to disappear; the mute mavis retires with her speckled throat and breast so beautiful into the forest gloom; the bold blackbird hides himself for a season, till the berries redden the holly-trees; and where have all the linties gone?

Are they too home-changing birds of passage? and have they flown ungratefully away with the swallows, to sunny southern isles?

Shepherd. He's mair poetical nor correck in his ornithology; yet it's better to fa' into siclike harmless errors in the study o' leevin' birds—errors o' a lovin' heart, and a mournfu' imagination—than to keep scientifically richt amang stuffed specimens sittin' for ever in ae attitude wi' bead een in a glass-case.

North. Blessings on thy ruby breast, sweet Robin, for thine own and those poor children's sake! A solitary guest of summer gloom; but at the first frost o' autumn, thou seek'st again the dwellings of men—"a household bird" all winter long—till soon-come spring invites thee to build another nuptial nest among the mossy roots of some old forest-tree! I see thee sitting there on the top-stone of the gable, as if the domicile were thine own; and thine own it is—for thou holdest it by the tenure of that cheerful song. "No better a musician than a wren!" So said sweet Willie—flattering the nightingale. But the wren now answering the robin—almost echo-like—from the bourtree bush in the garden—with his still small voice, touches the heart that knoweth how to listen—more tenderly, more profoundly, than Philomela's most richly-warbled song!

Tickler (within the shed). What have you been about with yourself, all day, my dear James?

Shepherd. No muckle. I left Altrive after breakfast—about nine—and the Douglass Burn lookin' gae temptin', I tried it with the black gnat, and sune creel'd some foure or five dizzen—the maist o' them sma'—few exceedin' a pund.

Tickler. Hem.

Shepherd. I fear, sir, you've gotten a sair thrott. Ane sune tires o' trooting at ma time o' life, sae I then put on a sawmon flee, and without any howp daunered doon to a favorite cast on the Yarrow. Sometimes a body may keep threshin' the water for a week without seein a snout—and sometimes a body hyeucks a fish at the very first thraw, and sae it happened wi' me—though I can gie mysel' nae credit for skill—for I was just watten my flee near the edge, when a new-run fish, strong as a white horse, rushed at it, and then oot o' the water wi' a spang higher than my head,

"My heart to my mooth gied a sten',"

and he had amaist rugged the rod oot my nieve; but I sune recovered my presence o' mind, and after indulgin' his royal highness in a few plunges, I gied him the butt, and for a quarter o' an hour keep't his nose to the grunstane. It's a sair pity to see a sawmon sulky, and I thocht—and nae doubt sae did he—that he had taen up his lodgings at the bottom o' a pool for the nicht—though the sun had just reached his meridian. The plump o' a stane half a hunder-wecht made him shift his quarters—and a sudden thocht struck him that he would make the best o' his way to the Tweed, and then doon to the sea at Berwick. But I bore sae hard on him wi' an aughteen feet rod, that by the time he had swam twa miles —and a' that time, though I aften saw his shadow, I seldom saw himsell—he was sae sair blawn that he cam to the surface o' his ain accord, as if to tak breath—and after that I had it a' my ain way—for he was powerless as a sheaf o' corn carried doon in a spate —and I launded him at the fuird, within a few hunder yards o' Altrive. Curious eneuch, wee Jamie was sittin' by himsel' on the bank, switherin' about wadin' across, and you may imagine the dear cretur's joy on seeing a twenty-pund fish—the heaviest ever killed wi' the rod in Yarrow—floatin' in amang his feet.

Tickler. You left him at home?

Shepherd. Where else soud I hae left him?

Tickler. Hem.

Shepherd. You really maun pit some flannen roun' that thrott—for at this time o' the year, when baith man and horse is saft, inflammation rapidly arrives at its height—mortification without loss of time ensues—and within the four-and-twenty hours I've kent a younger chiel than you, sir, streekit oot——

Tickler. What?

Shepherd. A corp.

Tickler. Any more sport?

Shepherd. Returnin' to the Loch, I thocht I wud try the otter. Sae I launched him on his steady leaden keel—twa yards lang—breadth o' beam three inches—and mountin' a hunder and fifty hyeucks——

Tickler. A first-rate man-of-war.

Shepherd. I've seen me in the season atween spring and summer secure ten dizzen wi' the otter at a single launch. But in October twa dizzen's no to be despised—the half o' them bein' about the size o' herrings, and the half o' the size o' haddocks—and ane—but he's a gray trout——

Tickler. Salmo Ferox?

Shepherd. As big's a cod.

Tickler. Well, James?

Shepherd. I then thocht I would take a look o' some night lines I had set twa three days syne, and began puin' awa' at the langest —wi' some five score o' hyeucks, baited for pike and eel, wi' troot and par-tail, frogs, chicken-heads, hen-guts, some mice, some moles, and some water-rats—for there's nae settin' bouns to the voracity o' thae sharks and serpents—and it was like drawin' a net. At length pike and eel began makin' their appearance—first a pike—then an eel —wi' the maist unerrin' regularity o' succession—just as if you had been puttin' them on sae for a ploy! "Is there never to be an end o' this?" I cried to mysell; and by the time that, walkin' backwards, I had reached the road, that gangs roun' the bay wi' a bend—enclosin' atween it and the water edge a bit bonny grass meadow and twa three trees—the same that your accomplished freen', George Moir, made sae tasteful a sketch o'—there, wull ye believe me—were lying five-and-twunty eels and five-and-twunty pikes—in all saxty—till I cou'd hae dream't that the meadow had been pairt o' the bay that moment drained by some sort o' subterraneous suction—and that a' the fishy life the water had contained was noo wallopin' and wrigglin' in the sudden sunshine o' unexpected day. I brak a branch aff an ash, and ran in amang them wi' my rung, lounderin' awa richt and left, and loupin' oot o' the way o' the pikes, some of which showed fecht, and offered to attack me on my ain element, and I was obliged to wrestle wi' an eel that speel'd up me till his faulds were wounded round my legs, theeghs, and body, in ever sae mony plies, and his snake head—och! the ugly auld serpent—thrust outowr my shouther—and hissin' in my face—till I flang him a fair backfa' and then ruggin' him frae me—fauld by fauld—strechtened him oot a' his length—and treddin' on his tail, sent his wicket speerit to soom about in the fiery lake wi' his father, the great dragon.

North (in the arbour). Ha! ha! ha! our inimitable pastor has reached his grand climacteric!

Tickler (in the shed). And where, my dear James, are they all? Did you bring them along with you?

Shepherd. I left the pikes to be fetched forrit by the Moffat carrier.

Tickler. And the eels?

Shepherd. The serpent I overthrew had swallowed up all the rest.

Tickler. We must send a cart for him—dead stomachs do not digest; and by making a slit in his belly we shall recover the rest little the worse for wear—and letting them loose in the long grass, have an eel-hunt.

North (in the arbour). Who can give me a bit of sticking-plaster?

Shepherd. I prophesied you wou'd cut yoursel'. There's nae stickin' plaister aboot the toun; but here's an auld bauchle, and if onybody will lend me a knife, I'se cut aff a bit o' the sole, and when weel soaked wi' bluid, it'll stick like a sooker—or I can cut aff a bit waddin' frae this auld hat—some tramper's left ahint her baith hat and bauchle—and it may happen to stainch the bludin'—or best of a', let me rug aff a bit o' this remnant o' an auld sheep's-skin that maun hae belanged to the foot-board o' some gig—and wi' the woo neist your skin, your chin will be comfortable a' the nicht—though it shou'd set in a hard frost.

(SHEPHERD *advances to the arbour—but after a single glance into the interior, comes flying back to his stance on the wings of fear.*)

North (in the arbour). James! James! James!

Shepherd. A warlock! A warlock! A warlock! The king o' the warlocks! The king o' the warlocks! The king o' the warlocks!

(*From the arbour issues* CHRISTOPHER *in the character of* LORD NORTH—*in a rich court-dress—bag and wig—chapeau-bras—and sword.*)

North (kneeling on one knee). Have I the honor to be in presence of Prince Charles Edward Stuart Hogg? My sovereign liege and no Pretender—accept the homage of your humble servant—too proud of his noble king to be a slave.

Shepherd (graciously giving his hand to kiss). Rise!

(*From the shed issues* TIMOTHY *in the regimentals of the Old Edinburgh Volunteers.*)

Tickler (kneeling on one knee). Hail! King of the Forest!

Shepherd (graciously giving his hand to kiss). Rise!—Let us—supported on the arms of our two most illustrious subjects—enter our palace.

(*Enter the Forest King and the two Lords in waiting into* TIBBIE'S.)

SCENE II.—*Interior of* TIBBIE'S—*Grand Hall or Kitchen Parlor*—NORTH, TICKLER, *and* SHEPHERD.

Shepherd. A cozey bield, sirs, this o' Tibbie's—just like a bit wren's nest.

North. Methinks 'tis liker an ant-hill.

Tickler. Bee-hive.

Shepherd. A wren's nest's roun', and theeckit wi' moss—sae is Tibbie's; a wren's nest has a wee bit canny hole in the side o't for the birdies to hap in and out o', aiblins wi' a hangin' leaf to hide and fend by way o' door, and sae has Tibbie's; a wren's nest's aye dry on the inside, though drappin' on the oot wi' dew or rain, and sae is Tibbie's; a wren's nest's for ordinar' bigget in a retired spat yet within hearin' o' the hum o' men, as weel's o' water, be it linn or lake, and sae is Tibbie's; a wren's nest's no easy foon', yet when you happen to keek on't, you wunner hoo ye never saw the happy housie afore, and sae is't wi' Tibbie's; therefore, sirs, for sic reasons, and a thousan' mair, I observed "a cozey bield this o' Tibbie's, just like a wren's nest." Sir?

North. An ant-hill's like some small natural eminence growing out of the green ground, and sae is Tibbie's; an ant-hill is prettily thatched with tiny straw and grass-blades, and leaves and lichens and so is Tibbie's; an ant-hill, in worst weather, is impervious to the elements, trembles not in its calm interior, nor—howl till ye split, ye tempests—at any blast doth Tibbie's; an ant-hill, spontaneous birth of the soil though it seems to be, hath its own order of architecture, and was elaborated by its own dwellers—and how wonderfully full of accommodation, when all the rooms at night become the rooms of sleep—just like Tibbie's; an ant-hill, though apparently far from market, never runs out of provisions—nor, when "winter lingering chills the lap of May," ever once doth Tibbie's; Solomon, speaking of an ant-hill, said, Look at the ant, thou sluggard—consider her ways and be wise,—and so now saith North, sitting in Tibbie's; so for these and a thousand other reasons, of which I mention but one—namely, that here too, as there, is felt the balmy influence of the mountain-dew—I said, "methinks 'tis like an ant-hill." Sir?

Tickler. A bee-hive is like a straw-built shed, loving the lowness, without fearing the wind, and standing in a sheltered place, where yet the breezes have leave to come and go at will, wafting away the creatures with whom work all day long is cheerful as play, outward or homeward bound, to or fro among the heathery hills where the wild honey grows—and these are pretty points of resemblance to Tibbie's; a bee-hive is never mute—for all that restless noise of industry sinks away with the setting sun into a steady murmur, fit music for the moonlight—and so is it, when all the household are at rest, in Tibbie's; a bee-hive wakens at peep of day—its inmates losing not a glint of the morning, early as the laverocks waukening by the daisy's side—and so, well knows Aurora, does Tibbie's; a bee-hive is the perfection of busy order, where, without knowing it, every worker by instinct obeys the Queen, and even so seemeth it to be in Tibbie's; so for these, and a thousand other reasons, of which I mention but two, that it standeth in a land overflowing with milk and honey, and wanteth but *an eke*, I said—Bee-hive. Sir?

Shepherd. A wren's nest grows cauld in ae single season, and then's seen stickin' cauld and disconsolate in amang the thorns o' the leafless hedge, or to the side o' the mooth o' some solitary cave or cell amang the dreepin' rocks; and where the twa pawrent birds and the well-feathered family—perhaps half a score or a dizzen—hae flown till, wha kens? No me, lookin' about and seein' nae wing, listenin' and hearin' nae note in the wilderness—a' mute and motionless in frost and sna'—as if a' singers and chirpers were dead! But, thank God! it's nae sae in Tibbie's; for in the deed o' winter, I've seen't lookin' mair gladsomer, if possible, than in the life o' spring; and though ane o' the auld birds be nae mair—yet that happened lang syne—here are the maist feck o' the young anes

—(the ithers hae yemigrated to America)—cantier and cantier ilka year. Whisht—has na the cretur a linty-like vice—that's Dolly—as she's cleanin' the dishes—no forgettin' that she's within ma' hearin'—singin' ane o' the auld Shepherd's sangs! Sir?

North. A drove of cattle tread the myriad-lifed ant-hill—the fairy palace with all its silent people—into the hoof-printed mire of death—but ruin is not like the blind bestial—James—and will spare Tibbie's—James—till with its contemporary trees—now a youthful brotherhood—many human ages hence it fades away with gradual, unperceived, and unpainful decay, while the wayfaring stranger pausing to eye the scene so still and solitary, shall know, not that he is looking on ruins, but suppose them to be but simple scatterings of rocks! Sir?

Tickler. Full to overflowing of honey and happiness, a hideous hound, without the fear of Huber before his eyes, hangs the hive over a pit of sulphur, and twenty thousand faithful subjects perish with their Queen! But no unhallowed hand—James—shall touch the rigging of Tibbie's roof—no stifling vapor shall ever fill these cells—and when he who shall be nameless—the Unavoidable—who never names his day—comes hither on his own visit—his first and his last—may he be taken by Tibbie for his brother sleep!

Shepherd. Noo—that's what I ca' poetical eemagerie applied to real life.

North. There cannot be a doubt that we three are three men of genius.

Shepherd. Equal to ony ither sax.

Tickler. Hem! How rarely is that endowment united with talent like ours!

North. Stuff. A set of nameless ninnies, at every stumbling step they take, painfully feeling their intellectual impotence, modestly abjure all claim to talent, of which no line is visible on their mild unmeaning mugs, and are satisfied in their humility that nature to them, her favored blockheads—her own daring dunces—and more especial sumphs—in compensation gave the gift of genius—the fire which of old Prometheus had to steal from heaven.

Shepherd. Bits o' Cockney creturs wi' mealy mooths, lookin' unco weak and wo-begone, on their recovery frae a painful confinement consequent on the birth o' a pair o' twuns o' rickety sonnets.

Tickler. A pair of twins. Four?

Shepherd. Na—twa sonnets that'll never in this warld be able to gang their lanes, but hae to be held up by leading strings o' red riband round their waists, or otherwise hae to be contented to creep or crawl like clocks.

North. You bring an ordinary blockhead to the test—talent he has none—sentence is recorded—and thenceforth he never passes the window of a wig-maker without a sympathetic sigh; but a genius looks at you with meek defiance in his lack-lustre eyes—nay, with compassion for the mean estate of a mere man of talent, who at the best can never hope to rise higher than the Woolsack—and like an immortal mingling with mortals, he steps into an omnibus, nor steps out till off the stones, on his journey towards the poetic visions swarming among the daisies and dandelions of Hampstead Hill.

Shepherd. My warst enemy canna accuse me o' bein' a metty-physician; yet I agree wi' Mr. Tickler, that a man may hae great talents, and nae genie—talents baith for the uptak and the layin' doon—and sae far frae despising sic men, I regard them wi' gratitude, for without them this warld cou'd na wag, and wou'd sune come to a staun still. Mental perception, clear, quick, and acute as ane's verra ee—conception prompt, vivid, and complete, as if the past and the present were a' ane, and the shadow o' reality as gude's the substance—memory like a great mirror o' plate-glass never bedimmed either by damp or frost, sae that a single keek shows you whatever you want to see owre again, and aiblins maks you ken't better than ever noo that it's but a vision—judgment, discriminating by lines o' licht a' the relations o' things and thochts by which they are at ance a' connecket, and a' separated in a way maist wondrous and beautifu' to behauld—reason sometimes arrivin' at conclusions by lang round-a-bout roads windin' up alang the sides o' michty mountains atween it and truth—which, like an engineer, it turns when unable to surmunt—and sometimes dartin' on them—strecht as a sunbeam or an eagle's swoop—and that's intuition—the mind sae endowed, I say, sirs, I contemplate, when at wark, wi' admiration and gratitude, because it is at ance great and good, glorious and useful, and if to a' that you add conscience, the illuminator, what is wantin' to the speeritual eemage o' a perfect man? What is wantin', I ask you again, sirs, but—ca' it by what name you wull—imagination—invention—genius—the power that keeps perpetually evolvin' the new frae the auld—sae that this life, and this warld, and these skies, are something different the day frae what they were yesterday—and will be something different the morn frae what they were the day—and sae on for ever and ever ad infineetum, while we are cooped up in clay—till the walls o' our prison-house shall be crumbled by a touch o' the same Almichty Hand that by a touch gave being and adherence to the dust?

Tickler. You astonish me, James.

Shepherd. I sometimes astonish mysel' wi' the thochts that come upon me at a Noctes. They dinna seem to arise within my mind, like fish lowpin out o' the water frae aneath stanes, and roots, and banks whare they had their birthplace amang the gravel, at the cluds o' insects blawn by the breezes in showers o' ephemeral beauty frae the simmer woods, but rather come waverin' on frae some far-aff region o' visionary isles and cloudy heedlauns, like a lang-winged visitation o' bonny snaw-white sea-birds dippin' doon in the green sunshine, and then first ane and then anither awa'—awa'—awa'—as if some speerit were ca'in' them back again to their ain nests—and the latest loiterer unwilling to forsake its pastime, but afraid to disobey that ca'—wheelin' for a wee while round and round about the same circle o' whitening billows, and then lettin' drap farewell in a saft touch frae the tip o' its pinions, disappearin' like the rest, and leavin' ahint it nane o' the beauty o' life on the lanesome sea.

Tickler. You astonish me, James.

Shepherd. And mair nor you wud be astonished, gin Gurney hadna been laid up wi' swalled face——

Voice from the Spence. Dr. Wilkie of Innerliethen yesterday pulled the tooth, and all's well.

Shepherd. That cretur's vice gars me a' grue. Is't true that he's a natural sin o' the Inveesible Girl?

North. Hush, Shepherd.

Tickler. The heir apparent of Echo.

Shepherd. A curious air-apparent—at times owdible—and it's faersome to think on Short-haun' out o' sicht extennin' his notts!

Enter BILLY *and* PALMER *with their game-bags, which they empty on their division of the floor.*

North. Not a bad day's sport, James?

Shepherd. Ye dinna mean to tell me that you and Soothside, this blessed day, slew a' that ggemm?

North. We did—and more.

Enter CAMPBELL *and* FITZ-TIBBIE *with their game-bags, which they empty on their division of the floor.*

Shepherd. You dinna mean to tell me that you and Soothside, this blessed day, slew a' that ggemm?

North. We did—and more.

Enter MON. CADET *and* KING PEPIN *with their game-bags, which they empty on their division of the floor.*

Shepherd. You dinna mean to tell me that you and Soothside, this blessed day, slew a' that ggemm?

North. We did—and more.

Enter SIR DAVID GAM *and* TAPPITOURIE *with their game-bags, which they empty on their division of the floor.*

Shepherd. You dinna mean to tell me that you and Soothside, this blessed day, slow a' that ggemm?

North. We do—and more.

Enter AMBROSE *and* PETER *with their game-bags, which they empty on their division of the floor.*

Shepherd. You dinna mean to tell me that you and Soothside, this blessed day, slew a' that ggemm?!! Soothside?

Tickler. I do—and more.

Shepherd. Then are ye twa o' the greatest leears that ever let aff a gun.

North. Or drew a long bow. How many brace?

Billy. A dizen, measter.

North. How many brace?

Campbell. Half-a-score, sir.

North. How many brace?

Mon. Cadet. Seven, and a snipe.

North. How many brace?

Sir David Gam. Eight and an owl.

North. How many brace?

Ambrose. Nine neat, my lord.

North. Tottle of the whole?

Voice from the Spence. Forty-six-brace—an owl and a snipe.

Shepherd. That cretur's vice gars me a' grue. Gold and silver's deadlier than lead. You've been bribin' Dalgliesh. Mair poachers nor ane has been at the fillin' o' thae pauches—but ma certes, here's a vast o' ggemm! Let's sort them. That's richt, lads—fling a' the black-cocks intil the east corner, a' the gray-hens intil the wast—a' the red groose intil the north corner, and a' the paitricks intil the south—gie Gurney the snipe for his share, and Awmrose the owl to stuff for the brace-piece o' his bed-chawmer.

North. Where the deuce are the hares?

Tickler. Where the devil are the rabbits?

Enter ROUGH ROBIN *and* SLEEK SAM *with their game-bags, which they empty on their division of the floor—that is on the table.*

Shepherd. Fourteen fuds! Aught mawkins, and sax borough-mongers, as I houp to be saved!

North. I read, with indignation and disgust, of the slaughter by one gun of five score brace of birds between eight o'clock and two.

Shepherd. A chiel might as weel pride himsel' on baggin' in a pootry-yaird as mony chickens, wi' here and there an auld clockin' hen and an occasional howtowdie—and to crown a', the bubbly-jock himsell, pretendin' to pass him aff for a capercailzie. But I ca' this sport.

North. Which corner, James, do you most admire?

Shepherd. Let's no be rash. That nyeuck o' paitricks kythes unco bonnie, wi' its mild mottled licht—the burnished broon harmoniously mixin' wi' the siller gray in a style o' colorin' understood but by that sweet penter o' still life, Natur'; and a body canna weel look, without a sort o' sadness, on the closed een o' the puir silly creturs, as their heads—crimsoned some o' them wi' their ain bluid, and ithers wi' feathers, bricht in the pride o' sex, auld cocks and young cocks—lie twusted and wrenched by the disorderin' haun o' death—ootoure their wings that shall whirr nae mair—rich in their radiance as flowers lyin' broken by the wund on a bed o' moss!

Tickler. James, you please me much.

Shepherd. That glow of groose is mair gorgeous, yet bonnier it may na be—though heaped up higher again the wa'—and gloomin' as weel as gleamin' wi' a shadowier depth, and a prouder pomp o' color lavished on the dead. There's something heathery in the hues there that breathes o' the wilderness—and ane canna look on their legs—mony o' them lyin' broken—sae thick cleed wi' close, white, saft feathers—without thinkin' o' the wunter-snaw! The Gor-Cock! His name bespeaks his nature—and o' a' the wild birds o' Scotland, nane mair impressive is to my imagination and my heart. Oh! how mony thoosan' dawns have evanished into the forgotten warld o' dreams, at which I hae heard him crawin' in the silence o' natur, as I lay in my plaid by mysel' on the hillside, and kent by that bold trumpeting that morning was at hand, without needin' to notice the sweet token o' her approach in the clearer licht o' the wee spring-well in the greensward at my feet!

North. James, you please me much.

Shepherd. Yet that angle o' black-cocks has its charms, too, to ma een, for though there's less variety in the colorin', and a fastidious critic might ca' the spotty heep monotonous, yet sullen as it seems, it glistens wi' a kind o' purple, sic as I hae seen on a lowerin' clud on a mirk day, when the sun was shinin' on the thunder, or on the loch below, that lay, though it was meridian, in its ain nicht.

Tickler. James, you please me much.

Shepherd. O! thae saft, silken, but sair ruffled backs and breists o' that cruelly kill'd crood o' bonny gray-hens and pullets—cut aff in their sober matronship and gleesome maidenhood—whilk tho mair beautiful, 'twould tak a mair skeely sportsman than the Shepherd to decide—I could kneel doon on the floor and kiss ye, and gather ye up in my airms, and press you to my heart, till the feel o' your feathers filled my veins wi' luve and pity, and I grat to think that never more would the hill-fairies welcome the gleam o' your plumage risin' up in the mornin' licht amang the green plats on the sloping sward that, dipping down into the valley, retains here and there amang the decayed birk-wood, as loth to lose them, a few small stray sprinklings of the heather-bells.

Tickler. James, you please me much.

North. I killed two-thirds of them with Old Trusty—slap—bang right and left, without missing a shot——

Tickler. Singing out, "that's my bird," on a dozen occasions when it dropped at least a hundred and fifty yards—right in an opposite direction—from the old sinner's nose.

Shepherd. What was the greatest nummer ye brocht doon at a single discharge?

North. One.

Shepherd. That's contemptible. Ye o' the auld Lake-school are never contented accepp ye kiver your bird, sae that if ye dinna tak them at the crossin', ye shoot a hail day without killin' a brace at a blow; but in shootin' I belang to the new Mountain-school, and fire wi' a general aim intil the heart o' the kivey, trusting to luck to gar three or four play thud; and its no an uncommon case to pick up half-a-dizzen, after the first flaught o' fire and feathers has ceased to dazzle ma een, and I hae had time to rin in amang the dowgs, and pu' the ggemm out o' the mooths o' the rabiators. It was nae farder back nor the day afore yesterday, that I killed and wounded nine—but to be sure that was wi' baith barrels—though I thocht at the time—for my een was shut—that I had only let aff ane—and wondered that the left had been sae bluidy—but baith are gran' scatterers, and disperse the hail like chaff frae the fanners on a wundy day. Even them on the edge o' the ootside are no safe when I fire intil the middle, and I've knawn me knock heels ower head mair nor ane belongin' to anither set, that had taken wings as I was ettlin' at their neighbors.

Tickler. I killed two-thirds of them, James.

Shepherd. That's faur-thirds atween you twa—and at whose door maun be laid the death o' the other half?

North. Kit with Crambo killed a few partridges in a turnip field. where they lay like stones—an old black-cock that had been severely, if not dangerously wounded by a weazel, and fell out of bounds, I suspect from weakness—an ancient gray-hen that flew at the rate of some five miles an hour—a hare sitting, which he had previously missed—and neither flying, nor sitting, but on the hover, that owl. How the snipe came into his possession I have not learned, but I have reason to believe that he found it in a state of stupor, and I should not be surprised, were you, James, to blow into his bill, to see Jack resuscitated——

Shepherd, (putting the snipe's bill into his mouth, and puffing into him the breath of life.) Is his een beginnin' till open?

North. Twinkling like a duck's in thunder.

Shepherd. He's dabbin'.

North. Hold him fast, James, or he'll be off.

Shepherd. Let doon the wundow, Tickler, let doon the wundow. Oh! ye clumsy coof! there he has struggled himsel' out o' my hauns, and's aff to the mairsh to leeve on suction!

(*Enter Tibbie and Dolly to lay the cloth, &c.*)

Tickler. Symptoms.

Shepherd. Wi' your leave, sirs, I'll gie Mr. Awmrose the hares to pit intil the gig. (*Gives Mr. Ambrose the hares, who disappears four-in-hand.*)

North. Whose gig, James?

Shepherd. Mine. I'm expectin' company to be wi' me a' niest week—and a tureen o' hare soup's no worth eatin wi' fewer than three hares in't—sae sax hares will just mak twa tureens o' hare-soop, and no owre rich either—and the third and fourth days we can devour the ither twa rosted; but for fear my visiters should get sta'd o' hare, and auld Burton, in his Anatomy,* ca's hare a melancholy meat—and I should be averse to ony body committin' suicide in my house—Tappy, my man, let me see whether you or me can gather up on our aught fingers and twa thoombs, the mais multitude o' the legs o' black-cocks, gray-hens, red groose, and paitricks—and gin ye beat me, you shall get a bottle o' whisky, and gin I beat you, I shall not put you to the expense o' a gill. (*Aside.*) The Pech has twa cases o' fingers, wi' airn-sinnies, and I never kent the cretur's equal at a clutch.

(*The Shepherd and Tappitourie emulously clutch the game, and carry off some twenty brace of sundries.*)

Tickler. James, you please me much.

North. You astonish me, James.

Shepherd. Some folk are easily pleased, and some as easily astonished—but what's keepin' the denner?

(*Enter Tibbie, and Dolly, and Shusey, Ambrose, Mon Cadet Peter, Campbell, Billy, Palmer, Rough Robin, Sleck Sam, King Pepin, Sir David Gam, and Tappitourie, with black grouse-soup, red grouse-soup, partridge-soup, hare-soup, rabbit-soup, potato-soup, pease-soup, brown-soup, white-soup, hotch-potch, cocky-leeky, sheep's-head-broth, kale, and rumble-te-thumps.*)

North. Ay—ay.

Tickler. Haigh!

Shepherd. Hech!—Noo, that we've a' three said grace, let's fa

* "The Anatomy of Melancholy," by Robert Burton, an English clergyman—a singular book filled with curious facts, not a few paradoxes, and much learning. Archbishop Herring described it as "the pleasantest, the most learned, and the most full of sterling sense," adding that the wits of the reigns of Anne and the first George were deeply indebted to Burton. In our time, it was in a manner almost unknown, until Byron quoted from and largely praised it, which led to its being reprinted, and it is, once more, a standard work.—M.

to—and to ensure fair play, let ilka ane fill his neighbor's plate, as in an ass-race ilka ane rides his neighbor's cuddy.

Tickler. And let no man say a good thing, except between courses.

Shepherd. Or a bad thing either. Agreed. Noo for a fair start —ance—twice—thrice—aff!

North. Stop.

Shepherd. Dowg on't—what noo?

North. Incessant refilling of plates is——

Shepherd. I confess fretsome.

North. Therefore, James, that we may preserve our equanimity, let us shove aside our trenchers, shallow and profound, and take, each man, his tureen, and then, each man according to the courses, his dish; and, without speculation on the doctrine of chances, let us draw cuts for choice

Tickler. Straws.

(*Billy presents in his paw straws of unequal lengths, and the Sortes Ambrosianæ yield the following results.*)

North. First by a finger. I take the red grouse tureen.

Tickler. Second by a thumb. I, partridge ditto.

Shepherd. Third by a nail. Essence o' gray-hens.

North. We may now speak *ad libitum.*

Shepherd. Wi' this proviso, sirs, that nane o' us proceeds to a second tureen, till we a' again draw cuts. For Tickler's sic a rapid rabiator, that he'll be for fastenin' on his second tureen afore either Mr. North or me has cleared out our first, and though it's far frae impossible or improbable either that we twa micht overtak him in the lang rin, still accidents micht happen, and gin he was to get the start o' us, say by half a tureen, the odds wou'd rise on him again' the field, and, in spite o' the additional wecht he wou'd then be carrying, and the known goodness o' his antagonist, Tickler, roarer as he is, wou'd be likely to wun the sweepstakes, beatin' North by a head and shouthers, and me by a head.

Tickler. Agreed.

North. Stop.

Shepherd. For nae man leevin or dead.

North. Gentle—men—we are—by—no means—the—gluttons—that—peo—ple—regard—ing—this—Noc—tes—might—be—par—don'd—for sup—sup—sup—posing—we were—

Shepherd. Sup—sup—sup—sup—pose—pose—poseing—we are glutt—glut—t—t—t—tons—whattt—the—the—dee—deevil then? Gurn—Gurn—Gurney—is girn—girn—girnin'—at us—

Voice. I'm not girning, Mr. Hogg.

North (*laying down his ladle.*)

"It is well to be off with the old love
Before we are on with the new!"

Nay, better to be true to our first—our sole tureen—than vainly seek to transfer our passions or our affections to a second, however attractive; therefore let the worthies in waiting—male and female—waft away the rest into the spence, and there collaterally enjoy them—till I cough—with my well-known hem—for the second course.

(*The fourteen worthies in waiting carry off, each with his and her own peculiar smile—ten tureens—four but with spoons and plates.*)

Shepherd. Oh, sir! but you've a profound knowledge o' human natur'! Eatin' at ane's ease, ane's imagination can flee up into the empyrean—like an eagle soaring up the lift wi' a lamb in his talons, and then fauldin' up his wings, far abune shot o' the fowler, on the tapmost o' a range o' cliffs, leisurely devourin't, while ever and anon, atween the rugs, he glances his yellow black-circled een far and wide owre the mountainous region, and afore and after every moothful, whattin' his beak wi' his claws, yells to the echoes that afar aff return a faint but a fierce reply.

Tickler. Does he spit out feathers and fur?

Shepherd. He spits out naething—devourin' bird and beast stoup and roup, bones, entrails, and a', and leavin' after his repast but a wheen wee pickles o' bluidy down, soon dried by the sun, or washed away by the rain, the only evidence there had been a murder.

North. The eagle is not a glutton.

Shepherd. Wha said he was a glutton?

North. Living constantly in the open air—

Shepherd. And in a high latitude.

North. Yes, James—for hours, every day in his life, sailing in circles some thousand feet above the sea.

Shepherd. In circles, noo narrowin', and noo widenin' wi' sweepy waftage, that seems to carry its ain wund amang its wings—noo speerally wundin' up the air staircase that has nae need o' steps, till you could swear he was soarin' awa' to the sun—and noo divin' doon earthwards, as if the sun had shot him, and he was to be dashed on the stanes intil a blash o' bluid; but, in the pride o' his pastime, and the fierceness o' his glee, had been that self-willed headlong descent frae the bosom o' the blue lift, to within fifty fathom o' the croon o' the greenwood—for suddenly slantin' awa' across the chasm through the mist o' the great cataract, he has already voyaged a league o' black heather, and, eein' another arc o' the meridian, taks majestic possession of a new domain in the sky.

Tickler. No wonder he is sharp set.

Shepherd. I was ance in an eagle's nest.

Tickler. When a child?

Shepherd. A man—and no sae verra a young ane. I was let down the face o' the red rocks o' Loch Aven, that affront Cairngorum, about a quarter o' a mile perpendicular, by a hair rape, and after swingin' like a pendulum for some minutes back and forret afore the edge o' the platform, I succeeded in establishin' mysell in the eyrie.

Tickler. What a fright the poor eaglets must have got!

Shepherd. You ken naething about eaglets. Wi' them fear and anger's a' ane—and the first thing they do, when taken by surprise amang their native sticks by man or beast, is to fa' back on their backs, and strike up wi' their talons, and glare wi' their een, and snap wi' their beaks, and yell like a couple o' hell-cats. Providentially their feathers werena fu' grown, or they wou'd hae flown in my face and driven me ower the cliff.

Tickler. Were you not armed?

Shepherd. What a slaughter-house! What a cemetery! Hale hares, and halves o' hares, and lugs o' hares, and fuds o' hares, and tatters o' skins o' hares, a' confused wi' the flesh and feathers o' muirfool and wild dyeucks, and ither kinds o' ggemm, fresh and rotten, undevoor'd and digested animal maitter mixed in blue-mooldy or bloody red masses—emittin' a strange charnel-hoose, and yet larder smell—thickenin' the air o' the eyrie—for though a blast cam sughin' by at times, it never was able to carry awa' ony o' the stench, which I was obliged to breathe, till I grew sick, and feared was gaun to swarf, and fa' into the loch that I saw, but couldna hear, far doon below in anither warld.

Tickler. No pocket-pistol?

Shepherd. The Glenlivet was ma salvation. I took a richt gude wullie waught*—the mistiness afore my een cleared awa'—the waterfa' in my lugs dried up—the soomin' in my head subsided—my stamach gied owre bockin'—and takin' my seat on a settee, I began to inspect the premises wi' mair preceesion, to mak' a verbal inventory o' the furnitur', and to study the appearance or character o' the twa guests that still continued lyin' back on their backs, and regardin' me wi' a malignity that was fearsome, but noo baith mute as death.

North. They had made up their minds to be murdered.

Shepherd. I suspect it was the ither way. A' on a sudden doon comes a sugh frae the sky—and as if borne each on a whurlwund—the yell and the glare o' the twa auld birds! A mortal mun daurin' to invade their nest! And they dashed at me as if they wud hae dung me intil the rock—for my back was at the wa'—and I was

* "And we'll tak' a right good willie-waught,
For auld lang syne."—M.

haudin' on wi' my hauns—and aff wi' my feet frae the edge o' the ledge—and at every buffet, I, like an insect, clang closer to the cliff. Dazed wi' that incessant passing to and fro o' plumes and pennons, and beaks, and talons, rushin' and rustlin' and yellin', I shut my een, and gied mysell up for lost; when a' at ance a thocht struck me that I wou'd cowp the twa imps owre the brink, and that the parent birds wou'd dive doon after them to the bottom o' the abyss.

Tickler. What presence of mind!

North. Genius!

Shepherd. I flang mysell on them—and I hear them yet in the gullerals. They were eatin' intil my inside; and startin' up wi' a' their beaks and a' their talons inserted, I flang aff my coat and waistcoat, and them stickin' till't, owre the precipice!

Tickler. Whew!

Shepherd. Ay—ye may weel cry whew! Dreadfu' was the yellin' for ae glaff and ae glint; far doon it deaden'd; and then I heard nocht. After a while I had courage to lay mysell doon on my belly, and look owre the brink—and I saw the twa auld eagles wheelin' and skimmin', and dashin' amang the white breakers o' the black lock, madly seekin' to save the drownin' demons, but their talons were sae entangled in the tartan, that after floatin' awhile wi' flappin' wings in vain, they gied owre strugglin', and the wreck drifted towards the shore wi' their dead bodies.

Tickler. Pray, may I ask, my dear Shepherd, how you returned to the top?

Shepherd. There cam the rub, sirs. My freens abune, seeing my claes, wi' the eagles flaffing, awa doon the abyss, never doobted that I was in them—and they set up sic a shriek! Awa roon they set to turn the right flank o' the precipice by the level o' the Aven that rins out sae yellow frae the dark-green loch, because o' the color o' the blue slates that lie shivered in heaps o' strata in that lovely solitude—hardly howpin' to be able to yield me ony assistance, in case they should observe me attemptin' to soom ashore—nor yet to recover the body gin I was droon'd. Silly creturs! there was I four hours on the platform, while they were waitin' for my corp to come ashore. At last, ashore cam what they supposed to be my corp, and stickin' till't the twa dead eaglets, and dashin' doon upon't, even when it had reached the shingle, the twa savage screamers wi' een o' lichtenin'!

Tickler. We can conjecture their disappointment, James, on findin' that there was no corpse.

Shepherd. I shooted—but nature's self seemed deaf—I waved my bannat—but nature's self-seemed blin'. There stood the great deaf, blin', stoopid mountains—and a' that I could hear was ance a laigh echolike lauchter frae the airn heart o' Cairngorum.

Tickler. At last they recognised the Mountain Bard?

Shepherd. And awa' they set again to the tap to pu' me up; but the fules in their fricht had let the rape drap, and never thocht o' lookin' for't when they were below. By this time it was wearin' late, and the huge shadows were stalkin in for the nicht. The twa auld eagles cam back, but sae changed, I could na help pityin' them, for they had seen in the feathers o' them they loo'd sae weel wrap up, a' drookit wi' death, in men's plaids—and as they keep't sailin' slowly and disconsolately before the eyrie in which there was naebody sittin' but me, they werena like the same birds!

North. No bird has stronger feeling than the eagle.

Shepherd. That's a truth. They lay but twa eggs.

North. You are wrong there, James.

Shepherd. Twa young ones, then is the average, for gin they lay mair eggs, ane's aften rotten, and I'm mistaken if ae eagle's no nearer the usual nummer than fowre for an eyrey to send forth to the sky. Then they marry for life—and their annual families bein' sma', they concentrate on a single sinner or twa, or three at the maist, a' the passion o' their instinct, and savage though they be, they fauld their wide wings oure the down in their "procreant cradle" on the cliff, as tenderly as turtle-doves on theirs, within the shadow o' the tree. For beautiful is the gracious order o' natur, sirs, and we maunna think that the mystery o' life hasna its ain virtues in the den o' the wild beast and the nest o' the bird o' prey.

Tickler. And did not remorse smite you, James, for the murder of those eaglets?

Shepherd. Aften and sair. What business had I to be let doon by a hair rape intil their birth-place? And, alas! how was I to be gotten up again—for nae hair rape cam' danglin' atween me and the darkenin' weather-gleam. I began to doot the efficacy of a death-bed repentance, as I tried to tak' account o' my sins a' risin' up in sair confusion—some that I had clean forgotten, they had been committed sae far back in youth, and never suspected at the time to be sins ava', but noo seemin' black, and no easy to be forgiven—though boundless be the mercy that sits in the skies. But, thank Heaven, there was an end—for a while at least—o' remorse and repentance—and room in my heart only for gratitude—for, as if let doon by hands o' angels, there again dangled the hair-rape wi' a noose-seat at the end o't, safer than a wicker-chair. I stept in as fearless as Lunardi,* and wi' my hauns aboon my head glued to the tether—and my hurdies, and a' aneath my hurdies, inter-

* A celebrated Aeronaut.—M.

laced wi' a net-wark o' loops and knots, I felt mysell ascendin' and ascendin' the wa's, till I heard the voices o' them hoistin' Launded at the tap, you may be sure I fell doon on my knees—and while my heart was beginnin' to beat and loup again, quaked a prayer.

North. Thank ye, James; I have heard you tell the tale better and not so well, but never before at a Noctes. Another tureen?

Shepherd. Na. Tibbie? The fish. (*Enter* TIBBIE *with a fish.*) You see, sirs, I wasna leein' about the sawmon. It cam' up in the seat o' the gig. Tibbie was for cuttin't into twa cuts, but I like to see a sawmon served up in his integrity——

Tickler. And each slice should run from gill to tail.

Shepherd. Alang the shouthers and the back and the line, in that latitude, for the thick; and alang the side and the belly and the line in that latitude, for the thin; but nae short-curd till in the mouth; and as for helpin yoursell wi' a fork and a bit breed—that's like some silly conceit o' a spiled wean—and I'm sure there's naebody here sae bairnly's to fear cuttin' their mooth wi' a knife. The kyeanne pepper—the mustard—the vinegar the catshop—the Hervey sass—the yest—and the chovios! Thank ye, Dolly, ma deer. Mair butter, Tickler. North—put the mashed potawtoes on the pairt o' ma plate near the sawt—and the round anes a bit ayont. Tappy—the breed; and meanwhile, afore yokin' to our sawmon, what say ye, sirs, to a bottle o' porter?

(*Three shots are heard—and three silver jugs, foam-crowned, are duly administered and drained.*)

North. I forget, James, the weight of this fish?

Shepherd. Twunty pund.

North. We shall scarcely get through it—I fear—at one sitting.

Tickler. I begin to see the ribs and spine of the side to windward—but remember our friends in waiting——

Shepherd. What, sir, cou'd induce ye to tak so mony gillies to the hill?

North. At this season you know, James, the birds are wild, and we should have had no sport without markers. We distributed our forces judiciously along the heights, and kept moving in a circle of scouts—that always commanded a wide prospect. The birds finding themselves outwitted on their widest flights, lost courage, and resorted to close-sitting—nor had we occasion half-a-dozen times the whole day to fly the kite.

Shepherd. What's that?

North. Ambrose, I believe, who, you know, is a Yorkshireman, was the first to introduce the kite into the Forest. He is constructed of paper, like the common kite, such as you see flying over cities; but more bird-like, both in form and color, and Ambrose has painted him so cunningly, that but for his length of tail, which is necessary to keep him steady, you would not scruple to take a shot at him for a glead. King Pepin and Sir David Gam work him to windward with much judgment by the invisible string; and he looks so formidable on the hover, now turning and now stooping, as if instinct with spirit, that as long as he is aloft, not even the boldest old blackcock of Thirlestane will dare to lift his head above the rushes or the heather. By a signal he is brought to anchor—Haco and Harold trot in—while all the dogs are baking one another—whirr—whirr—slap—bang—and thud after thud—right and left—from four blazing barrels—tumble the three and four poundders, to the delight of Tappitourie, who fastens on them like a weasel.

Shepherd. I ca' that poachin'. It's waur nor the real leeving gemm-hawk—for the kivey hae to contend wi' poother and lead, for-bye that pented deevil in the air—and half-dead wi' fricht, hoo can it be expeckit that a single ane 'll be able to mak his escape? We'll be hearin' o' you usin' the net neist, alang wi' the broon-paper pented Yorkshire kite o' Awmrose. Confoun' me, but the verra first time I catch him beatin' to windward, gin I dinna fire at him, and bring him waverin' down, broken-backed, wi' his lang tail amang the rashes.

Tickler. What say you, Shepherd, to a glass of Champagne?

Shepherd. That the best o't 's aboot equal to middlin' sma' yill

Tickler. National prejudice. Tibbie?

(TIBBIE *fills each man's longshank with a shower of diamonds.*)

Shepherd. Na, but that is prime—na, but that is maist delishous—only it's a shame to drink ootlandish liquors at half-a-guinea a bottle, when you can get the best mawt whusky for less nor twa shillings. It's the duty.

North. You need not make yourself uneasy about the price, James, for I can afford it.

Shepherd. It's weel for you, sir.

North. Prime cost, James—corks included—is sixpence a bottle; and now, sir, you have tasted TIBBIE'S GREEN GROZET ST. MARY, what are the vine-covered hills and gay regions of France to the small, yellow, hairy gooseberry-gardens of your own Forest!

Shepherd. I'll nae draw back frae what I said in commendation o't, but a' hame-made wines, and maist foreign anes, are apt to gie me a pain in the stammack, and therefore if you be wise, sirs, you'll join me in a caulker o' the cretur by way o' a sedative. I ken you deal wi' my freen Richardson o' Selkirk, and there's no purer speerit than Richardson's best in a' the south—for it's a composition o' a' the prime whuskys he can collect, mixed up in due proportions, according to the relative qualities o' each, and maist savory and salutary is the ultimate result.

North. Tibbie, a bottle of Richardson's ULTIMATE RESULT.

(*They attend to the Result.*)

Shepherd. Noo, I ca' this a meeting of the True Temperance Society. We are three auldish men, and hae had a hard day's wark o' amusement—and it canna be denied that we hae earned baith our meat and our drink. Fowl and fish we hae wan frae air and water by our ain skill, and naebody 'll be the puirer on account o' this day's pastime, or this night's—no even gin we had ta'en each o' us anither tureen. It's heartsome to hear the gillies launchin' at their vittals, in their ain dinin' room, and frae this day Mr. Awmrose may date his lease o' a new life. That's right, Tibbie—tak' them ben the sawmon, and put you down the aipple-pie, the can o' cream and the cheese. (TIBBIE *takes them ben the salmon, and puts down the apple-pie, the can of cream, and the cheese.*) I'll defy a man to be a glutton as lang's he's obedient to the dictates o' a healthy natural appeteet, inspired by air and exercise in the Forest, and though I'm an enemy to the mixin' o' mony different dishes in the stammach at ae diet, yet sic soups, and sic saummon, and sic aipple-pie, and sic cheese, will a' lie amicably thegether, nor is there ony sense in sayin' that sic porter will jummle wi' sic cream. The champagne has been rectified, and a's safe. I ca't a plain, simple, manly, substantial, Forest dinner, in Tibbie's ain unpretendin' style, and hadna we limited it to our ain killin', I ken we should hae had the hin' quarter o' a sheep that's been in pickle syne the last day o' hairst, and a breast o' veal frae Bourhope, as white's a hen. (TIBBIE *sets down, with a smile, her own two dishes of mutton and veal, with a fresh peck of potatoes from the dripping-pan, and ditto of mashed turnips.*)

North. *Excellent creature!*

Shepherd. She's a' that—sir.

North. How virtuous is humble life! Question, if any one but a Conservative can understand the domestic life of the poor.

Shepherd. Nane else in our day has observed it in Scotland.

North. It is sustained by contentment—a habit of the heart—and continuous custom seems essential to the formation of that happiest of all habits which grows out of the quiet experiences of days—weeks—months—years—all so like one another in their flow, that the whole of life is felt, with its occasional breaks and interruptions, to be one, and better for them that under Providence enjoy it, than any other lot which at times their hearts may long for, and their imaginations picture.

Shepherd. The same stream flawin' alang channels and greener banks and braes.

North. Changes for the better, let us believe, and I do believe it, are almost invariably taking place in such conditions, as society at large progresses in knowledge, and as there opens before all minds a wider and higher sphere of feeling and of thought accessible through instruction.

Shepherd. In many respects, sir, the instruction is better.

North. Such belief is consolatory to all who love their kind, and lament to know that there is so much wretchedness in this weary world.

Shepherd. Edication in the rural districts o' Scotland, I doubt not, is mair carefu' and comprehensive than it was forty years ago; would that it were as sure, sir, that the hearts o' young and auld are as sensible to the habits and duties o' religion! It may be sae —yet, methinks, there is no the same earnestness and solemnity in the furrowed faces o' the auld—the same modesty and meekness in the smooth faces of the young sitters in the kirk on Sabbath, which I remember regarding sae reverently and sae affectionately half a century ago! I fear there are mair lukewarm and cauldrife Christians in the Forest wha consider Gospel truths like ony ither truths, and the Bible like ony ither gude book—not the book in comparison wi' which a' ithers were worthless—for not effectual like it to shed licht on the darkness o' the grave! Yet, I may be mista'en; for a' sweet thochts are sweeter, and a' haly thochts are halier, that carry my heart back to the mornin' o' life! And as the dew-draps seem to my een to hae then been brichter and purer than they are noo—though that can scarcely be—and the lang simmer-days far langer, as well as the gloamings langer too—which was no possible—sae human life itself may be as fu' o' a' that's gude noo as it was then —and the change—a sad and sair ane as I sometimes feel—in me, and no in them about me—and the same lament for the same reason continue to be made by all that are waxin' auld—to the end o' time.

North. Ay, James, memory so beautifies and sanctifies all we loved in youth with her own mournful light, that it is not in our power—we have not the heart—to compare them with the kindred realities encircling our age; but for their own dear, sweet, sad sakes alone—and for the sake of the grass on their graves—we hold them religiously aloof from the affections and the objects of our affections of a later day—in our intercommunion with them it is that we most devoutly believe in heaven.

Shepherd. You're growin' oure grave, sir, and maunna gie way to the mood, lest it get the better o' you—though it's natural to you, and, I confess, sits weel on your frosty prow. The warld's better acquainted the noo wi' the character o' Christopher North than it was some score o' years syne—and the truth is, that, like a' them that's been baith wutty and wise, he is constitutionally a melancholy man, and aften at the verra time that he seems to be writin' wi' a sunbeam, "draps a sad, serious tear upon his playfu' pen!"

North. The philosophy of truth, James, is pensive; it is natural religion, and, therefore, humane; hence all that is harsh falls away from it, all that is hateful; when purest and highest it becomes poetry—and——

Shepherd. Wheesht, you mystic—and eat awa' at your mutton.

North. I am at a loss to know, James, what the friends of the people really think is the character of the people of England?

Shepherd. Sae am I.

North. They tell us—if I do not mistake them—that this is the most enlightened age that has ever shone on life. They seem to apply the praise in the first place to mind. It is an age of useful and entertaining knowledge. But mind enlightens heart—and the two together elevate soul—and the three, like an angelic band floating in air, connect earth with heaven by an intermediate spirit of beauty and of bliss.

Shepherd. Is that what they say? For if it be, they maun be fine fallows, and I put down my name as a member o' the union.

North. They assert that knowledge is not only power, but virtue.

Shepherd. It is neither the ane nor the other necessarily; and I could pruve that they dinna understaun' their ain doctrine.

North. Not now, James. Let us admit their doctrine—and rejoice to know that we are the most enlightened people—physically, morally, intellectually, spiritually—that ever flourished on the face and bosom of the dædal earth.

Shepherd. I fear you and me's twa exceptions—at least I can answer for mysell—for aften when walkin' in what seems to me essential licht, through the inner warld o' thocht, a' at ance it's pitch-dark! I'm like a man blindfaulded, and obliged to grope his way oot o' a wood by the trees, no able to tell, but by a rough guess at the rind, whether he's handlin' an aik or an ash, or an elm, or a pine, or a beech, or a plane—and whatever they may be, gi'en himsell mony a sair knock on the head, and losin' his hat amang the branches that make you desperate angry by floggin' you on the face, and ruggin' out your hair, as your legs get entangled amang the briers. The enlightened age—the spirit o' the age—shouldna hollow till it gets oot o' the wood, sir.

North. Good, James. But what am I to think of the panegyrists of the spirit of the age, when I am told by the same oracles that there is not a virtuous woman among the lower orders in all England?

Shepherd. You have only to think that they are a set o' inconsistent and contradictory idiwits, and a base gang o' calumniators and obscene leears.

North. But I'm a moderate man, and wish to have the inconsistency explained—or removed—the libel made less loathsome—and some apology offered to the sex.

Shepherd. Wha said it, and whare?

North. Parliament.

Shepherd. The Reform Bill, then, it seems, is no a feenal measure, sir?

North. There is no mob now-a-days, James—no rabble—no swinish multitude——

Shepherd. I hate that epithet.*

North. So do I. No scum—but the wives, daughters, and sisters of all the working-men of England—are prostitutes.

Shepherd. A damm'd lee.

North. An infernal falsehood.

Shepherd. Yet the verra same brutes that hae said that o' a' the English lassies in laigh life, wull break oot on me and you for swearin' at a Noctes?

North. We have heard the Lord Chancellor of England, and the Lord Bishop of London,† announce this article of the Christian creed—which unless we all hold, verily we cannot be saved—that the sin of incontinence is infinitely worse in a woman than in a man.‡

Shepherd. I thocht we had gude authority for believing woman to be the weaker vessel.

North. That authority is discarded; for be it now known to all men that they—not the maidens by whom they have been woo'd—are the victims of seduction.

Shepherd. That doctrin'll no gang doon; the kintra's no ripe for't yet; the verra pride o' man 'ill no alloo him to bolt it; the unregenerate sinner, wicked as he is, daurna, even in his seared conscience, sae offend again' the law o' nature written by the finger o' God ineffaceably on his heart.

North. If the sin be so great in woman, why does man suffer her to commit it?

Shepherd. Ay, ye may ask that at the Chancellor and the Bishop, and pause till doomsday for a reply. She canna commit it by hersell; he is airt and pairt; no merely an accessary afore and after the act; but——

North. Blind, brutal balderdash, born of the brother.

* First applied by Edmund Burke.—M.

† Lord Brougham and Dr. Blomfield.—M.

‡ This really was one of the principles of the Poor Law, as amended by the Whigs—viz. that if a woman had illegitimate offspring, she had no claim on the father, toward its maintenance, for that she ought not have allowed herself to be seduced! The previous custom had been, when the parish officers saw that 'Coming events cast their shadows before,' to summon the lady before a magistrate (as being in a condition, if unmarried, to become burthensome on the poor-rates) and compel her to state, upon oath, who was the author of the anticipated little responsibility. This was the cause of a great deal of perjury, no doubt, whereby affiliations were laid at the doors of innocent men. On one occasion a female was brought before the justice, and, in reply to the usual question, stated she was married.—"Where is your husband?"—"In India."—"How long has he been there—when did you last see him?"—"Two years ago," said the sobbing sinner, "but *I've had a many very moving letters from him!*"—M.

Shepherd. In a far waur place—situate in a darker region than the darkest lane in a' Lunnon.

North. Thus fortified by Law and Religion, a Christian legislature sets itself solemnly to work, to guard and save the victims of seduction from suffering any pecuniary loss from their misfortune, and enact that we poor, weak, deluded males shall not henceforth be burdened by the support of the illegitimate offspring we have been bedevilled to beget, but that where the *chief* crime lies, there shall be dree'd the *sole* punishment, and that the female fiends must either suckle their sin-conceived at their own dugs, dry-drawn by penury, or toss them into a workhouse!

Shepherd. Strang—strang—strang.

North. One Bishop there was, James—an illustrious man—who brought that doctrine to the test, and then held it up in his eloquent hand—like withered fruit of nightshade. "Show me a text—show me a text," was the cruel cry. No—I show all mankind the New Testament; and opening the leaves according to the *Sortes Virgilianæ*,* I read almost the first verse that meets mine eye, and may I never meet them I love in heaven, if the spirit of that verse, and of every verse, one merciful context, does not declare it to be the will of our God and our Saviour, that sinful man—and we are all in such eyes sunk in sin—shall sustain in life his own offspring—if he will not seek for himself eternal condemnation by profaning with his lips those few words of our Divine Preceptor, "Give us this day our daily bread!"

Shepherd. Say nae mair, sir, say nae mair. You ken I dinna think sae very muckle o' your writings, either by way o' prose or verse; but whether in preevat or in public, when you choose to let yoursell oot, O, man! but you are an orator—the orator o' the human race.

North. They say I cannot reason.

Shepherd. That's a lee. There lies your glory; for you deal oot intuitive truths, ane after anither, till the tenor o' your speech is like a string o' diamonds.

North. They say I have no logic.

Shepherd. You dinna condescend to chop logic wi' the adversary—but if he be a man, ye gang up to him—face to face—and knock him doon wi' ae blow on the head, and anither on the heart—if he be a shape o' Satan, you launch at him a thunderbolt, and the sinner is reduced to ashes.

North (*blushing like a pink*). Then, James, the English are all drunkards—and, day and night, worship Belial in the Tem-

* The *Sortes Virgilianæ* originally consisted in opening Virgil, at hazard, the first sentence on which the eye rested, being taken as prophetic. Some curious instances of such productions and fulfilments (there is solemn silence on the unfulfilled ones) are on record.—M.

ple of Gin—and Beelzebub in the House of Heavy-Wet—and Lucifer in the Abode of Brandy; and who says so, my dear Shepherd?

Shepherd. But the children o' Mammon.

North. Yes, James; who from the sweat of slaves, worked to death in his sultry mines, extract the ether on which they sustain their celestial lives, and the gorgeous dies with which they engrain their garments, as they sweep along the high places, and take their seats on thrones within palaces, and affront high heaven with blasphemy, forgetful in their pride that they themselves are but worms.

Shepherd. Strang—strang—strang.

North. Great Britain is constantly drunk—therefore, let there be no distillation from grain—let that spirit of the age be all bottled up in Apothecaries' shops, and labelled—poison, or medicine.

Shepherd. Like arsenic for rats or men.

North. If the English be, indeed, all irreclaimable drunkards, some such remedial and preventive law seems to be demanded—but by whom shall it be enacted? In the two sober Houses of Parliament by general cock-crow? By steady representatives, returned by constituents not able to stand?

Shepherd. Ach! the wine-bibbers!

North. If all the women in England who live by wages are prostitutes—and all the men drunkards—I can imagine but one event desirable for her good—an earthquake that shall give her to be swallowed up by the sea.

Shepherd. Or fire frae Heaven that destroyed Sodom and Gomorrah.

North. But such, thank God, is not yet the condition—distressful though, alas, in much it be—of what was once merry England.

Shepherd. And I'll swear in the parritch face o' Silk Buckingham,* and a' the lave o' the milk and water committee, that it's no the condition o' bonny Scotland.

North. Nor ever will be while she has a Christian church.

Shepherd. Hark hoo the voice o' the Forest—at this hoor sae saft and sweet—breathes o' contentment frae the soun', healthy, heart o' the happy hills! The Flowers o' the Forest are no' a' wede away—nor hae they been changed into weeds; and although I lament to alloo that in towns and cities, where countless croods o' Christian creturs are congregated thegither, and whare wark set them by wealth suffers them too short and seldom to pray, they owre aften seek renovation to their exhowsted bodies by means o' what's even mair hurtfu' to their wearied sowls, and thus fa' into

* James Silk Buckingham was in Parliament from 1832 (the first General Election under the Reform Bill), until 1835, and vainly attempted to carry a measure for the suppression of drunkenness. He made out such a strong case of intemperance against Scotland (where the consumption of ardent spirits was shown to be double of that in Ireland) that the Scotch were seriously offended.—*M.*

the arms o' vice, the leper, wha hauns them to death, the skeleton; yet seein' as clearly as that cluds are the cause o' rain, and cluds themsells vapors frae the undrained earth and the undrainable sea, that the great manufacturin' and commercial system o' the kintra is the cause o' a' their sins, sufferings, and sorrows, and that in spite o' the ruination, multitudes, oh! might I say the majority, hold fast their integrity, and slaves as they are, show their tyrants and task-masters virtues which they hae nae the grace to comprehend, far less to imitate; I do not despair that a Law, far beyond the sphere o' sic legislators as we hae been speakin' o', a Law originating in Heaven, and sanctioned in the heart, will yet rule wi' a saving sway ower sic doleful regions, for doleful they may weel be ca'd, since there famished folk forget their hunger in their thirst, and flee to cursed gin for relief rather than to blessed bread;—the Law o' Love and Religion, that was frae the beginning o' the warld, and was given to us again aughteen hundred years ago, in brichter licht than to the first Adam, to us, the children o' Adam, and though obscured and troubled by man's passions, that mak a' men at times seem waur nor mad, shall yet shine through the huge city smoke that the material day-spring canna penetrate, and establish an illumination, not on the spires, and steeples, and towers alone o' churches and cathedrals, although ever may they be held sacred, but on the low-roof'd houses o' the puirest o' the puir, wherever twa or three are gathered together to worship the Giver o' a' mercies, or to enjoy his mercies—say the frugal meal industry has earned and piety blessed, or the hard bed that seems saft to the sleep that nae evil conscience ever haunts;—bed and sleep, emblems indeed o' death and the grave, but only o' their rest, for a lamp burns beside them, let down frae the skies, which they hae but to feed wi' gude warks and trim wi' the finger o' faith, and when they will wauken at last in Heaven, they will know it was the lamp o' Eternal Life.

North (*looking up at the cuckoo*). Eight o'clock! It is Saturday night—and Tickler and I have good fourteen miles to drive to the Castle of Indolence.

"O blest retirement! friend to Life's decline!"

Our nags must be all bedded before twelve—for there must be no intrusion on the still hours of Sabbath. James, we must go.

Shepherd. I declare I never observed Tibbie takin' awa the rosts! Sae charmed, sir, hae I been wi' your conversation, that I canna tell whether this be my first, second, or third jug?

North. Your second.

Shepherd. Gude nicht.

(*They finish the second jug, but seem unwilling to rise.*)

North. God bless you, my dearest James!

Shepherd. You're a kind hearted cretur, sir.

North. I cannot lend my sanction, James, to sumptuary laws.

Shepherd. What kind o' laws may they be? I never heard tell o' them afore—but if they be laws anent eatin' and drinkin' ony particular sort o' vivres, I gee ma vote for beginnin' wi' wine.

North. On what principle, James?

Shepherd. On the principal o' principles—Justice. Our legislators—that's the maist feck o' them—belang to the upper ranks—at least, members o' Parliament are seldom seen hedgin' and ditchin', or knappin' stanes—accepp it may be for their ain amusement—in avenues and the like; and still seldomer working at the haunloom, or takin' tent o' the power-loom, or overlookin' ony great instrumental establishment o' spindles obedient to the command o' steam.

North. Steam is a tyrant.

Shepherd. He's a' that—and his subjects are slaves. But what I was gaun to say was this—that our legislators maun be better acquainted wi' the good and evil o' their ain condition o' life than wi' them o' that aneath it, for personal experience is the surest teacher o' truth. Now, sir, hard-workin' folk dinna for ordinar' drink wine, and I dinna pity them, for to my taste, wine's wersh, and it aye sours on my stomach, and bein' made o' mere frute it can hae nae nourishment. Still the gentry like it, and get fou' on't—or if no fou', they drink daily sufficient to sap thoosans o' constitutions—forby injuring their fortunes by the annual expense o' importation. Let a' foreign wines then be excluded by ack o' Parliament, makin' it felony, punishable by transportation for life, to hae abune half-a-dizzen o' ony ae kind in a private cellar—wi' a provision legaleezin' the sale thereof in Apothecaries' shops alang wi' ither droogs—to be selt in thummlefu's, per permit. After an experiment o' a few years' trial, the gentry will be able to judge, not only hoo they like the law, but hoo its operations agrees wi' their health. They will then be able, wi' a gude grace, to ca' the attention o' the lower orders to the temperance o' the higher—and as the example o' our superiors is powerfu', sobriety will be seen descendin' by degrees through all grawds till it reaches even the tinklers—and then the ack may be extended to speerits frae sugar and grain, withoot ony national convulsion, but a slicht sneeze.

North. I grieve to think that the lower orders should be so addicted to this most pernicious vice. But like all other evil habits, it can be prevented or cured but by moral influences—and, in my opinion, to expect to see that done by Act of Parliament, betrays a lamentable ignorance of human nature.

Shepherd. Waur than that—cruel injustice in them who seek to hae recourse to sic measures. They will not suffer ony interference in their ain vices—or rather they ken that mony o' them in which they shamelessly indulge, are o' a kind that nae law can weel tak haud o'—and while they enjoy their ain luxuries without stint, their ain vices and their sins, they froon on the far mair excusable frailties o' the poor, exaggerate them oot o' a' measure, and to prevent excesses which all good men must deplore, would without compunction, cut awa' comforts frae that condition, which, rather than curtail, a good man would put baith hauns into the fire.

North. Luxury hardens the heart.

Shepherd. Makes it fat or fosey—fu' o' creesh or wund,

North. How did the Drunken Committee vote on the Malt Tax?

Shepherd. I really canna say. But I fear thae beer-houses are bad places; and I'm sure that folk are no like to mak themsells fou on hame-brewed yill—for the speerit of domestic comfort's a sober speerit, though a gladsome—and the master o' the mawte, at his ain fireside, has every reason to preserve moderation at the cheerful, hamely meal, enlivened by the liquor flowing frae the produce o' his ain farm. But the incidence o' taxation's a kittle problem—and, I confess, no for a shepherd to solve. Only this is sure, that taxation is a burden that a' ought to bear alike, accordin' to the strength o' their shouthers; sae that your political economists maun begin wi' ascertaining the strength o' folk's shouthers, or they will alloo thousans and tens o' thousans to walk wi' their backs straught and no an ounce on the nape o' their necks, while they oppress as mony mair beneath a hunder wecht, that lang ere the close o' this life's darg bows their foreheads to the dust.

North. James, a little while ago you delivered one of the longest sentences of perfect grammatical construction I remember since the days of Jeremy Taylor.*

Shepherd. Was't grammatical? That's curious, for I never learned grammar.

North. One seldom hears a speaker get out of a long sentence till after the most fearful floundering——

Shepherd. Perhaps 'cause he has learned what grammar is, without haein' acquired the power o' observin't; whereas the like o' me wha kens naething about it, instinctively steers clear o' a' difficulties, and comes out at the end, bauldly shakin' his head, like a stag from a wood, hungry for the mountains.

North. James, the days are fast shortening—alas! alas!

Shepherd. Let them shorten. The nights 'll be sae muckle the langer—and "mortal man, who liveth here by toil," hae mair time for wauken as well as for sleepin' rest. Wunter, wild as he sometimes is, is a gracious Season—and in the Forest I hae kent him

* *Ante*—pages 339, 340.—M.

amaist as gentle as the Spring. Indeed, he seems to be gettin' safter and safter in his temper ilka year. Frost is his favorite son —and I devoutly howp there'll never be ony serious quarrel atween them twa; for Wunter never looks sae cherry as when you see him gaun linkin' haun in haun wi' fine black Frost. Snaw is Frost's sister, and she's a bonnie white-skinned lassie, wi' her characte without speck or stain. She came to see us last Christmas, but stayed only about a week, and we thocht her lookin' rather thin; but the mornin' afore she left us, I happened to see her on the hill at sunrise—and oh! what a briest!

North. Like that of the sea-mew or the swan.

Shepherd. Richt. For o' a' the birds that sail the air, thae twa are surely the maist purely beautifu'. Then they come and they gae just like the snaw. You see the mew fauldin' her wings on the meadow as if she was gaun to be for lang our island guest—you see the swan floatin' on the loch as if she had cast anchor for the wunter there—you see the snaw settled on the hill as if she never would forsake the sun who looks on her with saftened licht—but neist mornin' you daunner out to the brae—and mew, swan, and snaw, are a' gane—melted into air—or flown awa to the sea.

North. These images touch my heart. Yet how happens it that my own imagination does not supply them, and that you, my dear Shepherd, have to bring them before the old man's eyes?

Shepherd. Because I hae genie.

North. And I, alas! have none.

Shepherd. Dinna look sae like as if you was gaun to fa' a greetin'—for I only answered simply a simple question—ane was far frae meanin' to deny that you had the gift.

North. But I canna write a sang, Jamie—I canna write a sang!

Shepherd. Nor sing ane verra weel either, sir; for, be the tune what it may, ye chant them a' to Stroudwater, and I never hear you without thinkin' that you wou'd hae made—a monotonous ane to be sure, but a pathetic precentor. O but hoo touchingly wou'd ye hae gien out the line!

North. Allan Cunningham, and William Motherwell, and you, my dear James, have caught the true spirit of the old traditionary strain —and, seek the wide world, where will there be found such a lyrical lark as he whom, not in vain, you three have aspired to emulate— sweet Robby Burns?

Shepherd. That's richt, sir. I was wrang in ever hintin' ae word in disparagement o' Burns' Cotter's Saturday Night. But the truth is, you see, that the soobject's sae heaped up wi' happiness, and sae charged wi' a sorts o' sanctity—sae national and sae Scattish—that beautifu' as the poem is—really, after a', naething can be mair beautifu'—there's nae satisfyin' either peasant or shepherd by ony delineation o't, tho' drawn in lines o' licht, and shinin' equally wi' genius and wi' piety. That's it. Noo, this is Saturday night at Tibbie's—and, though we've been sae funny, there has been naething desecratin' in our fun', and we'll be a' attendin' divine service the morn—me in Yarrow, and you, Mr. North, and Mr. Tickler, and the lave o' you, in Ettrick kirk.

North. And, James, we can no where else hear Christianity preached in a more fervent and truthful spirit.

Shepherd. Naewhere. Do you see, sir, that splendid and magnificent assemblage o' towers and temples far ben in the heart o' that fire o' peat and wood? See! see! how they sink and settle doon in the flames! I prophesy the destruction o' baith Houses o' Parliaments.* O spare, thou devourin' element! O, spare, I beseech thee, that ancient Ha'; spare, oh, spare, that ancient Abbey, where the banes o' the michty dead repose—nor lick up wi' ony ane o' thy thousan forked tongues the holy dust on their tombs!

North. Thou seer!

Shepherd. Noo, mind my words. I dinna say that they're burnin' at this very minute—for that spectacle may either be shadowin' forth the past or the future—but I say that they are either burning, or hae been burned, or will be burned within a week's time, and

"That the blackness of ashes shall mark where they stood."

The Lords' House and the Commons' House—but that the fire shall spare the auld Ha', and the auld Abbey—for look! look! how they stand unscathed, while all about them smoulders! And see na you, sir, that globe o' safter licht hangin' owre them, as if it were the image o' the moon, happy to see them safe frae her watchtower in the sky?

North. Where? where?

Shepherd. A's gane. Tickler has seen naething o' this prefigurin' revelation. That comes o' fa'n' asleep.

North. I shall awake him—(*vainly shaking Timothy*).

Shepherd. Whattt?

North. Let him sleep.

Shepherd. Oh! sir! but yon was a delichtfu' meeting at New-Inn, Tushielaw. His lordship 'll no be sorry to hear o't in Cheena—or as Bourhope weel ca'd it out o' the poet, "far Cathay;" for the account, when it reaches him, will shaw that "though absent lang and distant far," he and his fair gude leddy, and their beautifu' family, are no forgotten in the Forest, but that a' hearts will keep

* Nothing can be more safe than to prophecy *after the fact.* Hogg did so, in this instance. The Burning of the Houses of Parliament, in London, took place in October, 1834. The expense of rebuilding on a scale of unexampled beauty and magnificence will exceed two million pounds sterling. The Lords and the Commons now sit in the new Chambers.—M.

beatin warmly towards them till their happy return.* Saw ye ever, sir, a mair enthusiastic pairty? It was a tribut—and nae humble ane either—to vertue; and the anniversary o' Lord Napier's birthday will be commemorated in the Forest wi' unceasin' kindness, ilka year till some bonnie ship, sailin' through the sunshine, or flingin' aff the storms frae her sails, brings them a' back again to Ettrick, and in a few weeks we forget that they ever were awa'. Here's their health wi' a' the honors.

North. The Master of Napier,† and his brother in Germany—

Shepherd. A'—a'—a'—God bless them!—the pawrent birds—and the weel-feathered young anes—o' baith sexes—wha hae flown in howp and beauty frae their sylvan hill-nest.

(*Shepherd's toast is drunk with all the honors.*)

Tickler (*starting up*). Hurra, hurra, hurra!—hip, hip, hip—hurra, hurra, hurra, hurra! hurra! hurra!

Shepherd. Gie's your haun, sir, Mr. Tickler—sense and feelin' are wi' you in your verra sleep.

Enter CAMPBELL *to tell the Gigs are at the door.*

North (*sub dio*). "How beautiful is night!"

Shepherd. That's Southey. In fowre words, the spirits o' the skies.

North. Not one star.

Shepherd. Put on your specs and you'll see hunders. But they are saft at him—though there is nae mist—only a kind o' holy haze—and their lustre is abated by the dews. I thocht it had been frost; but there's nae frost—or they would be shinin' clearly in thousans——

North. Like angel eyes.

Shepherd. A common comparison—yet no the waur for that—for a' humanity feels, that on a bricht starry nicht, heaven keep watch and ward over earth, and the blue lift is instinct wi' love.

North. Where's the moon?

Shepherd. Lookin' at her a' the time wi' a gratefu' face, that

* Lord Napier, a Scottish peer, was an officer in the British Navy, who, in 1833, was appointed Superintendent of the trade and interests of the British nation in China. He reached Macao in July, 1834, but the Governor of Canton appeared desirous of preventing him from going up to Canton, until the Imperial pleasure on that head had been received from Pekin. Lord Napier persevered, went to the British factory at Canton, on July 24, 1834, and refused to comply with the Governor's edicts that he should return to Macao. On this, commercial relations between the British and Chinese merchants were prohibited by the Governor. Two British frigates, the Imogine and Andromache, which Napier sent up the Boyne river, were fired upon by the Chinese forts. In return, the frigates battered down the forts, on September 7th. On that day week, Napier became seriously indisposed—ordered the British ship-of-war to "move out of the river," returned to Macao, and died there on the 11th of October, 1834. The events in which he thus took part, were assigned as justification of the war subsequently waged by Great Britain upon China.—M.

† In Scotland, where the eldest son of a peer has not a distinctive title (and those of Viscounts and Barons have not), he is called "The Master." Thus Lord Arbuthnot, Forbes, Napier, &c., would have their eldest sons respectively called The Master of Arbuthnot, Forbes and Napier.—M.

smiles in her licht! as if you were gaun to sing a sang in her praise, or to say a prayer.

North. No halo.

Shepherd. The white Lily o' the sky.

North. No rain to-morrow, Shepherd.

Shepherd. Not a drap. 'Twull be a real Sabbath-day. Ye see the starnies noo—dinna ye, sir? Some seemin' no farrer awa nor the moon—and some far ahint and ayont her, but still in the same region wi' the planet—ithers retiring and retired in infinitude—and sma' as they seem, a' suns! Awfu' but sweet to think on the great works o' God!—But the horses 'll be catchin' cauld—and a' that they ken is, that it's a clear nicht. Lads, tak care o' the dowgs, and they dinna break the couple, and worry sheep. You'll be at the Castle afore Mr. North—for it's no abune five mile by the cut across the hills—and no a furlon short o' fourteen by the wheelrod. —(*They ascend their Gigs.*)—For Heaven's sake, take tent o' the Norways! Haco's rearin', and Harold's funkin'—sic deevils!

Tickler. Whew! Whew! Whew! *D. I. O.* North! *Do—Da —Do—Tibi Gratias!* Farewell—thou Bower of Peace!

No. LXIX.—DECEMBER, 1834.

SCENE—*Old Blue Parlor, Ambrose's, Gabriel's Road.—Present,* NORTH, TICKLER, SHEPHERD.

Shepherd. What'n a nicht! Only hear to that lumm—as if a park o' artillery were firin' a salute in the sky. But a salute or salvo seldom consists o' mair than a hunder guns, and there aërial engines hae been cannonadin' for hours on end, as if the north und the east wuld were fechtin' a pitched battle wi' the South and the West for the Empire o' Darkness. In such a hurricane, I could pity the Moon—but then to be sure she has her ain Cave o' Peace. starroof'd, in a region sacred frae a' storms.

North. Poetry!

Shepherd. There goes an auld woman frae the chumley-tap, rattling down the sklates, to play crash among the cats in the area.

Tickler. Painting!

Shepherd. Blash awa', Sleet! thou wishy-washy faced dochter o' Rain and Snaw! Blatter awa', Rain! thou cloud-begotten son o' Uranus! Drift awa', Snaw! thou flaky fàmily o' Dew and Frost, embracing on their air-bed in the lift wi' mirk curtains, and stock ice-congealed yet thaw-drippin—and aften sinkin' doon till it settle on some mountain-tap where the pine trees daurna grow!

North. Fancy! Imagination!

Shepherd. O the power o' Glass! Yet what is't to the power o' the human Ee! Licht, I'm tauld, is driven frae the sun to the earth some hunder million o' miles or thereabouts in minutes fewer in nummer than my fingers—and yet hoo saftly it solicits the een o' mortal creturs, for whom it was there prepared! And what pleasure it gies the pupil devoutly learnin' to read the sky!

Tickler. Philosophy!

Shepherd. It's just the nicht, sirs, for het toddy and caller oysters.

(*Enter* MR. AMBROSE *with the Natives.*)

North. Ambrose! In the Blue Parlor met once more!

"Three blither hearts
You may not find in Christiandie."

(AMBROSE *deposits the Barrel, and rushes out quite overpowered by his emotions.*)

Shepherd. Puir fallow!—he's the verra child o' Sense and Sensibility!—Whatt? You're greetin' too! The tears rap, rap, rappin' doon your nose like hail-stanes, and jumpin' on the rug!

North (*wiping his eyes*). Old times so hurried upon my heart——

Shepherd. That you could but gasp—and glower like a Goshawk or a Hoolet.

North. Here was writ the Chaldee MSS.! Here—in that closet sat Gurney—a novice from Norwich—taking down NOCTES AMBROSIANÆ, No. I.! And now they have almost reached the natural term of man's life—Threescore and Ten!

Voice. Seventy but One.

Shepherd. That cretur's voice aye gars me a' grue. Fule that I was to save him free droonin' in the Yarrow! But a braw time's coming, and the auld saw will be confirmed. Short-haun' 'll be Lang-Neck afore he gies up the ghost.

Tickler. I never heard of the rescue.

Shepherd. He enjoined silence—but you see, sirs, naething wud satisfy the cretur, when you were a' in the Forest, but that he too maun try the Fishin'. Sae takin' a baggy-mennon-net, he sallies oot ae mornin' afore the smoke had left the lumm, and awa' doon to Yarrow-brigg for what he ca'd bait for the swivel. Our rivers, ye ken, are rather deceptive to strangers, and Girmy thocht yon saft, smooth flawin' o' liquid licht a fuird! He never considered that a brigg's never built owre a fuid; sae in he gangs intil what seemed to his ee some sax inch deep o' water, just coverin' the green glimmerin' gravel—and at the second step—plump outowre head and ears, like a pearl-diver or water-hen.

Tickler. Who saw him dive?

Shepherd. I saw him dive. I had happened to rise early, and was leanin' owre the ledge, spittin' wafers into the water. My first fear was that he was committin' suicide, and I stood switherin' for a while whether or no to prevent him effectin' his purpose, for he has lang been the plague o' my life, and his death wud be a great riddance. By and by, he makes his appearance on the surface, shootin' and gullerin' like a hoolet on a dyeuck's back, and then doon again, wi' his dowp in the air, and up again five or sax times, as if he had been gamesome, and was takin' a recreation to whet his appeteet for the barley scones, and fresh butter at breakfast. I couldna but wonder at his activity, for it seemed equal to that o' ony otter. This couldna hae lasted abune some ten minutes or less, when he began to wax weakish, and to stay rather langer at a time aneath than seemed consistent wi' prudence; sae I walked hooly doon to the bank, and cried on him to come oot, unless he was set on *felo-de-se.* I do not believe that he heard me, for he was now lyin' yellow at the bottom, as still as a salmon.

North. You listered him?

Shepherd. I did.

Tickler. And resuscitated him according to the rules prescribed by the Humane Society.

Shepherd. I hate a' new-fangled schemes o' resuscitation, or ony thing else; and acted as my forefathers o' the Forest hae done for a thousan' years. I just took him by the heels, and held him up wi' his head doonmost, to alloo the water an opportunity o' rinnin' oot his mouth—and I can assure you, sirs, that the opportunity was no neglected, for it gushed as if frae the stane mouth o' the image o' a fountain, and ran back into the Yarrow like a wee waterfa'. You can imagine what a relief it was to the cretur's stammack, and he began to spur. But I knew better than to reverse his position, and held him perpendicular to the last drap. I then let him doon a' his length on his back; and the sun coming out frae behind a cloud, rekindled the spark o' life, till it shone on his rather insignificant features, relaxing into a smile. He then began to bock dry—was convulsed—drew up his legs—streekit them oot again—flang about his arms—clenched his hauns—whawmmled hissell owre on his groof—bat the gerss—opened his een—muttered—and lo! there was my gentleman sittin' on his dowp, and starin' at me as if I had been the deil. We got him carried up into the Gordon Arms—pit'n into the blankets—wi' bottles o' het water at his soles—and rubbed him owre wi' sawte, till he was as red as a labster. What'n a breakfast did na he devoor!

Voice. A true bill.

North. Ah! Gurney! those were happy days in the Forest. How different now our doom!

Shepherd. You're no like the same man, sir. Oh! but you were a buirdly auld carle in yon Peebles plush sportin' jacket, Galashiels tartan troosers, Moffat hairy waistcoat, Hawick rig-and-fur stockins, and Thirlstane trampers a' studded wi' sparables, that carried destruction amang the clocks. On the firm sward you carried alang wi' you an earthquake—and as ye strode alang the marshes, how the quagmires groaned!

North. I stilted the streams in spate, James, as the heron stilts the shallows in midsummer drought.

Shepherd. And noo ye hirple alang the floor like the shadow o' a hare by moonlicht, and you sit on your chair like a ghaist leanin' on its crutch! O-hon-a-ree!

North. James!

Shepherd. Forgie me sir, but tenderness will tell the truth. Embro' does na agree wi' you, sir. Pitch your perennial tent, sir, in the Forest, and you will outlive the crow.

North (*showing a toe*). Are these spindle shanks?

Shepherd. Frae the bottom o' my sowle I wuss they were—but, alas! they are but wunnlestraes! The speeder wou'd na trust himsell to what's sae slender—the butterfly wou'd fear to sit doon on sic a fragile prap. You're a wee, wizened, wrinkled, crunkled, bilious bit body, that the wund could carry awa' wi' a waff. And a' the wark o' ae single month! Come and keep your Christmas at least wi' your freens in the Forest—

Tickler. Curse the country in winter.

Shepherd. Wheesht—wheesht—wheesht! That's a fearsome sentiment. Eat in your words, sir—eat in your words; for though I ken you're no serious, and only want to provoke the Shepherd, I canna thole the thocht o' impiety toward the hoary year.

Tickler. I am an idiot. Your hand, my dear James.

Shepherd. There's them baith.

North. This was the Shortest Day—you remember this year's longest day, James?

Shepherd. And wull till I dee!

North. It resembles some one or other of those Longest Days that, half a century ago, used to enshroud us in the imagery of some more celestial sphere than our waning life now inhabits—when, between sunrise and sunset, lingeringly floated by what was felt in its bliss and beauty to be a whole Golden Age!

Shepherd. I shouldna hae been sorry to hae said that mysell, sir, for it's rather—verra—beautifu'; and the expression, while it is rich, is simpler than your usual style, which, I canna help thinkin', has a tendency to the owre-ornate.

North. You think no such thing, James. But let the foolish world persist in the utterance of any bit of nonsense, and even men of genius, in spite of their hearts, will begin to repeat the cry.

Shepherd. I daursay you're richt. Tak Time, and stretch it out till it becomes an invisible line, and then is felt to break, yet shall ye not be able to lengthen out a day now into the endurance o' an Hour,

"In life's morning march, when the spirit was young.'

North. I recoil from the very imagination of those interminable day dargs of delight, when earth's realities were all splendid as dreams, and yet dreams there were that extinguished even those lustrous realities, in which we took our seats upon thrones among the Sons of the Morning, and felt privileged in our pride to walk through the Courts of Heaven.

Shepherd. But our verra dreams, sir, are dulled noo—on their breakin', we do not feel noo as we used to do then, as if fallen to eerth frae sky! The warld o' sleep is noo but different frae the wauken warld in being somewhat sadder, and somewhat mair confused; and ane cares but little noo, sir, about either lying doon or rising up, for some great change has been wrocht within the mysterious chambers o' the brain and cells o' the heart, and life's like a faded flower, scentless and shrivelled. yet are we loath to part with it, and even howp against a howp that baith color and brightness may revive. But inexorable is the law o' the Dust.

North. Cheer up—cheer up, James!

Shepherd. But you'll no let me—for your face is a' wintry-like as if it had never known a simmer smile. Lauch, sir—lauch—and I'll do my best to be happy.

North (smiling). Time and place are as nothing to a wise man. My mind my kingdom is—and there I am monarch of all I survey.

Shepherd. Weel quoted. But is nae the Forest exceedin' fair? and may na the joy o' imagination, broodin' open'-eyed on its saft silent hills—ilka range in itsell like a ready-made dream—blend even wi' that o' conscience—till the sense o' beauty is felt to be almost ane wi' the sense o' duty, sae peacefu' is all around in nature, and all within the Shepherd's heart! I felt sae last Sabbath as we were comin' frae the kirk—for though the second Sabbath o' November—a season when I've kent the weather wild—sae still was the air, and in the mild sun sae warm, that but I missed the murmur o' the bee, I could hae thocht it simmer, or the glimpsing spring.

North. I have heard it said, my dear James, that shepherds and herdsmen, and woodsmen, and peasants in general, have little or no feeling of the beauty of Nature. Is that true?

Shepherd. It canna weel be true, sir, seein' that it's a lee. They hae een and ears in their heads, and a' the rest o' the seven senses—and is't denied that they hae hearts and sowles? Only grant that they're no a' born blin' and deaf—and that there's a correspondency atween the outward and the inward warlds—and then believe if you can that the sang o' a bird, and the scent o' a flower, or the smell o't, if it ha' nae scent, is no felt to be delightfu' by the simplest, ay, rudest heart, especially after a shower, and at the coming out o' the rainbow.

North. Help yourself, my dear James.

Shepherd. They dinna flee into raptures at rocks, like town folks, for that's a' folly or affectation; nor weary ye wi' nonsense about sunrise and sunset, and clouds and thunder, and mist stealin' up the hills, and sic like clishmaclavers—but they notice a' the changes on nature's face, and are spiritually touched—believe me, sir—by the sweeter and the mair solemn—the milder or the mair magnificent—for they never forget that nature is the wark o' an Almighty hand—and there is nae poetry like that o' religion.

North. Go on, James.

Shepherd. Is there nae description o' the beauty o' nature in the Bible? All the Christian world mair dearly loves the lily o' the field, for sake o' a few divine words. None but poor men now read the New Testament. By none—I mean too few—they who do chiefly live in rural places—and how can they be insensible to the spirit breathing around them from the bosom of the happy earth?

North. Go on, my dear James.

Shepherd. Wha wrott a' our auld sangs? Wha wrott a' the best o' our ain day? In them is there nae love o' nature? Wha sing them? Wha get them by heart that canna sing? Lads and lassies o' laigh degree—but what signifies talkin'—only think on that ae line,

"The Flowers o' the Forest are a' wede awa!"

North. You need say no more, James.

Shepherd. Simple folk, sir, never think o' expatiatin' on the beauties o' nature. A few touches suffice for them; and the more homely and familiar and common, the dearer to their hearts. The images they think of are never far-fetched, but seem to be lying about their very feet. But it is affection or passion that gives them unwonted beauty in their eyes, and that beauty is often immortalized by Genius that knows not it is Genius—believing itself to be but Love—in one happy word.

North. James, what is Beauty?

Shepherd. The feeling o' Pure Perfection—as in a drop o' dew, a diamond, or a tear. There the feeling is simple; but it is complex as you gaze on a sweet-brier arrayed by Morn in millions o' dew-draps—or on a woman's head, dark as night, adorned wi' diamonds as wi' stars—or on a woman's cheek, where the smile canna conceal the tear that has just fallen, in love or pity, frae her misty een, but the moment afore bright-blue as the heavenliest spot o' a the vernal skies.

Tickler. Here come the oysters.

(*Enter* MR. AMBROSE, *solus, with more Natives.*)

Shepherd. What newspaper's that?

North. Bell's Life in London*—worth all the other Weeklies in a bunch—Examiner, Spectator, Atlas, and the rest.

Shepherd. Dinna say sae, sir.

North. Well—I won't. Indeed, it is not true; for the papers I have mentioned—though I hate their politics as I hate the gates of hell—are in much admirable—and the three ablest of the kind ever published in Britain. But "Bell's Life in London" is the best sporting paper that ever flourished, and will circulate all over the Island

* Edited for many years by Vincent Dowling (who died in 1852) one of the best sporting men in England, and an infallible authority on all matters connected with field or other sports. From his great height, he was called "The Long Scribe." There is one such in every city.—M

long after many a philosophical penny-wiseacre, that pretends to despise it, has gone the way of all flesh.

Shepherd. Mair nor ane o' our farmers takes it in—and it used to be weel thoomb'd by your friend the Flying Tailor. Indeed, he had it filed for some years, and it brocht a great price at the sale o' his leebrary. Puir fallow! wi' what pride he used to turn up the leaf in ane o' the files, containin' the account o' his beatin' Christopher North at hap-step-and-loup!

North. That's a lie, James. Bell's Life in London had then no existence.

Shepherd. Sae you confess he beat you?

North. It never was in his breeches—but I merely said, "that's a lie—Bell's Life in London had then no existence." We leapt, it is true——

Shepherd. And he beat ye a' to sticks. But what for said ye "that's a lie?" I'm never sae rude. I only say, when you happen to deviate frae the truth, "that's a lee." Noo there's an essential difference atween thae twa words. "That's a lie"—pronounced in what tone you will—is aye felt to be rather insultin'; "that's a lee"—especially if pronounced wi' a sort o' a lauch—is but a britherly intimation that you shou'd tak tent o' what you're sayin; for that, if you do not, every body mayna choose to answer ye sae ceevilly, but may even impeach your veracity in direct terms.

North. It is a Chronicle—and a fair, and faithful, and most animated—of the manly amusements of the gentleman and the people of England—the Turf—the Chase—and all the sports and games of the field.

Shepherd. It's a curious fact, sir, o' my idiosyncrasy——

North. Your what, James?

Shepherd. Na—catch me, after gettin' safely through a word o' sax syllables, tryin' the adventure again the same nicht. But it's a curious fact o' my peculiar conformation o' character, that I tak the intensest interest in reading about actions and events that I wou'd na gang a mile o' gate to see. There's horse-racin', on a regular coorse at Musselburgh, for purse, plate, or steaks. Naething to me mair wearisome in this wearisome world.

North. The Caledonian Hunt!

Shepherd. There sit the leddies in the grand-stann, sae high up, that for ony thing you can tell they may a' hae bairds.

North. Ho! ho! you never look at the race.

Shepherd. The blaw o' the bonnets is bonny aneuch, and sae is a tulip-bed; but if a man in a booth below bids ye admire the beauty in the pink pelisse, they hae a' pink pelisses, or purple anes, which is just the same thing; and your een, after a' their glowerin', are just as likely as no to fa' on the blowzey face o' some auld dowager.

Tickler. A just punishment.

Shepherd. I've seen some gay bonny faces in the hired landaws alang the rapes—and the lasses in them are aye ready to gie a body a nod or a wink—but sic vehicles, it seems, are no reckoned genteel, though fu' o' parasols.

Tickler. They cannot possibly be vulgar, James, if full of parasols.

Shepherd. I thocht he had been sleepin'. I gie a penny for a bill, and try to mak oot the color o' the horses and their riders. But a's initials. Why no prent meres, geldings, staigs, fillies, colts, and the rest o' the rinnin' horses, at full length, to prevent confusion? I've compared them severally wi' the paper, ane after anither, as they cantered by the staun afore the start, and never yet cou'd identify a single naig wi' his description. The uniform o' the jockies is even mair puzzlin'—sae that the minute after layin' a croon, nae idea had I on what beast I hae betted, when aff they set, a haudin' in, as if the race was to be won by the hindmost, and I tell my neighbor to let me ken when they are beginnin' to mak' play.

North. That you may hedge?

Shepherd. I have aye had mair sense. For what's the use o' hedgin' on a green jacket when he comes in a black ane? or on a black mere when she comes in a broon horse? or cryin' "Crimson for a croon," meanin' him that's a hundred and fifty yards afore a' the lave, when, after the heat, a wee wicket vretch, wi' long waistcoat and tap-boots, taps you on the shouther, and hauds oot his haun, swearing that Purple has won in a canter, and that him that was really Crimson had broke doon, and was limpin' by the distance post?

North. On what principle do you make up your book?

Shepherd. What'n book?

North. Your bet-book.

Shepherd. Catch me wi' a pocket-book o' ony kind on a race-grun'. But the race was to hae been in heats. Ae horse wuns ae heat—and anither horse wuns anither—but never by ony accident him or her I was supposed to be bettin' on, though I was not; and now, after a lang delay, and frequent ringin' o' bells, comes what a' men are justified in believing to be the heat decisive o' the stakes. The horses do indeed seem most uncommon sleek and dry, and their colors not only to have brichtened up most uncommon, but to have undergone a great change—for, lo and behold! an iron-gray and a chestnut, which I had never observed in the twa first heats—and, mair extraordinary still, and as appears to me no fair, five horses in the whole in place o' foure—that set aff like a whurlwund! I cry, "Purple a pound!" certain that I am takin' the naig that wun the last heat in a canter. The twa miles are ran in little mair than three minutes—and the same wee wicket vretch wi' the lang waist-coast and tap-boots taps me again on the shouther, and hauding out his open haun, swears that nae Jockey wore purple—and I discover, to my consternation, that this was a different race—atween different horses, wi' different riders—and for different stakes—for that the ither race was as gude as dune;—fand there by-and-by comes Purple to canter the coorse by himsell, as the condition was heats.

North. Done brown, James, on both sides, like a bit of dry toast.

Shepherd. O' the twenty thousan' folk present, I dinna believe abune five hunder ken, o' their ain knowledge, wha wuns or wha loses a single stake.

North. Your losses have soured you, James, with the Turf.

Shepherd. I alloo my losses hae been considerable—for I canna hae lost at Musselburgh, during the last five years, less than five punds sterling.

North. Per annum?

Shepherd. Heaven forbid! A'thegither. Frae which you may deduct fifteen shillings won frae a lang clever chiel' o' your acquaintance in spectacles—wha's sand-blin'—and mistook a bricht bay for a mouse color, and because he happened to hae a rat-tail.

North. Well—it cannot be said, after all, that you have dearly purchased your experience and disgust.

Shepherd. I hae cheaply purchased my delicht in the turf. I tak in the New Sporting Magazine.

North. That is right. So do I. The editor is a gentleman—of that his very name is an assurance—and he also is a scholar.

Shepherd. And the Auld Sportin' Magazine too.

North. That is right. So do I. I have taken it for nearly forty years! Hambletonian and Diamond! That was a race. Sir Joshua and Filho da Puta! That was another. The first is now an old story—nor the second a new one—there were racers in those days.

Shepherd. And are now.

North. Plenipo? Bah! Bah! Bah!

Shepherd. But, sir, wasna ye gaun to defend "Bell's Life in London" frae the charge o' blackguardism brocht lately against it by some writers, or writer, in the United Service Journal and the New Monthly Magazine?

North. Not I. I greatly admire both those periodicals—and have no wish (at present) to break a lance with any knight who chooses in those lists to challenge another adversary—and not me, who am known to be a man of peace.

Shepherd. Knicht! Lance!

North. Well—well—James—fight him yourself with a rung. But don't hit him on the head.

Shepherd. What for no?

North. You may guess.

Shepherd. Ay—ay—I understand. Can you comprehend, sir, the horror many worthy folk feel for fechtin' wi' the nieves?

North. I candidly declare that I cannot. The whole question, James, lies in a nut-shell.

Shepherd. But a cocoa-nut-shell, sir.

North. Well. The English have for ages chosen to decide their personal quarrels by an appeal to the fist.

Shepherd. It's the custom o' the kintra—a natural characteristic—a trate o' mainners—and I howp that a pastime sae truly popular will never be discountenanced by them who love the people, and see in all their manly amusements an expression of the inborn energies o' the sons of Liberty.

North. The fist is a national weapon, and always at hand.

Shepherd. That's a truism.

North. Nor though formidable, is it often fatal.

Shepherd. A swurd's a deadly weapon—and still deadlier a dirk—but he would indeed be a coof that would say that the human haun'——

North. You have but to look at your knuckles to know that a knock-down blow must be a casualty of frequent occurrence during a fair stand-up fight between two powerful and courageous men—and most of the men of England are powerful—according to their length and inches—and all the men of England are courageous as mastiffs, bull-dogs, game-cocks, or lions.

Shepherd. Modern naturals assert the lion's a cooard.

North. Modern naturals are idiots.

Shepherd. I'm glad to hear ye say sae, sir, for I would be ashamed o' my country had she chosen to emblazon her banner wi' an animal that was a cooard.

Tickler.

> "And in the vault of heaven serenely fair,
> The Lion's fiery mane floats through the ambient air."

North. "Victorious Judah's Lion-Banner rose."

Tickler. "Lord of the Lion-heart and eagle eye."

Shepherd. Ye need na accumulate authorities, for a true Tory, though he gies up the doctrine o' the divine richt o' human king's, haulds firm to the ancient faith, that by the fiat o' Him who created the dust o' the desert, courage, the regal virtue, has his residence in the lordly heart o' the King o' Beasts.

North. Gray, in the famous ode, speaks of the "Lion port" of Queen Elizabeth—for the poet thought of her addressing her heroes on the heart-rousing alarm of the Armada, and the image was characteristic of the glorious bearing of the Virgin Queen—for she was indeed a Lioness—worthy to rule over that race, of whom another poet has said,

> "Pride in their port, defiance in their eye,
> I see the lords of human kind pass by."

Shepherd. Yon's no the roar o' a cooard, sirs, when he puts his dreadfu' mooth to the grun', and for miles roun' spreads sic a thundrous earthquake, that troops o' deers and antelopes are seen boundin' up frae the groanin' sands, and fear drives the whole desert aflight, frae the majestic auld male elephant, risin' up in his seraglio like a tower amang turrets, and trumpeting in terror that the lion is on his walk, up to the insignificant ape, incapacitated by a shiverin'-fit frae chatterin', and clingin' in desperation, not only wi' his paws but his tail, to the very tapmost twig o' a tree.

North. People calling themselves Christians should be shy of applying the name "brutal" to the actions of men—and these men Englishmen. The English are not a brutal race—yet they are a race of boxers. Sir Charles Bell* has written a treatise—the best of all the Bridgewater Treatises—except Whewell's—on the Hand—and we happen to know that Sir Charles Bell, so far from thinking that the Hand is degraded by being doubled up into a bunch of fives, and quick as light applied to the *os frontis* of Sampson Agonistes, delights in the *beau idéal* of a fist such as Jem Belcher's, and regards pugilism as one of the chief causes and effect of BRITISH SPIRIT.

Shepherd. I like a fine manly fallow o' a philosopher that cares na about ae chiel gien anither chiel a clour on the head, but rather encourages them to set to, kennin' that the lettin' o' liquid in that way's far healthier than in ony ither, and that a dash on the nose, dispassionately considered, though it does for the time occasion a determination o' bluid to the heed, maun ultimately be a great relief, especially to a man o' a sanguine temperament; and unless a man be o' a sanguine temperament, tak ma word for't, he'll be nae great fechter.

North. It seems, then, to be admitted on all hands, that the English are the most courageous people in the world, and that they have chosen, of their own accord, to settle such disputes as cannot otherwise be settled, by the fist. He, therefore, who calls that custom a

* Sir Charles Bell, the eminent anatomist, had been Professor of Surgery in Edinburgh University, and went to reside in London, in 1806. Here he became, first a lecturer on anatomy and surgery at the academy founded by William and John Hunter, and subsequently a Professor of the Royal College of Surgeons. Whenever or wherever he lectured, the benches were crowded with attentive auditors. He published many professional works of high character, but is chiefly esteemed for discoveries in connection with the nervous system. William IV. knighted him. One of the Bridgewater Treatises was his production. He died in 1842, and his widow, who was left in distressed circumstances, has been put on the pension list.—M.

cowardly custom, should be kicked out of this island as a calumniator of the character of the inhabitants.

Shepherd. The sea would spew him back.

North. I laid emphasis, James, on the words BRITISH SPIRIT, and I lay emphasis on the words FAIR PLAY.

Voice. I have underlined them both—capitals—sir.

Shepherd. That cretur's vice gars me a' grue.

North. Gurney is an Englishman—a pretty sparrer with the gloves —and for his weight——

Shepherd. For his wecht! He can be nae wecht—nae heavier than his bowk in air.

North. FAIR PLAY is a synonyme for HONOR and HUMANITY. Often in hot, seldom in bad blood, the challenge is given and accepted—the booths stand tentless, and the wake forms a ring on the village green, a circle perfect as sun or moon, with a pleasant halo symptomatic of a squall, soon to be succeeded by a calm. The men strip and meet at the scratch—toe to toe—face to face—eye to eye —and as they *shake hands*—anger subsides into resolution—and hatred—if such a passion could for a moment possess an English yokel's breast—expires in the generous glow that warms his heart and illumines his countenance as he inwardly says—"now, it will be seen which is the better man." They set to—and after a merry battle of half-an-hour, a hit on the jugular, or a cross-buttock, gives the victory to our friend with the red whiskers. In five minutes, the man who lost the fight feels himself not a whit the worse—the conqueror treats him and his second to a gallon of cider—and during the evening you see them both figuring in the same dance, with faces that would shame the rainbow.

Shepherd. Freens for life—nay brithers—for they inveet ane anither to ane anither's houses, and mutually marry ane anither's sisters.

North. Fair play, which I have rightly called Honor and Humanity, could not thus prevail among any people—not even the English —without the aid of laws. Therefore laws were enacted—in the spirit and letter of justice—and these are the LAWS OF THE RING. They are few and simple—in theory and in practice equally sanctioned by nature—and form a code purer and higher far than was ever fabricated by Vattel, Puffendorf, or Grotius.

Shepherd. International law—that is, the law o' nations—seems to me nae better than a systematized and legalized scheme o' rape, robbery, piracy, incendiarism, and murder.

North. Quite correct. Such combats, thus guarded by laws passed by the people, keep alive the sentiments in which the laws originated; and thus in England we see the working of a Spirit of Laws that was beyond the experience, and above the comprehension of President Montesquieu.

Shepherd. Tickler's sleepin'.

North. Thus no man need fight at all unless he chooses—and no man need fight a moment longer than he chooses—and hence are the English—in the boxing counties—the least quarrelsome of the nations of Europe.

Shepherd. The boxin' coonties?

North. Yes, James, the boxing counties. Unfortunately, in some of the northern counties, THE LAWS OF THE RING are unknown—and the up-and-down system—savage as in Kentucky—prevails to an extent that may well make a Briton blush black while he weeps. What maimings and murderings then befall? More loss of life and limb in one year than over all the rest of England in twenty, in fair stand-up fight—though who will say that the men of the North are not naturally as brave as their brethren who live under better laws—and with whom, as I said, fair play is honor and humanity?

Shepherd. That's deceesive.

North. Juries in vain threaten capital conviction—judges in vain declare capital conviction shall certainly be followed by execution—but evil customs are the most inveterate—they laugh at penal law, and defy its terrors—and at every assize the calendar is crammed with the names, and the prison with the bodies of such criminals—must I say the word—when speaking of Englishmen?—I must—with ruffians.

Shepherd. Nefawrious.

North. Thus far I have been speaking the sentiments of the wisest man I ever had the happiness to know—I need not say the humanest too; but there are fools—and I suspect that eke are they—who, while they have not the audacity to libel the whole people, nor choose to have their own filthy lick-spittle blown back in their faces from the

> "Bold peasantry, their country's pride,"

assembled at rural feast, and fair, and festival, all over merry England—squirt their venom, like toads from holes, at the LONDON RING, and seem to suppose that the Legislature will listen to the croak of incarcerated reptiles.

Shepherd. Taeds is the only leevin cretur I canna thole.

North. Extinguish the London Ring and you extinguish all the Rings in England. In it the laws are settled as in a Court of Judicatory of the last resort. In it the best men contend—London against all England, and all England, with London against the world. The provinces look up to the capital in all things—Westminster Hall, St. Stephens, Covent Garden, Moulsey Hurst. What a people of pettifoggers we should be, were there no woolsack softly soliciting the sitting-down thereon of an Eldon, a Lyndhurst, or a Vaux! What odd oratory would be ours, if there were no grander field for its display than the Green of Glasgow, by Glasgow's gander cackled and hissed over from the Calton to the Goosedubs? In provincial towns the genius of Kemble and Cook and Kean would have fretted and strutted its little hour in vain; and but for the London Ring, pitched on fair Moulsey Hurst, by Thames's silver side, no such glorious title would have been known as "Champion of England"—and Jem Belcher gone down to the grave without his fame.

Shepherd. You give me much pleasure, Mr. North.

North. I am speaking, my dear James, of mere amusements—

Shepherd. Mere amusements—such is the word—o' the people are no' to be shackled on licht gruns—much less put down by the arm o' the law.

North. Good. In this hard-working world, the people are entitled to their amusement—the sweeteners of life and solders of society—and they *will have them,* James, in spite of cant, hypocrisy, and falsehood—never rifer than now in the spite of the mean malignants, never before so numerous or so noisy, who, in utter ignorance of the nobility of their nature, would shear away the privileges of the people—and by a base outcry against gin-drinking, and Sabbath-breaking, and dancing, and wrestling, and cudgelling, and boxing—which are huddled together—with many more—as equal and kindred enormities—and made crimes at all but by liars' license and liars' logic—would fain persuade us that Albion is a sink and sewer—filled with the foul vices of slaves—the scum of the earth—whereas all the wide world knows that

> "Though some few spots be on her flowing robe
> Of stateliest beauty,"

she is worthy still to wear the title she won of yore, and is crowned still with her towery diadem—Queen of the Sea.

Shepherd. There's a flicht!

North. A person in Parliament—if the reporters are to be trusted—and they seldom misrepresent any man—some months ago rose up in a sudden fit of humanity, justice, and religion, and vehemently asked if the House would take no steps in consequence of a MURDER that had lately been perpetrated under circumstances of peculiar atrocity at Andover. I forget whether he uttered these words before or after the trial. If before the trial, then he cruelly and impiously prejudged the case of a fellow-citizen and a fellow Christian—whose life he believed was at stake—far wickeder behaviour than if I were now—with Gurney at work in the closet—to denounce any M. P. as a dishonest man, supposing that his conduct had ever been subjected to such a charge, and before he could refute that charge, tell all Europe that he was a swindler. If after the trial, then he not only lied against an innocent man, but libelled jury, judge, and law; for Owen Swift, so far from having been convicted of murder under circumstances of peculiar atrocity, was found guilty of manslaughter under circumstances of peculiar alleviation—and his conduct all through the unfortunate fight with his antagonist Anthony Noon—the Pocket Hercules—and especially towards its close, when Swift refrained from striking him—and seconds, bottle-holders, umpire, referee, and all the ring, did what they could to prevent that poor fellow from rushing in—was declared, by as enlightened a judge as ever dignified the seat of justice, Judge Patteson, to have been "fair, manly, and *humane!*"

Shepherd. He'll be a Sant—a crocodile.

North. Saint, crocodile, or shark, he is one of your speakers at meetings in Free Masons' Hall in the cause of humanity—and while he would have wept to flog a negro convicted of setting fire to a plantation, seemed in haste to hang a white for an offence which, notwithstanding the lamentable result, was pronounced by the common sense of the people of England one of the lightest in the calendar at that assize.

Shepherd. I can excuse occasional inconsistency in politics, for nae mortal man is aboon the influence o' party speerit, and selfishness will at times sway the maist upright; but in penal legislation I can conceive naething mair wicked—because naething mair cruel—than to deal out undue severity o' punishment to particular offences, while we let ithers as bad, or far waur, gang free—legislating noo in a tender, and noo in a truculent speerit, and thus showing that your guides and monitors are no at a' times that reason and that conscience to which you avow before the public ye are aye, under religion, humbly obedient, but just as aften prejudices, and bigotries, and wilfulnesses, and blindnesses o' birth and breeding, at biddin' o' which, instead o' temperin' justice wi' mercy, you harden mercy into a mood misnamed o' justice, and thereby are seen ae day fentin at the sicht—na the thocht—o' the sheddin' o' the bluid o' the maist atrocious criminal who may hae outlawed and excommunicated himsel' frae human nature by some horrid ack, and are heard neist day, imprecatin' the last human punishment on some unfortunate fellow, who, after having been severely beaten in a fair fight, has happened, not only contrary to his own wish, but against his own will, to cause the death o' his too obstinate antagonist. Sic Justice is no blin', but she squints, and wi' sic obliquity o' visions she mauna be trusted wi' the swurd in her haun'.

North. I have walked over the beautiful fields of England——

Shepherd. The boxing counties.

North. ——and mixed familiarly with all grades of life—but

never with disreputable society, high, middle, or low—and never did I receive a wanton insult from any man.

Shepherd. Nor ever, I'm sure, sir, gied ane.

North. Never. I have seen many a turn-up, and some pitched battles among the yokels; and though one or two were rather too sanguinary for my taste, no serious mischief was done; and I pronounce the English—with the exception of the barbarous practice already lamented and censured—a most peaceable people—a nation of humane heroes. Let no legislators, then, by their busy intermeddling with the national customs, endanger the stability of the national character. It would be sad and ludicrous indeed if John Bull were to be emasculated by Miss-Mollyism. Let the Miss Mollies wear stays and be thankful—no one expects them to strip.

"Let Dares beat Entellus black and blue,"

while the feebles and the fribbles paint their cheeks after their own fashion, and knit purses. Away with the wishy-washy school of sentiment in which a knock-down argument is thought of with the same horror as a knock-down blow! It might be cruel perhaps to impale such insects, and pin them down on paper, but not to brush them away; yet, if they will persist in biting, the midges must be murdered at last.

Shepherd. I can forgie a' creturs o' that kind, but no the blusterin' fallows that ca' a' folk blackguards wha happen to like to look at twa men fechtin', and extend their abuse to a' athletics whatsomever, as if the powers o' the body were na intended to be brocht intil play for our amusement and pastime as weel's the powers o' the mind.

North. All athletic sports are nearly allied—they all flourish together—with the commonalty in England, boxing is the guardian of them all; and I do not hesitate to affirm, that even cricket-matches—that glorious game—would not be, among what are rightly called the lower ranks, the bloodless contests they now are, were it not for the operation of the ever-present principle of Fair-Play, which in all matters of amusement reigns in England, and derives its permanent power from, and makes its ultimate appeal to, the practice of the Ring.

Shepherd. I've heard there are desperate battles at the Hurlin' Matches in Ireland.

North. I love and admire the Irish. But what think ye, James, of O'Connell holding up his hands in horror at the death of one English pugilist before the superior prowess of his honorable and humane antagonist in single combat, and vowing before heaven that he would bring in a bill to amend the law of England and the character of the men of England—by making such manslaughter in all cases murder! He who, in Ireland, would indict capitally magistrate or policeman, for having been compelled to act in defence of their own lives, or the lives of others murderously attacked by an organized army of infuriated madmen, indiscriminately knocking out the brains of men, women, and children, with stones and staves—treading their flesh into the mire—driving their adversaries—adversaries from some senseless feud of which the parties know neither the origin nor the cause—into a lake or river—and not only seeing them drowning and drowned without pity—but frightening away the boats that went to rescue the battered wretches from death!

Shepherd. Alas! for Ireland.

North. From the depth of my heart a voice responds—alas! for Ireland.

Shepherd. Can naething, think ye, sir, be dune for her—the Gem o' the Sea?

North. It would seem to require the touch of some angel's hand—not to burnish up the gem, for it is green as any emerald—not to wipe away the stains of blood that often ruefully redden the verdure when at its brightest—but to heal the heart-wounds and the soul-sores, from which the poison flows—and which seem incurable by human skill, festering, and inflaming, and mortifying, till on all hands are misery, madness, and death.*

Shepherd. Strang—strang—strang.

North. Words weak as water. Two murders a-day!

Shepherd. Wha are the murderers?

North. Almost all Catholics.

Shepherd. The murdered?

North. Almost all Catholics.

Shepherd. It canna be their religion.

North. God forbid I should say it was their religion.

Shepherd. What can be the cause?

North. The wickedness of the heart, infuriated by superstition. The horrid delusion has been long gathering over their conscience, till it has become black as night—and now the eye of the soul—as Conscience has been called—sees not the sanctity of the house of life—and hands break through its walls—without pity and without remorse.

Shepherd. But their priests pray and preach against all such violation o' the first great law o' Nature—they are humane men—and withhold absolution from sinners who come to the confessional dipped and dyed up to the elbows in blood.

* The late Sir Isaac Coffin, a British Admiral (of American descent) excited a laugh in the House of Commons, on one occasion, by declaring that "the only way to pacify Ireland was to put her under water for four-and-twenty hours." It was strange that, years afterwards, he should meet his own death by drowning.—M.

North. Of that I know nothing. But this I know, that if the priests have done their duty, there must be something more dreadful in man's heart than was ever revealed to my own even in the delirious dreams of god-forsaken sleep.

Shepherd. Oh, sir!

North. I take the hint, and cease.

Shepherd. I did na mean, sir, to stap you—but to induce you to strike a less fearsome key—for that ane jarred my heartstrings and my brain—and I was growing sick.

North. Down with the Church is the cry.

Shepherd. And I'm no surprised that it is—for the Church does na deserve to staun when sic atrocities are rife beneath its shelter or its shadow, and prosper among the services of its most faithful and devoted Ministers. I never liked the Popish Church; but then, to be sure, I am a Protestant—and, what is worse, a Presbyterian bigot.

North. Down with the Protestant Church in Ireland!—that is the cry.*

Shepherd. Fools.

North. Madmen—and worse than madmen. Knowledge is Power—Knowledge is Pleasure—Knowledge is Wealth—Knowledge is Virtue—Knowledge is Happiness—

Shepherd. Oh! that it were! and earth in time might be an image of Heaven in Eternity!

North. Hymns and odes—had I the genius—would I sing in praise of Knowledge—for from Heaven descended the voice that said, "KNOW THYSELF."

Shepherd. Try.

North. No—dumb am I at those divine words—as in presence of a spirit—as in hearing of a spirit's voice. The minds of men were kindled—and lo! the REFORMATION dawned, and in that dawn was disclosed the true aspect of the skies. And scorn we now that light—now that it has climbed high up in heaven, and far and wide spread the blessing of meridian day?

Shepherd. Sir?

North. Tithes—tithes—tithes—abuses—abuses—abuses—are now the watchword and reply. And by whom are they yelled?

* The Irish law-established Protestant Church, immensely wealthy, had comparatively few members, the bulk of the nation holding a different, and, indeed, a hostile faith. The Conservatives claimed that the Irish Church should not be interfered with:—The moderate Reformers urged that, after all necessary ecclesiastical purposes had been provided for, the surplus should be applied to public education;—the ultra-Liberals demanded that the Church property should be wholly confiscated for the benefit of the State, every man paying his own pastor, on the voluntary system:—the Ministry steered a middle course, giving satisfaction to none. They lent (what finally became a gift) the sum of £1,000,000 to the Irish clergy, in lieu of the arrears of tithes which the Catholics refused to pay, and they abolished two Arch-bishoprics and ten bishoprics, but declined pushing the measure for appropriating the great surplus Church revenue to purposes not purely ecclesiastical.—M.

Not by poor, naked, hungry, ignorant, misconstructed, superstitious savages alone—nor by the fierce and reckless agitators that drive them into convulsions—for then we could understand the folly we deplored, and the wickedness we abhorred—but by men holding the Protestant faith—of which the cardinal belief is—that all good which man can enjoy on earth must be generated by the light of the Christian religion—and that that light is in the Bible as in a Sun.

Shepherd. It's an awfu' thing to think o' wide districts, sprinkled wi' touns and villages, and clachans, and thousands o' single houses, a' crowded wi' human beings, and no' ane o' them, for fear o' divine displeasure, suffered to read the Word o' God!

North. Dismal. And in that land a war waged against Protestantism by Christian statesmen! The Protestant Church is the cause of all this darkness, all this distraction, all this guilt! Therefore, let its altars be desecrated—its ministers despoiled—its services destroyed—its pride brought low with all its towers—and that meek, humble, and holy faith substituted and restored, which diffused peace and good-will to men, wide as day, from the Seven Hills on which it sat so long enthroned in simplicity, and as with an angel's voice did "indicate the ways of God to man!"

Shepherd. I wush you was Prime Minister.

North. What, in place of Lord Melbourne?

Shepherd. Wha's he? I never heerd o' him afore.

North. Nay, James. Stanley and Graham—

Shepherd. I've read some o' their speeches—

North. ——ought to have seen long before they did that their colleagues were a gang of church-robbers.* I have always admired both the men—but I cannot comprehend how they, eagle-eyed, were stone-blind to what was visible to the very moles.

Shepherd. They had unwittingly been hoodwinked—but as for moles being blin', you would hear a different story were you to ask the worms.

North. Therefore they resigned—and all the church-robbers in the kingdom shouted aloud for joy.

Shepherd. What think ye, sir, made Lord Grey resign? Was it a voluntary descent or a forced fa'?

North. A little of both.

Shepherd. I did na see your name, sir, in the list o' stewards—was you at the great Grey Denner?

North. Sir, Eh? What?

Shepherd. But tell me—though you was na there—was it a failure or a succeed?

* Mr. Stanley, Sir James Graham, and the Duke of Richmond, members of the Reform Ministry, resigned office rather than accede to the proposal for appropriation of surplus Church property, in Ireland, to secular purposes.—M.

North. Much folly and falsehood, I am sorry to say, all parties are guilty of, in describing Political Meetings got up by their adversaries; and so far from thinking that we Conservatives are less liable to the charge than the Destructives, be they Whigs or Radicals, I shall not be surprised to see myself taken to task, by the low-flying Tories, for declaring that in my opinion, the Edinburgh Dinner to Lord Grey was, on the whole, honorable to him, and creditable to our reformers.

Tickler. On the whole! Reformers!

North. With ten points of scornful admiration, if you please—for I do not believe that a greater mass of ignorance, prejudice, bigotry, stupidity, and vulgarity, were ever collected together under one roof.

Shepherd. Dinna ye?

Tickler (roused). Dishonesty and malignity.

North. Two-thirds of the two thousand five hundred males there assembled were of the lowest intellectual grade, and in the meanness of their moral nature, into which not one ennobling sentiment has ever been inspired by education or experience, incapable of comprehending any one of the great principles on which is founded the stability of a constitution in Church or State.

Shepherd. Ye're speakin' o' the Radicals.

North. No. Of the blind leading the blind—their name is Legion, for there are many—and not a few Radicals are among them—but far the greater number are Whigs.

Tickler. In Edinburgh there are ten Whigs for one Radical in good society——

Shepherd. What ca' ye gude society?

North. I presume the society of honest men.

Tickler. Right. But, as regards our argument, James, I mean by good society, the society of honest men of the middle ranks—for below that I fear most men at present suppose that they are Radicals—and I presume there were not many of that class at the dinner to Lord Grey.

Shepherd. They had mair sense than to get up a guinea for a cauld denner and a bottle o' cork'd port.

North. Eight hundred men—I calculate on data not to be denied by any one acquainted with Scotland—were present at that dinner, worthy to welcome to Scotland, and to Edinburgh, any Statesman.

Tickler. I agree with you, North. You and I do not lay any great stress on what is called the nobility and gentry present on that occasion—for they, though respectable, were sparse—but without excluding such sprinklings—and acknowledging with pleasure the high character of the Noble Chairman—we declare that the strength of the assemblage lay in those citizens who had either raised themselves from a humble condition to what is rightly called a high—or added lustre to the condition in which they happened to have been born—by their own moral and intellectual worth—or by the endowment of genius.

Shepherd. Genius?

North. Yes, genius. Henry Cockburn—now a Judge—which I am glad of—did not, to be sure, write the Queen's Wake—nor is Sir Thomas Dick Lauder the Editor of Blackwood's Magazine—nor did Andrew Skene write Adam Blair—nor Andrew Rutherford the Lights and Shadows of Scottish Life—nor Robert Jamieson the Trials of Margaret Lindsay—but have they not done far more difficult things—if not as good, or better? And think ye that the same powers that have raised them (the Painter and Poet of the great Morayshire Floods, out of politics, is one of ourselves, James, and though we need not vail our bonnets to him, we wear them in his presence but as equals*) to the highest eminence in law, might not, if directed into that pleasanter channel have won them as high a place in literature?

Shepherd. No in poetry, sir, no in po——

Tickler. Poo upon poetry! Fire away, Kit.

North. The educated classes in Scotland—and I allow a wide latitude to the term educated—were much divided on the question of reform. All true Conservatives abhorred the bill—many—nay, all moderate Whigs—feared it in much—and the wildest disliked some of its most improvident provisions—it was welcomed in its reckless radicalism but by the Destructives.

Shepherd. Truth uttered by Wisdom.

Tickler. Therefore not even the eighth hundred could have been unanimous in their approbation of the statesmanship of Lord Grey.

North. No, indeed. Not even had they been all the most violent of Whigs; but of the six hundred Whigs worthy the name—for I skim away the scum—a half at least had all their lives—as you well know, Tickler—deprecated such reform—a quarter of them at least had long abjured its principles—while the remaining fourth—with the exception of such men as Mr. Greenshiels, and a few other grave enthusiasts—men of talent and virtue—were either worthy old fogies, who took a pride in seeing doctrines triumphant in their age, which they had vainly battled for in a pedantic war of words in their youth, or worthy young fogies, whom—as I do not wish to be personal—I shall not name at a Noctes—following in their train, and fondly imagining themselves all the while to be leaders—or unworthy young fogies—yet still of reputable character——

* Sir T. D. Lauder.—M.

Tickler. *Yawp* for the loaves and fishes.

Shepherd. And what say ye o' the respectable Radicals?

North. Of the eight hundred, they may have composed about two; and though I do not well know what they would be at, I do know that, if they speak the truth, they now think very little of Lord Grey.

Tickler. I think, North, you may, in round numbers, say a thousand. For a half-a-dozen from this place—and half-a-score from that—and so on in proportion to the size of the clachan—having no political principles at all—but entertaining a certain vague admiration of what are called liberal opinions—and admirers in a small, but not insincere way, of something they choose to call consistency—and having been assured by the wise men of the village, well read in Annual Registers, that Lord Grey carried into effect the same plan of reform in 1831 that he had advocated in 1792—at great inconvenience, considerable expense, and some danger, came on outside places by heavy coaches to the great Grey dinner, and astonished their families on their return with descriptions of the Immense Wooden Erection, and the great lustre from the Theatre-Royal, dependent from the centre of the roof, and lighted with gas by pipes laid on purpose in cuts from the main conduit—a Fairy Palace!

North. My friend Hamilton is a man of skill, taste, and genius; and I am told the Pavilion was beautiful.

Shepherd. Was the denner really in great part devoor'd afore Yearl Grey took his seat by the side o' your worthy freend, the Lord Provost?

Tickler. Not in great part devoured, James. The enemies of the Church began collecting their tithes. Perhaps a dozen tongues, as many howtowdies, half a score hams, two or three pigeon and some fifty mutton-pies were gobbled up without grace—and I believe a few buttocks of beef met with the same premature fate; but there was nothing like a general attack—and I wish that to be known in England, for the credit of my countrymen.

Shepherd. Abstinence under sic circumstances did them immortal honor—for imitation and sympathy are twa o' the strangest active principles in human nature; and the wonder is, that in ten minutes they did no soop the board. Cry "Fire" in a crooded kirk, and the congregation treads and chokes itsell to death in makin' for the doors. Cry "Fa' to" in a crooded Pavilion, and at the first clatter o' knife and fork on the trencher, what cou'd hae been expected but that twa thoosand five hunder Reformers would hae been ruggin' awa at fish, flesh, and fule, afore they discovered that it was a false alarm?

Tickler. The justification is complete.

Shepherd. Besides, them that did fasten on the vittals—by your account few in number—perhaps no abune a hunder or twa—havin' been in the open air a' day, assistin' at the Procession, maun hae been desperate hungry—and few temptations are waur to resist than a sappy ham.* Whigs, too, are great gluttons——

North. We Tories again are epicures.

Shepherd. As may be seen at a Noctes, where we eat little, but very fine.

North. I cannot charge my memory with a case of ante-benediction gluttony at a great public Conservative dinner. Can you, James?

Shepherd. I never hear the grace at a great public denner—though I sometimes see an auld body at a distance haudin' up his haun—but I certainly canna charge my memory wi' ony instance o' ony pairt o' ony Christian company consumin' tongues, howtowdies, hams, pigeon and mutton-pies, and buttocks o' beef, afore the arrival o' the guest in whase honor, and in whase presence, it was intended the denner should be devoor'd—to say naething o' his participation. Sic behaviour is in fact mair like beasts than men—and I dinna believe ony thing like it ever took place even in a doug-kennel. Jowlers are vorawcious brutes, but they sit on their hurdies wi' waterin' chaps, till the whupper-in or the huntsman gies the signal—or cries, Soss! Soss! Soss! and then with one accord the canines crunch their cracklines.

North. Lord Grey spoke well—his demeanor was dignified—and he was listened to and looked at—as he deserved by his friends—with respect and admiration.

Shepherd. By you?

North. My dear Shepherd, I was not there—but I had an account of the evening from a Whig friend, on whose face I never can look without believing that he is a Tory. To my mind, Lord Grey disgraced himself by his vile misrepresentation of the sentiments that had been lately expressed by many distinguished Irish Protestants, lay and clerical, respecting the state of the Church and its affairs—and they are closely interwoven with the vital interests of the whole community—sentiments honorable to their character as men, and perfectly consistent with all Christian charities—but the expression of which had been grossly falsified by base reporters, who had been exposed by the calumniated to universal scorn. In this Lord Grey showed obstinate ignorance, at once comtemptible and hateful; and on reading it, I covered my face with my hands to hide the burning blushes of shame that tingled there for sake of

* A great dinner was given to Lord Grey, at Edinburgh, in the autumn of 1834, at which Brougham, Durham, and other leading liberals were present. The greater portion of the viands were eaten up, by the hungry ticket-purchasers, before the guests had entered the pavilion!—M.

Lord Brougham, who chimed in with the peevish and malignant reproach—while he had the brazen assurance to declare, that he had heard then for the first time of the shocking outrage, by fierce Protestant bigotry, on the meek Popish spirit of love—for that he, forsooth, had not read the sevenpenny newspapers for some time back—an absurd and indeed incredible inconsistency in the grim genitor of the Twa-Bawbee Magazine.*

Shepherd. Me and Hairy Brumm's great freens, and batin' yoursell, sir, he's the grandest companion I ken, either in a mixed company o' ordinar dimensions, or at a twa-haun' crack. He seems to hae made a kind o' triumphal progress or procession through Scotland in a post-chaise, and nae doot occasionally fowre horses; and I was glad to see for my ain sake, that the Lord Chancellor received the freedom o' the same burgs that, twenty years sin' syne, had conferred that honor on me for the Queen's Wake.

Tickler. Scotland has reason to be proud of your friend, James; for with her he passed his brilliant youth, and within the walls of our own College, and of our own old Parliament House, was first seen fitfully shining that mental fire which ere long burst into so bold and bright a blaze, and illumined his high career in the English Courts of Law, and the greatest Legislative Assembly in the world.

Shepherd. He was a real orator.

Tickler. He led the Commons—and had no equal but Canning.

North. He never led the Commons, and he was no match for Canning.

Shepherd. What ails the Times at Hairy Brumm?

North. Hang me if I know.

Shepherd. They'll no be able to rin him doon, sir.

North. The Times hits hard—fights at points—is good with both hands—up to all the manœuvres of the London Ring—always in tip-top condition—and in a close seldom fails in getting the fall either by back-lock or cross-buttock. He can lick all London dailies—though some of them are strong wiry chaps—and very ugly customers—all but the Standard—and the fine science and great strength of the Standard have given him the championship of the press.†

Shepherd. They say the Times fechts booty?

North. They who said so lied—he is above a bribe—and by his own power purchases his own gold. But there are other passions besides the "auri sacra fames"—other devils besides Mammon.

* *Bawbee*—a penny (or two cents) hence the name here given to the Penny Magazine, published by the Society for the Diffusion of Useful Knowledge, of which Brougham was founder and president.—M.

† Of the Tory press;—not otherwise.—M.

Shepherd. I weel ken that. There's Belial—and there's Beelzebub—and there's Lucifer—and there's——

North. These three are sufficient—you need not mention any more—and they are all gentlemen of the press.

Shepherd. And a' against Hairy Brumm?

North. Certainly not—unless they have lost all regard for consistency of character. Lucifer and he are friends for life.

Shepherd. I smell brimstone.

Tickler. Merely candle-snuff. One cannot choose but smile, to hear the Times telling how he patronized Brougham, and made him Lord Chancellor of England. Yet the boast is not without truth. The Press was a powerful auxiliar to his own great power—and in his favor the Times for years led the Press. It cut down his foes—it cleared his way—it cheered him on—it "bound his brows with victorious wreaths;" and now that "the winter of its discontent" hath come—the question is, will it have the force of frost or blight to wither them?

Shepherd. Na.

North. But it is base in Brougham to abuse the Press, merely because it now abuses him; for, during all the many long years it bore him up on its strang wings—yet he of himself could fly and soar—the Press, he well knew was systematically maligning better men, his rivals in the race, and never one word did he utter in its dispraise, till he had laid his own hand on the goal—and then, on an unwonted and unwelcome clamor assailing his ears—loud, indeed, but less truculent than had, to his great satisfaction, tormented superior spirits—superior inasmuch as Wisdom is a nobler gift than Wit, and TALENT but the servant of Virtue—then he turned round, with "visage all inflamed"——

Shepherd. "Sawtan dilated stood"——

North. ——and told the people of England, that he regarded the Press with contempt and scorn!

Shepherd. Hairy shou'd na' had said that—for o' a' the steam-engines that ever clattered, the maist like a leevin' giant is the Printing Machine.

North. With all his sins, Lord Brougham is worth a coal-wagon-train-full of Durhams. It is too ludicrous for laughing to see Lambton pitting himself against such a man. True, he confesses his inferiority in powers of speech; but in the very confession his poor pride is apparent; for by that candor he thinks he proves his claim to superior worth. Now the truth is, that the Coalmaster* approaches nearer to the Chancellor in eloquence than in any other natural or acquired gift; for it is wonderful how well he speaks, and he possesses no despicable power of jaw. He is a third-rate radical

* Lord Durham's property, which was large, consisted principally of coal-mines.—M.

rhetorician, and has a command of loose, lumbering language, very unpleasant to listen to, which he can atrabilariously keep delivering for a trying extent of time. But in powers of thought, he is a mere man of the multitude; in his harangues nobody looks for ideas; and his very admirers direct you, for proofs of his abilities, to his forehead and his face. Both are indeed beautiful—but "fronti nula fides" is an old saw and a wise one—and he would soon become indeed a jaundiced observer, who appealed to the color of his cheeks. Brougham is no beauty; but his mug is a book, in which men may read strange matters—and take him as he stands face and figure, and you feel that there is a man of great energy—and commanding intellect. His brain swarms with ideas—of which some have been almost magnificent—and his heart has been often visited by high and generous emotions, which but for a restless temper might have found there an abiding place; and but that conscience has too often been overcome by ambition, might have made him morally as well as intellectually great, and one of the most illustrious worthies of England.

Shepherd. Was na't Lord Durham that flew intil sic a fury again' the newspapers for sayin' something aboot the flag o' his pleesur yatt—and was for finin' and imprisonin' folk for some folly o' theirs aboot some folly o' his, somehoo or ither conneckit wi' the three-colore, and the Cherburgh rods, and the Tyne Louisa, and the Newcastle colliers, and some nonsense about depopulation o' a village, and breakin' doon some rails in the Isle o' Wight, and compromiseen some act, by payin' the law expenses, and makin' affidavits aboot falsehoods, and——

North. It was—and I am only astonished, James, at your retaining so distinct a recollection of so many pitiable exposures made of himself by the Champion and Guardian of the Liberty of the Press.*

Shepherd. Whether, sir, did you admire maist the Grey Festival here in Embro', or the Durham Demonstration yonder in Glasgow?

North. Ask Tickler.

Tickler. For your opinion? Hem. Pray, Kit, what was demonstrated by the Durham Demonstration?

North. That the stomachs of the Glasgow Radicals revolt from wine.

Shepherd. Was that a'?

North. Not all—but the most important point, established by the plainest proofs.

Shepherd. I could hae telt that before-haun'; for wine's waur nor wersh in the mooth to workmen, either in toon or kintra;—and forbye bein' waur nor wersh in the mooth, it's sickening to the

* Lord Durham's yacht had hoisted the tri-color over the British flag, and he prosecuted the *Newcastle Journal* (a Tory paper) for chronicling the fact.—M.

stammach, and it's irritatin' to the temper, and gars folk throw up ither things in folk's faces than mere indigested political maitters. I've seen that happen even amang Tories in the Forest, and we never thocht o' ca'in't by ony ither than the ordinar' idiomatic name; but noo we shall adopt that grand-soundin' descriptive phraseology—Durham Demonstration.

Tickler. Your justification of the Glasgow Radicals is as complete, James, as your justification of the Edinburgh Whigs.

Shepherd. It's founded sir, on the same constitutional principles —and in baith cases the chief blame lies at the door o' the fresh air. Fifeteen hunder men o' the hunder and fifety thoosan'—I like roun' nummers—to whose care and custody Lord Durham said he was willing to intrust his property and his life (I wunner hoo mony years' purchase they wou'd in that case be worth), comin' frae the caller air o' the open Green intil the foul air of the close-box o' the Pavilion, and sookin' port, cou'dna be expeckit to get wi' impunity to the dregs at the bottom o' the bottle. But the Men o' the Wast are a strang generation, and no sune cowpit—sae they kept their seats in spite o' the soomin' roun' o' the wa's—and a' attempts o' the seats theirsells to steal a march oot frae beneath them—and opened their mouths for—a public Durham Demonstration on a great scale. They made, in fack, a virtue o' necessity; and as it is wrang to hide your talent under a napkin, they exhibited the fruits o' theirs on the table.

Tickler. By way of dessert.

Shepherd. They were determined, sirs, that every thing should be aboon boord——and disdainin' to keep down their risin' emotions, to mak a clean briest. In this way, it may be said, by a metonymy——

Tickler. A metonymy!

Shepherd. ——that they discharged their consciences, and were entitled, with as good a grace as Lord Brougham, to hauld them up and exclaim, "These hands are clean."

North. It must have been a proud sight for the wives and daughters of the Demonstrators, and that anonymous class of ladies whom the Gander alluded to, as dearer even than wives and daughters—

Shepherd. Wha are they?

North. He best knows. I should have felt for Lord Durham at the shockingly insulting stop put to his return of thanks on an occasion on which I verily believe no man was ever so interrupted before—not even at a supper after the Beggars' Opera in Poossie Nancy's—had he not had the ineffable baseness to exclaim, "That comes from a Tory—there's an enemy in the camp." It required no readiness to improvise such a foolish falsehood—and he must have been ashamed of himself for venting it, when, sick of the scene, he retired from the Pavilion, in vain attempting to pick his steps among the *disjecta membra* of the Durham Demonstration, that had for hours been oozing through the joints of the deal-tables, till they adorned the floor.

Shepherd. "O laith! laith! was the Durham Lord,
To wat his high-heeled shoon."

North. Lord Grey exultingly asked the wise men of the East, if any symptoms of reaction were visible in that magnificent show; Lord Brougham told them, that he had been all over the north, and could assure them that there were none visible to the naked eye, on hill or dale; and to crown all, Lord Durham—with the most extraordinary symptoms of reaction before him ever disclosed to the human senses—declared there was none in the West; and yet these three very Lords were all the while at loggerheads and daggers-drawing, about men and measures—and two of them—the learned Lord and the unlearned Lord—objects of mutual hatred—that feeling in the one being mitigated by contempt, and in the other exasperated by envy.

Tickler. Brougham insidiously ousts Grey, and Grey indignantly cuts Brougham.

North. Brougham sneeringly glances at Durham, and Durham savagely growls at Brougham.

Tickler. Brougham accuses Durham of clipping and paring the Bill of Reform.

North. And Durham—had his father-in-law not told him that only bad boys broke oaths and told lies—would have accused Brougham of proposing to castrate it.

Tickler. And after all this vulgar bickering, at once anile and childish, we are told the nation is unanimous.

North. And a Whig-Rad government the object of its holy reverence and undying love!

Shepherd. What wou'd the warld say if we three cast oot in that gate?

North. Easier far for a new set of men to carry on the government than the Noctes Ambrosianæ.

Shepherd. That's just what the warld wou'd say gin it heard on the same day that the Whig government and the Tory magazine had been baith dissolved.

Mr. Ambrose (*entering in full tail, and looking into his hat in hand*). I have this moment, sir, received—by express—a single copy of the Sun newspaper*—and I have—the honor and happiness—of being the first to announce—to Mr. North—that the Melbourne ministry is dissolved and that—his Majesty—has been——that—his Majesty—has—been—graciously pleased—to intrust—

* Famous, at that time, for its rapid transmission of news, by express.—M.

his Grace the Duke of Wellington—with the formation of a Conservative Government.

(*Exeunt* AMBROSE *and Tail, with a bow and a wag.*)

Shepherd. That's a curious coincidence.

Tickler. What is?

Shepherd. I was just opening my mouth to predict the doonfa' o' the Whiggamores, when in cam the express!

Tickler. A prophet should never sit with his mouth open, for more than five minutes at a time, on the eve of an intended prediction; for "when great events are on the gale," one of them may fly, as it did now, into the aperture, to the discredit of the craft.

Shepherd. Did na I see the conflagration o' baith Houses o' Parliament foretokened in the ribbs at Tibbie's?

Tickler. You certainly did, James.

Shepherd. A King's messenger came for me frae Lunnon to tak me up for examination before the Preevy Council; but I kent better than to gang; for the black ggemm were packin', and by firin' out o' the study-wundow, I cou'd murder a dizzen at ae discharge.

Tickler. O thou Murderer and Incendiary!

Shepherd. Sae I enticed the Cockney to tak a look at the graymare's tail on our way to Moffat for the mail-cotch, and while he was glowerin' at the water-preevilege—as the Americans ca't—I slippet intil yon cozey cave, kent but to the Covenanters o' auld, and noo but to the shepperds—and left him sair perplexed to think that he had been apprehending a speerit.

Tickler. I trust, James, you had no hand in the fire?

Shepherd. I shanna say. It seems rather tyrannical in a Whig Preevy Cooncil to send doon an offisher a' the way to the Forest to apprehend the Shepherd for hain the second sicht. But they hae met wi' their punishment. They're oot.

Tickler. Such events are seldom attributed at the time to the true causes—and ages may elapse before another D'Israeli, in the course of his indefatigable researches, discover that it was the Ettrick Shepherd who overthrew this brazen-faced Dagon with leathern body and feet of clay.

Shepherd. Unless Girrney let the cat oot o' the bag.

Small thin Voice. Hip—hip—hip—hurra! hurra! hurra!

Shepherd. Only look, Mr. Tickler, at North! lyin' back on his chair—wi' shut een—that thoughtfu' face o' his calm as a cloud—wi' his hauns faulded on his briest—pressed palm to palm—the fingers pintin' towards ye like the tips o' arrows—and the thoombs like javelins! Wheesht! he's gaun till utter.

North. There will be much brutal abuse of the King. The Whigs hated George the Good, and they had not hearts capable of disinheriting the Son, of the curses with which they clothed the

Sire. That hatred was first transferred to George the Graceful; and then it hovered like a hornet round the head of William the Brave. Lured by the scent of prey, it flew off for a while—but now it will return, hot as hell, and settle, if it be not scared away, on the royal brow. Nay, the filthy fly will attempt the temples of the Queen,* and its venomous sting will threaten veins translucent with purest and hallowed blood.

Shepherd. Damn them—I beg my pardon—that was wrang—will they blackguard Queen Adelaide?

North. What they did they will do again.

Shepherd. The dowgs will return to their vomit.

North. The lowest of the Radicals will join in that charge—nor will the highest gainsay the ribaldry of the rabble—but like philosophers, as they all pretend to be, let human nature take its course. But the PEOPLE OF BRITAIN will not suffer the slander—and high up above the reach of foulest vapors, before their eyes will our Queen be seen shining like a star.

Shepherd. God bless the people o' Britain! Wi' a' their fawtes—and they are great and mony—shaw me sic anither people on the face o' the yearth.

North. As for his Most Gracious Majesty he has been in fire before now—and our King, who never turned his head aside for hissing balls and bullets, will hold it erect on the Throne of the Three Kingdoms, as he did on the quarterdeck of a man-of-war, nor heed, if he hear, the vain hurtling of windy words.

Tickler. There is little loyalty in the land now, North.

North. Little—compared with that elevating virtue as it breathed in many million bosoms some twenty or thirty years ago—but more than lives in the heart of any other people towards their chief magistrate—for that now—though a somewhat cold—is the correct and accredited word. In other, and perhaps in nobler times, there was much in common between loyalty to a king, patriotism to a country, and the zeal of the martyrs of religion.

Shepherd. I ca' that a true Holy Alliance.

North. But we must make the best of our own times; and every man do his utmost to uphold the powers and principles that constitute the strength of our national character.

Shepherd. Enumerate, sir.

North. Not now. Our ideas and feelings of loyalty, however, we must not adopt from them who were last week his Majesty's ministers, nor from the double-faced, double-tongued crew that will be

* *The Times* announced "The Ministry are out. THE QUEEN HAS DONE IT ALL."—The fact was, William IV. had become timid, seeing the ministerial measures denounced by the majority of the House of Lords, and the Queen (a strong partisan) was always at hand to prophecy ruin to the empire if the Whigs continued in office. This was her gratitude to the country for voting her £100,000 per annum, for life, besides rent free and tax free Palaces, and other pickings.—M.

seizing on their dismissal as an occasion for venting their rage against him whom, for four years, they have been hypocritically worshipping for their own base purposes, and incensing with perfumery that must have long stunk in the royal nostrils.

Tickler. The Modern Alfred! Alfred the Second!

North. Faugh! let us speak as we feel of our king, in a spirit of truth. True loyalty scorns the hyperbole, and is sparing of figures of speech. To the patriot statesman, whom true loyalty inspires, history is no old almanack; for an old almanack is the deadest of all dead things—and more useless than dust. To him history is a record ever new—all its pages are instinct with life—and its examples show the road to honor on earth, and happiness in heaven. Let us not fear to compare our King with his Peers. The place assigned him by posterity will be a high one; and among his many noble qualities will be reckoned scorn of sycophancy, and intolerance of falsehood. As long as his servants served him according to their oath—in its spirit as well as its letter—he was willing to make sacrifice of some thoughts and feelings that to him were sacred, of some opinions so deeply rooted he could not change, though he could give them up—but as soon as he saw and knew that he must not only sacrifice feelings, and relinquish opinions, but violate his conscience, he exerted his prerogative—a prerogative bestowed by God—and called on that MAN,* who had been the Saviour of his country, again to rescue her from danger—by the weight of his wisdom, and the grandeur of his name, to bear down her internal enemies, as, by his valor and his genius, he had crushed or scattered all foreign foes—so that the land, by a succession of bloodless, and, therefore, still more glorious victories, might again enjoy that liberty which consists in order and peace.

Shepherd. You dinna fear, sir, I howp, that there will be ony very serious disturbances in the kintra, on account o' the change o' Ministry?

North. I think there will be a great deal of very ludicrous disturbances in the country, on account of the change of Ministry, and that the People will find it so difficult to assume a serious countenance, on the kicking out of the Whigs—if kicking out it has been—that they will almost immediately give over trying it, and join in a good-humored, yet perhaps a rather malicious, peal of hearty laughter.

Shepherd. That's a great relief to my mind. But are ye sure, sir, o' the Political Unions?

North. Quite sure. It is not improbable that they may be revived

* Wellington, who declined the Premiership, but did the work of all the different departments, in the three weeks which elapsed from the time when Peel was sent for, to Italy, and his return to England.—M.

in a small sort of way, but half a million of men will not march up to London from Birmingham, as about half a dozen men talked of their intending to do in the delirium of the Bill-fever.

Shepherd. It maun be a populous place, that Brummagem, as the Bagmen ca't.

North. Very. For my own part, I rather liked the Whig government.

Shepherd. Whatttt?

North. For it is an amiable weakness of mine to feel kindness towards any man or body of men whom I see the object of very general contempt or anger. No ministry in my time was ever so unpopular—to use the gentlest term—as the one t'other day turned to the right about—and as for my Lord Melbourne, though you, James, say you never heard of him—I know him to be one of the most amiable and accomplished men—and that is saying much—in the Peerage. So that I am sorry that any Ministry, of which he was the head, should have been so universally despised when living, and so universally ridiculed when dead.

Shepherd. That seems to me a new view o' the subject.

North. However, it is the true one. I am disposed to think they were not kicked out—but that they backed out, in a state of such weakness, that had there been any rubbish in the way, they would have fallen over it, and injured their organs of philoprogenitiveness and Number One. All the world has known for some time that they intended to resign on the meeting of Parliament—for they had got quarrelsome in their helplessness—as teething childhood, or toothless age.

Tickler. I wish your friend Brougham, James, would publish his epistolary correspondence with the King during his Lordship's late visit to Scotland.

Shepherd. But wou'dna that be exposing family—that is, Cabinet secrets? And Hairy wou'd never do that, after the dressin' he is thocht to hae gi'en Durham on that point. Besides, it wou'd be awfu' to publish the King's letters to him without his Majesty's consent!

Tickler. I think I can promise him his Majesty's permission to publish all the letters the Lord Chancellor ever received in Scotland from his most gracious Master.*

* Lord Brougham made a tour through Scotland in the autumn of 1834, and was very well received. On one or two occasions he is reported to have said, in acknowledgment of this kindness, that when next he wrote to the King, he should certainly mention their loyalty, as partly evinced by their reception of himself, the first officer of the Crown. It is probable that he did *not* say any thing of the sort, but it was so reported, and was said to have reached the ears of William IV., who was also said to be displeased with the familiarity it indicated. In a few weeks after this, (November 14, 1834) the Melbourne Ministry were literally turned out of office, on a very slight pretext, by William IV., who commissioned Wellington to form an administration. At his recomendation that task was confided to Peel, who was then on a tour in Italy. He was sent for, and it may be remarked, as corroboratory of *The Times'* strong statement, on the dis-

North. Umph. The vol. would sell—title, "Letters from the Mountains."

Shepherd. Na—that wou'd be stealin' the title o' a delichtfu' wark o' my auld freen Mrs. Grant's.

North. I think I can promise him Mrs. Grant's permission to pub lish under the title of what you justly call, James, her very delightful work,* all the letters the Lord Chancellor ever wrote to his Most Gracious Majesty from Inverness, Elgin, Dundee, Edinburgh, or Hawick.

Shepherd. A' impediments in the way o' publication being thus removed, I shall write this verra nicht—sae that my letter may leave the post-office by to-morrow's post—to Lord Brumm to send down the MSS.—and they maun be a' holographs in the parties' ain haun-writing—to Messrs A. and R. Blackwood—and I shall stay a month in Embro', that I may correct the press mysell—in which case I houp there may be a black frost, that at leisure hours we may hae some curlin'.

North. The Grey Ministry, in its best days, was never, somehow or other, inordinately admired by the universal British nation.

Tickler. That was odd. For the nation, I have heard it said, was for Reform to a man.

North. All but some dozen millions or thereabouts—but people are never so prone to discontent as when they have had everything their own way—especially when, as it happened in this case, not one in a thousand knows either what he had been wanting, or what he has got, or what else he would wish to have, if at his bidding or beck the sky were willing that moment to rain it down among his feet.

Tickler. They surely were the most foolish financiers that ever tried taxation.

North. Of not one of them could it be sung,

> "That even the story ran that he could gauge."

They were soon seen to be equally ignorant and incapable on almost all other subjects; nor—except with Brougham—was there a gleam of genius—nor a trait of talent beyond mediocrity—to make occasional amends for their deplorable deficiencies as men of no-

solution of the Melbourne Ministry, "The Queen has done it all," that the confidental messenger sent for Peel was Mr. Hudson, *one of the Queen's pages*—who, by the way, was this introduced into public life, and had risen in 1852 (the last time his name crossed me) to the position of Envoy Extraordinary and Minister Plenipotentiary from England to the Court of Tuscany. Peel's government, resisted by the Whigs, whom O'Connell, a few days previously, had denounced as "base, bloody, and brutal," was broken up in April, 1835. The Melbourne Cabinet was recalled—with the sole exception of Lord Chancellor Brougham—and this pointed omission was said to have been made by special desire of the King, who had recollected what had been said, in the previous autumn, of the letter writing from Scotland.—M.

* Mrs. Grant of Laggan, whose "Memoirs of an American Lady" are well known in this country, wrote a variety of other works, among which her "Letters from the Mountains" take the lead. She died in 1838, aged seventy-seven.—M.

business habits, and of non-acquaintance equally with principles and with details.

Tickler. Hollo! we are forgetting Stanley and Graham.

North. So we are, I declare—but I hope they will forgive us—since they too often, or rather too long, forgot themselves—and I should be happy to see them—whether Ins or Outs—at a Noctes. Their secession left the Reform Ministry in a state of destitution more pitiable than that of any pauper-family under the operation of the new Poor Law.

Tickler. Strange how it contrived to stand for the last six months—yet all of us must have many a time seen a tree, Kit, lopped, barked, grubbed—remaining pretty perpendicular during a season of calm weather—by means of some ligature so light as to be invisible—till a brisk breeze smites the skeleton, and down he goes—whether with or against his own inclination you can hardly say—so resignedly among the brushwood doth he lay his shorn and shaven head.

Shepherd. Haw—Haw—Haw! But it's no lauchin' maitter. I'm glad after a', sir, that at this creesis you're no Prime Minister. The Duke 'll hae aneuch to do to get a'richt—and to keep a'richt—and I only wuss Sir Robert were hame again frae Tureen.

North. So do I. A Conservative Ministry can now be formed, stronger in talent, knowledge, eloquence, integrity, power, and patriotism, than any ministry the country has had within the memory of man.

Shepherd. Then whare's the difficulty wi' the Duke?

North. I will tell you, James, some night soon. The difficulties are strong and formidable—and there must be a dissolution.

Tickler. The Ex-Chancellor has assured us that the Press has lost all its power—so the elections will not be disturbed by that engine. The Whigs disdain to use bribery and corruption—and the Rads, for sufficient reasons, seldom commit such sins. No Reformer would condescend to receive a consideration from a Tory. A fair field, therefore, lies open to all parties—and, though not of a sanguine but melancholious temperament, I will bet a barrel of oysters with any man that the new House of Commons will back the Duke.

North. He will carry by large majorities, all his measures of Conservative Reform in Church and State.* He did so before the Bill was the law of the land—and he will do so now that he is the law of the land—but, to speak plainly, gentlemen, I am getting confounded sleepy; and I feel as if I were speaking in a nightcap.

* Peel knew, on taking office in 1834, that it was impossible to govern except on the principle of Progress. He was prepared with measures of Reform in Church and State, but the unexpected alliance of the Whigs with the O'Connellites turned the scale and threw him out of office.—M.

Shepherd. And I as if there were saun in ma een—sae gie's your airm, sir, and I sall be the chawmermaid that lichts you till your bed. It's wice in you to lodge in the Road sic a nicht.—Do ye hear him—"tirlin' the kirks?" Be a good boy, and never forget to say your prayers.

(*Exeunt the Tres.*)

No. LXX.—JANUARY, 1835.

SCENE—*Old Blue Parlor, Ambrose's, Gabriel's Road. Time, Eight—Present,* NORTH, TICKLER, *and the* SHEPHERD.

North. Yes, James! I do indeed love my country with a passionate devotion—of all my heart, all my soul, and all my mind—far beyond the imagination of your citizen of the world, or your——

Shepherd. Imagination! Your citizen o' the warld hasna abune an inch thick o' soil on his sowle; and the substratum is a cauld till, that keeps the vegetation shiverin' on the surface in a perpetual ague.

Tickler. Good.

Shepherd. Yet vegetation's owre strang a name for the meagre mixtur o' weeds and moss mopin' aloof frae the happy gerss an' floueres—aye wat wi' a sickly sweat—unvisited by bee or butterfly—and only at times travelled in haste by the lang-legged speeder, or the ask that has lost his way——

Tickler. The ask?

North. Or lizard.

Shepherd. They say they're harmless; but I never liked them, sin' we used to bash them wi' stanes, whan we were callants.

Tickler. A most poetical and Christian prejudice.

Shepherd. Is't? I'm thinkin' you're about an equal judge o' poetry and o' Christianity, sir. But what for spoil a feegurative expression? Never be critical in conversation, but accepp what's said—be't the sma'st triffle—frae a man o' genius—and be thankfu'. Noo, you've interuppit the flaw o' my ideas, and lost an illustration that you micht hae committed to memory, and passed it aff as an original ane o' your ain at the card-club.

North. The climate of Scotland is the best in the whole circle of the sky.

Shepherd. And the maist beautifu'. Wha daured to say that the gerss o' Scotland's no green? Is the cheese o' the moon green? Is a grossert green? Is a guse green? Is a fairy's mantle green? Are the een o' an angry cat green? Is a mermaid's hair green? Are the edges o' the Orange islands green, that lie in a sea o' purple and vermilion around the setting sun?

Tickler. There he goes, North.

Shepherd. But no sae green as the gerss o' the Forest, when June makes his bed on the embodied dews o' May, and haps himsell up in a coverlet "o' wee modest crimson-tipped floures"—

North. Daisies.

Shepherd. Just sae—daisies, and their kith and kin—that by their bauld beauty repel the frosts, and gar them melt awa' in tears o' very shame, pity, and repentance, for havin' thocht o' withrin' the earliest gifts o' Flora, profusely scattered owre bank and brae—the sweet-scented, bright-hued embroidery o' nature—

"The simmer to nature, my Willie to me!"

Oh sirs! what a line! I could ban Burns for hae'n said it—instead o' me! But ban I will not—I will bless him—for by it he has made a' Scotland, and a' the daughters o' Scotland, lovelier and mair delightfu' to every Scottish heart.

North. There he goes, Tickler.

Shepherd. Green indeed! Put on a pair o' green specs, and you'll ken whether or no the gerss o' Scotland be green. The optician embues them wi' as intense a glower o' green as science can impart to the assisted human ee—but though they change the snaw into verdure without dissolvin't—they add nae deeper hue to the sward, sir—ma' faith, that's ayont the force o' ony artificial focus—for a green licht is native in every blade on which balances the dewdrap—green licht sae saft, sae tender, sae delicate, that you wonder hoo at the same time it should be sae vivid—sae dazzlin' I had amaist said—and I will say't—sae dazzlin'—for when the sun, seein' some sicht o' mair especial sweetness far doon below on the happy earth, canna help breakin' oot into a shinier smile, aimed frae his throne on high at the heart o' the verra spat where that sweetness lies—oh! but that spat grows insupportably beautifu'! A paradise within a paradise—like—like—like——

Tickler. Like what, James? Don't stutter.

Shepherd. Like a bonnie Sabbath among the bonnie week-days—when they are lovely as the earthly on-goings o' time can ever be—but it's a heavenly floatin' by wi' something mair sacred in the blue skies, and something mair holy in the whiter clouds.

North. God bless you, my dear James.

Tickler. Ditto.

Shepherd. Your hauns, chiels. The English are severe on our cleemat, and our cleemat, when it catches a Cockney in't, is still severer on them—lauchin' a' the while at the cretur's astonishment, when a blash o' sleet suddenly blind his face, or a hail-dance peppers him—a wee bit malicious whurlwund havin' first reversed his umbrella, and then whuppin it oot o' his haun', carried it to the back o' beyond—to be picked up as a curiosity frae Lunnun by some shepherd in anither glen—in anither glen where a' is loun as faery-lawn, and the willow leaves, wi' untwinkling shadows, are imaged in the burnie that has subsided into sleep, and is scarcely seen, no heard ava', to wimple in its dream.

North. I do not remember, James, ever to have seen you under an umbrella.

Tickler. Nor I, James, with ever so much as one under your arm —or used as a walking-stick.

Shepherd. A daft-like walkin'-stick indeed is an umbrella! gie me a gude black thorn, wi' a spike in't. As for carryin' an umbrella aneath ma oxter—I hae a' my life preferred the arm o' a bit lassie cleikin' mine—and whenever the day comes that I'm seen unfurlin' an imbrella, as I'm walkin' or sittin' by mysell, may that day be my last, for it'll be a proof that the pith's a' oot o' me, and that I'm a puir fusionless body, ready for the kirkyard, and my corp no worth the trouble o' howkin' up. Nae weather-fender for the Shepherd but the plaid! I look out intil the lift, and as Tamson shooblimely says—

> "See the deep fermenting tempest brewed
> In the grim evening sky."

But what care I for the grim brewer? What's his browst? Rain or snow—or thunner and lichtenin'—or a' fowre thegither, or what's ca'd elemental war? Thunner and lichtening's gae owsome in winter, I confess; and it's an eerie thing, sirs, to see a whurlwund heepin' up a snaw-drift, by the glare o' heaven's angry ee, that for a moment alloos you a look intil the nicht! And nae man kens what thunner is, wha hasna heard it deadened intil sullen, wrathfu' groans—for they're no peals—they're no peals yon—again' the sides o' hills, snaw-shrooded—that groan in their turns—but in fear, no in anger—as if some strange judgment had found oot the damned in their hour of respite, and were ordering them to rise up again to dree the trouble of the guilty dead. It's nae exaggeration, sir. Lord safe us, what'n a howl?

Tickler. James, send round the jug.

Shepherd. I'll dae nae sic thing, Timothy. The jug's mine ain—but I'll gie you a glass frae my jug if yours is dune, or gotten cauld——

Tickler. That's unconscionable. Pray, when did you discover that the jug was your own? Till now it has been common property during the evening.

North. It has, indeed, my dear James.

Shepherd. Then why didna you mention that sooner? for I've been treatin't as individual property this last half hour——

North. And I, seeing with what a resolute grasp you held the handle, have been taking an occasional taste of the Glenlivet, in a succession of small drams such as King Oberon might turn up his little finger to, as he raised to his lips the rose-chalice, trembling to the brink with dewdrops brightening in the lustre of Titania's eyes, as she longed for the genial hour of love, soon about to be ushered in by the moonshine already beginning to smooth their nuptial bed on that bank of violets.

Shepherd. Eh? Say you the Glenlivet smells like violets? (*puts the Tower of Babel to his nose.*) It does that—a perfect nosegay.

North. No land on earth like Scotland for the landscape-painter. Skies! I have lived for years in Italy—and——

Shepherd. And speak the language like a native, I'll answer for that—for I never understood Dante, till I heard you read up the greatest part o' Hell ae nicht in your ain study. Yon's fearsome. The terzza rima's an infernal measure—and you let the lines rin intil ane anither wi' the skill o' a Lucifer. When every noo and then you laid doon the volumm on your knees—mercy on us! a great big volumm wi' clasps just like the Bible—and receeted a screed that you had gotten by heart—I could hae thocht that you was Dante himsell—the great Florentine—for your vice keipt tollin' like a bell—as if some dark spirit within youre breist were pu'in' the rope—some demon o' which you was possessed; till a' at once it grew saft and sweet in the soun' as the far-aff tinkling o' the siller bells on the bridle-reins o' the snaw-white palfrey o' the Queen o' the Fairies—as I hae heard them i' the Forest—but that was lang, lang syne—for my ears, in comparison wi' what they were when I was a mere child, are as if they were stuffed wi' cotton—then they could hear the gerss growin' by moonlicht—or a drap o' dew slipping awa' into naething frae a primrose-leaf.

North. Most episodical of Shepherds! Much nonsense has been written about Italian skies—true that they are more translucent than ours—and that one sometimes feels as if he not only saw higher up into heaven, but as if he were delightfully received into it, along with the earth, so perfectly pure the ether that it spiritualizes all the imagery, as well as the being of him who gazes on it, and are all united together in the beautiful repose of joy, as if the dewy prime of nature were all one with the morning of life!

Shepherd. Haena I felt a' that and mair in the Forest?

North. You may, James—but, then, James, you are a Poet—and I am not——

Shepherd. That's true.

North. To feel so I had to go to Italy. That clime worked so even upon me, who am no poet. What then would be its effect on the Ettrick Shepherd?

Shepherd. I shou'd grow licht in the head—as I did the first time I blew saip-bubbles frae a pipe.

Tickler. How was that, James? I never heard that tale.

Shepherd. I hae nae tale ta tell; but it sae happened that I had never heard tell o' blawin' saip-bubbles frae a pipe till I was aught year auld—the maist poetical epok perhaps in the life o' a great untaucht original genius.

Tickler. Millions of poets are cut off ere they reach that epoch.

Shepherd. And mony million mair by teethin'——

Tickler. And the gripes.

Shepherd. That's tautology—teethin' includes the gripes—though you may hae forgotten it—but great wits hae short memories—that's proverbial—sae let me proceed.

Tickler. Wet your whistle.

Shepherd. My whistle's never dry. I had seen a lassie doin't, and though she could na do't well, yet even sic bubbles as she blew—she was a verra bonnie bit lassie—appeared to my imagination mair beautifu' than ony ither sicht my een had ever beheld—no excepting the blab o' hinny that I used to haud up atween me and the licht, afore I soaked it, after I had flung awa', in twa halves, the bum-bee that had gathered it partly frae the clover and partly frae the heather-floures.

Tickler. How amiable is infant-cruelty!

Shepherd. And how detestable the cruelty of auld age! That verra day I took up the saip—I remember the shape and size o' the cut at this moment—and bat a bit aff—makin' it appear by the nibblin' o' my teeth, as if the thief had been a mouse.

Tickler. How amiable is infant hypocrisy!

Shepherd. Whare was ye last nicht, you auld Archimawgo? I then laid hauns on a new pipe my father had brocht frae Selkirk in a present for my mother—for the cutty was worn doon to an inch, and had owre strong a smell even for the auld wives; but as for my mother, she was then in the prime o' life, and reckoned verra like the Duchess; and havin' provided mysell wi' a tea-cup and a drap water, I stole out intil what ance had been the garden o' Ettrick ha', and sat down aneath ane of the elm-trees, as big then as they are noo—and in solitude, wi' a beatin' heart, prepared my suds. I quaked a' the same as if I had been gaun to do something wicked—

North. Shaksperean.

Tickler. Nothing equal to it in Massinger.

Shepherd. Wi' a trummlin' heart—indeed a' in a trummel—I put the mouth o' the pipe as gently's I cou'd on the precious saip and water, and it sooked in the wee bells till they a' made but ae muckle bell, on which depended a' my happiness for that day at least, for in my agitation I let the tea-cup fa'—though thank God it didna break—and a' my hopes were in the bole o' that pipe, and it was limited to that ae single charge! I drew in my breath—and I held in my breath—wi' the same sort o' a shiver that a wean gies afore gaen into the dookin'—and then I let out ae sigh after anither sigh—hainin' my breath—when, oh! ineffable and inconceivable happiness! the bells grew intil bubbles! and the bubbles intil balloons! and the balloons intil meteors! and the meteors intil moons! a' irradiated wi' lustre, a thousan' times mair mony-colored than the rainbow—each in itsell a wee glorious globe o' a warld—and the beautifu' series followin' ane anither up the air, as if they were sailin' awa' to heaven. I forgot utterly that they were saip-suds, and thocht them what they seemed to be—creturs o' the element! Till first ane and then anither—ah, waes me! gaed oot—and left me staunin' forloon wi' my pipe in my haun' aneath the auld elm-tree, as if the warld I breathed in was altered back intil what it was before—and I, Jamie Hogg, again at ance a schoolboy and a herd—likely to get his licks baith frae Mr. Beatie the dominie, and auld Mr. Laidlaw—instead o' muntin' up to heaven as the bubbles munted up to heaven—to find our hame in the sky! I looked sideways to the houses—and there was my mother fleein' towards me—shaking her nieve, and callin' me "Sorrow"—and demandin' hoo I daured to meddle wi' that pipe? The stalk, at that moment, broke into ten pieces in my hand! and the head of the pipe, pale as death, trundled at my feet. I felt my crime to be murder—and without a struggle submitted to my mother, who gave me my paiks, which I took as silent as a fox. Severe disenchantment! Yet, though my ears tingled, when I touched them, till bedtime, I was an unreformed sinner in sleep—and blew dream saip-bubbles frae a visionary pipe up the ether of imagination, uninterrupted, unterrified, and unpunished by any mortal mother—dream saip-bubbles far transcending in purest loveliness even them for which I had wept—and is na't a strange thocht, sirs, to think that the sowle in sleep's capable o' conceivin' what's even mair beautifu' and mair evanescent than the first perfect heavenly joy that a puir wee bit poetic laddie like me ever experienced in the waukin' warld?

North. What better have we been pursuing all our lives?

Shepherd. Said ye pursuin'? I did na pursue them—I stood rooted to the grund—I gazed on them as glories that I knew a breath would destroy—I feared to breathe for fear the air would break their pictured sides—for ilka ane as it arose glistened wi' changefu' pictures—painted a' roun' and roun' wi' wee clouds, and as I thocht wee trees—the globes seemin' rather to contain the scenery within them like sae mony floatin' lookin'-glasses—and some o' them shinin' wi' a tiny sun o' its ain—the image it micht be

—the reflected image—o' the great sun that illumines not only this world but the planetary system.

North. Well, James! what better have we been gazing at all our lives?

Tickler. That ROUND OF BEEF, Kit.

Shepherd. Timothy's speakin' sense, and we twa hae been speakin' nonsense—and yet that Round of Beef, though there's nae fear, I houp, o' his floatin' awa' up the air and meltin' in a drap o' saip and water, is but a bubble in his way too, and corned though he be, look for him to-morrow, and you will find him not.

Tickler. Yet is he a prize buttock.

North. Transitory as a prize poem.

Shepherd. In Eternity as short will be the date of that still larger round—the Earth.

North. Not any more mustard, Timothy. (TICKLER *hands a substantial sandwich across the table to* NORTH.) Thank ye, Tim. Depth three half inches—the middle layer in a pepper and salt coat, rather the thinnest of the three—no fat but round the edges—and confound crust. There's a recipe for a beef sandwich; and if you ask to take a lesson how to eat one, pray observe the mode of opening the mouth like a gentleman—wide, without gaping—and, having fixed that in your memory, attend to the difference between a civilized swallow and a barbarous bolt. There! that was a civilized swallow; and by the law of contrast, you have already, in fair imagination, a barbarous bolt. But we are rambling; and I remember we were discussing the skies of Italy in comparison with those of Scotland. Saw ever Italy such storms as Scotland sees?

Shepherd. In some spat or ither amaist every day o' her life.

Tickler. Yes, she does; and such storms, too, as Scotland never sees. For all our volcanoes are dead; and, except now and then a slight shiver about Comrie, she never had an earthquake.

North. Shelley says grandly,

> "As when some greater painter dips
> His pencil in the gloom of earthquake and eclipse."

I forget whether the word is earthquake or thunder.

Shepherd. An' it's nae great maitter.

North. Is there any great picture of an earthquake? or of an eclipse?

Shepherd. Ye mean in iles or canvass?

North. I do. I know of none—but, were there fifty, I stake my credit on the assertion, that all of them together would not do the business to imagination so perfectly as one line and a half in Milton—

> "Disastrous twilight sheds, with fear of change
> Perplexing monarchs."

Shepherd. I've written as gude a line and a half as thae—but I've forgotten a' my poetry, except some sangs. But keep to the pint.

North. Great painters will rarely seize, I think, on the throes of mother Earth, or on the agonies of father Uranus. In earthquake, she seems to be too ruefully rent—in eclipse, he seems to be too disastrously darkened—for us, their children, to desire to see one or other so painted; but poetry can sublime them both by some mighty moral, gathering up the supernatural trouble into a few words, and then by applying it illustratively to human life, magnifying both images—making them both more portentous and prodigious by their natural reaction on the imagination.

Shepherd. I suspect, sir, that's verra gude. After a', there's naething like poetry.

North. And no poets like the poets of Britain. But the truth is, James, that there is no country like Britain; and that her children far excel all the rest of mankind equally in imagination and in intellect.

Shepherd. Are you sure o' that, sir, and can you pruv't?

North. I am sure of it, and I can prove it in one sentence, to the dissatisfaction of all the rest of mankind. What mortal man, in universality of genius, ever equalled Shakspere?

Shepherd. That's a poser. I defy the rest o' mankind, leevin' or dead, to parry that thump. You've knocked them a' doon, sir, wi' ae hit on the universal jugular.

North. What mortal man ever equalled Newton?

"God said, Let Newton be—and all was light!"

Shepherd. Nane. That's a sickener on the stamach.

North. What mortal man ever equalled Bacon?

Shepherd. What, auld Roger?

North. No, James,—Francis.*

Shepherd. Oo ay,—Francie!—In whattt? Howsomever that's a settler on the kidneys.

North. What mortal man in majestic wisdom of moral imagination—that is, "in the vision and the faculty *divine*," ever equalled Milton?

Shepherd. The shooblimest o' a' poems, though a silly shepherd says sae, assuredly is Paradise Lost. The blin' bard was a seraph.

North. I have done; and merely ask, where are we to look for the equals of Spenser and Wordsworth?

Shepherd. Dinna weaken your argument, sir, nor shall I, or I micht ask where we are to find a Scott and a Byron—or a Burns —or——

* Francis Bacon, Lord Verulam,
"The wisest, greatest, meanest of mankind."—M.

Tickler. An Ettrick Shepherd.

Shepherd. Dinna indulge in personalities, Mr. Tickler. I'm satisfied to be the Scottish Theocritus.

(*Enter, in two columns, the Ambrosial brethren, with their tails, and the usual supplies.*)

North. How are you, gentlemen?

Omnes (*in all kinds of voices*). Pretty bobbish.

Shepherd. What kind o' an answer's that to make to Mr. North, ye neerdoweels? And it maun be preconcerted—for wha ever heard tell o' twa columns o' waiters, each wi' its ain maister at its head, without preconcert, and in perfect unison, cryin' out in tenor, treble, and base, "Pretty bobbish?" For shame o' yoursells! answer me that wiselike. Hoo's a wi' ye, lads?

Omnes (*in all kinds of voices*). All alive and kicking.

(*They deposit the dishes, and deploy out of the room in gallopade, Tappitourie, to the great delight of the family, hitting his hurdies* with his heels, and disappearing in a Somerset.*)

Shepherd. I've lang gien up wonderin' at ony thing; but there couldna weel be fewer than twa score. Mony faces glowered on me, as the columns deployed, some wi' goggle and some wi' pig een—some wi' snouts and some wi' snubs—and think you yon black-a-viced man wi' the white teeth could be a blackamoor?

North. The truth is, my dear James, that thousands of strangers in Edinburgh—many of them from foreign countries—are perennially dying to see the Ettrick Shepherd in all his glory at a Noctes—and I lately discovered, by the merest accident, that Ambrose, out of the purest humanity—for you know he is above all selfish motives—has been in the practiee—since we resumed our sittings—to admit as many of the more distinguished as the parlor can prudently hold, on account of the flooring, into his Tail, and into the Tail, too, of Mon. Cadet. The black-a-viced gentlemen is, as you conjectured, a blackamoor. The Duke of Lemonade—fresh from St. Domingo.

Shepherd. And the Tawney?

North. That was the Marquis of Marmalade, the duke's eldest son, by a French countess, who survived the Great Massacre, and was the beauty of Port-au-Prince.

Shepherd. I houp Mr. Awmrose 'll be kind to the duke and marquis in the bar, and no let them want for ony thing reasonable in the way o' drink. Noo, sirs, dinna distract my attention frae the boord, for it requires as meikle thocht to play a supper o' this complicated character as a game at chess. You twa are at liberty to speak to ane anither, but no to me, and mind that ye converse in a

* *Hurdies*—buttocks.—M.

laigh or at least moderate key, that ye dinna wax warm and smite the table or your thees, and abune a' things else that ye flee na up in ane anither's faces in a rage, and gie ane anither the lee. Be temperate, for I canna help fearin' the kintra's in a predicament. Thir are prime.

North. You may perhaps remember, Mr. Hogg, that at last Noctes, in reply to a question of yours, if I thought there would be any serious disturbance in the country on account of the dissolution of the Ministry, I said, that I thought there would be a great deal of ludicrous disturbance, and that the people would experience so many difficulties in preserving a grave countenance, that they would very soon desist from the attempt, and find relief in general laughter.

Shepherd. I'm no hearkenin', and your words in my lugs seem to follow ane anither wi' that kind o' connection that might be expected amang written slips o' paper read, as they cam to haun, out o' a hat.

North. Has it not been even so, Tickler? I see "in the *Sun* a mighty angel stand" waving a broadsword all over Scotland.

Tickler. On such occasions the London papers, in the adverse faction, always tell the people of England to look at Us. We are always in a flame of patriotism—the conflagration spreads over the country like a thousand fires in the season of heather burning, when every hill has its beacon.

North. And in the smoke the stars are stifled like bees in brimstone, and fall hissing into the lochs.

Tickler. I contemplated the meeting in the Grassmarket from one of the eyes of the White Hart, and felt ashamed of Auld Reekie. In that vast area I have seen fifty thousand people, all gazing intently on one man, who was making them a speech. "Ladies and gentlemen," said the orator, with hands impressively folded across his breast, "on rising to address you on this occasion, I feel it to be a duty incumbent on me to deviate from the usual practice of my predecessors in the chair, and to declare with a voice that will be heard all over Scotland, that so far from charging the fair sex with having been the cause of my downfall—which is now near at hand—for I am about to relinquish the situation which I have for a good many years held in this city—I have ever found them the best of friends—and that had I taken their advice earlier in my career, although my life might not have been one of such adventure—and, without presumption, I may even say, achievement—nor my death witnessed by so numerous and highly respectable an assemblage of my fellow-citizens—(and here he bowed all round) I might on the whole have been a happier man. With my last words, therefore, I beg the ladies to accept the assurance of my sincerest gratitude, highest respect and warmest affections." And so saying, he dropped the handkerchief, and in air danced the usual solo.

Shepherd. Was na the rubber a sodger?

Tickler. When I thocht of that orator and that audience, and the sublime sympathy that stilled the vast assemblage while he spoke —and then looked at the pitiful crew standing on the shabby scaffold, all of them like criminals guilty of no particular crime, but somehow or other invested with the mean air of servants out of livery and out of place—I could not but painfully feel the disheartening and humiliating contrast; nor was my shame for the degeneracy of my countrymen not exacerbated by the miserable and wretched speeches emitted in voices that alternately played cheep! and peep! or sputtered out in syllables that seemed composed of slaver, and left most of their fluency on the waistcoats of the delirious idiot drivelling about Claverhouse and Bothwell-bridge.

North. Why, he is their crack orator.

Tickler. The mob near the scaffold was very far indeed from resembling the swell mob. It looked like the last relics of a meal mob, that had scattered on the streets what it should have put in its stomach—or rather like a general meeting of your friends the old clothesmen.

North. My friends the old clothesmen—I beg you to be civil.

Tickler. You know you always knock them down simply for popping the question. But they were far from being enthusiastic.

North. You seldom find united in one and the same individual the extremes of enthusiasm and hunger.

Tickler. I did not say they all looked hungry—though I do not doubt many of them were so—but they almost all looked as if they had been drunk the night before, and kept spitting till they stood in a puddle of phlegm. 'Twas rather a raw day, and the afternoon of a raw day toward the end of November, in the Grassmarket, is not favorable to noses. The cheekery got sallower and sallower as the light declined, and the mob began to snifter, and wipe its nose on its sleeve—dangerous symptoms of anger and disgust. It then began to swear and to cut jokes, and only wanted spirit for a row. "Spunks—spunks—spunks—who will buy my spunks?" cried an errant voice with a beseeching earnestness that wershified the insipidity of the patriot at that moment advising his Majesty to look to his crown, and Jock's appeal to the sympathy of the shiverers excited an abortive guffaw.

Shepherd. Wha leuch?

Tickler. The meanest of mankind are yet susceptible of shame, and from the outskirts of the mob I saw slinkings away into closes, and heard sulky proposals, such as "Come awa', Jamie—for I never heard sic haverers—come awa' and let's join for a dram."

Shepherd. Wi' a' my heart. Your health, sir.

Tickler. There had not at the thickest been more than a couple of thousand near the scaffold, and as the mob thinned, and you could see through "its looped and windowed raggedness," you could not help admiring how the lowest rabble in Scotland contrive to have such fair skins.

North. Cutaneous diseases are now chiefly confined to England.

Tickler. True, I seldom go there now for fear of catching the itch.

North. 'Tis a retribution on them for all their wit on the Scotch fiddle.

Tickler. Had these poor fellows attended to their own business instead of the affairs of the State, they might all, with the regular wages going, have clad themselves decently on week days, and had a Sunday suit; whereas, you never saw out of Ireland such apologies for breeches; and one radical at a distance I mistook for a Highland-man, whose imagined kilt of the Macgreggor tartan, on somewhat nearer inspection appeared in its true colors—those of a dirty shirt.

Shepherd. I hae been tryin' a' I could to hear you—but I hae been obliged, whether I would or no, to follow the threed o' your discourse, like a speeder waverin' apparently again' his wull in the wund—

North. On a line of his own spinning. James—but, Shepherd, you are like the fly, unwittingly caught in the spider's web.

Shepherd. I dinna like to hear you abusin' puir folk.

North. Come—come, James, much as I esteem you, I shall not suffer you to utter such stuff.

Shepherd. Weel—weel, then—I eat in my words.

North. I love the people of Scotland, and they know it. A nobler race never toiled for bread. Abuse the poor, indeed! No—

"An honest man's the noblest work of God"—

And Scotland is full of them—of men in low degree, on whose hearts Nature has set her own badge of highest merit, that to my eyes shines brighter than any silver star. The commonalty of Scotland has produced many of her greatest geniuses and most heroic patriots—and will continue to produce them; but independently of such produce rich and rare, I love the people for the sake of the virtues of their own condition, on which the country, equally in time of peace and of war, for her happiness and her safety mainly relies. And now that the political privileges of the people have been extended—though to such extension I was adverse, and gave reasons for my opposition which never yet have been refuted—so far from finding fault with their exercise of those privileges, I would despise them now whom I have heretofore admired, were they not to value them highly, and to consider every case in which they think themselves called to use their rights, as a case of conscience.

Shepherd. Sound doctrine that—and high sentiment too—just like yoursell!

North. Nay, I shall always make great allowance for them in times of excitement, and the moment you hear me call them mob or rabble, get me cognosced, and confined, and let the Lodge be let.

Shepherd. I should in that case hae nae objections to sit in't rent-free, provided the trustees would only pay the taxes, and the wages o' the gardener for keepin' up the place, and the gravel walks tidy, for a' things on the yerth I do maist detest and abhor chicken-weed and sic like trailin' trash chokin' up the boxwood and ither odoriferous plants, sae that you might mow the avenue wi' a scythe, and put up into cocks a kind o' coorse product, atween hay and straw and rashes, that stirks in wunter wad eat rather than starve.

North. But no friends, James, of the people are they who collect such ragamuffin congregations of the dregs of the lowest canaille as that which disgraced the Grassmarket, and libel the lower orders by addressing the insignificant assortment of small gangs, as if they represented the worth and intelligence, and industry, and patriotism of the Working Classes. Why, Tickler tells me that the few scores belonging to that excellent order stood aloof in knots with their aprons on, for a short while regarding the proceedings with indifference or contempt, and then walking away, with a laugh or a frown, to their afternoon's work. It is a stupid mistake, and shows utter ignorance of their characters, to believe that the respectable mechanics of Edinburgh like to see magistrates and gentlemen descending to a level on which they themselves would scorn to stand. They think and say—I have heard more than one of them say so—that they wonder how their superiors in station can submit to such degradation as they themselves, humble men as they are, would spurn; and are surprised how they are permitted to do so by their wives.

Shepherd. The wives o' the workin' classes, I ken, aye set their faces against their husbands attendin' sic riff-raffery affairs; for in nae ither class o' society hae honest men's wives mair becoming pride, and in amaist every woman's breist there is a natural repugnance to a' pursuits—except it be an occasional ploy—that tak her man frae his wark or his fireside—and especially to sic as embitter and exasperate his temper, which politics, as they're ca'd, are certain sure to do, and to mak him a domestic tyrant at last.

North. What cruel wickedness is involved in those two words—Domestic Tyrant!

Shepherd. The chiel, frae abusin' the misgovernment o' the kintra, and the misdirection o' public affairs, and a' things whatsomever in the wide warld—the hail system, in short, sir, o' our foreign and domestic policy—acquires a habit o' fawte-findin' that he applies to the mismanagement o' the hame department within his ain door-cheeks—and the neebours hear him flyting on the gudewife, like a tinkler, till at last he takes to the harlin' o' her alang the flure by the hair o' the head—and some nicht the polish enter at the cry o' murder, and carry the Radical Reformer to the shells.

North. Strang—strang—strang—James.

Shepherd. Mind ye, sirs, I'm no sayin' this is the common character o' Radical Reformers amang mechanics. It's an extreme case —the cry o' murder. For a woman will thole a hantle o' ill-usage afore she breaks out either in fury or fear at her husband, rememberin' the days o' their youth. But the peace o' the fireside may be sair disturbed without things comin' till that extremity; and I manteen it's no in the nature o' things that ony hard-workin' contented, decent, douce, domestic chiel wi' a wife, and of coorse weans, can lang busy himsell wi' correctin' the abuses o' church and state, without suner than he suspecks becomin' rather idlish, gae sour, no just sae ceevil in his mainer as he used to be, upsettin', and proud o' bein' the cock o' the company whare ilka bit bantam maun hae its craw—instead o' happy in bein' the cock o' his ain roost, chucklin' by the saft side o' his ain chuckin' hen, as bonnie as if she were yet an yearock, though she has been aften cluckin', and has bred up chickens that are some o' them doin' for themsells, and the rest cheerfully runnin' about and pickin' crumbs frae the floor.

North. Tickler, how pleasingly he illustrates his political and economical views!

Shepherd. Safe us! what's become o' a' the oysters! You hae aye been a great freen', sir, o' the educatin' o' the People.

North. Always. I shall give my support to no ministry that does not strive with all its might and main to effect that object. The late ministry deserved praise for what they did; and we shall show ourselves a strange nation indeed if we grudge any grant of the public moneys, however magnificent, to be employed in spreading and establishing knowledge in the land.

Shepherd. Was na't twenty thousand pounds?

North. And too little. What if it were a hundred thousand? The mind of the people would repay it—in hard cash—a thousandfold. Even as an Utilitarian, I say—at any cost—let our twenty-four millions have education.

Shepherd. That's a man.

North. But let us know what we are about—and what we are to expect—and what are the possibilities of education. I am willing to believe that a constant progress is making towards truth, and that this must be for happiness; but any one who looks at the world and its history may satisfy himself that for some reason or another this truth was not intended to come all at once. Either in the human understanding, or the positive state of the human will, there is some ground wherefore this should not be. It is not possible then, nor meant to push mankind forwards at once into the possession of the inheritance. There are degrees and stages; and seeing this, a wise man is patient and temperate.

Shepherd. Like yoursell.

North. Many men fall into this error, James, by a miscalculating impatience to bring on at once the reign of truth—that they foolishly imagine that small portions of truth communicated, which it is in their power to communicate, are the reign of truth brought on earth!

Shepherd. Coofs!

North. The truth which is in their power, is that which regards definite relations, as mathematics, and the science of matter. Their hasty and enthusiastic imagination seizes on parcels of this truth, and upon plans for communicating them, and to judge from their manner of speaking, it foresees consequences of a magnitude and excellence, conceivable only if all truth were to have possession of the human heart.

Shepherd. You are gettin' rather beyond my depth—yet by drappin' my foot I feel grund—only tak tent you dinna droon me in some plum.

North. In judging the past, James, we are not to condemn errors, simply because they were errors. They were many of them, the necessary guidance of man!

Shepherd. Alas! for puir man, if he had had nae sic Christianity even as the Roman Catholic religion afforded him in the dark ages.

North. Alas! for him indeed, my dear Shepherd. Neither are we to judge the total effect of the error by the effect of the excess of that error.

Shepherd. Eh?

North. Not, for instance, to judge the total effect of monastic orders by the worst pictures of sloth and vice which monasteries have afforded—not the total effect of Aristotle's dialectics—if erroneous or erroneously used—by the most frivolous and vain of the school-subtleties—not the effect of the Roman Catholic religion at a Spanish or English *auto-da-fe.*

Shepherd. I canna but agree wi' you. But look at Tickler, (*yawning,*) is na he sleepin'?

North. Our business, my dear pastor, is not to hunt error out of the world, but to invite and induce truth. It is a work not of enmity but of love; and, with all my admiration of Lord Brougham,

I cannot think his temper and method as a moral teacher so good as those of Socrates.

Shepherd. You'll forgie me, sir—but I never can help suspectin' that a man's getting a wee dullish or sae—even if that man should happen to be yoursell—when I experience a growing diffeeculty in keepin' up my lids. What think you noo, sir, o' the prospects o' the Government?

North. The same I thought of them at last Noctes. Sir Robert Peel had not then arrived from Rome—but I knew he would be Premier—Wellington Foreign Secretary—and Lyndhurst Chancellor—and I said that the strongest ministry would be formed the country had seen since the time of Pitt. I added there would be a dissolution, and that the government would have many formidable difficulties to encounter and overcome in the new Parliament.

Shepherd. Sagawcious.

North. I heard a gentleman, who, I presume, has studied politics, and declares that he belongs to the *juste milieu*, prophesy—that was his word—that in two months the King would, much against his will, send for Lord Stanley, and request him to form a ministry, and I wish Gurney to record the prophecy, that this philosopher of the golden mean may enjoy through life the halo that will glorify his brows ever after its fulfilment.

Shepherd. Wha was't? And what said ye till the man o' mediocrity?

North. I never mention the names of private persons at a Noctes, and I said nothing to him, for I make it a rule never to disturb any friend's self-complacency, so long as his remarks are innocent.

Shepherd. And that, sir, was indeed as innicent a remark as ever was lisped by a babby about a change o' kittens.

North. The greater and indeed the lesser prophets were inspired direct from heaven—and I do not believe that my worthy friend, who is such an enemy to extremes, thought of claiming Elijah's mantle, or that he imagined he had had communion with the spirit

> "That touch'd Isaiah's hallowed lips with fire."

To another class of prophetic personages, called seers, he could not well suppose he belonged, as they are always Highlanders. But he was born of Lowland parents in the Luckenbooths—so he cannot have the second sight—nor to his eyes "coming events cast their shadows before." Milton, again, speaks of the sages whose

> "Old experience doth attain
> To something like prophetic strain;"

but my friend is not forty, and his experience has been circumscribed within a somewhat narrow circle. He could not, therefore, have been in Milton's eye.

Shepherd. He maun o' necessity then belang till that class o' prophets that are ca'd simple conjecturers—because they're nae conjurers. He'll hae just knowledge aneuch to ken frae the newspapers that Lord Stanley did na quite like the noo to join Ministers, and that he has been praised for hangin' back by the Whiggamores, though between you and me, sir, he's nae favorite noo with them, and like to be less sae afore seed-time.* And as nae man o' mediocrity wad ever dream o' Durham's being Premier, the simple conjecturer could na weel help prophesying—sae he was determined to prophesy—that Stanley would be the man.

North. I believe you have hit it—James. But was not two months too short a term?

Shepherd. Ratherly. But the simple conjecturer, though nae conjurer, had seen in the papers that the new Ministry would be refused the supplies by the new House—and takin' that for gospel, he fixed his time, and I only wonner he alloo'd Sir Robert to be Premier abune sax weeks. But what think ye, sir?

North. I think that nothing could be more amusing than the serious view taken by part of the press of the temporary dictatorship of the Duke of Wellington. The "wearifu' woman" of the Morning Chronicle for three weeks, without one moment's intermission, kept up a mumbling and maundering vituperation of the Duke, whom for lengthiness she classically called Dictator, for having put all the seals of office, in a bunch, into his pocket,† and being resolved to keep them there as long as he chose, to the indignation, disgust, and horror of the entire British nation, who, she said, at such an unconstitutional spectacle, rose up as one man. As one man, however, it appeared, that the entire British nation almost immediately sat down again—much to the "wearifu' woman's" exasperation, who insisted still more vociferously that the entire British nation should once more get on its legs.

* Stanley did not join Peel's Ministry, in 1834–5. When Peel again became Premier, in 1841, Stanley was his Colonial Secretary, but resigned, in the autumn of 1845, when Peel had determined to abolish all duties on the importation of corn. In February, 1852, Stanley (who had become Earl of Derby, by his father's death), became head of the British Government, but—the Whigs and the Irish party combining, as they had done in 1835—was defeated in the House of Commons, and resigned in December, 1852.—M.

† It is a fact that, in the three weeks which elapsed between the dismissal of the Melbourne Ministry, and the arrival of Sir Robert Peel, from Italy, to form another, the entire duties of the Executive Government were performed by the Duke of Wellington, without any apparent deficiency in, or detriment to, the public service. The Whig newspapers were indignant—as became them, being partisans—at this "Dictatorship," but the People did not trouble themselves about it, being rather pleased than otherwise, at the efficiency of "The Duke," who had recovered the popularity he lost in 1830–2. It is proper to mention, as the matter has been misrepresented and exaggerated, that, in June, 1831, when the Duke "made a fortress of Apsley House" (as has been gravely writ in History), all he actually did was to put up *jalousies*, or outer window blinds, such as are common to most houses in the principal cities of Europe and America, but had not then been introduced into England. They are generally made of wood, whereas those at Apsley House were manufactured of iron, which had the advantage of durability, and are probably musket-proof when closed.—M.

Shepherd. She might have mumbled till she was black in the face.

North. The best-natured old woman in the world would lose her temper, James, if nobody were to listen to her, or even so much as to pretend not to see her, but if every body were to walk by, as if in the still of the evening silence accompanied their steps. The "wearifu' woman" was irritated even to madness by such usage. Like an aged clergyman of our acquaintance—now, alas! no more—who, in a brain fever, preached in his bed—supported by pillows and supposing himself in a succession of pulpits—the same sermon twenty-seven times in twenty-seven hours—each time fondly believing it to be a different discourse—so snoozed away—column after column of the same eternal lamentation—for she seemed at last more in sorrow than in anger—though much in both—the "wearifu' woman" of the Chronicle of the rosy-fingered Morn. Incredible as it may be held—from extracts of her distraction cruelly published in the Sun—in her own broad-sheet they were only printed—there is but too good reason to fear that she thinks she is but entering on her career, and if such steps are not taken as humanity suggests, she may keep at it well on into the ensuing year!

Shepherd. The wonner's no in the words; for memory—though it never surveeves the ither faculties—and here it appears they are a' dead—can continue to repeat it by rote to the very last—as I ascertained in the case o' an auld parrot, that after a brain fivver becam a sort of idiwit. As for teachin' him a new word—if it had been but a single syllable—you micht as weel hae tried to teach a stuffed specimen the unknown tongue. You may judge o' his imbecility frae ae fact, that he had forgotten the way to eat. Yet, like your freen the minister, sir, and the "wearifu' woman," he keepit a command o' his vocabulary to the last—but I daurna tell you the words that fell out frae atween his big tongue and his dry pallet the verra minute afore he expired—but they were fearsome!—and the only excuse for the cretur was, that he had picked them up at sea. But what think ye o' the prospects o' the new Government?

North. Sir Robert's address to his constituents is all that the nation could desire—and the policy announced in it may be supported, without either sacrifice or compromise of a single principle, by all Conservatives.*

Shepherd. That's aneuch for me. You've said it, and whatever you say is richt.

* This was his address to the electors of Tamworth, a lengthy and explicit statement of his political views as Prime minister. With one exception—a resolution to devote the surplus (if any) of the Irish Church revenue to none but strictly ecclesiastical purposes—it was such a programme as Lord Grey or Lord Melbourne, or any other professed Liberal, might have issued to the satisfaction of the public, after the passing of the Reform Bill. Why, then, did not Parliament allow him to carry out his views?—because though principle be the *eidolon* of Party, personal interest is the substance. Not measures, but men make the rallying point in England.—M.

North. Oh, shame to the selfishness—the pelf rather than the power-craving selfishness, that instigates needy or greedy knaves to be such fools as to say, that no statesman that opposed the bill of Parliamentary Reform should ever be suffered to take part in the affairs of the nation!

Shepherd. Hoots, toots! you're fechtin' the wund. That never was said, sir?

North. Yes—James—and it will be acted on by thousands. Many of the Whig Candidates have already, in addresses to their Constituents, called on them to choose representatives according to that creed. For any baseness, however barefaced and brazenfaced, we must have been long prepared, in the degenerate Whigs of Scotland. But not till I see that opinion acted on by the Whigs of England, many of whom seem yet to possess many of the political virtues of their forefathers, who were illustrious patriots in their day, shall I believe that Whig is now indeed a word for all that is most despicable and hateful in the heart of man. If this be indeed now a Whig Principle—there is another word of the same number of letters—"letters four do form its name"—the name not of a principle but of a place—to which I devoutly trust all Whigs will in good time be sent, there to form his Majesty's Opposition.

Shepherd. What place is that? It canna be Coventry—for that's a dissyllable. Oo ay! Oo ay! Oo ay! I hae ye now, sir. Wi' a' my heart.

North. Sir Robert Peel, in a few calm words sets this principle in its true light. "The King, in a crisis of great difficulty, required my services. The question I had to decide was this: shall I obey the call, or shall I shrink from the responsibility, alleging as the reason that I consider myself, in consequence of the Reform Bill, as laboring under a sort of moral disqualification which must preclude me and all who think with me, both now and for ever, from entering into the official service of the Crown? Would it, I ask, be becoming in any public man to act on such a principle? Was it fit that I should assume that either the object or the effect of the Reform Bill has been to preclude all hope of a successful appeal to the good sense and calm judgment of the people; and so to fetter the prerogative of the crown, that the King has no free choice among his subjects, but must select his Ministers from one section, and one section only, of public men?"

Shepherd. Hoo sensible—hoo dignified—hoo true!

North. Faction will cling with desperate tenacity to the objection to any Conservative government, thus disposed of in a few simple words. But we must cut off its paws. They who now urge it know of a surety that the measures of the New Ministry will be of the most enlightened and liberal kind. Ay—the epithet liberal—so long misused and abused—will recover its rightful meaning, and that meaning be illustrated by a policy that on foundations of law and order shall establish peace.

Shepherd. There has been nae peace in men's minds lately, sir; and Earl Grey himself spak' wi' mair than seriousness o' the pressure frae without. What is't?

North. It was the pressure of some hundreds of thousands, perhaps millions, savagely seeking to squeeze the life out of the government, that they might usurp the rule of the state. These were the very millions to whom the government had given power. I speak not now of the Reform Bill—though the evils it has perpetuated stand before my eyes in all their magnitude—but of the encouragement directly afforded by the whole spirit—and a truckling spirit it was—of their 'havior to them who soon became their inveterate and their victorious enemies. The Radicals destroyed the Melbourne Ministry. I say so on the authority of Lord Melbourne.

Shepherd. Eh me! Is that possible? On the authority, sir, o' Lord Melbourne!

North. Yes. What care I—what cares any man of common sense—for such explanations as the late Ministry may choose to give the country—and I do not believe one of them, unless it be Littleton,* would speak what he did not think the truth—of the circumstances attending their dismission?

Shepherd. No a button.

North. The causes are patent to the whole world. The "pressure from without" had produced a great difficulty of breathing, and sadly affected their speech. Nay, there was a manifest pressure on the brain—the patient looked at once apoplectic and paralytic—black-blue in the face, while the power of one side of the body at least was gone! How could it be expected that such a ministry were to carry on the government of a great country?

Shepherd. They stoitered again the kirk.

North. Has not Lord Melbourne told the country, in his answer to the Derby address, that the chief embarrassments of the ministers were occasioned by the wild outcry that had been yelled against the church? And how ought Ministers to have dealt with such dangerous enemies? Put them down by union among themselves, and by an open determination to guard our sacred establishments from the touch even of the little finger of any leader or follower of that impious crew. Instead of that, they parleyed with the enemy, and seemed sorry that they could not make all the concessions he demanded; while among themselves was one certainly—perhaps more than one—who, though he was "not prepared to say that there

* Now Lord Hatherton. When Mr. Littleton, he had been Chief Secretary for Ireland.—M.

should be no alliance between church and state"—nay, though he was prepared to say, after much apparent hesitation, or at least delay, that the alliance should be preserved—had frequently said that he was ready to rob the church—for that the alienation of her property to secular purposes is robbery I shall not think it at all presumptuous in me to affirm, in spite of the dictum to the contrary of my Lord John Russell.

Shepherd. And think ye, sir, there has been a wide and deep reaction? For unless it has been sae, it'll do nae gude.

North. Reaction of what on what? Millions of people anticipated from the Reform Bill peace—order—industry—contentment—and above all, increased attachment to all our institutions—and a clearer conviction and deeper feeling of the sanctity of property, guarded as it then would be by equal laws, and by measures sanctioned by the true representatives of the people.

Shepherd. And hae they begun to change their opinions!

North. Ay, many is the number of those who have done so—but I shall not insist on that, for the Reform Bill is the law of the land. But some millions of those many millions now see that, whether to be laid at the door of the Bill or not, society is now threatened by evils which, three years ago, they would have smiled in your face had you hinted at--and I did more than hint at them—I described them in colors only less dark than the truth; and my trust is, that a great majority of the people of England, seeing many things in a very different light now, will support the Conservative Government of which Sir Robert Peel is head.

Shepherd. I ca' that moderation.

North. And when heard you, or any man, anything but moderation from my lips? I cannot doubt that the good sense and good feeling of the country will prevail, and that it will be found to be out of the power of faction to act, to any wide extent, on a principle of such unutterable baseness as that the Government must be opposed, however excellent its measures, and with a fury proportioned to their excellence. That many elections will be carried in a spirit of pure hatred of Conservatism I believe; but in the House the Destructives will be made to quail; and England, expecting that every man will do his duty there who loves her institutions, will speak with another voice, should any great number of the representatives of the people there dare to vote against measures they have always approved, merely because they are the measures of Government.

Shepherd. There assuredly will be a reaction again' ony pairty that lang ack sae—were it but on account o' the impudence o' sic behaviour. I howp Tickler's no gaun till rat; but this obstinate somnolency is suspicious, and hae na ye been observin' that there has been little or nae snore? When a man sleeps in company without snorin', there's reason to think his mind may be takin' tent o' things drapped in conversation, and that he may use what he hears anither day. (*Burns paper below* TICKLER'S *nose.*) Gif he be awake, he maun be stimulatin', and o' strang resolution. But he is true as steel to the back-bone. (*Smacks* TICKLER *with both hands on the back, and then shakes him with all his might by the shoulders.*) Fire! Fire! Fire!

Tickler (*starting up, and staring wildly around*). Water! Water! Water!

Shepherd. Whusky! Whusky! Whusky! (*Enter* AMBROSE.)

North. Is Peter in the house, Mr. Ambrose? Give me your arm.

Ambrose. Ay—ay, sir.

(*Exeunt omnes.*)

No. LXXI.—FEBRUARY, 1835.

SCENE—*Penetralia of the Lodge—Time, ae wee short hour ayont the Twal—Present,* NORTH *and* SHEPHERD.

Shepherd. It was nae safe in you, sir, to gie a' your domestics the play for a hale month in hairst, and to leeve incog a' alane by your single sel' in this Sanctum, like the last remainin' wasp in its nest, at the close o' the hummin' season;—for what if you had been taken ill wi' some sort o' paralysis in your limbs, and been unable to ring the alarm-bell for succor? Dinna ye see that you might hae expired for want o' nourishment, without the neighborhood ha'in' had ony suspicion that a great licht was extinguished, and that you micht hae been found sittin' in your chair, no a corp in claes, but a skeleton? You should really, sir, hae mair considera-tion, and no expose your freens to the risk o' sic a shock. Wull ye promise?

North. You forget, James, that the milk-lassie called every morn-ing, and eke the baker's boy—except, indeed, during the week I subsisted on ship-biscuit and fruitage.

Shepherd. You auld anchorite!

North. Such occasional abstraction, my dear James, I feel to be essential to my moral and intellectual well-being. I cannot do now without some utter solitude.

Shepherd. But folk 'll begin to think you crazy—and I'm no sure if they would be far wrang.

North. At my time of life, James, it matters not much whether I be crazy or not,—indeed one so seldom sees a man of my age who is not a little so, that I should not wish to be singular—though, I confess, that I have a strong repugnance to the idea of dotage. Come, now, be frank with your old friend, and tell me, if the oil in the lamp be low, or if the lamp itself but want trimming?

Shepherd. Neither. But the lamp's o' a curious construction—a self-feedin', self-trimmin' lamp—and, sure aneuch, at times in the gloom it gies but a glimmer—sae that a stranger micht imagine that the licht was on its last legs—but would sune start to see the room on a sudden bricht as day, as if the window-shutters had been opened by an invisible hand, and let in a' the heavens.

North. I never desire to be brilliant.

Shepherd. Nor does the day.

North. Nor the night.

Shepherd. There lies the charm o' their beauty, sir, just as yours. There's nae ostentation either in the sun, or in the moon, or in the stars, or in Christopher North.

North. Ah, you quiz!

Shepherd. There's the sun. Hoo aften does he keep out o' sight through the greatest part even o' a lang simmer day! True, ye aye ken, withouten ony science, whereaboots he is in the sky; for that face o' his canna be sae entirely hidden that our een dinna hear it silently speak.

North. A mixed image, James—a——

Shepherd. Saft, sweet, laigh murmur, as it were, o' licht. I'm alludin' the noo, to the sun far ben in heaven on a serene day—when, if you could suppose a human ee openin' for the first time on natur, the human being would think the air was the sun o' which he had read in the Bible, and perhaps imagine that St. Mary's loch was what was ca'd licht! Or possibly he micht include in his idea the greenness o' the hills, out or in the water; but whatever he thocht or felt we canna doubt that he would be happy as a seraph, and utter a thanksgiving to the Invisible.

North. My dear Shepherd, I forget and forgive your banter in the beauty of such images—so purely Scottish.

Shepherd. Whare's the sun in a thunner-storm! You micht absolutely believe he was afraid o' bein' struck by the lichtnin'.

North. That's an original thought, if ever there was one. Ha! ha! ha! James.

Shepherd. Wha the deevil ever heard a man afore lauchin' at the shooblime?

North. Why, that's another! I must begin to look serious.

Shepherd. Knawin', like a great chemist as he is, that water's a non-conductor, and naturally abhorred by the electric fluid—when the tempest's at its hicht, and threatens to tak' the sky by storm—

North. That is the third.

Shepherd. ——and to escalade the verra citadel into which he has retired——

North. Fourth.

Shepherd. ——the sun commands the clouds to become rain and droon the lichtnin'!——

North. Fifth.

Shepherd. ——And then sallyin' frae the dungeon-vaults of that celestial stronghold, he shows his unharmed head all glittering wi' golden hair, mair beautifu' than an angel's, while earth lauchs back to heaven, and from all her groves hymneth the Lord of Light and

Love in choirs of gratulation that gladden the blue lift and the green hills wi' holy echoes!

North. The half-dozen.

Shepherd. O' whattt?

North. Of original ideas.

Shepherd. Na—you're turnin' the tables on me noo, sir.

North. Well—well—let it be so.

(*By his thumb on the rim* NORTH *makes revolve the Circular, so that he and the* SHEPHERD *exchange jugs.*)

Shepherd. I ca' that selfish. A drap cauld wesh drags at the bottom o' yours, and mine fu' to the brim o' het, strang, stingin' toddy! But ae gude turn deserves anither. (*Imitates* NORTH *in his management of the orrery, and restores the planetary system into its former position in space.*)—Is that you, my bonnie jug! Let me kiss your hinnie mou! That's a kind cretur!

North. Then the moon, James.

Shepherd. Why, sir, she aften comes out o' her bower when the sun is shinin' frae pure modesty and bashfulness, that nane may see her takin' a walk, happy to be eclipsed into obscurity by that omnipotent licht.

North. Seven.

Shepherd. In that resemblin' yoursell, sir, wha are fond o' my society in a' its splendor, that, like the Leddy Moon in presence o' the Lordly Sun, you may escape notice, in your ain quate and cozey neuck, contented wi' your ain somewhat pallid face, while the general gaze is concentrate on mine glowing wi' mair roseate colors.

North. Eight.

Shepherd. And hae na ye seen her an a clear blue nicht, when she couldna help rejoicin' in her beauty, and there could be nae use in denyin' that she knew hoo exceedin' fair she was, Mother o' Pearl o' the Firmament—

North. Nine.

Shepherd. Ha na ye seen her then acceleratin' her pace to meet the lagging clouds, and divin' intil the heart o' the first mass she met, carin' naething for the disappointment o' the shepherds sprinkled owre the hills, sae that she enjoy for a while her beloved retirement, like a princess shunnin' a people's gaze, and layin' hersell doon in a bed wi' white curtains, and white sheets, but no half sae white as her ain lovely limbs, for they are o' lilies—and what whiteness is like that o' lilies, whether they grow in the garden, or in the loch?

North. Ten.

Shepherd. And yet she's no aye sae blate—for hae na you and me aften seen her shinin' in the sky, mair like the sun than the moon, brichtenin' and brichtenin' while we continued to gaze, as if she were resolved in her queenly heart to domineer—I had amaist said to tyrannize—in the divine power o' her beauty over all upward eyes —outfacing her worshippers till they wink't, if no under her lustre yet under her loveliness—and turned awa' perhaps quite overcome —to relieve their hearts by a look o' the Evening Star?

North. Eleven.

Shepherd. What's a' the ships that ever sailed the sea to her— what's a' the isles that slumber on the sea—what's a' the birds, though God kens they are beautifu', that, on the bosom o' that sea or o' thae isles, alicht and fauld up their pennons spotless as the snaw! She heeds them not—for to her the sea is but a mirror in which her heart is gladdened by the beauty o' her countenance; and that she may enjoy her gaze on hersell she chains in saft, shinin' fetters the charmed warld o' waves!

North. The dozen, by Diana!

Shepherd. As for the stars—never cou'd my heart decide whether they were fairest risin', seittin', or studded, stationary sparkles, in the sky, like diamonds on the sclate-roof o' a human dwellin'.

North. Second Series. Number One.

Shepherd. I'm glad to see ye dinna start at the comparison. For what's bonnier than the yellow glintin' diamonds on the blue sclate-roof o' a human dwellin'—laigh though the riggin' be? And what forbids that they should be likened to the starry splendor on the cope o' highest heaven?

North. Nothing.

Shepherd. The same hand formed those in the earthen mine, that hung these on the celestial vault—and then methinks, sir, that the laigher roof, as the heart keeps narrowin' and hallowin' its feelings in domestic peace, is something even mair sacred—seein' that God gied us such shelter that aneath it we might sing his praise—than the far-aff roof star-spangled—the roof, as it were, o' the boundless universe. For 'tis the roof o' ane's ain wee dearest warld, whare every thing is suitable in its significance—I had amaist said insignificance—but ae great thocht made me change the word—for are we not immortal—though born to die!

North. I have lost count, my dearest Forester, of the original and delightful ideas you have been pourin' forth this last half hour, and hope this shovel of oysters will be to your taste. Nothing, after all, like the open-stitch shovel for roasting natives.

(*Scrapes off half a hundred natives on the* SHEPHERD'S *plate— and half a hundred on his own.*

Shepherd. Prime. As I look on a risin' star I feel the same as if listenin' to a soarin' laverock—I wud think, as the star sets ahint the hill, I saw the bird drappin' earthward to its nest.

North. Love you best, James, to gaze on them clear or in mist—in scores or in thousands?

Shepherd. I seldom noo, sir, gaze on them ava. It is sufficient to ken that they are there—their presence abune is impressive on my heart, though my een be on the grund as I am trudging hame outowre the hills, or atween my yad's lugs as I'm trottin' alang the bridle-roads wi' a tight rein for fear he comes doun and breaks his knees—nae unusual occurrence. If they're dimmish, which they may be without bein' misty, that's nae positive sign that it will rain the morrow—but when wannish it will surely be wat, and as I never yet kent rain thrown awa in the Forest, I'm aye glad to see them wannish; for sae far frae being then sickly, 'tis a symptom o' health, and indeed diseases there are nane amang the heavenly lichts, nor did a single ane o' them a' ever send down to earth but a blessing on man and beast. I canna thole noo to luik lang on a refulgent star—it makes me sae melancholy—but frequently sic a ane obleeges me to see it—singlin' itsell out frae the rest if it wished a' the warld below to admire it, and then I pause, and wi' a sigh give it a silent benediction. When they hae ta'en possession o' the skies in thousans—and that tens o' thousans are aften visible at ance to my naked een, I shall continue to believe in spite o' a' the astronomers that ever peep't through telescops—'tis then that I hae nae fear to tak a lang steady look at the nocturnal heavens. A's sae cheerfu' as weel's sae serene—sae merry, I had amaist said, as weel's sae majestic—a' sae gay, sir, as weel's sae glorious—that a temper'd joy diffuses itsell through a' my bein', and the man admires like a child the illuminated sky palace o' nature.

North. The Material Universe! and is there nothing beyond? Where is the abode of spirits? And what is spirit?

Shepherd. O sir! surely ye are no a materialist?

North. No, indeed, James. It has been argued by materialists that we know nothing at all about what we call Spirit—but believe me, my dear friend, that we know as much of it as we do of Matter.

Shepherd. Do ye say sae, sir!

North. In the first place, James, it is probable that we have generally included in the notion that may have been in our mind at any time we have been meditating on our inner being, the idea of some action proceeding; that we have not conceived of Spirit as something in a state of utter rest, but rather in motion, or with thought awake in it, or with inclination of love or aversion, or under the affection of pleasure or pain, or as exercising agency on some other being?

Shepherd. Be sae gude as to speak affirmatively, sir, if you please, and no interrogatively—for it's my desire no to teach but to learn.

North. Well—James—that act—the idea of which I conceive has commonly been in our minds when we have spoken of Spirit—was not conceived of by us as impressed on this being at the instant by some other being; if it was motion, we did not think that the being was merely driven along by a force extraneous to itself, in which it had no participation, but that it moved itself; if the act conceived of was agency exercised upon some other being—the Spirit exercising it was not thought of as a mere passive instrument transmitting that agency from some other being, not as a mere powerless, will-less medium of agency, but as itself operating; if it was an act of thought, we did not suppose it merely carried on in it by extraneous energy without its participation, but as proceeding by faculty of its own; if it was a movement of love, aversion, will in any kind, we still thought of it, however called forth, as proceeding from itself; if imagined in the mere passive state of impressed pleasure or pain, we considered that passion as terminating on sense of its own—in a word, as centring on itself; nay, do not rub your forehead, as if you were perplexed, for I appeal to your consciousness, is it not even so?

Shepherd. Dinna ask me—but go on, sir.

North. Now, James, these are all ideas, I affirm, of very strong, positive, and most important realities. What then may that be which always appears to our minds the deficiency in our conception of Spirit—which makes the conception to our reflection appear unsatisfactory—nay, which at times makes us doubt if indeed we have it at all?

Shepherd. Clear up that to my contentment, sir, and you'll mak me happy a' the rest o' the nicht.

North. We say, then, that we can conceive a notion of the being of matter, but not a notion of the being of Spirit.

Shepherd. The materialists say sae.

North. What conception then, I ask, have we of the being of Matter? Probably there comes before our mind the image of something extended and opake?

Shepherd. Just sae.

North. If we make the conception a little more intense, then the conception of that property by which body is displaced or displaces is superadded?

Shepherd. Just sae.

North. If we were to think farther, quality after quality is superadded, till the idea is of some definite known substance?

Shepherd. This table.

North. Just so, James. Or by effort of the mind we may proceed in the other direction, endeavoring to abstract the idea to the utmost; we can dismiss the idea of opacity, and conceive Matter as transparent; we can reduce the idea of extension to the most indivisible atom. In all such cases it is obvious that our conception of Matter is the mere recovery to the mind of some remains of actual impression made on the sense.

Shepherd. It would seem sae—just sae, sir.

North. The conclusion, I apprehend, must be, that the conception we think we have of the being of Matter, is a conception either of past impressions of sense, or of an apprehended power to affect the sense with impressions; but the moment we attempt to conceive of that Something having power to affect the sense—to conceive of it in any way absolutely distinct from the remembered impression of sense, we find that we are entirely unable to shape such a conception—and we acknowledge, that of the being of Matter itself, we really have no more conception than of the being of Spirit?

Shepherd. That seems sound logic.

North. Therefore, my dear Shepherd, we cannot call it an imperfection in our conception of Spirit, that we do not conceive its mode of being, since you see we do not conceive it even of Matter.

Shepherd. Conclusive.

North. What we miss, then, in the conception of Spirit, is I believe, nothing else than that shadowy image of Matter, derived from sense, which unavoidably attends upon the conception of Matter.

Shepherd. Even o' a ghost.

North. A good illustration. If this be true, then, all that is really deficient in our conception of Spirit is that which it could not by any possibility include, namely, the image of an impression on sense!

Shepherd. Let the materialists answer that. That's a bane for them to mumble till their jaws are sair.

North. But, my dear James, I claim your ear for a few minutes more.

Shepherd. You'll no be angry if I keep eatin' awa' at the oysters?

North. Not at all. If the two conceptions of Matter and Spirit be examined in more particular comparison, it will perhaps be found that what to our first apprehension of them makes the difference of the power of conceiving them so indissoluble, are the two circumstances—first of the excessive complexity of impressions—the body of impressions, if it may be called so—that we derive from the forms of material being with which we are most familiar—and, secondly, that the great qualities of its weight and impenetrability make such powerful and overcoming impressions upon those bodies from which the mind receives the materials of all its conceptions. These are circumstances in the conception of material being which must needs affect strongly the opinion of the mind which has not been practised to analyze its conceptions, but which it puts away, one by one, as it becomes familiar with the process of resolving its complex impressions into their elements.

Shepherd. My genius is rather synthetical, than analytic, I suspeck, but I'm no carin'.

North. Now, Spirit, James, presents no such complex aggregate of impressions embodied together, and therefore does not rise as a full conception to the mind, but has to be slowly produced. Thus, it appears to me that there is nothing defective in the conception of Spirit which it could possibly include. All that is defective, in our knowledge of it, is, that its properties are not manifested to sense; but that is the very ground of its character, and its essential distinction from Matter, of which the sole character that we can give is, that it is being, of which the properties are manifested to sense.

Shepherd. If that's no truth, then welcome falsehood.

North. Spirit is conscious of itself, and that consciousness is the sole ground of our belief in its being.

Shepherd. And what else would fules seek?

North. Firmer than all rocks. Oh! what is the whole life of the human creature but continual self-consciousness, varied in ten thousand times ten thousand ways? This Spirit, united by life to material being, sees no spirit but itself; but it sees living bodies like its own—warm in life—springing with motion—gestures, look, voice, speech answering to its own; and it believes them to bear Spirits like itself—beings of will, love, wrath, tears.

Shepherd. Dinna rin aff into description; but haud up your head, and stick to the soobject, like a Scots thrissle, tall as a tree.

North. We believe, then, in a kind of being distinct from Matter, because we cannot help it. We have no other resource, and we choose to call it Spirit. That there is power, energy, will, pleasure, pain, thought, we know; and that is all that is necessary to the conception of Spirit, except one negation—that it is not cognizable to sense. All we have now to ask ourselves is, "Is this being, that feels, wills, thinks, cognizable by sense? If so, by what sense? If there is no account to be given, that this thinking, willing, feeling being was ever taken cognizance of by sense, it seems at least a hard assertion to say it *is* so cognizable—an assertion at least as hazardous as to say it is not.

Shepherd. Ten thoosand million times mair sae.

North. If you consider, then, my dearest Shepherd, what is our reasoning when we form to ourselves a belief of Spirit, it is simply this—"Here is Matter which I know by my senses. There is nothing here which appears to me like what I know in myself. My senses, which take cognizance of Matter, show me nothing of the substance which thinks, or wills, or feels. I believe, then, that there is being, which they cannot show me, in which these powers reside. I believe that I am a spirit.

Shepherd. "Plato, thou reasonest well."

North. From the moment the child is conscious of power within himself, of thought, sense, love, desire, pain, pleasure, will, he is beginning to gather together in one the impressions, feelings, and recollections which he will one day unite in conception under the name of Spirit.

Shepherd. Mysterious life o' weans!

North. Ah! that deep and infinite world, which is gradually opened up within ourselves, overshadowed as it is with the beautiful imagery of this material world, which it has received into itself and cherishes! Ah! this is the domain of Spirit. When our thoughts begin to kindle, when our heart dilates, the remembrances of the works of Spirit pour in upon us: let me rather say, my Shepherd, the Sun of Spirit rises in its strength, and consumes the mist, and we walk in the joy of his light, and exult in the genial warmth of his life-glorifying beams.

Shepherd. Simpler, simpler, simpler, sir.

North. Oral need not be so correct as written discourse. But I take the hint, and add, if it be asked why it is hard to us to form the conception, why we nourish it with difficulty, why our minds are so slow to reply when they are challenged to speak in this cause, it is because they are dull in their own self-consciousness.

Shepherd. That's a better style.

North. The Spirit, which feeds the body with life, itself languishes. It has not learnt to awaken and cherish its own fires. It is only when strong conception seizes upon its powers, and swells them into strength, that it truly knows, and vividly feels itself, and rejoices, like the morn, in its own lustre.

Shepherd. Eyeing the clouds as ornaments, and disposin' them as fits its fancy in masses, or braids, or specs—a' alike beautifu'.

North. Illustrating the line in Wordsworth—

> "This morning gives us promise of a glorious day."

Shepherd. Weel—weel—aye quottin' Wordsworth.

North. Oh the blind breasts of man! Because in the weakness of our nature we cannot rend ourselves enough from sense, we often seek to clothe the being of Spirit in the vain shadows of material form! But we must aspire to a constant conviction that at the verge and brink of this material nature in which we stand, there is an abyss of being unfathomable to all our thoughts! Unknown existences incomprehensible of an infinite world! Of what mighty powers may dwell there—what wonders may be there disclosed—what mutation and revolution of being or what depths of immutable repose, we know nothing. Shut up in our finite sense, we are severed for a while, on our spot of the universe, from those boundless immortalities. How near they may be to us we know not, or in what manner they may be connected with us—around us or within us! This vast expanse of worlds, stretching into our heavens many thousand times beyond the reach of our powerfullest sight—all this may be—as a speck of darkness!

Shepherd. I wuss Dr. Chaumers heard ye, sir.

North. I wish he did. And may we, with our powers, fed on Matter and drenched in Sense, think to solve the question of what being may be beyond? Take upon us impiously to judge whether there be a world unsearchable to us, or whether this Matter on which we stand be all? And by the measure of our Sense circumscribe all the possibilities of creation, while we pretend to believe in the Almighty? If where we cannot know, we must yet needs choose our belief, oh! let us choose with better hope that belief which more humbles ourselves; and in bowed down and fearful awe, not in presumptuous intelligence, look forth from the stillness of our souls into the silence of unknown Being!

Shepherd. I may weel be mute, sir. Sit nearer me, sir, and gie me your haun'—and lay't on my shouther, if you're no quite dune.

North. I would fain speak to the youth of my native land, James—

Shepherd. And dinna they a' read the Noctes?

North. ——and ask them—when the kindling imagination blends itself with Intellectual Thought—when the awakened, ardent, aspiring intelligence begins in the joy of young desire to lift itself in high conception to the stately minds that had lived upon the earth —when it begins to feel the pride of hope and power, to glow with conscious energy, to create thoughts of its own of the destinies of that race to which it rejoices to belong—do not then, I ask them, all the words which the mighty of old have dropped from their kindling lips concerning the Emanation of the Eternal Mind, which dwells in a form of dust, fall like sparks, setting the hope of immortality in a blaze—

> "The sudden blaze
> Far round illumines *heaven*?"

If, while engaged in the many speculations in which our studious youth have been involved, they suffer themselves to be dragged for a time from that primal belief, do they find a weight of darkness and perplexity come over them, which they will strive in vain to shake off? But as soon as they reawaken to the light of their first conviction, that heavy dream will be gone. "I can give no account"—such an one might say—"nor record of this conviction. I drew it from no dictate of reason. But it has grown upon me through all the years of my existence. I cannot collect together the arguments on which I believe, but they are for ever rising round me anew, and in new power, every moment I draw my breath. At every step I take of inquiry into my own being, they burst upon me in different unexpected forms. If I have learned to lean to the side of the material philosophy, every thing that I understood before was darkened—my clearest way was perplexed. I believed at first, because the desire of my soul cleaved to the thought of its lofty original. I believe now, because the doctrine is a light to me in the difficulties of science—a clew in labyrinths otherwise inextricable."

(*Knocking at the front door and ringing of the front-door bell, as if a section of guardians of the night were warning the family of fire, or a dozen devils, on their way back to Pandemonium, were wreaking their spite on Christopher's supposed slumbers.*)

Shepherd. Whattt ca' ye' thattt?

North (*musing*). I should not wonder were that Tickler?

Shepherd. Then he maun be in full tail as weel's figg, or else a Breearious. (*Uproar rather increases.*) They're surely usin' sledge-hammers! or are they but cain' away wi' their cuddie-heels? We ocht to be gratefu', howsomever, that they've settled the bell. The wire rop's brak.

North (*gravely*). I shall sue Southside for damages.

Shepherd. Think ye, sir, they'll burst the door?

North (*smiling contemptuously*). Not unless they have brought with them Mons Meg.* But there is no occasion for the plural number—'tis that singular sinner Southside.

* From the Bomb Battery of Edinburgh Castle, is a fine view of the New Town, the environs, the Firth of Forth, and the coast of Fife. On the Argyle battery, beneath it, now stands an ancient piece of ordnance called MONS MEG. It is a gun, composed of long bars of beat iron, hooped together by a close series of rings. It measures twenty inches in the bore and is supposed to have been fabricated under the auspices of James IV., who, in 1498, employed it at the siege of Norham Castle, on the borders of England. It was rent in 1682 when firing a salute, since which time it has been quite useless. In 1745, it was removed to England and deposited in the Tower of London. It is mentioned in Drummond's Macaronics

—Sicuti Mons Megga crackasset.

When George IV. was in Edinburgh in 1822, he visited the Castle, and after he had stood upon the bastion whereon Mons Meg had formerly stood, Scott so earnestly solicited the restoration of the old and useless gun, that his Majesty consented. However, it was not brought back for several years, it appearing by Scott's diary, under date March 9, 1829, that great solemnity was used on the occasion. His memorandum is:—"Went about one o'clock to the Castle, where we saw the *auld* murderess, Mons Meg, brought up in solemn procession to reoccupy her ancient place on the Argyle Battery. Mons Meg is a monument of our pride and poverty. The size is enormous, but six smaller guns would have been made at the same expense, and done six times as much execution as she could have done. There was immense interest taken in the show by the people of the town, and the numbers who crowded the Castle Hill had a magnificent appearance. About thirty of our Celts [the Celtic Club, composed of men of rank and fortune] attended in costume; and as there was a Highland Regiment for duty, with dragoons and artillery-men the whole made a splendid show. The style in which the last manned and wrought the windlass

Shepherd. Your servants maun be the Seven Sleepers

North. They have orders never to be disturbed after midnight.

Enter PETER, *in his shirt.*

Peter, let him in—show him ben—and (*whispers Peter, who makes his exit and his entrance, ushering in* TICKLER *in a Dreadnought, covered with cranreuch.** NORTH *and the* SHEPHERD *are seen lying on their faces on the hearth-rug.*)

Peter. Oh! dear! oh! dear! oh! dear! what is this! what is this! Hae I leeved to see my master and Mr. Hogg lyin' baith dead!

Tickler (*in great agitation*). Heavens! what has happened! This is indeed dreadful.

Peter. Oh! sir! oh! sir! it's that cursed charcoal that he wou'd use for a' I cou'd do—the effluvia has smothered him at last. There's the pan—there's the pan! But let's raise them up, and bear them into the back-green.—(PETER *raises the body of* NORTH *in his arms*—TICKLER *that of the* SHEPHERD.)—Stiff! stiff! stiff! cauld! cauld! cauld! dead! dead! dead!

Tickler (*wildly*). When saw you them last?

Peter. O, sir, no for several hours! my beloved master sent me to bed at twelve—and now 'tis two half-past.

Tickler (*dreadfully agitated*). This is death.

Shepherd (*seizing him suddenly round the waist*). Then try Death a wrastle.

North (*recuperated by the faithful* PETER). Fair play, Hogg! You've hold of the waistband of his breeches. 'Tis a dog-fall.

(*The* SHEPHERD *and* TICKLER *contend fiercely on the rug.*)

Tickler (*uppermost*). You deserve to be throttled, you swineherd, for having wellnigh broke my heart.

Shepherd. Pu' him aff, North—pu' him aff—or he'll thrapple me! Whr—whr—rrr—whrrr——(SOUTHSIDE *is choked off the* SHEPHERD *and takes his seat on the sofa with tolerable composure. Exit* PETER.)

Tickler. Bad taste—bad taste. Of all subjects for a practical joke, the worst is death.

Shepherd. A gran' judge o' taste! Ca' you't good taste to break folk's bell-rops, and kick at folk's front doors, when a' the city's in sleep?

Tickler. I confess the propriety of my behaviour was problematical.

Shepherd. Problematical! You wad hae been cheap o't, if Mr. North out o' the window had shot you dead on the spat.

which raised Old Meg, weighing seven or eight tons, from her temporary carriage to that which has been her basis for many years, was singularly beautiful, as a combined exhibition of skill and strength." It had been customary to fire bullets of stone from Mons Meg, which were afterwards economically sought for, and picked up for future use. Some of those are now piled alongside of the old gun, which the Scotch consider a kind of National palladium!—M.

* Cranreuch—hoar-frost.—M.

North (*leaning kindly over* TICKLER, *as* SOUTHSIDE *is sitting on the sofa, and insinuating his dexter hand into the left coat-pocket of* TIMOTHY'S *Dreadnought.*) Ha! ha! Look here, Mr. Hogg! (*Exhibits a bell-handle and brass knocker.*) Street robbery!

Shepherd. Hamesucken!

North. An accomplished cracksman!

Tickler. I plead guilty.

Shepherd. Plead guilty! What brazen assurance! Caught wi' *corpus delicti* in the pouch o' your wrap-rascal. Bad taste—bad taste. But sin' you repent, you're forgi'en. Whare hae you been, and whence at this untimeous hour hae you come! Tak' a sup o' that. (*Handing him the jug.*)

Tickler. From Duddingstone Loch. I detest skating in a crowd—so have been figuring away by moonlight to the Crags.

Shepherd. Are you sure you're quite sober?

Tickler. Quite at present. That's a jewel of a jug, James—But what were you talking about?

Shepherd. Never fash your thoomb—but sit doon at the side-table yonner.

Tickler. Ha! The ROUND! (*Sits retired.*)

Shepherd. I was sayin', Mr. Tickler, that I canna get rid o' a belief in the mettaseekozies or transmigration o' sowles. It aften comes upon me as I'm sittin' by mysell on a knowe in the Forest; and a' the scenery, steadfast as it seems to be before my senses as the place o' my birth, and accordin' to the popular faith where I hae past a' my days, is then strangely felt to lose its intimate or veetal connection wi' my speerituality, and to be but ae dream-spat amang mony dream-spats which maun be a' taken thegither in a bewilderin' series, to mak' up the yet uncompleted mystery o' my being or life.

North. Pythagoras!

Shepherd. Mind that I'm no wullin' to tak my Bible-oath for the truth o' what I'm noo gaun to tell you—for what's real and what's visionary—and whether there be indeed three warlds—ane o' the ee—ane o' the memory, and ane o' the imagination—it's no for me dogmatically to decide; but this I wull say—that if there are three, at sic times they're sae circumvolved and confused wi' ane anither, as to hae the appearance and inspire the feelin' o' their bein' but ae world—or I should rather say, but ae life. The same sort of consciousness, sirs, o' my haen experimentally belanged alike to them a', comes owre me like a threefauld shadow, and in that shadow my sowle sits wi' its heart beatin', frichtened to think o' a' it has come through, syne the first far-awa glimmer o' nascent thocht connectin' my particular individuality wi' the universal creation. Am I makin' mysell understood?

Tickler. Pellucid as an icicle that seems warm in the sunshine.

Shepherd. Yet you dinna see my drift—and I'm at a loss for words.

Tickler. You might as well say you are at a loss for oysters, with five hundred on that board.

Shepherd. I think on a cave—far ben, mirk always as a midnight wood—except that twa lichts are burnin' there brichter than ony stars—fierce leevin lichts—yet in their fierceness fu' o' love, and therefore fu' e' beauty—the een o' my mother, as she gently growls o'er me wi' a pur that inspires me wi' a passion for milk and bluid.

Tickler. Your mother! The man's mad.

Shepherd. A lioness, and I her cub.

North. Hush—hush, Tickler.

Shepherd. I sook her dugs, and sookin' I grow sae cruel that I could bite. Between pain and pleasure, she gies me a puff wi' her paw, and I gang head owre heels like a bit playfu' kitten. And what else am I but a bit playfu' kitten! For we're o' the Cat kind —we Lions—and bein' o' the royal race o' Africa, but ae whalp at a birth. She taks me mewin' up in her mouth, and lets me drap amang leaves in the outer air—lyin' down aside me and enticin' me to play wi' the tuft o' her tail, that I suppose, in my simplicity, to be itsell a separate hairy cretur alive as weel as me, and gettin' fun, as wi' loups and springs we pursue ane anither, and then for a minute pretend to be sleepin'. And wha's he yon? Wha but my Father? I ken him instinctively by the mane on his shouthers, and his bare tawny hurdies—but my mither wull no let him come ony nearer, for he yawns as if he were hungry, and she kens he would think naething o' devourin, his ain offspring. Oh! the first time I heard him crunch! It was an antelope—in his fangs like a mouse —but that is an after similitude—for then I had never seen a mouse —nor do I think I ever did a' the time I was in the great desert.

North (*removing to some distance*). Tickler, he looks alarmingly leonine.

Shepherd. I had then nae ee for the picturesque—but out o' thae materials then sae familiar to my senses, I hae mony a time since constructed the landscape in which my youth sported—and oh! that I could but dash it off on canvass!

North. Salvator Rosa, the great Poussin, and he of Duddingstone, would then have to "hide their diminished heads."

Shepherd. A cave-mouth, half-high as that o' Staffa; but no fantastic in its structure like the hexagonals—a' ae sullen rock! Yet was the savage den maist sweet—for frae the arch hung doun midway a mony-colored drapery, leaf-and-flower-woven by nature, who delights to beautify the wilderness, renewed as soon as faded, or else perennial, in spite o' a' thae suns and a' thae storms! Frae our roof strecht up rose the trees, wi' crowns that touched the skies. There hung the umbrage like clouds—and to us below how pleasant was the shade! From the cave-mouth a green lawn descended to a pool, where the pelican used to come to drink—and mony a time hae I watched crouchin' ahin' the water-lilies, that I micht spring upon her when she had filled her bag—but if I was cunnin' she was wary, and aye fand her way back unskathed by me to her nest. A' roun' was sand; for you see, sirs, it was an oasis—and I suspect they were palm-trees. I can liken a leaf, as it cam waverin' doon, to naething I hae seen sin' syne but a parachute. I used to play with them till they withered, and then to row mysell in them, like a wean hidin' itsell for fun in the claes, to mak its mither true it was na there—till a' at ance I loupt oot on my mither the Lioness, and in a mock-fecht we twa gaed gurlin' down the brae—me generally uppermost—for ye can hae nae idea hoo tender are the maist terrible o' animals to their young—and what delicht the auld she ane has in pretendin' to be vanquished in even-doon worryin' by a bit cub that would be nae mair than a match for Rover there, or even Fang. Na—ye need na lift your heads and cock your lugs, my gude douggies, for I'm speakin' o' you and no to you, and likenin' your force to mine when I was a Lion's whalf.

Rover and Fang (*leaping up and barking at the* SHEPHERD). Wow—bow—wow—bow—wow—wow.

North. They certainly think, Tickler, that he must be either Wallace or Nero.

Shepherd. Sae passed my days—aud a happier young hobbletehoy of a Lion never footed it on velvet pads alang the Lybian sands. Only sometimes for days—na weeks—I was maist desperate hungry—for the antelopes and sic like creturs began to get unco scarce—pairtly frae bein' feared awa'—and I've kent us obleeged to dine, and be thankfu', on jackal.

Tickler. Hung up in hams from the roof of the cave.

Shepherd. But that was no the worst o't—for spring cam—as I felt rather than saw—and day or nicht—sleepin' or waukin'—I cou'd get nae rest—I was verra feverish and verra fierce, and keepit prowlin' and growlin' about——

Tickler. Like a lion in love——

Shepherd. I couldna distinctly tell why—and sae did my mither. wha lookit as if in gude earnest she wad tear me in pieces.

Tickler. Whattt?

Shepherd. She wou'd glare on me wi' her green een, as if she wanted to set fire to my hide, as you may hae seen a laddie in a window wi' a glass settin' fire to a man's hat on the street, by the power o' the focus—and then she wou'd wallow on the sand, as if to rub aff ticks that tormented her—and then wi' a shake, garrin' the piles shower frae her, wou'd gallop down to the pool as if aboot to droon hersell, and though no in general fond o' the water, plowter in't like the verra pelican.

Tickler. "Just like unto a trundling mop
Or a wild goose at play."

Shepherd. The great desert grew a' ae roar! and thirty feet every spang cam lowpen, wi' his enormous mane, the Lion my father, wi' his tail, tuft and a', no perpendicular like a bull's, but extended horizontally ahint him, as stiff's iron, and a' bristlin'—and fastened in his fangs in the back o' the Lioness my mother's neck, wha forthwith began caterwauling waur than a hunder roof fu's o' cats, till I had amaist swarfed through fear, and forgotten that I was ane o' their own whalps.

Tickler. "To show how much thou wast degenerate."

Shepherd. Sae I thocht it high time to leave them to devoor ane anither, and I slank aff, wi' my tail atween my legs, intil the wilderness, resolved to return to my native oasis never mair. I looked back frae the tap o' a sand-hill, and saw what micht hae been, or not been, the croons o' the palm-trees—and then glided on till I cam to anither "palm-grove, islanded amid the waste"—as Soothey finely says—where instinct urged me to seek a lair, and I found ane —no sae superb, indeed, as my native den—no sae magnificent—but in itsell bonnier and brichter and mair blissfu' far—safter, far and wide a' around it, was the sand to the soles and pawms o' my paws—for an event befell me there that in a day elevated me into Lionhood, and crooned me wi' the imperial diadem of the Desert.

Tickler. As how?

North. James!

Shepherd. In the centre o' the grove was a well—not dug by hands—though caravans had passed that way—but formed naturally in the thin-grassed sand by a spring that in summer drought cared not for the sun—and round about that well were some beautifu' bushes, that bore flowers amaist as big's roses, but liker lilies——

Tickler. Most flowery of the feline!

Shepherd. But, oh heavens! ten thousand million times mair beautifu' than the gorgeous bushes 'neath which she lay asleep! A cretur o' my ain kind! couchant! wi' her sweet nose atween her forepaws! The elegant line o' her yellow back, frae shouther to rump, broken here and there by a blossom-laden spray that depended lovingly to touch her slender side! Her tail gracefully gathered up amang the delicate down on which she reposed! Little of visible but the tender tuft! Eyes and lips shut! There slept the Virgin of the Wild! still as the well, and as pure, in which her eemage was enshrined! I trumbled like a kid—I heard a knock-in', but it did na wauken her—and creepin' stealthily on my gruff, I laid mysell, without growlin', side by side, a' my length alang hers—and as oor fur touched, the touch garred me at first a' grue, and then glow as if prickly thorns had pleasurably pierced my verra heart. Saftly—saftly pat I ae paw on the back o' her head, and anither aneath her chin—and then laid my cheek to hers, and gied the ear niest me a wee bit bite! When up she sprang higher in the air, Mr. Tickler, than the feather on your cap when you was in the Volunteers; and on recoverin' her feet after the fa', without stayin' to look around her, spang by spang tapped the shrubs, and afore I had presence o' mind to pursue her, round a sand-hill was out o' sicht!

North. Ay, James—joy often drops out between the cup and the lip—or, like riches, takes wings to itself and flies away. And was she lost to thee for ever?

Shepherd. I lashed mysell wi' my tail—I trode and tore up the shrubs wi' my hind paws—I turned up my jaws to heaven, and yowled in wrathfu' despair—and then pat my mouth to the dust, and roared till the well began to bubble—then I lapped water, and grew thirstier the langer I lapped—and then searched wi' a' my seven senses the bed whare her beautifu' bulk had lain—warmer and safter and sweeter than the ither herbage—and in rage tried to bite a bit out o' my ain shouther, when the pain sent me bounding aff in pursuit o' my lovely lioness—and lo! there she was stealin' alang by the brink o' anither nest o' bushes, far aff on the plain, pausin' to look back—sae I thocht—e'er she disappeared in her hiding-place. Round and round the brake I careered, in narrowing circles, that my Delicht should not escape my desire, and at last burst crashin' in upon her wi' ae spang, and seized her by the nape o' the neck, as my father had seized my mother, and pinned her down to the dust.* But I was mercifu' as I was strang; and being assured by her, that if I wou'd but be less rampawgeous, that she would at least gi'e me a hearin', I released her neck frae my fangs, but keepit a firm paw on her, till I had her promise that she wou'd agree to ony proposal in reason, provided my designs were honorable—and honorable they were as ever were breathed by bosom leonine in the solitary wilderness.

North. "I calmed her fears, and she was calm,
And told her love with virgin pride;
And thus I won my Genevieve,
My bright and beauteous bride."

Shepherd. We were perfectly happy, sir. Afore the hinny-moon had filled her horns, mony an antelope, and not a few monkeys,

* In the tragedy of Douglas, Horne has the line,
"I'll woo her as the lion does his bride."—M.

had we twa together devoored! Oh, sirs! but she was fleet! and sly as swift! She would lie couchin' in a bush till she was surrounded wi' grazin' edibles suspectin' nae harm, and ever and anon ceasin' to crap the twigs, and playin' wi' ane anither, like lambs in the Forest, where it is now my lot as a human cretur to leeve! Then up in the air and amang them wi' a roar, smitin' them dead in dizzens wi' ae touch o' her paw, though it was safter than velvet —and singlin' out the leader by his horns, that purrin' she micht leasurely sook his bluid—nor at sic times wou'd it hae been safe even for me, her lion and her lord, to ha'e interfered wi' her repast. For in the desert, hunger and thirst are as fierce as love. As for me, in this respect, I was mair generous, and mony is the time and aft that I hae gi'en her the tid-bits o' fat frae the flank o' a deer o' my ain killin' when she had missed her aim by owrespringin't—for I never ken't her spang fa' short—without her so much as thankin' me—for she was owre prood ever to seem gratefu' for ony favor— and carried hersell, like a Beauty as she was, and a spoiled Bride. I was sometimes sair tempted to throttle her—but then, to be sure, a playfu' pat frae her paw could smooth my bristles at ony time, or mak' me lift up my mane for her delicht, that she might lie down bashfully aneath its shadow, or as if shelterin' there frae some object o' her fear, crouch pantin' amang that envelopment o' hairy clouds.

Tickler. Whew!

North. In that excellent work the Naturalists' Library,* edited by my learned friend Sir William Jardine, it is observed, if I recollect rightly, that Temminck, in his monograph, places the African Lion in two varieties, that of Barbary and that of Senegal—without referring to those of the southern parts of the continent. In the southern parts there are two kinds analogous, it would seem, to the northern varieties—the yellow and the brown, or, according to the Dutch colonists, the blue and the black. Of the Barbary Lion, the hair is of a deep yellowish brown, the mane and hair upon the breast and insides of the fore-legs being ample, thick, and shaggy; of the Senegal Lion, the color of the body is of a much paler tint, the mane is much less, does not extend so far upon the shoulders, and is almost entirely wanting upon the breast and insides of the legs. Mr. Burchel encountered a third variety of the African Lion, whose mane is nearly quite black, and him the Hottentots declare to be the most fierce and daring of all. Now, my dear James, pardon me for asking whether you were the Senegal or Barbary Lion, or one of the southern varieties analogous to them, or the third variety, with the mane nearly black, that encountered Mr. Burchel?

* Published in Edinburgh.—M.

Tickler. He must have been a fourth variety, and probably the sole specimen thereof; for all naturalists agree that the young males have neither mane nor tail-tuft, and exhibit no incipient symptoms of such appendage till about their third year.

Shepherd. Throughout the hale series o' my transmigration o' sowle I hae aye been equally in growth and genius extraordinar' precocious, Timothy; and besides, I dinna clearly see hoo either Buffon, or Civviar, or Tinnock, or Sir William Jarrdinn, or Jeems Wulson, or even Wommle himsell, familiar as they may be wi' Lions in plates or cages, should ken better about their manes and the tuft o' their tails, than me wha was ance a Lion *in propria personâ*, and hae thochts o' writing my ain Leonine Owtobiography wi' Cuts. But as for my color, I was neither a blue, nor a black, nor a white, nor a red Lion—though you, Tickler, may hae seen sic like on the signs o' inns—but I was the TERRIBLE TAWNEY O' TIMBUCTOO!!!

Tickler. What! did you live in the capital?

Shepherd. Na—in my kintra seat a' the year roun'. But there was mair than a sugh o' me in the metropolis—mony a story was tauld o' me by Moor and Mandingo—and by whisper o' my name they stilled their cryin' weans, and frichtened them to sleep. What kent I, when a lion, o' geography? Nae map o' Africa had I ever seen but what I scrawled wi' my ain claws on the desert dust. As for the Niger, I cared nae whether it flawed to meet the risin' or the settin' sun—but when the sun entered Leo, I used instinctively to soom in its waters, and I remember, as if it had been yesterday, loupin' in amang a bevy o' black girlies bathin' in a shallow, and breakfastin' on ane o' them, wha ate as tender as a pullet, and was as plump as a paitrick. It was lang afore the time o' Mungo Park—but had I met Mungo I wou'd na hae hurt a hair o' his head—for my prophetic sowle would hae been conscious o' the Forest, and however hungry, never wou'd I hae harmed him wha had leeved on the Tweed.

North. Beautiful. Pray, James, is it true that your Lion prefers human flesh to any other—nay, after once tasting it, that he uniformly becomes an anthropophagus?

Shepherd. He may or he may not uniformly become an anthropophagus, for I kenna what an anthropophogus is; but as to preferring human flesh to ony ither, that depends on the particular kind o' human flesh. I presume, when I was a Lion, that I had the ordinar' appetencies o' a Lion—that is, that I was rather abune than below average or par—and at a' events that there was naething about me unleonine. Noo I cou'd never bring my stammach, without difficulty, to eat an auld woman—as for an auld man that was out o' the question, even in starvation. On the whole I preferred, in the long run, antelope ever to girl. Girl dootless was a delicacy ance a fortnicht or thereabouts—but girl every day would hae been——

Tickler. *Toujours perdrix*.

Shepherd. Just sae. Anither Lion, a freen' o' mine, tho', thocht otherwise, and used to lie in ambuscade for girl, on which he fed a' through the year. But mark the consequence, why he lost his senses, and died ragin' mad!

Tickler. You don't sae so!

Shepherd. Instinctively I ken't better, and diversified my dinners wi' zebras and quaggas, and such small deer, sae that I was always in high condition, my skin was aye sleek, my mane meteorous; and as for my tail, wherever I went, the tuft bore aff the belle.

North. Leo—are you, or are you not a cowardly animal?

Shepherd. After I had reached the age o' puberty my courage never happened to be put to ony verra severe trial, for I was aye faithfu' to my mate—and she to me—and jealousy never disturbed our den.

Tickler. Any cubs?

Shepherd. But I cou'dna hae wanted courage, since I never felt fear. I aye took the sun o' the teegger; and, though the rhinoceros is an ugly customer, he used to gie me the wa'; at sicht o' me the elephant become his ain trumpeter, and sounded a retreat in amang the trees. Ance, and ance only, I had a desperate fecht wi' a unicorn.

North. So he is not fabulous?

Shepherd. No him, indeed—he's ane o' the realest o' a' beasts.

Tickler. What may be the length of his horn, James?

Shepherd. O' a dagger.

Tickler. Shape?

Shepherd. No speerally wreathed like a ram's horn—but stretcht, smooth, and polished, o' the yellow ivory—sharper than a swurd.

Tickler. Hoofs.

Shepherd. His hoofs are no cloven, and he's no unlike a horse. But in place o' nicherin' like a horse, he roars like a bull; and then he leeves on flesh.

Tickler. I thought he had been omnivorous.

Shepherd. Nae cretur's omnivorous but man.

North. Rare?

Shepherd. He maun be verra rare, for I never saw anither but him I focht. The battle was in a wood. We're natural enemies, and set to wark the moment we met without ony quarrel. Wi' the first pat o' my paw I scored him frae shouther to flank, till the bluid spouted in jettees. As he ran at me wi' his horn I jookit ahint a tree, and he transfixed it in the pith—sheathen't to the verra hilt.

There was nae use in flingin' up his heels, for wi' the side-spang I was on his back, and fastenin' my hind claws in his flank and my fore-claws in his shouthers, I began at my leisure devooring him in the neck. She sune joined me, and ate a hole into his inside till she got at the kidney—but judgin' by him, nae animal's mair tenawcious o' life than the unicorn—for when we left him the remains were groanin'. Niest mornin' we went to breakfast on him, but thae gluttonous creturs, the vulturs, had been afore us, and he was but banes.

North. Are you not embellishing, James?

Shepherd. Sic a fack needs nae embellishment. But I confess, sirs, I was, on the first hearin' o't, incredulous o' Major Laing's bain' found the skeleton stickin' to the tree!

North. Why incredulous?

Shepherd. For wha can tell at what era I was a Lion? But it pruves that the banes o' a unicorn are durable as airn.

North. And Ebony an immortal wood.

Tickler. Did you finish your career in a trap?

Shepherd. Na. I died in open day in the centre o' the great square o' Timbuctoo.

Tickler. Ha, ha! baited?

Shepherd. Na. I was lyin' ae day by mysell—for she had disappeared to whalp amang the shrubs—waitin' for some wanderin' waif comin' to the well—for thirst is stranger than fear in them that dwall in the desert, and they will seek for water even in the Lion's lair—when I saw the head o' an unknown animal high up amang the trees, browsin' on the sprays—and then its lang neck—and then its shouthers—and then its forelegs—and then its body droopin' down into a tail like a buffalo's—an animal unlike ony ither I had ever seen afore—for though spotted like a leopard, it was in shape liker a unicorn—but then its een were black and saft, like the een o' an antelope, and as it licket the leaves, I kent that tongue had never lapped bluid. I stretched mysell up wi' my usual roar, and in less time than it takes to tell't was on the back o' the Giraffe.

Ambo. Oh! oh! oh! oh! oh! oh!

Shepherd. I happened no to be verra hungry—and my fangs—without munchin'—pierced but an inch or twa deep. Brayin' across the sand-hills at a lang trot flew the cameleopard—nor for hours slackened she her pace—till she plunged into the Black river——

Tickler. The Niger.

Shepherd. ——Swam across, and bore me through many groves into a wide plain, all unlike the wilderness round the Oasis we had left at morn.

North. What to that was Mazeppa's ride on the desert-born!

Shepherd. The het bluid grew sweeter and sweeter as I drank—

and I saw naething but her neck, till a' at ance staggerin' she fell doon—and what a sicht! Rocks, as I thocht them—but they were houses—encirclin' me a' round—thousan's o' blackamoors, wi' shirts and spears and swurds and fires, and drums, hemmin' the Lion—and arrows—like the flyin' dragons I had seen in the desert, but no, like them, harmless—stingin' me through the sides intil the entrails, that when I bat them brak! You asked me if I was a cooard? Was't like a cooard to drive, in that condition, the hale city like sheep? But a' at ance, without my ain wull, my spangin' was changed into sprawlin' wi' my fore feet. I still made them spin—but my hind legs were useless—my back was broken—and what I was lappin', sirs, was a pool o' my ain bluid. I had spewed it as my heart burst—first fire grew in my een and then mist—and the last thing I remember was a shout and a roar. And thus, in the centre o' the great square o' Timbuctoo, the Lion died.

North. And the hide of him, who is now the Ettrick Shepherd, has for generations been an heir-loom in the palace of the Emperor of all the Saharas!

Shepherd. Nae less strange than true. Noo, North, let's hear o' ane o' your transmigrations.

North. "Some Passages in the Life o' a Merman?"

Shepherd. If you please.

North. Another night, James; for really, after such painting and such poetry——

Shepherd. Weel, weel, sir. I never insist. Oh! hoo I hate to hear a hash insist! Insistin' that you shall tell a story—insistin' that you shall sing—insistin' that you shall tak anither jug—insistin' that you shall sit still—insistin', in short, that you shall do the verra thing, whatever it happens to be, that ye hae declared a dizzen times that you will be danged if you do—dang him! droon him! deevil droon him! canna he haud his foul tongue, and scarte his sawte head without ony interruption, and be thankfu'—and no—

North. James! James! James!

Shepherd (*laughing*). Beg your pardon, sir; but only yestreen at a pairty I was "sae pestered wi' a popinjay," that I'm ashamed to say I forgot mysell sae far as to dash a jug o' het water in his face—and tho' he made an apology, I fin' I hae na forgi'en him yet—was I red in the face?

North. Ratherly.

Shepherd. What's this? What's this? See, the floor's in an inundation! Is that your doin', Mr. Tickler?

Tickler. What the deuce do you mean, Hogg? My doing?

Shepherd. Yes—it is your doin'. A stream o' water comin' frae you a' owre the Turkey carpet—and reachin'—see tull't—the rim o' the rug. What sort o' mainners is this, to force your way at midnicht into an honest man's house, and spile a' his furnitur'? There you sit at the Round, in your dreadnoucht, like a Norway bear, and never thocht hoo the snaw, and the cranreuch, and the icicles hae been meltin' this last hour, till the floor's a' soomin'!

Tickler. You can cross at the ford.

North. James—let it seep. Shall we have some beef-à-la-mode, James?

Shepherd. Eh?

North. Thus.

(NORTH *flings into the bright smokeless element slice after slice of the Round, previously well-salted and peppered—they fizz—fry—and writhe like martyrs in the fire.*)

Shepherd. There's a bould, a daurin' simplicity in that, sir, that reminds ane o' the first elements o' cookery, as yet no an airt, far less a science, anterior to the time o' Tubal-Cain.

North. They have a flavor when done so, James, superior far to that imparted by the skill of a Kitchener or an Ude. They are more thoroughly searched by the fire—and in fact imbibe the flavor of fire.

Shepherd. I wuss they mayna be smeekit!

North. Try.

(NORTH *extricates the fry from the fire with the tongs, and deposits them in layers on a platter.* TICKLER *forsakes the side-table—joins the circular—and as he is helping himself to beef-à-la-mode, the* SHEPHERD *entangles his fork with* SOUTHSIDE'S, *and pins down the savory slice.*)

Shepherd. I despair o' meetin' wi' gude mainners in this rude and boisterous warld.

North. By the way, my dear James, I should like to hear you on National Manners.

Shepherd. The mainners o' a' nations are equally bad.

North. That may be true, but surely they are different—and I desire to hear the Shepherd on their distinctive qualities, and on the causes that have modified—

Shepherd. And transmogrified the original Adam?

North. You have it, James.

Shepherd. And you ken sae little o' human nature, or mak sae little allooance for its infirmities, as seriously to expeck me to enter into sic a feelosophical and historical inquery wi' this fry afore me?—wi' my mouth comin' into unremittin' contact wi' the maist dalicious o' a' dishes—beef *à-la-mode*, according to Christopher—or, as I micht ca't, North's *feu-de-joy*?

North. We shudder at the enormity of American manners, and bless our stars that we were born in Scotland; yet are we little better than savages—

Shepherd. Little better than savages, said ye, sir?

North. Come, don't fly into a passion, James.

Shepherd. We're no half sae gude. Savages, as far as mainners are concerned, are your only gentlemen.

North. Right.

Shepherd. Wha ever heard tell o' a Red Indian takin' the word oot o' your mooth, or contradictin' ye in a lood vice, or telling ye to your face that you was an ignorawmus—a bundle o' exploded prejudices—ane o' the auld schule, whase day was gane by—ahint the age by half a sentry—in plain terms, a fule?

North. No white man.

Shepherd. Nae Red Indian, whether Cherokee, Iroquois, or Mohawk, ever disgraced himself by insultin' you in that gate—as I hae been mony hunder times insulted by some upsettin' whalp o' a bit sma' Embro shopkeeper, a' his life occupied a' day in tyin' broon paper parshels wi' twine.

North. I cannot sit still, and hear you abuse the shopocracy—the most enlightened constituency——

Tickler. Waur hawk, Ponto! No politics, Kit.

Shepherd. Ten-pounder, indeed! The whalp's no even a clerk—and sweeps the shop he serves—yet has the imprudence to cock his snub nose in the face o' the Ettrick Shepherd.

North. Whose genius has swept the Forest.

Shepherd. But let's soar higher up society, and tak' the Embro' shopkeepers as a class—and there's nane ither mair respectable—what say ye till their mainners?

North. The manners of many—of almost all I know—at least with whom I dine—are as agreeable as their minds are enlightened.

Shepherd. Are ye satarical, sir?

North. I should be ashamed of myself if I were.

Shepherd. But then, sir, your freens are the *élite*.

North. Why, I believe that is true—though they are not all Tories.

Shepherd. Oh, sir! if you kent some that I ken—you would fent.

North. Is the smell so very strong?

Shepherd. I was na thinkin' o' the smell—though, noo that you mention't, it is sometimes strong indeed—but o' their a' roarin' through ither as if they were gawn to fa' to the fechtin'—wi' their een starin' in their head—and their faces, red, blue, and purple—excepp the lad in the jaundice—and this they ca' arguin'! Na, a' the while they're a' arguin' on the same side. For you see, sir, they're Whigs and Radicals, and a' unanimously insistin' on sinkin' a' minor differences, and bringin' a' their energies to bear on the common enemy—that is us, sir, you, and me, and Sir Robert Peel, and the Duke o' Wellington——

Tickler. Waur hawk, dogs!

Shepherd. I cou'd forgie them their tenets—for the're only seekin' to overturn Church and State—and every noo and then a bit sticket minister-lookin' cretur—but wha's a clerk in some excise or custom-house—cries out. wi' a vice like a corn-craik—"It's a speculative question, Mr. Hogg." Speculative or practical, I cou'd forgi'e them their tenets, and without ony symptom o' impatience, hear them drive the Bishops out o' the House o' Lords—then destroy the House o' Lords itself, that is, the Peerage as a legislative body—na, banish the King and the Royal Family to Van Diemen's Land, and set up a Republic, wi' a President—wha micht be dear aneuch at that soom—wi' three hundred pounds sterling per annum and a free house, including coal and candle. I repeat, I cou'd forgive their tenets—for I'm a leeberal, and can range wi' pleasure through a' latitudes o' opinion on the sphere o' thocht—but oh! sir! are na sic *mainners* maist offensive? And wou'd I be a Christian if I were na indignant wi' a company that a' nicht lang never ance lost the opportunity o' my openin' my mouth, without thrustin' their rotten Radicalism doon my thrott?

North. Why visit?

Shepherd. Whattt? wou'd ycu hae me to refuse an invitation to denner frae an auld freen—to meet a wheen auld freens—merely, 'cause their mainners are no sae polished as ane cou'd wish, and thae clever chiels no sae considerate as might be expectit frae their education, o' ane's feelin's as connected wi' his political principles?

North. Pray what has been their education?

Shepherd. They can read and write, and keep byeuks. I'm no denyin' their preevilege to lay down the law on government and religion, nor their ability to do sae—I was only compleenin' o' their *mainners*—which is the soobject o' our present disconrse—and agreein' wi' you that the tone in mony a tradesman's parlor in the modern Athens—as far as mainners are concerned—is probably rather below that o' the cabin o' an American steamboat on the Mississippi.

North. Do not say, James, that you agree with me in that opinion—for I have not said a single word about the matter.

Shepherd. What say ye, then, sir, to the mainners o' leeterary men?

North. If you mean, James, literary men by profession—regular authors—then we must speak first of those who conduct the periodical press, and latterly of those who devote themselves to what are called Works.

Shepherd. You'll hae some diffeeculty, sir, in makin' oot that distinction wi' a difference; for whare's the author of what is ca'd a wark that has nae dabbled mair or less wi' the dailies, the weeklies. the monthlies, and the quarterlies?

North. Let me consider—(*putting his finger to the organ of Memory*).

Shepherd. If there be ony such, they'll pruve a set o' auld fogics, that hae passed their lives in writin' what naebody reads; and wi' a due estimation o' the worth o' posthumous fame, I think that maun be a disconsolate occupation, and likely to bring down their gray heads wi' sorrow to the grave.

North. I could mention a few who have established a reputation by works that are in every good library. But——

Shepherd. There's Southey, the first man of letters in Europe, now that Sir Walter is gone—poet, historian, and philosopher——

North. He is—but I give up the distinction, and speak now simply of writers who have achieved a high place in literature. The manners of all such men, as far as my experience goes, are delightful, and, at the same time, their superiority as conspicuous in the intellectual intercourse of social life as in the productions of their genius.

Shepherd. Are you serious, sir?

North. Perfectly so, James. Dugald Stewart, indeed, has written that he seldom or never found that a great philosopher excelled in conversation, and that as for poets, or men of genius in the realms of imagination, he had almost always been painfully impressed by their comparative inferiority when not under the inspiration of the Muse, who visited them, it would appear, only during the hours of composition. At all other times they were dullish, or idiotic, or, at best, commonplace.

Shepherd. I daursay the Professor was na far wrang in the case o' great philosophers; but what great poets, may I ask, did he number amang his acquaintance?

North. I cannot say—I believe—for one—Thomas Campbell.

Shepherd. And is he na bricht?

North. Why, his conversation is not pitched on the same key as his Ode to the Mariners of England, or Lochiel's Warning.

Shepherd. Heaven forbid!

North. But he is one of the wittiest of the witty—when in spirits, lavish of happy thoughts—elegant in his illustrations, and in his manner, I should say graceful; his easy and unambitious talk characteristic at once of the scholar and the man of the world.

Shepherd. Thamas Cammel, a man of the warld!

North. Yes, James. For in what society would not the author of the Pleasures of Hope be welcome—in what sphere or circle the Poet of Wyoming not be a shining star?

Shepherd. True, sir.

North. A man of genius is always a man of genius, and unless he has been too much of a recluse, pleasant and instructive in all companies worthy of him, but he rarely desires to play first fiddle——

Shepherd. There should never be a first fiddle in a private concert.

North. Right.

Shepherd. Nae Paganini. Yet it's nae unusual thing to hear some Cockney o' a cratur—an Embro' Cockney—(what for, sir, dinna ye cut up the Embro' Cockneys?)—no only playin' first fiddle—but solo fiddle—and whether in ambition or imbecility, restrictin' himsell to ae string. But the true Musicianer—that is the man o' real genie, or tawlent, or learnin', or wisdom—for a' sic are nature's musicianers—interexchange instruments in harmonious amity—and without byeuks afore them—but by a natural ear for music, wi' which heaven has endowed their souls—keep for ever a' in perfect tune, whatever be the piece they may be performin'—and if ane is left in a solo by himsell, it's because the rest hae ceased to play, in order that they may hear some spontaneous strain in which his peculiar genie is known to excel, and at its close, a' the company, till then still and silent, expresses its gratitude by a gentle murmur, the sweetest sort o' applause.

North. Tickler—is not that happy? Asleep.

Shepherd. Dozin' in a dreadnocht! But for his face you micht suppose him a bear—and but for his figure you micht take him for a Whaup. For it's mair like a neb nor a nose.

North. Without literature or manners, I hardly see how a man can be a gentleman.

Shepherd. Nor me. But mony a man has a sufficient share o' literatur' that does na like to let it oot, especially in presence o' you or me, sir; but it colors his conversation for a' that, and there's a charmin' modesty, sir, in some men o' fine edication, that gies a mild yet manly character to a' they inobtrusively say in the course o' an evenin', leavin' on the minds o' them that kens what's what, a far stranger impression o' their leeterary abeelities and information, than the lang harangues o' your declamatory chiels, wha, frae an owre-anxiety to appear somebody abune common, only succeed in showing you that they are sumphs.

North. There is something, James, to my mind, not a little laughable in the exclusive idea many minds have formed and expressed of good society.

Shepherd. Something no a little laithsom. Them that uses the term are contemptible coofs.

North. Not always coofs, James—though I grant contemptible. Of late years, one hears even of men of genius—who in their works write for the whole world—yet who would be uneasy to be seen familiarly mixing in the circles of the middle ranks.

Shepherd. Wha were their pawrents?

North. People in trade—and in a small way—in the soft or hard line—sugar or shagreen—retail dealers in treacle or tin—collaterally connected, perhaps by blood, with a Dean of Guild or a Provost, whose memory still survives in their native borough, after the lapse of a quarter of a century, and whose title is still legible on a decent freestone slab in its kirkyard. They affect "good society," forsooth—and strut before splendid mirrors in "fashion's most magnificent saloons," forgetful of the far happier days, in which their only "mirror for magistrates" was a pail of water, in whose stream—before washing its face and hands—the household set its cap or shaved.

> "Who would not weep, if such a man there be?
> Who would not weep, if Atticus were he?"

Shepherd. Wha's Atticus?

North. All society—every society—is good—that is composed of men and women of good character, good manners, and good education—and there are many millions of such men and women.

Shepherd. And, thank Heaven! the number's increasin' in Britain every year.

North. Among them there are, it is true, degrees rather than distinction of rank, and every person of common sense knows his proper place on one or other of the levels of the social system, to which, by birth or profession, he more peculiarly belongs; and *there* lies "the haunt and main region" of his life. *There*—are his habitualities—his familiarities—his domesticities.

Shepherd. I dinna dislike thae words, though rather oot o' the common usage.

North. As long as he cherishes them, and prefers them to all else, he is true to his order.

Shepherd. Gude, sir—verra gude.

North. Should he desert them, he is a traitor.

Shepherd. A sowleless sumph.

North. At least a heartless slave; and on his neck erelong he will experience the tyrant's heel. Men of genius, James, lose all the glory it can confer on personal character, by separating themselves from their natural connexions, when these happen to be comparatively humble, to associate with the great in power, the high in rank, or the opulent in riches; and for such distinction as "good society" can confer, or such enjoyment as "good society" can impart, sacrifice that feeling of independence which accompanies *propriety;* a comprehensive term, including many observances, which, though when taken singly, are but small, yet collectively are of mighty import for happiness and virtue.

Shepherd. I wou'dna be asleep the noo, like Tickler, for ten pounds.

North. James, a man may degrade himself equally by leaving his own sphere, either for a higher or a humbler than that to which he properly and mainly belongs; and if to him a kind Providence has assigned the golden mean, by all that is most sacred to the human heart, let him adhere to his lot with unspeakable gratitude, best shown by fidelity without a flaw to the persons and the things (and for sake of persons, how holy things become!) that compose it, and constitute it a happy little world, circumscribed by lines of light that make it at once a prison and a paradise.

Shepherd. No for twenty pounds.

North. I shall not say another word, my dear James, on the effect on the whole character of the man inevitably produced—and that, too, in no long time—by an exclusive or undue association with *coteries*—and they deserve no better name—that absurdly assume to themselves the irrational title of "good society," though I have, in the little I have said, merely hinted it; and I need not be more prolix on the——

Shepherd. Prolix! You're at ance fluent and conceese.

North. ——on the evil as inevitably produced to the moral and intellectual frame, by stepping out of our own sphere into what, without offence, may be called an inferior one—a lower one—in respect to the habits and mental cultivation, at least, of those who properly belong to it, and in it are respectable and worthy the respect of all men. Intimacies with our inferiors in station—and we have all our stations—are not unfrequently even of an endearing kind, when they have originated in some of those pleasant circumstances that in early life bring naturally together those whom in after-life here would have occurred nothing to unite, but whom, indeed, all the ordinary usages of the world keep but too much asunder. O, sweet companionship is boyhood between the children of the poor and rich, the high and the humble!

Shepherd. At schule!

North. A thousand thoughts, James, are crowding in upon my mind—a thousand feelings stealing in upon my heart—when I——

Shepherd. They're no croodin' in and stealin' in, sir, but they're risin' up, linked thegether, frae the inner recesses o' brain and briest.

North. ——when I think, James, of the character of our countrymen, and the great changes, for good or for evil——

Shepherd. Haply, sir, for baith—that are likely to tak place in't, frae the great changes wrocht, and no yet owre, on the Constitution by the Bill o' Reform, which, to tell you the truth, I never hae read. Pray, Mr. North, where can a body get a copy?

Tickler. Waur sheep! Hector.

Shepherd. Huts-tuts. Mayna we take a pick at politics?

Tickler. No, sir. Obey the law.

North. I trust we shall for ever love our country, hap what may —and that shaken as they are, we Conservatives——

Shepherd. A michty band.

North. ——shall be able to support our Institutions——

Shepherd. Secular and religious—o' Church and State. I've seen a spire, though built o' granite, trummle in the tempest, like a fishin'-rod—yet there was nae mair danger—whatever micht be the fear—o' its bein' blawn owre than Tintock. There's the Eddystane Lichthouse, that I never saw, but I hae read Smeaton's account o't —him that was the arkitect—and it's construckit after the bole o' a tree. They say it is felt by the folk high up in the licht-room to shake as if it swayed, when ae great sea after anither rides owre the tap o't, and the foam cries hurraw as it thinks it droons the Star. But there it stauns in spite o' a' the wildest wunters, and will stan' for centuries, shinin' in its steady smiles on gratefu' ships. Sae wull it be wi' the religious institutions o' our sea-beat isle. Oh, sir! if they were tappled doon in ruins, the laun' wou'd be waur than the sea—and darker and stormier—and then the verra state itsell, sir, would suffer—shipwrack—though that may be an Eerish bull—and no a single life-boat—though that may be another—wou'd put aff to save us a' frae sinkin' into perdition.

North. I cannot yet think that our countrymen are irreligious—but I trust that they are still united more closely and firmly than they know, by many sacred sympathies that will yet survive all this hubbub, and stabilitate the structure of social life, by preserving in extremity that of our political and pious institutions, that for ages have breathed back on the natural character the spirit out of which they arose.

Shepherd. What is Love o' Kintra but an amalgamated multitude o' sympathies in brethren's hearts!

North. Yes, James, you speak well. The love of our country is not so much an attachment to any assignable object, as it is our participation in that whole Spirit which has breathed in the breast of that whole race of which we are sprung.

Shepherd. Yes, Christopher, you speak well. It is the Sympathy of Race.

Tickler. Philosophers!

North. All patriotism roots itself round those objects by which we are most essentially bound to our race—of our own and of past generations. How sacred the ties by which we are bound to our

Mother Country! Think of a party of poor Indians, forced to quit their homes, bearing with them the dear bones which, reburied in their new place of settlement, would make it, by that mighty magic, holy to them, even as their Natale Solum! Think of the People, who, when upbraided with continually flying before Alexander, said, "Let him pursue us to the Tombs of our Fathers, and he will then know whether we always fly!"

Shepherd. The Sceethans, said ye? Faith, there they wad hae shawn Sandy hoo till fecht.

Tickler. Alexander the Great called Sandy by the Ettrick Shepherd at a Noctes Ambrosianæ!

Shepherd. I care nae mair for Alexander the Great than I do for Tappitourie.

North. Hence the Arab with his roving tent has yet a country.

Shepherd. And in his seal-skin breeks the Eskymaw.

North. Hence with the Romans that feeling kept pace with their destinies—from their mud huts to their marble palaces—

Tickler. Dum Domus Æneæ capitoli immobile saxum
Accolet, imperiumque Pater Romanus habebit.

North. Ah! Timothy! why didst thou not recite the two preceding lines, so beautiful—

Tickler. Fortunati ambo! si quid mea carmina possint
Nulla dies unquam memori vos eximet aevo!

North. Thank you, my friend. Ay—the desire and the forethought of the sympathy of others, in its own consciousness of itself, may be more easily conceived of those whose genius exercises itself in pacific arts, than of those whose glory begins in desolation. We can well imagine that the sculptor or the painter, while he looks himself with delight on the beautiful forms that are rising into life beneath his hand, feels rejoicingly that other spirits framed by Nature with souls like his own, will look with the same emotion on the same forms, and thank him to whose genius they owe their enjoyment. And most of all with the great poets! What a divine emotion must have been the consciousness which Virgil felt of the pleasure which his verse would inspire, when, having celebrated in one of the most beautiful passages of all his poetry, the perilous and fatal adventure of those two friends, and closed their eyes in death, his heart broke forth into that affecting and sublime ejaculation! He prophesied falsely of the duration of the Roman greatness; but he committed no error in prophesying his own fame; and as the delight which he felt himself in the tender and heroic picture he had drawn, is felt as he believed it would be by numberless spirits, and will be felt till the end of time. He knew too that he should win from all ages, with love for his fallen heroes, some fond and grateful affection for him who had sung so well the story of their fortunes—

he saw the everlasting light of glory shining through his own transient tears.

Shepherd. Gude. But are na ye wannerin' frae the soobject?

North. No. I am diverging circularly but to return. When warriors of Forest Germany, James, had met in some central spot in their annual assembly, they returned each to his own home, more bound to his country, because one and all had participated in an act of the people.

Shepherd. Our Saxon progenitors!

North. If all the circumstances, James, are considered which mix in this passion—

Shepherd. What'n passion, sir?

North. Patriotism! such as the attachment to old institutions, to manners, to national peculiarities of speech and dress, it will be found that they have all their power by means of sympathy.

Shepherd. As I said.

North. As you said, and with even more than your usual eloquence. It is not simply that old recollections are gathered upon them—

Shepherd. Though that's much—

North. ——but that by them each man feels himself with vivid reality to belong to his people. On any other ground on which patriotism may be founded it may seem to have something unsubstantial and illusory; but once shown to be founded thus, it is apparent that it can only decay when one of the most important principles of our nature is in decay.

Shepherd. Sympathy, or the power o' feelin' alang wi' a' our brethren o' mankind, but mair especially them that hae flourished and faded awa' amang the flowers of our ain soil, in a' the best emotions o' natur' continuous in their characteristic current frae the cradle to the grave.

North. Good. How else, my dear Shepherd, can we comprehend that extraordinary passion of patriotism felt in old times! You know—nobody better—what infinite causes concurred in such states to give immense power to that sympathy by which each man felt himself united to all his countrymen. We thus understand the importance attached by the Greeks to their national games, which otherwise would appear extravagant, or even absurd—the price to the first-fallen of the war—of their civic funeral, and their oration pronounced in the hearing of all the people of Athens.

Shepherd. A' the nation lamentin' and exultin' for sake o' ae man!

North. We understand the value of pillars, on which their names were inscribed and read—of statues, in which their features were still looked upon by thousands of living eyes—

Shepherd. Glowerin' on the eemages o' the glorious dead, till they too kindled wi' the houp o' ae day bein' glowered at by heroes yet unborn! Posthumous fame! posthumous fame! Oh, sirs! but it's a mystery that nae patriot wou'd seek to analeeze, but rather alloo't to remain in its shooblime simplicity, conneckit wi' a feelin' shooblimer still, the immortality o' the soul.

North. Think on the feelings a nation of heroes entertain for their greatest hero.

Shepherd. Far, far ayont their individual part in the cause or the success, but no ayont the dilatation o' spirit and power ilka ane o' them feels frae his ain union wi' the power and the will o' a' thae conquerin' myriads whom he heads! He, their leader, sir, is the centre roun' which a' their passions revolve, like planets roun' the sun.

Tickler. Hollo, James!

Shepherd. Whattt! Do you think, you coof, that their attachment is a' for himself alane? Na. In him, sir, a' their ain micht and their ain majesty is bund up in ae veesable eemage. He is your only true, and, at the same time, ideal representative o' his kintramen; and at mention o' him, their hearts burn within them, and the licht o' patriotism illumines the land far and wide—and, in danger is concentrated intil fire, that rins alang the earth, devoorin' a' that wou'd resist it like stubble, till the rear-guard o' the invaders is extinguished wi' a fizz in the sea. O heavens! at sic a time hoo the pressure o' common mortality is thrown aff! hoo its bands hae fallen awa'! The fears, the pains, the sorrows, the anguish, that tak hold on weak natur, hae at once ceased, when all are sustained and strengthened by ae consentin' passion, fearsomer to faes than thunner growlin' frae the sky it blackens—gladsomer to freens than the lauch o' morn—

Tickler. ——"Seems another morn,
Risen on mid-day."

Shepherd. Gude! Milton.

North. Yes, James, that is our country—not where we have breathed alone; not that land which we have loved, because it has shown to our opening eyes the brightness of heaven, and the gladness of earth; but the land for which we have hoped and feared—that is to say, for which our bosom has beat with the consenting hopes and fears of many million hearts; that land, of which we have loved the mighty living and the mighty dead; that land, the Roman and the Greek would have said, where the boy had sung in the pomp that led the sacrifice to the altars of the ancient deities of the soil.

Shepherd. And therefore, when a man he wou'd guard them frae profanation, and had he a thousan' lives, would pour them a' oot for sake o' what some micht ca' superstition, but which you and me and Southside, sittin' there wi' his great gray een, wou'd fear na', in the face o' heaven, to ca' religion.

Tickler. Hurra!

Shepherd. I but clench my nieves.

North. James, the Campus Martius and the Palæstra——

Shepherd. Sir?

North. ——where the youth exercised Heroic Games, were the Schools of their Virtue; for there they were taking part in the passions, the power, the life, the glory that flowed through all the spirit of the nation.

Shepherd. O' them, sir, the ggemms at St Ronan's are, but on a sma' scale, an imperfect eemage.

North. Old warriors and gowned statesmen, that frowned in marble or in brass, in public places, and in the porches of noble houses—trophied monuments, and towers riven with the scars of ancient battles—the temple raised where Jove had stayed the Flight—or the Victory whose expanded wings still seemed to hover over the conquering bands—what were all these to the eyes and the fancy of the young citizen, but characters speaking to him of the great secret of his Hopes and Desires—in which he read the union of his own heart to the heart of the heroic nation of which he was One?

Shepherd. My bluid's tinglin' and my skin creeps. Dinna stap.

North. And what, James, I ask you, what if less noble passions must hereafter take their place in his mind?—what if he must learn to share in the feuds and hates of his house or of his order? Those far deeper and greater feelings had been sunk into his spirit in the years when it is must susceptible, unsullied, and pure, and afterwards in great contests, in peril of life and death, in those moments of agitation or profound emotion in which the higher soul again rises up, all those high and solemn affections of boyhood and youth would return upon him, and consecrate his warlike deeds with the noblest name of virtue that was known to those ancient states.

Shepherd. What was't? Eh?

North. Patriotism.

Shepherd. Oo ay. Say on, sir.

North. Therefore how was the Oaken Crown prized which was given to him who had saved the life of a citizen!

Shepherd. And amang a people too, sir, whare every man was willin' at a word to die.

North. Perhaps, James, he loved not the man whom he had preserved; but he had remembered in the battle that it was a son of his country that had fallen, and over whom he had spread his shield. He knew that the breath he guarded was part of his country's being.

Shepherd. Mr. Tickler saw ye ever sic een?

North. Look at the simple incitements to valor in the songs of that poet who is said to have roused the Lacedemonians, disheartened in unsuccessful war, and to have animated them to victory. "He who fights well among the foremost, if he fall shall be sung among his people; or if he live, shall be in reverence in their council; an old man shall give place to him; his tomb shall be in honor, and the children of his children."

Shepherd. Simple incitement, indeed, sir, but, as you said richtly, shooblime.

North. Why, James, the love of its own military glory in a warlike people is indeed, of itself, an imperfect patriotism.

Shepherd. Sir? Wull ye say that again, for I dinna just tak it up.

North. Believe me, my dear Shepherd, that in every country there is cause for patriotism, or the want of such a cause argues defects in the character and condition of the country of the grossest kind. It shows that the people are vicious, or servile, or effeminate——

Shepherd. Which only a confounded leear will ever say o' Scotsmen.

North. The want of this feeling is always a great vice in the individual character; for it will hardly ever be found tó arise from the only justifiable or half-justifiable cause, namely, when a very high mind, in impatient disdain of the baseness of all round it, seems to shake off its communion with them. I call that but half-justifiable.

Shepherd. And I, sir, with your leave, ca't athegither unjustifiable, as you can better explain than the simple Shepherd.

North. You are right, James. For the noblest minds do not thus break themselves loose from their country; but they mourn over it, and commiserate its sad estate, and would die to recover it. They acknowledge the great tie of nature—of that house they are—and its shame is their own.

Shepherd. O, sir! but you're a generous noble-hearted cretur!

North. In all cases, then, the want of patriotism is sheer want of feeling; such a man labors under an incapacity of sympathizing with his kind in their noblest interests. Try him, and you shall find that on many lower and unworthier occasions he feels with others—that his heart is not simply too noble for this passion—but that it is capable of being animated and warmed with many much inferior desires.

Shepherd. A greedy dowg an' a lewd and—in the ae case, snarlin' for a bane—an' in the ither, growlin' for the flesh. I scunner at the sinner.

North. Wo to the citizen of the world.

Shepherd. Shame—shame—shame!

North. The man who feels himself not bound to his country can have no gratitude.

Shepherd. Hoo selfish and cauld-hearted maun hae been his verra childhood!

North. I confess that, except in cases of extreme distress, I have never been able to sympathize with——emigrants.

Shepherd. I dinna weel ken, sir, what to say to that—but mayna a man love, and yet leave his country?

North. My dear James, I see many mournful meanings in the dimness of your eyes—so shall not pursue that subject—but you will at least allow me to say, that there is something shocking in the mind of the man who can bear, without reluctance or regret, to be severed from the whole world of his early years—who can transfer himself from the place which is his own to any region of the globe, where he can advance his fortune—who, in this sense of the word, can say, in carrying himself, "omnia mea mecum porto."

Shepherd. That's na in my book o' Latin or Greek quottations.

North. Exiles carry with them from their mother-country all its dearest names.

Shepherd. And a wee bit name—canna it carry in it a wecht o' love!

North. Ay, James, the fugitives from Troy had formed a little Ilium, and they had, too, their little Xanthus.

Tickler. "Et avertem Xanthi cognomine rivum."

Shepherd. You're twa classical scholars, and wull aye be quottin' Greek. But for my pairt,—after a' those eloquent diatribes o' yours on the pawtriotism o' the auncients, I wud na desire to stray for illustrations ae step oot o' the Forest.

Tickler. Aren't ye all Whigs?

Shepherd. Some o' a' sorts. But it's an epitome o' the pastoral warld at large—and the great majority o' shepherds are Conservatives. They're a thinkin' people, sir, as ye ken; and though far frae bein' inspeculative, or unwillin' to adopt new contrivances as sune's they hae got an insicht intil the principle on which they wark, yet a newfangle in their een's but a newfangle; and as in the case o' its bein' applied to a draw-well, they wait no only to see how it pumps up, but hae patience to put its durability to the proof o' a pretty lang experience, sae in the political affairs o' the State—they're no to be ta'en in by the nostrums o' every reformer that has a plan o' a new, cheap constitution to shaw, but they fasten their een on't as dourly as on a dambrodd; and then begin cross-questionin' the chiel—quack or else no—on the vawrious bearings o' the main-springs, wheels, and drags; and as sune's they perceive a hitch, they cry ha! ha! ma lad! I'm thinkin' she'll no rin up hill—and if ye let her lowse at the top o' ane, she'll rattle to the deevil.

North. And such too, my dear sir, don't you think, is the way of thinking among the great body of the agriculturists?

Shepherd. I could illustrate it, sir, by the smearin' o' sheep.

Tickler. And eke the shearing.

Shepherd. Say clippin'. The Whugs and Radicals assert tounfolks are superior in mind to kintra folks. They'll be sayin' neist that they're superior to them likewise in body—and speak o' the rabble o' the Forest as ither people speak o' the rabble o' the Grassmarket. But the rural riff-raff are in sprinklings' in sma' families, and only seen lousin' ane anither on spats formin' an angle on the road-sides. Findlay o' Selkirk has weel nigh cleaned the coonty o' a' sic—but in great toons, and especially manufacturin' anes, there are hale divisions hotchin' wi' urban riff-raff, and it's them ye hear at hustins routin' in a way that the stots and stirks o' the Forest would be ashamed o' theirsells for doin' in a bare field on a wunter day, when something had hindered the hind frae carryin' them some fodder to warm their wames in the snaw. The salvation o' the country, sir, depends on the———

Tickler. This will never do, North—this is too bad. See, 'tis six!

North (*rising, and giving his guests each his candle*). We shall hear you another time, my dear Shepherd—but now—

Shepherd. The salvation o' the kintra, sir, depends on the—

North (*touching first one spring and then another, while fly open two panels in the oak wainscotting*). You know your rooms, gents. The alarm bell will ring at twelve—and at one, lunch will be on the table in the Topaz. I wish you both the nightmare—(*touches a spring, and vanishes.*)

Shepherd. Mr. Tickler! I say the salvation of the country—baith gane! I'm no sleepy—but I'll rather sleep than soliloqueeze.

(*Vanishes, while Gurney comes out like a mouse, and begins to nibble cheese.*)

END OF THE NOCTES.

GENERAL INDEX.

INDEX TO THE POETRY.

CPSIA information can be obtained
at www.ICGtesting.com
Printed in the USA
LVHW100424110522
718424LV00003B/74

9 783375 004736